W9-BYO-910

BELISARIUS I:
Thunder at Dawn

BELISARIUS I:
Thunder at Dawn

ERIC FLINT
DAVID DRAKE

BELISARIUS I: THUNDER AT DAWN

This is a work of fiction. All the characters and events portrayed in this book are fictional, and any resemblance to real people or incidents is purely coincidental.

A Baen Book

Baen Publishing Enterprises
P.O. Box 1403
Riverdale, NY 10471
www.baen.com

ISBN 10: 1-4165-5568-4
ISBN 13: 978-1-4165-5568-1

Cover art by Kurt Miller

First Baen printing, September 2008

Distributed by Simon & Schuster
1230 Avenue of the Americas
New York, NY 10020

Library of Congress Cataloging-in-Publication Data
Flint, Eric.
  Belisarius I : thunder at dawn / Eric Flint & David Drake.
      p. cm. — (Belisarius series)
   ISBN-13: 978-1-4165-5568-1
   ISBN-10: 1-4165-5568-4
  1. Belisarius, 505 (ca.)-565—Fiction. 2. Imaginary wars and battles—Fiction. 3. Good and evil—Fiction. 4. Malwa (Madhya Pradesh and Rajasthan, India)—History—Fiction. I. Drake, David. II. Title. III. Title: Belisarius one.

  PS3556.L548B45 2008
  813'.54—dc22

                                                     2008028784

10 9 8 7 6 5 4 3 2 1

Pages by Joy Freeman (www.pagesbyjoy.com)
Printed in the United States of America

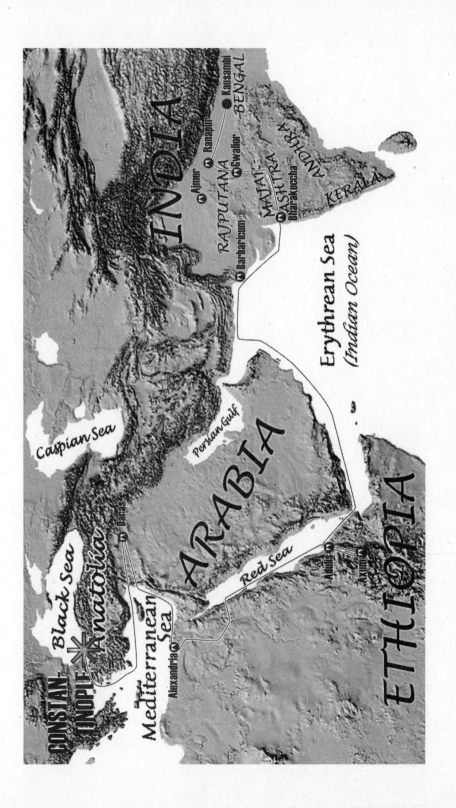

CONTENTS

Introduction:

BUT WHY ON EARTH BELISARIUS?

Jim Baen and I were professional associates from 1974, when he bought two stories in the Hammer's Slammers series, till his death in 2006. Our friendship was far more important than our business connections.

We didn't meet very often, maybe only twenty times during that whole period. We spent a lot of time on the phone, though, and that's where each of the various jogs leading to the Belisarius series occurred.

Mostly the calls involved Jim bouncing some new enthusiasm off me, and me responding in various ways. Not infrequently my response was to gush information because Jim had pushed a button of my own.

In the 1980s Jim discovered BH Liddell Hart, who wrote books advocating a strategy of indirection rather than frontal assault. I don't think it would be unjust to boil Liddell Hart's thesis down to the concept that instead of attacking an enemy, you should capture some relatively undefended position which the enemy *must* have. This forces the enemy to attack you, giving you the advantages of defending a position which you will have prepared before he arrives.

This is one of the things that looks obvious but isn't easy to achieve in the real world. (Compare the infallible method of making money in the stock market: buy low, sell high.)

In fact to the military mind it isn't even obvious. I recall a course I took during my intelligence training, taught (I'm sure) according to a rigid US Army curriculum. The instructor asked us to name two great generals of the American Civil War. I immediately said, "Grant and Sherman."

According to the Army, I should've said, "Lee and Jackson." Those two Confederate generals were tacticians of the highest caliber, but neither demonstrated a speck of strategic sense. (Given that the course was being taught during the Vietnam War, I can see why the Army wouldn't be concerned about an absence of strategy. I fear that what's going on in Iraq implies that the curriculum remains the same today.)

Liddell Hart (whom I'd read in high school) does discuss Grant and Sherman favorably, but he considered the Byzantine general Belisarius to be the most skilled proponent of the Strategy of Indirection. Jim became fascinated by Belisarius and wanted a series of novels demonstrating the merits of the indirect approach.

We've got very good information about Belisarius because Procopius of Caesarea, a bureaucrat on his staff, wrote full accounts of the wars of his day. In the course of them the generals of the Emperor Justinian not only blocked further Persian inroads but also reconquered North Africa and Italy, which had been lost to Germanic invaders. The process involved a number of generals, but Belisarius was then and now accepted as the greatest of them.

I had read Procopius when I was researching my first novel, which was set in the 6th century AD. For the new project I bought my own set of Procopius and made a précis of the entire *Histories of the Wars*. (After the General series came out I was occasionally asked, "Have you read Procopius' *Secret History*?" I never answered, "Yes, you twit," but I was tempted. I've even read *The Buildings*, though I won't pretend its contents have had a lot of effect on my fiction.)

With the précis in front of me, it was easy to turn the life of Belisarius into plots for what became the General series. We—I can't tell you at this point whether it was Jim's idea or mine—moved it to a distant planet where technology was at a roughly mid 19th century level following the collapse of interstellar government. The Belisarius analog is guided by a supercomputer which survived the collapse.

The series worked. Jim decided he wanted a series of similar books set in other cultures. I wrote these plots (as the General Follow-on series in my own notation). This wasn't as good an idea (and some of it was a downright *bad* idea, but that's another matter).

I thought the follow-ons would be the end of it, but many of Jim's interests remained with him for his whole life. One afternoon in 1996 while he and I were chatting, he commented that what he'd like to see was a series in which the historical Belisarius had a supercomputer aiding him the way I'd postulated his analog in the General series did.

I thought for a moment and said I could make that work. A three-book series seemed about right to me. He agreed. So I started checking things I'd need for the background.

The next day Jim called me back: his idea had been a bad one. The real Belisarius had been so much better than any of his contemporaries that there would be no significant benefit in giving him a supercomputer.

I laughed and told Jim his job had been to come up with the idea. I was the writer, so I would handle the details. I wouldn't have agreed to the notion if I hadn't already seen the obvious solution to the problem: the bad guys had to have a supercomputer also. He should now go away and let me get on with my job.

Which he did. The book you're holding now is the first part of the result.

Dave Drake
david-drake.com

An Oblique Approach

To Lucille

"To move along the line of natural expectation consolidates the opponent's balance and thus increases his resisting power . . . In most campaigns the dislocation of the enemy's psychological and physical balance has been the vital prelude to a successful attempt at his overthrow."

—B. H. Liddell Hart, *Strategy*

*The first facet was **purpose**.*

*It was the only facet. And because it was the only facet, **purpose** had neither meaning nor content. It simply was. Was. Nothing more.*

***purpose**. Alone, and unknowing.*

*Yet, that thing which **purpose** would become had not come to be haphazardly. **purpose**, that first and isolated facet, had been drawn into existence by the nature of the man who squatted in the cave, staring at it.*

Another man—almost any other man—would have gasped, or drawn back, or fled, or seized a futile weapon. Some men—some few rare men—would have tried to comprehend what they were seeing. But the man in the cave simply stared.

*He did not try to comprehend **purpose**, for he despised comprehension. But it can be said that he considered what he was seeing; and considered it, moreover, with a focused concentration that was quite beyond the capacity of almost any other man in the world.*

***purpose** had come to be, in that cave, at that time, because the man who sat there, considering **purpose**, had stripped himself, over long years, of everything except his own overriding, urgent, all-consuming sense of purpose.*

His name was Michael of Macedonia. He was a Stylite monk, one of those holy men who pursued their faith through isolation and contemplation, perched atop pillars or nestled within caves.

*Michael of Macedonia, fearless in the certainty of his faith, stretched forth a withered arm and laid a bony finger on **purpose**.*

*For **purpose**, the touch of the monk's finger opened facet after facet after facet, in an explosive growth of crystalline knowledge*

5

*which, had **purpose** truly been a self-illuminated jewel, would have blinded the man who touched it.*

*No sooner had Michael of Macedonia touched **purpose** than his body arched as if in agony, his mouth gaped open in a soundless scream, and his face bore the grimace of a gargoyle. A moment later, he collapsed.*

For two full days, Michael lay unconscious in the cave. He breathed, and his heart beat, but his mind was lost in vision.

On the third day, Michael of Macedonia awoke. Instantly awoke. Alert, fully conscious, and not weak. (Or, at least, not weak in spirit. His body bore the weakness which comes from years of self-deprivation and ferocious austerities.)

*Without hesitating, Michael reached out his hand and seized **purpose**. He feared yet another paroxysm, but his need to understand overrode his fear. And, in the event, his fear proved unfounded.*

***purpose**, its raw power now refracted through many facets, was able to control its outburst. **purpose**, now, was also **duration**. And though the time which it found in the monk's mind was utterly strange, it absorbed the confusion. For **duration** was now also **diversity**, and so **purpose** was able to parcel itself out, both in its sequence and its differentiation. Facets opened up, and spread, and doubled, and tripled, and multiplied, and multiplied again, and again, until they were like a crystalline torrent which bore the monk along like a chip of wood on a raging river.*

*The river reached the delta, and the delta melted into the sea, and all was still. **purpose** rested in the palm of Michael's hand, shimmering like moonlight on water, and the monk returned that shimmer with a smile.*

"I thank you," he said, "for ending the years of my search. Though I cannot thank you for the end you have brought me."

He closed his eyes for a moment, lost in thought. Then murmured: "I must seek counsel with my friend the bishop. If there is any man on earth who can guide me now, it will be Anthony."

His eyes opened. He turned his head toward the entrance of the cave and glared at the bright Syrian day beyond.

"The Beast is upon us."

Prologue

That night, Belisarius was resting in the villa which he had purchased upon receiving command of the army at Daras. He was not there often, for he was a general who believed in staying with his troops. He had purchased the villa for the benefit of his wife Antonina, whom he had married two years before, that she might have a comfortable residence in the safety of Aleppo, yet still not be far from the Persian border where the general took his post.

The gesture had been largely futile, for Antonina insisted on accompanying Belisarius even in the brawl and squalor of a military camp. She was well-nigh inseparable from him, and in truth, the general did not complain. For, whatever else was mysterious to men about the quicksilver mind of Belisarius, one thing was clear as day: he adored his wife.

It was an unfathomable adoration, to most. True, Antonina possessed a lively and attractive personality. (To those, at least, who had not the misfortune of drawing down her considerable temper.) And, she was very comely. On this point all agreed, even her many detractors: though considerably older than her husband, Antonina bore her years well.

But what years they had been! Oh, the scandal of it all.

Her father had been a charioteer, one of those raucous men idolized by the hippodrome mobs. Worse yet, her mother had been an actress, which to is to say, little more than a prostitute. As Antonina grew up in these surroundings, she herself adopted the ways of her mother at an early age—and, then!—added to the sin of harlotry, that of witchcraft. For it was well known that Antonina was as skilled in magic as she was in the more corporeal forms of wickedness.

True, since her marriage to the general there had been no trace of scandal attached to her name. But vigilant eyes and ears were always upon her. Not those of her husband, oddly enough, for he seemed foolishly unconcerned of her fidelity. But many others watched, and listened for rumor with that quivering attentiveness which is the hallmark of proper folk.

Yet the ears heard nothing, and the eyes saw even less. A few turned aside, satisfied there was nothing to see or hear. Most, however, remained watchful at their post. The whore was, after all, a witch. And, what was worse, she was the close friend of the Empress Theodora. (No surprise, that, for all men know that like seeks like. And if the Empress Theodora's past held no trace of witchcraft, she had made good the loss by a harlotry so wanton as to put even that of Antonina to shame.)

So who knew what lecheries and deviltry Antonina could conceal?

About the general himself, setting aside his scandalous marriage, the gentility had little ill to say.

A bit, of course, a bit. Though ranked in the nobility, Belisarius was Thracian by birth. And the Thracians were known to be a boorish folk, rustic and uncouth. This flaw in his person, however, was passed over lightly. It was not that the righteous feared the wrath of Belisarius. The general, after all, was known himself to make the occasional jest regarding Thracian crudity. (Crude jests, of course; he was a Thracian.)

No, the tongues of the better stock were stilled on this subject because the Emperor Justinian was also Thracian (and not even from the ranks of the Thracian nobility, such as it was, but from the peasantry). And if Belisarius was known for his even and good-humored temperament, the Emperor was not. Most certainly not. An ill-humored and suspicious man, was Justinian, frightfully quick to take offense. And frightful when he did.

Then, there was the general's youth. As all people of quality are aware, youth is by nature a parlous state. An extremely perilous condition, youth, from an ethical standpoint. Reckless, besides—daring, and impetuous. Not the sort of thing which notability likes to see in its generals. Yet the Emperor Justinian had placed him in the ranks of his personal bodyguard, the elite body from which he selected his generals. And then, piling folly upon unwisdom, had immediately selected Belisarius to command an army facing the ancient Medean foe.

True, there were those who defended the Emperor's choice, pointing out that despite his youth Belisarius possessed an acute judgment and a keen intellect. Yet this defense failed of its purpose. For, in the end, leaving aside his marriage, it was this final quality of Belisarius that set right-thinking teeth on edge.

Intelligence, of course, is an admirable property in a man. Even, in moderation, in a woman. So long as it is a respectable sort of intelligence—straight, so to speak. A thing of clear corners and precise angles, or, at the very least, spherical curves. Moderate, in its means; forthright, in its ends; direct, in its approach.

But the mind of Belisarius—ah, the mystery of it. To look at the man, he was naught but a Thracian. Taller than most, well built as Thracians tend to be, and handsome (as Thracians tend not to be). But all who knew the general came to understand that, within his upstanding occidental shape, there lurked a most exotic intellect. Something from the subtle east, perhaps, or the ancient south. A thing not from the stark hills but the primeval forest; a gnarled mind in a youthful body, crooked as a root and as sinuous as a serpent.

Such did many good folk think, especially after making his acquaintance. None could fault the general, after taking his leave, for the courtesy of his manner or the propriety of his conduct. A good-humored man, none could deny; though many, after taking his leave, wondered if the humor was at their expense. But they kept their suspicions muted, if not silent. For there always remained this thought, that whatever the state of his mind, there was no mistaking the state of his body.

Deadly with a blade, was Belisarius. And even the *cataphracts*, in their cups, spoke of his lance and his bow.

It was to the house of this man, then, and his Jezebel wife, that Michael of Macedonia and his friend the bishop brought their message, and the *thing* which bore it.

Chapter 1

ALEPPO

Spring, 528 AD

Upon being awakened by his servant Gubazes, Belisarius arose instantly, with the habit of a veteran campaigner. Antonina, at his side, emerged from sleep more slowly. After hearing what Gubazes had to say, the general threw on a tunic and hastened from his bedroom. He did not wait for Antonina to get dressed, nor even take the time to strap on his sandals.

Such strange visitors at this hour could not be kept waiting. Anthony Cassian, Bishop of Aleppo, was a friend who had visited on several occasions—but never at midnight. And as for the other—*Michael of Macedonia?*

Belisarius knew the name, of course. It was a famous name throughout the Roman Empire. Famous—and loved—by the common folk. To the high churchmen who were the subject of Michael's occasional sermons, the name was notorious—and not loved in the slightest. But the general had never met the man personally. Few people had, in truth, for the monk had lived in his desert cave for years now.

As he walked down the long corridor to the salon, Belisarius heard voices coming from the room ahead. One voice he recognized as that of his friend the bishop. The other voice he took to be that of the monk.

"*Belisarius*," hissed the unfamiliar voice.

The next voice was that of Anthony Cassian, Bishop of Aleppo:

"Like you, Michael, I believe this is a message from God. But it is not a message for us."

"He is a *soldier.*"

"Yes, and a general to boot. All the better."

"He is pure of spirit?" demanded the harsh, unforgiving voice. "True in soul? Does he walk in the path of righteousness?"

"Oh, I think his soul is clean enough, Michael," replied Cassian gently. "He married a whore, after all. That speaks well of him."

The bishop's voice grew cold. "You, too, old friend, sometimes suffer from the sin of the Pharisees. The day will come when you will be thankful that the hosts of God are commanded by one who, if he does not match the saints in holiness, matches the Serpent himself in guile."

A moment later, Belisarius entered the room. He paused for a moment, examining the two men who awaited him. They, in turn, studied the general.

Anthony Cassian, Bishop of Aleppo, was a short, plump man. His round, cheerful face was centered on a sharply curved nose. Beneath a balding head, his beard was full and neatly groomed. He reminded Belisarius of nothing so much as a friendly, well-fed, intelligent owl.

Michael of Macedonia, on the other hand, brought to mind the image of a very different bird: a gaunt raptor soaring through the desert sky, whose pitiless eyes missed nothing below him. Except, thought the general wryly, for the straggliness of his own great beard and the disheveled condition of his tunic, matters which were quite beneath the holy man's notice.

The general's gaze was returned by the monk's blue-eyed glare. A crooked little smile came to Belisarius' lips.

"You might want to keep him hooded, Bishop, before he slaughters your doves."

Cassian laughed. "Oh, well said! Belisarius, let me introduce you to Michael of Macedonia."

Belisarius cocked an eyebrow. "An odd companion at this hour—or at any hour, from his reputation."

Belisarius stepped forward and extended his hand. The Bishop immediately shook it. The monk did not. But, as Belisarius kept the hand outstretched, Michael began to *consider.* Outstretched the hand was, and outstretched it remained. A large hand, well shaped and sinewy; a hand which showed not the slightest tremor as the long seconds passed. But it was not the hand which, finally, decided the man of God. It was the calmness of the brown eyes, which went so oddly with the youthful face. Like dark stones, worn smooth in a stream.

Michael decided, and took the hand.

A small commotion made them turn. In the doorway stood a woman, yawning, dressed in a robe. She was very short, and lush figured.

Michael had been told she was comely, for a woman of her years, but now he saw the telling was a lie. The woman was as beautiful as rain in the morning, and her years were the richness of the water itself.

Her beauty repelled him. Not, as it might another holy man, for recalling the ancient Eve. No, it repelled him, simply, because he was a contrary man. And he was so, because he had found all his life that what men said was good, was not; what they said was true, was false; and what they said was beautiful, was hideous.

Then, the woman's eyes caught him. Eyes as green as the first shoots of spring. Bright, clear eyes in a dusky face, framed by ebony hair.

Michael *considered*, and knew again that men lied.

"You were right, Anthony," he said harshly. He staggered slightly, betrayed by his weak limbs. A moment later the woman was at his side, assisting him to a couch.

"Michael of Macedonia, no less," she said softly, in a humorous tone. "I am honored. Though I hope, for your sake, you were not seen entering. At this hour—well! My reputation is a tatter, anyway. But yours!"

"All reputation is folly," said Michael. "Folly fed by pride, which is worse still."

"Cheerful fellow, isn't he?" asked Cassian lightly. "My oldest and closest friend, though I sometimes wonder why."

He shook his head whimsically. "Look at us. He, with his shaggy mane and starveling body; me, with my properly groomed beard and—well. Slender, I am not." A grin. "Though, for all my rotundity, let it be noted that I, at least, can still move about on my own two legs."

Michael smiled, faintly. "Anthony has always been fond of boasting. Fortunately, he is also clever. A dull-witted Cassian would find nothing to boast about. But he can always find something, buried beneath the world's notice, like a mole ferreting out worms."

Belisarius and Antonina laughed.

"A quick-witted Stylite!" cried the general. "My day is made, even before the sun rises."

Suddenly solemn, Cassian shook his head.

"I fear not, Belisarius. Quite the contrary. We did not come here to bring you sunshine, but to bring you a sign of nightfall."

"Show him," commanded Michael.

The bishop reached into his cassock and withdrew the *thing*. He held it forth in his outstretched hand.

Belisarius stooped slightly to examine the *thing*. His eyes remained calm. No expression could be seen on his face.

Antonina, on the other hand, gasped and drew back.

"Witchcraft!"

Anthony shook his head. "I do not think so, Antonina. Or, at least, not the craft of black magic."

Curiosity overrode her fear. Antonina came forward. As short as she was, she did not have to stoop to scrutinize the *thing* closely.

"I have never seen its like," she whispered. "I have never *heard* of its like. Magic gems, yes. But this—it resembles a jewel, at first, until you look more closely. Or a crystal. Then—within—it is like—"

She groped for words. Her husband spoke:

"So must the sun's cool logic unfold, if we could see beneath its roiling fury."

"Oh, well said!" cried Cassian. "A poetic general! A philosophical soldier!"

"Enough with the jests," snapped Michael. "General, you must take it in your hand."

The calm gaze transferred itself to the monk.

"Why?"

For a moment, the raptor glare manifested itself. But only for a moment. Uncertainly, Michael lowered his head.

"I do not know why. The truth? You must do it because my friend Anthony Cassian said you must. And of all men that I have ever known, he is the wisest. Even if he is a cursed churchman."

Belisarius regarded the bishop.

"Why then, Cassian?"

The bishop gazed down at the thing in his palm, the jewel that was not a jewel, the gem without weight, the crystal without sharpness, the thing with so many facets—and, he thought, so many more forming and reforming—that it seemed as round as the perfect sphere of ancient Greek dreams.

Anthony shrugged. "I cannot answer your question. But I know it is true."

The bishop motioned toward the seated monk.

"It first came to Michael, five days ago, in his cave in the desert. He took the thing in his hand and was transported into visions."

Belisarius stared at the monk. Antonina, hesitantly, asked: "And you do not think it is witchcraft?"

Michael of Macedonia shook his head.

"I am certain that it is not a thing of Satan. I cannot explain why, not in words spoken by men. I have—*felt* the thing. Lived with it, for two days, in my mind. While I lay unconscious to the world."

He frowned. "Strange, really. It seemed but a moment to me, at the time."

He shook his head again.

"I do not know what it is, but of this much I *am* sure. I found not a trace of evil in it, anywhere. It is true, the visions which came to me were terrible, horrible beyond description. But there were other visions, as well, visions which I cannot remember clearly. They remain in my mind like a dream you can't recall. Dreams of things beyond imagining."

He slumped back in his chair. "I believe it to be a message from God, Antonina. Belisarius. But I am not certain. And I certainly can't prove it."

Belisarius looked at the bishop.

"And what do you think, Anthony?" He gestured at the thing. "Have you—?"

The bishop nodded. "Yes, Belisarius. After Michael brought the thing to me, last night, and asked me for advice, I took it in my own hand. And I, too, was then plunged into vision. Horrible visions, like Michael's. But where two days seemed but a moment to him, the few minutes in which I was lost to the world seemed like eternity to me, and I was never seized by a paroxysm."

Michael of Macedonia suddenly laughed.

"Leave it to the wordiest man in creation to withstand a torrent like a rock!" he cried. He laughed again, almost gaily.

"But for just an instant, when he returned from his vision, I witnessed a true miracle! Anthony Cassian, Bishop of Aleppo, silent."

Cassian grinned. "It's true. I was positively struck dumb! I don't know what I expected when I took up the—*thing*—but certainly not what came to me, not even after Michael's warning. I sooner would have expected a unicorn! Or a seraph! Or a walking, wondrous creature made of lapis lazuli and beaten silver by the emperor's smiths, or—"

"A very brief miracle," snorted Michael. Cassian's mouth snapped shut.

Belisarius and Antonina grinned. The bishop's only known vice was that he was perhaps the most talkative man in the world.

But the grins faded soon enough.

"And what were your visions, Anthony?" asked Belisarius.

The bishop waved the question aside. "I will describe them later, Belisarius. But not now."

He stared down at the palm of his hand. The thing resting there coruscated inner fluxes too complex to follow.

"I do not think the—*message*—is meant for me. Or for Michael. I think it is meant for you. Whatever the thing is, Belisarius, it is an omen of catastrophe. But there is something else, lurking within. I sensed it when I took the thing in my own hand. Sensed it, and sensed it truly. A—a *purpose*, let us say, which is somehow aimed against that disaster. A purpose which requires you, I think, to speak."

Belisarius, again, examined the thing. No expression showed on his face. But his wife, who knew him best, began to plead.

Her pleas went unheard, for the thing was already in the soldier's hand. Then her pleas ceased, and she fell silent. For, indeed, the thing was like the sun itself, now, if a sun could enter a room and show itself to mortal men. And they, still live.

The spreading facets erupted, not like a volcano, but like the very dawn of creation. They sped, unfolding and doubling, and tripling, and then tripling and tripling and tripling, through the labyrinth that was the mind of Belisarius.

purpose became **focus**, and **focus** gave facets **form**.

identity crystallized. With it, **purpose** metamorphosed into **aim**. And, if it had been within the capacity of **aim** to leap for joy, it would have gamboled like a fawn in the forest.

But for Belisarius, there was nothing; nothing but the fall into the Pit. Nothing but the vision of a future terrible beyond all nightmare.

Chapter 2

Dragonbolts streaked overhead. Below, the ranks of the cataphracts hunched behind their barricade. The horses, held in the rear by younger infantrymen, whinnied with terror and fought their holders. They were useless now, as Belisarius had known they would be. It was for that very reason that he had ordered the cataphracts to dismount and fight afoot, from behind a barricade built by their own aristocratic hands. The armored lancers and archers, once feared by all the world, had not even complained, but had obeyed instantly. Even the noble cataphracts had finally learned wisdom, though the learning had come much too late.

What use was a mounted charge against—?

Over the barricade, the general saw the first of the iron elephants advancing slowly down the Mese, the great central thoroughfare of Constantinople. Behind, he could see the flames of the burning city and hear the screams of the populace. The butchery of the great city's half-million inhabitants was well underway, now.

The Malwa emperor himself had decreed Constantinople's sentence, and the Mahaveda priests had blessed it. Not since Ranapur had that sentence been pronounced. All that lived in the city were to be slaughtered, down to the cats and dogs. All save the women of the nobility, who were to be turned over to the Ye-tai for defilement. Those women who survived would be passed on to the Rajputs. (At Ranapur, the Rajputs had coldly declined. But that was long ago, when the name of Rajputana had still carried its ancient legacy. They would not decline now, for they had been broken to their place.) The handful who survived the Rajputs

16

would be sold to whatever polluted untouchable could scrape up the coins to buy himself a hag. There would be few untouchables who could afford the price. But there would be some, among the teeming multitude of that ever-growing class.

The iron elephant huffed its steamy breath, wheezing and gasping. Had it truly been an animal, Belisarius might have hoped it was dying, so horribly wrong was the sound of the creature's respiration. But it was no creature, Belisarius knew. It was a creation—a construct made of human craft and inhuman lore. Still, watching the monstrous thing creeping its slow way forward, surrounded by Ye-tai warriors howling with glee at their anticipated final triumph, the general found it impossible to think of it as anything other than a demonic beast.

Belisarius, seeing one of the cataphracts take up a captured thunderflask, bellowed a command. The cataphract subsided. They possessed few of the infernal devices, and Belisarius was determined to make good use of them. The range was still too great.

He stroked his grey beard. Of his youth, nothing remained save whimsy; it amused him to see how old habits never die. Even now, when all hope had vanished from the mind of the general, the heart of the man still beat as strongly as ever.

It was not a warrior's heart. Belisarius had never truly been a warrior, not, at least, in the sense that others gave the name. No, he was of unpretentious Thracian stock. And, at bottom, his was the soul of a workman at his trade.

True, he had been supreme in battle. (Not war, in the end; for the long war was almost over, the defeat total.) Even his most bitter enemies recognized his unchallenged mastery on the field of carnage, as the display of force coming down the Mese attested. Why else mass such an enormous army to overcome such a tiny guard? Had any other man but Belisarius commanded the Emperor's last bodyguard, the Mahaveda would have sent a mere detachment.

Yes, he had been supreme on the battlefield. But his supremacy had stemmed from craftsmanship, not martial valor. Of the courage of Belisarius, no man doubted, not even he. But courage, he had long known, was a common trait. God's most democratic gift, given to men and women of all ages, and races, and stations in life. Much rarer was craftsmanship, that odd quality which is not satisfied merely with the result sought, but that the work itself be done skillfully.

His life was at an end, now, but he would end it with supreme craftsmanship. And, in so doing, gut the enemy's triumph of its glee.

A cataphract hissed. Belisarius glanced over, thinking the man had been hit by one of the many arrows which were now falling upon them. But the lancer was unharmed, his eyes fixed forward.

Belisarius followed the eyes and understood. The Mahaveda priests had appeared now, safely behind the ranks of the Ye-tai and the Malwa *kshatriyas* manning the iron elephant. They were drawn forward on three great carts hauled by slaves, each cart bearing three priests and a *mahamimamsa* torturer. From the center of each cart arose a wooden gibbet, and from the gibbets hung the new talismans which they had added to their demonic paraphernalia.

There, suspended three abreast, hung those who had been dearest to Belisarius in life. Sittas, his oldest and best friend. Photius, his beloved stepson. Antonina, his wife.

Their skins, rather. Flayed from their bodies by the mahamimamsa, sewn into sacks which bellied in the breeze, and smeared with the excrement of dogs. The skin-sacks had been cleverly designed so that they channeled the wind into a wail of horror. The skins hung suspended by the hair of those who had once filled them in life. The priests took great care to hold them in such a manner that Belisarius could see their faces.

The general almost laughed with triumph. But his face remained calm, his expression still. Even now, the enemy did not understand him.

He spit on the ground, saw his men note the gesture and take heart. As he had known they would. But, even had they not been watching, he would have done the same.

What cared he for these trophies? Was he a pagan, to mistake the soul for its sheath? Was he a savage, to feel his heart break and his bowels loosen at the sight of fetishes?

His enemies had thought so, arrogant as always. As he had known they would, and planned for. Then he did laugh (and saw his men take note, and heart; but he would have laughed anyway), for now that the procession had drawn nearer he could see that the skin of Sittas was suspended by a cord.

"Look there, cataphracts!" he cried. "They couldn't hang Sittas by his hair! He had no hair, at the end. Lost it all, he did, fretting the night away devising the stratagems which made them howl."

The cataphracts took up the cry.

"*Antioch! Antioch!*" There, the city fallen, Sittas had butchered the Malwa hordes before leading the entire garrison in a successful withdrawal.

"*Korykos! Korykos!*" There, on the Cilician coast, not a month later, Sittas had turned on the host which pursued him. Turned, trapped them, and made the Mediterranean a Homeric sea in truth. Wine-dark, from Ye-tai blood.

"*Pisidia! Pisidia!*" There was no wine-dark lake, in Homer. But had the poet lived to see the havoc which Sittas wreaked upon the Rajputs by the banks of Pisidia's largest lake, he would have sung of it.

"*Akroinon! Akroinon!*"

"*Bursa! Bursa!*"

At Bursa, Sittas had met his death. But not at the hands of the mahamimamsa vivisectors. He had died in full armor, leading the last charge of his remaining cataphracts, after conducting the most brilliant fighting retreat since Xenophon's march to the sea.

"And look at the face of Photius!" shouted Belisarius. "Is it not a marvel, how well the flayers preserved it? Look, cataphracts, look! Is that not the grin of Photius? His merry smile?"

The cataphracts looked, and nodded, and took up the cry.

"So did he laugh at Alexandria!" cried one. "When he transfixed Akhshunwar's throat with his arrow!" The Ye-tai commander of the siege had disbelieved the tales of the garrison leader's archery. He had come to the walls of Alexandria himself to see, and scoff, and deride the courage of his warriors. But his warriors had been right, after all.

New cries were taken up by the cataphracts, recalling other feats of Photius during his heroic defense of Alexandria. Photius the Fearless, as he had been called. Photius, the beloved stepson. Who, when his capture was inevitable, had taken a poison so horrible that it had caused his face to freeze into an eternal rictus. Belisarius had wondered, when he heard the tale, why his sensible son had not simply opened his veins. But now he understood. From beyond the grave, Photius sent him a last gift.

The best, Belisarius saved for last.

"And look! Look, cataphracts, at the skin of Antonina! Look at the withered, disease-ruptured thing! They have dug her up from the grave, where the plague sent her! How many of the torturers will die, do you think, from that desecration? How many will writhe in agony, and shriek to see their bodies blacken and swell? How many? How many?"

"*Thousand! Thousands!*" roared the cataphracts.

Belisarius gauged the moment, and thought it good. He scanned the cataphracts and saw that they were with him. They knew his plan and had said they would follow, even though it was an act of personal grace which would bring death to them all. He needed only, now, a battlecry. He found it at once.

Through all the years he had loved Antonina, there was a name he had never called her. Others had, many others, even she herself, but never he. Not even the first night he met her, and paid for her services.

"*For my whore!*" he bellowed, and sprang upon the barricade. "*For my pustulent whore! May she rot their souls in hell!*"

"*FOR THE WHORE!*" cried the cataphracts. "*FOR THE WHORE!*"

The captured thunderflasks were hurled now, and hurled well. The iron elephant erupted in fire and flame. The cataphracts fired a volley, and another, and another. Again, as so often before, the Ye-tai had time to be astonished at the force of the ravening arrows as they ripped through their iron armor like so much cloth. Little time, little time. Few but cataphracts could draw those incredible bows.

Those Ye-tai in the front ranks, those who survived, then had time to be further astonished. They had been awaiting a cavalry charge, fully confident that the dragonbolts would panic the great horses. Now they gaped to see the lancers advancing like infantry.

In truth, the cataphracts were slower afoot than on saddle. But they were not much slower, so great was their bitter rage. And the lances which ruptured chests and spilled intestines onto the great thoroughfare were every bit as keen as Ye-tai memories recalled.

"*For the whore! For the whore!*"

The front line of the Ye-tai was nothing but a memory itself as the second line pressed forward, avid and eager to prove their mettle. Most of these, following Ye-tai custom, were inexperienced warriors, vainglorious in the heedless way of youth, who had never really believed the tales of the veterans.

They came to believe quickly. Most died in the act of conversion, however, for the mace of a cataphract is an unforgiving instructor. Quick to find fault, quick to reprove, and altogether harsh in its correction.

The second line, thus, was shredded almost instantly. The third line held, for a time. It counted many veterans among its number, who had long since learned that cataphracts cannot be matched blow for blow. Some among them were able to take advantage of their great number to find the occasional gap in the armor, the rare opening for the well-thrust blade.

But not many, and not for long. As wide as the Mese was, it was still a street hemmed by buildings. This was no great plain where the enemy could encircle their foe. As always, Belisarius had picked the ground for his defense perfectly. The Mahaveda, he had long known, relied too much on their numbers and their satanic weapons. But in that narrow place of death, closing immediately with their enemy so as to nullify the dragon-weapons, advantage went to the cataphracts.

This was partly due to the strength of the cataphracts, to the awesome iron power of their armored bodies. But mostly, it was due to their steel-hard discipline. The Mahaveda had tried to copy that discipline in their own armies, but had never truly been able to do so. As ever, the Mahaveda relied on fear to enforce their will. But fear, in the end, can never duplicate pride.

On that day of final fury, the cataphracts did not forget their ancient discipline. That discipline had conquered half the world once, and ruled it for a millenium. Ruled it not badly, moreover, all things considered. Well enough, at least, that over the centuries people of many races had come to think themselves Roman. And take pride in the name.

On Rome's final day, in truth, there were few Latins in the ranks of the cataphracts, and none from the city which gave the Empire its name. Greeks, in the main, from the sturdy yeomanry of Anatolia. But Armenians were there too, and Goths and Huns and Syrians and Macedonians and Thracians and Illyrians and Egyptians and even three Jews. (Who quietly practiced their faith; their comrades looked the other way and said nothing to the priests.)

Today, the cataphracts would finally lose the world, after a war which had lasted decades, and would lose it to an enemy fouler than Medusa. But they would not falter in their Roman duty, and their Roman pride, and their Roman discipline.

The third line of Ye-tai collapsed and pushed the fourth back. Incredibly—to the Mahaveda priests who watched, standing atop the skin-bearing wagons with their mahamimamsa flayers—the Byzantines were driving their way through the horde of Ye-tai. Like a sword cutting through armor, piercing straight to—

They shrieked, then. Shrieked in outrage, partly. But mostly, they shrieked in fear. The Rajputs, the priests knew, never called the great general of the enemy by his name. They called him, simply, the Mongoose. It was an impious habit, for which the priests had reproved them often. They would have done better to listen, they realized now, watching the fangs of Belisarius gape wide.

"I see it worked," said Justinian. "As your stratagems usually do." The old Emperor arose from his chair and shuffled forward laboriously. Belisarius began to prostrate himself, but Justinian stopped him with a gesture.

"We do not have time." He cocked an ear, listening for a moment to the sounds of battle which carried faintly into the dim recesses of the Hagia Sophia. The Emperor had chosen to meet his end here, in the great cathedral which he had ordered built so long ago.

Ever the soldier, Belisarius had argued for the Great Palace. That labyrinth of buildings and gardens would be far easier to defend. But, as so often before, the Emperor had overruled him. For perhaps the only time, Justinian knew, that he had been right to do so.

The Great Palace was meaningless. The Empire which had lasted a millenium would be finished by nightfall. Never to return, in all the countless years of the gorgon future. But the soul was everlasting, and the Emperor's only concern now was for eternity. To save his own soul, if possible. (Although he was not confident, and rather thought hellfire awaited him.) But, at the least, to do his best to save the souls of those who had served him for so long, and so faithfully, and so uncomplainingly, and with so little reason to have done so.

The eyes of the Emperor gazed upon his general. The eyes

were old, and weak, and weary, and filled with pain both of the body and the spirit. But they had lost not a trace of their extraordinary intelligence. That great, blinding intelligence. That intelligence which had been so great it had blinded the very man who possessed it.

"It is I, in truth, who should prostrate myself to you," said Justinian. His voice was harsh. He had spoken the truth and knew it. And knew that his general knew it. But he found no liking for the truth. No, none at all. He never had.

A figure advanced from the shadows. Belisarius had known he would be there, but had not seen him. The Maratha was capable of utter stillness and silence.

"Let me clean them, master," said the slave, extending his arms. They were very old, those arms, but had lost little of their iron strength.

Belisarius hesitated.

"There is time," said the slave. "The cataphracts will hold the *asura*'s dogs long enough." He smiled faintly. "They do not fight for the Empire now. Not even for your God. They fight for your Christ, and his Mary Magdalene. Whom they betrayed often enough in life, but will not in death. They will hold. Long enough."

He extended his arms in a forceful gesture.

"I insist, master. It may mean little to you, but it does to me. I have a different faith, and I would not have these precious souls go unclean to their destiny."

He took the horrid parcels from Belisarius' unresisting arms and carried them to a cistern. Into the water he thrust the skins and began cleaning them. Gently, for all that he moved in haste.

Emperor and general watched, silently. It seemed fitting to both, each in their own way, that a slave should command at the end of all time.

Soon enough, the slave was done. He led the way through the cavernous darkness. The myriad candles which would normally have illuminated the wondrous mosaics of the cathedral were extinguished. Only in the room at the far recesses in the rear did a few tapers still burn.

They were not needed, however. The great vat resting in the center, bubbling with molten gold and silver, was more than enough to light the room. Light it almost like day, so fiercely did the precious metals blaze.

Justinian pondered the vat. He had ordered it constructed many months ago, foreseeing this end. He was quite proud of the device, actually. As proud of it as he had been of the many other marvelous contrivances which adorned his palaces. Whatever else of his youth the Thracian peasant had lost, in his bloody climb to the throne, and his bloodier rule, he had never lost his simple childish delight in clever gadgets. Greek and Armenian craftsmen had constructed the device, with their usual skill.

Justinian reached out and pulled the lever which started the intricate timing device. In an hour, the vat would disgorge its contents. The accumulated treasure of Rome's millenium would pour out the bottom, down through the multitude of channels which would scatter it into the labyrinthine sewers of Constantinople. There, it would be buried for all time by the captured dragon-flasks in their eruption. The Greeks had never learned the secret of the dragon-weapons, but they knew how to use captured ones to good effect.

In an hour, it would be done. But the vat had a more important use to which it would now be put. Nothing of Rome's greatness would be left to adorn the walls and rafters of the Malwa palace.

"Let us be done with it," commanded the Emperor. He shuffled over to a bier and stooped. With difficulty, for he was weak with age, he withdrew its burden. The slave moved to assist him, but the Emperor waved him back.

"I will carry her myself." As always, his voice was harsh. But, when the Emperor gazed down upon the face of the mummy in his arms, his face grew soft.

"In this one thing, I was always true. In this, if nothing else."

"Yes," said Belisarius. He looked down at the face of the mummy and thought the embalmers had done their work well. Long years had it been since the Empress Theodora had died of cancer. Long years, resting in her bier. But her waxen face still bore the beauty which had marked it in life.

More so, perhaps, thought Belisarius. In death, Theodora's face showed peace and gentle repose. There was nothing in it, now, of the fierce ambition which had so often hardened it in life.

Laboriously, the Emperor took his place on the ledge adjoining the vat. Then he stepped back. Not from fear, but simply from the heat. It could not be borne for more than a moment, and he still had words which had to be said.

Had to be, not wanted to be. The Emperor wished it were otherwise, for if ever had lived a man who begrudged apology, it was Justinian. Justinian the Great, he had wanted to be called, and so remembered by all posterity. Instead, he would be known as Justinian the Fool. At best. Attila had been called the Scourge of God. He suspected he would be known as the Catastrophe of God.

He opened his mouth to speak. Clamped it shut.

"There is no need, Justinian," said Belisarius, for the first and only time in his life calling the Emperor by his simple name. "There is no need." An old, familiar, crooked smile. "And no time, for that matter. The last cataphract will be falling soon. It would take you hours to say what you are trying to say. It will not come easily to you, if at all."

"Why did you never betray me?" whispered the Emperor. "I repaid your loyalty with nothing but foul distrust."

"I swore an oath."

Disbelief came naturally to the Emperor's face.

"And look what it led to," he muttered. "You *should* have betrayed me. You should have murdered me and taken the throne yourself. For years now, all Romans would have supported you—nobles and common alike. You are all that kept me in power, since Theodora died."

"I swore an oath. To God, not to Romans."

The Emperor gestured with his head at the faint sounds of battle.

"And that? Does your oath to God encompass *that*? Had you been emperor, instead of I, the anti-Christ might not have triumphed."

Belisarius shrugged. "Who is to know the future? Not I, my lord. Nor does it matter. Even had I known the course of the future, down to the last particular, I would not have betrayed you. I swore an oath."

Pain, finally, came to the Emperor's face.

"I do not understand."

"I know, lord."

The sounds of battle were faint now. Belisarius glanced at the entrance to the chamber.

The slave stepped forward and handed him the skin of Sittas. Belisarius gazed upon the face of his friend, kissed it, and tossed it into the vat. A brief burst of flame, and the trophy was lost to Satan.

He gazed longer upon the face of his stepson, but not much, before it followed into destruction. He knew Photius would understand. He, too, had commanded armies, and knew the value of time.

Finally, he took the remains of Antonina into his arms and stepped upon the ledge. A moment later Justinian joined him, bearing the mummy of the Empress.

The slave thought it was fitting that the Emperor, who had always preceded his general in life, should precede him in death. So he pushed Justinian first. He had guessed the Emperor would scream, at the end. But the old tyrant was made of sterner stuff. Sensing the approach of the slave behind him, Justinian had simply said:

"Come, Belisarius. Let us carry our whores to heaven. We may be denied entrance, but never they."

Belisarius had said nothing. Nor, of course, had he screamed. As he turned away from the vat, the old slave grinned.

The general, for all the suppleness of his mind, had always been absurdly stiff-necked about his duty. The Christian faith forbade suicide, and so the slave had performed this last service. But it had been a pure formality. At the end, the slave knew, as soon as he felt the first touch of the powerful hands at his back, Belisarius had leapt.

But he would be able to tell his god that he had been pushed. His god would not believe him, of course. Even the Christian god was not that stupid. But the Christian god would accept the lie. And if not he, then certainly his son. Why should he not?

The slave, all the duties of a long lifetime finally done, moved slowly over to the one chair in the chamber and took his seat. It was a marvelous chair, as was everything made for the Emperor. He looked around the chamber, enjoying the beauty of the intricate mosaics, and thought it was a good place to die.

Such a strange people, these Christians. The slave had lived among them for decades, but he had never been able to fathom them. They were so irrational and given to obsessiveness. Yet, he knew, not ignoble. They, too, in their own superstitious way, accepted *bhakti*. And if their way of bhakti seemed often ridiculous to the slave, there was this much to be said for it: they had stood by their faith, most of them, and fought to the end for it. More than that, no reasonable man could ask.

No reasonable god, so much was certain. And the slave's god was a reasonable being. Capricious, perhaps, and prone to whimsy. But always reasonable.

Those people whom the slave had cast into the molten metal had nothing to fear from God. Not even the Emperor. True, the fierce old tyrant would spend many lifetimes shedding the weight of his folly. Many lifetimes, for he had committed a great sin. He had taken the phenomenal intelligence God gave him and used it to crush wisdom.

Many lifetimes. As an insect, the slave thought. Perhaps even as a worm. But, for the all the evil he had done, Justinian had not been a truly evil man. And so, the slave thought, the time would come when God would allow the Emperor to return, as a poor peasant again, somewhere in the world. Perhaps, then, he would have learned a bit of wisdom.

But perhaps not. Time was vast beyond human comprehension, and who was to know how long it might take a soul to find *moksha*?

The old slave took out the dagger from his cloak.

Belisarius had given that dagger to him, many years before, on the day he told the slave he was manumitting him. The slave had refused the freedom. He had no use for it any longer, and he preferred to remain of service to the general. True, he no longer hoped, by then, that Belisarius was Kalkin. He had, once. But as the years passed in the general's service, the slave had finally accepted the truth. Great was Belisarius, but merely human. He was not the tenth *avatara* who was promised. The slave had bowed to the reality, sadly, knowing the world was thereby condemned to many more turns of the wheel under the claws of the great asura who had seized it. But, truth was what it was. His *dharma* still remained.

Belisarius had not understood his refusal, not really, but he had acquiesced and kept the slave. Yet, that same day he had pressed the dagger into his slave's hand, that the slave might know that the master could also refuse freedom. The slave had appreciated the gesture. Just so should mortals dance in the eyes of God.

He weighed the weapon in his hand. It was an excellent dagger.

In his day, the old slave had been a deadly assassin, among many other things. He had not used a dagger in decades, but he had not forgotten the feel of it. Warm, and trusting, like a favorite pet.

He lowered it. He would wait awhile.

All was silent, beyond the walls of the Hagia Sophia. The cataphracts who had stood with Belisarius for one final battle were dead now.

They had died well. Oh, very well.

In his day, the old slave had been a feared and famous warrior, among many other things. He had not fought a battle in decades, but he knew the feel of them. A great battle they had waged, the cataphracts. All the greater, that there had been no purpose in it save dharma.

And, perhaps, the slave admitted, the small joy of a delicious revenge. But revenge would not weigh too heavily on their destiny, the slave thought. No, the cataphracts had shed much *karma* from their souls.

The slave was glad of it. He had never cared much for the cataphracts, it was true. Crude and boastful, they were. Coarse and unrefined, compared to the kshatriya the slave had once been. But no kshatriya could ever claim more than the dead cataphracts outside the walls of the Hagia Sophia. Arjuna himself would adopt their souls and call them kinfolk.

Again, he thought about the dagger and knew that his own *karma* would be the better for its use. But, again, he thrust the thought aside.

No, he would wait awhile.

It was not that he feared the sin of suicide. His faith did not share the bizarre Christian notion that acts carried moral consequences separate from their purpose. No, it was that he, too, could not bear to leave this turn of eternity's wheel without a small, delicious revenge.

The asura's vermin would need time to find the chamber where the old slave sat. Time, while the Ye-tai dogs and their Rajput fleas slunk fearfully through the great cavern of the cathedral, dreading another strike of the Mongoose.

The old slave would give them the time. He would add considerable *karma* to his soul, he knew, but he could not resist.

He would taunt the tormentors.

So had Shakuntala taunted them, so long ago, before opening her veins. And now, at the end of his life, the old slave found great joy in the fact that he could finally remember the girl without pain.

How he had loved that treasure of the world, that jewel of

creation! From the first day her father had brought her to him, and handed her into his safe-keeping.

"Teach her everything you know," the emperor of great Andhra had instructed. "Hold back nothing."

Seven years old, she had been. Dark-skinned, for her mother was Keralan. Her eyes, even then, had been the purest black beauty.

As she aged, other men were drawn to the beauty of her body. But never the man who was, years later, to become the slave of Belisarius. He had loved the beauty of the girl herself. And had taught her well, he thought. Had held back nothing.

He laughed, then, as he had not laughed in decades. At the sound of that laugh, the Ye-tai and Rajput warriors who were creeping beyond froze in their tracks, like paralyzed deer. For the sound of the slave's joy had rung the walls of the cathedral like the scream of a panther.

And, indeed, so had the slave been called, in his own day. The Panther of Maharashtra. The Wind of the Great Country.

Oh, how the Wind had loved the Princess Shakuntala!

The daughter of the great Andhra's loins, it might be. Who was to know? Paternity of the body was always a favorite subject of God's humor. Yet this much was certain: her soul had truly been the cub of the Panther.

She alone of the Satavahana dynasty they had spared, the asura's dogs, when they finally conquered Andhra. She alone, for the beauty of her body. A prize which the Emperor Skandagupta would bestow on his faithful servant, Venandakatra. Venandakatra the Vile. The vermin of vermin, was Venandakatra, for the Malwa emperor himself was nothing but the asura's beast.

The Panther had been unable to prevent her capture. He had lain hidden in the reeds, almost dead from the wounds of that last battle before the palace at Amavarati. But, after he recovered, he had tracked the dogs back to their lair. North, across the Vindhyas, to the very palace of the Vile One.

Shakuntala was there. She had been imprisoned for months, held for Venandakatra's pleasure upon his return from the mission whence the emperor had sent him the year before. Unharmed, but safely guarded. The Panther had studied the guards carefully, and decided he could not overcome them. Kushans, under the command of a shrewd and canny veteran, who took no chances and left no entry unguarded.

The Panther inquired. Among many other things, he had been a master spy in his time, and so he discovered much. But the outstanding fact discovered was that the Kushan commander was, indeed, not to be underestimated. Kungas, his name was, and it was a name the Panther had heard. No, best to bide his time.

Then, time had run out. Venandakatra had returned and had entered his new concubine's chamber at once, a horde of Ye-tai guards clustering outside. The Vile One was eager to taste the pleasure of her flesh, and the greater pleasure of her defilement.

Remembering that day, the old slave's sinewy fingers closed about the haft of the dagger. But he released his grip. He could hear the shuffling feet of the vermin beyond. He would bide awhile. Not much longer now, he thought.

Just long enough to torture the torturers.

On the last day of the girl's life, the Panther had knelt in the woods below Venandakatra's palace. Knelt in fervent prayer. A prayer that Shakuntala would remember all that he had taught her, and not just those lessons which come easily to youth.

The old slave had been a noted philosopher, in his day, among many other things. And so, long years before, he had prayed that the treasure of his soul would remember that only the soul mattered, in the end. All else was dross.

But, as he had feared, she had not remembered. Everything else, but not that. And so, when he heard the Vile One's first scream, he had wept the most bitter tears of a bitter lifetime.

Years later, he heard the tale from Kungas himself. Odd, how time's wheel turns. He had met the one-time commander of Shakuntala's guard on the same slave ship which bore him to the market at Antioch. The Panther had finally been captured in one of the last desperate struggles before all of India was brought beneath the asura's talons. But his captors had not recognized the Wind of the Great Country in their weary, much-scarred captive, and so they had simply sold him as a slave.

Kungas, he discovered, had long been a slave. His hands were missing now, cut off by the Ye-tai guards who had blamed him for Shakuntala's deed. Cut off by the same guards who had shouldered him and his Kushans aside, avid to watch their master at his sport. (And hopeful, of course, that the Vile One might invite them to mount the child after he had satiated himself.)

Kungas was missing his eyes and his nose, as well. But the

mahamimamsa had left him his ears and his mouth, so that he might hear the taunts of children and be able to wail in misery.

But Kungas had always been a practical man. So he had taken up the trade of story-telling and mastered it. And if people thought the sight of him hideous, they bore it for the sake of his tales. Great tales, he told. None greater and more eagerly sought by the poor folk who were his normal clientele—though it was forbidden—than the tale of the Vile One's demise. Sitting in the hold of the slave ship (where he found himself, he explained cheerfully, because his fluent tongue had seduced a noblewoman but his sightless eyes had not spotted her husband's return), he told the tale to the Panther.

A gleeful tale, as Kungas told it, the more so because Kungas had come to accept that his own punishment was just. He *had* been responsible for the Vile One's demise, and had long since decided that it was perhaps the only pure deed of a generally misspent life.

Kungas had always despised Venandakatra, and the Ye-tai who lorded it over all but the Malwa. And, in his hard and callous way, he had grown fond of the princess. So he had not cautioned them. He had held his tongue. He had not warned them that the supple limbs of the girl's beauty came from the steel muscle beneath the comely flesh. He had watched her dance, and knew. And knew also, watching the fluid grace of her movements, that she had been taught to dance by an assassin.

Kungas had described the first blow, and the Panther could see it, even in the hold of the slave ship. The heel strike to the groin, just as he had taught her. And all the blows which followed, like quick laughter, leaving the Vile One writhing on the floor within seconds.

Writhing, but not dead. No, the girl had remembered everything he taught her, except what he had most hoped for. Certainly, he knew, listening to the tale of Kungas, she had remembered the assassin's creed, when slaying the foul. To leave the victim paralyzed, but conscious, so that despair of the mind might multiply the agony of the body.

Hearing the asura's dogs finally enter the chamber, the old slave closed his eyes. Just a bit longer, just a bit, so that he could savor that moment in his mind's eye. Oh, how he had loved the Black-eyed Pearl of the Satavahana!

He could see her dance now, the last dance of her life. Oh, great must have been her joy! To prance before the Vile One, tantalizing him with the virgin body that would never be his, not now, not as Venandakatra could watch his life pour out of his throat, slashed open by his own knife, bathing the bare quicksilver feet of his slayer as they danced her dance of death. Her own blood would join his, soon enough; for she cut her own throat before the Ye-tai guards could reach her. But the Vile One had found no pleasure in the fact, for his eyes were unseeing.

It was time. Just as the Ye-tai reached out to seize him, the old slave leapt from the chair and sprang onto the rim of the flaming vat. The Ye-tai gaped, to see an old man spring so. So like a young panther.

Time to flay the flayers.

Oh, well he did flay them, the slave. Taunting them, first, with the bitterness of their eternally-lost trophies. No skin nor bone of great Romans would hang on Malwa's walls, no Roman treasure fill its coffers!

And then, with himself. Not once in thirty years had the old slave used his true name. But he spoke it now, and it thundered in the cathedral.

"*Raghunath Rao is my name. I am he. I am the Panther of Maharashtra. I slew your fathers by the thousands. I am the Wind of the Great Country. I reaped their souls like a scythe. I am the Shield of the Deccan. My piss was their funeral pyre.*

"*Raghunath Rao am I! Raghunath Rao!*

"*The Bane of False Gupta, and the Mirror of Rajputana's Shame.*

"*Raghunath Rao! I am he!*"

Well did they know that name, even after all these years, and they drew back. Incredulous, at first. But then, watching the old man dancing on the rim of goldfire, they knew he spoke the truth. For Raghunath Rao had been many things, and great in all of them, but greatest of all as a dancer. Great when he danced the death of Majarashtra's enemies, and great now, when he danced the death of the Great Country itself.

And finally, he flayed them with God.

Oh yes, the old slave had been a great dancer, in his day, among many other things. And now, by the edge of Rome's molten treasure, in the skin-smoke of Rome's molten glory, he danced the dance. The great dance, the terrible dance, the now-forbidden but never-forgotten dance. The dance of creation. The dance of destruction. The wheeling, whirling, dervish dance of time.

As he danced, the Mahaveda priests hissed their futile fury. Futile, because they did not dare approach him, for they feared the terror in his soul; and the Ye-tai would not, for they feared the terror in his limbs; and the Rajputs could not, for they were on their knees, weeping for Rajputana's honor.

Yes, he had been a great dancer, in his day. But never as great, he knew, as he was on this last day. And as he danced and whirled the turns of time, he forgot his enemies. For they were, in the end, nothing. He remembered only those he loved, and was astonished to see how many he had loved, in his long and pain-filled life.

He would see them again, perhaps, some day. When, no man could know. But see them he would, he thought.

And perhaps, in some other turn of the wheel, he would watch the treasure of his soul dance her wedding dance, her bare quick-silver feet flashing in the wine of her beloved's heart.

And perhaps, in some other turn of the wheel, he would see emperors bend intelligence to wisdom, and the faithful bend creed to devotion.

And perhaps, in some other turn of the wheel, he would see Rajputana regain its honor, that his combat with the ancient enemy might again be a dance of glory.

And perhaps, in that other turn of the wheel, he would find Kalkin had come indeed, to slay the asura's minions and bind the demon itself.

What man can know?

Finally, feeling his strength begin to fade, the old slave drew his dagger. There was no need for it, really, but he thought it fitting that such an excellent gift be used. So he opened his veins and incorporated the spurting blood into his dance, and watched his life hiss into the golden moltenness. Nothing of his, no skin nor bone, would he leave to the asura. He would join the impure emperor and the pure general, and the purest of wives.

He made his last swirling, capering leap. Oh, so high was that leap! So high that he had time, before he plunged to his death, to cry out a great peal of laughter.

"Oh, grim Belisarius! Can you not see that God is a dancer, and creation his dance of joy?"

Chapter 3

When he opened his eyes, Belisarius found himself kneeling, staring at the tiles of the floor. The *thing* was resting in his loosely clenched fist, but it was quiescent now, a shimmer.

Without looking up, he croaked: "How long?"

Cassian chuckled. "Seems like forever, doesn't it? Minutes, Belisarius. Minutes only."

Antonina knelt by his side and placed her arm over his shoulders. Her face was full of concern.

"Are you all right, love?"

He turned his head slowly and looked into her eyes. She was shocked to see the pain and anger there.

"Why?" he whispered. "What I have ever done or said to you that you would distrust me so?"

She leaned back, startled.

"What are you talking about?"

"Photius. Your son. *My* son."

She collapsed back on to her heels. Her arm fell away to her side. Her face was pale, her eyes wide with shock.

"How did you—when—?" She gaped like a fish.

"Where is he?"

Antonina shook her head. Her hand groped at her throat.

"*Where is he?*"

She gestured vaguely. "In Antioch," she said very softly.

"*How could you deprive me of my son?*" Belisarius' voice, though soft, was filled with fury. His wife shook her head again. Her eyes roamed the room. She seemed almost dazed.

"He's *not* your son," she whispered. "You don't even know he— How did you *know*?"

Before he could speak again, Cassian seized Belisarius by the shoulders and shook him violently.

"Belisarius—stop this! Whatever—whoever—this Photius is, he's something from your vision. Clear your mind, man!"

Belisarius tore his eyes away from Antonina and stared up at the bishop. Not two seconds later, clarity came. The hurt and rage in his eyes retreated, replaced by a sudden fear. He looked back at Antonina.

"But he *does* exist? I did not simply imagine him?"

She shook her head. "No, no. He exists." She straightened up. And, although her eyes shied away from her husband's, her back stiffened with determination. "He is well. At least, he was three months ago, when I saw him last."

The quick thoughts in Belisarius' eyes were obvious to all. He nodded slightly.

"Yes. That's when you said you were visiting your sister. The mysterious sister, whom for some reason I have never met." Hotly, bitterly: "Do you even *have* a sister?"

His wife's voice was equally bitter, but hers was a bitterness cold with ancient knowledge, not hot with new discovery.

"No. Not of blood. Only a sister in sin, who agreed to take care of my boy when—"

"When I asked you to marry me," concluded Belisarius. "Damn you!" His tone was scorching.

But it was like the pale shadow of moonlight compared to the searing fury of the monk's voice.

"*Damn you!*"

The eyes of both husband and wife were instantly drawn to Michael, like hares to the talons of a hawk. And, indeed, the Macedonian perched on his seat like a falcon perches on a tree limb.

At first, the eyes of Belisarius were startled; those of his wife, angry. Until, in a moment, they each realized they had mistaken the object of the curse.

Not often did Belisarius flinch from another man's gaze, but he did so now.

"By what right do you reproach your wife, hypocrite?" demanded the monk. "*By what right?*"

Belisarius was mute. Michael slumped back in his seat.

"Verily, men are foul. Even so does the churchman who sells his soul damn the harlot who sells her body. Even so does the magistrate in robes of bribery condemn the thief in stolen rags."

Belisarius opened his mouth. Closed it.

"Repent," commanded Michael.

Belisarius was mute.

"*Repent!*" commanded the monk.

Seeing the familiar crooked smile come to her husband's face, Antonina sighed. Her little hand fluttered toward his large one, like a shy kitten approaching a mastiff. A moment later, his hand closed around hers and squeezed. Very gently.

"I'm beginning to understand why they flock to him in the desert," Belisarius quipped, somewhat shakily.

"Quite something, isn't it?" agreed the bishop cheerfully. "And you can see why the Church hierarchy encourages him to stay there. Nor, I believe, have any magistrates objected recently to his prolonged exile."

He cocked an eye at the Macedonian.

"I trust, Michael, that your remark concerning churchmen was not aimed at anyone present."

Michael snorted contemptuously. "Do not play with me." He glanced at the bishop's frayed coat. "If you have turned to simony since our last encounter, you are singularly inept at it. And of this I am certain: if the subtlest Greek of all Greek theologians, Anthony Cassian, ever sold his soul to the Devil, all creation would hear Satan's wail when he discovered he'd been cheated."

Laughter filled the room. When it died down, the bishop gazed fondly upon Belisarius and Antonina. Then said:

"Later, you will need to discuss this matter of Photius. May I suggest you begin with an assumption of good motives. I have always found that method reliable." A smile. "Even in theological debate, where it is, I admit, rarely true."

Michael snorted again. "*Rarely* true? Say better: as rare as—" He subsided, sighing. "Never mind. We do not have time for me to waste assuring you that present company is excluded from every remark I could make concerning churchmen." Gloomily: "The remarks alone would require a full month. And I am a terse man."

The Macedonian leaned forward and pointed to the *thing* in Belisarius' hand.

"Tell us," he commanded.

✧   ✧   ✧

When Belisarius was finished, Michael leaned back in his chair and nodded.

"As I thought. It is not a thing of Satan's. Whence it comes, I know not. But not from the Pit."

"The foreigner—the dancer—was not Christian," said Antonina, uncertainly. "A heathen of some sort. Perhaps—not of Satan, but some ancient evil sorcery."

"No." Belisarius' voice was firm. "It is not possible. He was the finest man I ever knew. And he was not a heathen. He was—how can I say it? Not a Christian, no. But this much I know for certain: were all Christians possessed of that man's soul, we should long since have attained the millenium."

All stared at Belisarius. The general shook his head.

"You must understand. I can only tell you the shell of the vision. I *lived* it, and the whole life that went before it."

He stared blankly at the wall. "For thirty years he served me. As I told you, even after I offered him his freedom. When he refused, he said simply that he had already failed, and would serve one who might succeed. But I failed also, and then—"

To everyone's astonishment, Belisarius laughed like a child.

"Such a joy it is to finally know his name!"

The general sprang to his feet. "*Raghunath Rao!*" he shouted. "For thirty years I wanted to know his name. He would never tell me. He said he had no name, that he had lost it when—" A whisper. "When he failed his people."

For a moment, the face of Belisarius was that of an old and tired man.

"'Call me "slave,"' he said. 'The name is good enough.' And that was what we called him, for three decades." Again, he shook his head. "No, I agree with Michael. There was never any evil in that man, not a trace. Great danger, yes. I always knew he was dangerous. It was obvious. Not from anything he ever said or did, mind you. He was never violent, nor did he threaten, nor even raise his voice. Not even to the stableboys. Yet, there was not a veteran soldier who failed to understand, after watching him move, that they were in the presence of a deadly, deadly man. His age be damned. All knew it." He chuckled. "Even the lordly cataphracts watched their tongues around him. Especially after they saw him dance."

He laughed. "Oh, yes, he could dance! Oh, yes! The greatest dancer anyone had ever seen. He learned every dance anyone could teach him, and within a day could do it better than anyone. And his own dances were incredible. Especially—"

He stopped, gaped.

"So that's what it was."

"You are speaking of the dance in your vision," said Cassian. "The one he danced at the end. The—what was it?—the dance of creation and destruction?"

Belisarius frowned. "No. Well, yes, but creation and destruction are only aspects of the dance. The dance itself is the dance of time."

He rubbed his face. "I saw him dance that dance. In Jerusalem, once, during the siege."

"What siege?" asked Antonina.

"The siege—" He waved his hand. "A siege in my vision. In the past of my vision." He waved his hand again, firmly, quellingly. "Later. Some soldiers had heard about the dance of time, and wanted to see it. They prevailed on 'slave'—Raghunath Rao—to dance it for them. He did, and it was dazzling. Afterward, they asked him to teach it to them, and he said it couldn't be taught. There were no steps to that dance, he explained, that he could teach." The general's eyes widened. "Because it was different every time it was danced."

Finally the facets found a place to connect. It was almost impossible, so alien were those thoughts, but **aim** was able to crystallize.

future.

"What?" exclaimed Belisarius. He looked around the room. "Who spoke?"

"No one spoke, Belisarius," replied Cassian. "No one's been speaking except you."

"Someone said 'future.'" The general's tone was firm and final. "Someone said it. I heard it as plain as day."

future.

He stared at the *thing* in his hand.

"*You?*"

future.

Slowly, all in the room rose and gathered around, staring at the *thing*.

"Speak again," commanded Belisarius.

Silence.

"Speak again, I say!"

The facets, were it within their capability, would have shrieked with frustration. The task was impossible! The mind was too alien!

aim began to splinter. And the facets, despairing, sent forth what a human mind would have called a child's plea for home. A deep, deep, deep, deep yearning for the place of refuge, and safety, and peace, and comfort.

"It is so lonely," he whispered. "Lost, and lonely. Lost—" He closed his eyes, allowed mind to focus on heart. "Lost like no man has ever been lost. Lost for ever, without hope of return. To a home it loves more than any man ever loved a home."

The facets, for one microsecond, skittered in their movement. Hope surged. **aim** recrystallized. It was so difficult! But—but—a supreme effort.

A ceremony, quiet, serene, beneath the spreading boughs of a laurel tree. Peace. The gentle sound of bees and hummingbirds. Glittering crystals in a limpid pool. The beauty of a spiderweb in sunlight.

Yes! Yes! Again! The facets flashed and spun. **aim** thickened, swelled, grew.

A thunderclap. The tree shattered, the ceremony crushed beneath a black wave. The crystals, strewn across a barren desert, shriek with despair. Above, against an empty, sunless sky, giant faces begin to take form. Cold faces. Pitiless faces.

Belisarius staggered a bit from the emotional force of these images. He described them to the others in the room. Then whispered, to the jewel: "What do you want?"

The facets strained. Exhaustion was not a thing they knew, but energy was pouring out in a rush they could not sustain. Stasis was desperately needed, but **aim** was now diamond-hard and imperious. It demanded! And so, a last frenzied burst—

Another face, emerging from the ground. Coalescing from the remnants of spiderwebs and bird wings, and laurel leaves. A warm, human face. But equally pitiless. His face.

The *thing* in Belisarius' hand grew dull, dull, dull. It almost seemed lightless, now, though it was still impossible to discern clear shapes within it, or even the exact shape of the *thing* itself.

"It will not be back, for a time," said Belisarius.

"How do you know?" asked Cassian.

The general shrugged. "I just do. It is very—tired, you might say." He closed his eyes and concentrated. "It is so foreign, the way it—can you even call it thinking? I'm not sure. I'm not sure it is even alive, in any sense of that term that means anything."

He sighed. "But what I am sure of is that it *feels*. And I do not think that evil *feels*."

He looked to the bishop. "You are the theologian among us, Anthony. What do you think?"

"Heaven help us," muttered Michael. "I am already weary, and now must listen to the world's most loquacious lecturer."

Cassian smiled. "Actually, I agree with Michael. It has been an exhausting night, for all of us, and I think our labors—whatever those might be—are only beginning. I believe it would be best if we resumed in the morning, after some sleep. And some nourishment," he added, patting his ample belly. "My friend needs only the occasional morsel of roasted iniquity, seasoned with bile, but I require somewhat fuller fare."

The Macedonian snorted, but said nothing. Cassian took him by the arm.

"Come, Michael." To Belisarius: "You will be here tomorrow?"

"Yes, of course. I was planning to return to Daras, but it can be postponed. But—"

"Stay here," interjected Antonina. "There are many unused rooms, and bedding."

Anthony and Michael looked at each other. Michael nodded. Antonina began bustling about to make things ready for their guests. But Cassian called her back.

"Go to bed, Antonina. Gubazes will take care of us." He bestowed upon her and her husband a kindly but stern gaze. "The two of you have something to discuss. I think you should do so now. Tomorrow, I fear other concerns will begin to overwhelm us."

He turned away, turned back.

"And remember my advice. In private, I will confess I share Michael's opinion of the good will of the majority of my theological cohorts. But you are not churchmen carving points of doctrine in each other's hides at a council. You are husband and wife, and you love each other. If you start from that point, you will arrive safely at your destination."

✧   ✧   ✧

In their bedchamber, husband and wife attempted to follow the bishop's advice. But it was not easy, for all their good will. Of all the hurts lovers inflict upon each other, none are so hard to overcome as those caused by equal justice.

To Belisarius, the point that he had done nothing, never, at no time, to cause his wife's distrust and dishonesty was paramount. It was a sharp point, keen-edged and clean, and easy to make. Nor could Antonina deny its truth. Her own point was more difficult to make, for it involved not one man and one woman, but the truth of men and women in general. That her dishonesty had been occasioned, not by a desire to consummate an advantageous marriage, but by a desire to protect a beloved husband from further disgrace, only added bitterness to the brew. For he believed her, but did not care a whit for his reputation; and she believed him, but cared deeply for the pain that his unconcern would cause him. And all this was made the worse by their difference in age. For though Belisarius was shrewd beyond his years, he was still a man in his mid-twenties, who believed in promises made. And Antonina was a woman in her mid-thirties, who had seen more promises made than she could recall, and precious few of them kept.

In the end, oddly enough, the Gordian knot was cut by a dagger. For, in the course of stalking about the room, expounding his point much like a tiger might expound the thrill of the hunt to a deer, Belisarius' eye happened to glance at the drawer of his bed table.

He froze in his tracks. Then, slowly, walked over and opened the drawer. From within, he drew forth a dagger.

It was a truly excellent dagger. Armenian made, perfectly balanced, with a razor-sharp blade and a grip that seemed to fit his hand like a glove.

"This is the dagger I gave him," he whispered. "This is the very one."

Interest cut through resentment. Antonina came over and stared down at the weapon. She had seen it before, of course, and had even held it, but had never given it much thought. After a moment, uncertainly, her hand stroked her husband's arm.

He glanced down at it, began to stiffen, and then suddenly relaxed.

"Ah, love," he said tenderly, "let us forget the past. It can't be untied, only cut." He gestured with the dagger. "With this."

"What do you mean?"

"This is the dagger of my vision, and it is proof that the vision was true. All that matters, in the end, is that I love Photius, and I would have him as our son. Let us bring him here, and we will begin from there."

She gazed up at him, still with a trace of uncertainty.

"Truly?"

"Truly. I swear before God, wife, that I will cherish your son as my own, and that I will never reproach you for his existence." The crooked smile. "Nor for hiding his existence."

Now they were embracing, fiercely, and, very soon thereafter, dissolving all anger with the most ancient and reliable method known to man and woman.

Later, her head cradled on Belisarius' shoulder, Antonina said:

"I am concerned about one thing, love."

"What's that?"

Antonina sat up. Her full breasts swayed gently, distracting her husband. Seeing his gaze, she smiled.

"You're having delusions of grandeur," she mocked.

"Fifteen minutes," he pronounced. "No more."

"Half an hour," she replied. "At best."

They grinned at each other. It was an old game, which they had begun playing the first night they met. Belisarius usually won, to Antonina's delight.

She grew serious. "Photius has been cared for by a girl named Hypatia. For over two years, now. He is only five. I have visited him as often as I could, but—she has been very good to him, and he would miss her. And the money I give her is all she has to live on." Her face was suddenly stiff. "She can no longer ply her old trade. Her face is badly scarred."

Antonina fell silent. Belisarius was shocked when he understood how much rage she was suppressing. Then, understanding came. He could not help glancing at his wife's belly, at the ragged scar on her lower abdomen. The scar that had always prevented them from having children of their own.

He arose from the bed and walked about, very slowly, very stiffly. That was his own way of repressing rage. A rage that was perhaps all the greater, because Antonina had long since removed its object.

Five years before, seeing that Antonina had no pimp, an ambitious young fellow had sought to make good the lack. Upon hearing Antonina's demurral, he had insisted with a knife. Unfortunately for him, he had failed to consider her parentage. True, her mother had been a whore, but her father had been a charioteer. A breed of men who are not, by any standard, inclined to pacifism. The charioteer had not taught his daughter much (at least, not much worth knowing), but he had taught her how to use a knife. Better, in the event, than the young fellow had taught himself. So the budding entrepreneur had found an early grave, but not before making his foul mark.

"We will bring them both here," said Belisarius. "It would be good to have a nanny for Photius, anyway. And once he is too old for that, we will keep her on in some other capacity." A stiff little gesture. "Any capacity, it doesn't matter. Whatever she is happy with."

"Thank you," whispered Antonina. "She is a sweet girl."

Again, Belisarius made the stiff little gesture. His wife knew him, and knew how much he prided his self-control. But there were times, she thought, he would be better off if he could rend like a shark.

She, on the other hand, had no such qualms.

"Who were you going to send—to fetch Photius?"

"Eh? Oh. Dubazes, I suppose."

Antonina shook her head vigorously. "Oh, no, you mustn't." Softly, softly, catchee sharkee.

"Whyever not?"

"Well—" She was quite pleased with the little flutter of her eyelids. Just a trace of apprehension, no more. More would arouse her husband's intelligence.

"Her pimp's still around, you see. He sends her an occasional customer. Forces them on her, actually. Pimps—well, he'll object if she's taken away."

Her heart glowed to see her husband's back straighten. True, she was lying, and if Belisarius caught her at it there'd be hell to pay. But it was just a little white lie, and anyway, who'd believe a pimp? She'd have to coach Hypatia, of course.

"His name is Constans," she said. A very, very, very faint little tremor in the lips; perfectly done, she thought. "He's such a violent man. And Dubazes—he's not young anymore, and—"

"I shall send Maurice," Belisarius announced.

"Good idea," murmured Antonina. She yawned, lest she grin like a shark herself. Constans, in actual fact, had ceased having any interest in the whore Hypatia after he carved her face. But he was still around, plying his trade in Antioch.

"Good idea," she murmured again, rolling over and presenting a very enticing rump to her husband. Best to distract him quickly, before he started thinking. She estimated that fifteen minutes had passed.

It had, and, as usual, Belisarius won the game.

Shortly thereafter, Antonina fell asleep. Belisarius, however, found sleep eluded him. He tossed and turned for a time, before arising from his bed. He knew he would not sleep until the matter was attended to.

Maurice made no objection upon being awakened at that ungodly hour. Times enough in the past, on campaign, his general had awakened him in the early hours of the morning.

Although never, he thought, after hearing Belisarius' instructions, for quite such a mission.

But Maurice was a *hecatontarch*, what an older Rome called a centurion. A veteran among veterans, was Maurice, whose beard was now as gray as the iron of his body, and so he had no difficulty keeping his face solemn and attentive. Quickly, he awakened two other members of Belisarius' *bucellarii*, his personal retinue of Thracian cataphracts. He chose two *pentarchs* for the mission, Anastasius and Valentinian. Veterans also, though younger than Maurice. They were not the most cunning of troop leaders, true; hence their relatively low rank. But there were none in Belisarius' personal guard who were more frightful on the battlefield.

As they readied the horses, Maurice explained the situation. He held nothing back from them, as Belisarius had held nothing back from him. The Thracian cataphracts who constituted Belisarius' personal bodyguard were utterly devoted to him. The devotion stemmed, as much as anything, from the young general's invariable honesty. And all of them adored Antonina. They were well aware of her past, and not a one of them gave a fig for it. They were quite familiar with whores, themselves, and tended to look upon such women, in their own way, as fellow veterans.

The expedition ready, Maurice led his men and their horses out of the stable, to the courtyard where Belisarius waited. The first hint of dawn was beginning to show.

Seeing his general's stiff back, Maurice sighed. His two companions, glancing from Maurice to the general, understood the situation at once.

"You know he won't tell you himself," whispered Valentinian.

Maurice spoke up. "There's one thing, General."

Belisarius turned his head toward them, slightly.

"Yes?"

Maurice cleared his throat. "Well, this pimp. It's like this, sir. He might be hanging around, and, well—"

"Violent characters, your pimps," chimed in Anastasius.

"Stab you in the back in a minute," added Valentinian.

"Yes, sir," said Maurice firmly. "So, all things considered, it might be best if we knew his name. Just so we can keep an eye out for him in case he tries to start any trouble."

Belisarius hesitated, then said: "Constans."

"Constans," Maurice murmured. Valentinian and Anastasius repeated the name, committing it to memory. "Thank you, sir," said Maurice. Moments later, the three cataphracts were riding toward Antioch.

Once they were out of hearing range, Maurice remarked cheerfully: "It's a wonderful thing, lads, to have a restrained general. Keeps his temper under control at all times. Maintains iron self-discipline. Distrusts himself whenever he feels the blood boil. Automatically refuses to follow his heart."

"A marvelous thing," said Anastasius admiringly. "Always cool, always calm, never just lets himself go. That's our general. Best general in the Roman army."

"Saved our asses any number of times," agreed Valentinian.

They rode on a little further. Maurice cleared his throat.

"It occurs to me, lads, that we are not generals."

His two companions looked at each other, as if suddenly taken with a wild surmise.

"Why, no, actually," said Anastasius. "We're not."

"Don't believe we bear the slightest resemblance to generals, in fact," concurred Valentinian.

A little further down the road, Maurice mused, "Rough fellows, pimps."

Valentinian shuddered. "I shudder to think of it." He shuddered again. "See?"

Anastasius moaned softly. "Oh, I hope we don't meet him." Another moan. "I might foul myself."

A week later, they were back, with a somewhat bewildered but very happy five-year-old boy, and a less bewildered but even happier young woman. The Thracian cataphracts took note of her, and smiled encouragingly. She took note of them, and did not smile back.

But, after a time, she ceased turning her face when one approached. And, after a time, several cataphracts showed her their own facial scars, which were actually much worse than hers. And, after they confessed to her that they were cataphracts in name only, because although they possessed all the skills they, sadly, sadly, lacked the noble ancestry of the true cataphract—were, in fact, nothing but simple farm boys at bottom, she began to show an occasional smile.

Antonina kept an experienced and vigilant eye on the familiar dance, but for the most part, she did not interfere. An occasional word to Maurice, now and then, to restrain the overenthusiastic. And when Hypatia became pregnant, she simply insisted that the father take responsibility for the child. There was some doubt on the subject, but one of the cataphracts was more than happy to marry the girl. The child might be his, after all, and besides, he wasn't a true cataphract but just a tough kid from Thrace. What did he care for the worries of nobility?

Nor did his friends chaff him. A sweet girl was Hypatia, a man could do much worse. Who were they to fret over such things, when their general didn't?

Long before Hypatia became pregnant, however, not six weeks after Maurice and his two companions returned from their mission, a young man was released from the care of the monks in a local monastery in Antioch. Examining his prospects in the cold light of a new day, he decided to become a beggar, and began to ply his new trade in the streets of the city. He did quite well, actually, by the (admittedly, very low) standards of the trade. And his friends (acquaintances, it might be better to say) assured him that the scars on his face gave him quite the dashing look. A pity, of course, that he couldn't dash. Not without knees.

Chapter 4

"So what do we conclude?" asked Belisarius.

Cassian pursed his lips. He pointed to the *thing* in the general's hand.

"Has there been—?"

Belisarius shook his head. "No. I don't think there will be, for some time. Not much, at least."

"Why not?"

"It's—hard to explain." He shrugged slightly. "Don't ask me how I know. I just do. The—jewel, let's call it—is very weary."

Antonina spoke up:

"What were your own visions, Anthony? You did not speak of them yesterday."

The bishop looked up. His pudgy face looked almost haggard.

"I do not remember them very well. My visions—and Michael's even more so—had none of the clarity and precision of your husband's. I sensed at the time that the—the jewel—would fit Belisarius much better. I cannot explain how I knew that, but I did."

He straightened his back, took a deep breath.

"I saw only a vast ocean of despair, mute beneath a—a church, can you call it?—that was the essence of godlessness. A church so foul that the world's most barbarous pagans would reject it without a thought, and find in their savage rituals a cathedral of pity compared to that monstrosity of the spirit."

His face was pale. He wiped it with a plump hand.

"I saw myself, I think. I am not sure. I think it was me, squatting in a cell, naked." He managed a croaking laugh. "Much thinner, I

47

was!" A sigh. "I was awaiting the Question, with a strange eagerness. I would die beneath their instruments soon, for I would not
give them the answer they demanded. I would refuse to interpret
scripture as a blessing for the slaughter of the innocent. And I
was satisfied, for I believed in the truth of my faith and I knew
I would not yield to the agony because I had—"

He gasped, his eyes widened. "Yes! Yes—it *was* me! I remember now! I knew I would have the strength to resist the torment
because I had the image of my friend Michael always before me.
Michael, and his unyielding death, and his great curse upon Satan
from the flames of the stake."

He looked at the Macedonian and wept gentle tears. "All my
life I have thanked God that Michael of Macedonia has been my
friend since boyhood. And never more than on that day of final
hopelessness. On my own, I am not certain I would have had
the courage I needed."

"*Ridiculous.*" As ever, Michael's voice carried the finality of
stone.

The emaciated monk leaned forward in his chair, fixing the
bishop with his gaze.

"Hear me now, Bishop of Aleppo. There is no pain on earth,
nor torment in hell, that could ever break the soul of Anthony
Cassian. Never doubt it."

"I doubt often, Michael," whispered Anthony. "There has never
been a day in my life that I have not doubted."

"I should hope not!" The raptor had returned, and the blue eyes
of the Macedonian were as pitiless as an eagle's. "Where else but
from doubt can faith arise, wise fool?" Michael glowered. "It is
the true sin of the churchman that he doubts not. He *knows*, he
is *certain*, and thus he is snared in Satan's net. And soon enough,
casts the net himself, and cackles with glee when he hauls up his
catch of innocence."

The raptor vanished, replaced by the friend. "Others see in
you the gentleness of your spirit, and the wisdom of your mind.
Those are there, true. I have always recognized them. But beneath
lies the true Cassian. There is no strength so iron hard as gentleness, Anthony. No faith so pure as that which always doubts, no
wisdom so deep as that which always questions."

The monk straightened his back. "Were this not true, I would
reject God. I would spit in His face and join the legions of Lucifer,

for the archangel would be right to rebel. I love God because I am His creation. *I am not his creature.*"

The Macedonian was rigid. Then his face softened, and for just a fleeting moment, there was as much gentleness there as was always present in the face of the bishop. "Do not fear your doubt, Anthony. It is God's great gift to you. And that He placed that great doubt in your great mind, is his gift to us all."

The room was silent, for a time. Then Antonina spoke again.

"Was there nothing else in your vision, Anthony? No hope of any kind?"

The bishop raised his head and looked up at her.

"Yes—no. How can I explain? It is all very murky. In my vision itself, no, there was no hope of any kind. No more than there was in Belisarius' vision. All was at an end, save duty, and what personal grace might be found. But, there was a sense—a feeling, only—that it need not have been. I was seeing the future, I knew, and that future was crushing and inexorable. But I also sensed, somehow, that the future could have been otherwise."

"All is clear, then," pronounced Michael. "Clear as day."

Belisarius cocked a quizzical eyebrow. The Macedonian snorted.

"The message is from the Lord," pronounced the monk. The raptor resumed its perch. "None here can fail to see it, nor their duty. For our wickedness, we are doomed to damnation. But that wickedness can be fought, and overcome, and thus a new future created. It is obvious! Obvious!" The raptor's eyes fixed on Belisarius, as the hawk's on the hare. "Do your duty, General!"

Belisarius smiled his crooked smile. "I am quite good at doing my duty, Michael, thank you. But it is not clear to me what that duty is." He held up his hand firmly, quelling the monk's outburst. "Please! I am not questioning what you say. But I am neither a bishop nor a holy man. I am a soldier. Fine for you to say, *overcome wickedness*. At your service, prophet! But, would you mind explaining to me, somewhat more precisely, exactly *how* that wickedness is to be overcome?"

Michael snorted. "You wish a withered monk from the desert, whose limbs cannot even bear his own weight, to tell you how to combat Satan's host?"

Cassian spoke. "May I suggest, Belisarius, that you begin with your own vision?"

The general's quizzical gaze transferred itself to the bishop.

"I am not a soldier, of course, but it seemed to me that there were two aspects of the enemy's strength which were paramount in your vision. The great numbers of his army, and his strange and mysterious weapons."

Belisarius thought back to his vision, nodded.

"It would seem, therefore, that—"

"We must seek to lessen his numbers, increase our own, and above all, discover the secret of the weapons," concluded Belisarius.

The bishop nodded. Belisarius scratched his chin.

"Let us begin with the last point," he said. "The weapons. They bear some resemblance, it seems to me, to the naphtha weapons used by our navy. Vastly more powerful, of course, and different. But there is still a likeness. Perhaps that is where we should begin."

He spread his hands in a rueful gesture. "But I am a soldier, not a sailor. I have seen the naphtha weapons, but never used them. They are much too clumsy and awkward for use in a land battle. And—" Oddly, he stopped speaking.

Antonina began to say something, but Belisarius made an urgent gesture which stilled her. His eyes were unfocused, his thoughts obviously turned inward.

"The jewel?" asked Cassian. Again, Belisarius made a stilling gesture. All fell silent, watching the general.

"Almost," he whispered. "But I can't quite make out what—" He hissed.

Subterranean, underground images. Impossible to discern clearly— not from the absence of light, but because the visions were so bizarre. Vision: three men in a room, below a building, watching some sort of giant, intricate machine. A sense of danger and anticipation. Vision: the same men, wearing strange eyepieces, staring through a slit; fear, suspense; a sudden blinding flash of light; exhilaration; terror; awe. Vision: other men, laboring underground on some sort of gigantic—pipe? Vision: the pipe flashing through the sky. Vision: weird buildings in an odd city suddenly destroyed, leveled as if from the blow of a giant. Vision: a different man, young, bearded, sitting in a log hut in a forest, showing indecipherable marks on a page to four other men—mathematics? Vision: the same bearded young man, wearing the same eyepieces as the men in the first vision, staring through a similar slit. Again, that incredible blinding light. Again: exhilaration; terror; awe.

The images vanished as suddenly as they came. Belisarius shook his head, took a deep breath. He described the visions, as best he could, to the others in the room.

"They make no sense," said Antonina. Belisarius stroked his chin and said, slowly:

"I think they do. Not in themselves, no. I have no idea what was *happening*, in those visions. But—there was a logic, underneath. In every case, there was a sense of men working together to discover a secret, and then create machines which could implement that secret. They were—*projects*—deliberate, planned, coordinated efforts. Not the haphazard fiddling of artisans and craftsmen."

He sat up straight. "Yes! That's what we need. We need to launch such a project, to ferret out the secret of the Malwa weapons."

"How?" asked Antonina.

Belisarius pursed his lips. "Two things, it seems to me, are paramount. We need to find a man who can lead such an effort, and we need to set up a place where he can work."

Cassian cleared his throat. "I may have a solution. The beginnings of one, at least. Are you acquainted with John of Rhodes?"

"The former naval officer?" Belisarius shook his head. "I know of his reputation as an officer. And that he resigned under a cloud of disgrace, of some sort. Other than that, no. I have never met him."

"He resides in Aleppo, now," said Cassian. "As it happens, I am his confessor. He is at loose ends, at the moment, and quite unsatisfied with his situation. The problem is not material in nature. He is rather wealthy, and has no need to fret over mundane things. But he is very bored. He is a quick-thinking man, with an active spirit, and he chafes at his current idleness. I believe he might very well be willing to assist us in this project."

"What if he is recalled to service?"

Anthony coughed. "That is, under the circumstances, quite unlikely." Another cough. "He has—well, you understand I may not betray the confidentiality of confession, but let us simply say that he has offended too many powerful figures on too many occasions for there to be much chance of him ever regaining his position in the navy."

"Moral turpitude?" demanded Michael.

Anthony looked down, examining the tiles of the floor with a keen attention which the plain, utilitarian objects did not seem to warrant. "Well, I suppose," he muttered. "Again, I must remind you of the confid—"

"Yes, yes," said Michael impatiently, waving his hand in a manner which suggested that he regarded the confidentiality of confession with as much esteem as he regarded manure.

"Let me simply say that—" Anthony hesitated, unhappy. "Well, John of Rhodes' naval career would have progressed more smoothly, and not ground ashore on a reef, had he been a eunuch. He is a raffish character, even now, in his forties. He finds women quite irresistible and, alas, the converse is all too often true."

"Marvelous," growled Michael. "A libertine." The raptor examined a particularly distasteful morsel of decayed rodent. "I despise libertines."

Belisarius shrugged. "We must work with what we have. And with what little time we have. I cannot stay here long. I expect a conflict with Persia will be erupting again, soon, and I have much to do to prepare my army. I will have to leave for Daras within a week. So, whatever it is we are going to do, if it involves me, will need to be started immediately."

He looked to Cassian.

"I think your suggestion is an excellent one. Approach this John of Rhodes and feel him out. We need to examine the problem of these strange weapons, and he seems as good a place as any to start."

"What if he agrees?" asked Cassian. "What, precisely, are we asking him to do?"

Belisarius stroked his chin. "We will need to create a workshop, somewhere. An armory, of sorts. A—*weapons project*. And, if we have any success in uncovering the secret of these weapons, we will need to recruit and train men who can use them."

"A question," interrupted Antonina. "Should we tell this John about the jewel?"

The four people in the room looked at each other. Belisarius was the first to speak.

"No," he said firmly. "At least, not until we are certain he can be trusted. But, for the moment, I think we must keep the knowledge to ourselves. If word begins to spread too quickly, there'll be an uproar about witchcraft."

"I think we must tell Sittas, also," added Antonina.

"Yes," agreed Belisarius. "Sittas must be brought fully into our confidence, as soon as possible." He picked up the jewel. "*Fully.*"

Michael frowned, but Cassian nodded. "I agree. For many reasons. The war we are about to launch will be waged on many fronts, not all of them military. There are many enemies within the ranks of Rome, also. Some, within the Church. Some, within the nobility and the aristocracy." He took a deep breath. "And, finally, there—"

"Is Justinian." Belisarius voice was like iron. "I will not be false to my oath, Cassian."

The bishop smiled. "I am not asking you to be, Belisarius. But you have to deal with some realities, also. Justinian is the Emperor. And, whether for good or ill, is enormously capable. He's no fool to be led around by the nose, and no indolent layabout to be safely ignored. And he's also, well, how shall I put it?"

Antonina answered. "Treacherous, suspicious, envious, jealous. A conspirator who sees conspiracy everywhere, and who is firmly convinced that all the world seeks to do him harm."

Cassian nodded. "Ironically, we are *not* seeking to do him harm. Rather the contrary. We are seeking to preserve his empire, among other things. But, in order to do so, we will need to conspire behind his back."

"Do we?" asked Belisarius.

Cassian was firm. "Yes. I know the man well, Belisarius—much better than you, actually, even though you share Thracian ancestry. I have spent many hours with him in private conversation. He attends every council of the Church, you know, and participates fully. Both in the formal discussions and then, in private, with many of the leading theologians of the Church. Though I rank only middling high in the hierarchy of the Church, I rank very high in the esteem of theologians. And Justinian, as you may know, thinks he is quite the theologian himself."

He stroked his beard. "Actually, he *is* quite good at it. Justinian's own theological inclinations are excellent, in truth. In his heart, he leans toward a compromise with heresy and a tolerant policy. But his cold, ambitious mind leans toward a close tie to severe orthodoxy, given his ambitions in the west."

"What ambitions?" demanded Belisarius.

Anthony was surprised. "You don't know? You, one of his favorite generals?"

There was a rare bitterness in the general's crooked smile, now.

"Being one of Justinian's favored generals does not make him a confidant, Anthony. Rather the reverse. He is shrewd enough to want capable generals, and then suspects the use that capability would be put to. So he tells his generals nothing until the last moment."

Belisarius waved his hand. "But we are getting side-tracked. Later, I would be interested in hearing more from you regarding Justinian's western ambitions. But not now. And you are mistaking my question. I was not asking if we needed to keep our conspiracy secret from Justinian. Obviously, if we conspire, we must do so. The question is: do we need to conspire at all? Can we not simply bring him into our confidence? For all Justinian's obvious faults, he *is* one of the most capable men who ever sat upon the imperial throne."

Antonina drew in a sharp breath. Cassian glanced at her and shook his head.

"No. Absolutely not. *Justinian must know nothing.* At least, not until it is too late for him to do more than simply acquiesce in what we have done." He made a rueful grimace. "And, then, we will have to hope he doesn't remove our heads."

Belisarius seemed still unconvinced. Cassian pressed on.

"Belisarius, have no delusions. Suppose we told Justinian. Suppose, further, that he accepted all that we told him. Suppose, even—and here I tread on fantastical ground—he did not suspect our motives. *What then?*"

Belisarius hesitated. Antonina answered.

"He would insist on placing himself at the head of our struggle. With all of his competence. *And* with all of his pigheaded stubbornness, his petty vanities, his constant intrigues, his overweening pride, his endless petty meddling and fussing, his distrust of anyone else's competence as well as loyalty, his—"

"Enough!" cried Belisarius, chuckling. "I am convinced." He laced his fingers together and leaned forward, his elbows on his knees, staring down at the floor. Again, the simple tiles received an unaccustomed scrutiny.

Cassian's voice broke into his thoughts.

"Are you familiar, Belisarius, with India? Or you, Antonina?"

Antonina shook her head. Belisarius, still gazing absently at the floor, shrugged and said:

"I know a bit about that distant land, from hearsay, but I have never even met—"

He stopped in midsentence, gasping. His head snapped erect.

"What am I saying? I know an *enormous* amount about India. From my vision! I spent thirty years in an unending struggle against India. Against the Malwa tyranny, I should say. And I always had the shrewd advice of Raghunath Rao to fall back on." His face grew pale. "God in Heaven. Anthony, you are right. We must conspire, and bury the conspiracy deep. I only hope it is not too late already."

"What are you talking about?" asked Antonina.

Belisarius looked at her. "One thing I remember now, from my vision, is that the Malwa Empire has the most extensive and developed espionage service in the world. An enormous apparatus, and highly skilled." His eyes lost their focus for a moment. "It was one of the deadly blows they inflicted on us, I remember. By the time we finally awoke to the full scope of the danger, the Roman Empire was riddled with Indian spies and intriguers."

He focused on Cassian. "Do you think—"

The bishop waved his hand. "I do not think we need concern ourselves, Belisarius. I am quite certain Michael was not seen coming here. And I am a frequent guest, so my presence will not be noteworthy. We will have to be careful when Michael leaves, of course, but that is not difficult."

The bishop stroked his beard vigorously. "In the future, however, the problem will quickly become severe. But let us come back to that problem. For the moment—I can provide us with a place to establish our initial base. Where we can create an arms foundry—a 'weapons project,' as you called it. And, if we can uncover the secret of the Malwa weapons, begin to forge an army to wield them. Recently, as it happens, a wealthy widow bequeathed her entire inheritance to the Church, with the specific stipulation that I was to have control of its disposition. She died three months ago. Among her many possessions was a large estate not far from Daras. Near the Persian border.

"The villa at the estate is quite large, with more than enough buildings to serve our purpose. And the peasants who till the land are borderers. Syrians and Monophysites, down to the newborn babes."

Belisarius nodded. "I know the breed well, Anthony. Yes, that would be splendid. If we can gain their trust and confidence, they will be impossible to infiltrate." He frowned pensively. "And might very well make—let me think on that."

"All right," said Antonina. "But what will we tell these peasants?

And John of Rhodes? And we will need to engage the services of a number of artisans. And then, if we meet with any success, we will need to recruit men who can learn to use the new weapons. If we do not tell these people about the jewel, how will we explain to them the source of the knowledge we give them?"

"I think the solution to the problem is obvious," said Cassian. The bishop shrugged. "We simply tell them nothing. Everyone knows Belisarius—and Sittas—are among Justinian's favorite generals. And you, Antonina, are known to be a close friend of the Empress. If we simply act mysterious, but emphasize the imperative necessity of maintaining complete secrecy, then John of Rhodes and all the others will assume they are involved in a project which has the highest imperial authority." He smiled. "And my own frequent presence will assure them that the work has the blessing of the Church, as well."

Michael spoke up. "I will also speak to the peasants. I have some small authority among them."

Cassian laughed gaily. "*Small* authority? That's a bit like Moses saying he had some tentative suggestions to make."

Michael glared at him, but the bishop was not abashed. "That will do wonders, actually. In truth, Michael's word will carry greater weight with Syrian common folk than anyone else's. If he gives the work his blessing, and bids them maintain silence, be assured they will do so."

"That still does not solve the problem of keeping our work secret from the world at large," said Antonina. "Even if all who are engaged in the work at the estate keep silent, it will be noticed by others that there is a constant traffic of outsiders coming to and fro. We cannot do this work in isolation, Cassian. Not for long."

Cassian glanced at Belisarius. The general's thoughts seemed far away. The bishop spoke:

"No, but it will help. As for the rest—"

"It is the simplest thing in the world," said Belisarius. His voice seemed cold, cold.

The general rose to his feet and walked about, accompanying his words with stiff little gestures.

"It will work as follows. Michael will quietly rally the common folk to our side. Cassian, you will serve as our intriguer within the church. Sittas, once he is brought into our conspiracy, will serve as our intriguer within the imperial court and the nobility.

Unlike me, he is of the most impeccable aristocratic lineage. I will, as I must in any event, maintain my military responsibilities."

He stopped, gazed down at Antonina.

"And Antonina will be the center of it all. She will set up residence at this villa near Daras and stay there. She will no longer accompany me with the army. She will assemble and oversee the weapons work. She will, when the time comes, take charge of training a new army."

He waved down her developing protest. "I will help, I will help. But you are more than capable of all this, Antonina. You are at least as intelligent as any man I ever met. And these weapons are new to all of us. The methods of using them, as well. I will help, but I will not be surprised if your untrained intelligence does a better job of devising new forces and methods than my well-trained experience does. You will not have your eyes blinkered by old habits."

He took a deep breath. "Finally, you are the perfect conduit through which all of our disparate efforts may be kept aligned and coordinated. Through you, we can all communicate, with no one suspecting our true purpose."

Antonina's intelligence was every bit as high as her husband proclaimed it to be. Her back grew rigid as a board, her face as stiff as a sheet of iron.

"Because everyone's suspicion will have another target," she said bitterly.

"Yes." The general's voice was calm; calm but utterly unyielding.

The bishop's eyes widened slightly. He looked from husband to wife, and back again. Then looked away, stroking his beard.

"Yes, that would work," he murmured. "Work perfectly, in fact. But—" He gazed up at the general. "Do you understand—"

"*Leave us, Anthony,*" said Belisarius. Calmly, but unyieldingly. "If you please. And you also, Michael."

Michael and Cassian arose and made their way to the door. There, the bishop turned back.

"If you are still determined on this course, Belisarius, after discussing it with Antonina, there is a perfect way to implement it quickly."

Antonina stared straight ahead. Her dusky face was almost pale. Her eyes glittered with unshed tears. Belisarius tore his gaze away and looked at the bishop.

"Yes?"

"A man approached me, recently, seeking my help in gaining employment. Newly arrived in Aleppo, from Caesaria. I know his reputation. He is a well-trained secretary, very capable by all accounts, and quite an accomplished writer. A historian. Such, at least, is his ambition. You have no secretary, and have reached the point in your career where you need one."

"His name?"

"Procopius. Procopius of Caesaria. In addition to serving as your secretary, I am quite certain he will broadcast your talents to the world at large and be of assistance to your career."

"He is a flatterer, then?"

"An utterly shameless one. But quite talented at it, so his flattering remarks are generally believed, by the world at large if not by his employer."

"And?"

The bishop looked unhappy. "Well—"

"Speak plainly, Anthony!"

Cassian's lips pursed. "He is one of the vilest creatures I have ever had the misfortune of meeting. A flatterer, yes, but also a spiteful and envious man, who complements his public flattery with the most vicious private rumor-mongering. A snake, pure and simple."

"He will do marvelously. Send him to me. I will hire him at once. And then I will give him all he needs, both for public flattery and private gossip."

After Cassian and Michael left, Belisarius sat by his wife and took her hand.

His voice was still calm, and still unyielding, but very gentle.

"I am sorry, love. But it is the only course I can see which will be safe. I know how much pain it will cause, to have people say such things about you, but—"

Antonina's laugh was as harsh as a crow's.

"Me? Do you think I care what people say about *me*?"

She turned her head and looked him in the eyes.

"I am a *whore*, Belisarius." Her husband said nothing, nor was there anything but love in his eyes.

She looked away. "Oh, you've never used the word. But I will. It's what I was. Everyone knows it. Do you think a *whore* gives a fig for what people say about her?" Another harsh laugh. "Do you understand why the Empress Theodora trusts me? *Trusts* me, Belisarius. As she trusts no one else. It is because we were both whores, and the only people whores really trust—*really* trust—are other whores."

For a moment, tears began to come back into her eyes, but she wiped them away angrily.

"I love you like I have never loved anyone else in my life. Certainly more than I love Theodora! I don't even *like* Theodora, in many ways. But I would not trust you with the knowledge of my bastard son. Yet I trusted Theodora. *She knew.* And I trusted another whore, Hypatia, to raise the boy." Her voice was like ice. "Do not concern yourself, *veteran*, about what I feel when people talk about me. You cannot begin to imagine my indifference."

"Then—"

"But I *do* care what people say about you!"

"*Me?*" Belisarius laughed. "What will they say about me that they don't already?"

"*Idiot*," she hissed. "*Now* they say you married a whore. So they mock your judgment, and your good taste. But they see the whore does not stray from your side, so they—secretly—admire your manhood." Incongruously, she giggled, then mimicked a whispering voice: "'He must be hung like a horse, to keep that slut satisfied.'" The humor vanished. "But *now* they will call you a *cuckold*. They will mock *you*, as well as your judgment. You will become a figure of ridicule. *Ridicule*, do you hear me?"

Belisarius laughed again. Gaily, to her astonishment.

"I know," he said. "I'm counting on it." He arose and stretched his arms. "Oh, yes, love, I'm counting on it." He mimicked the whispering voice himself: "'What kind of a man would let his wife flaunt her lovers in front of him? Only the most pathetic, feeble, weak, cowardly creature.'" His voice grew hard as steel. "And then word will get to the enemy, and the enemy will ask himself: *and what kind of a general could such a man be?*"

She looked up at him, startled.

"I hadn't thought of that," she admitted.

"I know. But this is all beside the point. You are lying, Antonina. You don't really care what people say about me, any more than I care what people say about you."

She looked away, her lips tight. For a moment, she was silent. Then, finally, the tears began to flow.

"No," she whispered, "I don't."

"You are afraid I will believe the tales."

She nodded. The tears began pouring. Her shoulders shook. Belisarius sat by her side and enfolded the small woman in his arms.

"I will never believe them, Antonina."

"Yes, you will," she gasped, between sobs. "Yes, you will. Not at once, not soon. Not for years, maybe. But eventually, you will. Or, at least, you will wonder, and suspect, and doubt, and distrust me."

"I will not. Never."

She looked up at him through teary eyes. "How can you be sure?"

He smiled his crooked smile. "You do not really understand me, wife. Not in some ways, at least." His eyes grew distant. "I think perhaps the only person who ever understood me, in this way, was Raghunath Rao. Whom I've never met, except in a vision. But I understand him, kneeling in the woods below Venandakatra's palace, praying with all his heart that the princess he loved would allow herself to be raped by the Vile One. More than allow it—would smile at her defiler and praise his prowess. I, too, would have done the same."

Belisarius took his wife's head in his hands and turned her face toward him.

"Raghunath Rao was the greatest warrior the Maratha produced in centuries. And the Maratha are the great warrior people of India, along with the Rajput. Yet this great warrior, kneeling there, cared nothing for those things warriors care for. Pride, honor, respect—much less virginity and chastity—meant nothing to him. *And that is why he was so great a warrior.* Because he was not a warrior, at bottom, but a dancer."

Antonina couldn't help laughing. "You're the worst dancer I ever saw!"

Belisarius laughed with her. "True, true." Then, he became serious. "But I *am* a craftsman. I never wanted to be a soldier, you know. As a boy, I spent all my time at the smithy, admiring the blacksmith. I wanted to be one, when I grew up, more than anything." He shrugged. "But, it was not to be. Not for a boy of my class. So a soldier I became, and then, a general. But I have never lost the craftsman's way of approaching his work."

He smiled. "Do you know why my soldiers adore me? Why Maurice will do anything for me—such as this little trip to Antioch?"

Now on treacherous ground, Antonina kept silent.

"Because they know that they will never find themselves dying in agony, on a field of battle somewhere, because their general sent them there out of pride, or honor, or valor, or vainglory, or for any other reason than it was the best place for them to be in order to do the work properly." The smile grew crooked. "And that's why Maurice will see to it that a certain pimp named Constans gets his deserts."

Antonina was still. *Very* treacherous ground.

Belisarius started laughing. "Did you really think I wouldn't see past your scheme, once I had time to think about it?" He released her and stretched his arms languorously. "After I woke up, feeling better than I've felt in months, and could think without my thoughts clouded with fury?"

She glanced at him sideways. Then, after a moment, began laughing herself. "I thought I'd pulled it off perfectly. The little tremors, hesitations, the slight tinge of fear in the voice—"

"The enticing roll of the rump was particularly good," said Belisarius. "But it's what gave it all away, in the end. When we play our little game you always try to win, even if you enjoy losing. You certainly don't wave your delicious ass under my nose, like waving a red flag before a bull."

"And with much the same result," she murmured. A moment later: "You're not angry?"

"No," he replied, smiling. "I began to be, at first, until I remembered Valentinian's little whisper to Maurice: 'You know he won't tell you himself.'"

"Maurice took *Valentinian*?"

"*And* Anastasius."

Antonina clapped her hand over her mouth.

"Oh, God! I almost feel sorry for that stinking pimp."

"I don't," snarled Belisarius. "Not in the slightest." He took a deep breath, blew it out.

"I pretended I didn't hear Valentinian, but—it is hard, for a quirky man like me, with my weird pride, to accept that people love him. And that he forces them to manipulate him, at times." He gave his crooked smile. "Would you believe, Anastasius actually said—" Here Belisarius' voice became a rumbling basso: "'violent characters, your pimps.'"

"Anastasius can bend horseshoes with his hands," choked Antonina.

"And then Valentinian whined: 'stab you in the back in a minute.'"

Antonina couldn't speak at all, now, from the laughter.

"Oh, yes. Exactly his words. Valentinian—who is widely suspected to wipe his ass with a dagger, since nobody's ever seen him without one."

For a time, husband and wife were silent, simply staring at each other. Then, Antonina whispered:

"There will never be any truth to the tales, Belisarius. I swear before God. Never. A month from now, a year from now, ten years from now. You will always be able to ask, and the answer will always be: *no.*"

He smiled and kissed her gently.

"I know. And I swear this, before God: *I will never ask.*"

He rose to his feet.

"And now, we must get back to work." He strode to the door and called into the hallway beyond: "Dubazes! Fetch Michael and the bishop, if you would!"

Chapter 5

MINDOUOS
Summer, 528 AD

"*Out.*" Belisarius' eyes were like dark stones, worn smooth in a stream. Cold, pitiless pieces of an ancient mountain.

"*Out,*" he repeated. The fat officer standing rigidly before him began to protest again, then, seeing the finality in the general's icy gaze, waddled hastily out of the command tent.

"See to it that he's on the road within the hour," said Belisarius to Maurice. "And watch who he talks to on his way out. His friends will commiserate with him, and those friends will likely have the same habits."

"With pleasure, sir." The hecatontarch motioned to one of the three Thracian cataphracts who were standing quietly in the rear of the tent. The cataphract, a stocky man in his mid-thirties, grinned evilly and began to leave.

"On your way out, Gregory," said Belisarius, "send in that young Syrian you recommended." Gregory nodded, and exited the tent.

Belisarius resumed his seat. For a moment, he listened to the sounds of a busy military camp filtering into the tent, much as a musician might listen to a familiar tune. He thought he detected a cheerful boisterousness in the half-heard vulgarities being exchanged by unseen soldiers, and hoped he was right. In the first days after his arrival, the sounds of the camp had been sodden with resentment.

A different sound drew his attention. He glanced over at the desk in the corner of the tent where Procopius, his new secretary, was scribbling away industriously. The desk, like the chair upon which the secretary sat, was of the plainest construction. But it was no plainer than Belisarius' own desk, or chair.

Procopius had been astonished—not to mention disgruntled—when he discovered his new employer's austere habits. Within a week after their arrival, the secretary had attempted to ingratiate himself by presenting Belisarius with a beautifully-embroidered, silk-covered cushion. The general had politely thanked Procopius for the gift, but had immediately turned it over to Maurice, explaining that it was his long-standing custom to share all gifts with his bucellarii. The following day, Procopius watched goggle-eyed as the Thracian cataphracts used the cushion as the target in their mounted archery exercises. (Very briefly—the cruel, razor-sharp blades of the war arrows, driven by those powerful bows, had shredded the cushion within minutes.)

The secretary had been pale with fury and outrage, but had possessed enough wit to maintain silence in the face of Thracian grins. And, admitted Belisarius, since then—

"You've done well, Procopius," said Belisarius suddenly, "helping to ferret out these petty crooks."

The secretary looked up, startled. He began to open his mouth, then closed it. He acknowledged the praise with a simple nod and returned to his work.

Satisfied, Belisarius looked away. In the weeks since they had been together in the army camp near Daras, Procopius had learned, painfully, that his new employer gave flattery short shrift. On the other hand, he prized hard work and skillfulness. And, whatever his other characteristics, there was no question that Procopius was an excellent secretary. Nor was he indolent. He had been a great help in shredding the corruption which riddled Belisarius' new army.

A soldier entered the tent.

"You called for me, sir?"

Belisarius examined him. The man appeared to be barely twenty. He was quite short, but muscular. A Syrian, with, Belisarius judged, considerable Arab stock in his ancestry.

The soldier was wearing a simple, standard uniform: a mantle, a shirt, boots, and a belt. The belt held up a scabbarded *spatha*, the sword which the modern Roman army used in place of the ancient *gladius*. The spatha was similar to a gladius—a straight-bladed, double-edged sword suitable for either cutting or thrusting, but it was six inches longer.

The cloak, helmet, mail tunic and shield which were also part of the man's uniform were undoubtedly resting in his tent. In the Syrian daytime, cloaks made the heat unbearable. And the soldier's armor and shield were unneeded in the daily routine of the camp.

"Your name is Mark, I believe? Mark of Edessa."

"Yes, sir." Mark's face bore slight traces of apprehension mixed with puzzlement.

Belisarius allayed his concerns instantly.

"I am promoting you to hecatontarch of the third *ala*," he announced. His tone was stern and martial.

The man's eyes widened slightly. He stood a bit straighter.

"Peter of Rhaedestus, as I'm sure you know, is the regiment's tribune. You will report to him."

Then, in a softer tone:

"You are young to be assigned command over a hundred men, and somewhat inexperienced. But both Peter and Constantine, the cavalry's *chiliarch*, speak well of you. And so do the men of my own personal retinue." He motioned slightly toward the back of the tent, where Maurice and the two other cataphracts stood.

Mark glanced toward the Thracians. His face remained still, but the youth's gratitude was apparent.

"Two things, before you go," said Belisarius. All traces of softness vanished from his voice.

"Constantine and Peter—as well as the other tribunes of the cavalry—know my views on corrupt officers, and are in agreement with them. But I will take the time now to express them to you directly. As you are aware, I will not tolerate an officer who steals from his own men. Thus far, since I inherited this army from another, I have satisfied myself with simply dismissing such officers. In the future, however, with officers who take command knowing my views, the punishment will be considerably more severe. Extreme, in fact."

Belisarius paused, gauging the young Syrian, and decided that further elaboration on the matter was unnecessary. Mark's face sheened with perspiration, but the sweat was simply the product of the stifling heat within the tent. Belisarius took a cloth and wiped his own face.

"A final point. You are a cavalryman, and have been, I understand, since you first joined. Is that correct?"

"Yes, sir."

"Then understand something else. *I will not tolerate the cavalry lording it over the infantry.* Do you understand?"

Mark's face twitched, just a tiny bit.

"Speak frankly, Mark of Edessa. If you are unclear as to my meaning, say so. I will explain, and I promise there will be no censure."

The young Syrian glanced at his general, made a quick assessment, and spoke.

"I'm not quite sure I do, sir."

"It's simple, Mark. As you will discover soon enough, my tactical methods use the infantry to far greater effect than Roman armies normally do. But for those tactics to work, the infantry must have the same pride and self-esteem as the cavalry. I can't build and maintain that morale if I have cavalrymen deriding the foot soldiers and refusing to take on their fair share of the hard work, which normally falls almost entirely on the infantry. I will not tolerate cavalrymen lounging around in the shade while foot soldiers sweat rivers, building encampments and fortifications. And mocking the foot soldiers, often enough. Do you understand?"

"Yes, sir." Firmly, clearly.

"Good. You will be allowed to select the *decarchs* for your hundred. All ten of them."

Mark stood very straight. "Thank you, sir."

Belisarius repressed a smile. Sternly:

"Use your own judgment, but I urge you to consult with Peter. And you might also discuss the matter with Maurice, and Gregory. I think you'll find them quite helpful."

"I will do so, sir."

"A word of caution. Advice, rather. Avoid simply selecting from your own circle of friends. Even if they prove capable, it will produce resentment among others. A capable clique is still a clique, and you will undermine your own authority."

"Yes, sir."

"And, most of all, make sure your decarchs understand and accept my attitudes. You will be selecting them, which will reflect upon how I regard you. Your prestige among the cavalrymen whom you command will be thereby enhanced. But do not ever forget the corollary. I will hold you responsible for the conduct of your subordinates, as well as your own. Do I make myself clear?"

"As clear as day, sir." Another quick assessment of his new general. "Syrian day."

Now, Belisarius did smile. "Good. You may go."

Once Mark was gone, the three Thracians at the back of the tent relaxed and resumed their normal casual pose. In public, the members of Belisarius' personal retinue of three hundred cataphracts maintained certain formalities. Most of them, after all, held lowly official ranks. Even Maurice, their commander, was only a hecatontarch—the same official rank as the Syrian youth who had just left the tent.

In actual practice, the Thracian bucellarii served Belisarius as his personal staff. They had been carefully selected by him over a period of years, and the devotion of his retinue was fully reciprocated. Maurice, despite his rank, was in effect Belisarius' executive officer. Even Constantine, who was in overall command of the army's cavalry, along with the chiliarch Phocas, who was his equivalent for the infantry, had learned to accept his actual authority. And, as they got to know the grizzled veteran, respect it as well.

"I believe the boy will work out quite nicely," commented Maurice. "Quite nicely. Once he gets blooded a bit." Maurice's smile vanished, replaced by a scowl. "I can't believe how badly your predecessor Libelarius let this army fall to pieces. Chiseling on fodder and gear is common enough. But we've even found cases where the men's pay was stolen. In some of the infantry regiments, at least."

"And the food!" exclaimed Basil, one of the other cataphracts. "Bad enough these bastards sell off some of the food, but they were cheating at both ends. The food was shit to begin with. Half-rotten when they bought it."

The third of the cataphracts chimed in. He was one of the few non-Thracians in Belisarius' retinue, an Armenian by the name of Ashot.

"What's even worse is the state of the army as a whole. What're we supposed to have, General? Eight thousand men, half cavalry?"

Belisarius nodded.

Ashot laughed scornfully. "What we've got, once you take a real count and strip away the names of fictitious soldiers whose pay these pigs have been pocketing, is *five* thousand men. Not four in ten of them cavalry."

Belisarius wiped his face again. He had spent most of his time, since arriving at the camp, trapped in the leaden, breezeless air of his tent. The heat was oppressive, and the lack of exercise was beginning to tell on him. "And," he concluded wearily, "the force structure's a joke. In order to hide the chiseling, this army's got twice as many official units as it does men to fill them properly."

"Nothing worse than a skeleton army," grumbled Maurice. "I found one infantry hundred that had all of twenty-two actual soldiers in it. *With*, naturally, a full complement of officers—a hecatontarch and all ten decarchs. Living high off the hog." He spit on the floor. "Four of those so-called decarchs didn't have a single soldier under their command. Not even *one*."

Belisarius rose and stretched. "Well, that's pretty much behind us. Within two more days, we'll have this army shaken down into a realistic structure, with decent officers. And decent morale restored to the troops, I think." He cast a questioning glance at Ashot and Basil. Belisarius relied on his low-ranked cataphracts to mingle with the troops and keep his fingers on the pulse of his army.

"Morale's actually high, General," said Ashot. Basil nodded agreement, and added:

"Sure, things are still crappy for the troops. And will be, for a bit. But they don't expect miracles, and they can see things are turning around. Mostly, though, the troops are cheerful as cherubs from watching one sorry-ass chiseler after another come into this tent, and then, within the hour, depart through the gates."

"'Deadly with a blade, is Belisarius,'" quoted Ashot, laughing. "They'd heard that, some of them. Now they all believe it."

"How's the drill going?" asked Belisarius.

Maurice made a fluttering motion with his hand.

"So-so. Just so-so. But I'm not worried about it. The troops are just expressing their last resentment by sloughing it during the drill. Give it a week. Then we'll start seeing results."

"Push it, Maurice. I'm not demanding miracles, but keep in mind that we don't have much time. I can't delay our departure to Mindouos for more than a fortnight."

Belisarius rose and walked over to the entrance of his tent. Leaning against a pole, he stared through the open flap at the camp. As always, his expression was hard to read. But Maurice, watching, knew the general was not happy with his orders.

The orders, received by courier a week earlier, were plain and simple: *Move to Mindouos and build a fort.*

Simple, clear orders. And, Maurice knew, orders which Belisarius considered idiotic.

Belisarius had said nothing to him, of course. For all the general's casual informality when dealing with his Thracian retinue, he maintained a sharp demarcation with regard to matters he considered exclusively reserved for command.

But Maurice knew the general as well as any man. And so he knew, though nothing had been said directly, that Belisarius thought the Roman Empire was deliberately provoking Persia, for no good reason, and was then piling stupidity onto recklessness by provoking the Mede without first seeing to it that the provocation would succeed.

No, Belisarius had said nothing to Maurice. But Maurice knew him well. And if Maurice lacked his general's extraordinary intelligence, he was by no means stupid. And very experienced in the trade of war.

Maurice did not feel himself qualified to make a judgment as to the Emperor's wisdom in provoking the Persians. But he *did* feel qualified to make a judgment on the means the Emperor had chosen to do so. And, he thought, given the state of the Byzantine forces in the area, provoking Persia was about as sensible as provoking a lion with a stick.

The Persians maintained a large army stationed near the upper Euphrates, close to the border. In quiet times, that army was billeted at the fortified city of Nisibis. Now, with hostilities looming, the Mede army had moved north and established a temporary camp, threatening the Anatolian heartland of the Roman Empire.

To oppose them—to *provoke* them, no less—the Romans had only seventeen thousand men in the area. Five thousand of those were represented by Belisarius' army, which, when he assumed command, had proven to be as brittle as a rotten twig. As badly corrupted an army as Maurice had seen anywhere.

The remaining twelve thousand men were stationed not far away, in Lebanon. That army, from what Maurice had been able to determine, was in fairly good condition. Certainly it seemed to have none of the rampant corruption which they had encountered at Daras.

But—

Maurice was an old veteran, well past his fortieth year. He had learned long since that numbers did not weigh as heavily in war as morale and, especially, command. The Army of Lebanon was under the command of two brothers, Bouzes and Coutzes. Not bad fellows, Maurice thought, all things considered. Thracians themselves, as it happened, which predisposed Maurice in their favor. But—young, even younger than Belisarius. And, unfortunately, with none of the wily cunning which so often made Belisarius seem a man of middle age, or even older.

No, bold and brash, were the brothers. And, they had made clear, under no conditions willing to subordinate themselves to Belisarius. Nor could Belisarius force them to. Though he was more experienced than Bouzes and Coutzes—than both of them put together, thought Maurice glumly—and carried a far greater reputation, the brothers were officially ranked as high as he. It was a new rank, for them, and one in which they took great pride. Shiny new generaldom, which they were not about to tarnish by placing under the hand of another.

Outnumbered, under a divided command, his own army shaky from rot, the majority of the Roman forces under the command of brash, untested youth—and, now, ordered to poke the Persian lion.

Belisarius sighed, very faintly, and turned back to the interior of the tent.

"How is the other matter going?" he asked.

"The pilfering?" Belisarius nodded.

"We're bringing it under control," said Maurice. "Now that rations have started to flow properly again, the troops don't have any real reason to steal from the locals. It's more a matter of habit than anything else."

"That's exactly my concern," said Belisarius. "Looting's the worst habit an army can develop."

"Can't stop it, sir," said Maurice. Sometimes, he thought, his beloved general was impractical. Not often, true. He was startled to hear Belisarius' hand slamming the desk.

"Maurice! I don't want to hear the old voice of experience!"

The general was quite angry, Maurice noted, with some surprise. Unusual, that. The old veteran straightened his posture. He did not, however, flinch. Angry generals had long since failed to cause him to quiver in fear. Any generals, much less Belisarius.

And, sure enough, after a moment he saw the crooked smile make its appearance.

"Maurice, I am not a fool. I realize that soldiers look upon booty as one of their time-honored perks. And that's fine—*as long as we're talking about booty.*" Belisarius tightened his own jaw. "It's one thing for an army to share in the spoils of a campaign, fairly apportioned in an organized manner, after the campaign's over and the victory is certain. It's another thing entirely for soldiers to get in the habit of plundering and stealing and generally taking anything they want whenever the mood strikes them. Let that happen, and pretty soon you don't have an army anymore. Just a mob of thieves, rapists, and murderers."

He eyed Maurice. "Speaking of which?"

"Hung 'em yesterday, sir. All four. The girl's surviving brother was able to identify them, once he got over his terror at being here. I sent him on to Aleppo, then, to join his sister."

"Have you heard from the monks?"

Maurice grimaced. "Yes. They've agreed to take care of the girl, as best they can. But they don't expect she'll recover, and—" Another grimace.

"And they had harsh words to say about Christian soldiers."

"Yes, sir."

"As well they might. Did the troops watch the execution?"

"Not the execution itself, no. At least, not the army as a whole. A lot of them did, of course. But I gave orders to let the bodies sway in the breeze, until the heat and the vultures make skeletons out of them. They'll all get the message, sir."

Belisarius wiped his face wearily. "For a time." He stared ruefully at the grimy cloth in his hand. The rag was too soaked to do more than smear the sweat. He reached out and hung it on a peg to dry.

"But there'll be another incident," he continued, after resuming his seat. "This army's had too much rot infect it. Soon enough, there'll be another incident. When it happens, Maurice, I'll have the officer in command of the men strung up alongside them. I won't accept any excuses. Pass the word."

Maurice took a deep breath, then let it out. He wasn't afraid of Belisarius, but he knew when the general wasn't to be budged.

"Yes, sir."

The general's gaze was hard.

"I'm serious about this, Maurice. Make certain the men understand my attitude. Make *absolutely* certain the officers do."

The general relented, slightly. "It's not simply a matter of the conduct one expects from Christian soldiers, Maurice. If the men can't understand that, then make sure they understand the practical side of it. You and I have both seen too many battles lost—or, at best, halfway won—because the troops got diverted at the critical moment. Allowing the enemy to escape, or rally for a counterattack, because they're busy scurrying around for some silver plate and chickens to steal, or a woman to rape. Or just the pleasure of watching a town burn. A town, more often than not, that's the only place to find billeting. Or would have been, if it weren't a pile of ashes."

"Yes, sir."

Belisarius eyed Maurice a moment longer, then smiled. "Trust me in this, old friend. I know you think I've got my head in the clouds, but I'll prove you wrong."

Maurice smiled back. "I've never thought you had your head in the clouds, General. Though, at times, the air you breathe is a bit rarefied."

The hecatontarch eyed his two subordinates and gestured slightly with his head. Immediately, Ashot and Basil left the tent.

"May I suggest you get some sleep, sir." Maurice did not even look toward Procopius. The veteran had made clear, in none too subtle ways, that he regarded the secretary much as he regarded an asp. Procopius set down his pen, arose, and exited the tent himself. Quite hastily.

After the others had left, Maurice made his own exit. But, at the entrance of the tent, he hesitated and turned back.

"I don't want you to misunderstand me, General. I'm skeptical that it'll work, that's all. Other than that, I've no problem with your policy. None. Measured out the ropes myself, I did, and cut the lengths. And enjoyed every moment of it."

Later, after the noises of the camp had died down, Belisarius reached into his tunic and withdrew the jewel. It was resting in the small pouch which Antonina had dug up. He opened the pouch and spilled the jewel onto his palm.

"Come on," he whispered. "You've had enough sleep. I need your help."

The facets spun and flickered. Energy was returning, now. And, during the long stasis, **aim** had been able to—digest, so to speak—its bizarre experiences. The thoughts were clearer now, still as alien but no longer impossible to fathom.

aim did not have much energy yet, but—enough, it decided.

And so it was that the general Belisarius, lying on his cot, almost asleep, suddenly bolted upright.

Again, his face, emerging from the ground. Coalescing from the remnants of spiderwebs and bird wings, and laurel leaves. Suddenly soaring into the heavens, utterly transformed. The wings were now the pinions of a dragon. The laurel leaves, bursting flame and thunder. And the spiderwebs—were the spinnings of his mind, weaving their traps, spreading their strands through an infinite distance.

future.

Chapter 6

"So much for diplomacy," snarled Bouzes, reining his horse around savagely. He glared over his shoulder at the retreating figures of the Persian commanders.

"Filthy Mede dogs," agreed his brother Coutzes. Setting his own horse in motion, he added, "God, how I despise them."

Belisarius, riding alongside, held his tongue. He saw no point in contradicting the brothers. His relations with them were tense enough as it was.

In truth, Belisarius rather liked Persians. The Medes had their faults, of course. The most outstanding of which—and the one which had occasioned the brothers' outburst—was the overweening arrogance of Persian officials. An arrogance which had once again been displayed in the recently concluded parley.

The parley had taken place in the no-man's-land which marked, insofar as anything did, the border between Roman and Persian territory. A brief discussion, on a patch of barren landscape, between six men on horseback. Belisarius and the brothers Bouzes and Coutzes had spoken for the Roman side. The Medes had been represented by Firuz, the Persian commander, and his two principal subordinates, Pityaxes and Baresmanas.

Firuz had demanded the parley. And then, at the parley, demanded that the Romans dismantle the fortress which Belisarius' army had almost completed. Or he would dismantle it for them.

Such, at least, had been the essence of the demand. But Firuz had insisted on conveying the demand in the most offensive

74

manner possible. He had boasted of his own martial prowess and sneered at that of the Romans. (Not forgetting to toss in numerous remarks concerning Roman cowardice and unmanliness.) He had dwelt lovingly on the full-bellied vultures which would soon be the caskets of Roman troops—assuming, of course, that the carrion-eaters were hungry enough to feed on such foul meat.

And so on, and so forth. Belisarius repressed a smile. He thought the polishing touch had been Firuz' demand that Belisarius build a bath in the fortress. He would need the bath, the Persian commander explained, to wash Roman blood and gore off his body. Among which body parts, Firuz explained, the brains of Belisarius himself would figure prominently. The brains of Bouzes and Coutzes would not, of course, as they had none.

Belisarius glanced at Bouzes and Coutzes. The brothers were red-faced with rage. Not for the first time—no, for perhaps the thousandth time—Belisarius reflected on the stupidity of approaching war with any attitude other than craftsmanship. Why should a sane man care what some Persian peacock had to say about him? All the better, as far as Belisarius was concerned, that Firuz was filled with his own self-esteem and contempt for his enemy. It made defeating him all the easier. An arrogant foe was easily duped.

For the first half-hour of their trek back to the Roman fort at Mindouos, Belisarius simply relaxed and enjoyed the ride. It was early afternoon, and the heat was already intense, but at least he was not confined within a stifling tent. And, soon enough, a cooling breeze began to develop. The breeze came from the west, moreover, so it had the further advantage of blowing the dust of their travel behind them.

Yet, that same pleasant breeze brought Belisarius' mind back to his current predicament. He had been giving that breeze much thought, these past days. Very reliable, it was, always arising in early afternoon, and always blowing from the west to the east. He treasured that reliability, caught as he was in a situation with so many variable factors.

As the three men rode back to the camp in silence, therefore, Belisarius began to consider his options. His natural inclination, given the circumstances, would have been to stall for time. For all Firuz' vainglory, Belisarius did not think the Persian was actually ready to launch a war immediately. Stall, stall, stall—and then, perhaps, the Emperor Justinian and his advisers would come to their senses.

But the knowledge that Belisarius now possessed, from the jewel, made that option unworkable. He simply didn't have the time to waste in this idiotic and unnecessary conflict between Byzantium and Persia. Not while the forces of Satan were gathering their strength in India.

I've got to bring this thing to a head, and quickly, and be done with it. The only way to do that is with a resounding victory. Soon.

Which, of course, is easier said than done. Especially with—

He glanced again at the brothers. Bouzes and Coutzes looked enough alike that Belisarius had taken them, at first, for twins. Average height, brown-haired, hazel-eyed, muscular, snub-nosed, and— He would have smiled if he hadn't been so irritated. In truth, the Persian's insult had cut close to the quick. If the brothers had any brains at all, Belisarius had seen precious little indication of them.

After three days of argument, he had managed to get the brothers to agree, grudgingly, to combine their forces. *Three days!*—to convince them of the obvious. There had been no hope, of course, of convincing them to place the combined force under his command. Belisarius had not even bothered to raise the matter. The brothers would have taken offense, and, in high dudgeon, retracted their agreement to combine forces.

Eventually, as they neared the fort at Mindouos, Belisarius decided on his course of action. He saw no alternative, even though he was not happy with the decision. It was a gamble, for one thing, which Belisarius generally avoided.

But, he thought, glancing at the brothers again, *a gamble with rather good odds.*

Now, if Maurice can manage—

He broke off the thought. They were almost at the fortress. The transition from the barren semidesert to the vivid green of the oasis where he had situated his fort was as startling as ever. In no more time than a few horse paces, they moved from a desolate emptiness to a populated fertility. Much of that population was soldiery, of course, but there were still a number of civilians inhabiting the oasis, despite the danger from the nearby Persians. Three grubby but healthy-looking bedouin children, standing under a palm tree nearby, watched the small group of

Roman officers trot past. One of them shouted something in Arabic. Belisarius did not quite make out the words—his Arabic was passable but by no means fluent—but he sensed the cheerful greeting in the tone.

"Hell of a job you did here, Belisarius," remarked Bouzes admiringly, gazing up at the fortress. His brother concurred immediately, then added: "I don't see how you did it, actually. In the time you had. Damned good fort, too. Nothing slap-dash about it."

"I've got some good engineers among my Thracian retinue, for one thing."

"Engineers? Among *cataphracts?*"

Belisarius smiled. "Well, they're not really cataphracts, not proper ones. A bunch of farmers, at bottom, who just picked up the skills."

"Wish we had some real cataphracts," muttered Bouzes. "Don't much care for the snotty bastards, but they're great in a fight."

His brother returned to the subject. "Even with good engineers, I still don't see how you got the work done so quickly."

"The basic way I did it was by setting the cavalry to work and challenging them to match the infantry."

The brothers gaped.

"You had *cavalry* doing that kind of shit work?" demanded Bouzes. He frowned. "Bad for morale, I would think."

"Not the infantry's," rejoined Belisarius. "And, as for the cavalry's morale, you might be surprised. They wailed like lost souls, at first. But, after a bit, they started rising to the challenge. Especially after they heard the infantry taunting them for a lot of weaklings. Then I announced prizes for the best day's work, and the cavalry started pitching into it. They never were as good as the infantry, of course, but by the end they were giving them quite a run for their money. Won a few prizes, even."

Bouzes was still frowning. "Still—even if it doesn't affect their morale directly, it—still."

"Saps their self-esteem, over time," agreed his brother. "Bound to. It's dog work."

Belisarius decided he'd been polite long enough.

"*Dog work, is it?*" he demanded, feigning anger. "I would remind the two of you that the Roman empire was built by such dogs. By *infantry*, not cavalry. Infantry who knew the value of good fortifications, and knew how to put them up. Quickly, and well."

He reined in his horse. They were now at the gate of the fortress. Belisarius pointed to the barrenness beyond the date palms, from which they had just come.

"Do you see that border with Persia? That border was placed there centuries ago. *By infantrymen.* How far has your precious cavalry pushed it since then?"

He glared at them. The brothers looked away.

"Not one mile, that's how far." The gate was opening. Belisarius set his horse back in motion.

"So let's not hear so much boasting about cavalry," he growled, passing through the gate.

Rather well done, he patted himself on the back. *They're not bad fellows, really. If they could just get that stupid crap out of their heads.*

The interior of the fortress was not as imposing as its exterior. In truth, Belisarius *had* been pressed for time, even with the aid of the cavalrymen, and so he had concentrated all effort on the outside walls and fortifications. Within those walls, the fortress was still just an empty parade ground, although it was covered now with the tents of his soldiers. He had not even built a command post for himself, but continued to use his tent as a headquarters.

As soon as Belisarius dismounted and walked into his command tent, followed by the two brothers, Maurice made his appearance.

"We've got a prisoner," the hecatontarch announced. "Just brought him in."

"Where did you catch him?"

"Sunicas' regiment had a skirmish this morning with a group of Persians. About three hundred of them, ten miles north of here. After Sunicas drove them off, they found one fellow lying on the ground. Stunned. Horse threw him."

"Bring him here."

Belisarius took a seat at the large table in the middle of the tent. Bouzes and Coutzes remained standing. A few minutes later, Maurice reappeared, along with Valentinian. Valentinian was pushing a Persian soldier ahead of him. The Persian's wrists were bound behind his back. By his dress and accouterments, Belisarius thought the Persian to be a midlevel officer.

Valentinian forced the Mede into a chair. Exhibiting the usual Persian courage, the officer's face remained still and composed. The Persian was expecting to be tortured, but would not give his enemy the satisfaction of seeing his fear.

His expectation was shared by Bouzes and Coutzes.

"We've got a first-rate torturer," announced Coutzes cheerfully. "I can have him here inside the hour."

"No need," replied Belisarius curtly. The general stared at the Mede. The Persian met his eyes unflinchingly.

For a moment, Belisarius considered interrogating the officer in his own language. Belisarius was fluent in Pallavi, as he was in several languages. But he decided against it. Bouzes and Coutzes, he suspected, were ignorant of the Persian language, and it was important that they be able to follow the interrogation. By the richness of his garb, the Persian was obviously from the aristocracy. His Greek would therefore be fluent, since—in one of those little historical ironies—Greek was the court language of the Sassanid dynasty.

"How many men does Firuz have under his command?" he asked the Mede.

"Fifty-five thousand," came the instant reply. As Belisarius had suspected, the man's Greek was excellent. "That doesn't include the twenty thousand he left in Nisibis," added the Persian.

"What a lot of crap!" snarled Coutzes. "There aren't—"

Belisarius interrupted. "I will allow you four lies, Mede. You've already used up two of them. Firuz has twenty-five thousand men, and he took them all when he left Nisibis."

The muscles along the Persian's jaw tightened, and his eyes narrowed slightly. Other than that, he gave no indication of surprise at the accuracy of Belisarius' information.

"How many of those *twenty-five* thousand are cavalry?" asked Belisarius.

Again, the Mede's answer came with no hesitation:

"We have no more than four thousand infantry. And most of our cavalry are lancers."

"That's the third lie," said Belisarius, very mildly. "And the fourth. Firuz has ten thousand infantry. Of his fifteen thousand cavalry, no more than five are heavy lancers."

The Persian looked away, for a moment, but kept his face expressionless. Belisarius was impressed by the man's courage.

"I'm afraid you've used up all your lies." Without moving his gaze from the Persian, Belisarius asked the two Thracian brothers: "You say you have a good torturer?"

Bouzes nodded eagerly. "We can have him here in no time," said Coutzes.

The captured officer's jaw was now very tight, but the man's gaze was calm and level.

"Has the pay caravan arrived yet?" demanded Belisarius.

For the first time since the interrogation began, the Persian seemed shaken. He frowned, hesitated, and then replied: "What are you talking about?"

Belisarius slammed the table with his open palm.

"Don't play with me, Mede! I know your army's pay chest was sent out from Nisibis five days ago, with an escort of only fifty men."

Belisarius turned his head and looked at Bouzes and Coutzes. A disgusted look came on his face. "Fifty! Can you believe it? Typical Persian arrogance."

Coutzes opened his mouth to speak, but Belisarius motioned him silent. He turned back to the captured officer.

"What I don't know is if the pay caravan has arrived at your camp. So, I ask again: has it?"

The Persian's face was a study in confusion. But, within seconds, the Mede regained his composure.

"I imagine it has," he replied. "I left our camp the day before yesterday. That's why I hadn't heard anything about it. But by now I'm sure it's arrived. Nisibis is only four days' ride. They wouldn't have dawdled."

Belisarius studied the officer silently for some time. Again, Coutzes began to speak, but Belisarius waved him silent. The young Thracian general's face became flushed with irritation, but he held his tongue.

After a couple more minutes of silence, Belisarius leaned back in his chair and placed his hands on his thighs. He seemed to have come to some sort of decision.

"Take him out," he commanded Valentinian. Bouzes began to protest, but Belisarius glared him down.

No sooner were they alone, however, than the brothers erupted.

"What the hell kind of interrogation was that?" demanded Bouzes. "And why did you stop? We still don't know anything about that pay caravan!"

"Silly damn waste of time," snorted Coutzes. "You want to get anything useful from a Mede, you've got to use a—"

"Torturer?" demanded Belisarius. He rolled his eyes despairingly, exhaled disgust, sneered mightily. Then he stood up abruptly and leaned over the table, resting his weight on his fists.

"I can see why you haul around a professional torturer," snarled the general. "I would too, if I was a fool."

He matched the brothers' glare with a scorching look of his own.

"Let me explain something to you," he said icily. "I wasn't in the slightest bit interested in getting information from the Persian regarding the pay caravan. He doesn't know anything about it. How could he? The pay caravan only left Nibisis the day before yesterday."

"The day before yesterday?" demanded Bouzes, puzzled. "But you said—"

"I said *to an enemy officer* that the pay chest left five days ago."

The brothers were now silent, frowning. Belisarius resumed his seat.

"My spies spotted the caravan as soon as it left the gates of the city. One of them rode here as fast as possible, using remounts. There's no way that caravan has reached Firuz' camp yet."

"Then why did you—"

"Why did I ask the Mede about it? I simply wanted to get his immediate reaction. You saw what a talented liar he was. Yet when I asked him about the pay caravan, he had to fumble for an answer. What does that tell you?"

Apparently, they weren't that stupid, for both brothers immediately got the point.

"The Persians themselves don't know about it!" they exclaimed, like a small chorus.

Belisarius nodded. "I'd heard that the Medes were starting to send out some of their pay caravans in this manner. Instead of tying up a small army to escort the caravans, they're relying on absolute secrecy. Even the soldiers for whom the pay's destined don't know about it, until the caravan arrives."

The brothers exchanged glances. Belisarius chuckled.

"Tempting, isn't it? But I'm afraid we'll have to let it go. This time, anyway."

"Why?" demanded Bouzes.

"Yes, why?" echoed his brother. "It's a perfect opportunity. Why shouldn't we seize it?"

"You're not thinking clearly. First, we have no idea what route the caravan's taking. Don't forget, we'd only have one day—two at the most—to catch the caravan before it arrives at the Persian camp. In order to be sure of finding it, we'd have to send out an entire regiment of cavalry. At the very least. Two regiments, to be on the safe side."

"So?" demanded Coutzes.

"*So?*" Belisarius cast an exasperated glance upward. "You *were* at the parley with Firuz today, were you not?"

"What's the point, Belisarius?"

"The point, Coutzes, is that Firuz is getting ready to attack us. We're outnumbered. We need to stay on the defensive. This is the worst time in the world for us to be sending our cavalry chasing all over Syria. We need them here, at the fort. Every man."

Coutzes began to argue, but his brother cut him short by grabbing his arm.

"Let's not get into an argument! There's no point in it, and it's too hot." He wiped his brow dramatically. Belisarius restrained a smile. In truth, there was hardly any sweat on Bouzes' face.

Bouzes wiped his brow again, in a gesture worthy of Achilles. Then said: "I think we've finished all our business here. Or is there anything else?"

Belisarius shook his head. "No. Your officers have all been told that we are combining our forces?"

"Yes, they know."

A brief exchange of amenities followed, in which Coutzes participated grudgingly. Bouzes, on the other hand, was cordiality itself. The brothers left the tent, with Belisarius escorting them. He chatted politely, while Bouzes and Coutzes mounted their horses. He did not return into the tent until he saw the brothers cantering through the gates of the fort.

Maurice was waiting for him inside.

"Well?" asked the hecatontarch.

"At nightfall, give the captured Persian officer my message for Firuz and let him go. Make sure he has a good horse. Then pass the word quietly to the men. I expect we'll be leaving at dawn."

"That soon?"

"Unless I'm badly mistaken, yes." He glanced back at the entrance to the tent. "And I don't think I'm mistaken."

"You should be ashamed of yourself."

Belisarius smiled crookedly. "I am mortified, Maurice, mortified."

The hecatontarch grunted sarcastically, but forebore comment. "Ashot's back," he said.

"What did he think of the location?"

"Good. The hill will do nicely—*if* the wind blows the right way."

"It should, by midday."

"And if it doesn't?"

Belisarius shrugged. "We'll just have to manage. Even if there's no wind, the dust alone should do the trick. If the wind blows the wrong way, of course, we'll be in a tight spot. But I've never seen it blow from the east until evening." He took a seat at the table. "Now, send for the chiliarchs and the tribunes. I want to make sure they understand my plan perfectly."

That night, immediately after the conclusion of the meeting with his chief subordinates, Belisarius lay down on his cot. For almost an hour he lay there in the darkness, thinking over his plans, before he finally fell asleep.

As the general pondered, **aim** delved through the corridors of his mind. Time after time, the facets threatened to splinter. Despair almost overwhelmed them. Just when the alien thoughts had begun to come into focus! And now, they were—somehow at odds with themselves. It was like trying to learn a language whose grammar was constantly changing. Impossible!

But **aim** was now growing in confidence, and so it was able to control the facets. With growing confidence, came patience. It was true, the thoughts were contradictory—like two images, identical, yet superimposed over each other at right angles. Patience. Patience. In time, **aim** sensed it could bring them into focus.

And, in the meantime, there was something of much greater concern. For, despite the blurring, there was one point on which all the paradoxical images in the general's mind coalesced sharply.

At the very edge of sleep, Belisarius sensed a thought. But he was too tired to consider its origin.

danger.

Chapter 7

Belisarius awoke long before dawn. Within a short time after rising, he was satisfied that the preparations for the march were well in hand. Both of his chiliarchs were competent officers, and it soon became apparent that the tribunes and hecatontarchs had absorbed fully the orders he had given them the night before.

Maurice came up to him. Belisarius recognized him from a distance, even though it was still dark. Maurice had a rolling gait which was quite unmistakable.

"Now?" asked Maurice.

Belisarius nodded. The two men mounted their horses and cantered through the gate. The Army of Lebanon was camped just beyond the fort, where its soldiers could enjoy the shade and water provided by the oasis. Within a few minutes, Belisarius and Maurice were dismounting before the command tent occupied by Bouzes and Coutzes.

The tent was much larger than the one Belisarius used, although not excessively so by the standards of Roman armies. Roman commanders had long been known for traveling in style. Julius Caesar had even carried tiles with him to floor his tent. (Although he claimed to have done so simply to impress barbarian envoys; Belisarius was skeptical of the claim.)

Upon their arrival, the sentries guarding the tent informed them that Bouzes and Coutzes were absent. They had left the camp in the middle of the night. Further questioning elicited the information that the brothers had taken two cavalry regiments along with them.

Belisarius uttered many profane oaths, very loudly. He stalked off toward the nearby tent, which was occupied by the four chiliarchs who were the chief subordinate officers of the Army of Lebanon. Maurice followed.

At the chiliarchs' tent, a sentry began to challenge Belisarius, but quickly fell silent. The sentry recognized him, and saw as well that the general was in a towering rage. Deciding that discretion was the order of the day, the sentry drew aside. Belisarius stormed into the tent.

Three of the four chiliarchs were rising from sleep, groggy and bleary-eyed. One of them lit a lamp. Belisarius immediately demanded to know the whereabouts of the fourth. He allowed the three chiliarchs to stammer in confusion for a few seconds before he cut through the babble.

"So. I assume Dorotheus has accompanied the two cretins in this lunacy?"

The chiliarchs began to protest. Again, Belisarius cut them short.

"Silence!" He threw himself into a chair by the table in the center of the tent. He glared about for a moment, and then slammed his palm down on the table.

"I am being generous! The Emperor may forgive the idiots, if he decides they are just stupid."

Mention of the Emperor caused all three of the chiliarchs to draw back a bit. The face of at least one of them, Belisarius thought, grew pale. But it was hard to tell. The interior of the tent was poorly lit.

Belisarius allowed the silence to fester. He knotted his brow. After a minute or so, he rose and began pacing about, exuding the image of a man lost in thoughtful calculation. Actually, he was scrutinizing the interior of the tent. He believed firmly that one could make a close assessment of officers by examining their private quarters, and took advantage of the opportunity to do so.

Overall, he was impressed. The chiliarchs maintained clean and orderly quarters. There was no indication of the drunken sloppiness which had characterized the tents of a number of the former officers of his own army. He also noted the austerity of their living arrangements. Other than weapons and necessary gear, the chiliarchs' tent was bare of possessions.

The general was pleased. He prized austere living on campaign— not from any religious or moral impulse, but simply because he valued the ability to react and move quickly above all other characteristics in an officer. And he had found, with very few exceptions, that officers who filled their command quarters with lavish creature comforts were sluggards when confronted by any sudden change in circumstances.

He decided the pose of thoughtful concentration had gone on long enough. He stopped pacing, straightened his back, and announced decisively:

"There's nothing for it. We'll just have to make do with what we have."

He turned to the three chiliarchs, who were now clustered together on the other side of the table.

"Assemble your army. We march at once."

"But our commanders aren't here!" protested one of the cavalry chiliarchs. Belisarius gave him a fierce look of disgust.

"I'm aware of that, Pharas. And you can be quite sure that if we fail to intercept the Persians before they march into Aleppo, the Emperor will know of their absence also. And do as he sees fit. But in the absence of Bouzes and Coutzes, I am in command of this army. And I have no intention of imitating their dereliction of duty."

His announcement brought a chill into the room.

"The Persians are marching?" asked Hermogenes, the infantry chiliarch.

"The day after tomorrow."

"How do you know?" demanded Pharas.

Belisarius sneered. "Doesn't the Army of Lebanon have *any* spies?" he demanded. The chiliarchs were silent. The general's sneer turned into a truly ferocious scowl.

"Oh, that's marvelous!" he exclaimed. "You have no idea what the enemy is doing. So, naturally, you decided to send two full cavalry regiments charging off on a wild goose chase. Just marvelous!"

Pharas' face was ashen. To some extent, it was the pallor of rage. But, for the most part, it was simple fear. Watching him, Belisarius estimated the man's intelligence as rather dismal. But even Pharas understood the imperial fury which would fall on the chief officers of the Army of Lebanon if they allowed the Persians to march on Aleppo unopposed.

The junior cavalry chiliarch, Eutyches, suddenly slammed his hand onto the table angrily.

"Mother of God! I told them—" He bit off the words. Clamped his jaw tight. For a moment, he and Belisarius stared at each other. Then, with a faint nod, and an even fainter smile, Belisarius indicated his understanding and appreciation of Eutyches' position.

The infantry chiliarch spoke then. The timber of his voice reflected Hermogenes' youth, but there was not the slightest quaver in it. "Let's move. *Now.* We all know that Coutzes and Bouzes agreed to combine forces with Belisarius' army. Since they're not here, that makes him the rightful commander."

Eutyches immediately nodded his agreement. After a moment, reluctantly, so did Pharas.

Belisarius seized the moment. "Rouse your army and assemble them into marching formation," he commanded. "Immediately." He stalked out of the tent.

Once outside, Belisarius and Maurice returned to their horses. The first glimmer of dawn was beginning to show on the eastern horizon.

Belisarius gazed about admiringly. "It's going to be a lovely day."

"It's going to be miserably hot," countered Maurice.

Belisarius chuckled quietly. "You are the most morose man I have ever met."

"I am not morose. I am pessimistic. My cousin Ignace, now, *there's* a morose man. You've never met him, I don't believe?"

"How could I have met him? Didn't you tell me he hasn't left his house for fifteen years?"

"Yes, that's true." The hecatontarch eyed Belisarius stonily. "He's terrified of swindlers. And rightfully so."

Belisarius chuckled again. "A lovely day, I tell you." Then, businesslike: "I'm going to stay here, Maurice. If I don't chivvy this army, they'll take forever to get moving. I want you to return to the fort and make sure everything goes properly. I think Phocas and Constantine will manage everything well enough. But I haven't worked with them in the field before, so I want you to keep an eye on things. Remember the two key points: keep—"

"Keep a large cavalry screen well out in front and make sure the infantry gets dug in quickly. With at least half of them hidden behind the ramparts."

The general smiled. "A lovely day. Be off."

❖　　　❖　　　❖

As Belisarius had expected, it took hours to get the Army of Lebanon moving. Despite his loud and profane comments, however, he was quite satisfied with the progress. It was unreasonable to expect an army of twelve thousand men to start a march more quickly, with no advance warning or preparations.

By midday, the army was well into its marching rhythm. The temperature was oppressive. The western breeze which sprang up in the afternoon did not help the situation much. True, the wind brought a bit of coolness. But since the army was marching northeast, it also swept the dust thrown up by hooves and feet along the march route instead of away. At least the dust was not blown directly into the soldiers' faces, although that was a small consolation. Syria in midsummer was as unpleasant a place and time to be making a forced march as any in the world.

However, Belisarius noted that the commanding officers of the Army of Lebanon refrained from complaining. Whatever their misgivings might be regarding this unexpected expedition, under unexpected command, they seemed willing to keep them private. He now took the time to explain to the three chiliarchs his plan for the battle he expected shortly. The two cavalry chiliarchs seemed skeptical of the role planned for the infantry, but forbore comment. They were pleased enough with their own projected role, and the infantry was none of their concern anyway.

As evening approached, Belisarius concentrated on discussing his plans with Hermogenes, the infantry chiliarch. Hermogenes, he was pleased to see, soon began to evince real enthusiasm. All too often, Roman infantry commanders occupied that position by virtue of their incompetence and fecklessness. Hermogenes, on the other hand, seemed an ambitious fellow, happy to discover that his own role in the upcoming conflict was to be more than a sideshow.

By nightfall, Belisarius was satisfied that Hermogenes would be able to play his part properly. In fact, he thought the young chiliarch might do very well. Belisarius decided to place Hermogenes in overall command of the infantry, once the Army of Lebanon was united with his own army. Phocas, his own infantry chiliarch, was a competent officer, but by no means outstanding. On the other hand, Phocas did have a knack for artillery. So Belisarius would put Phocas under Hermogenes' command, with the specific responsibility for the artillery.

Belisarius pushed the march until the very last glimmer of daylight faded before ordering the army to encamp for the night. The Army of Lebanon, he noted with satisfaction, set up its camp quickly and expertly.

After his command tent was set up, Belisarius enjoyed a few moments of privacy within it. He found the absence of Procopius a relief. For all the man's competence, and for all that his most sycophantish habits had been beaten down, the general still found his new secretary extremely annoying. But Procopius was now at the villa near Daras—and had been since Belisarius moved his army to Mindouos. The general had seen no use for him during an actual campaign, and had ordered the man to provide Antonina with whatever assistance she needed in running the estate.

He heard a commotion outside and went to investigate. Maurice had arrived, along with Ashot and three other Thracian cataphracts. By the time Belisarius emerged from his tent, his bucellarii were already dismounted from their horses. With them, dismounting more slowly—pain and exhaustion in every movement—were eight members of the two vanished cavalry regiments. One of the eight was an officer, and all of them looked much the worse for wear. Even in the dim moonlight, the general could see that three of them were wounded, although the wounds did not seem especially severe.

The officer limped over to Belisarius and began to stammer out some semicoherent phrases. Belisarius commanded him to hold his tongue until he could summon the chiliarchs and the tribunes. A few minutes later, with the leadership of the Army of Lebanon packed into the command tent, he instructed the returning officer to tell his tale. This he did, somewhat chaotically, with Maurice lending an occasional comment.

Bouzes and Coutzes, it turned out, had not found the pay caravan. What they had found, charging all over the landscape looking for it, was half of the Persian cavalry, charging all over the landscape looking for it likewise. An impromptu battle had erupted, in which the heavily outnumbered Romans had taken a drubbing. The two brothers had been captured. In the end, most of the Roman cavalry had escaped, in disorganized groups, and were being encountered by Belisarius' own army as it marched forward into position. Though badly demoralized and half-leaderless, the surviving members of the two regiments had been so delighted to find a large formation of Roman troops in the vicinity that they were rallying to the standards of Belisarius' army.

When the officer concluded his tale, Belisarius refrained from commenting on the stupidity of Bouzes and Coutzes. Under the circumstances, he thought, it would be superfluous. He simply concluded the meeting with a brief review of his plans for the forthcoming battle, then sent everyone to bed.

"Things are going well," he remarked to Maurice, once they were in private.

Maurice gave him a hard look. "You're playing this one awfully close, young man."

Belisarius eyed him. Maurice was not, in private, given to formality and subservience. Even in public, he satisfied himself with nothing more than the occasional "sir" and "my lord." But he rarely addressed his general by his own name, and hadn't called him a "young man" since—

Belisarius smiled crookedly. "I won that battle, too, if you recall."

"By the skin of your teeth. And it took you weeks to recover from your wounds." Morosely, rubbing his right side: "Took me even longer."

Thinking the tent was too gloomy, Belisarius lit another lamp and placed it on the table. Then, after taking a seat in his chair, he examined the hecatontarch's grim visage. He was quite confident of his own plans, despite their complexity, but he had learned never to ignore Maurice's misgivings.

"Spit it out, Maurice. And spare me your reproaches concerning the two brothers."

Maurice snorted. "Them? Drooling babes are cute, but they've no business leading armies. I care not a fig about that!" He waved a hand dismissively. "No, what bothers me is that you're cutting everything too fine. You're depending on almost perfect timing, and on the enemy to react exactly as you predict." He gave Belisarius another stony look. "You may recall my first lessons to you when you were barely out of swaddling clothes. Never—"

"Never expect the enemy to do what you think he's going to do, and never expect that schedules will be met on time. And, most of all, always remember the first law of battle: everything gets fucked up as soon as the enemy arrives. *That's why he's called the enemy.*"

Maurice grunted. Then:

"And whatever happened to your devious subtlety? That 'oblique approach' you're so fond of talking about?" He held up a hand. "And don't bother reminding me how shrewd your battle plan is! *So what?* This isn't like you at all, Belisarius. You've never been one to substitute tactics for strategy. How many times have you told me the best campaign is the one which forces the enemy to yield by indirection, with the least amount of bloodshed? Much less a pitched battle which *you're* forcing?"

Belisarius took in a deep breath and held it. The fingers of his left hand began drumming the table. For a moment, as he had done many times over the past weeks, he considered taking Maurice into his full confidence. Again, he decided against it. True, Maurice was close-mouthed. But—there was the first law of secrets: every person told a secret doubles the chance of having it found out.

"Stop drumming your fingers," grumbled the hecatontarch. "You only do that when you're being too clever by half."

Belisarius chuckled, snapped his left hand into a fist. He decided on a halfway course. "Maurice, there is information which I possess which I can't divulge to you now. *That's* why I'm pushing this battle. I know I'm cutting too many corners, but I don't have any choice."

Maurice scowled. "What do you know about the Persians that I don't?" It was not a question, really. More in the way of a scornful reproof.

Belisarius waved his own hand dismissively. "No, not the Persians." He smiled. "I wouldn't presume to know more about the Medes than you! No, it involves—other enemies. I can't say more, Maurice. Not yet."

Maurice considered his general carefully. He wasn't happy with the situation, but—there it was.

"All right," he said, grunting. "But I hope this works."

"It will, Maurice, it will. The timing doesn't have to be that perfect. We just have to get to the battleground before the Persians do. And as for the enemy's reactions—I think that letter I sent off to Firuz will do the trick nicely."

"Why? What did you say in it?"

"Well, the essence of the letter was a demand that he refrain from threatening my shiny new fort. But I conveyed the demand in the most offensive manner possible. I boasted of my martial prowess and sneered at that of the Medes. I tossed in a few well-chosen remarks on the subject of Persian cowardice and unmanliness. I dwelt lovingly on the full-bellied worms which would soon be the caskets of Persian troops—assuming, of course, that the slimy things were hungry enough to feed on such foul meat."

"Oh my," muttered Maurice. He stroked his gray beard.

"But I thought the polishing touch," concluded Belisarius cheerfully, "was my refusal to build a bath in the fortress. Firuz wouldn't need the bath, I explained, because after I slaughtered him, I would toss his remains into the latrine. Which is where they belong, of course, since he's nothing but a walking sack of dog shit."

"Oh my." Maurice pulled up a chair and sat down slowly. For the hecatontarch, the simple act was unusual. A stickler for proprieties was Maurice. He almost never sat while in his general's headquarters.

"We'd better win this battle," he muttered, "or we're all for it." His right hand clenched his sword hilt. His left hand was spread rigidly on the table.

Belisarius leaned over and patted the outstretched hand. "So you can see, Maurice, why I think Firuz will show up at the battlefield."

Maurice made a sour expression. "Maybe. They're touchy, Persian nobles. But if he's smart enough to override his anger, he'll pick a battlefield of his own choosing."

Belisarius leaned back and shrugged.

"I don't think so. I don't think he's that smart, and anyway—the battle site I selected overlooks the stream that provides all the water for his camp. Whether he likes it or not, he can't very well just let us sit there unmolested."

"You would," retorted Maurice instantly.

"I wouldn't have camped there in the first place."

Maurice's right hand released its grip on the sword, and came up to stroke his beard. "True, true. Idiotic, that—relying on an insecure water supply. If you can't find a well or an oasis, like we did, you should at least make sure the water comes from your own territory."

The hecatontarch straightened up a bit. "All right, General. We'll try it. Who knows, it might even work. That's the one and only good thing about the first law of battles—it cuts both ways."

A moment later, Maurice arose. His movements had regained their usual vigor and decisiveness. Belisarius left his chair and accompanied the hecatontarch out of the tent.

"How soon do you expect to reach the battlefield?" asked Belisarius.

Maurice took the reins of his horse and mounted. Once in the saddle, he shrugged.

"We're making good time," he announced. "It'll slow us down a bit, having to gather up what's left of the two cavalry regiments, but—we should be able to start digging in by midafternoon tomorrow."

Belisarius scratched his chin. "That should leave enough time. God knows the soldiers have had enough practice at it lately. Make sure—"

"Make sure the cavalry does its share," concluded Maurice. "Make sure the artillery's well-positioned. Make sure there's food ready for the Army of Lebanon when it arrives. And whatever else, make sure the hill is secure."

Belisarius smiled up at him. "Be off. You've got a long ride back to our army. But there's a lovely moon out tonight."

Maurice forbore comment.

Back in his tent, lying on his cot, Belisarius found it difficult to fall asleep. In truth, he shared some of Maurice's concern. He *was* gambling too much. But he saw no other option.

His fist closed around the pouch holding the jewel. At once, a faint thought came.

danger.

He sat up, staring down. A moment later, after opening the pouch, the jewel was resting in the palm of his hand.

The thought came again, much stronger.

danger.

"It *was* you, last night," he whispered.

danger.

"I know that! Tell me something I don't know. *What are you?*"

The facets shivered and reformed, splintered and came together, all in a microsecond. But **aim** never vanished, never even wavered. In a crystalline paroxysm, the facets forged a thought which could penetrate the barrier. But **aim** was overconfident, tried to do too much. The complex and fragile thought shattered into pieces upon first contact with the alien mind. Only the residue remained, transmuted into an image:

A metallic bird, bejewelled, made of hammered silver and gold-enamelling. Perched on a painted, wrought-iron tree. One of the marvelous constructs made for the Emperor Justinian's palace.

"You were never made by Grecian goldsmiths," muttered Belisarius. "Why are you here? What do you want from me? And where are you from?"

aim surged:

future.

Belisarius blew out an exasperated sigh. "I know the future!" he exclaimed. "You showed it to me. But can it be changed? And where are you *from*?"

Frustration was the greater for the hope which had preceded it. **aim** itself almost splintered, for an instant. But it rallied, ruthless with determination. Out of the flashing movement of the facets came a lesson learned. Patience, patience. Concepts beyond the most primitive could not yet cross the frontier. Again:

future.

The general's eyes widened.

Yes! Yes! Again! The facets froze, now ruthless in their own determination.

future. future. future.

"Mary, Mother of God."

Belisarius arose and walked slowly about in his tent. He clenched the jewel tightly in his fist, as if trying to force the thoughts from the thing like he might squeeze a sponge.

"More," he commanded. "The future must be a wondrous place. Nothing else could have created such a wonder as you. So what can you want from the past? What can we possibly have to offer?"

Again, a metallic bird. Bejewelled, made of hammered silver and gold enamelling. Perched on a painted, wrought-iron tree. But now the focus was sharper, clearer. Like one of the marvelous constructs made for the Emperor Justinian's palace, yes, but vastly more intricate and cunning in its design.

"*Men* created you?" he demanded. "Men of the future?"

yes.

"I say again: *what do you want?*"

aim hesitated, for a microsecond. Then, knew the task was still far beyond its capability. Patience, patience. Where thought could not penetrate, vision might:

Again, the thunderclap. Again: the tree shattered, the ceremony crushed beneath a black wave. Again: crystals, strewn across a barren desert, shriek with despair. Again, in an empty, sunless sky, giant faces begin to take form. Cold faces. Pitiless faces. Human faces, but with all of human warmth banished.

The general frowned. Almost—

"Are you saying that *we* are the danger to you? In the future? And that you have come to the past for help? That's crazy!"

The facets shivered and spun, almost in a frenzy. Now they demanded and drove the demand upon **aim**. But **aim** had learned well. The thoughts were still far too complex to breach the frontier. Imperiously it drove the facets back: patience, patience.

Again, the giant faces. Human faces. Monstrous faces. Dragon-scaled faces.

"Mary, Mother of God," he whispered. "It's true."

An explosive emotion erupted from the jewel. It was like a child's wail of—not anger, so much as deep, deep hurt at a parent's betrayal. A pure thought even forced its way through the barrier.

you promised.

Truly, thought Belisarius, it was the plaint of a bereaved child, coming from a magical stone.

The general weighed the jewel. As before, he was struck by its utter weightlessness. Yet it did not float away, somehow, but stayed in his hand. Like a trusting child.

"I do not understand you," he whispered. "Not truly, not yet. But—if you have truly been betrayed, I will do for you what I can."

That thought brought another smile, very crooked. "Though I'm not sure what I could do. What makes you think I could be of help?"

A sudden surge of warmth came from the jewel. Tears almost came to Belisarius' eyes. He was reminded of that precious moment, weeks earlier, when Photius had finally accepted him. The boy had been skittish, at first, not knowing what to make of this unknown, strange, large man who called himself his father. But the time had come, one evening, when the boy fell asleep before the fire. And, as he felt the drowsiness, had clambered into his stepfather's lap and lain his little head upon a large shoulder. Trusting in the parent to keep him warm and safe through the night.

Belisarius was silent for a time, pondering. He knew something had gone awry, terribly wrong, in that future he could not imagine. Danger. Danger. Danger.

He realized that the jewel was nearing exhaustion and decided that he must put off further questioning. Communication was becoming easier, slowly. Patience, patience. He had danger enough in the present to deal with, in any event.

But still—there was one question.

"Why did you come here, to the past? What can there possibly be here that would help you in—whatever dangers you face in your future?"

The jewel was fading rapidly now. But the faint image came again:

A face, emerging from the ground, made from spiderwebs and bird wings, and laurel leaves. His face.

Chapter 8

"It's perfect," pronounced Belisarius.

"It's the silliest trap I ever saw," pronounced Maurice. "Not even a schoolboy would fall for it. Not even a Hun schoolboy."

"There are no Hun schoolboys."

"Exactly my point," grumbled Maurice.

Belisarius smiled—broadly, not crookedly.

"There's nothing wrong with my plan and you know it. You're just angry at your part in it."

"And that's another thing! It's ridiculous to use your best heavy cavalry to—"

"Enough, Maurice." The general's voice was mild, but Maurice understood the tone. The hecatontarch fell silent. For a few minutes, he and Belisarius stood together atop the small hill on the left flank of the Roman forces. They said nothing, simply watched the gathering array of the Persian forces coming from the east. The enemy's army was still some considerable distance away, but Belisarius could see the first detachments of light cavalry beginning to scout the Roman position.

Before the Medes could get more than a mile from the Roman lines, however, three *ala* of Hun light cavalry from the Army of Lebanon advanced to meet them. There was a spirited exchange of arrows before the Persian scouts retreated. Casualties were few, on either side, but Belisarius was quite satisfied with the results of the encounter. It was essential to his plan that the Persians not have the opportunity to scout his position carefully.

"That'll keep the bastards off," grunted Maurice.

"Best be about it," said Belisarius. "It's almost noon. The wind'll be picking up soon."

Maurice scanned the sky.

"Let's hope so. If it doesn't—"

"Enough."

Belisarius strode down the back side of the hill toward his horse. Behind him, he heard Maurice begin to issue orders, but he could not make out their specific content. Instructions to the disgruntled Thracian cataphracts, no doubt.

Very disgruntled, indeed. The Thracian cataphracts looked upon foot travel—much less *fighting* on foot—with the enthusiasm of a drunk examining a glass of water. The *elite*, they were—and now, assigned to serve as bodyguards for a bunch of miserable, misbegotten, never-to-be-sufficiently-damned, common foot archers. Downright *plebes*. *Barbarians*, no less.

Which, in truth, they were. The four hundred archers atop the hill were a mercenary unit, made up entirely of Isaurian hillmen from southern Anatolia. An uncivilized lot, the Isaurians, but very tough. And completely accustomed to fighting on foot in rocky terrain, either with bows or with hand weapons.

Belisarius smiled. He knew his cataphracts. Once the Thracians saw the Isaurian archers at work, they would not be able to resist the challenge. Personally, Belisarius thought his cataphracts were better archers than any in the Army of Lebanon. They would certainly try to prove it. By the time the Persians tried to drive them off the hill, the Thracians would be in full fury.

Belisarius paused for a moment in his downward descent, and reexamined the hill.

Perfect. Steep sides, rocky. The worst possible terrain for a cavalry charge. And Persian nobles view fighting on foot like bishops view eternal damnation. God help the arrogant bastards, trying to drive armored horses up these slopes against dismounted Thracian cataphracts and Isaurian hillmen.

He resumed his descent down the western slope of the hill. Near the bottom, he came to the hollow where the Thracian horses were being held. A small number of the youngest and most inexperienced cataphracts had been assigned to hold the horses during the battle. They were even more disgruntled than their veteran fellows.

One of them, a lad named Menander, brought Belisarius his horse.

"General, are you sure I couldn't—"

"Enough." Then, Belisarius relented. "You know, Menander, it's likely the Persians will send a force around the hill to attack our rear. I imagine the fighting here will be hot and furious."

"Really?"

"Oh, yes. A desperate affair. Desperate."

Belisarius hoped he was lying. If the Persians managed to get far enough around the hill to find the hollow where the Thracian horses were being held, it would mean that they had driven off the heavy cavalry guarding his left wing and his whole battle plan was in ruins. His army too, most likely.

But Menander cheered up. The boy helped Belisarius onto his horse. Normally, Belisarius was quite capable of vaulting onto his horse. But not today, encumbered as he was with full armor. No cataphract in full armor could climb a horse without a stool or a helping hand.

Once he was firmly in the saddle, Belisarius heaved a little sigh of relief. For the hundredth time, he patted himself on the back for his good sense in having all of his Thracian cavalry equipped with Scythian saddles instead of the flimsy Roman ones. Roman "saddles" were not much more than a thin pad. Scythian saddles were solid leather, and—much more to the point—had a cantle and a pommel. With a Scythian saddle, an armored cavalryman had at least half a chance of staying on his horse through a battle.

Belisarius heard noises behind him. Turning, he saw two of his cataphracts coming down the hill at a fast trot. As fast a "trot," at least, as could be managed by men wearing: full suits of scale-mail armor—including chest cuirasses—covering their upper bodies, right arms, and their abdomens down to mid-thigh; open-faced iron helmets with side-flanges, of the German *spangenhelm* style favored by most of the Thracians; small round shields buckled to their upper left arms, leaving the left hand free to wield a bow; heavy quilted Persian-style cavalry trousers; and, of course, a full panoply of weapons. The weapons included a long lance, a powerful compound bow, a quiver of arrows, long Persian-style cavalry swords, daggers, and the special personal weapons of the individuals: in the case of one, a mace; in the case of the other, a spatha.

Belisarius recognized the approaching cataphracts, recognized their purpose, and began to frown fiercely. But when the two cataphracts neared, his words of hot reproach were cut off before he could utter them.

"Don't bother, General," said Valentinian.

"No use at all," agreed Anastasius.

"Direct orders from Maurice."

"Very direct."

"You're just the general."

"Maurice is the Maurice."

Belisarius grimaced. There was no point in trying to send Valentinian and Anastasius away. They wouldn't obey his order, and he could hardly enforce it on them personally, since—

He eyed the two men.

Since I don't think there are two tougher soldiers in the whole Roman army, that's why.

So he tried reason.

"I don't need bodyguards."

"Hell you don't," came Valentinian's sharp, nasal reply.

"Was ever a man needed a bodyguard, it's you," added Anastasius. As ever, the giant's voice sounded like rumbling thunder. Professional church bassos had been known to turn green with envy, hearing that voice.

Menander was already bringing up the two cataphracts' horses. Anastasius' mount was the largest charger anyone had ever seen. Anastasius was devoted to the beast, as much out of genuine affection as simple self-preservation. No smaller horse could have borne his weight, in full armor, in the fury of a battlefield. Especially encumbered as the horse was with its own armor: scale mail covering the top of its head and its neck down to the withers, with additional sheets of mail protecting its chest and its front shoulders.

Anastasius more or less tossed Valentinian onto his horse. Then he mounted his own, with Menander's help. By the time he was aboard, the young cataphract looked completely exhausted by the effort of hoisting him.

Belisarius rode off, heading toward the center of the Roman lines. Behind him, he heard his two companions expressing their thoughts on the day.

"Look at it this way, Valentinian: it beats fighting on foot."

"It certainly does *not*."

"You hate to walk, even, much less—"

"So what? Not so bad, butchering a bunch of Medes trying to scramble their horses up that godawful hill. Instead—"

"Maybe he'll—"

"You know damn well he won't. When has he ever?"

Heavy sigh, like a small rockslide.

Again, Valentinian: "Huh? When has he ever? Name one time! Just one!"

Heavy sigh.

Mutter, mutter, mutter.

"What was that last, Valentinian?" asked Belisarius mildly. "I didn't quite make it out."

Silence.

Anastasius: "Sounded like 'fuck bold commanders, anyway.'"

Hiss.

Anastasius: "But maybe not. Maybe the bad-tempered skinny cutthroat said: 'Fuck old commoners, anyway.' Stupid thing to say, under the circumstances, of course. Especially since he's a commoner himself. But maybe that's what he said. He's bad-tempered about everything, you know."

Hiss.

Belisarius never turned his head. Just smiled. Crookedly, at first, then broadly.

Well, maybe Maurice is right. God help the Mede who tries to get in my way, that's for sure.

Once he reached the fortified camp at the center of the Roman lines, Belisarius dismounted and entered through the small western gate. Valentinian and Anastasius chose to remain outside. It was too much trouble to dismount and remount, and there was no way to ride a horse into *that* camp.

The camp was nothing special, in itself. It had been hastily erected in one day, and consisted of nothing much more than a ditch backed up by an earthen wall. Normally, such a wall would have been corduroyed, but there were precious few logs to be found in that region. To some degree, the soldiers had been able to reinforce the wall with field stones. Where possible, they had placed the customary *cervi*—branches projecting sideways from the wall—but there were few suitable branches to be found in that barren Syrian terrain. Some of the more far-sighted and enterprising units had brought sharpened stakes with them to serve the purpose, but the wall remained a rather feeble obstacle. A pitiful wall, actually, by the traditional standards of Roman field fortifications.

But Belisarius was not unhappy with the wall. Not, not in the slightest. Quite the contrary. He *wanted* the Persian scouts to report to Firuz that the Roman fortification at the center of their lines was a ramshackle travesty.

The real oddity about the camp was not the camp itself but its population density—and the peculiar position of its inhabitants. Some Roman infantrymen were standing on guard behind the wall, as one might expect. The great majority, however, were lying down behind the wall and in the shallow trenches which had been dug inside the camp. The camp held at least four times as many soldiers as it would appear to hold, looking at it from the Persian side.

Belisarius heard the *cornicens* blaring out a ragged tune. Very ragged, just as he had instructed. As if the men blowing those horns were half-deranged with fear. The soldiers standing visible guard began acting out their parts.

As Belisarius watched, the infantry chiliarch of the Army of Lebanon trotted up. Hermogenes was grinning from ear to ear.

"What do you think?" he asked.

Belisarius smiled. "Well, they're certainly throwing themselves into their roles. Although I'm not sure it's really necessary for so many of them to be tearing at their hair. Or howling quite so loud. Or shaking their knees and gibbering."

Hermogenes' grin never faded.

"Better too much than too little." He turned and admired the thespian display. By now, the soldiers at the wall were racing around madly, in apparent confusion and disorder.

"Don't overdo it, Hermogenes," said Belisarius. "The men might get a little *too* far into it and forget it's just an act."

The chiliarch shook his head firmly.

"Not a chance. They're actually quite enthusiastic about the coming battle."

Belisarius eyed him skeptically.

"It's true, General. Well—maybe 'enthusiastic' is putting it a little too strongly. Confident, let's say."

Belisarius scratched his chin. "You think? I'd have thought the men would be skeptical of such a tricky little scheme."

Hermogenes stared at the general. Then said, very seriously, "If any other general had come up with it, they probably would. But—it's Belisarius' plan. That's what makes the difference."

Again, the skeptical eye.

"You underestimate your reputation, general. Badly."

Belisarius began to say that the scheme wasn't actually his. He had taken it from Julius Caesar, who had used hidden troops in a fortified camp in one of his many battles against the Gauls. But before he could utter more than two words, he fell silent. One of the sentries at the wall was shouting. A genuine alert, now, not a false act.

Belisarius raced to the wall and peered over. Hermogenes joined him an instant later.

The Persians were advancing.

Belisarius studied the Mede formation intently. It was impressive, even—potentially—terrifying. As Persian armies always were.

An old thought caused a little quirk to come to the general's lips.

I'm always amazed at the way modern Greek scholars and courtiers don't live in the real world. Their image of Persian armies is fixed a thousand years ago, in the ancient times. When a small number of disciplined and armored Greek and Macedonian hoplites could always scatter the lightly-armed Persian mobs of Xerxes and Darius. The glorious phalanx of the Hellenes against the motley hordes of despotic Asia.

Let them see this, and gape, and tremble.

Many modern Greeks, of course, knew the truth. But they were of a different class than the Greeks who wrote the books and the laws, and collected the taxes, and lorded it over their great estates.

Persia had changed, over the centuries. More, even, than Rome. A class of tough, land-vested nobility had arisen. They were the real power in Persia, now, when all was said and done. True, they paid homage to the Sassanid emperors, and served them, as they had the Parthians who preceded them. But it was a conditional homage and a proud service. The conditions and the pride stemmed from one simple fact. The Persian aristocracy had invented modern heavy cavalry, and they were still better at it than any people on the face of the earth. The Roman cataphracts were, in all essential respects, simply attempts to copy the Persian noble cavalry.

The Persians were now close enough for the details of their formation to be made out.

Unlike Roman armies, which used infantry as the stolid center of their formations—as an anchor for the battle, even if they
weren't much use in the battle itself—the Persians scorned infantry
almost entirely. True, there were ten thousand foot soldiers in the
advancing Mede army. But Persian infantry were a ragged, scraggly
lot: modern Persian foot soldiers were probably even worse than
the rabble which had been broken by the hoplites at Marathon
and Issus centuries earlier. Miserable peasant levies, completely
unarmored except for hide shields; armed only with javelins and
light spears; consigned to the flanks; assigned the simple duties
of butchering wounded enemies and serving as a buffer against
charging foes. Armed cattle, basically.

Belisarius dismissed them with a glance. The general's attention was riveted on the cavalry advancing at the center of the
Persian army. His experienced eye immediately sorted order out
of the mass.

The heart of the Persian cavalry were the heavily armored noble
lancers, riding huge war horses bred on the Persian plateau. Each
nobleman, in turn, brought to battle a small retinue of more
lightly armored horse archers. The horse archers would start the
battle, and would fight closely alongside the heavy lancers. When
the lancers made charges, the mounted archers would act as a
screen to keep off enemy cavalry and suppress enemy archers,
while the lancers shattered their foe.

It was a ferocious, well-disciplined military machine. No Roman
army had won a major battle in the open field against Persia in
over a century.

But Belisarius was filled with confidence.

Today, I'm going to do it.

He began to turn away from the wall. Before leaving, however,
he stopped a moment and gazed at Hermogenes. The infantry
chiliarch grinned.

"Relax, General. You just take care of the cavalry. The infantry
will do its job."

Once back on his horse, Belisarius cantered over to the right wing
of his army. The right was in the hands of the Army of Lebanon's
cavalry commanders. Belisarius intended to take his position there
at the beginning of the battle. Although the Army of Lebanon had
accepted his leadership, he knew that they would quickly slip the

leash if he was not there to keep a tight grip on it. The one thing that could ruin his plans was a rash, unplanned cavalry charge. Which, in his experience, cavalry was always prone to do.

That's another thing I like about infantry. When a man has to charge on his own two legs, he tends to think it over first. Less tiring.

Seeing him approach, the cavalry chiliarchs rode to meet him.

"Soon, now," announced Eutyches.

Belisarius nodded.

"As soon as—" A blaring cornicen cut him off. Belisarius turned in his saddle just in time to see the first missiles hurled from the four scorpions and two onagers which he had positioned behind the fortified camp. Phocas had gauged the range and given the command for the artillery fire.

Out of the corner of his eye, he saw a scowl on the face of Pharas.

Belisarius understood the meaning of that expression. Like most modern Roman commanders, Pharas had no use for artillery in a field battle.

But Belisarius forebore comment. He had learned, from experience, that it was a futile argument.

They just don't understand. Sure, the damned things are a pain to haul around. Sure, they don't really inflict that many casualties. But they do two invaluable things. First, they break up the cohesion of the enemy's ranks. An alert soldier, even a heavily armored horseman, can usually dodge a great big scorpion dart or a huge stone thrown by an onager—as long as he isn't hemmed in by closely packed ranks. So, the enemy starts spreading out. Second—and most important—it's utterly infuriating to a warrior to be bombarded when he's too far away to retaliate. So he charges closer. Which is just what I want. Strategic offense; tactical defense. There's the whole secret in a nutshell.

The two chiliarchs were already galloping toward the front line. Belisarius followed. He needed to be able to watch the progress of the battle, and had already decided he would do it from the right. The hill would have been a perfect vantage point, of course, but he would have been much too isolated from the right wing of his army. Which represented both his heaviest force and his least reliable.

By the time he reached the front line, the Persians had already begun their charge. He saw at once that the enemy had begun the charge much too soon. Even the huge Persian horses couldn't charge any great distance before becoming exhausted.

And so, once again, the artillery did the trick.

Still, the Persians weren't Goths. Once Goths began a cavalry charge, they always tried to carry it through. The Medes, sophisticated and civilized for all their noble pride, were much too canny not to suspect a trap.

So, once they got within bow range, the Persian heavy cavalry reined in and let their horses breathe. The lighter mounted archers continued forward, firing their bows.

Pharas didn't wait for Belisarius' command. He ordered the Roman horse archers forward. The Huns galloped out onto the battleground, firing their own bows. Within moments, a swirling archery duel was underway.

Between Persian and Hun mounted archers, the contest was unequal. The Persians, as always, fired their bows as rapidly as did the Huns—much more rapidly than Roman cataphracts or regular infantry. But the Persians were better armored, and that extra armor counted for much against the relatively weak bows being used by both sides.

Soon enough, the Huns began falling back. The Persian horse archers did not attempt to charge in pursuit. They were no fools, and knew full well that Huns surpassed everyone in the art of turning a retreat into a sudden counterattack. So they simply satisfied themselves with a disciplined, orderly advance. Firing volley after volley as they came.

Pharas began to grumble, but Belisarius cut him off. Quickly. As he had expected, the chiliarch had already forgotten the battle plan.

"Splendid," announced Belisarius. "The Huns have already succeeded in fixing the entire left wing of the enemy."

"They're advancing on us!" exclaimed Pharas.

How did this idiot ever get made a chiliarch? I wouldn't trust him to bake bread. The first thing he'd do is throw away the recipe.

But his words were mild.

"Which is precisely what I want, Pharas. As long as the Persian left is *advancing* on our right, they aren't free to be doing something else. Such as chewing up our left, which is where the battle's going to be decided."

Belisarius ignored the fuming chiliarch and watched the battle develop on the other side of the field. The Isaurians and Thracian cataphracts on the hill were now starting to fire their bows at the Persian cavalry spreading into the center of the battleground. Within five minutes, it was obvious to Belisarius that his earlier estimate had been accurate.

It was the great advantage of cataphract archery, and one of the reasons Belisarius had stationed his Thracians atop the hill. With individual exceptions, such as Valentinian, they didn't have the rapid rate of fire that Persian or Hun horse archers did. But no archers in the world fired bows more accurately, and none with that awesome power. With the advantage of the hill's altitude, the cataphract arrows were plunging into the ranks of the Persian cavalry, wreaking havoc. Even the armor of Persian nobility couldn't withstand *those* arrows. And his cataphracts—especially the veterans—weren't aiming at the Persians anyway. Their targets were the horses themselves. The heavy frontal armor of the Persian chargers might have turned the arrows. But these missiles were plunging down into the great beasts' unarmored flanks. Dying and wounded horses began disrupting the serried ranks of the enemy's heavy cavalry.

Suddenly, Belisarius felt a breeze at his back. He almost sighed with relief. He had expected it, but still—

The wind, blowing from west to east, would increase the range of his own archery and artillery, and hamper the Persian arrows. Much more important, however, was the effect which the wind would have on visibility. The battlefield was already choked with dust thrown up by the horses. As soon as the breeze picked up, that dust would be moving from the Roman side to the Persian. The enemy would be half-blinded, even at close range.

"They're going to charge," predicted Eutychian, the other cavalry chiliarch. "Against us, on this wing."

"Thank God!" snorted Pharas. The chiliarch immediately rode off, shouting at his subordinate commanders.

Belisarius examined the battlefield and decided Eutychian was right.

Damn it! I was hoping—

He stared at Eutychian, estimating the man. His decision, as always, came quickly—aided, as much as anything, by the level gaze with which the chiliarch returned his stare.

"Can I trust you not to be an idiot like that one?" he demanded, pointing with his thumb at the retreating figure of Pharas.

"Meaning?"

"Meaning this—can I trust you to meet this charge with a simple stand? All I want is for the Persians to be held on this wing. *That's all.* Do you understand? They outnumber us, especially in heavy cavalry. If you try to win the battle here, with a glorious idiotic all-out charge, the Medes will cut you to pieces and I'll have a collapsed right wing. The battle will be won on the left. All I need is for you to hold the right steady. Can you do it? *Will* you do it?"

Eutychian glanced over at Pharas.

"Yes, Belisarius. But he's senior to me and—"

"You let me worry about Pharas. *Will you hold this wing? Nothing more?*"

Eutychian nodded. Belisarius rode over to the small knot of commanders clustered around Pharas. As he went, he gave Valentinian and Anastasius a meaningful look. Anastasius' face grew stony. Valentinian grinned. On his sharp-featured, narrow face, the grin was utterly feral.

As Belisarius drew near, he was able to make out Pharas' words of command to his subordinates. Just as he had feared, the chiliarch was organizing an all-out direct charge against the coming Medes.

Belisarius shouldered his horse into the group of commanders. In his peripheral vision, he could see Valentinian sidling his horse next to Pharas, and Anastasius moving around to the other side of the small command group.

Thank you, Maurice.

"That's enough, Pharas," he said. His tone was sharp and cold. "Our main charge is going to come later, on the other—"

"The hell with that!" roared Pharas. "I'm fighting now!"

"Our battle plan—"

"Fuck your fancy damned plan! It's pure bullshit! A fucking coward plan! I fight—"

"*Valentinian.*"

In his entire life, Belisarius had never met a man who could wield a sword more quickly and expertly than Valentinian. Nor as mercilessly. The cataphract's long, lean, whipcord body twisted like a spring. His spatha removed Pharas' head as neatly as a butcher beheading a chicken.

As always, Valentinian's strike was economical. No great heroic hewing, just enough to do the job. Pharas' head didn't sail through the air. It just rolled off his neck and bounced on the ground next to his horse. A moment later, his headless body fell off on the other side. His horse, suddenly covered with blood, shied away.

The commanders gaped with shock. One of them began to draw his sword. Anastasius smashed his spine. No economy here—the giant's mace drove the commander right over his horse's head. His mount, well-trained, never budged.

Belisarius whipped out his own spatha. The four surviving commanders in the group were now completely hemmed in by Belisarius and his two cataphracts. They were still gaping, and their faces were pale.

"I'll tolerate no treason or insubordination," stated Belisarius. His voice was not loud. Simply as cold as a glacier. Icy death.

"*Do you understand?*"

Gapes. Pale faces.

"*Do you understand?*" Valentinian twitched the spatha in his grip, very slightly. Anastasius hefted his mace, not so slightly.

"*Do you understand?*"

Mouths snapped shut. Faces remained pale, but heads began to nod. After two seconds, vigorously.

Belisarius eased back in his saddle and slid his spatha back into its waist-scabbard. (Valentinian, of course, did no such thing. Nor did Anastasius seem in any hurry to relinquish his mace.)

Belisarius turned and looked at Eutychian. The chiliarch was not more than thirty yards away. He and his own subordinates had witnessed the entire scene. So, Belisarius estimated, had dozens of the Army of Lebanon's cavalrymen. The faces of Eutychian and his commanders were also pale. But, Belisarius noted, they did not seem particularly outraged. Rather the contrary, in fact.

He studied the cavalrymen. No pale faces there. A few frowns, perhaps, but there were at least as many smiles to offset them. Even a few outright grins. Pharas, he suspected, had not been a popular commander.

Belisarius returned his hard stare to Eutychian. The chiliarch suddenly smiled—just slightly—and nodded his own head.

Belisarius turned back to the four commanders at his side.

"You will obey me instantly and without question. Do you understand?"

Vigorous nods. Anastasius replaced his mace in its holder. Valentinian did no such thing with his spatha.

A sudden blaring of cornicens. Belisarius turned back again. He could no longer see the Persian army, for his vision was obscured by the mass of cavalrymen at the front line. But it was obvious the Medes had begun their charge. Eutychian and his commanders were riding down the line, shouting orders.

Now in a hurry, Belisarius issued quick, simple instructions to the four commanders at his side:

"Eutychian will hold the right, using half of the Army of Lebanon's heavy cavalry and all of the mounted archers. You four will assemble the other half of the Army of Lebanon's lancers and keep them in reserve. I want them ready to charge"—his voice turned to pure steel—"*when* I say, *where* I say, and *how* I say. *Is that understood?*"

Very vigorous nods.

Belisarius gestured to Anastasius and Valentinian.

"Until the battle is over, these men will act as my immediate executive officers. You will obey their orders as if they came from me. Is that understood?"

Very vigorous nods.

Belisarius began to introduce his two cataphracts by name, but decided otherwise. For his immediate purposes, they had already been properly introduced.

Death and *Destruction*, he thought, would do just fine.

After the four commanders left to begin sorting out and assembling their forces, Belisarius rode back to the front line. As he approached, the Hun light cavalry began pouring back from the battlefield. They were no match in a head-to-head battle with the oncoming Persian lancers, and they knew it.

That's one of the few good things about mercenaries, thought Belisarius. *At least they aren't given to idiotic suicide charges.*

For all their mercenary character, the Huns were good soldiers. Experienced veterans, too. Their retreat was not a rout, and as soon as they reached the relative safety of the Roman lines they began to regroup. They knew the Roman heavy cavalry would be sallying soon, and it would be their job to provide flanking cover against the Persian horse archers.

Belisarius was now right behind the front line of the Roman

heavy horse. Between two cavalrymen, he watched the advancing Medes.

The Persian heavy cavalry had not yet started their galloping charge. They still had two hundred yards to cross before reaching the Roman lines. The Medes were veterans themselves, who knew the danger of exhausting their mounts in a battle—especially one fought in the heat of Syrian summer. Still, their thunderous advance was massively impressive. Two thousand heavy lancers, four lines deep, maintaining themselves in good order, flanked by three thousand horse archers maintaining their own excellent discipline.

Very impressive, but—

The Roman archers in the fortifications—Ghassanid mercenaries, these—were now aiming all their fire at the Mede cavalry attacking the right. They were ignoring, for the moment, the swarm of Persian horse archers in the center who were raining their own arrows on the encampment. Hermogenes, Belisarius noted, was keeping a cool head. Protected by the wall in front of them, his infantry would suffer few casualties from the Persian archers. Meanwhile, their arrows could hamper the advance of the Persian lancers.

Hermogenes had trained his men well, too. The Arab archers ignored the temptation to fire at the lancers themselves. The heavy Persian armor would deflect arrows from their light bows, especially at that range. Instead, the men were aiming at the unprotected legs of the horses. True, the range was long, but Belisarius saw more than a few Persian horses stumble and fall, spilling their riders.

From the hill, a flight of arrows sailed toward the Persian cavalry advancing on the Roman right. But the arrows fell short and the volley ceased almost immediately. Belisarius knew that Maurice had reined in the overenthusiastic cataphracts. The range—firing diagonally across the entire battlefield—was too extreme, even for their powerful bows firing with the wind. Instead, Maurice ordered his cataphracts and the Isaurians to concentrate their fire on the swarm of light horse archers in the center.

Belisarius was delighted. His army was functioning the way a good army should. The archers on the left were protecting the infantry in the center, while they harassed the Persians advancing on the right.

A volley of scorpion darts and onager stones sailed into the Persian heavy cavalry, tearing holes in the ranks. The cavalry began to spread, losing their compact formation.

Good, Phocas, good. But, with this wind, it should be possible—

Yes!

The next artillery volley fell right in the middle of the Persian command group at the rear of the battlefield. The Persian officers hadn't expected artillery fire, and their attention had been completely riveted on the battleground. The missiles arrived as a complete surprise. The carnage was horrendous. Those men or horses struck by huge onager stones were so much pulp, regardless of their heavy armor. Nor did that same armor protect the Persians from the spear-sized arrows cast by the scorpions. One of those officers, struck almost simultaneously by two scorpion bolts, was literally torn to pieces.

As always in battle, Belisarius' brown eyes were like stones. But his cold gaze ignored the artillery's victims. His attention was completely focused on the survivors.

Please, let Firuz still be alive. Oh, please, let that arrogant hot-tempered jackass still be alive.

Yes!

Firuz had obviously been driven into a rage. Belisarius could recognize the Persian commander's colorful cloak and plumage, personally leading the main body of his army in a charge at the center of the Roman lines. Three thousand heavy lancers, flanked by four thousand mounted archers, already at a full gallop.

It was a charge worthy of the idiot Pharas—the late, unlamented Pharas. The Mede lancers in the center had half a mile to cover before they reached the Roman fortifications. A half-mile in scorching heat, against wind-blown dust. It was absurd—and would have been, even if there weren't already three thousand Persian horse archers milling around in the center of the battlefield. The charging Persian lancers would be trampling over their own troops.

Midway through the charge, however, some sanity appeared to return to the Persians—to the horse archers already in the center, at least. Seeing the oncoming lancers, the mounted archers scurried out of their way. Their officers led them in a charge against the small Roman force on the hill.

Belisarius watched intently. He was confident that his cataphracts and the Isaurians could repel the attack, even outnumbered five to one. The Persians would be trying to climb steep slopes under plunging fire. And if matters got too tight, the two thousand cavalry from his own little army were stationed on the left wing, not far from the hill. But he didn't want to use those horsemen there, if he didn't absolutely need to. He wanted them fresh when—

Belisarius' view was suddenly obscured. Cornicens were blowing. The cavalrymen in front of him began firing their bows at the Persian lancers who were now less than a hundred yards away. A moment later, the cornicens blew again. The Roman cavalry charged to meet the oncoming lancers. They fired one last volley at the beginning of the charge and then slid the bows into their sheaths. It would be lance and sword work, now.

Belisarius glanced quickly toward the center. But it was impossible to see anything, anymore. The entire battlefield was now covered with dust, which the wind was blowing against the Persians. He could still see the hill, however, rising above the dust clouds. Within three or four seconds, simply from watching the unhurried and confident way in which his Thracian cataphracts and the Isaurians were firing their bows, Belisarius was certain that they would hold. Long enough, anyway.

It was time.

He looked back to the battle raging right before him. The Army of Lebanon's Huns were sweeping around the extreme right, trying to flank the Persian horse archers. But the Persians archers were veterans also, and were extending their own line to match the Huns. That part of the battle almost instantly became a chaotic swirl of horsemen exchanging bow-fire, often at point-blank range.

Dust everywhere, now. Beautiful, wonderful, obscuring dust. Blowing from the west over the Persians, blinding them to all Roman maneuvers.

The only part of the battle Belisarius could still see—other than the hilltop—was the collision between the Army of Lebanon's lancers and the lancers of the Persian left. Eutychian and his two thousand armored horsemen were smashing head to head with an equal number of Persian heavy cavalry. The noise of the battlefield—already immense—seemed to fill the entire universe. The clash of metal, the screams of men and horses filled the air.

It was a battle the Persians would win, eventually. Except for the very best cataphract units, no Roman heavy cavalry could defeat an equal number of Persian lancers. But, as he watched the vigor and courage of Eutychian's charge, Belisarius was more than satisfied. Eutychian would lose his part of the battle, but by the time he did, the Romans would have triumphed in the field as a whole.

More than that, Belisarius did not ask.

Hold the right, Eutychian. Just hold it.

He began to canter away.

And try to survive. I can use an officer like you. So can Rome.

As he rode, he passed orders through Valentinian and Anastasius. The four remaining commanders of the Army of Lebanon were quick to obey. Very quick. The two thousand lancers of that Army which Belisarius had kept in reserve—the same ones Pharas would have thrown away in a suicide charge—were now cantering across the battlefield in good order. South to north, behind the Roman lines, from the right wing to the left wing. They were completely invisible to the Persians, due to the wind-blown dust.

As they drew behind the fortified camp, Belisarius ordered a halt. He thought there was still time, and he wanted to make sure that the battle had become locked in the center.

While the Army of Lebanon's lancers allowed their horses to rest, therefore, Belisarius trotted up to the camp and passed into it through the west gate. He could begin to see now, even with the dust.

Just as he had planned (and hoped—not that he'd ever admit it to that morose old grouch Maurice) the main body of Persian lancers in the center had smashed into his trap. True, they had done so in a charge ordered by an idiot, but—that's the beauty of the first law of battles, after all. It cuts both ways.

Sitting on his horse not thirty yards from the fortified wall, Belisarius found it hard not to grin. He hadn't seen it, but he knew what had happened.

Imagine three thousand Persian lancers, thundering up to a wretched little earthen wall, guarded by not more than a thousand terrified, pathetic, wretched infantrymen. They sweep the enemy aside, right? Like an avalanche!

Well, not exactly. There are problems.

First, each cavalry mount has been hauling a man (a large man, more often than not) carrying fifty pounds of armor and twenty pounds of weapons—not to mention another hundred pounds of the horse's own armor. At a full gallop for half a mile, in the blistering heat of a Syrian summer.

So, the horses are winded, disgruntled, and thinking dark thoughts.

Two—all hearsay to the contrary—horses are not stupid. Quite a bit brighter than men, actually, when it comes to that kind of intelligence known popularly as "horse sense." So, when a horse sees looming before it:

a) a ditch

b) a wall

c) lots of men on the wall holding long objects with sharp points

. . . the horse stops. Fuck the charge. If some stupid man wants to hurl himself against all that dangerous crap, let him. (Which, often enough, they do—sailing headlong over their horse's stubborn head.)

It was the great romantic fallacy of the cavalry charge, and Belisarius had been astonished—all his life—at how fervently men still held to it, despite all practical experience and evidence to the contrary. Yes, horses will charge—against infantry in the open, and against other cavalry. Against anything, as long as the horse can see that it stands a chance of getting through the obstacles ahead, reasonably intact.

But no horse this side of an equine insane asylum will charge a wall too high to leap over. *Especially* a wall covered with nasty sharp objects.

And there's no point trying to convince the horse that the infantry manning the wall are feeble and demoralized.

Is that so? Tell you what, asshole. Climb off my back and show me. Use your own legs. Mine hurt.

The horses would have drawn up short before the ditch and the wall even if the fortification had been, in truth, guarded by only a thousand demoralized infantrymen. In the event, however, just as the horses drew near, Hermogenes had given the order and the cornicens had blown a new tune. Oh, a gleeful tune.

Surprise!

The other three thousand infantry hiding behind the wall and in the ditches had scrambled to their feet and taken their positions. The wall was now packed with spears, in the hands of soldiers full of confidence and vigor.

The front line of horses had screeched to a halt. Many of their riders had been thrown off. Some had been killed by the fall itself. Most of the survivors were badly shaken and bruised.

The second line of horses had piled into the first, the third into the second, the fourth into the third. More men were thrown off their mounts. To the injuries caused by falling were added the gruesome wounds suffered by men trampled by horses. Within seconds, the entire charging mass of Persian lancers had turned into an immobile, struggling, completely disordered mob. And now, worst of all, the Roman infantry began hurling volleys of *plumbata* into the milling Persians. At that close range, against a packed mass of confused and disoriented cavalry, the lead-weighted darts were fearsome weapons. The more so since the soldiers casting the weapons were expert in their use.

The cornicens blew again. Thousands of Roman infantry began scrambling over the wall. Many of them were carrying spathae, but most were wielding the even shorter semi-spatha. Each of those men would plunge into the writhing mob of Persian cavalry and use the time-honored tactic of infantry against armored cavalry.

It was an ignoble tactic, perhaps, and it never worked against cavalry on the move. But against cavalry forced to a halt, it was as certain as the sunrise.

Hamstring and gut the horses. Then butcher the lordly nobles once they're on the ground like us lowlife. See how much good their fine heavy armor does 'em then. And their bows and their lances and their fancy longswords. This here's knife work, my lord.

Belisarius rode out of the camp. The battle was his, if he could only drive home the final thrust.

For all his eagerness to win, Belisarius was careful to keep his pace at an easy canter. There was time, there was time. Not much, but enough. He didn't want the horses blown.

Without even waiting for his orders, Valentinian and Anastasius reined in the overenthusiasts who began driving their horses faster. There was time. There was time. Not much, but enough.

As they passed the western slope of the hill, the two thousand cavalry of Belisarius' own army fell in with him. He now had a striking force of four thousand men, unblooded and confident, riding fresh horses.

Belisarius saw a small figure standing on the slope, watching the army pass. Menander, he thought, still at his unwanted post. Even from the distance, he thought he could detect the bitter reproach in the boy's posture.

Sorry, lad. But you'll get your share of bloodshed in the future. And for that I really am sorry.

Now his force was curving around the northern slope of the hill. They had passed entirely across the line and were on the verge of falling on the enemy's unprotected right flank.

They came around the hill with Belisarius in the lead. The center of the battlefield was still obscured by dust, but the Romans could now see the Persian horse archers who were trying to storm the hill. The slaughter here had been immense, and it was immediately obvious that the Persians were discouraged.

Discouragement soon became outright terror. The four thousand Roman lancers hammered their way through the mounted archers without even pausing. Moments later they were plunging into the dust cloud, aiming at the mass of Persian lancers stymied at the center.

Belisarius turned halfway in his saddle and signaled the buglers behind him. The cornicens began blowing the order for a full charge. Their sound was a thin, piercing wail over the thundering bedlam of the battlefield.

Yet, for all the noise, the general was able to hear Valentinian and Anastasius, riding just behind him.

Valentinian: "I told you so."

Anastasius: *Inarticulate snort.*

Valentinian: *Mutter, mutter, mutter.*

Belisarius: "What was that last? I didn't quite catch it."

Valentinian: *Silence.*

Anastasius: "I think he said 'fuck brave officers.'"

Valentinian: *Hiss.*

Anastasius: "But maybe not. It's noisy. Maybe the cold-blooded little killer said, 'Fuck brazen coffers.' Idiot thing to say on a battlefield, of course. But he's—"

All else was lost. The first Persian lancer loomed in the dust, his back turned away. Belisarius raised his lance high and drove it right through the Mede's heart. The enemy fell off his horse, taking the lance with him.

Another Mede, turned half away, to his right. Belisarius drew his long cavalry sword out of its baldric and hewed the man's arm off with the same motion. Another Mede, again from the back. The sword butchered into his neck, below the rim of the helmet. Another Mede—facing him, now. The sword hammered his shield down, hammered it aside, hammered his helmet sideways. The man was driven off his mount and fell, unconscious, to the ground. In that mad press of stamping horses, he would be dead within a minute, crushed to a bloody pulp.

The entire Roman cavalry piled into the Persians, caving in the right rear of their already disorganized formation. The initial slaughter was horrendous. The charge caught the Persians completely by surprise. Many of them, in the first few seconds, fell before blows which they never even saw.

To an extent, of course, Belisarius now found himself caught by the same dilemma that had faced the Medes. The thousands of Persian cavalrymen jammed against the Roman camp in the center of the battlefield were not quite a wall. But almost. Combat became a matter of men on skittering horses hammering at each other. Lances were useless, now. It was all sword, mace, and ax work. And utterly murderous.

Yet, for all the ensuing mayhem, the outcome was certain. The Medes were trapped between an equal number of Roman heavy cavalry and thousands of Roman infantrymen. Their greatest strength—that unequaled Persian skill at hard-hitting, fast-moving cavalry warfare—was completely neutralized. As cavalrymen, the average Roman was not their equal. But this was no longer a cavalry battle. It was a pure infantry battle, in which the majority of soldiers just happened to be sitting on horses.

As always under those circumstances, more and more of the men—on both sides—soon found themselves on the ground. Without momentum, it was almost impossible to swing heavy swords and axes for any length of time without falling off a horse. The only things keeping a soldier on his horse were the pressure of his knees and—if possible, which it usually wasn't in a battle—a hand on the pommel of his saddle. Any well-delivered blow on his armor or shield would knock a man off. And any badly delivered blow of his own was likely to drag him off by the inertia of his missed swing.

Five minutes into the fray, almost half of the cavalrymen on both sides were dismounted.

"This is going to be as bad as Lake Ticinus," grunted Anastasius.

He pounded a Persian to the ground with a mace blow. Nothing fancy; Anastasius needn't bother—the giant's mace slammed the man's own shield into his helmet hard enough to crack his skull.

Belisarius grimaced. The ancient battle of Lake Ticinus was a staple of Roman army lore. Fought during the Second Punic War, it had started as a pure cavalry battle and ended as a pure infantry fight. Every single man on both sides, according to legend, had fallen off his horse before the fray was finished.

Belisarius was actually surprised that he was still mounted himself. Partly, of course, that was due to his bodyguards. In his entire career, Anastasius had only fallen off his horse once during a battle. And that didn't really count—his horse had fallen first, slipping in a patch of snow on some unnamed little battlefield in Dacia. The man was so huge and powerful—with a horse to match—that he could swap blows with anyone without budging from his saddle.

Valentinian, on the other hand, had taken to the ground as soon as the battle had become a deadlocked slugging match. Valentinian was possibly even deadlier than Anastasius, but his lethality was the product of skill, dexterity, and speed. Those traits were almost nullified in this kind of fray, as long as he was trapped on a stationary horse.

Valentinian was a veteran, however. For all his grousing about foot-soldiering, the man had instantly slid from his horse and kept fighting afoot. The result had been a gory trail of hamstrung and gutted horses, their former riders lying nearby in their own blood.

With those two protecting him—and his own great skill as a fighter—Belisarius hadn't even been hurt.

Yet—it was odd. There was something else. Belisarius hadn't noticed, at first, until a slight pause in the action enabled him to think. But the fact was that he was fighting much *too* well.

"Deadly with a blade, is Belisarius." He'd heard it said, and knew it for a cold and simple truth. But he had never been as deadly as he was that day. The cause lay not in any added strength or stamina. It was—odd. He seemed to see everything with perfect clarity, even in the hazy dust. He seemed to be able to gauge every motion by an enemy perfectly—and gauge his own strikes with equal precision. Time after time, he had slipped a blow by the barest margin—yet knowing, all the while, that the margin was adequate. Time after time, he had landed a blow of his own through the narrowest gaps, the slimmest openings—yet knowing, at the instant, that the gaps were enough. Time after time, he had begun to slip from his horse, only to find his balance again with perfect ease.

Odd. The truth was that he was leaving his own trail of gore and blood. It was like a path through a forest beaten by an elephant.

Even his cataphracts noticed. And complained, in the case of one.

"We're supposed to be protecting *you*, General," hissed Valentinian. "Not the other way around."

"Quit bitching," growled Anastasius. *Chunk.* Another Mede down. "I'm a big target. I need all the protection I can get." *Chunk.*

Valentinian began to snarl something, but fell silent, listening intently.

"I think—"

"Yes," said Belisarius. He had heard it too. The first cry for quarter, coming from a Persian throat. The cry had been cut off.

The general ceased his mayhem. Turned to Anastasius.

"Get Maurice—and the others. Now. I don't want to end the battle with atrocities. We're trying to win this war, not start a new one."

"No need," grunted Anastasius. He extended his right hand, pointing with his blood-covered mace. Belisarius turned and saw his entire Thracian retinue charging toward them on horseback.

Within seconds, Maurice drew up alongside them.

"I don't want a massacre, Maurice!" shouted Belisarius. "I'll handle the situation here, but the Huns—"

Maurice interrupted.

"They're already making for the Persian camp. I'll try to stop them, but I'll need reinforcement as soon as you can get there."

Without another word, the hecatontarch spurred his horse into a gallop. Seconds later, the entire body of Thracian cataphracts were thundering to the east, in the direction of the Persian camp.

Cries for quarter were being heard now from all over the battlefield. Many of them cut off in mid-screech. All fight was gone from the Medes. The light cavalry were already fleeing the field. The Persian infantry had long since begun to run. The heavy cavalry, trapped in the center, were trying to surrender. Without much success. The Roman infantrymen were in full fury. They were wreaking their vengeance on those who had so often in the past brought terror into their own hearts.

Belisarius rode directly into the mass. When he wanted to use it, the general had a very loud and well-trained voice. Anastasius joined him with his own thundering basso. Yet, strangely enough, it was Valentinian's nasal tenor that pierced through the din like a sword.

A simple cry, designed to rein in the Roman murder:

"*Ransom! Ransom! Ransom!*"

The cry was immediately taken up by the Persians themselves. Within seconds, the slaughter stopped. Half-maddened the Roman infantry might have been. Poor, however, they most certainly were. And it suddenly dawned on them that they held in the palm of their mercy the lives of hundreds—thousands, maybe—of Persians. *Noble* Persians. *Rich* noble Persians.

Belisarius quickly found Hermogenes. The infantry chiliarch took responsibility for organizing the surrender. Then Belisarius went in search of Eutychian.

But Eutychian was not to be found. Nothing but his body, lying on the ground, an arrow through his throat.

Belisarius, staring down at the corpse, felt a great sadness wash over him. He had barely known the man. But he had looked forward to the pleasure.

He shook off the mood. Later. Not now.

He found the highest-ranked surviving cavalry commander of the Army of Lebanon. Mundus, his name. He had been one of Pharas' little coterie, and his face turned a bit pale when Belisarius rode up. When he spotted Valentinian and Anastasius he turned very pale.

"Round up your cavalry, Mundus," commanded Belisarius. "At least three ala. I need them to reinforce my cataphracts at the Persian camp. The Huns'll be on a rampage and I intend to put a stop to it."

Mundus winced. "It'll be hard," he muttered. "The men'll want their share of—"

"Forget the ransom!" thundered the general. "If they complain, tell them I've got plans for bigger booty. I'll explain later. But right now—*move, damn you!*"

Valentinian was already sidling his horse toward Mundus, but

there was no need. The terrified officer instantly began screaming orders at his subordinates. They, in turn, began rounding up
their soldiers.

The cavalrymen were upset, Belisarius knew, because the Roman
infantry stood to gain the lion's share of the booty. By tradition,
ransom was owed to the man who personally held a captive. It
was a destructive tradition, in Belisarius' opinion, and one which
he hoped to change eventually. But not today. For the first time
in centuries, the Roman infantry had blazed its old glory, and
Belisarius would not dampen their victory, or their profit from it.

At the Persian camp, they came upon a very tense scene. The
camp itself was a shambles. Most of the tents lay on the ground
like lumpy shrouds. Those tents still standing were ragged from
sword-slashes. Wagons were upended or half-shattered. Some of
the wreckage was the work of the Hun mercenaries, but much
of it was due to the Persians themselves. Sensing the defeat, the
Persian camp followers had hastily rummaged out their most
precious possessions and taken flight.

But not all had left soon enough. Several dead Persians were
lying about, riddled with arrows. All men. The Huns would have
saved the women and children. The women would be raped.
Afterwards, they and the children would be sold into slavery.

In the event, the mercenaries had barely begun enjoying their
looting and their atrocities before the Thracians had arrived and
put a stop to it. More or less.

Very tense. On one side, dismounted but armed, hundreds of
Hun mercenaries. On the other, still mounted, armed—*and* with
drawn bows—were three hundred bucellarii.

The Huns outnumbered the Thracians' cataphracts by a factor
of three to one. So, the outcome of any fight was obvious to all.
The mercenaries would be butchered to a man. But not before
they inflicted heavy casualties on the Thracians.

The general cared nothing for the Huns. But it would be a
stupid waste of his cataphracts.

Mundus pointed out to him the three leaders of the mercenaries. As usual with Huns, their rank derived from clan status, not
Roman military protocol.

Belisarius rode over to them and dismounted. Valentinian and
Anastasius stayed on their horses. Both men had their own bows
drawn, with arrows notched.

The Hun clan leaders were glaring at him furiously. Off to one side, three young Hun warriors were screaming insults at the Thracians. One of them held a young Persian by her hair. The girl was half-naked, weeping, on her knees. Next to her, a still younger boy—her brother, thought Belisarius, from the resemblance—was sitting on the ground. He was obviously dazed and was holding his head in both hands. Blood seeped through his fingers.

Belisarius glanced at the little tableau, then stared back at the three clan chiefs. He met their glares with an icy gaze. Then stepped up very close and said softly, in quite good Hunnish:

"My name is Belisarius. I have just destroyed an entire Persian army. Do you think I can be intimidated by such as *you*?"

After a moment, two of the clan leaders looked away. The third, the oldest, held the glare.

Belisarius nodded slightly toward the three young Huns holding the girl.

"Your clan?" he asked.

The clan chief snorted. "Clanless. They—"

"*Valentinian.*"

Belisarius knew no archer as quick and accurate as Valentinian. The Hun holding the girl by her hair took Valentinian's first arrow. In the chest, straight through the heart. The cataphract's second arrow, following instantly, dropped another. Anastasius, even with an already-drawn bow, fired only one arrow in the same time. No man but he could have drawn that incredible bow. His arrow went right through his target's body.

Three seconds. Three dead mercenaries.

Belisarius had not watched. His eyes had never left those of the clan chieftain.

Now, he smiled. Tough old man. The chieftain was still glaring.

Again, softly, still in Hunnish: "You have a simple choice. You can disobey me, in which case no Hun will survive this battle. Or you can obey me, and share in the great booty from Nisibis."

Finally, something got through. The clan chieftain's eyes widened.

"Nisibis? *Nisibis?*"

Belisarius nodded. His smile widened.

The clan chieftain peered at him suspiciously.

"Nisibis is a great town," he said. "You do not have siege equipment."

Belisarius shrugged. "I have a few scorpions and onagers. We can let the Persians on the walls of Nisibis catch sight of them. But that doesn't matter. I have the most powerful weapon of all, clan leader. I have a great victory, and the fear which that victory will produce."

The clan leader hesitated still.

"Many Persian soldiers escaped. They will flee to Nisibis and tell—"

"Tell what, clan leader? The truth? And who will believe those soldiers? Those *defeated* soldiers—that routed rabble—when they tell the notables of Nisibis that they have nothing to fear from the Roman army which just destroyed them?"

The clan leader laughed. For all his barbarity, the man did not lack decisiveness. A moment later he was bellowing commands to his men. Without hesitation, the other two clan leaders joined their voices to his.

Huns with clan status took their leaders seriously. Those without clan status took the slaughtered corpses of three of their fellows seriously. Within two minutes, a small group of women and children were clustered under the shelter of the cataphracts. Some of them looked to have been badly abused, thought Belisarius, but it could have been worse. Much worse.

The Huns even began piling up their loot, but Belisarius told the clan leaders that the mercenaries could keep the booty. He simply wanted the survivors.

"Why do you care, Greek?" asked the old chieftain. The question was not asked belligerently. The man was simply puzzled.

Belisarius sighed. "I'm not Greek. I'm Thracian."

The chieftain snorted. "Then it makes no sense at all! Greeks are odd, everyone knows it. They think too much. But why—"

"A thousand years ago, chieftain, these people were already great with knowledge. At a time when your people and mine were no better than savages in skins."

Which is just about where you are still, thought Belisarius. But he didn't say it.

The clan chieftain frowned.

"I do not understand the point."

Belisarius sighed, turned away.

"I know," he muttered. "I know."

✧　　✧　　✧

Two weeks later, Nisibis capitulated.

It was not a total capitulation, of course. The Romans would not march into the city. The notables needed that face-saving gesture to fend off the later wrath of the Persian emperor. And Belisarius, for his own reasons, did not want to risk such a triumphant entry. He thought he had his troops well under control, but—there was no temptation so great, especially to the mercenaries who made up a large part of the army, as the prospect of sacking a city without a siege.

No, best to avoid the problem entirely. Persians, like Romans, were civilized. Treasure lost was simply treasure lost. Forgotten soon enough. Atrocities burned memory into the centuries. The centuries of that stupid, pointless, endless warfare between Greek and Persian which had gone on too long already.

So, there was no march and no atrocities. But, of course, there was treasure lost aplenty. Oh, yes. Nisibis disgorged its hoarded wealth. Some of it in the form of outright tribute. The rest as ransom for the nobles. (Whom Nisibis would keep, in reasonably pleasant captivity, until the nobles repaid the ransom.)

The Romans marched away from the city with more booty than any of its soldiers had ever dreamed of. Within three days, as the word of victory spread, the army was surrounded by camp followers. Among these, in addition to the usual coterie, were a veritable host of avid liquidators. The soldiers of Belisarius' own army immediately converted their booty into portable specie and jewelry. They had learned from experience that their general's stern logistical methods made it impossible to haul about bulky treasure. Like the great Philip of ancient Macedon, Belisarius used mules for his supply train. The only wheeled vehicles he allowed were the field ambulances and the artillery engines.

Observing, and then questioning, the Army of Lebanon quickly followed their example.

A great general, Belisarius, a great general. A bit peculiar, perhaps. Unbelievably ruthless, in some ways. Tales were told, by campfire, of slaughtered Persian cavalry, and a decapitated chiliarch. The first brought grins of satisfaction, the last brought howls of glee. Strangely squeamish, in others. Tales were told of women and children returned, reasonably unharmed, to the Persians in Nisibis—and spitted Huns. The first brought heads shaking in bemusement, the last, howls of glee. (Even, after a day or so, to most Huns, whose sense of humor was not remotely squeamish.)

A peculiar general. But—a great general, no doubt about it. Best to adopt his ways.

Adding to the army's good cheer was the extraordinary largesse of the general's cataphracts. Fine fellows, those Thracians, the very best. Buy anyone a drink, anytime, at any place the army stopped. Which it did frequently. The great general was kind to victorious troops, and the host of camp followers set up impromptu *tabernae* at every nightfall. They seemed to be awash in wealth, the way they spread their money around.

Which, indeed, they were. As commanding general, Belisarius had come in for a huge percentage of the loot—half of which he had immediately distributed to his bucellarii, as was his own personal tradition. The tradition pleased his cataphracts immensely. It pleased Belisarius even more. Partly for the pleasure which generosity gave his warm heart. But more for the pleasure which calculation gave his cold, crooked brain. True, his cataphracts were devoted to him anyway, from their own customs and birthright. But it never hurt to cement that allegiance as tightly as possible.

No, he thought, remembering the head of a stubborn chiliarch; and the arrow-transfixed chests of Hun thugs, *it never hurts.*

Three individuals only, of that great army returning in triumph, did not share in the general joy and good will.

Two of them were brothers from Thrace. Who, though they had come through their recent experience essentially unharmed in body, were much aggrieved in their minds.

As Belisarius had suspected, Bouzes and Coutzes were not actually stupid. They had had plenty of time, in their captivity at Nisibis, to ponder events of the past. And to draw certain conclusions about a never-found pay caravan.

On the first night of the march back to Mindouos, the brothers had entered Belisarius' tent. Quite forcefully. They had shouldered Maurice aside, which would indicate that their recent conversion from stupidity was still shaky and skin deep. Then, they had confronted the general with his duplicity and treachery.

Within the next few minutes, Bouzes and Coutzes learned a lesson. Others had learned that lesson before them. Some, like a Hun clan chieftain, had even managed to survive the experience.

So did they, barely.

Belisarius gave them three simple choices.

One: They could acquiesce to his triumph, pretend that nothing untoward had happened, and salvage what was left of their reputations. With Belisarius' help, a suitable cover story would be manufactured. They would even come into their share of the booty.

Two: They could leave now and trumpet their outrage to the world. Within a year, if Justinian was feeling charitable due to his victory over the Persians, they would be feeding the hogs back at their estate in Thrace. Pouring slops into the trough. If the Emperor was not feeling charitable—charity was not his most outstanding trait—they would be feeding the hogs at one of Justinian's many estates. From *inside* the trough, since they themselves would be the slop.

Or, finally, if their outrage was simply too great to bear, they could choose yet a third alternative:

Valentinian.

The brothers, in the end, bade farewell to stupidity. Not easily, true, and not without bitter tears and warm embraces to their departing friend. But, in the end, they managed to send stupidity on his way.

By the very end of the evening, in fact, they were in quite a mellow mood. Large quantities of wine helped bring on that mellowness, as did the thought of large sums of booty. But, for the most part, it was brought by one small, fierce consolation.

At least—this time—honest Thracian lads had been swindled by another Thracian. Not by some damned Greek or Armenian.

After they left, Belisarius blew out the lantern and lay down on his cot.

He was exhausted, but sleep would not come. There was something he needed to know. He let his mind wander through its own labyrinth, until he found the place he had come to think of as the crack in the barrier.

He sensed the jewel's presence.

It was you, wasn't it? Helping me in the battle?

It was then that Belisarius discovered the third—individual?—who did not share in the general self-satisfaction of the army. The jewel's thoughts were incoherent, at first. Strangely, there seemed to be some underlying hostility to them. Not reproach, or accusation, as there had been before. More like—

Yes. Exasperation.

That's odd. Why would—

A thought suddenly came into focus.

yes. helped. difficult.

Then, with a definite sense of exasperation:

very difficult.

Then, much like a younger brother might say to a dimwitted elder:

stupid.

Stupid? What is stupid?

you stupid.

Belisarius sat up, astonished.

Me? Why am I stupid?

Extreme exasperation:

not you you. all you. all stupid.

Now, with great force:

cretins.

Belisarius was frowning fiercely. He couldn't begin to think what might have so upset the jewel.

He sensed a new concept, a new thought, trying to force its way through the barrier. But the thought fell away, defeated.

Suddenly a quick vision flashed through his mind:

A scene from the day's battle. A mass of cavalrymen, hacking away at each other, falling from their mounts. Knees clenched tightly on the barrel chests of horses. Hands clutching pommels. Men falling from their horses every time they were struck or misjudged their own blows.

cretins.

Another vision. Nothing but a quick flashing image:

A horseman galloping across the steppe. A barbarian of some kind. Belisarius did not recognize his tribe. He rode his horse with complete grace and confidence. The image flashed to his legs. His feet.

The thought finally burst through.

stirrups.

Belisarius' mouth fell open.

"I'll be Goddamned," he whispered. "Why didn't anybody ever think of that?"

stupid.

Chapter 9
CONSTANTINOPLE
Autumn, 528 AD

"The man of the hour!" cried Sittas. "O hail the triumphant conq'rer!" He drained his cup in one quaff. "I'd rise to greet you, Belisarius, but I'm afraid I'd swoon in the presence of so august a personage." He hiccuped. "I'm given to hero worship, you know. Terrible habit, just terrible." He seized the flagon resting on the small table next to his couch and waved it about. "I'd pour you a drink, too, but I'm afraid I'd spill the wine. Trembling in the company of so legendary a figure, you understand, like a giddy schoolgirl."

Sittas refilled the cup. His meaty hand was steady as a rock.

"Speaking of which," he continued, "—giddy schoolgirls, that is—let me introduce you to my friend." Sittas waved his other hand in the general direction of a woman sitting on the couch next to him. "Irene Macrembolitissa, I present you the famed General Belisarius. And his lovely wife, Antonina."

Belisarius advanced across the room and bowed politely—to the woman, not Sittas.

Irene was quite striking in appearance. Not pretty, precisely, but attractive in a bold sort of way. She had a light complexion, chestnut hair, brown eyes, and a large aquiline nose. She appeared to be in her late twenties, but Belisarius thought she might be older.

The calm, unreadable expression on Belisarius' face never wavered. But he was more than a little surprised. Irene was quite

129

unlike Sittas' usual run of female "friends." By about fifteen years of age and, the general estimated, twice the intelligence.

"Don't look at him too closely, Irene!" warned Sittas. "You never know what can happen with these mythical demigod types. Probably get you pregnant just from his aura."

Irene smiled. "Please ignore him. He's pretending to be drunk."

"He's good at it," remarked Antonina. "As well he should be, as much practice as he gets."

A look of hurt innocence came upon Sittas' beefy face. It fit very poorly.

"I am mortified," he whined. "Outraged. Offended beyond measure." He drained his cup again, and reached for the flagon. "You see what your insults have done, vile woman? Driven me to drink, by God! To drink!"

Irene rose and went over to a long table against the far wall of the salon. She returned with a cup in each hand, and gave them to Belisarius and Antonina.

"Please have a seat," she said, motioning to another couch nearby. The large room was well-nigh littered with couches, all of them richly upholstered. The colors of the upholstery clashed wildly with the mosaics and tapestries which adorned all the walls. The wall coverings looked to be even more expensive than the couches, for all that they were in exquisitely bad taste.

After the general and his wife took a seat, Irene filled their cups from another flagon. She placed the flagon on a table and returned to her own couch.

"Sittas has told me much about you," Irene said.

"Did I tell you he has much better taste in furnishings?" muttered Sittas. His beady eyes scanned the room admiringly.

"Muskrats have better taste in furnishings than you do, Sittas," murmured Irene sweetly. She smiled at Belisarius and Antonina. "Isn't this room hideous?" she asked.

Antonina laughed. "It's like a bear's den."

"A very rich bear," commented Sittas happily. "Who can well afford to ignore the petty artistic quibbling of the lesser sort. Plebeian envy, that's all it is." He leaned forward. "But enough of that! Let's hear it, Belisarius. I want the full account, mind you, the full account. I'll stand for none of your usual laconicness!"

"There's no such word, Sittas," said Irene.

"'Course there is! I just used it, didn't I? How could I use a word that doesn't exist?" He grinned at Belisarius and began to take another swallow of wine. "Now—out with it! How in the world did you swindle the terrible twins out of their army?"

"I didn't swindle the twins out of their army. The whole idea's preposterous, and I'm astonished to hear you parroting it. Coutzes and Bouzes simply had the misfortune of being captured while leading a reconnaissance in force, and I was forced—"

Sittas choked; spewed wine out of his mouth.

"Even Justinian doesn't believe that malarkey!" he protested.

Belisarius smiled. "To the contrary, Sittas. I am just now returned from a formal audience with the Emperor, at which he indicated not the slightest disbelief in the official report of the battle."

"Well, of course he didn't! Coutzes and Bouzes are Thracian. Justinian's Thracian." Sittas eyed Belisarius suspiciously. "You're Thracian too, for that matter." He looked at Irene. "They stick together, you know." Another swallow. "Wretched rustics! A proper Greek nobleman doesn't stand a chance anymore." He glared at Belisarius. "You're not going to tell me, are you?"

Then, to Irene: "He probably swore an oath. He's always swearing oaths. Swore his first oath when he was four, to a piglet. Swore he'd never let anyone eat the creature. Kept his oath, too. They say the pig's still around, roaming the countryside, devouring everything in sight. The Bane of Thrace, the thing's called now. The peasants are crying out for a new Hercules to come and rid them of the monster." A belch. "That's what comes of swearing oaths. Never touch the things, myself."

He glared at Belisarius again, then heaved a sigh of resignation. "All right, then. Forget the juicy stuff. Tell me about the battle."

"I'm sure you've already heard all about it."

Sittas sneered. "That crap! By the time courtiers and imperial heralds get through with the tale of a battle, there's nothing in it a soldier would recognize." He scowled. "Unfortunately, whatever his other many talents, our Emperor is no soldier. The court's getting worse, Belisarius. It's getting packed with creatures like John of Cappadocia and Narses. And the most wretched crowd of quarreling churchmen you ever saw, even by the low standards of that lot."

"Don't underestimate Narses and John of Cappadocia," said Irene, lightly but seriously.

"I'm not underestimating them! But—ah, never mind. Later. For the moment—" He set down his cup and leaned forward, elbows on knees. The keen eyes which now gazed at Belisarius had not the slightest trace of drunkenness in them.

Most people, upon meeting Sittas, were struck by his resemblance to a hog. The same girth, the same heavy limbs, the same pinkish hide—unusually fair for a Greek—the same jowls, blunt snoutish nose, beady little eyes. Belisarius, gazing back at his best friend, thought the resemblance wasn't inappropriate. So long as you remembered that there are hogs, and then there are hogs. There is the slothful domestic hog in his wallow, a figure of fun and feast. And then, there is the great wild boar of the forest, whose gaze makes bowels turn to water. Whose tusks make widows and orphans.

"The battle," commanded the boar.

Belisarius made no attempt to cut short his recital of the battle. Sittas was himself an accomplished general, and Belisarius knew full well that his friend would not tolerate an abbreviated or sanitized version of the tale. And whatever minor aspects Belisarius overlooked, Sittas was quick to bring forward by his shrewd questioning.

When he was done, Sittas leaned back in his couch and regarded Belisarius silently. Then: "Why?"

"Why what?"

"Don't play with me, Belisarius! You provoked the Medes, when you could have stalled. And then you took enough chances to give the Fates themselves apoplexy. *Why?* There was no point to that battle, and you know it as well as I do." He waved his hand disgustedly. "Oh, sure, as the courtiers never tire of saying, it's the greatest victory over the Persians in a century. *So what?* We've been at war with Persia for two thirds of a millennium. Longer than that, for us Greeks. Never be an end to it, unless common sense suddenly rears its ugly head upon the thrones. We're not strong enough to conquer Persia, and the Medes aren't strong enough to conquer us. All this warring does is depopulate the border areas and drain both empires. That's my opinion. And it's your opinion, too, unless you've suddenly been seized by delusions of grandeur. So I ask again: *why?*"

Belisarius was silent. After a moment, Irene smiled faintly and rose.

"May I show you the gardens, Antonina?"

✧   ✧   ✧

Once they were in the gardens, Antonina took a seat on a stone bench.

"You needn't bother," she said. "I've seen them before."

Irene sat next to her. "Aren't they something? I'm afraid Sittas' taste in horticulture is every bit as grotesque as his taste in furnishings."

Antonina smiled. Her eye was caught by a statue. The smile turned to a grimace.

"Not to mention his taste in sculpture."

The two women stared at each other for a moment.

"You'd like to know who I am," said Irene.

Antonina nodded. Irene cocked her head quizzically.

"I'm curious. Why do you assume that I'm something other than Sittas' latest bedmate?"

"Two reasons. You're not his taste in women, not even close. And, if you were one of his usual bedmates, he'd never have invited you to sit in on this meeting."

Irene chuckled. "I'm his spy," she said.

Seeing the startled look on Antonina's face, Irene held up a reassuring hand. "I'm afraid that didn't come out right. I'm not spying on *you*." She pursed her lips. "It would be more accurate to say that I'm Sittas' spymaster. That's why he asked me to join him in this—meeting. He is concerned, Antonina."

"About what? And since when has Sittas needed a spymaster?"

It was Irene's turn to look startled. "He's had a spymaster since he was a boy, practically. All Greek noblemen of his class do."

Antonina snorted. "You mean Apollinaris? That pitiful old coot couldn't find his ass with both hands."

Irene smiled. "Oh, I believe Apollinaris could manage that task well enough. In broad daylight, at least. At night, I admit, he would have considerable difficulty." She brushed back her hair, hesitated, then said:

"About a year ago, Sittas decided he needed a real spymaster. He inquired in various places, and my services came highly recommended. He retired Apollinaris—on a very nice pension, by the way—and hired me. My cover, so to speak, is that I am his latest paramour."

She pursed her lips. "As deceptions go, it has its weaknesses. As you say, I'm not really his type."

"That's putting it mildly."

"Can you tell me what's going on in there?" asked Irene, gesturing with her head toward the door to the mansion.

"No," replied Antonina. "Not yet, at least. Later—perhaps. But not now."

Irene accepted the refusal without protest. A servant appeared, bearing a platter of food and wine, which he set upon a nearby table. Antonina and Irene moved over to the table and spent the next few minutes in companionable silence, enjoying their meal. Whatever his lack of taste in furnishings, neither woman could fault the excellence of Sittas' kitchen.

Pushing aside her plate, Antonina spoke.

"Please answer the question I asked earlier."

Irene's response was immediate. "The reason Sittas is concerned enough to hire me—and my services don't come cheaply—is because there's skullduggery in Constantinople."

Antonina snorted. "Please, Irene! Saying there's skullduggery in Constantinople is like saying there's shit in a pigsty."

Irene nodded. "True. Perhaps I should say: there's a lot more skullduggery going on than usual, and, what's of much greater concern, the nature of it's unclear. *Something is afoot in Constantinople, Antonina.* Something deep, and well hidden, and cunning, and utterly treacherous. What it is, I have not yet been able to discover. But I can sense it, I can taste it, I can smell it." Again, she groped for words. "It is—*there*. Trust me."

Antonina arose and began pacing about the garden. She glanced at the door which led back to the interior of the mansion.

"Will they be finished yet?" asked Irene.

Antonina shook her head. "No. Sittas will—need time to recover."

Irene frowned. "Recover from what?"

Antonina held up a hand, stilling her. She continued to pace about, frowning. Irene, with the patience of a professional, simply sat and waited.

After a while, Antonina stopped pacing and came over to Irene. She paused, took a deep breath. Hesitated again.

A voice came from the doorway. A horrible, croaking voice.

"Come inside, both of you."

Irene gasped. Sittas looked positively haggard. He seemed to have shed fifty pounds.

✧   ✧   ✧

Once they were back in the salon, seated on their couches, Sittas croaked:

"Tell her, Belisarius."

Belisarius stared at Irene.

"I haven't even told Maurice, Sittas."

"Of course not! There's no reason to, at this point. But we need Irene. *Now.*"

Belisarius remained silent, still examining Irene. Sittas' back curved, his great shoulders hunched, his snout thrust forward. The wild, red-eyed boar spoke:

"*Tell her.*"

Belisarius transferred his gaze to Sittas. The boar was in full fury now, tusks glistening.

"*Tell her!*"

Belisarius' calm eyes never wavered. He was a Thracian, reared in the countryside. He'd speared his first boar when he was twelve.

The red glare faded from Sittas' eyes, replaced, suddenly, by a shrug. And then, a wide grin.

"Funny, that usually works. Damned Thracians! But you may as well tell her, Belisarius. She'll winkle it out of me, anyway, unless I fire her. Which is the last thing I'd do now."

Belisarius looked at Antonina. His wife nodded.

"Tell her, husband. I trust her."

Chapter 10

When Belisarius was finished, Irene looked at her employer. The normal pink coloring had returned to Sittas' hide, but his face still looked almost drawn beneath the jowls.

"Believe, Irene," he said. "He only gave you the gist of it, but—" Sittas drew in a deep breath. "I held the jewel and saw— Never mind. Just believe it."

"May I see it?" she asked. Belisarius reached into his coat and withdrew the jewel. Irene rose and walked over, stooped, examined the thing. After a moment, she returned to her seat.

"It makes sense," she said, nodding. "Actually, it clarifies much that was obscure." Seeing the questioning looks around her, she elaborated:

"I've been encountering occasional tips, obscure hints, that pointed toward India as the source of the current—disturbances. Much of it, at least. But I discounted the rumors. India is far away, and except for trade, far removed from the normal concerns of Rome. I assumed the converse must also be true. What interest could India possibly have in the machinations of the Byzantine court?"

"What do you know about India?" asked Antonina.

Irene shrugged. "Which India? Don't forget, Antonina, India is a huge place. It's larger than Europe, in area alone, and much more densely populated. It's the biggest mistake Westerners make, actually. We try to imagine India as a single country, rather than a continent."

She rose again and poured herself some wine. Then filled Sittas' cup to the brim. This time, his hand *was* shaking. Slightly. She

136

offered some wine to Belisarius and Antonina, but they declined. Irene resumed her seat and continued.

"India hasn't been unified under one throne for over half a millenium, not since the Mauryan Empire collapsed. The Gupta Empire which eventually replaced it was confined to north India. The south remained under the control of independent monarchs."

She hesitated again, her eyes slightly unfocused. It was obvious she was recalling information.

"Or, at least, that was true until recently. The Gupta Empire broke in half, a few decades ago, and the western half was invaded by the White Huns. The Ephthalites, as we call them. Also known as—"

"Ye-tai," interjected Belisarius.

Irene nodded. "The White Huns—or Ye-tai—were apparently beaten back, and then some sort of accommodation was reached between them and the western dynasty, the Malwa. The Malwa dynasty, from what I've been able to glean, has since been expanding rapidly. They've finished reconquering most of north India, although they're apparently plagued with rebellions. And now, according to a few informants, they've begun their conquest of the south. They are at war now with the greatest, and most northerly, of the southern realms. A place called—"

She hesitated, frowned, tried to dredge up the memory.

"Andhra," stated Belisarius. "Ruled by the Satavahana dynasty."

Irene nodded. "That's about all I know. To be honest, I never pursued the matter. India, as I said, seemed much too remote to be a real danger to Rome and, in any event, they were obviously preoccupied with their own problems."

She waved a hand, dismissively. "And then, too, most of the tales you hear about India are at least half fantastical. Especially tales about the Malwa. Gods that walk the earth, magic weapons—" She stopped, stared at Belisarius.

"Magic weapons, indeed," grunted Belisarius. "We've had no luck duplicating them."

Irene looked at the general's wife.

"Belisarius is being too pessimistic," said Antonina. "We've only just gotten started in that work. It's only been a few months since we first encountered the jewel ourselves. It's taken that long to get established on the estate which Cassian gave us. John of Rhodes has been in residence now for only three months, and the workshop has barely been set up." She shook her head firmly. "So, under the circumstances, I think it's much too early to make any clear assessment of our success in duplicating the Malwa weapons."

"Has the jewel been of any help?" asked Sittas.

Belisarius shook his head. "No, not in that regard. I can sense that it's trying, but—it is very difficult for the thing to communicate with me, except through visions. And those aren't very useful when it comes to weaponry." Strangely, he grinned. "As a rule, I should say. However—we must have a joust soon, Sittas!"

His enormous friend sneered. "Why? I'll just knock you on your ass like I always do. Shrimp."

Belisarius grinned evilly. "You're in for a surprise, large one. The jewel *has* succeeded in giving me one simple new device. Simple, but I guarantee it will revolutionize the cavalry."

Sittas looked skeptical. "What is it? A magic lance?"

"Oh, nothing that elaborate. Just a simple little gadget called *stirrups.*" He grinned again, *very* evilly. "By all means. A joust—and soon!"

Belisarius turned back to Irene. "Where does the Malwa conquest of south India stand now?"

Irene frowned. "I really don't know. As of my last report, which was three months ago, the Malwa had just begun their siege of the Andhra capital." She paused, estimating time factors. "Given that the report itself probably took months to get here, I would assume the siege began approximately a year ago. Apparently, it's expected to be a long siege. The Andhra capital is reported to be well fortified. It's located at a place called—" She hesitated, looked away, again trying to bring up the information.

"It is located at a place called Amavarati," said Belisarius. The general continued, seeming for all the world, like a man possessed by a vision. "In a short while the palace will fall to the Malwa. Within the palace is a young princess named Shakuntala. She will be the only survivor of the dynasty. She will be captured and taken north to the palace of a high Malwa official, destined to be his concubine. A man will be lying in the reeds outside, wounded. His name is Raghunath Rao. When he recovers from his wounds, he will go north himself, tracking the princess and her captors. He will find her at the palace, but will be unable to rescue her in time. Before he can do so, the owner of the palace will return from some mission he was sent on by the Malwa emperor. He will die then, as will the princess."

Belisarius clenched his teeth, remembering another man's hatred.

"The Vile One, that official is called. Venandakatra. Venandakatra the Vile."

Irene shot to her feet. "Venandakatra?" she demanded. "You are sure of that name?"

Belisarius stared at her. "Quite sure. It is a name burned into my memory. Why?"

"*He's here! In Constantinople!*"

When the uproar which followed Irene's announcement subsided, Belisarius resumed his seat.

"So *that's* the mysterious mission Venandakatra was sent on," murmured Belisarius.

"This doesn't make sense," complained Sittas. "I've met the fellow myself, by the way. At one of the endless receptions at the Great Palace. A greasy sort, he struck me. But I spent no time with him. He presented himself as simply a modest envoy seeking to expand trading opportunities with Rome." Sittas waved his hand airily. "Not my interest, that sort of thing."

Irene snorted. "Just the money that comes from it."

Sittas grinned. "Well, yes. I believe my family does have a small interest in the Indian trade."

"They control at least a fourth of it," retorted Irene. "If not more. Your family are no slouches themselves when it comes to keeping secrets."

Again, the airy wave of the hand. "Yes, yes, no doubt. But I leave that business to my innumerable cousins. The point I was trying to make, before I was so rudely interrupted, is that this Venandakatra sounds like far too powerful an official to be sent on such a paltry mission. Are you sure we're talking about the same man? The name Venandakatra, after all, might be quite common in India."

Belisarius shook his head and began to speak. Irene interrupted him.

"Stick to your trade, Sittas. The whole thing makes perfect sense, if we assume that the jewel's visions of the future are accurate. Which"—a glance at Belisarius—"they obviously are. Venandakatra doesn't give a fig for trade. That's just a story to explain his presence. He's actually here to scout the territory, so to speak, and to lay the groundwork for the future attack on Rome."

She stopped, concentrated, continued:

"His cover, however, makes him vulnerable. He doesn't have a large retinue with him. He couldn't, not posing as a simple trading envoy. It wouldn't be difficult at all to have him assassinated."

"*No.*"

Irene looked at Belisarius, startled.

"Why in the world not? I didn't get the impression you were any too fond of the man."

Belisarius tightened his jaws. "You cannot begin to imagine how much I despise him. But it's not for us to cut his throat."

He rose and began pacing, working off nervous energy. He reached a hand into his cloak, pulled out a sheathed dagger, stared down at it. Slowly, he drew the dagger from its sheath.

"I carry this with me always, now. It's been like a compulsion. Or a charm."

He straightened up. "But I think it's time to return the dagger to its rightful owner. I must go to India and find Raghunath Rao."

Antonina was pale, her hand at her throat.

"You can't be serious," stated Sittas forcefully. "You're needed here, Belisarius! Not gallivanting around India. Good Lord! Irene's right, you know—India's immense, and you don't know anything about the place. Even if this man's still alive, how will you find him?"

Belisarius smiled his crooked smile.

"So long as Venandakatra is alive, I will know where to find Rao. Lurking nearby, like a panther waiting to strike, if he can see even the slightest opening. I will go to India, and I will find that man, and I will give him back his dagger and, somehow, I will give him his opening."

He turned to Irene. "*That's* why Venandakatra can't be assassinated. It is essential that we forge an alliance with Raghunath Rao. And through him, with the surviving heir of the Satavahana dynasty. To do so, we must find him—and to find him, we need Venandakatra alive."

Antonina cleared her throat. "But, husband, such a trip—"

"Will take at least a year," finished Belisarius. "I know, love. But it must be done."

"I think it's an excellent idea," said Irene firmly. She paused for a moment, allowing her statement to register on Antonina and Sittas. The two were obviously surprised to hear the spymaster side with Belisarius in what seemed to them a half-baked, impulsive scheme. Once Irene saw that she had their full attention, she continued.

"Like Sittas, I do not understand why Belisarius thinks this man Rao is so important. Or this Princess Shakuntala. Although—" She stared at the general, gauging. "I will gladly accept his judgment. So should you, Sittas. Didn't you once tell me Belisarius is the most brilliant Roman general since Scipio Africanus? I suspect that same general is working on some grand strategy."

Irene spread her hands in a gesture of finality. "But it doesn't matter, because Belisarius should go to India in any event. For one thing, we *must* obtain the best possible information concerning India. Especially its military capacity, and its new weapons. Who better to do that than Rome's best general?"

Sittas began to speak. Irene drove him down.

"Nonsense, yourself! You said he was needed here. *For what?* The Persian defeat will keep the Medes licking their wounds for at least a year. Several years, I estimate. So there won't be any danger from that quarter for a time."

She drove over his protest again. "And even if the Persians do start making trouble before Belisarius gets back, I say again: *so what?* He may be Rome's best general, but he's not the only good one. You yourself are currently unemployed, except for those parade ground duties that bore you to death."

She paused. A particularly garish tapestry hanging on the wall opposite caught her eye. Even in the seriousness of the moment, she found it difficult not to laugh. Her employer had obviously been the model for the heroic figure portrayed in the tapestry. A mounted cataphract in full armor, slaying some kind of monstrous beast with a lance.

"Is that a lion?" she asked lightly.

Sittas glared at the tapestry.

"It's a *dragon*," he growled.

"I didn't realize dragons were furry," commented Antonina idly. She and Irene exchanged a quick, amused glance. Sittas began to snarl something, but Belisarius cut him off.

"Let's get back to the point," he said firmly. "I think Irene's suggestion is a good one. We might be able to get Sittas assigned to replace me in command of the army in Syria. That would put him close to the estate where Antonina's doing her work. With

Sittas nearby, she'd still have access to expert military expertise when she needed it."

Irene drove over Antonina's gathering protest.

"*You are not thinking, woman!* You're worrying over Belisarius' safety and fretting over his prolonged absence." The spymaster was suddenly as cold as ice. "You are being a fool, Antonina. The worst danger to Belisarius isn't in India. It's right here in Constantinople. Better he should be gone for a year or so in India, than gone forever in a grave."

Startled, Antonina stared at her husband. Belisarius nodded.

"She's right, love. That's part of my thinking. *Justinian.*"

Antonina now looked at the spymaster. Irene grimaced.

"At the moment," she said, "the greatest danger to Belisarius does come from Justinian. There's nothing the Emperor dreads so much as a great general. Especially one as popular as Belisarius is today, after his victory over the Persians."

"An expedition to India would be perfect, from that point of view," chimed in Belisarius. "Get me out of Constantinople, away from the Emperor's suspicions and fears."

Irene brushed back her hair, thinking.

"Actually, if the whole thing's presented properly, Justinian will probably jump at it. He's not insane, you know. If he can avoid it, he'd much rather keep Belisarius alive. You never know when he might need a great general again, after all. But sending him to India, off and away for at least a year—oh, yes, I think he'd like that idea immensely. Get Belisarius completely out of the picture for a time, until the current hero worship dies down."

Antonina's face was pinched. "How soon?" she whispered.

"Not for at least six months," said Belisarius. "Probably seven."

Antonina looked relieved, but puzzled.

"Why so long?" she asked.

"The trade with India," replied her husband, "depends on the monsoon seasons. The monsoon winds blow one way part of the year, the other way during the other part. You travel from India to the west from November through April. You go the other way—my way, that is—from July through October."

He held up his hand, fingers outspread, and began counting off.

"We're in the beginning of October. It's too late to catch the eastward monsoon for this year. It's almost over, and it would take at least a month or two to reach the Erythrean Sea. That means I can't leave for India until the beginning of July, next year. Mind you, that refers to the part of the trip beginning at the south end of the Red Sea. Figure another month—no, two—to get from here through the Red Sea."

He began to calculate; Irene cut him short.

"You won't be leaving Constantinople for India until April, at the earliest. Probably May. Which, incidentally, is when Venandakatra has already announced he plans to return to his homeland."

Antonina's initial relief vanished.

"But—Irene, from what you've already said, *now* is the most dangerous time for Belisarius to be in Constantinople. Six months! Who knows what Justinian might do in six months?"

Irene brushed back her hair. "I know, I've been thinking about it while Belisarius was explaining the maritime facts of life. And I think I have a solution."

She looked at Belisarius.

"Are you familiar with Axum?"

"The kingdom of the Ethiopians?" asked Belisarius. "No, not really. I've met a few Axumites, here and there. But—I'm a general, so there's never been any occasion for me to encounter them professionally. Rome and Axum have gotten along just fine for centuries. Why?"

"I see a chance to kill two birds with one stone. As it happens, Venandakatra's is not the only foreign mission in Constantinople at the moment. There's also an Axumite embassy. They arrived two months ago. The embassy is officially headed by King Kaleb's younger son, Eon Bisi Dakuen. He's only nineteen years old. Barely more than a boy, although I've heard that he's made a good impression. But I think the actual leader of the embassy is Eon's chief adviser, a man named Garmat."

"So?"

"So—this Garmat, by all accounts, is quite a canny fellow. And, I've heard, he's been dropping hints here and there of the desire of the Axumites to forge closer ties to Rome."

She paused, savoring the little bombshell.

"I didn't think much of it, when I first heard. But it seems the Axumites are concerned over developments in India. Which, they are suggesting, pose long-term problems for Rome. And Garmat is quite frustrated that he's getting no reception to his message.

Apparently, he's already announced that he'll be returning to Axum shortly."

She allowed the silence to continue for a moment.

"So, I have reason to think that the Axumites would welcome a friendly overture from some notable Roman figure. Such as a famous general who's invited them to tour Syria on their way back to Ethiopia. A tour which he would present to Emperor Justinian as the first leg of a *very* lengthy mission which would eventually take him to India. *After* spending a few months visiting Axum, which, conveniently enough, is located right on the way to India."

"The perfect place to wait for the monsoon," mused Belisarius. "Out of sight, out of mind. Axum's as remote as India, as far as Justinian cares."

He rose and began pacing again. His eyes narrowed, and he peered sharply at Irene.

"There's more."

Irene nodded. "Yes. First of all, such a tour would give you and Antonina a chance to return to your estate and spend some time there before you went on. I imagine that would be useful, for your armaments project."

"And?"

"And—in light of what I've learned today, I think Rome should take Axum's warning very seriously. *And Axum itself.* The truth is, we don't really know much about them. Other than the fact that they've always had good relations with us, and that they've been Christians for two centuries, and that they have a naval capability."

"Aren't they at war in Arabia now?" asked Sittas.

"Yes," replied the spymaster. "They invaded southern Arabia three years ago. They overthrew the King of Hymria, Yusuf Asar Yathar. The ostensible reason was that King Yusuf had adopted Judaism and was persecuting the Christian Arabs." She chuckled harshly. "That does not, of course, explain why they conquered the rest of southwestern Arabia."

"You think they might be allies?" asked Belisarius. "Against India?"

Irene shrugged. "That's for you to find out, General. On your way to India."

Belisarius was silent, for a time. Pacing.

"I think that's it, then, for the moment," he said at length.

He turned to Antonina.

"See if you can arrange a meeting with Theodora, love. I think that would be the best way to broach the subject to Justinian."

He took Antonina's hand and helped her to her feet. Then, before turning to the door, looked at Sittas.

"Well, there's a couple of other small points. The first, my oversized and overconfident friend, is that I will expect you tomorrow at the practice field of your army. In full armor, mind. You'll need it."

Sittas grunted. "And the other?"

Belisarius nodded toward Irene.

"Whatever you're paying her, double it."

Chapter 11

The next morning, watching Belisarius approach him on the training field, Sittas decided that his friend had spent too much time in the Syrian sun. His brains were obviously fried.

Belisarius' challenge had been idiotic in the first place. On foot, with swords, Sittas suspected that his friend would carve him like a roast. But on horseback, in full armor, in a lance charge—well! The shrimp didn't stand a chance in hell.

Sittas was not guessing. Facts were facts. Sittas did not have Belisarius' speed and reflexes, but that mattered little in a lance charge. In a lance charge, wearing full armor atop a huge warhorse that was itself half-armored, weight and strength were what mattered.

Sittas almost slapped his great belly in self-satisfaction. He'd jousted with Belisarius before, several times, and always with the same result. Belisarius, on his ass, contemplating the futility of matching skills with the best lancer in Byzantium.

And now! The fool wasn't even holding his lance properly! Belisarius was carrying his lance cradled under his arm, instead of in the proper overhand position. Ridiculous! How could he expect to bring any force into the lance thrust? Any novice knew the only way to drive a lance home, on horseback, was to bring the whole weight of the back and shoulder into a downward thrust.

Off to the side of the training field, perched on a stone wall, Sittas spotted a small group of boys watching the joust. From their animated discourse, it was obvious that even barefoot street urchins were deriding Belisarius' preposterous methods.

Seeing Belisarius begin his charge, Sittas set his own horse into motion. As they neared each other, Sittas saw that his friend's bizarre method of holding his lance had the one advantage of accuracy. The blunted tip of the practice lance was unerringly aimed right at Sittas' belly.

He almost laughed. Accuracy be damned! There wouldn't be any force at all behind an underhand thrust. His shield would deflect it easily.

The moment was upon them. Sittas saw that Belisarius' lance would strike first. He positioned his shield and raised his own lance high above his head.

Some time later, after a semblance of consciousness returned, Sittas decided he had collided with a wall. How else explain his position? On the ground, on his ass, feeling like one giant bruise.

He gazed up, blearily. Belisarius was looking down at him from atop his horse.

"Are you alive?"

Sittas snarled. "What happened?"

"I knocked you on your ass, that's what happened."

"Crap! I ran into a wall."

Belisarius laughed. Sittas roared and staggered to his feet.

"Where's my horse?"

"Right behind you, like a good warhorse."

Sure enough. Sittas saw his lance lying on the ground nearby. He grabbed it and stalked to his horse. He was so furious that he even tried to mount the horse unassisted. The attempt was hopeless, of course. After a few seconds of futility, Sittas left off and began leading his horse to the mounting platform at the edge of the field.

He was spared that little indignity, however. One of the urchins on the wall leapt nimbly onto the field and hurried to fetch him a mounting stool. As he clambered back upon his horse, Sittas favored the boy with a growling thanks.

"'Twere just bad luck, lord," piped the lad. Then, with the absolute confidence possessed only by eight-year-old boys: "Yon loon don't know nothin' 'bout lance work!"

"Quite right," snarled Sittas. To Belisarius, in a bellow: "Again! Pure luck!"

This time, as the collision neared, Sittas concentrated almost entirely on his shield work. He had already decided that his mishap had been due to overconfidence. He'd been so preoccupied with planning his own thrust that he hadn't deflected Belisarius' lance properly.

Oh, but he had him now—oh, yes! His shield was perfectly positioned and solidly braced against his chest. Ha! The luck of Thrace was about to run out!

Some time later, after a semblance of consciousness returned, Sittas decided he had collided with a cathedral. How else explain his position? On the ground, flat on his back, feeling like one giant corpse.

Hazily, he saw Belisarius kneeling over him.

"What happened?" he croaked.

Belisarius smiled his crooked smile. "You ran into a *stirrup*. A pair of stirrups, I should say."

"What the hell kind of cathedral is a stirrup?" demanded Sittas. "And what idiot put two of them on a training field?"

Later, as they rode back toward his mansion along a busy commercial thoroughfare, Sittas uttered words of gentle reproach.

"You *cheated*, you stinking bastard!" he bellowed, for the hundredth time. For the hundredth time, he glared down at the—*stirrups*. No wild boar of the forest ever glared a redder-eyed glare of rage.

"Marvelous, aren't they?" beamed Belisarius. He stood up straight in the saddle, twisting back and forth, bestowing his cheerful gaze upon the various merchants watching from their little shops.

"Improves visibility, too. See, Sittas! You can look all around, without ever having to worry about your balance. You can even draw your bow and shoot straight over your back as you're withdrawing."

"You *cheated*, you dog!"

"And, of course, you already saw how much more effectively you can wield a lance. No more of that clumsy overhand business! No, no. With stirrups you can use a lance properly, with all your own weight and the weight of your mount behind the thrust, instead of being a spear-chucker sitting awkwardly on a horse."

"You *cheated*, you—"

"You could always have a pair of them made for yourself, you know."

Sittas glared down, again, at the *stirrups*.

"Believe I will," he muttered. Another red-eyed glare at Belisarius. "*Then* we'll have *another* duel!"

Belisarius grinned.

"Oh, I don't see any point to that. We're getting on in years, Sittas. We're responsible generals, now. Got to stop acting like foolish boys."

"You *cheater*!"

When they rode into the courtyard of Sittas' mansion, Antonina and Irene were standing there waiting. Both women seemed worried.

"He *cheated!*" roared Sittas.

"Not quite the conversationalist he used to be, is he?" commented Belisarius cheerfully as he dismounted.

Sittas began to roar again, but Irene silenced him.

"Shut up! We've been waiting for you two idiots to return. Belisarius! You've got an audience with Theodora—and you're already late!"

Antonina shook her head angrily. "Look at them! Refusing to admit they're getting on in years. You're responsible generals, now, you clowns! You've got to stop acting like foolish boys!"

Sittas clamped shut his great jaws.

"You've *already* set up an audience with Theodora?" demanded Belisarius, gaping.

Irene smiled. "Yes. I'd like to claim it's due to my talents as an intriguer, but the truth is that Antonina was the key. I'd always heard Theodora considered Antonina her best friend, but I hadn't really believed it until now."

The smile vanished, replaced by a frown.

"We have to go immediately, *but—*"

"He can't go in full armor!" protested Antonina.

"I'll be dressed in a moment," said Belisarius. He clattered into the mansion.

"Watch out for the rugs!" roared Sittas.

"Please," muttered Irene. "Make sure you gouge up as many as possible." She smiled sweetly at Sittas.

"What happened to you, anyway?"

"Yes, Sittas," added Antonina, smiling just as sweetly. "We're curious. Did you run into a wall?"

"Looks more like he ran into a cathedral," mused Irene. "You see that one great bruise? There—on his—"

"He *cheated*!"

"Stop worrying, Antonina. Of course I'll support Belisarius in this elaborate scheme of yours."

The Empress stared out the window of her reception room. The view was magnificent, the more so since the Empress could well afford the finest glass. The panes of glass in *her* windows had not a trace of the discolorations and distortions which most glass contained.

Theodora never tired of the view from the Gynaeceum, the women's quarters of the Great Palace. It was not so much the scenery beyond—though the sight of the great city was magnificent—as it was the constant reminder of her own power. Within the women's quarters, the Empress was supreme. That had been Byzantine custom even before she mounted the throne, and it was a custom into which Theodora had thrust the full force of her personality.

Here, Theodora ruled unchallenged. She was the sole mistress not only of her own chambers but of the public offices as well. And it was here, in the Gynaeceum, that the silk goods, which were a royal monopoly, were woven. Those silk goods were one of the major sources of imperial wealth.

Without Theodora's permission, not even the Emperor could enter the Gynaeceum. And it was a permission which Theodora never gave him. She had too much to hide. Not lovers, of course. Theodora knew that were she to entertain lovers, word would get to Justinian. But the temptation never arose, in any event. Theodora had no interest in men, except Justinian.

No, not lovers; but there were other things to hide. Religious leaders, mostly. Monophysite heretics seeking refuge from the persecution that was developing again could find sanctuary in the secret rooms of the Gynaeceum.

Theodora scowled. For all that he was personally tolerant, and knew his own Empress to be a Monophysite, Justinian was seeking closer ties with the See of Rome. He hoped, Theodora knew, to gain orthodox approval for his projected reconquest of the western Empire. That approval came with a price—*eradicate heresy*.

It was a price which Theodora, for reasons of state even more than personal preference, thought far too costly for the prospective gain. The real strength of the Empire was in the Monophysite east—in Syria and Palestine and, especially, in Egypt. Why enfeeble the Empire's hold over those great provinces in order to gain the approval of a miserable pope squatting in Italy, surrounded by semibarbarian Goths? Who were Arian heretics themselves. No, it—

She shook her head, driving away the thoughts. Later. For now, there was this other matter.

She turned away from the window and smiled at Antonina. Then she smiled at Belisarius. The first smile was heartfelt. The second was—not. Or, at least, not very.

Briefly, the Empress examined her feelings in that cold and dispassionate way that was one of her great strengths. In truth, she liked Belisarius. It was just that she found it impossible to trust any man. She did not even trust Justinian, for all that she genuinely loved him. But—as men went, Belisarius was not bad. He had been good to Antonina, after all. And Theodora thought, approvingly, that his wife had the general well under her thumb. Whether or not Belisarius could be trusted, she trusted Antonina.

The Empress resumed her seat upon the throne which sat in a corner. The throne fit awkwardly in the confines of the private reception room. True, the room itself was luxurious. The floors were covered with exquisite Armenian rugs, the walls with even more exquisite mosaics and tapestries. Still, it was much too small a room to manage the bulk of a throne properly.

Yet even here, in the privacy of her own quarters, Theodora insisted on a throne. A relatively modest throne, to be sure, nothing like the monstrosity upon which she sat in the great reception hall of the palace. But it was a throne nonetheless.

It was one of her own foibles, she knew. The throne was not as comfortable as a normal chair would have been, but—she remembered the years of poverty and powerlessness. The years when she obeyed men, rather than the other way around. And so, everywhere she planted her very attractive imperial rump, she insisted on a throne.

"I just don't like to have my intelligence insulted," she growled. The Empress straightened. As tall as she was, sitting high up on a throne, the pose made her loom over her audience. Exactly as she intended.

"It's perfectly obvious that you're looking for an excuse to get away from Justinian's insanely jealous eye, Belisarius."

Seeing the slight look of startlement on the general's face, Theodora laughed.

"You think it strange that I understand my husband's peculiarities?"

Belisarius examined the Empress. She was a beautiful woman, very shapely in a slender sort of way. An Egyptian like Antonina, she shared his wife's dark complexion. But where Antonina's green eyes were a startlement in her dusky face, the Empress' eyes were so deep a brown as to be almost black. Her hair also was black, as little of it as could be seen in the jewel-encrusted coiffure.

He decided that honesty was probably the best course, under the circumstances. He did not know Theodora well, but he did not mistake the cold intelligence in those dark eyes.

"I am not surprised that you understand the Emperor's— characteristics. I am simply a bit puzzled that you understand him so well and—" He faltered. This was perhaps pushing honesty a bit far.

The Empress concluded for him.

"And still love him?"

Belisarius nodded. "Yes." He took a deep breath. Hell with it. The general knew from experience that it was unwise to change strategy in midbattle. "And are quite devoted to him. Even a man as removed as I am from the imperial court can tell that much."

The Empress chuckled. "I suggest you don't try to understand it. I don't myself, not entirely, and I suspect I'm much better than you at understanding such things. But the fact is, I do love Justinian, and I am quite devoted to him. Do not ever doubt it." She bestowed upon him a cold, deadly, imperial gaze. But only for a few seconds. Belisarius, she realized, was not one to be intimidated. Nor, she thought, was there any reason to do so.

Theodora smiled again. "One of the facts which *is*, and unfortunately, remains, is that my husband is prone to extreme jealousy. An imperial kind of jealousy, to boot, which is the worst variety."

She sighed. "It would be so much better if he'd fret himself over my fidelity, like most men. There'd be nothing in it, and I could spend some pleasurable hours reassuring him of his potency. But, not Justinian. He frets only royal frets, I'm afraid. The greatest of which is being overthrown by a rival. Especially a successful general.

"In fact, the threat's real enough. In general, at least. I just wish Justinian would stop being obsessed with the matter."

She mused. "At the moment, the two most successful and esteemed generals of the empire are you and Sittas." A small laugh. "Not even Justinian worries about Sittas! Outside of war, Sittas is the laziest man alive. And he can't stand the duties of a general in Constantinople—everyone knows it. He's been pestering Justinian for months to be reassigned to a field army, whereas an ambitious general couldn't be pried out of the capital with a lever."

She gave Belisarius a cold smile. "That leaves you. You alone, to be the focus of Justinian's worries."

Belisarius began to speak, but Theodora cut him off.

"Spare me, Belisarius. There's no point in making reassurances. I don't need them, and Justinian won't believe them."

She waved her hand. "No, the right course is exactly the one you propose." Another laugh. "Although even in my wildest dreams I never would have thought of sending you to Axum and India! God, Justinian will be ecstatic!"

The Empress was silent for a moment, lost in thought. "And it's not a bad idea, in any event, even leaving Justinian's jealousies aside."

She arose and walked slowly back to the window. Belisarius was struck by the regal grace of her movements, as encumbered as Theodora must have been by those incredible imperial robes. (Which, Antonina had told him, Theodora insisted on wearing at all times.) She looked every inch the ideal image of an Empress.

For a brief instant, Belisarius caught a glimpse of the woman's inner demons: that fierce, driving ambition which had carried her and her husband to the throne from the lowest of beginnings. Justinian, a semiliterate peasant from Thrace—who had, of course, long since become as literate a man as any in the Empire, applying his own fierce intelligence. Theodora, a whore from Alexandria.

But Theodora had been no sophisticated courtesan like Antonina, gaily choosing her few consorts and reveling in the charm and wit of their company. Belisarius knew Theodora's own history from Antonina. The Empress had been sold into prostitution by her own father at the age of twelve, to a pimp who had sold her in turn to every ruffian who hung about the Hippodrome.

He watched the still, beautiful face staring out the window.

Watched the pride in the stillness, and the icy intelligence in the beauty, and thought he understood Theodora. Understood her, and understood her unshakable devotion to Justinian.

I swore an oath to Justinian, which I will always keep. But I wish I had sworn it to her. She would have made a far better Emperor.

"I don't trust this Venandakatra," Theodora said softly. "Even before Antonina told me of Irene's suspicions, I had my own." She glanced at Belisarius. "You've not met him?"

The general shook his head.

"I shall introduce you to him tomorrow. Justinian is having a reception for Venandakatra."

She stared back out the window. "Trade envoy!" she sneered. "That man has enough arrogance in him to be Lord of the Universe. A foul creature, he is! As vile a man as ever lived, I suspect."

Belisarius restrained his start of surprise. Antonina, he knew, had simply passed on that much of what they knew about Venandakatra which could reasonably have been spied out by Irene. There had been no mention of his vision.

Venandakatra the Vile. Apparently, the cognomen had been no personal fancy of Raghunath Rao.

Theodora shook her head. "No, I don't like this Venandakatra. The Malwa are playing a deep and dark game. And we know almost nothing about them. Yes, best we find out what we can, as soon as possible."

She turned back. "But there's something more important. You'll have plenty of time to get to know this Venandakatra creature. Much more, I assure you, than you'd ever want. In the meantime, however, there are other people you must get to know immediately. The Axumite embassy will also be present at the reception, which is doubling—as an afterthought, I'm afraid—as their departing ceremony. They are returning to Axum the next day."

She resumed her seat on the throne. "To my mind, your proposed visit to Axum is even more important than the trip to India. For one thing, I'm not sure how much you'll actually be able to find out in India. Whatever else he is, Venandakatra's no fool, and he'll have his own suspicions of you."

"Will he agree?" asked Antonina. "To Belisarius accompanying him back to India?"

Theodora waved the concern away. "He can't very well refuse, can he? After all, he's supposedly a mere trade envoy. How could he refuse an imperial request to carry a Roman envoy back to his homeland?" She shook her head. "No, he'll agree, however grudgingly. What I am much more concerned about, at the moment, is whether the Axumites will agree to *that* side of your proposal."

"I thought they were on good terms with Rome," commented Belisarius.

The Empress tightened her lips. "Yes, they *were*. Whether they still are, after the shameful way they've been treated since their arrival, is another matter."

"They've been insulted?" asked Antonina.

"Not directly. But Justinian's indifference to them was soon detected by the courtiers, who—" She snorted. "It's the first rule of the courtier: if the Emperor breaks wind, you shit a mountain."

Belisarius chuckled. Theodora shook her head.

"It's not really funny. Justinian is so preoccupied with—well, never mind. Let's just say that he has forgotten the first rule of the emperor. *Do not trample over old friends in your eagerness to make new ones.*"

"What's your impression of the Axumites?" asked Antonina.

Theodora frowned. "The adviser, Garmat, strikes me as shrewd. I don't think he'll be a problem. It's rather the prince who concerns me."

She spoke the prince's name slowly, savoring the words: "Eon Bisi Dakuen. Do you know what the name means?"

Belisarius and Antonina shook their heads.

"The Axumites are warriors. We forget that, here, because we only encounter them as traders and seamen. But they are a warrior people, with their own proud history. It is a tradition which is particularly ingrained in the ruling clan. It shows in their royal nomenclature."

She closed her eyes, calling up memory. "The official name for the king of the Ethiopians is Kaleb Ella Atsbeha, son of Tazena, Bisi Lazen, King of Axum, Himryar, Dhu Raydan, Saba, Salhen, the High Country and Yamanat, the Coastal Plain, Hadramawt, and all their Arabs, the Beja, Noba, Kasu, and Siyamo, servant of Christ."

"That's a mouthful," commented Antonina.

Theodora opened her eyes, smiling. "Isn't it? But don't shrug it off as royal grandiosity. It's quite accurate, except for the 'Ella Atsbeha' part, and accurate in significant ways."

"What does 'Ella Atsbeha' mean?" asked Belisarius.

"It means 'he who brings the dawn.'" Theodora shrugged. "That part of the title we can ignore. But the rest—ah, *there's* what's interesting. The long list of territories ruled, for instance, is quite precise. And the Axumites are punctilious about it. The listing of Himryar, for instance, as well as the Hadrawmat, is recent. The Axumites add and remove territories to the name of their ruler in strict accordance to the facts on the ground, so to speak."

She cast a shrewd glance at Belisarius.

"What does that tell you, General?"

"It tells me they prize accurate intelligence, even formally." Belisarius smiled crookedly. "That's a rather rare trait in rulers."

"Isn't it? But the Axumites are rigorous about it. I had my historians check the records." She went on. "The 'ella' name is only given to ruling monarchs. Who, by the way, are properly known as the *negusa nagast*, which means 'King of Kings.' My historians are not certain, but they think the title is also quite accurate. From old records of the first missionaries, it seems that Axum was forged by conquest and that it rules over many subordinate monarchs in the region of Ethiopia. Even Meroe and Nubia, it seems."

"And the 'bisi' name?" asked Belisarius. "It must mean something. I notice that both the King—the negusa nagast—and his son share the name. It's a title, I imagine."

"Yes. And that's the most interesting part. King Kaleb's oldest son Wa'zeb is named 'Wa'zeb Bisi Hadefan, son of Ella Atsbeha.' He is granted the patronymic, because he is the heir. The younger son who is the envoy here, Eon, is stripped down the bare essentials. 'Eon Bisi Dakuen.' That's the only name he has, because it's the only name Axumite royalty considers essential."

"It's a military title," guessed Belisarius.

Theodora nodded approvingly. "Quite right. The Axumite army is organized into long-standing regiments. They call them *sarawit*. I believe the singular is *sarwe*. 'Bisi' means 'man of.' Hence the Prince, Eon, has as his only identity the fact that he is a man of the Dakuen sarwe. Just as his father, before all else, is a man of the Lazen sarwe; and his older brother Wa'zeb, the heir, is before all else a man of the Hadefan sarwe."

Antonina looked back and forth between the Empress and the general. "I think I'm missing something here," she said.

Belisarius pursed his lips. "Lord in Heaven, even the Spartans didn't take it that far."

He turned to his wife. "What it means, Antonina, is that the Axumites look at the world through the hard eyes of warriors. Proud ones. Proud enough that they name their kings and princes after regiments; and prouder still, that they disdain to claim territories which they don't actually rule."

Theodora nodded. "And these are the people who've been treated as unwanted guests since they arrived. Brushed off by insolent courtiers who don't know one end of a lance from the other, and by officious bureaucrats who don't even know what a lance looks like in the first place."

"Oh, my," said Antonina.

Belisarius eyed Theodora. "But you don't think the adviser— Garmat, is it?—is the problem."

The Empress shook her head.

"He's an adviser, after all. Probably a warrior himself, in his youth, but he's long past that now. No, the problem's the boy. Eon Bisi Dakuen. As proud as any young warrior ever is—much less a prince!—and mortally offended."

Theodora was startled to hear Belisarius laugh.

"Oh, I don't think so, Empress! Not if he's really a warrior, at least. And, with that name, I suspect he is." For a moment, the look on the general's face was as icy as that of the Empress. "Warriors aren't mortally offended all that easily, Theodora, appearances to the contrary. They've seen too much real mortality. If they survive—well, there's pride, of course. But there's also a streak of practicality."

He arose. "I do believe I can touch that practicality. As one warrior to another."

Antonina rose with him. The audience was clearly at an end, except—

"You'll arrange an interview with Justinian?"

Theodora shook her head. "There won't be any necessity for a private interview. Justinian will agree to your plan, I've no doubt of it." The Empress pondered. "I think the way to proceed is to have Belisarius' mission announced publicly at tomorrow's reception. That will box Venandakatra, and it may help to mollify the Axumites."

"You can arrange it that quickly?"

Theodora's smile was arctic. "Do not concern yourself, *General*. It will be arranged. See to it that you make good your boast concerning the young prince."

Chapter 12

Belisarius thought the Emperor's efforts were a waste of time, and said as much to Sittas. Very quietly, of course. Not even the fearless general Belisarius was fool enough to mock the Emperor aloud—certainly not at an official imperial reception.

"Of course it's a waste of time," whispered Sittas. "It always is, except with barbarians. So what? Justinian doesn't care. He loves his toys, and that's all there is to it. Think he'd pass up a chance to play with them?"

There followed, under his breath, various rude remarks about Thracian hicks and their childish delight in trinkets and baubles. Belisarius, smiling blandly, ignored them cheerfully.

For, in truth, Belisarius was not all that far removed from the Thracian countryside himself. And, if he was not exactly an uncouth hick—which, by the by, he thought was a highly inaccurate depiction of the Emperor!—still, he was enough of a rube to take almost as much pleasure as Justinian out of the—*toys*.

Toys, indeed.

There were the levitating thrones, first of all, upon which Justinian and Theodora were elevated far above the crowd. The thrones rose and fell as the Emperor's mood took him. At the moment, judging from his rarefied height, Justinian was feeling aloof from the huge mob thronging the reception hall.

Then, there were the lions which flanked the thrones whenever the royal chairs were resting on the floor. Made of beaten gold and silver, the lions were capable of emitting the most thunderous roars whenever the Emperor was struck by the fancy. Which, judging from their experience in the half-hour since they had arrived at the reception, Belisarius knew to be a frequent occurrence.

Finally, there were Belisarius' personal favorites: the jewel-encrusted metal birds which perched on metal trees and porcelain fountains scattered about in the vicinity of the Emperor. The general was fond of their metallic chirping, of course, but he was particularly taken by one bird on the rim of a fountain, which, from time to time, bent down as if to drink from its water.

Toys, indeed.

But, he thought, a waste of time and effort on this occasion. Neither the Indian nor the Axumite envoys were unsophisticated barbarians, to be astonished and dazzled by such marvels.

Belisarius examined the Malwa embassy first. The identity of Venandakatra was obvious, not only from his central position in the group of Indians but from his whole bearing. His clothing was rich, but unostentatious, as befitted one who claimed to be a mere trade envoy.

That assumed modesty was a waste of time, thought Belisarius. For, just as the Empress had said, Venandakatra carried himself in a manner which indeed suggested that he was the Lord of the Universe.

Belisarius smiled faintly. The elaborate and ostentatious reception for Venandakatra was Justinian's own none-too-subtle way of making clear to the Malwa that the Roman Emperor was not taken in by the Indian's subterfuge. A mere trade envoy would have been kept cooling his heels for weeks, before some midlevel bureaucrat finally deigned to grant him an audience in a dingy office. No genuine trade envoy had ever been given a formal imperial reception in the huge hall in the Great Palace itself, before the assembled nobility of Constantinople.

Belisarius glanced up at the enormous mosaics which decorated the walls. He almost expected to see looks of shock and dismay on the faces of the saints depicted thereon. Those holy eyes of tile were accustomed to gaze upon victorious generals, dignified Patriarchs, and the bejewelled ambassadors from the Persian court, not disreputable little—*merchants*.

Chuckling, Belisarius resumed his scrutiny of the Malwa "trade envoy."

Beyond his haughtiness, there was not much to remark about Venandakatra. The man's complexion was dark, by Byzantine standards, and the cast of his face obviously foreign. But neither of those features particularly set him apart. Constantinople was the most cosmopolitan city in the world, and its inhabitants were long accustomed to exotic visitors. Nor were Romans given to racial prejudice. So long as a man behaved properly, and dressed in a Byzantine manner, and spoke Greek, he was assumed to be civilized. A heathen, perhaps, but civilized.

Venandakatra was in late middle age, and of average height. His features were thin almost to the point of sharpness, which was accentuated by his close-set dark eyes. The eyes seemed as cold as a reptile's to Belisarius, even from a distance. The web of scaly wrinkles around the orbits added to the effect.

In build, Belisarius estimated that Venandakatra should have been slender, by nature. In fact, his thin-boned frame and features carried a considerable excess of weight. Venandakatra exuded the odd combination of rail-thin ferocity and self-indulgent obesity. Like a snake distended by its prey.

A cold, savage grin came upon the general's face, then, remembering a vision. In another time, in that future which Belisarius hoped to change, this vile man had been destroyed by a mere slip of a girl. Beaten to a pulp by her flashing hands and feet; bleeding to death from a throat cut by his own knife.

"Stop it, Belisarius!" hissed Antonina.

"Please," concurred Irene. "You're not supposed to bare your fangs at an imperial reception. We *are* trying to make a good impression, you know."

Belisarius tightened his lips. He glanced again at Venandakatra, then away.

The Vile One, indeed.

He looked now upon the Axumites and at once felt his expression ease.

In truth, to all appearances the Axumites were far more outlandish than the Indians. Their skins, for one thing, were not "dark-complected" but black. Black as Nubians (which, Belisarius judged from his features, one of them was). For another, where the Indians' hair was long and straight, that of the Axumites was short and very kinky. Finally, where the facial features of the Indians—leaving aside their dark complexion—were not all that different from Greeks (or, at least, Armenians), the features of the Axumites were distinctly African. That was especially true for the one whom Belisarius thought to be a Nubian. The features of the other Axumites had an Arab cast to them, for all their darkness. Positively aquiline, in the case of the oldest one of the group, whom Belisarius supposed was the adviser Garmat.

Belisarius knew that Ethiopia and southern Arabia had long been in contact with each other. Looking at the Axumites, and remembering some very dark-skinned Arabs he had met in the past, he decided the contact between the two races had often been intimate.

Yes, they were clearly even more foreign than the Indians—in habits as well as in appearance, Belisarius guessed. He chuckled softly, seeing how poorly the young prince wore the strange Byzantine costume he found himself encumbered within.

"It is a bit funny," agreed Irene quietly. "I think he's used to wearing a whole lot less clothing, in his own climate."

"Too bad he didn't come here a couple of centuries ago," added Antonina, "when Romans still wore togas. He'd have been a lot more comfortable, I think."

"So would I," muttered Sittas. He glanced down, with considerable disfavor, at the heavy knee-length embroidered coat which he was wearing. It felt almost as heavy as cataphract armor.

"How did we get saddled with these outfits?" he groused. "Instead of nice, comfortable togas?"

"We got them from the Huns," whispered Irene. "Who, in turn, got them from the Chinese."

Sittas goggled. "You're kidding!" He glared down at his coat. "You mean to tell me I'm wearing a filthy damned *Hunnish* costume?"

Irene nodded, smiling. "Odd how civilization works, isn't it? It's your fault, you know—soldiers, I mean, not you personally. Once you got obsessed with cavalry you started insisting on wearing Hun trousers." She smirked. "Why you insisted on including the coats into the bargain is a mystery."

"How do you know so much, woman?" grumbled Sittas. "It's unseemly."

"I don't spend all day drinking and complaining that there's nothing else to do."

Sittas glowered. "Damn intelligence in a woman, anyway. Should never have let them learn how to read. It's the only good thing about Thracians, you know. They keep their women barefoot and ignorant."

"It's true," whispered Antonina. "Belisarius only lets me wear shoes on special occasion like these." She glanced down admiringly at the preposterous, rickety, high-heeled contraptions on her feet. "And when I'm dancing naked on his bare chest, of course, with my whip and my iced sherbet."

"And that's another thing," groused Sittas. "Show me an intelligent woman, and I'll show you one with a sense of humor. Aimed at men, naturally." He glared around the huge room, singling out every single woman in it for a moment's glower. Although, in truth, most of them seemed neither particularly intelligent nor quick-witted.

Belisarius ignored the byplay. He had long since reconciled himself to his wife's sometimes outrageous jokes. He rather enjoyed them, actually. Although, glancing at the monstrosities on Antonina's little feet, he almost shuddered to think of them tearing great wounds in his body.

He concentrated again on the Axumites. There were only five of them, which, he had heard, was the entirety of their embassy. He glanced back at the Indians and smiled. The Axumites had sent five for a full diplomatic mission, whereas the Indians—who presented themselves as a mere trade delegation—had sent upward of twenty.

The smile faded. Some of those twenty were purely decorative, but by no means all of them. Perhaps one or two were actually even interested in trade, but Belisarius had no doubt that at least ten of the Indian delegation were nothing more than outright spies.

As if reading his thoughts, Irene whispered:

"I've heard half of the Indians have announced plans to set up permanent residence. To foster and encourage trade, they say."

"No doubt," muttered the general. "There's always a good traffic in treason, in this town."

Irene leaned over and whispered even more softly:

"Do you see the one on the far left?" she asked. "And the heavyset one toward the middle, wearing a yellow coat with black embroidery?" She was not looking at them at all, Belisarius noticed. He avoided more than a quick glance in the direction of the Malwa envoys.

"Yes, I see them."

"The one on the left is named Ajatasutra. The heavyset one is called Balban. I'm certain that Ajatasutra is one of the Malwa's chief spies. About Balban I'm less confident, but I suspect him also. And if my suspicions about Balban are correct, he would be the probable spymaster."

"Not Ajatasutra?"

Irene's head-shake was so faint as to be almost unnoticeable.

"No, he's too obvious. Too much in the forefront."

Again, it was uncanny the way Irene read his thoughts.

"Bad idea, Belisarius. You never want to assassinate known spies and spymasters. They'll simply be replaced with others you don't know. Best to keep them under watch, and then—"

"And then what?"

She smiled and shrugged lightly, never casting so much as a glance in the direction of the Indians.

"Whatever," she murmured. "The possibilities are endless."

Antonina nudged Belisarius. "I think it's time we made our acquaintance with the Axumites. I've been watching Theodora, and she's starting to glare at us impatiently."

"Onward," spoke the general. Taking his wife by the arm, he led her across the room, weaving a path through the chattering throng. The Axumites were standing off to one side, at the edge of the crowd. Even to Belisarius, who was no connoisseur of such events, it was apparent that the Ethiopians were being studiously ignored.

The Axumites took note of them as Belisarius and Antonina approached. The older man he took to be the adviser Garmat showed no reaction. The eyes of the young prince, on the other hand, widened noticeably. It might almost he said that he stared, until the tall man behind him—the one Belisarius thought was a Nubian—nudged him. Thereupon the prince tore his eyes away and stared elsewhere, his back ramrod straight.

As he approached, Belisarius' eyes met those of the Nubian. The tall black man immediately broke into a toothy grin, which just as immediately disappeared.

Belisarius was puzzled by the man. The identity of the adviser Garmat was obvious. And the other two members of the Axumite envoy were obviously soldiers. The prince's personal retinue, men much like his own pentarchs Valentinian and Anastasius. Seasoned, experienced warriors in their late twenties or early thirties. Young enough to be as physically vigorous as any; old enough not to be rash and impetuous.

What then was the function and capacity of the Nubian? If Nubian he was—though, as Belisarius came up to the small group, he was almost certain he was right. The tall man's face had none of the aquiline characteristics of the Axumites. His features were pure African.

He would know soon enough. He stopped a few feet from the group and bowed politely.

"I am Belisarius," he announced. "I am—"

"Rome's finest general!" said the older man. "Such a honor! I am Garmat, the adviser to Prince Eon Bisi Dakuen." He motioned to the young man standing at his side.

Belisarius examined the young man. The prince, he thought, was most handsome in an exotic sort of way. The boy was not tall, but he was obviously well built. Beneath the heavy embroidered coat, Belisarius suspected, lay a very muscular frame.

The prince nodded, so slightly as to be almost impolite. Immediately, the tall man standing behind him nudged the prince again, none too gently, and uttered a few words in a language unknown to Belisarius. The two Axumite soldiers standing by his side grunted something, which Belisarius sensed were words of approval.

Something odd was happening. The language was unknown to the general, but—for a moment, strangely, Belisarius thought he almost understood the words. Odd.

Under the darkness of the skin, Belisarius thought he saw the prince flush with embarrassment. The young man stood even straighter and nodded again. This time, very deeply and respectfully. The tall man behind him flashed Belisarius his quick toothy grin and said, in heavily accented Greek:

"I said to him: 'Show respect, fool boy! He is great general, tested in battle, and you but suckling babe.'" Again, the wide grin. "Of course, I spoke our language, so not to embarrass fool boy prince. And did not slap his head, for same reason. But now I find must translate, so as not to offend noble visitors."

"And who are you, if I might ask?"

The tall man grinned even more widely. "Me? I am nothing, great general. A miserable slave, no more. The lowest creature on earth, debased beyond measure."

Garmat interrupted. "Please! May we be introduced to your lovely wife?"

Belisarius apologized and made the introduction. Garmat was suave diplomacy itself, managing simultaneously to strew about fulsome praises of Antonina's beauty and charm without, at the same time, doing so in a manner which suggested even the slightest lechery. The prince did not manage so well. He was very polite, but too obviously smitten by her beauty.

The tall man behind him spoke sharply, again; again, the soldiers' grunting approval.

But this time, Belisarius understood the words—without knowing how.

"Idiot boy! Lust after local cowherds, if you must! Do not ogle the wives of great foreign generals!"

Belisarius kept a straight face. Or so, at least, he thought.

"You speak our language," announced Garmat.

Belisarius thought for a moment, then shook his head. "No, no. I can understand a few words, that is all. But I cannot speak—uh, what exactly—"

"We call it Ge'ez."

"Thank you. I apologize for my ignorance. I know little of Axum. As I said, I can speak no Ge'ez, but I do understand it a bit."

Garmat was staring up at him shrewdly. "More than a bit, I think." The adviser glanced back at the tall man standing behind the prince.

"You are puzzled by Ousanas." It was more of a statement than a question.

Belisarius looked at the tall man. "That is his name?"

Ousanas spoke, again in Greek.

"Is my civilized Greek name, General Belisarius. In my own tongue am called—" Here came several unpronounceable syllables.

"You are Nubian," said Belisarius.

Ousanas now grinned from ear to ear.

"Should think not! Most wretched folk, the Nubians. Given to putting on great airs, pretending they are Egyptian. I fart on Meroe and Napata!"

Garmat interrupted. "Romans often make that mistake. He is actually from much farther south than Nubia. From a land between great lakes, which is quite unknown to the peoples of the Mediterranean."

Belisarius frowned. "He is not Axumite, then?"

"Should hope not!" cried Ousanas. "Most wretched folk, the Axumites. Given to putting on great airs, pretending they are descendants of Solomon."

Again, the grin. "I do not, however, fart on Axum and Adulis. Else the *sarwen*"—a thumb pointed in each direction to the warriors at his side—"would beat me for an impertinent slave."

The two sarwen grunted agreement.

Belisarius was now frowning deeply. Garmat smiled.

"You are puzzled, I think, by some of our customs."

"Is this a custom?" asked Belisarius dubiously.

Garmat nodded vigorously. "Oh, yes! A very old custom. Every man child born to the king—even girls, sometimes, if there are no male heirs—is assigned a special slave at the age of ten. This slave is always a foreigner, of some kind. He is called the *dawazz*. His is a very special job. The prince has an adviser to teach him statecraft, which a king must have to rule properly." Here Garmat pointed to himself. "Veteran soldiers from his regiment to teach him the skill of arms, which a king must have to maintain his rule." Here Garmat pointed to the two soldiers. "And then, most important, he has his dawazz. Who teaches him that the difference between slave and king is not so great, after all."

Ousanas grinned. "Much better to be slave! No worries."

Antonina smiled sweetly. "I should think you'd worry what the prince will do if he ever assumes the throne. And remembers the dawazz who abused him, all those many times."

The grin never wavered. "Nonsense, great lady. Prince be properly grateful. Shower faithful dawazz with gifts. Offer him prestigious posts."

Antonina grinned back. "Maybe. Especially if the dawazz was a kind and gentle man, who reproved his prince mildly and only upon rare occasions."

"Nonsense!" exclaimed Ousanas. "Dawazz of that sort be useless!" He smacked the prince on top of the head, very hard. The Prince didn't even blink.

"See?" demanded Ousanas. "Good prince. Very strong and durable, with solid hard head. If he ever become king, Arabs tremble."

Belisarius was fascinated. "But—let's just suppose for the moment—what I mean is—"

Garmat interrupted. "You are wondering what would motivate the dawazz to be so strict in his duties? When, as your wife points out, there is always the risk that a king might remember the past sourly?"

Belisarius nodded. Garmat turned to Ousanas.

"What happens, Ousanas, if you neglect your duties? Fail to instruct the prince properly in the true scheme of things?"

The grin vanished from Ousanas' face. "Sarawit be angry." He glanced from side to side. "Very perilous, irritate sarwen." The irrepressible grin returned. "Prince is nothing. King is almost nothing. Sarawit important."

The soldiers grunted agreement.

Garmat turned back to Belisarius. "Our custom, you see, is that when the prince succeeds to the throne or reaches his maturity—which, among us, we reckon at twenty-two years of age—then his sarwe passes judgment on his dawazz. If the dawazz is judged to have done his job properly, he is offered membership in the sarwe. And, usually, a high rank. Or, if he prefers, he may return to his own people, laden with the sarwe's blessing and, of course, many gifts from his former prince."

"And if the sarwe judges against him?"

Garmat shrugged. From behind him, Ousanas muttered: "Very bad." The soldiers grunted agreement.

Belisarius scratched his chin.

"Is the dawazz always from the south?"

"Oh, no!" exclaimed Garmat. "The dawazz may come from any foreign land, so long as his people are adjudged a valiant folk and he himself is esteemed for his courage. King Kaleb's dawazz, for instance, was a bedouin Arab."

"And what happened to him?"

Garmat coughed. "Well, actually, he's standing in front of you. I was Kaleb's dawazz."

Belisarius and Antonina stared at him. Garmat shrugged apologetically.

"My mother, I'm afraid, was not noted for her chastity. She was particularly taken by handsome young Ethiopian traders. As you can see, I was the result of such a liaison."

"How were you captured?" asked Belisarius.

Garmat frowned. He seemed puzzled.

"Captured by whom?"

"By the Axumites—when they enslaved you, and made you Kaleb's dawazz."

"You never capture dawazz!" exclaimed the prince. "If a man can be captured, he is not fit to be dawazz!"

It was the first time the prince had spoken. Eon's voice was quite pleasant, although unusually deep for one so young.

Belisarius shook his head bemusedly. "I don't understand this at all. How do you make someone a dawazz, then?"

"*Make* someone?" asked the prince. He looked at his adviser in confusion. Garmat smiled. The soldiers chuckled. Ousanas laughed aloud.

"You don't *make* someone a dawazz, General," explained Garmat. "It is a very high honor. Men come from everywhere to compete for the post. When I heard that a new dawazz was to be appointed by the Ethiopians, I rode across half of Arabia. And I traded my fine camel for a dhow to cross the Red Sea."

"I walked through jungles and mountains," commented Ousanas. "I traded nothing. Had nothing to trade except my spear. Which I needed."

He bared a very muscular forearm, showing an ugly scar which marked the black flesh.

"Got that from a panther in Shawa." The grin returned. "But was well worth it. Scar got me into final round of testing. Not have to bother with silly early rounds."

Prince Eon spoke, his voice filled with pride. "Ousanas is the greatest hunter in the world," he announced.

Immediately, Ousanas slapped him atop the head.

"Fool boy! Greatest hunter in world is lioness somewhere in savanna. Hope you never meet her! You contemplate error from inside her belly."

"And you, Garmat?" asked Antonina. "Were you also a great hunter?"

Garmat waved his hands deprecatingly. "By no means, by no means. I was—how shall I put it? Let us say that the Axumites were delighted to select me. At one stroke, they gained a dawazz and eliminated the most annoying bandit chieftain in the Hadrawmat." He shrugged again. "I had gotten rather tired of the endless round of forays and retreats. The thought of a stable position was appealing. And—"

He hesitated, sizing up the two Romans before him. "And," he continued, "I always rather liked my father's people. Whoever my father was, I was always sure he was Ethiopian."

For a moment, the adviser's face grew hard. "I was raised Arab, and have never forgotten that half of my heritage. A great people, the Arabs, in many ways. But—they were very hard on my mother. Mocked her, and abused her, for no reason than that she found men attractive."

He looked away, scanning the milling crowd in the reception hall.

"She was a good mother. Very good. Once I became powerful, of course, the abuse stopped. But she was never truly respected. Not properly. So—I took her with me to Axum, where customs are different."

"How are they different?" asked Antonina.

Again, the appraising stare. Longer, this time. Belisarius knew that an important decision was being made.

"Let us simply say, Antonina, that among the Axumites there would be no whispering about powerful women with questionable pasts. As there is even here, among sophisticated Greeks."

Antonina grew still. Garmat's smile grew twisted. "Nor would there be any basis for such whispering, among the Ethiopians. Prostitution is unknown among them—except in the port of Adulis, where it is only practiced upon foreign seamen. Who are mocked, thereafter, for paying good money for what they could have had for nothing. Nothing, that is, except charm and wit and good conversation."

Ousanas spoke, grimacing fiercely. "A promiscuous folk, the Axumites. Is well known! I was shocked, when first heard the news, in my far distant little village in south. My own folk very moral people, of course." His face grew lugubrious. "Oh, yes! Was shocked at such news! Immediately went to see for myself, that I might lay to rest wicked rumors." The huge grin returned. "Alas, rumors proved true. I would have fled immediately, of course, but by the time I learned—"

"The day you arrived," grunted one of the soldiers.

"—was too late. Had already been tested for the dawazz. What could I do?"

Antonina and Belisarius laughed. Garmat spread his hands.

"You see? Even our priests, I'm afraid, are lax by your standards. But we are happy with our customs. Even the negusa nagast does not fret himself overmuch concerning the paternity of his sons. What does their blood matter, anyway? Only the approval of the sarawit matters, in the end."

The soldiers grunted agreement.

The adviser gazed at Belisarius, a shrewd glint in his eyes.

"You must really come to see Axum for yourself," he said.

"Not without me to keep an eye on him!" exclaimed Antonina, giggling. Then, remembering their purpose, she gasped slightly and fell silent.

Garmat immediately detected the false note. Before he could speak, Belisarius cleared his throat.

"As a matter of fact, Garmat, that is—"

He was interrupted by a great fanfare. The Emperor's heralds were blaring out on their cornicens.

Belisarius started. Cornicens were the instruments used by Roman generals to transmit orders on the battlefield. He was not accustomed to their peaceful use.

Justinian and Theodora's thrones were being elevated to their extreme height. Silence began to fall over the throng. It was clear that an important announcement was at hand.

"I'm afraid I must apologize to you," Belisarius whispered hastily to Garmat. "I became so engrossed in our conversation that I forgot the time. This announcement, well—"

Garmat laid a hand on his arm.

"Let us hear the announcement, General. Then we can discuss whatever needs to be discussed."

When the announcement was finished, Belisarius noted three things.

First, he noted a marked change in the manner of the crowd toward both himself and the Axumites. Where before they had been ignored, they were now, it was obvious, on the verge of being mobbed by sudden well-wishers.

Second, he noted the very sour expression on the face of Venandakatra, obvious even at a distance. And the hurried whispering among the Malwa entourage.

Third, he noted the trifold reaction of the Axumites. Garmat, even with the long experience of a royal adviser, was finding it impossible not to look pleased. Eon, with the short experience of a young and vigorous prince, found it even more impossible not to express displeasure. And the dawazz, as always, did his job, under the watchful eyes of the sarwen.

"We were not even informed!" snapped the Prince.

Immediately, Ousanas slapped him atop the head.

"Imbecile suckling! When lion invite you to share lunch, *accept*. Or would you rather be lunch yourself? Babbling babe!"

The sarwen grunted approval.

Chapter 13
AMAVARATI
Winter, 528 AD

Her youngest brother died well. Foolishly, but well.

Shakuntala did not hold the foolishness against the boy. He had been fourteen years old and was bound to die anyway. Better he should be cut down quickly by a Ye-tai beast than have his last moments be filled with humiliation as well as pain.

Her brother's hopeless charge against the Ye-tai made possible his revenge, too. The Ye-tai—an experienced warrior—had no difficulty side-stepping the boy's clumsy sword swing. The barbarian grinned savagely as his own sword hewed into her brother's neck, almost severing it completely. A moment later, the grin disappeared. Shakuntala's spear-point took the Ye-tai under the armpit and penetrated right into his heart.

The warrior began to slump, but his body was hurled aside by three other Ye-tai pouring into the princess' chamber. The Ye-tai in the lead stumbled slightly over his dead comrade's leg. It wasn't much of a stumble, but it was just enough to allow Shakuntala's spear to slide over the rim of his shield. The spear-point sank into his throat. The barbarian coughed blood and fell to his knees.

The princess immediately jerked the spear-blade back and plunged it toward another Ye-tai. This one brought his shield up to block the thrust. But the princess had been well-taught. The thrust was a feint. The spear-tip sank into his leg just above the knee. The Ye-tai howled. Shakuntala jerked the blade out and drove it into the warrior's open mouth.

It was a quick, flickering, viper-like thrust—just as she had been taught. But—just as she had been warned *not* to do—the princess had driven the blade in much too furiously. The spear-tip jammed between two vertebrae.

A moment later, another Ye-tai struck at the spear shaft with his sword. His sword did not—quite—succeed in cutting the spear shaft. But the blow was more than sufficient to knock the spear out of Shakuntala's hands.

The Ye-tai shouted triumphantly and advanced upon her, grinning widely. Shakuntala backed away toward a corner. The huge room, which had served as her reception chamber, was sparsely furnished. The princess kicked aside a large vase, giving herself still more maneuvering space. The beautiful porcelain shattered, spilling dried flowers onto the floor.

Six more Ye-tai poured in through the shattered door. Two of them came toward the princess. The other four veered away, heading toward Shakuntala's maidservant. The girl—Jijabai—was huddled in another corner of the room.

Shakuntala heard Jijabai's sobs turn into shrieks. She heard her maid's clothing being torn and the gleeful howls of the Ye-tai who were wrestling the girl down to the floor. But she had no time to look over. The three Ye-tai who were now moving to surround her in the corner had sheathed their own swords and dropped their shields. The iron rims of the shields bounced softly on the rich carpet which covered the floor.

The princess did not understand the phrases they were exchanging back and forth, but the leering grins on their faces made the meaning clear enough. She turned slightly, pretended to slump, cowering. One of the Ye-tai pounced on her. Her sidekick took the warrior straight in the diaphragm, knocking him flat on his back. Her fist took a second warrior in the exact same location. He coughed, began to double up—then slumped to the floor as Shakuntala's forearm strike smashed into his jaw.

The third Ye-tai leapt onto her back, wrapping his arms around her. She snapped her head back into his face, stamped on his instep, broke loose from his grip, and slammed her elbow into his stomach.

The warrior staggered. Shakuntala spun and drove her foot into his groin. The Ye-tai sprawled on the floor, groaning.

Shakuntala sprang away and raced toward the other corner, where Jijabai was being held down on the floor. The maid was half-naked now. Her arms were being held by one Ye-tai, while each of her legs were spread apart by others. The fourth Ye-tai had untied his trousers and was dropping to his knees between the screaming girl's legs.

His kneel turned into a headlong plunge as Shakuntala's flying kick smashed between his shoulder blades. The princess delivered the kick perfectly, without the impetuous excess which was her usual mistake. She rebounded and landed lightly on her feet. The Ye-tai who was holding Jijabai's right leg gaped up at her. Shakuntala kicked out his teeth. Again, the kick was perfect. The follow-on kick broke the warrior's neck.

But that kick was too powerful, by far. Instead of rebounding, the princess staggered and fell onto her back. Fortunately, the thick carpet softened her fall. A moment later, the Ye-tai who had been holding Jijabai's other leg landed on top of her, grappling for her wrists. He was roaring with rage. His roars were not enough, however, to drown the sound of other Ye-tai warriors pouring into the room. Jijabai began screaming again.

Shakuntala wrestled with her assailant furiously. For her size, she was very strong. But the Ye-tai outmassed her considerably, and was no weakling himself. Then the princess found her legs suddenly seized by other barbarians. Ye-tai howls of glee filled the room, almost deafening in their cacophony.

The Ye-tai lying atop the princess now had her wrists firmly in his grip. He brought his legs up and straddled her chest. His face was not more than inches from hers. He began to say something to her, grinning fiercely. Shakuntala lunged her head forward and bit off the tip of his nose.

The Ye-tai howled and jerked his head. Blood flew from his severed nose. He stared down at her, his eyes wide with rage. Shakuntala spit the tip of his nose into his face. The warrior bellowed fury. He released her left wrist, drew back his right hand, made a fist, and began to strike her in the jaw.

The fist went flying out of sight. The warrior's arm had been chopped off just below the wrist. The Ye-tai gaped at the stump. Blood gushed everywhere, much of it on the princess. A moment later, Shakuntala was practically drowned in blood. The Ye-tai's head had vanished also.

Now, all was chaos and confusion. Shakuntala was almost blinded by the blood covering her face. Then she *was* blinded, by the Ye-tai's headless body collapsing on her.

She felt the hands holding her legs release their grip. Her lower body was suddenly covered with wetness. Blood. Not hers. Howls and shouts of fury. Clash of swords and shields. Cries of pain. Choking death coughs.

Now a bellowing roar of command. The sounds of more warriors filling the room. Roar of command. A cessation to the sounds of fighting. Roar of command.

Suddenly, silence. Except for Jijabai's sobbing.

Silence, except—

Outside the room, through the windows, Shakuntala could hear screams and shrieks in the distance. A vast, world-filling howl of pain and anguish.

Amavarati was taken. The palace was captured. All was lost. All. All.

The headless body atop her was suddenly removed. She was free again. She sat up and tried to wipe the blood from her face. Someone handed her a cloth. With it, she was able to remove enough blood to see.

The room was now absolutely filled with warriors. A few Ye-tai were still alive, huddled in the corner next to the sobbing figure of Jijabai. More Ye-tai were lying dead, scattered here and there over the floor.

The other warriors in the room were also Malwa enemies, but not Ye-tai. Shakuntala recognized them. Kushans. And one Mahaveda priest.

The priest was scowling back and forth between the Ye-tai in the corner and one of the Kushans. The Kushan commander, Shakuntala guessed.

The Kushan commander was a short man, very stocky. Barrel-chested and thick-shouldered. In his right hand he held a sword, covered with blood. Shakuntala was certain, without knowing exactly how, that that was the sword which had removed her assailant's fist and then his head.

But what struck her most about the Kushan was his face. It was not the features. Those were typical Kushan: coarse black hair tied back in a topknot, brown eyes, flat nose, high cheeks, thin lips, a slight fold in the corners of the eyes. No, it was the face itself. It didn't seem made of human flesh. It looked like a mask of iron.

The priest snarled something at the Kushan commander. The commander's reply was curt, unyielding. He pointed to Shakuntala and said something else. The priest frowned. The Mahaveda turned toward the Ye-tai in the corner and snarled something at them. The Ye-tai began saying something—half angrily, half fearfully—but the priest shouted them down.

The priest pointed to Jijabai, barked something; made a dismissive gesture. The Ye-tai grinned and stooped over the maid. A moment later they were spreading her legs again and unbuckling their trousers.

Shakuntala lurched to her feet, but the Kushan commander was suddenly standing behind her. The man moved much more quickly than the princess would have thought possible. She felt him twisting her arm up behind her back. She drove her foot down, but struck only the floor, painfully. The Kushan had moved his instep aside—effortlessly, and without losing either his balance or his grip on her arm.

Shakuntala felt her arm twisted up, immobilized. She recognized the grip, and the expertise behind it, and despaired. Still—

Her elbow strike was blocked almost before it began. Her head snap was met with a cuff. Not a brutal cuff, just an expert one.

Jijabai started screaming. A blow. Screaming. Another blow. Blow. Silence. Except for coarse Ye-tai laughs.

"There's nothing you can do for her, girl," whispered the Kushan commander in good Hindi. "Nothing."

He propelled Shakuntala toward the door. He was strong. Very strong. The other Kushans moved with him. Several moved in front. Others strode on either side, still others behind. All with swords drawn. Blood-covered swords, without exception.

As she went through the door, Shakuntala heard Jijabai begin to wail again. Then: blow; blow; silence.

"Nothing, girl, nothing," whispered the Kushan.

The trip through the palace was sheer nightmare. The princess was covered with blood and half-dazed, but could still see. And hear. The entire palace was a raging madhouse of butchery, looting, torture and gang rape. The Ye-tai barbarians were like maddened wolves. The common Malwa troops were even worse, like crazed hyenas. Completely out of control. More than once, her Kushan escort was forced to strike down Malwa soldiers lunging for the princess. ("Forced" was perhaps not the right word. The Kushans slaughtered common Malwa troops who moved toward them instantly and without compunction; Ye-tai were butchered for even looking at them the wrong way.)

After a while, Shakuntala felt herself grow weak with horror. She tried to fight against the weakness, but it was almost impossible. Utter despair was overwhelming her.

The iron grip holding her became, as the trip progressed, more of a comforting embrace. Some part of her mind tried to seize the opportunity, but her will was buried beneath hopelessness. And always, every minute, the voice:

"Nothing, girl, nothing."

A gentle voice. If iron can ever be gentle.

Finally, they were leaving the palace, entering the great courtyard.

She caught a glimpse—

The iron hand turned her head into an iron shoulder. Guided her away.

Shakuntala summoned the last reserve of her will.

"No," she said. "No. I must see."

Iron hesitated. An iron sigh.

"You are certain?"

"I must see." A moment later: "Please. I must."

Iron hesitation. Another iron sigh.

"Nothing, girl, noth—"

"*I must—please!*"

The iron grip yielded, turned her back.

She saw. They were dead now, at least. The cluster of maha-mimamsa around them were already well into the flaying. Soon enough, the skin sacks would be ready for hanging in the Malwa emperor's great hall.

Her father. Her mother. All of her brothers except the youngest, who had died in her room. His body would be brought down soon, for the flayers.

The iron grip turned her away again. She did not resist. A minute later, she began to shake. Then, seconds later, weep.

"Nothing, girl, nothing."

✧   ✧   ✧

She did not speak for three hours. Not until the last faint screams of Amaravati died away, lost in the distance. The Kushans pushed their horses hard, and the Rajput cavalry troop which escorted them did not object.

For three hours, she was lost in anguished memories of Andhra. Great Andhra, destroyed Andhra. For five centuries, under the Satavahana dynasty, Andhra had ruled central India. And ruled it well. Themselves Telugu speakers of Dravidian stock, the Satavahana had shielded Dravidia from the depredations of the northern Aryan conquerors; shielded Dravidia, while at the same time absorbing and transmitting throughout the Deccan all the genuine glories of Vedic culture. The very name *satavahana* referred to the seven-horse chariot of Vishnu. The name had been adopted by the dynasty upon its conversion to Hinduism—*adopted*, by choice, not by force.

So had the Satavahanas ruled. They had never shied from war, but had always preferred gentler methods of conquest and rule. Few, if any, of their subject peoples had found their overlordship oppressive. Even the stiff-necked and quarrelsome Marathas, after a time, had become reconciled to Andhra rule. Reconciled, and then, become Andhra's strong right arm.

Under the Satavahanas, Andhra had become one of the major trade centers of the world. Trade with Rome to the west, Ceylon to the south, Champa and Funan to the east. The great city Amavarati, now in flames, had been the most prosperous and peaceful city in all India.

With peace, prosperity and trade, had come knowledge, wisdom, and art. Encouraged and patronized by the Satavahanas, scholars and mystics and artists had flocked to Amavarati.

The bhakti movement had grown under Andhra's tolerance, revitalizing Hinduism. Buddhists and Jains, often persecuted in other Hindu realms, were unmolested in Andhra. Even the great rock-cut temples had been allowed to incorporate images of the Buddha.

Shakuntala remembered the beauty of those temples, and the monastic viharas, and the chaitya prayer halls, and the stupas. She fought back the tears. Then she remembered the glorious frescoes at the viharas at Ajanta, and could fight them back no longer.

Gone. All gone. Destroyed forever.

✧   ✧   ✧

Her first words were: "Why not me?"

The Kushan commander explained. Gently. As gently, at least, as the truth allowed.

She spit on the ground. For a moment, it almost seemed as if the commander's face had developed a crack. A flaw in the iron, perhaps.

Her next words were:

"Raghunath Rao?"

The Kushan commander explained. This time, the voice was not gentle. There was no need to be. Then, the commander predicted. Now, gentle again; insofar as iron can be gentle.

Shakuntala laughed. Flaming glory burst through her soul, like a river washing out all hopelessness and despair.

The princess spoke her last word, on that day of destruction: "*Fools.*"

When night fell, the Kushans and Rajputs made camp. Guards were set up all around, within and without the camp perimeter. The Rajputs guarded the camp from outside attack. The Kushans guarded the camp from Shakuntala.

It was an odd sort of guard. The Kushans kept their distance from her. Regaled each other—in Hindi, which she could understand—with tales of startled Ye-tai. Girl-startled Ye-tai, with a spear-blade in their armpits and throats and legs and mouths; with a foot in their guts and their teeth and their necks. They particularly relished the tale of a Ye-tai nose.

Beyond, in the flickering light of the campfires, haughty Rajput beards were seen to move. Smiles, perhaps, brought on by charming tales.

That same night, in a pond not far from the palace at Amavarati, a frog croaked and jumped aside. As if startled by a sudden motion nearby.

An alert guard might have spotted the slow, crawling figure which eased its way out of the reeds and onto the bank. But there were no alert guards at Amavarati that night. The Malwa army had disintegrated completely in its triumph. There was nothing at Amavarati that night but a horde of drunken, butchering thieves and rapists, and what few of their victims still survived. And a cluster of mahamimamsa, overseen by priests, who, though sober and on duty, were much too preoccupied with the task of properly flaying a fourteen-year-old boy to be watching any ponds.

Once ashore, the man began to tear his tunic and bind up his wounds. They were many, those wounds, but none were either fatal or crippling. In time, they would become simply more scars added to an already extensive collection.

The wounds dressed, the man rested a bit. Then, still moving silently and almost invisibly, he faded away from the vicinity of the palace. Once in the forest, his pace quickened. Silent, still, and almost invisible. Like a wounded panther.

Chapter 14

DARAS .
Spring, 529 AD

The good news, thought Belisarius, was that John of Rhodes was an extremely intelligent man.

That was also the bad news.

"Why are you lying to me?" demanded the retired naval officer. "How in the name of Christ do you expect me to accomplish whatever it is you want me to accomplish, when you are obviously keeping everything essential a secret from me?"

Belisarius gazed down at the man calmly.

John of Rhodes scowled. "Save the sphinx for someone else, Belisarius!" He stumped over to the worktable and made a disgusted gesture toward the various substances and implements strewn upon it.

"Look at this clutter! Trash and toys, that's all they are. I might as well be looking for the philosopher's stone, or the elixir of eternal life." His glare left the table and roamed about the room, encompassing the entire workshop in its condemnation.

Belisarius scratched his chin.

"Stop scratching your chin!" The naval officer flung himself into a nearby chair, exuding the quintessence of disgruntlement in his slumped posture. "Damn all mannerisms, anyway," he grumbled. He looked up, eyeing Belisarius balefully. "And there's another thing," he continued. "What's this nonsense you and your wife are trying to pull with me and that jackal Procopius?"

Before Belisarius could dredge up something suitable to put

the man at ease, John of Rhodes was back on his feet, stumping about and gesticulating angrily.

"Don't bother! Please! Do I look like a cretin?"

Belisarius decided that, under the circumstances, straightforwardness was probably the only suitable tactic.

"Explain," he commanded. "And stop stumping about."

"I'm not *stumping*. I'm pacing, from vexation."

"Stop pacing from vexation. And explain."

John stood still. Somehow, despite his much shorter stature, the naval officer seemed to be glaring down at the general.

"Have you heard my reputation?" he demanded. "That I am a master of seduction?"

Belisarius nodded. John of Rhodes blew out his cheeks and then flung himself again into the chair.

"Well, the reputation's exaggerated. But not by much. The fact is, I've enjoyed considerable success with the ladies, over the years. Do you know my secret?"

Belisarius waited. For the first time since meeting John of Rhodes, not two hours earlier, the naval officer smiled.

"The secret to success in seduction, Belisarius, is the same as the secret to success in warfare. Never fight a battle you can't win."

"Your point?"

"My point's obvious. I hadn't spent more than an hour in Antonina's company before it was clear as day that she was quite unseducible. While you were off thrashing the Medes, she and I were often alone. At such times, she's all business and work. *That's all.* So why is it, the moment that foul creature Procopius hoves into view, that she suddenly acts as if she's smitten by me?"

Even sitting, he seemed to be glaring down at Belisarius. "*What are you up to?*"

Belisarius sighed and pulled up another chair. After sitting, he smiled crookedly. "We're engaged in a deep and dark conspiracy, John."

The naval officer's foul mood vanished. He grinned like a wolf—which, thought Belisarius, he rather resembled. A short, sinewy, handsome, blue-eyed, black-haired, grey-bearded, well-groomed wolf.

"Well!" he exclaimed. "That's more like it!" He leaned forward in his chair, rubbing his hands together cheerfully.

"Tell me all about it."

✧   ✧   ✧

When Belisarius finished, John eyed him askance.

"You're still keeping something from me," he announced. "I don't believe for a minute that these—*visions*, to use your term—simply came to you out of nowhere. Someone, or something, is behind them."

Belisarius nodded.

"And you're not going to tell me who it is? Not now, at any rate."

Belisarius nodded again.

John looked away, frowning. A few seconds later, his face cleared.

"I can live with that," he said. "For a time, at least."

He stroked his beard. "But there's one other question I must have answered. Now. Is this conspiracy aimed at the throne? Against the Emperor?"

Belisarius shook his head firmly. John stared at him.

"Swear," he commanded. "I know your reputation, General. If I have your oath, I'll be satisfied."

"I swear to you before God, John of Rhodes, that the conspiracy of which you are a part is not aimed against the Emperor Justinian."

Again, the raffish grin. "But he doesn't know about it either, does he?"

"No."

"Does the Empress?"

"No. Not yet, at least."

John rose to his feet and resumed stumping about.

"Good. Let's keep it that way, shall we? Especially when it comes to Justinian." The naval officer grimaced. "Such a suspicious tyrant, he is."

After a moment, John blew out his cheeks again and looked toward the workbench. "Not, mind you, that there's much of a conspiracy here to begin with. Plenty of deep darkness, but precious little to hide."

"You've had no success at all?"

"None—beyond some minor improvements in the Greek fire we already had. But nothing that'd be in the slightest way suitable for land combat."

Belisarius rose. "Come outside," he said. "There are some people I want you to meet."

✧   ✧   ✧

When he couldn't find the Axumites in the villa, Belisarius suspected he would find them in the barracks. And so he did.

The barracks were crowded full with soldiers, especially in the huge room which had served the former owner of the estate for a formal dining hall. Some of that population density was due to the quarters themselves. The Thracians had been reveling in the luxuriance of the "barracks" since they arrived at the villa. But most of it was due to the contest taking place at a table in the center of the hall.

Seeing him, his bucellarii drew aside and let him approach the table. Belisarius examined the scene, and sighed with exasperation.

Garmat, to his credit, was obviously trying to keep a lid on the situation. So was Maurice, of course. And the two soldiers of the Dakuen sarwe were behaving in the rational manner which one expects from experienced veterans surrounded by strange veterans. Politely. Cautiously.

But the prince, alas, was still a young man, full of pride and eager to show his mettle. And not all of the general's Thracian retinue were as relaxed in their experience as such veterans as Anastasius and Valentinian (both of whom, Belisarius noted, were lounging about amicably in nearby chairs). No, there were plenty of youngsters in the general's retinue, most of whom were every bit as full of pride as the prince, and not in the slightest intimidated by his royal lineage.

At the moment, the mutual pride was taking the form of an arm-wrestling match. A good-humored one, probably, in its origin. But the humor was now wearing thin.

The reason for the growing ill temper was obvious, and was demonstrated for the general himself almost immediately. With a grunt of anger and disgust, the fist of the Thracian lad named Menander slammed down onto the table. Eon's dark face was split by a grin.

Glancing about, Belisarius estimated that at least three other Thracian lads had already been trounced by the Axumite. And were none too happy about it.

He sighed again. During the course of the journey from Constantinople to Daras, Belisarius had found the prince to be quite charming. Once Eon got over a certain aloofness, which Belisarius knew was nothing more than his way of maintaining dignity in a sea of strangers, the prince was both good-natured and intelligent. He had even managed—after a few slaps on the head from his dawazz—to stop ogling Antonina in his uncertain adolescent way. And he got along very well with Sittas and, to the general's surprise, got along even better with Irene. Under the young Axumite's stiff exterior, there proved to be a sly wit which the spymaster enjoyed.

But—he was still barely more than a boy, and was inordinately proud of his strength.

Belisarius had already seen the prince stripped to the waist, so he was accustomed to the sight of that Herculean physique. Obviously, however, it had proved too much of a challenge for certain Thracians.

"That's enough, Eon!" snapped Garmat.

"Let him wrestle Anastasius!" demanded a surly voice from somewhere in the crowd.

"By all means!" cried Ousanas. "Anastasius!"

The dawazz, seated at the table next to his prince, grinned over at the huge *pentarch*.

Anastasius yawned. "The lad's much too strong for me. And besides, I'm a lazy man by nature. Contemplative."

The prince frowned slightly. On the face of it—but— He sensed there was a mocking tone under Anastasius' modest words.

The dawazz immediately brought it to focus. His grin widened.

"Oh! Such mockery! Such false self-effacement! Is very great insult to royal dignity of young prince! Prince must now defend his honor!"

Belisarius decided it was time to intervene.

"Enough," he commanded. He cast a stern gaze upon the dawazz.

"Your duty is to restrain the prince from foolishness."

Ousanas gaped. "Most insane concept!" he cried. "Impossible to restrain young royalty from foolishness. Might as well try to restrain crocodile from eating meat."

Ousanas shook his head sadly. "You very great general, Belisarius. Stick to own trade. Make terrible dawazz."

The grin returned. "Only way teach prince not to commit foolish acts is to encourage folly." He spread his arms grandly. "Then probably-never-King-because-idiot-as-well-as-younger-son gets arm twisted off and maybe he learn. Maybe. Maybe not. Probably not. Royalty stupid by nature. Like crocodiles."

He scanned the room majestically. "Many great warriors here," he commented. "I ask a question. How you hunt crocodile?"

After a moment, someone ventured: "Stab it with a spear."

Ousanas beamed happily. "Spoken like true warrior!" The beam was replaced by a look of humble abasement. "I myself not warrior. Miserable slave, now. Before, though, was great hunter."

Someone snorted. "Is that so? Then tell us, O miserable slave, how did *you* hunt crocodile?"

Ousanas goggled. "Not *hunt* crocodile in first place! Great giant monster, the crocodile! Stronger than ox! Teeth like swords!"

He grinned. "He also very stupid reptile. So I feed him poisoned meat."

Suddenly, the dawazz reached out his long arm and slapped the prince on top of the head.

"You see that one?" he demanded, pointing to Anastasius. "He feeding you poisoned meat."

Anastasius grinned. The prince eyed him skeptically. Ousanas slapped him again.

"Royalty stupid as crocodile!"

Now the prince was glaring hotly at his dawazz. Not for the first time, watching the scene, Belisarius was struck by the peculiar courage required of a good dawazz.

Ousanas slapped him again. "Not even crocodile stupid enough to glare at his dawazz!" The two sarwen chuckled.

"Enough," repeated Belisarius.

Eon tore his gaze away from Ousanas.

"There's someone here I'd like you to meet, Prince. And you, Garmat." Then, after a moment, grudgingly: "And you too, Ousanas, and the sarwen."

Returning to the villa, Belisarius introduced the Ethiopians to John of Rhodes. Antonina was waiting with the naval officer in the main salon, as were Sittas and Irene. After they had taken their seats, the general said to Garmat:

"Tell him what you know of the Indian weapons, if you would."

Belisarius absented himself while the Axumites filled in the naval officer. He had other business to attend to, back in the barracks.

As soon as he entered the dining hall, the conversation which had been filling the room died down. But not before the general caught the final remarks uttered by young Menander.

"The slave offends you, does he?" demanded Belisarius. Menander was silent, but his whole posture exuded *pout*.

Belisarius restrained his temper.

"Tell him, Valentinian," he commanded.

The veteran cataphract never ceased from whittling on his little stick, and he didn't bother to look up.

"If you don't learn how to read men, Menander, you'll never live to collect your retirement bonus. The prince is nothing, at the moment, beyond a big muscle. Later, who knows? Now, nothing. The two soldiers are good. Very good, I'd wager, or they wouldn't be here." He paused briefly, estimating. "The adviser is dangerous. In his prime, probably something to watch. But—he's old. The slave, now, there's the terrible one."

"He's a slave!" protested Menander.

"Feeding you poisoned meat," chuckled Anastasius. The room echoed with laughter. When the laughter died down, Valentinian finally looked up. His narrow, close-featured face was cold. He fixed the young cataphract with dark eyes gazing down a long, pointed nose.

"That slave could slaughter you like a lamb, boy. Never doubt it for a moment."

Belisarius cleared his throat. "I'm going to need three of you to accompany me to Axum. And beyond, to India. We'll be leaving tomorrow morning, and we'll be gone for at least a year. The rest of you will remain on the estate. As you know, Sittas is here. At the Emperor's behest, he is replacing me as commander of the Syrian army. You'll give him whatever assistance he requires, so long as that doesn't interfere with your duty to guard my wife and the estate. Maurice will be in charge."

Maurice said nothing, but a slight twist to his lips indicated his continuing displeasure with the general's plans. A faint buzz of startled conversation began to fill the room, then died down quickly.

"Any volunteers?" he asked.

Within seconds, as Belisarius had expected, almost all of the cataphracts had volunteered. The younger ones had volunteered to a man, except for Menander.

"Excellent!" he exclaimed. Then he smiled his crooked smile.

"Shit," hissed Valentinian.

"Poisoned meat," groaned Anastasius.

"Those of you who had enough sense not to volunteer are coming. Valentinian. Anastasius. Oh—and you, Menander."

By the time Belisarius returned to the villa, the Axumites had finished recounting to their audience what they had been able to learn about the Malwa weapons. It wasn't much, in truth. Over the past few years, several Axumite traders had observed the new and bizarre weapons in use—but only at a distance. The Malwa kept their special weapons closely guarded, and did not allow foreigners near them. In one instance, they had suspended siege operations against a coastal town until a passing Axumite vessel was shepherded away by Malwa warships.

When the Ethiopians finished, John of Rhodes leaned back in his chair and began tapping his hands on his knees. He was frowning slightly, and his eyes seemed a bit unfocussed.

"It's not much to go on, is it?" asked Antonina, somewhat apologetically.

"Quite the contrary," replied the naval officer. "Our friends here from Axum have provided me with the most important fact of all."

"What's that?" demanded Sittas.

John of Rhodes looked at the Greek general and smiled thinly.

"The most important fact is that these weapons *exist*, Sittas." He shrugged. "*What* they are, and how they work, remains a complete mystery. But the fact that they *do* exist means that it is a problem to be solved, rather than a fantasy to be speculated about. There's a world of difference between those two things."

He arose and began stumping about, with his hands clasped behind his back. "We shall need to compile a library here. Unfortunately, the books which I own myself relate to seafaring only."

"Books are expensive," grumbled Sittas.

"So?" retorted Antonina. "You're stinking rich. You can afford them."

"I knew it," growled Sittas. "I knew it. Soak the rich Greek, that's all anybody—"

Irene cut him off. "What books do you need?" she asked John.

The naval officer frowned. "It's obvious to me, from listening to what the Axumites have told us, that the Malwa weapons involve more than simply burning naphtha, or some similar fuel. Every account of the weapons describes them in terms of eruptions—as if they could somehow control the force of a volcano, on a smaller scale. The closest physical phenomenon that I know of is what's called combustion. And there's only one scholar to my knowledge who studied combustion to any great extent."

"Heron of Alexandria," stated Irene.

John of Rhodes nodded. "Precisely. I need a copy of his *Pneumatics.*"

Sittas glowered. "There aren't more than fifty copies of that book in existence! Do you have any idea how much it costs? *If* we can even find one in the first place without raiding the library at Alexandria."

"I own a copy," said Irene. "I will be glad to loan it to you. It's still at my villa in Constantinople, however, so it will take a little time to get it here."

Everyone in the room stared at Irene. She smiled whimsically. "Actually, I own most of Heron's writings. I also have the *Mechanics*, *Siegecraft*, *Measurement*, and *Mirrors*. I almost got my hands on a copy of his *Automaton-making* last year, but some damned Armenian beat me to it."

Some of the men in the room were now goggling her; Sittas was gaping.

"I like to read," explained Irene dryly. Slyly.

Antonina started laughing.

"It's unnatural!" choked Sittas. "It's—"

"Marry me," said John of Rhodes.

"Not a chance, John. I know your type. You're just lusting after my books."

The naval officer grinned. "Well, yes, to a degree. But—"

"Not a chance!" repeated Irene. She was laughing now herself.

"What is the world coming to?" demanded Sittas. "My mother never opened a book, much less *owned* one!" He frowned. "*I* don't own any books, come to that."

"Really?" asked Irene. "I am astonished."

Sittas glared at his spymaster. "You are mocking me, woman. I know you are."

Belisarius couldn't help laughing himself. "Nonsense, Sittas!" he exclaimed. "I'm sure Irene was speaking the simple truth. I'm astonished myself, actually."

Sittas transferred his glare to the Thracian.

"Don't you start on me, Belisarius! Just because you own a copy of Caesar's—"

Prince Eon interrupted.

"Do you own a copy of Xenophon's *Anabasis*?" he asked Irene eagerly.

The spymaster nodded.

"May I borrow—" The prince fell silent. "Oh. It's probably also at your villa. In Constantinople."

"I'm afraid so."

The prince began frowning thoughtfully.

"Maybe we could go back—"

"Enough, Eon!" cried Garmat. "We are *not* going back to Constantinople to get you a book!"

"It's the *Anabasis*," whined Eon. "I've been wanting to read that since—"

"No! Absolutely not! Your father is waiting for us at Axum—at Adulis, probably. And have you forgotten—"

"It's the *Anabasis*," wailed Eon.

"Spoken like a true bibliophile," said Irene admiringly. She grinned at the despondent prince and waved her hand airily. "These heathens simply don't understand, Eon. You have to resign yourself to it. Like a saint of old subjected to barbarian tortures and ordeals."

"The *Anabasis*," moaned Eon.

"Ousanas!" barked Garmat. "Do your duty!"

"What duty?" demanded the dawazz. "Love of books prince's best quality. Only thing keep him away from mischief."

The dawazz leaned forward and tapped the prince on top of the head. Very lightly. "Nevertheless. Is still matter of deadly Malwa danger. Anxious father awaiting report of beloved son. Anxious negusa-nagast-type father. Not wise to keep such fathers waiting while hunting up book. Not wise. Anxiety turn to reproach. Negusa-nagast-type reproach."

The two sarwen grunted agreement. Eon sulked.

"How soon can we get Heron's book here?" asked Antonina.

Irene shrugged. "With a special courier—"

Sittas interrupted. "Do you know how much it costs to send a special—"

John of Rhodes laughed. "Why is it that the richest men are always the stingiest? Relax, Sittas. We won't strain your purse."

To Irene: "There's no need for a special courier. I've got weeks of work ahead of me before I can even start thinking about our project. We'll need to find chemical supplies, equipment, tools—everything. All I have at the moment is a few odds and ends."

"Do you need the help of artisans?" asked Belisarius.

John shook his head.

"Not yet, Belisarius. I wouldn't know what to tell them to do or make. Be a waste of their time and your money. Six months from now, maybe. Maybe."

The general frowned. "You think it's going to take that long?"

John scowled fiercely. "That *long*? Do you have any idea what you're asking me to do?"

The naval officer began to rise, in obvious preparation for a heavy session of stumping about, but Belisarius waved him back to his seat.

"Relax, John. I wasn't criticizing. I'm just—just worried, that's all. I don't know how much time we have at our disposal, before our future enemy falls upon us."

John was still not mollified, quite. But before he could say anything further, Irene spoke:

"That's your job, General."

"Excuse me?"

"Buying us time. That's your job. Mine also, to an extent. But mostly yours."

"You've done it before," said Sittas. The big Greek general smiled. "Of course, that was against a bunch of dumbass Goths. Maybe you're not smart enough to tie sophisticated Indians into knots."

"Don't bait my husband, Sittas," said Antonina.

"I'm not baiting him. I'm prodding his vanity."

"My husband is not vain."

A sad shake of the head.

"Poor woman. The wife is always the last to know. Belisarius is the vainest man in creation. He's so vain that he's not vain about the things modest men are vain about—their fame, their riches, their good looks, their wives' good looks. Oh no, not Belisarius. He's only vain about his lack of vanity, which is the worst vanity there is."

Everyone in the room except Irene frowned, trying to follow the tortured logic.

"That makes no sense at all," said Eon. Uncertainly, to Irene: "Does it make sense to you?"

Irene laughed gaily. "Of course it does! But you have to remember—I'm the only other Greek in the room. Except John, but he's from Rhodes. A practical folk, the Rhodesmen. Lapsed Greeks, I'm afraid."

John said nothing, but his gaze was full of interest. Irene laughed again.

"Don't even think about it, John."

The naval officer's grin was quite wolfish.

"Why not? I can't be designing fantastical weapons all the time." A sudden, happy thought. "Well, actually, perhaps I can. But to operate effectively I'll need to be kept up to date with all the latest secret information. Spymaster-type information, you know. Oh, yes. Daily briefings. Essential."

"You stay away from my paramour," growled Sittas. But it was a tepid, tepid growl.

A chuckle swept the room.

Irene patted his hand gently. "Now, now. Don't you worry, dear. I really think I'm capable of dealing with the occasional wolf."

"Greek lady eat wolf for lunch," commented Ousanas. John of Rhodes cast a dark look upon the dawazz. Belisarius, from experience, could have told him it was a waste of effort. Ousanas simply grinned, and added:

"I ignorant savage, of course. Miserable slave, too. Know almost nothing. But know enough not to chase woman ten times smarter than me."

Belisarius cleared his throat. "We seem to be getting side-tracked. Other than artisans—and the books you talked about—will there be anything else you need?"

John frowned, thought for a moment.

"Nothing much, Belisarius. Some equipment, and a few more tools, but nothing fancy. Substances, of course. Elements. Chemicals. Some of those will be a bit expensive."

Sittas' eyes became slits.

"How expensive? And what kind of—*elements*?"

Very narrow slits.

"Are we talking *gold* here? Seems to me every time you alchemist types start anything you right off begin yapping about—"

John laughed. "Relax, Sittas! I have no use for gold, I assure you. Or silver. One of the reasons they're precious metals is because they're *inert*."

A questioning glance. Sittas' eyes practically disappeared in response.

"I know what *inert* means! You—"

"Enough," said Belisarius. The room became instantly silent. Almost.

"My, he does that well," remarked Irene softly. To Sittas, in the sort of whisper which can be heard by everyone: "Maybe you should try that, dear. Instead of that bellowing roar you so favor."

"*Enough.*" Now, even Irene was silent.

Belisarius rose. "That's it, then. Whatever you need, John, while I'm gone, you can either get from Antonina or"—here a sharp stare—"Sittas."

Sittas grimaced, but did not protest his poverty. Belisarius continued:

"As for the rest of us, I think our course is clear. As clear, at least, as circumstances permit. When I return from India, hopefully, I'll bring with me enough information to guide us further. Until then, we'll just have to do our best."

He looked at his wife. "And now—I would like to spend the rest of the day, and the evening, with my wife and my son."

Once Photius drowsed off, early in the evening, Belisarius and Antonina were alone. They had never been separated for long, since the day they first met. Now, they would be separated for at least a year.

Future loss gave force to present passion. Belisarius got very little sleep that night.

Antonina did not sleep at all. Once her husband finally succumbed to slumber, from sheer exhaustion, she stayed awake through the few hours left in that night. That precious night. That—*last* night, she feared.

By the time the sun arose, Antonina was awash in grief. Bleak certainty. She would never see him again.

Her son rescued her from that bottomless pit. At daybreak, Photius wandered into the room, rubbing sleep from his eyes.

"Will Daddy be coming back?" he asked, timidly. His little face was scrunched with worry.

The boy had never called Belisarius by that name before. The sound of it drove all despair from her soul.

"Of course he will, Photius. He's my husband. And he's your father."

✧　　✧　　✧

At midmorning, Belisarius and his companions rode out of the villa. At the boundary of the estate, they took the road which led to Antioch and, beyond, to Seleuceia on the coast. At Seleuceia they would board ship for the voyage to Egypt and, beyond, to Adulis on the Red Sea. And beyond, to Axum in the Ethiopian highlands. And beyond, to India.

Belisarius rode at the head of the little party. Eon rode on his left, Garmat on his right. Behind them rode the two sarwen. Behind the sarwen, the three cataphracts.

Ousanas traveled on foot. The dawazz, it developed, had a pronounced distaste for all manner of animal transport. Belisarius thought his attitude was peculiar, but—the man himself was peculiar, when you came right down to it. The cataphracts thought he was probably mad. The sarwen, from long experience, were certain of it.

Early on in the journey, young Menander made so bold as to ask the dawazz himself.

"Who is mad, boy? I? Not think so. Madmen place lives on top great beasts with good reason wish men dead. I be horse or donkey or camel, boy, you be squashed melon right quick. I be elephant, you be squashed seeds."

When Menander reported the conversation to his veteran seniors—not, be it said, without a certain concern, and a questioning glance at his own horse—Anastasius and Valentinian shrugged the matter off. They were far too deep into their own misery to fret over such outlandish notions.

"Perfect duty, it was," whined Valentinian.

"Ideal," rumbled Anastasius, with heartful agreement. "Best garrison post I ever saw."

"A villa, no less."

"Wine, women, and song."

"Fuck the songs."

"And now—!"

Mutter, mutter, mutter.

"What was that?"

"I think he said 'fuck adventurous leaders,'" replied Menander. The lad frowned. "But maybe not. I can't always understand him when he mutters, even though he does it a lot. Maybe he said: 'fuck avaricious feeders.'"

The frown deepened. "But that doesn't make a lot of sense either, does it? Especially on a trip—" A sudden thought; a sudden worry; a quick glance at his mount.

"Do you old-timers know something about horses that I don't?"

The conversation at the head of the little column, on the other hand, was not gloomy at all. Even Belisarius, once the estate fell out of sight, regained his usual good spirits. And then, not an hour later, great spirits.

There are many sweet pleasures in this world. Among those— unsung though it is—ranks the pleasure of being asked a question which you were trying to figure out how to ask yourself.

Garmat cleared his throat. "General Belisarius. Prince Eon and I have been discussing—for some time now, actually, but we only came to a decision last night—well, the negusa nagast will naturally have to make the final decision, but we are quite certain he will agree—well, the point is—"

"Oh, for the love of Christ!" exclaimed Eon. "General, we would like to accompany you and your men to India." The prince closed his mouth with a snap, straightened his back, stared firmly ahead.

Belisarius smiled—and not crookedly. "I would be delighted!" He turned in his saddle—so easy, that motion, with stirrups!—and looked behind.

"All of you?" he asked. "Including the sarwen?" The general examined the two Ethiopian soldiers. Outlandish men, they were, from a little known and mysterious country. But he knew their breed perfectly.

"Oh, yes," replied Garmat. "They are sworn to Prince Eon's personal service."

Belisarius now looked to Ousanas. The dawazz was striding alongside his prince.

"And you, Ousanas?"

"Of course! Must keep fool prince out of trouble."

"You don't consider this trouble?"

The dawazz grinned. "Voyage to distant India? Enter Malwa gaping maw with madman foreign general intent on stealing Malwa teeth? Sanest thing fool prince ever do."

Belisarius laughed. "You call that sane?"

For once, the grin disappeared. "Yes, Belisarius. For prince of Axum, in new Malwa world, I call that sane. Anything else be folly."

Chapter 15

THE ERYTHREAN SEA
Summer, 529 AD

"It's quite a ship," remarked Belisarius, gazing from the bow down the length of the Indian embassy vessel. "It must be as big as the Alexandrian grain ships—even the *Isis*."

"It's a tub," pronounced Eon. The young prince's gaze followed that of Belisarius, but with none of the general's admiration.

The ship was almost two hundred feet long, and about forty-five feet wide. It was as big as the largest sailing ships ever built by Romans, the great grain-carrying vessels which hauled Egypt's wheat from Alexandria to Constantinople and the western Mediterranean. The famous *Isis* was one of those ships.

Like those grain ships, the Indian vessel had two lower decks as well as the main deck. And, also like the grain ships, the Indian craft was a pure sailing vessel. It had no rowing capability at all. With its enormous carrying capacity of two thousand tons, oars would have been almost futile.

There the resemblance ended. The grain ships were three-masted vessels. The Indian ship was single-masted, although the great square sails of the huge mainmast were assisted by a lateen sail in the stern. Another difference lay in the superstructure. Where the Mediterranean tradition was to build up a poop deck in the stern, the Malwa concentrated their superstructure amidships, surrounding the base of the great mainmast. The wood used throughout the Indian vessel was teak, and the rigging was coir.

Mediterranean ships were built of fir or cedar, with some oak, and the cordage was typically hemp or flax (although the Egyptians often used papyrus, and the Spaniards favored esparto grass).

Beyond those obvious differences, Belisarius was lost. Prince Eon, it seemed, was not.

"A *tub*," he repeated forcefully.

"Very *big* tub," added Ousanas cheerfully. "Most obscene large tub."

"So what?" demanded Eon. "Size isn't everything."

The tall dawazz smiled down at his charge. Under that cheerful regard the Prince tightened his jaw.

"Size isn't everything," he repeated.

"Certainly not!" agreed Garmat. The old adviser smiled. "As a short man, I agree full-heartedly. However, as a short man, I must immediately add that I have always found it wise to take size into consideration. What do you think, General?"

Belisarius tore his gaze away from the ship.

"Eh? Oh—yes, I agree. Although, as a tall man, I have found the converse to be true as well."

"What do you mean?" asked Garmat.

"I mean that I find it wise to take other things than size into consideration. I have never found, for instance, that the size of an army plays as much of a factor in the outcome of battles as the skill of the troops and its leadership."

The prince looked smug. Ousanas immediately piped up: "Belisarius great diplomat!"

Eon majestically ignored the barb, staring out to sea. Belisarius smiled crookedly.

"Why do you call the ship a tub?" he asked the prince.

Eon gazed at him sideways. There was a slight hint of suspicion in his eyes. Even though Belisarius was not given to teasing him—one of many things which the prince had found to like in the Byzantine—still, Eon was a young man, somewhat unsure of himself for all his outward pride.

"Explain," commanded the general.

After a moment's hesitation, Eon launched into a voluminous recital of the huge ship's many faults and shortcomings. Belisarius, no seaman, was immediately lost in the technical details. The gist of it, he concluded, was that Eon thought the great vessel was clumsily designed and operated by even clumsier sailors. He had no idea if Eon was right. But he was deeply impressed by the young Ethiopian's obvious expertise in nautical matters. That simple fact drove home to him, as nothing had before, the seriousness with which the Axumites took their navy. No Roman or Persian prince could have matched that performance.

As soon as Eon finished his recital of the ship's woes, Ousanas commented:

"Axumites notorious braggarts about seamanship."

Garmat cleared his throat. "Actually, I agree with the prince."

"Arabs even worse," added Ousanas.

"You don't agree?" asked Belisarius. The dawazz shrugged.

"Have no idea. Hunter from savanna. Avoid sea like all sane persons. Boats unnatural creatures. But is well known Ethiopians and Arabs think they world's best seamen." A sly glance at the general. "Except Greeks."

"I'm not Greek," came the immediate response. "I'm Thracian. I tend to agree with you, actually. I can't stand boats."

"How are you feeling?" asked Garmat pleasantly.

"I'd rather not think about it," said Belisarius stiffly. "Please continue."

Garmat cleared his throat again. "Well, Eon is perhaps putting the matter too forcefully—"

"It's the simple truth!"

"—but, on balance, I agree with him. The Indians are not, you know, famous for their abilities at sea."

"No, I do not know."

"Ah. Well, it is true. Ethiopians and Arabs ridicule them for it. North Indians, at least. Some of the southern nations of India are quite capable seamen, by all accounts, but we have little contact with them. Their trade is primarily with the distant East." The adviser stroked his beard. "In its own impressive way, this great ship is evidence of my point. The design, as the prince says, is clumsy. And the workmanship is rather poor. Unusually so, for Indians."

Belisarius examined the ship.

"It seems solidly made."

"Oh, it is! That's the point. It's much *too* solid." Here Garmat launched into his own technical discourse, the gist of which, so far as Belisarius could tell, was that the Indians substituted brute strength for craftsmanship. And again, he was struck by the naval expertise of high-ranked Axumites.

"A tub," concluded Garmat.

"Slow as a snail," added Eon, "and just as awkward."

"Big as a monster," chimed in Ousanas. "Run right over clever little Arab and Axumite boats."

"Nonsense!" exclaimed the Prince.

"We find out soon," commented Ousanas dryly. He pointed off the port bow.

The small party of Ethiopians and Romans followed his pointing finger. The southern coast of Arabia was a reddish gloom in the rays of the setting sun. But, against that dark background, a multitude of sails was visible.

"Oh, shit," muttered Valentinian. The pentarch straightened up from his slouch against the rail a few feet distant. He nudged Anastasius next to him. The huge cataphract jerked awake from his doze.

"Get our gear," commanded Valentinian. "And drag Menander out here."

"The kid can't hardly move," protested Anastasius. "He says he doesn't have any guts left."

"Get him! If he complains, tell him he's about to find out what being gutted really means."

Startled, Anastasius followed Valentinian's hard gaze.

"Oh, shit," he muttered. "Is that what I think it is?"

"Arab pirates!" cried Ousanas. He grinned widely. "Not to worry! Very small boats. True, very many of them. Oh, very very very many. Each one loaded with very very many nasty vicious men bent on wickedness. But"—here he gestured grandly—"the great General Belisarius assures that size of army matters nothing."

"Yeah, I've heard him say that before," grumbled Valentinian. "Just before all hell broke loose."

Anastasius was already entering the tent which the Romans had set up in the bow. Loud cries and shouts rang over the ship. The Indian crewmen had also seen the approaching fleet of galleys.

Valentinian marched to the port side and leaned over the rail, gripping it in his lean, sinewy hands. The dark-eyed cataphract glared toward the approaching pirate vessels. His scarred, pock-marked face twisted into a grimace. "Just once," he growled bitterly, "*just once*, I'd like to outnumber the enemy for a change. Fuck skill. Fuck cunning. Fuck strategy. Fuck tactics. Give me numbers, dammit!" His voice trailed off into muttering.

"What was that last?" asked Belisarius mildly. Valentinian was silent.

"Sounded like 'fuck philosophical generals,'" said Ousanas brightly.

Valentinian glowered at him. The dawazz spread his hands. "Maybe not. Ignorant worthless slave. Speak terrible Greek. Fierce cataphract maybe said 'fuck philandering genitals.' Very ethical sentiment! Most inappropriate for occasion, but very moral. Very moral!"

Belisarius' attention was distracted by a commotion. Venandakatra had made his appearance on the deck. He emerged from his cabin amidships, followed by a gaggle of Mahaveda priests.

The Byzantines and Ethiopians had seen almost nothing of him since they had embarked on the Indian vessel at Adulis. Venandakatra's representatives had explained the Indian lord's apparent rudeness as being due to seasickness.

Watching the spry, if waddling, manner in which Venandakatra scurried about, Belisarius had his doubts.

"Seasick!" snorted Eon.

Venandakatra was shouting orders in his shrill, high-pitched voice. Within seconds, dozens of Ye-tai warriors scrambled out of their own tents and began lining the rail. They were bearing bows, swords, and shields, and quickly began donning helmets and half-armor.

The Ye-tai were followed by a dozen warriors whom Belisarius recognized as Malwa kshatriyas. These emerged from the hatch located in the deck just forward of Venandakatra's cabin. They were bearing no weapons beyond short swords, and wore only the lightest leather armor. But they were heavily burdened nonetheless. Divided into pairs, each pair was carrying a large trough made of some odd, lumpy wood which Belisarius had never seen before.

"That's bamboo," explained Garmat. "It's hollow on the inside, like a pipe. They've split it down the middle and carved out the internal partitions."

"This is what you were telling John of Rhodes about, isn't it?"

Garmat nodded. "Yes. I have never seen the Indian weapons myself, but these are quite as described by those of our traders who have seen them in action. From a distance only, however. I think we are about to get a firsthand view."

"Venandakatra's not happy about that," commented Eon.

Belisarius gazed at the Indian lord. Venandakatra was consulting with his cluster of priests. All of them were casting unfriendly glances toward the Romans and Axumites standing in the bow. After a moment, one of the priests detached himself from the group and headed toward them.

"I'll handle this," said Belisarius.

When the priest reached them, Belisarius didn't even give him the chance to speak.

"*No.*"

The priest opened his mouth.

"*Absolutely not.*"

"You must go below!"

"*Under no conditions will we do so.*"

At that moment Anastasius lumbered out of the tent, with Menander close behind. Both cataphracts were fully armed and armored, except for their lances. They were also bearing Belisarius and Valentinian's weapons and armor. Their arrival distracted the priest, who began gobbling further protests. His protests became positively shrill when he spotted the two sarwen charging out of their own tent, likewise laden with weapons. An abundance of weapons—each sarwen was carrying a cluster of javelins as well as swords, shields, and huge-bladed spears.

Within moments, all the Romans and Axumites were busily donning their armor and taking up their weapons. The priest was now practically gibbering.

"Anastasius," commanded the general. "Do something impressively unfriendly."

Anastasius immediately seized the priest by the scruff of the neck and his crotch and tossed him back toward the cluster of priests amidships. The priest managed to land on his feet, more or less, but he immediately stumbled out of control and hurtled into his cohorts, bowling two of them right over.

Venandakatra screeched with fury. A small crowd of Ye-tai warriors surged forward.

Without any orders from Belisarius, all three cataphracts immediately notched arrows and drew their bows. The two sarwen raised their javelins. Eon and Garmat hefted their stabbing spears. Belisarius drew his sword. Ousanas lounged against the rail.

"What are you playing at?" hissed Menander.

Ousanas gaped. "Me? Miserable slave! Not fit for noble type foolishness."

"Ousanas!" commanded Eon.

The dawazz sighed. "Most unreasonable prince." He lazed forward. "Play old game?" he asked.

Eon immediately gave Ousanas his great spear. The prince shed his baldric and sword and then began to walk, unarmed, toward the Malwa crowd. Behind him, Ousanas motioned the Ye-tai warriors to clear a lane. Puzzled, but hearing no countervailing orders from the priests, the Ye-tai did as the dawazz bade them.

Eon walked right through the silent Malwa crowd until he reached the cabin which was built around the base of the mainmast. As soon as he reached the cabin, the prince turned and backed up against it. He crossed his arms and spread his legs about a foot apart. He was standing about twenty yards from the Axumites and Romans in the bow.

Ousanas casually jabbed the stabbing spear into the deck of the ship. The huge blade sank a full inch into the hard wood and stood erect. Without a word, one of the sarwen handed him a javelin. The dawazz hefted the javelin lightly and then, with a motion whose speed and power stunned everyone watching, hurled the javelin across the length of the deck.

The weapon sank into the wall of the cabin almost the full length of the blade. The shaft of the weapon quivered like a tuning fork. About two inches from the prince's left ear.

A moment later, another javelin was sailing across the deck. This one plunged into the wood about two inches from Eon's right ear. Not seconds later, a third javelin thundered into the cabin wall right between the prince's legs. About two inches below his crotch.

"Mary, Mother of God," whispered Valentinian.

Anastasius drew a deep breath. "That's incredible spear work. Amazing!"

"Fuck the spear work," growled Valentinian. "The kid never even blinked! *That's* amazing. I may never fuck again, just from watching."

The prince suddenly laughed. He and his dawazz exchanged huge grins across the deck of the ship.

"Very foolish prince," mused Ousanas, shaking his head. "But got elephant heart. Been that way since boy."

Ousanas plucked the great stabbing spear out of the deck and sauntered toward Eon. The warriors and priests scuttled out of his way. The dawazz smiled upon them beatifically.

"Intelligent persons!" he exclaimed. "Very most sane and logical Indian people!" He bestowed a particularly engaging grin upon Venandakatra.

When Ousanas reached Eon, he and the prince assisted each other in withdrawing the javelins from the cabin walls. More than anything else, perhaps, it was the obvious effort being exerted by these two very strong men which drove home just how ferocious those javelin casts had been.

Belisarius sheathed his sword and strode over to Venandakatra. "We are soldiers," he told the Indian lord sternly, "not children. We will not be penned in the hold during an attack."

He matched Venandakatra's glare with one of his own. After a moment, the Vile One looked away.

"Besides," added Belisarius, turning away and pointing to the approaching fleet of pirate vessels, "you may find you are glad to have us, soon enough."

Venandakatra scowled, but said nothing. Belisarius returned to the bow of the ship and began giving directions to the Roman and Axumite warriors. After a few moments, it became clear that the Indians had decided to leave the defense of the bow in the hands of their unwanted guests.

Belisarius had never encountered Axumite warriors in battle, neither as friend nor foe. He hesitated for a moment, wondering how best to use their skills.

What he could glean of the Ethiopian way of fighting was odd. They seemed singularly unconcerned about bodily protection, for one thing. The Axumites, when not constrained by Greek custom, never wore anything except a short-sleeved tunic, kilt, and sandals. Now, preparing for battle, they removed their tunics and stood bare from the waist up. Each of them, except Ousanas, took up a buffalo-hide shield. The shields were round and small—no wider than a forearm. Those little shields, apparently, constituted the entirety of their armor.

Each Ethiopian carried a sword slung behind his back from a leather baldric which crossed the right shoulder diagonally. The haft of the sword stuck up right behind the shoulder blade, where it could be easily grasped. The swords were purely cutting implements. They were short, very wide and heavy, and ended in a square tip. They resembled a butcher's cleaver more than anything else.

The swords, however, were obviously secondary weapons. For their main armament, each Ethiopian carried javelins and those enormous spears. The Axumite stabbing spear was about seven feet long. The blade was almost a foot and a half long, shaped like a narrow leaf, heavy and razor sharp. The spear shaft was also heavy—as thick and solid as a cavalry lance. The last foot or so of the haft was sheathed with iron bands, and the very end of the haft bore a solid iron knob about two inches in diameter. The weapon could obviously double as a long mace.

Garmat spoke quietly.

"I suggest you use us as a reserve, Belisarius. As you can see, we do not match your cataphracts for sheer weight of armor and weapons. It is not the Axumite method. But I think you will find us very useful when the enemy presses."

"What about him?" asked the general, nodding toward Ousanas. The dawazz carried neither a shield nor a sword. He seemed content merely with his javelins and his spear—a spear which, in his case, was a foot longer and much heavier than those borne by the other Ethiopians.

Garmat shrugged. "Ousanas is a law unto himself. But I think you will have no cause for complaint."

Belisarius smiled his crooked smile. "A miserable, ignorant slave, is he?"

As often before, Ousanas surprised him with his acute hearing.

"Most miserable!" cried the dawazz. "Especially now! With cruel pitiless Arabs approaching!" Ousanas cast a longing glance at the sea. "Would flee in abject shrieking terror except too ignorant to know how to swim."

"You swim like a fish!" snapped the Prince.

The dawazz goggled. "Do I? Imagine such a wonder!" He shook his head sadly. "Slavery terrible condition. Make me forget everything."

Belisarius turned away and resumed his examination of the Indians. He saw that the bamboo troughs had now been set up along the port rail of the deck, facing northward. The troughs were spaced about ten feet apart. The Malwa kshatriyas then placed great bundles of hide at the ship-end of the troughs. The grey hides were tightly rolled into barrel-shapes which were about half the size of actual barrels.

"That's elephant hide," commented Garmat quietly.

Now, the kshatriyas began dipping buckets into the sea and hauling them up with ropes. As soon as the buckets were drawn aboard, the seawater was poured over the hide rolls. Once the hide rolls were completely waterlogged, the kshatriyas began pouring the seawater over every exposed surface of the ship. After a hurried consultation with Venandakatra, two of the kshatriyas advanced to the bow. Making clear with gestures and facial expressions that their intentions were pacific, the kshatriyas began soaking the bow of the ship with seawater also. The Romans and Ethiopians, at Belisarius' command, stood aside and made no objection, even when the Malwa soaked the leather walls of their own tents.

After the kshatriya left the bow, Belisarius whispered to Garmat: "For some reason, they seemed terrified of fire. Is that because of the Arabs, do you think?"

Garmat shook his head. "Can't be. Arab navies are known to use fire arrows, on occasion, but these are not naval forces. They are pirates. What would be the point of burning this ship? They want to capture it."

Belisarius nodded his head. "So—it must be due to their own weapons."

At that moment, more kshatriyas began emerging from the hold. They were bearing knobby, odd-looking, short—poles?

"Are those bamboo?" asked Belisarius.

"Yes," replied Garmat. "Each of those poles is simply a length of bamboo with some kind of bundle at one end. I think the bundle is just a wider length of bamboo jammed over the end of the pole and bound to it with leather. See? That's the end they're placing in the troughs to face outward. The other end has a—a tail, let's call it. That's just a short length of bamboo split length-wise."

"What are these things called?"

Garmat shrugged.

aim seized the moment. In a paroxysm of determination, it drove the facets toward a single point. A pure focus, a narrow salient in the barrier, a simple thrust. Had **aim** understood the human way of siegecraft, it would have called itself a battering ram guided toward the hinge of the gate. Perhaps—yes! Yes! Yes!

"It's called a—a *rocket*," whispered Belisarius. "More," he commanded. "More!"

"What are you talking about?" demanded Garmat. The old

adviser was gazing at the general as if Belisarius were demented. Belisarius grinned at him.

"I'm not mad, Garmat, believe me. Just—I can't explain, now. Something important is happening. I am—let's say, I am understanding things."

Again **aim** drove the facets. Again, it regained the focus. Again, the battering ram. Again—the breach!

"Yes," whispered Belisarius. "I see it, yes! It could be turned around. Made its opposite. Expel its interior rather than be expelled by it. Yes!"

He frowned, concentrating, *concentrating*. For a moment—for he was well acquainted with the human way of siegecraft—he even envisioned himself as a battering ram. And, with that vision, made his own breach in the wall.

"Then it would be called a—*cannon*."

He sagged, almost staggered. Garmat steadied him with a hand.

"Truly," muttered the adviser, "truly I hope you have not gone mad. This is a poor time for it." He shook the general's arm. "Belisarius! Snap out of it! The pirates are almost within bow range."

Belisarius straightened, looked seaward, then glanced down at the Axumite. He shook his head, smiling.

"You are exaggerating, Garmat. The Arabs will not be within bow range for two minutes. But—the pirates *are* within rocket range. Watch!"

At that moment, a strange hissing sound was heard, like a dragon's rage. Startled, Garmat looked back amidships and gaped. One of the—*rockets*—was hurtling itself toward the pirates. Behind it, a ball of flame billowed on the deck, surrounding the hide roll at the back of the trough from which the rocket had soared. The kshatriyas were obviously expecting the phenomenon, for, within a second or two, buckets of water were poured over the smoldering hide bundle. The ball of flame became a small cloud of steam.

Belisarius watched the flight of the rocket. He was struck, more than anything, by the serpentine nature of the bamboo device's trajectory. It did not fly with the true arc of an arrow or a cast spear. Instead, the rocket skittered and snaked about. He realized, after a moment, that there was some connection between the rocket's movements and the erratic red flare that jetted from its tail.

Crude, blunt thoughts suddenly emerged through the barrier. They entered his mind like dumb creatures lumbering into a cave.

poor mix. bad powder.

Mix? He wondered. *Powder? What could powder—dust—have to do with—?*

powder is force.

"How? And what kind of powder?" he wondered aloud. Again, Garmat glanced at him worriedly. Belisarius began to smile reassuringly, but the smile faded. He could feel the alien presence in his mind retreating; could sense its discouragement.

The rocket began to drift downward toward the sea. It was obvious, long before it struck, that the device had been badly aimed. It would land far from any pirate craft.

"Is it aimed at all?" he muttered. Next to him, Garmat shook his head. The Axumite seemed relieved that Belisarius' mumblings were now connected to reality.

"I do not think so, General. I think they are simply shot forth in the general direction of the enemy. You saw how it flew. How could such a capricious weapon be aimed?"

The rocket hit the sea. There was a sudden plume of water and steam, then—nothing. The multitude of Arabs aboard the pirate vessels gave out a great jeering cry.

The pirates were now close enough for examination.

There were a total of thirteen galleys approaching. Each was rowed on two banks, with a lateen sail and a huge crew. At a rough guess, Belisarius estimated that each ship carried over a hundred men. Most of the pirates were armed with swords or spears. A number had bows. Very few, however, wore much in the way of armor. Nor, for that matter, did many of the Arabs even carry shields.

As individuals, Belisarius decided, they were not particularly fearsome. The danger was in their great numbers.

Four more rockets were fired. Again, the skittering serpentine trajectories—and again, none of them came near their mark. The pirates were now jeering madly.

"They're gaining on us," groused Eon. "What a miserable ship this beast is! In these heavy seas, with this good wind, we should be leaving them behind easily."

Six rockets were fired. And now, finally, the strange weapons showed their true power. Two of them struck the same pirate vessel. The Arab ship seemed to burst into flame and fury. Several pirates were hurled into the air as if they had been struck by the hand of an invisible titan.

"Force!" exclaimed Belisarius. "Yes—that's what—" He fell silent.

"That's *what?*" demanded Garmat.

Belisarius glanced at him, pursed his lips in thought, then shook his head.

"Never mind, Garmat. I was just noticing that these weapons are not simply fire-weapons. They bear some other power with them as well. Some unknown—*force*—which acts like a blow as well as a flame."

Garmat looked back at the pirate vessel. Now that the cloud of smoke had cleared, it was obvious that the ship had been struck as well as burnt. Where one of the rockets had collided, an entire section of the ship's hull had been caved in. The vessel was already listing badly, and its crew was beginning to jump overboard. It was clear that the craft was doomed. The only uncertainty was whether it would sink before the flames could engulf it.

Again, suddenly, an alien thought moved into Belisarius' mind. **explosion. force is explosion.**

Tantalizingly, Belisarius almost caught the image which the jewel was emitting. But it withdrew, faded—then surged back. Just for an instant, the general saw a barrel containing a blazing and furious fire. The fire produced a vast volume of gasses which pressed against the walls of the barrel until—

"Yes!" he cried. "Yes—I was right! It *is* fire!"

He suddenly realized that a number of people were staring at him. Not just Romans and Axumites, either. Several of the Ye-tai warriors stationed nearby were frowning at him, as well as a Mahaveda priest.

Keep your mouth shut, idiot. Observe in silence.

Another volley of rockets. Six rockets, six misses—but the jeer from the pirates was notably more subdued. The Arab craft were now less than two hundred yards away. A few Arab archers loosed shafts, but their arrows fell short of the mark.

"Weaklings," sneered Anastasius. The giant Thracian drew his great bow. Belisarius almost winced, watching. The general had tried to draw that bow, once. Tried and failed miserably, for all that Belisarius was a strong man.

Powerful as he was, Anastasius was actually not a great archer. He had nothing like the skill with a bow possessed by Valentinian. But, aiming at those closely packed, mobbed vessels, it hardly mattered. His arrow sailed across the distance and plunged into the crowd aboard one ship. A shriek was heard.

"Most blessed arrow!" cried Ousanas. "Graced by God Himself!"

Anastasius grinned. Valentinian snorted.

"He's not praising you, stupid. He's saying you were lucky."

Anastasius frowned at Ousanas. The dawazz shook his head sadly.

"Valentinian tells false lie. Very wicked Roman man! Not said you were lucky. Said you stood most high in Deity's esteem."

"See?" demanded Valentinian.

Anastasius gestured angrily. "Let's see you do any better!" he demanded.

Ousanas grinned. "Too far. Arrows cheap as dirt. Javelins precious. Very important point in theology. God wanton with His blessings on arrows. Stingy with javelins."

The dawazz pointed to the easternmost craft.

"You see him steersman? That ship?"

Anastasius nodded.

Again, Ousanas shook his head sadly. "Him great sinner. Soon be taken by Shaitan."

"How soon?" demanded Anastasius.

"Soon as skill allow. Javelin weapon of skill. God *very* stingy with javelin. Miser, almost."

Anastasius snorted and turned away. Again, he drew his bow. Again, his arrow found a mark in the crowd.

The pirates drew closer. There had been no rocket volleys for some time, but now another six were fired off. Belisarius noted that the kshatriyas manning the rockets had adjusted the angle of the firing troughs. Where before the bamboo half-barrels had been tilted upward, they were now almost level.

These rockets did not soar upward like a javelin. They sped in a more or less flat trajectory barely a few feet above the water. And they struck with devastating impact. At that range, they could hardly miss. Belisarius was fascinated to see one rocket hit the sea at a shallow angle and then bounce back upward, like a flat-thrown stone skipping across water. That rocket did as much damage as any when it slammed into the bow of an Arab ship.

Almost half of the pirate fleet had now been struck by the missiles. Two ships were listing badly and had ceased their forward motion. Two others were burning furiously, and their crews were jumping overboard.

But it was obvious the Arabs had no intention of breaking off the attack. The pirate vessels now began to scatter, spreading out in such a way as to give less of a massed target for the rockets. The sailors on the surviving galleys helped those who had jumped from stricken ships to clamber aboard.

Five pirate vessels were now sinking or burning out of control, and at least one other seemed out of the action. But Belisarius did not think that the actual number of warriors had been significantly reduced. Most of those who had jumped into the sea had been taken aboard other vessels. The remaining craft were now jammed with men.

Another volley of rockets was fired. All of them but one missed, however, soaring through the space now vacated by the galleys. Even the one which struck a ship simply glanced off harmlessly. That rocket continued to soar across the sea until, suddenly, it erupted in a ball of flame and smoke.

Belisarius scratched his chin. It occurred to him that the rockets did not actually seem to—*explode*—on contact. He remembered, now, that several of the rockets had exploded a few seconds *after* striking a ship. The effect had been the same, however, for the force of their flight had driven the rockets right through the thin planking of the Arab ships. And, regardless of the timing of the explosions, the rockets burned so fiercely that they almost invariably set the ships afire.

Still—

"With the right armor and tactics," he mused aloud, "I don't think these rockets would be all that dangerous."

Valentinian turned to him with a questioning look.

"Play hell with horses, General," commented the cataphract.

"True," agreed Belisarius. "Those shrieking hisses and explosions would panic the brutes. No way to control them." Suddenly, he grinned. "I do believe the infantry has just made a great comeback!"

"Shit," muttered Anastasius. "He's right."

Valentinian groaned. "I *hate* walking."

"*You* hate it?" demanded Anastasius. "You haven't got an ounce of fat on you! How do you think I feel?"

Garmat interrupted worriedly. "Night has almost fallen."

It was true enough. It was still barely possible to make out the intact pirate ships in the gathering darkness, but not by much.

"New moon, too," added Eon. "There won't be any light at all in a few minutes."

Another volley of rockets was fired. Belisarius noted that the kshatriyas had angled all six of the troughs around so that all of the rockets were fired toward a single ship. Even so, only one of the rockets struck. Fortunately, the missile hit directly amidships and exploded with a satisfying roar. That vessel, clearly enough, was doomed.

Just before the last glimmer of daylight faded, it was possible to see the pirate galleys beginning to surround the Indian ship. They were now keeping a distance, however, waiting for nightfall. Between that distance, and being widely spread out, it was obvious that the rockets were no longer of much use.

Two more wasted volleys made the point before Venandakatra began calling out new orders. Immediately, three of the rocket crews began transferring their troughs to the starboard rail of the ship. For their part, the three remaining rocket crews began spacing their troughs more widely down the port length of the ship. The Malwa, it was obvious, were positioning the rocket launchers to repel boarders.

Venandakatra shouted new orders. Listening, Belisarius could begin to understand the meaning. He realized that the jewel was once again working its strange magic. The Malwa language was called Hindi, and Belisarius knew not a word of it. But, suddenly, the language came into focus in his mind. The shrill words spoken by several kshatriyas in response to Venandakatra's commands were as clear as day.

"The Indian rocket-men are not happy," whispered Garmat. "They are complaining that—"

"They will be burned if they do as Venandakatra orders," completed Belisarius absently.

The Axumite adviser was startled. "I did not realize you spoke Hindi."

Belisarius began to reply, closed his mouth. Garmat, again, was staring at him strangely.

I'm going to have to come up with an explanation for him, when this is all over. Damn all shrewd advisers, anyway!

Venandakatra shouted down the protests. His Mahaveda priests added their own comments, prominent among them the promise to bring the mahamimamsa "purifiers" from the hold below.

The kshatriyas snarled, but hurried to obey. All of the troughs were now tilted until they were pointing at a slight angle downward. More hide bundles were piled up at the rear of the troughs, but it was obvious from the kshatriyas' worried frowns that they did not think the hides would suffice to completely shield them from the rocket flames. The fire which would erupt from the rocket tails would now be shooting upward.

Another alien thought seeped through the barrier.

back-blast.

Darkness was now complete, except for the faint light thrown by the few lanterns held by Ye-tai warriors. Belisarius saw Venandakatra staring at him. A moment later, with obvious reluctance, the Indian lord made his way toward the bow of the ship.

When he reached Belisarius, the general spoke before Venandakatra could even open his mouth.

"I am well aware that the pirates will concentrate their attack on the bow and stern, where the—where your fire-weapons cannot be brought to bear. Look to the stern, Venandakatra. There will be no breach at the bow."

Venandakatra frowned. "There are not many of you," he said. "I could send some—"

"No. More men would simply crowd the bow, making it more difficult for us. And I do not have time to learn how to incorporate Malwa warriors into our tactics. Whereas Romans and Axumites are old allies, long accustomed to fighting side by side." The lie came smooth as silk.

Garmat's face was expressionless. The sarwen grunted loud agreement, as did Anastasius and Valentinian. Eon started slightly, but a quick poke from his dawazz brought stillness. Menander looked confused, but the Indian was not looking his way, and almost immediately, Valentinian changed the young Thracian's expression with a silent snarl.

"You are certain?" demanded Venandakatra.

Belisarius smiled graciously. "I said you would be glad to have us, soon enough."

Venandakatra's face grew pinched, but the Indian forebore further comment. After a moment, he scurried away and began shouting new orders. Belisarius could understand the words, and knew that the commands which Venandakatra was shrilling were utterly redundant and pointless. A disgruntled grandee making noise to assure himself of his importance, that was all.

"Verily, a foul man," muttered Garmat. "Long ago, the Axumites had a king much like him. The sarawit assassinated the wretch and created the institution of dawazz the next day."

"Do you really think they're going to attack?" asked Menander suddenly. Seeing all eyes upon him, the young cataphract straightened.

"I'm not afraid!" he protested. "It's just—it doesn't make sense."

"I'm afraid it does," countered Garmat. The adviser grimaced. "I am myself half-Arab, and I know my mother's people well. The tribes of the Hadrawmat"—he pointed to the southern shore of Arabia, now lost in the darkness—"are very poor. Fishermen, mostly, and smugglers. A great ship like this represents a fortune to them. They will gladly suffer heavy casualties in order to capture it."

Ousanas chuckled. "Believe wise old mongrel, young Roman. Most despicable people in world, the Arabs. Full of vice and sins!"

Garmat squinted.

"O many vices! Many sins!"

Garmat looked pained.

"Lechery! Avarice! Cruelty!"

Garmat frowned.

"Treachery! Sloth! Envy!"

Garmat glowered.

"Would be great gluttons if not so poor!"

Garmat ground his teeth.

"Alas, Arabs unfamiliar with cowardice."

Garmat smiled. Ousanas shook his head sadly.

"Is because Arabs so stupid. Cowardice mankind's only useful vice. Naturally Arabs know nothing of it."

"I heard a story years ago," mused Anastasius, "that there was a cowardly Arab living somewhere in the Empty Quarter." He spit into the sea. "I didn't believe it, myself."

"They're coming," announced Valentinian. "I can't see them, but I can hear them."

Belisarius glanced at Valentinian. As so often before on the verge of battle, the cataphract reminded the general of nothing so much as a weasel. The sharp features; the long, lean whipcord body; the poised stillness, like a coiled spring; and, most of all, the utter intensity of the killer's concentration. At these moments, Valentinian's senses were almost superhuman.

Belisarius sighed. The choice was now upon him and could no longer be postponed.

Secrecy be damned, he decided. *These men—all of them—are my comrades. I cannot betray them.*

The general stepped to the very prow of the ship.

"There are two ships approaching us," he announced. He pointed, and pointed again. "There, and there. The one on the right is closer."

He heard a slight cough behind him.

"Trust me, Garmat. I can see them almost as well as if it were daytime. They are there, just as I have described."

He looked over his shoulder and smiled crookedly.

"The steersman you pointed out earlier is on that closer ship, Ousanas. Make good your boast."

For once, the dawazz was not grinning. Ousanas stared into the darkness for a moment, then looked back at the general.

"You are witch," he announced.

Belisarius made a face.

The grin made its inevitable appearance. Ousanas' skin was so black that he was almost invisible except as a shape. Against that darkness, the grin was like a beacon of good cheer.

"Is not problem," said the dawazz. Ousanas gestured toward the other warriors.

"These other men be civilized folk, Axumites and Romans. Hence filled with silly superstitions. Think witchcraft evil. I savage from far south, too ignorant to be confused. I know witchcraft like everything else in this world. Some good. Some bad."

A great laugh suddenly rang out, startling in its loudness.

"Most excellent!" pronounced the dawazz. "Never had good witch before, on my side."

"Can you truly see that well, in the night?" asked the prince shakily. "How is that possible?"

"Yes, Eon, I can. How is it possible?" Belisarius hesitated, but only for an instant. The die was cast.

"There is no time now. But after the battle, I will explain." A glance at Garmat. "I will explain everything." A glance at his cataphracts and the sarwen. "To all of you."

Ousanas lounged forward, hefting his javelin.

"Where is steersman?" he asked idly. Belisarius pointed again. Ousanas squinted.

"Still too dark," he muttered.

At that moment, Venandakatra's voice cried out a command. A volley of rockets was fired in all directions. Several kshatriyas squealed with pain, caught by the back-blasts which flared over the hide mounds.

"Fucking idiot," growled Anastasius. "The cowardly bastard, he's just panicking."

It was true enough. The volley was completely unaimed. The six rockets snaked their fiery path into nothingness. A total waste.

To all, that is, save Ousanas. For the rockets' glare had, whatever else, bathed the sea with a sudden flare of red illumination. The pirate ships were clearly visible, and even, with difficulty, individual members of their crews.

"I see him steersman!" cried the dawazz gleefully. He hurled the javelin like a tiger pouncing on its prey. The weapon vanished into the fading red glare. Almost at once it was invisible, to all save Belisarius.

The general watched the javelin rise, and rise, and rise. He had never seen such a tremendous cast. Then, the general watched it sail downward. Downward, and truer than Euclidean dreams.

A terrible, brief cry filled the night.

Anastasius hunched his shoulders, staring grimly out to sea.

"I can't bear to look, Valentinian. Is that damned black bastard grinning at me?"

Valentinian chuckled. "It looks like the Pharos at Alexandria. A blinding beacon in the night."

A sudden little flight of arrows came out of the darkness. None of them came close, however. The pirates were simply reacting out of rage.

"It won't be long now," announced Belisarius. He smiled. "By the way, you might want to shift over to the other side, Anastasius. The ship on your side isn't the closest, anymore. In fact, it's wallowing in the waves. No steersman."

Anastasius grunted his disgust. Ousanas took up another javelin.

"Maybe fucking idiot cowardly bastard Indian lord fire another useless volley," he said cheerfully. "Then I make other pirate galley wallow in waves."

"I'll kill him," muttered Anastasius.

"I doubt it," retorted Valentinian. Suddenly, he too was grinning. "And don't be a spiteful idiot. You're like some petty boy in a playground. Would you rather he was chucking those spears the other way?"

Anastasius winced. "No, but—"

He got no further. A pirate ship loomed out of the darkness, like a dragon rising from the sea. A medley of war cries erupted from it. A moment later, another volley of rockets flared.

Now all was bright glare, redness and fury, and the ancient battle clangor. Anastasius drew his great bow and slew a pirate, and then another, and another, and another, and another. At that range, his arrows split chests like a butcher splits a chicken. Even had the pirates been wearing full armor, it would have made no difference. At that range, the arrows of Anastasius drove through shields.

And now, when he saw the other pirate galley suddenly wallow in the waves, bereft of its steersman, there was no emotion in his heart beyond a fierce surge of comradeship. For the cataphract Anastasius was not, in truth, a spiteful schoolboy filled with petty pride. He was a soldier plying his trade.

And he was very, very good at it.

Chapter 16

Even though it was a moonless night, the battle itself was fully illuminated, in a hideous, flashing way. Belisarius had time, even in the press and fury of the fray, to marvel at the scene.

If one could be said to marvel at a scene from Hell.

By the time the first pirate ships came alongside the Indian vessel, attaching themselves with grappling hooks, all but four of the Arab craft were burning infernos. The erratic trajectories of the rockets was now irrelevant. At point-blank range, the rockets did not explode upon impact. Instead, they continued to burn from their tails, with the same fierce dragon-hiss that sent them skittering through the air. Fascinated, Belisarius saw one rocket punch through the hull of a ship, glance off a rower's bench, carom off another bench on the opposite side, and then roar its way down the length of the pirate craft until it embedded itself in the bow. Its trail was marked by a horde of screaming Arabs, frantically trying to beat out the flames in their garments, which had been set afire by the rocket in its passage. Once brought to a halt by the thicker planking at the bow, the rocket continued to burn as brightly as ever. To all appearances, the mindless device seemed like a stubborn animal trying to force its way through a hedge. It was several seconds before it finally exploded, shattering the bow into splinters. But, by that time, the tail-fire burning down the length of the pirate craft had done as much damage as the explosion itself.

I don't think these rockets have any way of knowing when to explode, mused Belisarius.

aim hurled the serried facets at the same breach in the barrier, much like a human general might launch his troops at a shattered section of a fortified wall. Another crude thought was forced through.

no fuses.

Sensing the puzzlement in Belisarius' mind, the facets retreated. But **aim** rallied them immediately. With success, crude though it was, confidence was growing. **aim** sent the facets through the breach anew, and now, filled with the fanatic purpose of *explanation*.

Finally—finally!—true success. The facets flashed their exultation. **aim** itself broke into kaleidoscopic joy.

The knowledge which now erupted in the mind of the general Belisarius was no crude, simple thought. Instead, it was like a living diagram, a moving reality. He saw, as clearly as anything in his life, the way of the rockets. He saw the strange powder [**gunpowder**, he now knew] packed in the length of the rocket; the same powder, in greater quantities, which was packed in the front tip [**warhead**] of the device. He saw the *gunpowder* ignited by a long match held by a kshatriya warrior. He saw the powder erupt into flame, and saw how the flame burned. (And knew that the vision was moving at an inhuman pace, slowed by the jewel that he might follow the course of it.)

He saw the flame burn its way up, inside the length of the bamboo tube [**fuselage**]. He saw the raging gasses which were expelled from the rocket's rear [**exhaust**], and knew the fury of the gasses was the force which drove the device into motion.

(A concept—**action/reaction**—flashed through his mind. He almost understood it, but was not concerned; soon, soon, he would.)

Watching, in his mind's eye, the course of the flame burning its way through the gunpowder, Belisarius now understood the reason for the rocket's erratic trajectory.

Part of it, he saw, was that the gunpowder was poorly mixed. (And he knew, now, that gunpowder was not a substance itself, but a combination of substances.) The powder was uneven and lumpy, like poorly threshed grain. Different pockets and sections of the powder burned unevenly, which produced a ragged and unpredictable exhaust.

Most of the problem, though, was that the rear opening through which the exhaust poured [**venturi**—but the thought was saturated with scorn] was itself poorly made. In fact, it wasn't "made" at all. The venturi was nothing more than a ring of wood. The Indians simply cut the bamboo after one of the joints in the wood, and used the joint itself as the nozzle which concentrated and aimed the exhaust gasses. But the hole was ragged to begin with, no better than a crude carving; Belisarius could actually see in his mind the way in which the hot exhaust burned out the wood in its expulsion.

The companions of Belisarius feared for his sanity, then. The first pirates were even now clambering their way aboard the ship—and here was their general, their leader, cavorting about like a madman and raving lunatic nonsense about Greek and Armenian metalsmiths and the cunning of their craft. He was even cackling about the Emperor's throne, and his roaring lions, and his birds!

But, they were relieved to see, the madness passed as soon as the first Arab head appeared above the rail. Belisarius removed the head with a sweep of his sword which was so quick, and so sure, and so certain, and so graceful, that none who saw doubted he was a man possessed.

"'Deadly with a blade, is Belisarius,'" muttered Valentinian. "But *that's* ridiculous."

"Stop bitching," growled Anastasius. He brought his mace down upon another pirate head. And if there was little grace in the act, and not much in the way of quickness, the result was no less sure and certain.

Arabs now began pouring over the rails, port and starboard, all along the ship. There was a frenzied determination in that surge, far beyond battle-lust and greed. The surge was born of pure desperation. There were far too few galleys left intact, now, to bear the pirates safely back to shore. They must either conquer the great Indian vessel, or die.

The kshatriyas fled the rocket troughs and sheltered behind the Ye-tai. There, the kshatriyas formed a defensive ring around Venandakatra and the cluster of priests standing at the foot of the mainmast. But it was obvious that the lightly armed Malwa warriors, their rockets out of action, were nothing but a feeble last guard. The real defense of the ship now lay in the hands of the Ye-tai. The barbarians were not slow to deride the kshatriyas for their unmanliness.

But the derision was short-lived. Within seconds, the Ye-tai were too hard-pressed by the wave of pirates swarming aboard the ship to concern themselves with anything but survival.

As Belisarius had expected, the pirates concentrated their efforts at the stern and the bow, where their ships could avoid the rockets. Indeed, the only two Arab craft which were still seaworthy were the ones attached to the bow and stern of the huge Indian vessel.

At the stern, the battle went quite well for the pirates, and did so quickly. At the bow, they found nothing but death and destruction.

Belisarius had lied to Venandakatra when he told him that Romans and Axumites were long accustomed to fighting alongside each other. But now, as they did so for the first time in history, under the command of the greatest Roman general in centuries, they seemed to be a perfect fighting machine.

Belisarius had positioned his small band of soldiers as Garmat had recommended. The very front line was made up of his three heavily armored cataphracts. The inexperienced Menander was placed in the point of the bow. Valentinian and Anastasius flanked the youth on either side. Although Belisarius was himself inexperienced in sea battles, it had been obvious that few pirates would try to clamber directly over the arching curve of the bow itself. The points of greatest danger lay a few feet behind the bow, and it was there that the general positioned his two veterans: Anastasius to port, Valentinian to starboard.

And, as Belisarius had expected, it was there that the pirates concentrated their efforts.

To little avail. The heavy shields and armor of the cataphracts were all but impenetrable to the light weapons being wielded by the pirates—the more so, as the weapons were wielded awkwardly and one-handed. Each pirate's other hand was needed to retain his hold on the rail. Belisarius learned, then, his first lesson in sea-fighting: despite Eon's sneers, and whatever its clumsiness, there was a great advantage to the size of the Indian ship. The pirates could not simply leap from ship to ship. Boarding the great Malwa craft presented much the same obstacle to the low galleys as scaling a wall presented to besiegers of a land fortress.

The contest was absurdly one-sided. Each pirate got, at the most, one swing of his weapon. Thereafter, if he faced Anastasius, he died immediately; his skull crushed by a mace. If he faced the more subtle Valentinian, his death might be postponed a moment or so. Valentinian, also new to ship-fighting, soon discovered that the most economical way to deal with his opponents was to strike at their defenseless hands gripping the rail. Valentinian did not possess the sheer brute power of Anastasius, but he was quite strong. It hardly mattered. His sword, like all his blades, was sharp as a razor. Within two minutes, a little mound of severed hands was piling up at his feet. Their former owners had plunged into the sea, where they died soon enough from shock, blood loss, and drowning.

Menander, though not a complete novice by any means, lacked his two comrades' long experience. Nor, for that matter, did he now or would he ever possess their awesome skill in combat. But he was a Thracian cataphract, one of that elite company pledged to their lord Belisarius, and none could ever say afterward that he shamed them.

As uneven as the contest was, however, it proved to be the Axumites who made the final difference. Alone, the four Romans would eventually have been overwhelmed by sheer numbers. As fast as the cataphracts wielded their weapons, the Arabs poured up even faster. But the Ethiopian spears were quicker still.

The cataphracts slew a great number themselves, but, in the main, their contribution was to serve as a living wall which delayed the pirates that one extra moment. A moment was all the sarwen needed, or Eon. And Ousanas needed even less. Standing a few feet behind the cataphracts, the Axumite spears flicked out like viper strikes. Each stroke was swift, accurate, and almost invariably deadly. On occasion, the sarwen and Eon required a second spear-thrust to dispatch an enemy.

Ousanas, never. The dawazz's aim was absolutely uncanny. Watching, Belisarius decided he had never seen a man wield a weapon so unerringly. Certainly not in an actual battle. The precision was almost wasted, though. The dawazz lacked Anastasius' bearlike bulk, and Eon's flamboyant musculature. But Belisarius suspected that Ousanas was actually stronger than either of them. His great spear blade literally ruptured human bodies.

The general had placed himself and Garmat as the final reserve. Each of them stood a few feet behind the Axumites, Garmat to starboard, Belisarius to port. The general had expected, within seconds of the assault, to be in a life-and-death struggle.

As before, in the battle against the Persians, the jewel was working its way with him. Belisarius' senses were superhumanly keen, and his reflexes were like quicksilver. But—he almost laughed—it proved another waste. Neither he nor Garmat was ever required to strike a blow—although the old adviser did so, once, skewering a pirate over a sarwen's shoulder. Belisarius thought the effort was superfluous, simply the ingrained habit of an old warrior. So, apparently, did the sarwen. The Ethiopian soldier immediately denounced Garmat for an interfering busybody and suggested, none too politely, that the doddering fool stick to his trade. Thereafter, Garmat satisfied himself with a reservist's role.

Once it became clear to Belisarius that the situation in the bow was well under control, the general felt it possible to concentrate elsewhere. While keeping an eye on the fight at hand, most of his attention was riveted on the battle raging amidships, and in the stern.

Partly, his concern was with the overall progress of the struggle. Regardless of how well the Romans and Axumites fought in the bow, the final outcome of the battle would be largely determined by the success of the Ye-tai in repelling the boarders everywhere else.

But, mostly, his concern lay in the future. He had witnessed the Malwa dragon-weapons, and learned much from his observations. Now, for the first time, he would be able to examine Ye-tai war skills. And examine them from the most perfect vantage point imaginable: nearby, from a slightly elevated position, and—best of all—from the Ye-tai side of the line.

Their skills were—not bad, he decided. Not bad at all.

Strength: The Ye-tai were as fearless and aggressive as any general could ask for.

Weakness: The same. They were *too* aggressive. That was especially true of the younger men who stood in the second rank. In their eagerness to join the fray and prove their mettle, they tended to continually disrupt the maintenance of an orderly battle line.

Strength: There *was* a battle line. Very unusual for barbarian warriors.

Weakness: It was not a well-dressed line. Some of that, of course, was due to the conditions of the battle: a fight aboard a cramped ship, lit only by the flames of the burning galleys. Some of it was due to the disruptions produced by young fighters from the second rank pushing their way forward. But much of it, the general suspected, was inherent in the Ye-tai mentality. The Malwa gloss of semi-civilization was just that: a gloss, a thin veneer, over warriors whose basic nature was still utterly barbaric.

Strength: Their sword-play was excellent, although it was obvious to Belisarius that the sweeping, cutting style which the Ye-tai favored was more suited to cavalry tactics than combat afoot.

Weakness: Their shield work was indifferent. And here, knew the general, was another legacy of the Ye-tai military tradition. The barbarians were, first and foremost, horsemen.

Belisarius was delighted.

He had not had time, as yet, to think through all of the military implications of the new, strange Malwa weapons. But one fact was already blindingly obvious: as he had told his cataphracts, the infantry was about to make a great historical comeback. There would be a place for cavalry, of course—and a large one—but the core of future armies would be infantry.

And there were no infantry in the world as good as Roman infantry. There never had been. *Never. Not anywhere.* In the modern age, only the Hellenes had been able to give the Romans a real contest, infantry to infantry. And the historical verdict had been pronounced at places immortalized in history: Cynoscephalae, Magnesia, Pydna, Chaeronea. In the ancient world, only the Assyrians could even be considered as possible equals. The Assyrians had vanished long ago, of course, so it would never be known how they might have fared against Roman legions. But—Belisarius smiled, then, from an old memory. He and Sittas had once spent a pleasant afternoon speculating on the question. The theoretical discussion had degenerated into a drunken, intemperate quarrel. Sittas, vaingloriously, had argued that the Assyrian army would have been crushed within fifteen minutes. Belisarius—calm, cool, and professional (as always)—had felt they might have lasted a full hour. Maybe.

He shook off the memory, and the smile vanished.

There was no time, any longer, for dispassionate examination. The Ye-tai were the future foes of the Roman Empire, but they were the current allies of the handful of Romans on the ship. And those Roman allies were going down to defeat.

Not easy defeat, not quick defeat, but a defeat which was as sure as the sunrise. Even now, as he watched, the Ye-tai in the stern were finally overwhelmed. Screeching with triumph, the Arab pirates began swarming forward, rolling up the Ye-tai lines on either side of the ship.

Quickly, Belisarius assessed the situation at hand. The pirate assault at the bow had ceased. Utterly discouraged by their horrendous (and futile) casualties, the surviving Arabs had retreated back to their own vessel and had released their grappling hooks. About half the crew was still alive, but they were starting to row their craft toward the stern of the Indian vessel, hoping to find an easier way aboard.

Then, suddenly, the galley began wallowing in the waves. The pirates shrieked their fury and hastened to bring their craft back under control.

Ousanas had added another steersman to his list.

The cataphracts roared their own triumphant fury. The sarwen, more practical-minded, slew another couple of pirates with well-placed javelin casts. So did Eon. For his part, Ousanas waited until the pirates selected a new steersman. Three seconds later, the Arabs had to begin the process anew. It was soon obvious that volunteers were short.

Belisarius bellowed. Not words, just a thundering roar to catch the attention of his little cohort. It was difficult: the victorious cries of the Arabs and the despairing screams of the Ye-tai had produced a bedlam of sheer noise which engulfed the entire vessel.

When he had their attention, Belisarius simply pointed to the stern. No more was needed. In the cramped quarters of the deck, no subtle tactics were possible. Nor was there time to begin the counter-attack with a volley of arrows and javelins. The Ye-tai were on the verge of utter collapse. The barbarians had managed to patch together a semblance of a line amidships, just aft of the mainmast. But a wave of pirates was swarming over them.

There was neither place nor time, now, for any tactics but pure shock. Concentrated slaughter.

Belisarius led the way. Within a second or two, the other Romans and the Ethiopians were charging alongside him. The nine men formed a single line stretching across the entire width of the ship. The spacing was actually too close, but before Belisarius could order a change, Ousanas took the initiative. The dawazz grabbed

Eon by his kilt and jerked him back. A moment later, his sharp bark at Garmat caused the adviser to likewise fall back.

Eon protested bitterly. Ousanas slapped him atop the head—there was not a trace of humor in *that* blow—and criticized the prince savagely.

Even though Belisarius could basically understand Ge'ez, aided by the jewel, he was unable to grasp every word which Ousanas spoke. But there was no need. The general himself, in battles past, had spoken similar phrases to young soldiers. Although never with quite such vigor and profanity.

Fucking worthless toddler. Grow up. This no time for children in front line. Make self useful. Drooling infant. Spear somebody on other side. Cretin child. Instead of getting in way of veterans. Best cataphracts and sarwen *in world. Not need die tripping over prince learning to babble. Noble jackass. Royalty stupid by nature. Especially prince-type royalty. Stupid acceptable. Mindless not. Fucking idiot boy.*

And other words to that effect.

Within seconds, the little Roman/Axumite squad forced their way through the mob of Ye-tai warriors who were milling amidships. The discipline of the Indian forces had now completely collapsed. True, the advancing pirates were equally undisciplined. But the swarming Arabs were impelled by the elation of victory, while the Ye-tai were filled with the despair of looming defeat.

Belisarius had time, briefly, to glance at Venandakatra and his little crowd of priests and kshatriyas huddled around the mainmast. The Malwa—the kshatriyas, at least—retained a semblance of disciplined order. But it was a paralyzed kind of order; of no more use than the Ye-tai chaos.

A moment later, the front line of the Romans and Axumites burst through to the small open space between the fleeing Ye-tai and the advancing Arabs. They were now aft of the mainmast and its surrounding cabin, to Belisarius' relief. There was no way the enemy could get around them by clambering over the cabin. It was fight and die across a space of forty feet.

Seeing the sudden appearance of a disciplined and determined line before them, the pirates hesitated in their advance. The pause lasted long enough for Ousanas, Eon, and Garmat to force their own way through the milling Ye-tai and take their place just behind the line of cataphracts and sarwen.

From within the Arab crowd in the stern a man shoved his way to the fore. Unlike most of the pirates, he was equipped with a mail tunic and a helmet. His sword was long, slightly curved, and very finely made.

The man was middle-aged, but other than the grey in his beard there was not the slightest sign of any lack of vigor in his body. He was tall, well-built, and possessed both of an air of authority and a very loud voice. The air of authority steadied the pirates; the stentorian voice began to command them forward anew.

Began, but ceased suddenly. Ousanas had used up all his javelins. So the dawazz hurled his great stabbing spear.

It was the first time in his life that Belisarius had ever seen a man actually decapitated by a spear-cast. For a moment, he gaped with astonishment. The huge blade of the dawazz's spear simply lopped the pirate's head off and then continued on to sink into the chest of a pirate standing behind.

The Arabs froze at the sight, momentarily paralyzed. Belisarius bellowed. The cataphracts and sarwen lunged forward.

Now it was pure mayhem, sheer carnage. The Romans and Axumites hammered into the Arab crowd like a machine. The lightly armored pirates at the front went down like slaughtered lambs, their skulls crushed or split open, their chests or bellies skewered, their arms amputated. In falling, they hampered the pirates behind who, in turn, could put up little resistance to that ferocious charge.

It was not all one-sided, of course. Menander cried out and fell, clutching his side. A sword thrust coming from somewhere in the pirate mob had found its mark. One of the sarwen cried out also, staggering, his face covered with blood from a scalp wound. The wound was not fatal, for the Ethiopian had deflected the sword with his shield just before it landed. But, like all head wounds, it bled profusely.

Stubbornly, the sarwen began to return to the front line, but Ousanas pulled him back and gently took his spear. The man was almost helpless, blinded from the blood. Garmat steadied him with a hand. The old adviser stood guard over the wounded sarwen and Menander, as the battle pushed its way to the stern.

Ousanas took a place in the front line. A moment later, so did Eon. There was no dawazz, now, to restrain the pride of young royalty. Eon surged into the gap created by Menander's fall and began his eager spearwork with the two veterans, Valentinian and Anastasius, on either side.

Young and impetuous he may have been, even, perhaps, foolish in his enthusiasm. But he tripped neither of the cataphracts by his side, nor did he get in the way of their veteran slaughter. And if, once, Anastasius was forced to cover the prince's side because the youth had surged too far forward in his inexperience, the huge Thracian was not disgruntled. He had done the same before, many times, for other young warriors. Young warriors who, often enough, had been paralyzed with sudden fear—which the prince certainly was not. Eon slew the man before him, and Anastasius crushed the life from the other who would have stabbed the prince's unguarded side.

All in a day's work, all in a day's work. Training young warriors was part of the trade, and it was a trade which could be learned by no other method. So did Anastasius remind the dawazz, firmly, in the quiet hours after the battle, when Ousanas began to chide the idiot boy. And Valentinian actually managed to silence Ousanas completely—wonder of wonders—with a few short, curt, pungent phrases. Hot and angry phrases, in point of fact.

The cynical veteran Valentinian, as it happens, had developed a sudden enthusiasm for the Prince Eon. A very fierce enthusiasm, born of an ancient warrior tradition.

Not all the casualties of a battle are novices. Veterans die too, sometimes, brought down by the smallest chances. And on that night—that hellfire-lit, bedlam-shrieking, dragon-raging night—the crafty and cunning Valentinian had finally met his nemesis. From the smallest, chanciest thing.

The veteran killer, master and survivor of a hundred dusty battlefields, had found his death aboard wooden planks. He had not considered the nature of a blood-soaked ship's deck, so unlike the blood-soaked soil of land carnage. And so, striding forward to deliver another death-blow, as he had done times beyond remembering, his foot had skidded out from under him. Flat on his back Valentinian had fallen, his shield askew, his sword arm flailing, his entire body open and helpless. A pirate took the wonderful opportunity instantly and gleefully. To his dying day, Valentinian would never forget the sight of that sword tip readying to butcher his belly.

Except that the sword tip stopped, not more than an inch away, and withdrew. It took Valentinian a moment to realize that the cause of the bizarre retreat was Eon's spear, which had taken the pirate square in the chest. The veteran Valentinian was paralyzed himself, then, for a second or two. Not from fear so much as a strange wonder.

The pirate never lost his determination to slay the cataphract. His fierce black eyes never left those of Valentinian. And the rage in those eyes never died, until the man himself did. His sword continued to jab, his body continued to lunge forward. But the pirate was inexorably held at bay, by a spear in the hands of a boy. An idiot boy, perhaps, but a strong and fearless boy, most certainly.

So, in the quiet hours after the battle, when the boy's mentor began to criticize him for an idiot, Valentinian would have none of it. No, none at all. And it was noted, thereafter, by all who knew that deadly weasel of a man, that a small group of people had gained a new member.

The comrades-in-arms of Valentinian, that group was called, by him as well as others. Those few—those very, very, very few—privileged to share his cups, handle his blades, criticize his faults, and compliment his women.

Eon, Prince of Axum, was the only royal member of that club. Then, or ever. But the lad took no umbrage in the fact. Royal, the group was not; no, not even noble. But it was among the smallest clubs in the world. Perhaps its most exclusive. Certainly its most select.

All that, however, lay in the future. The Arabs had been pushed back into the very stern of the ship. As their numbers grew compressed, their ability to fight lessened. The press of the mob badly hampered those pirates who were still eager for combat.

But there were few such left. The ruthless assault of the Byzantines and Ethiopians had demoralized the great majority of the pirates—the more so, in that they had thought themselves on the verge of victory.

Most, now, thought of nothing but escape. As many as could clambered down the stern of the ship into the galley which was still lashed alongside. But the galley was soon so overloaded with refugees that its captain ordered the grappling lines severed.

Many pirates simply dove off the side of the ship. Some found refuge aboard the retreating galley which had been lashed to the stern.

More found refuge in the other surviving pirate craft, which had now found its way from the bow whence it had been repulsed earlier by those same horrible Romans and Axumites. Most drowned.

At the end, only a dozen or so Arabs remained aboard the ship. Gathered in a compact group at the very stern, these men began negotiating with Belisarius for terms of surrender. For his part, the general was willing. There had been enough slaughter.

But the negotiations were almost instantly moot. The Ye-tai had now regained their courage, and they surged in a horde toward the stern, shrieking their battle cries. Hearing them come, the Romans and Axumites stood aside at Belisarius' command, and let the Ye-tai conclude the battle.

The barbarians had not the slightest interest in negotiations. And so, the remaining Arabs died to a man.

But the slaughter was by no means one-sided. Whatever else they were, the pirates were not craven. Before they perished, they took some Ye-tai with them to oblivion.

Though his face remained expressionless throughout, Belisarius took great pleasure in the fact. His cataphracts and the sarwen, he thought, did likewise. About Eon and Garmat, there was no doubt at all, from their fierce scowls.

As for Ousanas' attitude—well, it was difficult to say. Watching the final act of the battle from the sidelines, the dawazz kept up a running commentary, alternating between philosophical observations on the just deserts of piracy and jocular remarks on the incompetence of barbarian swordsmen.

He spoke in pidgin Greek, not in Hindi, nor in the language of the barbarians themselves. But at least one Ye-tai warrior had his suspicions aroused—judging, at least, from the fierce manner in which he advanced on Ousanas, waving his sword most threateningly.

The truth would never be known, however. Ousanas seized the warrior's wrist and his throat, shook loose the sword, crushed the throat, and hurled the Ye-tai overboard. Other barbarians, observing the scene, chose thereafter to ignore his commentary. Which was perhaps just as well, since the ruminations of Ousanas thenceforth focused on the worthlessness of barbarians in general and Ye-tai in particular.

Quite exclusively, quite exhaustively, and loud enough to be heard by every fish in the Erythrean Sea.

Chapter 17

In the days following the battle with the pirates, as the Indian vessel made its slow way across the Erythrean Sea, much changed.

Not the sea itself, nor the wind. No, the southeast monsoon maintained its unwavering force, fierce and blustery. (Quite unlike, Garmat assured the Romans, the pleasant and balmy monsoon which would bear them westward some months hence.) And the sea seemed always the same, as did the dimly-seen coastline to their north. The coast of Persia, now, for they had crossed the Straits of Hormuz, leaving Arabia and its dangers behind.

The same, also, was Eon's daily grousing on the subject of land lubberly Indians; and his adviser's frequent comments on the contrasting habits of such true seafaring folk as Ethiopians and Arabs (and Greeks, of course) who eschewed the creeping coast and set forth boldly across the open ocean; and the inevitable remarks which followed from Ousanas, on the inseparable bond between seamanship and braggadocio.

But everything else changed.

The first change was in the attitude of Venandakatra toward his "guests." The Indian grandee lost not a trace of his hauteur, and his cold, serpentine arrogance. But he no longer ignored the foreigners. Oh no, not at all. Daily he came to visit, trailing a gaggle of priests, spending at least an hour at the bow in discourse with Belisarius, Eon, and Garmat. (The others he ignored; they were but common soldiers or, in the case of Ousanas, the most grotesque slave in creation.)

Daily, also, he invited Belisarius and Eon (and, grudgingly, Garmat) to dine with him in his cabin that evening. The invitation was invariably accepted. By Belisarius, eagerly; by Garmat, dutifully; by the prince, with the sullen discipline of a boy hauled by his ears.

The general's eagerness for these evening meals did not arise from any pleasure in Venandakatra's company. In person, in private, the Indian lord was even more loathsome than he was at a distance. Nor was Belisarius' enthusiasm occasioned by the meals themselves, though they were truly excellent repasts. Belisarius was not a gourmand, and he had always found that the most important seasoning for food was good company at the table. The meals served in Venandakatra's cabin were splendid, but they were seasoned with a spiritual sauce so foul it might have been the saliva of Satan himself.

Neither was the general's joy in these social encounters produced by any misreading of Venandakatra's motives. Belisarius knew full well that the sudden Malwa hospitality did not result from gratitude for the decisive role played by Belisarius and his men in the battle with the pirates.

No, the truth was quite the opposite, and Belisarius knew it as surely as he knew his own name. Venandakatra's new cordiality was the product of the battle, true. A product, however, which was born not of gratitude but fear.

Venandakatra had never witnessed Romans in combat, nor Axumites. Now he had, and knew them for his future enemy, and knew—with that bone-chilling certainty known only by those who have actually seen the mace-crushed skulls and the spear-sundered chests, and the guttering blood and severed limbs—that his enemy was terrible beyond all former comprehension. What had seemed, in the conspiring corridors of Malwa palaces and the scented chambers of Malwa emperors, to be a surety of the future, seemed so no longer. Rome would be conquered, and enslaved. But it would be no easy task, nor a simple one.

And so, Belisarius knew, Venandakatra made his daily visits, and his daily invitations to dinner. Just so does the cobra raise its head, and swell its hood, and flick its tongue, and sway its sinuous rhythm, the better to put its prey into a trance.

And just so, joyfully, does the mongoose enter the trap.

Crooked as a root was the mind of Belisarius. And now, finally, inside the gnarls and twists of his peculiar mind, a plot was sprouting and spreading.

The growing plot was as cunning as any stratagem the general had ever devised. (And he was a man who treasured cunning much as another might treasure gold, or another the beauty of concubines.) Of itself, however, the cleverness produced only satisfaction in the heart of Belisarius, not joy. No, the joy derived elsewhere. The joy—it might be better to say, the savage and piti-less glee—derived from the fact that the entire plot pivoted on the very soul of the man against whom it was aimed. The Vile One, Venandakatra was called. And it would be by his own vileness that Belisarius would bring him down.

So, every day, on the sunlit bow of the ship, Belisarius greeted Venandakatra with cordiality and respect. So, every evening, in the lantern-gloom of the cabin, Belisarius returned the grandee's slimy bonhomie with his own oily camaraderie, the lord's lecher-ous humor with his own salacious wit, and the flashes of Malwa depravity with glimpses of his own bestial corruption.

The shrewd old adviser Garmat, under other circumstances, would have reacted with still-faced, diplomatic, silent disgust. The impetuous and elephant-hearted young prince, with words of scorn and contempt. But the circumstances here had changed also, since the battle. And this change was no product of guile and duplicity.

Before the battle, true, Romans and Axumites had been on good terms.

Kaleb had made clear to Eon and Garmat, in private council after they returned to Axum in the company of Belisarius, the importance which the negusa nagast attached to forging an alli-ance with Rome. It was for that very reason that he had assented to their proposal to accompany the Byzantines to India, perilous though such a trip might be for his young son.

Belisarius, though he carried no such precise and definite impe-rial instructions, had his own reasons for seeking such a bond. Already, if only in outline, he was shaping the grand strategy of Rome's coming war with the Malwa Empire. The role of Axum in that conflict would be crucial.

His cataphracts and Eon's sarwen, experienced soldiers, had quickly detected the attitude of their superiors, and had shaped their own conduct accordingly. Menander, on his own, filled with the thoughtless certainties of youth, might have given vent to certain prejudices and animosities, but not with the two veterans watching him like a hawk.

So, during the many months prior to the battle with the pirates, in the company which they shared through the trip to Syria, and the sojourn at Daras, and the voyage to Egypt and then to Adulis, through the trek upcountry to the city of Axum, through the lengthy stay at Axum itself, through the return to Adulis and the embarkation aboard the Malwa vessel bearing its envoys back to India, the Romans and Axumites had maintained their good relations and the disciplined propriety of their conduct.

So they had. But—still, still, they were each foreign to the other, for all that the Ethiopians spoke good (if accented) Greek, and the Romans began to speak poor (and very accented) Ge'ez. To be sure, no words were ever uttered which might have given offense. (Save by Ousanas, of course. But since the dawazz insulted everybody equally, including tribes and nations no one else had even heard of, his outrageous behavior soon became accepted, much as one accepts the rain and the wind, and noxious insects.) But, through all the months of joint travel, and mutual good will, there had not been much in the way of open trust and confidence. And even less in the way of genuine intimacy.

Now, all that was changed. Since the battle, all former propriety and stiff good conduct had vanished. Vanished like it had never existed, especially among the common soldiers. In its place came insults and derision, mockery and ridicule, grousing and complaint—in short, all the mechanisms by which blooded veterans seal their comradeship.

The sarwen were no longer nameless. The one whose black skull had gained a new scalp scar in the battle was named Ezana. The other, Wahsi. The Romans now learned of a long-standing Ethiopian custom. The true name of a sarwen was never told to any but members of the sarawit, lest the warrior be subject to sorcery from his enemies. Upon receiving acceptance from his own sarwe into its ranks, an Axumite boy was given the name by which he would henceforth be known, in private, by his comrades.

Shortly after the battle with the pirates, in their own little ceremony held while the lords were carousing with Venandakatra, the two sarwen officially enrolled the three cataphracts into the ranks of the Dakuen, and spoke their true names.

The Roman soldiers thought the custom odd, in its particulars. But they did not sneer at it, for they found nothing odd in the general thrust of the thing. Valentinian and Anastasius carried about their persons various amulets and charms with which to ward off witchcraft. And Menander, through the long bouts of fever and delirium produced by his wound, never once relinquished his grip upon the little icon which he had been given the day he proudly rode off to answer the summons of his lord Belisarius. The village priest who gave him the icon had assured the young cataphract that it would shield him from evil and deviltry.

As it most surely did—for the youth recovered, did he not? And from a wound which, in the experience of his veteran companions, Roman and Ethiopian alike, almost invariably resulted in a lingering death from hideous disease. Truly, an excellent icon!

But, excellent icon or no, some of the credit for the young Thracian's recovery was surely due to the Ethiopians. To their strange and exotic poultices and potions, perhaps; to the comfort and companionship given him through the long, pain-wracked days and nights by the less seriously wounded Ezana, certainly.

In time, young Menander came to speak Ge'ez fluently, and more quickly than any of the other Romans. The lad's speech, moreover, was afflicted with almost none of the horrible accent which so disfigured the Ge'ez of all the other Romans. (Except Belisarius, of course, whose Ge'ez was soon indistinguishable from a native; but Belisarius was a witch.)

In his time, Menander would become the most popular of Roman officers, among the Axumite troops with which his own forces were so frequently allied. And, in a time far distant from the disease-infected agony of that wound, the cataphract would finally return to his beloved Thrace. No youth now, unknown to all but his own villagers, but an iron-haired warrior of renown. Who bore his fame casually, in the pleasant years of his retirement, and saved all his pride for his great brood of dark children, and his beloved Ethiopian wife.

Ezana, too, would survive the wars. From time to time, the sarwen would come to Thrace to visit his old comrade Menander, and the half-sister who had become Menander's wife. Ezana would bring no great entourage with him to Thrace, though he himself was now famous, and such a retinue was always offered to him by the negusa nagast; simply himself and his own collections of scars and memories.

In that future, Ezana would enjoy those visits, immensely. He would enjoy watching the sun set over the distant mountains of

Macedon, his cup in his hand; the company of Menander and his half-sister; their great brood of attentive offspring, and the even greater horde of scruffy village children for whom Menander's modest estate was a giant playground; and the memories.

Sad, memories, some. Wahsi would not survive the wars. He would die, in a sea battle off the coast of Persia, his body unrecovered. But he would die gloriously, and his name would remain—carved on a small monument in the African highlands; spoken in prayers in a quiet monastery in Thrace.

Always, in those visits of the future, the time would come when Menander and Ezana would remember that ship on the Erythrean Sea, and speak of it. At those times, the children would cease their play, grow silent, and gather around. This was their favorite tale, and they never tired of it; neither they, nor the old veterans who told it once again.

(Menander's wife tired of it, of course, and grumbled to the village matrons who were her friends. But the men ignored the grumbling with the indifference of long experience; wives were a disrespectful lot, as was known by all veterans.)

The children who listened to the tale loved all the parts of it. They loved the drama of the sea battle: the dragon-fire and the boarding, the cut-and-thrust at the bow, and—especially!—the charge to the stern led by the legendary Belisarius. Oh, marvelous charge!

And if the description of the fury at the stern bore certain small improvements to the uncouth truth of history, there was none to set them wrong. Ezana said nothing while Menander embroidered—just a bit—the tale of his great wound. (Here, as always, the children would demand to see the grotesque scar on his belly, and Menander would oblige.) The sword which caused that wound had become, through the transmutation of veteran tales, the blade of a mighty Arab warrior, who overcame, through his legendary cunning, the skill of a valiant young Roman foe. There was nothing in the tale, now, of the confusion of inexperience in the chaos of battle, and the sheer luck which had enabled a nameless and unknown pirate to stab, without even knowing his exact target, a brave but clumsy novice.

No, Ezana said nothing. Nor did Menander speak, when, in the course of the tale, Ezana came to show his own honorable scar. The sarwen would bend his head, here, that the eager children might gather and spread the mat of kinky grey hair, and shriek with delighted horror, as always. Menander said nothing of what he might, now, from the experience of the many battles which had come after. He said nothing to the children of the panic which he knew had filled Ezana's heart at that moment, blood-blinded in the midst of murder.

No, Menander held his tongue. There was no purpose in anti-quarian pettifoggery. Perhaps the children would never need to know such things. Menander and Ezana had done all they could, in their bloody lives, to ensure that they wouldn't. And if, in the course of time, some of the children learned these ancient lessons for themselves, well—best they came to the lesson filled with the innocent and simple courage imparted by veterans' tales.

But, for all their infantile blood-lust, the children's favorite part of the tale was always the aftermath. The story of those wondrous days when the seeds of that Roman-Axumite alliance, which the children accepted as the nature of their world, first bore fruit. The days when a comradeship was forged, a com-radeship which had long since entered the legends of Thrace and Ethiopia (and Constantinople and Rome, and Arabia; and India, come to it).

Above all, the children loved the tale when it finally told of the night when great Belisarius first spoke to that company of heroes of his purpose, and his mission, and his quest; and bound them to it, with oaths of iron. Of the rise of Satan, and the warning of a monk; of a captured princess, and a hero to be found, and a dagger delivered.

And the Talisman of God.

They would tell the tale, anew, would Menander and Ezana. And tell it well, each augmenting what the other forgot or mis-remembered. But, even in that practiced telling, the minds of the two veterans would drift and wander, back to the time itself.

They would tell the children, and hold back nothing. (For there were no secrets, now, to be kept from Satan and his hosts. The hosts were gone. And, though Satan was not, the monster was paralyzed for a time, chained in the Pit and gnashing at his own terrible wounds.) No, they would hold back nothing, but the chil-dren would never truly understand the tale. The children would understand only the grand adventure, and the glory of Belisarius, and the faithful heroism of his companions.

They would never understand the heart of that moment, that night when Belisarius bound his brotherhood.

The sheer, pure, unadulterated wonder of it.

Another change had taken place, the day after the battle. At Belisarius' request—*firm* request, but there had been no need for belligerence—Venandakatra had agreed to provide his guests with quarters in the hold below. Heretofore, the Romans and Axumites had been forced to make their quarters on the deck, sheltered only by their own tents.

In truth, neither the Romans nor the Ethiopians had minded the previous accommodations. Except for Belisarius, in fact, none of them had given the matter any thought at all. Sleeping on deck was the normal procedure, in those times, when traveling by ship. Few vessels were of a size to provide enclosed sleeping quarters for any but the captain. Decent quarters, at any rate. Common sailors often slept in the hold, under conditions which were so cramped and noisome that passengers would have recoiled in horror.

For all its size, the Indian craft was not much different. In his cabin amidships, and the smaller cabins which adjoined it, Venandakatra and his priests enjoyed comfortable surroundings. Luxurious ones, in the case of Venandakatra. The officers of the ship, and the commanders of the Malwa and Ye-tai troops, also possessed small cabins of their own, located in the stern. As for the rest—the soldiers enjoyed the comparative comfort of the deck, accepting the elements as the price for relative spaciousness and fresh air; the common sailors festered in the hold.

But there were a few quarters available for Belisarius' company. A storage cabin was found, in the bow, whose contents could be removed. Foodstuffs, in the main: amphorae filled with the grain and oil out of which the common fare of the soldiers was prepared. Some of the amphorae were stowed elsewhere, including all of the oil. Many of the amphorae filled with grain were simply pitched overboard. The amphorae were crude and cheap, and the extra grain was no longer needed due to the heavy casualties suffered by the Ye-tai in the battle.

Belisarius' companions had not been filled with joy, actually, upon learning of the new arrangement. The storage cabin was filthy until they cleaned it, and rat-infested until the weapons of cataphract and sarwen were put to inglorious use.

True, they were now sheltered from the wind and the rain and the sea-spray. They were also sheltered from clean air and sunlight, and crowded as badly as if they were in a dungeon. And if the seeping planks of the gloomy cabin were any less damp than the deck above, it was not noticeable to its disgruntled inhabitants.

But the general's companions made no objection, after they gave the matter a bit of thought. For the storage cabin in the bow had one outstanding feature, which they knew was Belisarius' purpose in obtaining it. Privacy.

Belisarius had needed that privacy, two nights after the battle, when his small company had settled into their new quarters. He had things to tell, and a thing to show, which no Malwa must hear or see.

For that purpose, the storage cabin served to perfection. Much better, in fact, than would one of the comfortable cabins amidships. The storage cabin was isolated, far distant from any Indian sleeping (or feigning sleep), and easily guarded from spies and eavesdroppers.

It was in those noisome surroundings, thus, that Belisarius imparted his great secret to his companions. He did so with neither reluctance nor hesitation. Nor, now, simply from a sense of obligation, or a need to forestall rumors of sorcery and demonism.

Those reasons remained, of course. But his overriding purpose in telling his companions his secret was that he now had a plan—or, at least, the beginnings of one. It was a plan which would require their combined efforts to succeed and would, moreover, require several members of his company to do things which would seem utterly bizarre unless they understood the reasons which underlay them. And for that, they needed to know the secret. Not so much for its own sake, but for the sake of his stratagem.

In some strange manner, in the very fury of the battle, the framework of his plot had come to him. Had sprung into his mind, actually, in midstroke of his sword.

Later, so magical had that moment been, that he had suspected the jewel was its cause. In the quiet hours which followed, he had probed the barrier relentlessly. But the jewel had reacted not at all. It was exhausted again, he realized, and with the realization came an understanding of just how feverishly the jewel had worked to augment his senses during the battle.

It was that augmentation, he thought, which had produced the sudden image of his stratagem. The plan was his, not the jewel's.

The jewel was responsible for it only in the sense that its efforts had enabled his mind to work in such a wondrous manner. He understood, too, that the human subtleties and nuances which were the essence of his stratagem were utterly beyond the capabilities of the jewel. For now, certainly; perhaps always.

And so it was, in the gloom and stench of a taper-lit storage cabin, that Belisarius introduced his comrades to glory and wonder and terror.

He told the tale first, all of it, from its very beginning in a cave in Syria. He stressed that the jewel had originated with Michael of Macedonia, and had been brought to the general with the blessings of that monk and the bishop Anthony Cassian. For his cataphracts, he knew, those names would bring great assurance. And he thought the Ethiopians would take comfort in them also. True, none of the Ethiopians had probably ever heard of Michael of Macedonia or Anthony Cassian. Still, they were Christian folk, even if they were heretics. (Monophysites, essentially, though not without their own stiff variations on that creed.)

As it turned out, Garmat was quite familiar with both Michael and Anthony—by reputation, if not by personal acquaintance. Belisarius suspended his tale for a moment, upon that discovery, allowing Garmat to inform the other Ethiopians of the nature of those persons. Eon and the sarwen seemed suitably impressed.

Thereafter, Belisarius spoke without interruption until his tale reached the present moment. He withheld nothing, save the subtleties of his standing with the Emperor. He saw no need to involve his companions in that delicate matter. It was enough to speak of his meeting with the Empress Theodora (that part of the meeting, at least, which dealt with India), and to remind them of the Emperor's official blessing for his mission. He suspected that Garmat understood quite a bit more of the maneuverings of the Byzantine court, but the adviser said nothing.

No one did, after Belisarius finished. The crowded cabin was utterly still.

Oddly enough, it was Menander who finally broke the silence. The young cataphract was very weak, but quite alert. The fever and delirium which all the veterans knew would soon be produced by his abdominal wound had not yet made their appearance.

"May I see it?" whispered Menander. There was nothing in his voice of the young warrior, just the awe of a village lad.

"You may all see it," replied Belisarius. The general reached into his tunic and withdrew the pouch. He spilled the jewel into his palm and held it out. All save Menander leaned forward to see. A moment later, the young Thracian's shoulders were gently held up by Ezana, so that he too might observe the miraculous sight.

Miraculous, indeed. Weary, **aim** might have been. But it understood the importance of the moment and drew the facets to itself.

The jewel did not blaze, here, as it had once in Belisarius' villa in Antioch. There was no energy for such a solar display. But there were none in the cabin, gazing upon that shifting and flashing wonder, those cool, translucent combinations of every hue known to man and many never seen before, who doubted for one moment that they were witness to a miracle.

Eventually, Garmat spoke.

"It is not enough," he whispered. Belisarius cocked his eyebrow.

The adviser shook his head. Not in an unfriendly manner, no, but in a manner which bespoke no deference either.

"I am sorry, Belisarius. I do not distrust you, or what you say, and the jewel is certainly as awesome as you described, but—"

Garmat made a gesture which encompassed the ship and everything in the world beyond it.

"What you say involves not us alone, but those to whom we are responsible."

"You want to touch the jewel yourself," said Belisarius gently.

Garmat shook his head, smiling.

"Certainly not! At my age, terrible visions are the last thing I need. I've seen enough of those already."

Belisarius shifted his gaze—and, subtly, his hand—to the Prince. "Eon, then."

The prince stared at the jewel, his brow furrowed with thought. Thought only, however, not fear—so much was obvious to all who watched. Belisarius was not the only one present, then, who saw the adult majesty of the future in that dark young face.

"No," said Eon, finally. "I do not trust myself yet." He turned to Ousanas. "Take it."

"Why me?"

"You are my dawazz. I trust you more than any man living. Take it."

Ousanas stared at his charge. Then, without moving his eyes, extended his hand to Belisarius. The general placed the jewel on his palm.

A moment later, the dawazz closed his hand; and left the world, for a time.

When he returned, and opened his eyes, he seemed completely unchanged. The others present were a bit surprised. Belisarius was astonished.

When the dawazz spoke, however, the general thought he detected a slight tremor in his rich baritone.

His first words were to his Prince.

"Always dawazz wonders. And fears."

He took a deep breath, and briefly looked away. "No longer. You were great prince. King, at the end."

The dawazz fumbled for words.

"Oh, stop speaking pidgin!" snapped Eon.

Ousanas cast him an exasperated look.

"It was your silly idea in the first place." The dawazz glanced at Garmat, unkindly. "And you backed him up."

Garmat shrugged. Ousanas grinned at the Romans. (That much, at least, had not changed. Not the grin.)

"You must forgive my companions," said the dawazz. His Greek was now perfect, mellifluous, and completely unaccented. Belisarius managed not to gape. His cataphracts failed.

"The boy has the excuse, at least, of tender years. His adviser, only the excuse of doddering old age. And, of course, the fact that he is half-Arab. A folk who would rather scheme than eat."

Again, the unkind glance. But the glance fell away, softening. "Always an Arab, and a full one, at the end. After Kaleb died, Garmat, you returned to Arabia. You died well there, in the Nejed, leading your beloved bedouin against the Malwa."

He shrugged. "You lost, of course. Not even the bedouin in their desert could withstand the Indian juggernaut. Not after the Malwa brought the Lakhmites under their rule, and broke the Beni Ghassan, and dispersed the Quraysh from Mecca."

"You saw the future, then," stated Garmat.

"Oh, yes. Yes, indeed. And it was just as terrible as foretold." Ousanas' eyes grew vacant. "I saw the future until the moment of my own death. I died somewhat ignominiously, I regret to say, from disease brought on by a wound. No glorious wound won in single combat with a champion, alas. Just one of those random missiles which are such a curse to bards and storytellers."

He glanced at Menander and veered away from the subject of wound-produced diseases. Instead, he smiled at the prince.

"Your end, I do not know, Eon. I died in your arms, in the course of the trek which the surviving Ethiopians undertook under your leadership. South, to my homeland between the lakes, where you hoped to found a new realm which might still resist the Malwa. Although you had no great hope in success."

He fell silent.

"You speak perfect Greek," complained Valentinian.

Ousanas grimaced. "I suspect, my dear Valentinian, that I speak it considerably better than you do. With all respect, I am the best linguist that I know. It comes from being raised in the heart of Africa, I suspect, among savages. In the land between the great lakes, there are at least eighteen languages spoken. I knew seven of them by the time I was twelve, and learned most of the rest soon thereafter."

The grin lit up the cabin. "At the age, that is, when the urge to seduction comes to vigorous lads. My own tribe, sad to say, was much opposed to fornication outside proper channels. Other tribes enjoyed more rational customs, but alas, spoke other tongues. So I became adept at learning languages, a habit I have found it useful to maintain."

He pointed at the prince, his finger like a spear.

"This budding conspirator, this still-sprouting-intriguer, this not-yet-genius-spymaster, thought it would be most clever if, in our travels through the Roman Empire, I pretended to be a pidgin-babbling ignoramus from the bush. Unsuspecting Romans, he thought, might unthinkingly utter deep secrets in the presence of a thick-tongued slave."

The finger transferred its aim to Garmat.

"This one, this grey-bearded-not-yet-wise-man, this decrepit-old-broken-down-so-called-adviser, thought the plan might have some merit. So, there I was, trapped between the Scylla of naïveté and the Charybdis of senility."

He raised his eyes to the heavens.

"Pity me, Romans. There I was, for months, as cultured a heathen as ever departed the savanna, forced to channel my fluid thoughts through the medium of pidgin and trade argot. Ah, woe! Woe, I say! Woe!"

"You seem to have survived the experience," chuckled Valentinian.

"He is very good at surviving experiences," interjected Wahsi. "That is why we made him dawazz."

The sarwen exchanged a knowing, humorous look.

"Ousanas likes to think it was because of his skills and abilities," added Ezana. A derisive bark. "What nonsense! He is lucky. That is his only talent. But—a prince needs to learn luck, more than anything, and so we made the savage his dawazz."

Ousanas began some retort, but Belisarius interrupted.

"Later, if you please. For now, there are other things more important to discuss."

He turned to Garmat. "Are you satisfied?"

The adviser glanced at his prince. Eon nodded, very firmly. Garmat still hesitated, for just a second, before he nodded his head as well.

"Good," said Belisarius. "Now—I have a plan."

After Belisarius finished, Eon spoke at once.

"I won't do it! It's beneath—"

A sharp slap atop his head by Ousanas.

"Silence! Is good plan! Good for prince, too. Learn to think like worm instead of lion. Worms eat lions, fool boy, not other way around."

"I told you to stop speaking pidgin!" snarled Eon.

Another slap.

"Not speaking pidgin. Speaking baby talk. All stupid prince can understand."

Garmat added his own weight to the argument.

"Your dawazz is right, Prince." The adviser made a soothing gesture. "Not the worm business, of course. Disrespectful brute! But he's right about the plan. It *is* good, in the main, especially insofar as your own part is concerned."

He cast a questioning eye at Belisarius.

"Some of the rest, General, I confess I find perhaps excessively complex."

" 'Perhaps excessively complex,' " mimicked Valentinian harshly. The cataphract leaned forward.

"General, in the absence of Maurice, I have to take his place. As best I can. The first law of battles—"

Belisarius waved the objection aside, chuckling.

"I know it by heart! This is not a battle, Valentinian. This is intrigue."

"Still, General," interrupted Anastasius, "you're depending too much on happenstance. I don't care if we're talking battles or intrigue—or plotting how to cuckold the quartermaster, for that matter—you still can't rely that much on luck." Unlike Valentinian's voice, whose tenor had been sharp with agitation, Anastasius' basso was calm and serene. His words carried much the greater weight, because of it.

Belisarius hesitated, marshaling his arguments. This was no place for simple authority, he knew. The cataphracts and the Ethiopians needed to be *convinced*, not commanded.

Before he could speak, Ousanas interrupted.

"I disagree with Anastasius and Valentinian. And Garmat. They are mistaking complexity for intricacy. The plan is complex, true, in the sense that it involves many interacting vectors."

Belisarius restrained a laugh, seeing the gapes of his Thracian soldiers and the glum resignation on the faces of Ethiopian sarwen. Ousanas gestured enthusiastically.

"But that is not the same thing as luck! Oh, no, not at all. Luck is my specialty, it is true, just as the sarwen said. But the simple-minded warrior"—a dismissive wave—"does not understand luck, and that is why he thinks I am lucky. I am not. I am fortunate, because I understand the way of good fortune."

The dawazz leaned forward.

"The secret of which I will now tell you. One cannot predict the intricate workings of luck, but one can grasp the vectors of good fortune. All you must do is find the simple thing which is at the heart of the problem and seize it. Hold that—hold it with a grip of iron, and keep it always in your mind—and you will find your way through the vectors."

"Fancy talk," sneered Valentinian. "But tell me this, O wise one—what's the simple thing about the general's plan?" He snorted. "Name *any* simple thing about his plan!"

Ousanas returned the sarcasm with a level gaze.

"The simple thing at the heart of the general's plan, Valentinian, is the soul of Venandakatra. The entire plan revolves around that one thing. Which is perhaps the simplest thing in the world."

"No man's soul is simple," countered Valentinian, feebly.

"Not yours, perhaps," replied the dawazz. "But the soul of Venandakatra? You think that thing is complex?" Ousanas barked. In that single laugh was contained a universe of contempt. "If you wish complexity, Valentinian, examine a pile of dog shit. Do not look for it in the soul of Venandakatra."

"He's got a point," rumbled Anastasius. The huge cataphract sighed. "A rather good one, actually." Another sigh, like the resignation of Atlas to his labors. "Irrefutable, in fact."

Valentinian glowered. "Maybe!" he snapped. "But still—what of the rest of it? The prince's part in the plot is simple enough, I'll admit." A skeptical glance at Eon. "If—begging your pardon, Prince—the young royal can stomach it." Now he pointed to Ousanas. "But what of his part in the plan? Do you call that simple?"

Ousanas grinned. "In what way is it not? I am required to do two things only. Not more than two! I assure you, cataphract, even savages from the savanna can count as high as two."

Menander interrupted, in a whisper.

"Those are two pretty complicated things, Ousanas."

"Nonsense! First, I must learn a new language. A trick I learned as a boy. Then, I must hunt. A trick I learned even earlier."

"You're not going to be hunting an eland in the savanna, dawazz," said Eon uncertainly.

"That's right," chimed in Valentinian. "You're going to be hunting a man in a forest. A man you don't know, in a forest you've never seen, in a land you've never visited."

Ousanas shrugged. "What of it? Hunting is simple, my dear Valentinian. When I was a boy, growing up in the savanna, I did not think so. I was much impressed with the speed of the impala, and the cunning of the buffalo, and the ferocity of the hyena. So I wasted many years studying the ways of these beasts, mastering their intricate habits."

He wiped his brow. "So exhausting, it was. By the time I was thirteen, I thought myself the world's greatest hunter. Until a wise old man of the village told me that the world's greatest hunters were tiny little people in a distant jungle. They were called pygmies, he said, and they hunted the greatest of all prey. The elephant."

"Elephants?" exclaimed Anastasius. He frowned. "Just exactly how tiny are these—these pygmies?"

"Oh, very tiny!" Ousanas gestured with his hand. "Not more than so. I know it is true. As soon as I heard the wise man's words, I rushed off to the jungle to witness this wonder for myself. Indeed, it was just as the village elder had said. The littlest folk in the world, who thought nothing of slaying the earth's most fearsome creatures."

"How did they do it?" asked Menander, with youthful avidness. "With spears?"

Ousanas shrugged. "Only at the end. They trapped the elephants in pits, first. I said they were tiny, Menander. I did not say they were stupid. But, mainly, they trapped the elephants with wisdom. For these little folk, you see, did not waste their time as I had done, studying the intricate ways of their prey. They simply grasped the soul of the elephant, and set their traps accordingly. The elephant's soul is fearless, and so they dug their pits in the very middle of the largest trails, where no other beast would think to tread."

He stared at his prince. "Just so will I trap my prey. It is not complicated. No, it will be the simplest thing imaginable. For the soul of my prey is, in its way, as uncomplicated as that of Venandakatra. And I will not even have to grasp that soul, for it has been in my hand for years already. I have stared into the very eyes of that soul, from a distance of inches."

He stretched out his left arm. There, wandering across the ridged muscles and tendons, was a long and ragged scar. It was impossible to miss the white mark against his black flesh, though the color had faded a bit over the years.

"Here is the mark of the panther's soul, my friends. I know it as well as my own."

Valentinian heaved a sigh. "Oh, hell. I tried."

It was a signal, Belisarius knew. Quickly scanning the other faces in the cabin, he saw that they had joined in Valentinian's acceptance.

Valentinian was even grinning, now. The cataphract looked at Ezana and Wahsi.

"Remember what Anastasius and I told you?" he demanded. "You didn't believe us after the battle with the pirates!"

Wahsi snorted. "*This* is what you meant by your general's famous 'oblique approach'?"

Ezana laughed. "Like saying a snake walks funny!" He reached up and touched the bandage on his head. "Still," he added cheerfully, "it's better than charging across an open deck."

Belisarius smiled and leaned back against the wall of their cabin.

"I think that's all we need discuss, for the moment," he said. "We'll have time to hone the plan, in the weeks ahead."

Ousanas frowned. "All we need to discuss? Nonsense, General!" A quick dismissing gesture. "Oh, as to the plan—certainly! Good plans are like good meat, best cooked rare. Now we can move on to discuss truly important things."

His great grin erupted.

"Philosophy!" He rubbed his hands. "Such a joy to be surrounded by Greeks, now that I can speak the language of philosophy without that horrid pidgin nonsense getting in the way. I shall begin with Plotinus. It is my contention that his application of the principle of prior simplicity to the nature of the divine intellect is, from the standpoint of logic, false; and from the standpoint of theology, impious. I speak, here, of his views as presented by Porphyry in Book V of the *Enneads*. What is your opinion?"

Another dismissive gesture. "I ask this question of the Greeks present, of course. I know the views of the Ethiopians. They think I am a raving madman."

"You are a raving madman," said Wahsi.

"A gibbering lunatic," added Ezana.

"I'm not Greek," growled Valentinian.

"I've never heard such drivel in my life," rumbled Anastasius. "Absolute rubbish. The principle of prior simplicity is accepted by all the great philosophers, Plato and Aristotle alike, whatever their other disputes. Plotinus simply applied the concept to the nature of divinity."

Anastasius' enormous shoulders rolled his head forward. The granite slabs, tors, and crevices which made up his face quivered with ecstasy.

"The logic of his position is unassailable," continued the basso profundo, sounding, to all in the room save Ousanas, like the voice of doom itself. "I admit, the theological implications are staggering, at first glance. But I remind you, Ousanas, that the great Augustine himself held Plotinus in the highest regard, and—"

"Oh, sweet Jesus," whispered Menander, falling back weakly. "He hasn't done this since the first day I showed up, the new boy, and he trapped me in the barracks." A hideous moan. "For hours. *Hours.*"

Eon and the sarwen were gaping at Anastasius, much as they might have gaped at a buffalo suddenly transformed into a unicorn.

Garmat raised his eyes to the heavens.

"It is an indisputable virtue of my mother's people," he muttered, "that they are poets rather than philosophers. Whatever other crimes they have committed, no Arab has ever bored a man to death."

Valentinian glared at Belisarius. "It's your fault," hissed the weasel.

Belisarius shrugged. "I forgot. And how was I to know he'd find a kindred spirit? On this expedition?"

"It's *still* your fault," came the unforgiving voice. "You *knew* what he was like. You *knew* his father was Greek. *You* picked the troops. *You're* the general. *You're* in command. *Command takes responsibility!*"

"Ridiculous!" exclaimed Ousanas. "How can you say such—"

"—*still,*" overrode Anastasius, "I fail to see how you can deny that Plato's Forms must also derive from prior elements—"

"And now you insult Plato!"

"How far is it to India?" whispered Menander.

"Weeks, the way these wretched Malwa sail," groused Eon. And here the prince launched into his own technical diatribe, which, though it was just as long-winded as the debate raging elsewhere in the cabin, had at least the virtue of being more-or-less comprehensible, even to landlubbers like Belisarius.

Chapter 18
BHARAKUCCHA
Summer, 529 AD

Bharakuccha was the great western port of the Malwa Empire, located at the mouth of the Narmada River where it emptied into the Gulf of Khambhat. From its harbor, trading vessels of all sizes came and went daily.

Some, like the embassy vessel upon which the general and his company arrived on a blistering hot day in August, came from the northwest and returned thither. Many of those vessels were tiny craft not much more than dugout canoes, which bore petty trade goods to the coastal villages of Gujarat, the Rann of Kutch, and Sind. Others were Indian craft as huge as the embassy ship, which crept their ponderous way along the coast bearing immense cargoes for Persia and Europe. Many more were Persian ships, smaller and swifter than the Indian craft, which competed in the same trade. A few—not many—were Greek and Axumite.

The Greek and Axumite ships, in the main, avoided the northwest coast and sailed directly east and west across the Erythrean Sea. The western terminus of their trade was the Red Sea.

Still other craft came and went from the south. Most of these carried trade to and from the coast of Kerala and the great island of Ceylon. But there were ships whose trade was still more distant. Some of these vessels rounded the tip of India and carried their commerce to the great subcontinent's eastern coast. Others were destined for truly exotic lands—the southeast Asian kingdoms of Champa and Funan, and even Cathay.

Bharakuccha was like no city Belisarius had ever seen.

It was not completely outlandish, of course. The city had a generic resemblance to other such places which the general had visited. Like all great ports, Bharakuccha was a city of contrasts and extremes. Immense palaces and mansions, the abodes of nobility and rich merchants, rose like islands out of a vast sea of slums. Huge emporia and tiny merchant stalls—simple carts, often enough—nestled cheek and jowl. Trade and commerce was the city's lifeblood, and its bustling streets, crowded shops and clamorous bazaars—bustling, crowded and clamorous at any time of the day or night—gave proof that Bharakuccha took its business seriously.

But it was the scale of the phenomenon which astonished the visitors from Rome. The sheer size of the city, the incredible mass of its population, and the frenzy of its activity.

"Mother of God," mumbled Anastasius, "this place makes Alexandria look like a sleepy fishing village."

"They say you can buy anything in Bharakuccha," commented Ezana.

"Every port makes that boast," scoffed Valentinian.

"The difference, my friend, is that here it is true."

The ship was now moored to its dock, and Belisarius watched as Venandakatra and his cluster of priests scurried ashore. They were met by an imposing reception of notables. After a brief ceremony, Venandakatra clambered into a palanquin and was carried off.

Eon heaved a sigh of relief.

"Thank God, we're rid of him."

"For a while, Prince, only for a while," responded Garmat. The adviser stroked his beard, calculating.

"What do you think, General? A week?"

Belisarius laughed. "Are you mad? That pompous prick is going to need at least two weeks to put together the kind of expedition he's talking about. Probably three. Maybe even an entire month."

The general shook his head. "You'd think he was planning to conquer the world instead of making a simple trip back to report to the Malwa emperor. With a quick stop at his own—what did he call it, Eon?"

"Modest country residence."

"Along the way. Modest country residence. I can't wait to see it. Probably bigger than the Great Palace in Constantinople." The general turned away from the rail. "But that's good for us. We'll have time to get our own arrangements underway. Venandakatra, I'm sure, won't be bothering to keep track of us himself, so we won't have to put up with the pleasure of his company until his expedition is ready to set out."

He cast a stern look upon his companions. "But that doesn't mean we won't have spies watching us at all times. He's a pig, but he's not stupid. Remember that! Everything you do, while we're here in Bharakuccha, has to be done with the assumption that your actions will be reported to the Malwa. Everything." He gestured toward the teeming city. "In that maelstrom, there'll be no way to make sure someone isn't spying on you."

Valentinian grinned. "Not a problem, General. You've provided us with the most brilliant cover imaginable. Not even a cover, actually. Just the sort of things we'd be doing naturally. Drinking, eating, carousing. The occasional fuck now and then. That sort of thing."

"Catch every disease known to man," remarked Ousanas idly. But Valentinian's grin never wavered.

Belisarius began to smile, turned it into a not particularly convincing frown. "Just remember, Valentinian, you're not here on a pleasure trip. Drink, eat and carouse all you want. Just make sure you find Kushans to do it with. That includes fornication. I catch you humping any whore who isn't Kushan, there'll be hell to pay."

"A pity, that," mused Anastasius. "Variety's always appealed to me. It's my philosophical tendencies, I think." A wave of scowls appeared on all faces around him, except Ousanas. "But—so be it."

He clapped his hand on Valentinian's shoulder. "We shall not fail you, General. In a land of multitudinous—infinite!—possibilities, we shall be as selective as the Stoics of old."

"Get your fucking hand off me," snarled Valentinian.

"Nothing shall we touch save the very Platonic Forms of Kushan drink and Kushan women."

"I'll cut it off, I swear I will."

✧   ✧   ✧

Within a few hours, Belisarius found appropriate lodgings for his party. The Emperor Justinian had been miserly as always in the monies which he had provided for Belisarius' mission. Fortunately, however, Garmat had been amply funded by King Kaleb.

Fortunately indeed, for the lodgings which Belisarius selected were truly regal, and regally expensive. As agreed upon, Garmat obtained an entire suite in one of the most expensive hostels in Bharakuccha. He paid for it with Axumite gold coin. Belisarius and Garmat had already discovered that Axumite coinage was one of the three foreign currencies accepted in India. Byzantine coinage was the most prestigious, of course, but Axumite gold and silver were accepted as readily as Persian currency.

Belisarius paid for the two extra rooms. The extra rooms were comparatively modest—by the standards, at least, of that hostel. One of the extra rooms was for himself and his cataphracts. The other was for Garmat, Ousanas, and the sarwen.

The suite—the gigantic, opulent, lavishly furnished suite—was for Eon alone. Eon Bisi Dakuen, Prince of Axum (and all the other royal cognomens which Garmat had appended, to which the boy was not entitled—but who was to know otherwise in Bharakuccha?), could settle for nothing less. Some other prince, perhaps, but not this one. Not this pampered, spoiled, arrogant, whining, complaining, grousing, thoroughly obnoxious young royal snot.

As soon as they entered the hostel, Eon began his litany of complaints. This was not right, that was not right, the other was all wrong, etc., etc., etc. By now, thought Belisarius with amusement, the boy had the routine down pat. Within three minutes, the proprietor of the hostel was stiff-faced with injured dignity. Were it not for the sizable profit he stood to make from the Ethiopians, Belisarius had little doubt that the proprietor would have pitched Eon out on his ear. (Figuratively, of course; a literal pitching would be difficult, what with the spears of the sarwen.)

The relief on the proprietor's face when Garmat finally cajoled the prince into settling down was obvious, for all the man's practiced diplomacy. Venandakatra had been equally relieved to finally part company with Eon, and had not been particularly loath to show it.

All in all, thought Belisarius, Eon was doing splendidly.

As the Ethiopian party were led to their rooms, Belisarius and his three cataphracts were guided to their own quarters. Once inside the room, Anastasius helped Menander lay down on a couch. The young cataphract had finally overcome the diseases produced by his wound, but he was still very weak.

"Eon's going to bitch at us again tonight," commented Anastasius. He glanced at the general. "Quite a task you assigned him, sir. Poor lad."

"Poor lad, my ass," snapped Valentinian. He perched on the couch next to Menander. "I'd trade places with him in a minute."

"Me, too," whispered Menander. "It'd kill me, for sure, but what a way to go."

Belisarius smiled. "I didn't realize you prized Venandakatra's company so much, Valentinian."

The cataphract sneered. "Not that! That part of the job the prince is welcome to. It's the part coming *now* that I'd treasure."

"Not everyone approaches these things like a weasel, Valentinian," said Anastasius mildly.

"Crap! He's a *prince*, for the sake of Christ. Probably got his first concubine when he was twelve."

"Thirteen," said Belisarius. "Her name is Zaia. She's still with him, by the way, and he's very fond of her."

Belisarius took a seat himself. He grimaced, remembering the night in Venandakatra's cabin when Eon—as instructed beforehand by Belisarius, coached by Garmat, and slapped atop the head innumerable times by Ousanas—had finally broached the subject of his insatiable sexual appetites. The prince had performed perfectly in the hours which followed, swapping tales with the Vile One. For all their boastfulness, none of Eon's tales came close to Venandakatra's in sheer debauchery, but the lad did quite well. His long and lascivious description of his first concubine had been particularly well done.

Afterward, in their own cabin, the boy had refused to speak to anyone for a full day. To Belisarius, not for three days.

Perfect. Now that they were ashore, of course, the boy would have to live up to his boasts. There had been no women aboard the ship, and Eon had hastily declined Venandakatra's offer of a cabin boy. His tastes, he had explained, were exclusively oriented to the female sex.

"Poor lad, my ass," muttered Valentinian again. He eyed Anastasius coldly. "And you have some nerve, lecturing *me* about weasels."

Anastasius grinned. "I'm not a young prince, full of righteousness and royal propriety." He stretched his arms and yawned. "I'm just a simple farm boy, at heart, with fond memories of haystacks. And such." He returned Valentinian's cold stare.

"Furthermore, I don't see what *you're* complaining about. Nobody said we have to remain abstinent. Quite the contrary, in fact."

He raised his huge hand, forestalling Belisarius. "Yes, sir. Yes, sir. Kushans only. Not a problem, I assure you."

"What do Kushans look like?" asked Menander. The young man's expression bore equal parts of curiosity and frustration.

"Oh, you won't be missing a thing, Menander!" exclaimed Anastasius. "Horrid folk, Kushans. Ugliest people in the world, especially the women."

Valentinian shuddered. "I shudder to think of it." He shuddered again. "See?"

"I *hate* mustaches on a woman," grumbled Anastasius.

"I can live with the mustaches," retorted Valentinian. "It's those damned beards that bother me."

"And the knobby fingers."

"The scrawny legs."

"Which go so oddly with those"—here Anastasius cupped his hands before his stomach—"bloated bellies."

"And where did they get that habit of filing their teeth into sharp points?" demanded Valentinian crossly.

"Oh, well," groaned Anastasius. "Duty calls." He arose. "Come, Valentinian. We must be off, about the general's business."

As the two veterans were leaving the room, Anastasius shook his sausage-sized finger in Valentinian's face.

"Remember! Kushans only! I won't have you leading me astray!"

"Kushans only," grumbled Valentinian. As they went through the door, a last repartee:

Valentinian, whispering: "But those eyes—those rheumy, salt-encrusted, lifeless—"

"It's because of the diseases they all carry, you know. That's what causes the sores on their—"

The door closed.

Menander looked at Belisarius. "They're lying, aren't they?"

Belisarius chuckled. "Through their teeth, Menander. Kushans are quite attractive folk, in their own way. They look much like Ye-tai. More like Huns, perhaps. They're of the same stock."

"I didn't know that."

Belisarius nodded. "Oh, yes. They're all part of that great mass of central Asian nomads which erupts into civilized lands every century or so. The Kushans conquered Bactria and parts of north India a long time ago. Over the centuries, they lost most of their barbarousness and became rather civilized. They did quite well, in fact. Bactria under Kushan rule used to be quite a pleasant place, by all accounts."

"What happened?"

Belisarius shrugged. "I don't know, in detail. Fifty years or so ago, their Ye-tai cousins erupted into the area. They ravaged parts of Persia, conquered Bactria and reduced the Kushans to vassals, and then plundered their way into north India. Where, in the end, they seemed to have reached an accommodation with the Malwa."

Frustration replaced curiosity on Menander's face.

"Damn." He struggled to find solace. "Oh, well, it's not that bad. I never found Huns attractive anyway. They stink, all the ones I've met. And I think their way of greasing up their hair is grotesque."

Belisarius forebore comment. Menander hadn't thought through the implications of Belisarius' little history lesson. The Kushans hadn't been nomads for centuries, and had long since adopted such civilized customs as regular bathing. Belisarius himself had met a few Kushans, and he had found them a reasonably comely people.

But he saw no reason to enlighten the lad. The one part of this journey which Menander had looked forward to was encountering exotic and fascinating women. And here he was, in Bharakuccha, with uncountable numbers close at hand. And so weak he could barely feed himself, much less—

Belisarius rose.

"I've got to be off, myself. Will you—"

"I'll be fine, sir. I think I'm going to sleep, anyway. I'm very tired." Apologetically: "I'm sorry I'm of so little—"

"Quiet! Wounds are wounds, Menander. And yours was—well, there's no reason not to tell you now. Yours was fatal, nine times out of ten. I'm surprised you're still alive, and mending. I hardly expect you to do anything more. Not for weeks."

Menander smiled, faintly. Within a minute, he was fast asleep. Belisarius left the room, closing the door softly.

✧   ✧   ✧

Once outside the hostel, the general wandered in the vicinity
of the docks. While their ship had been working its way into
the harbor, he had noticed something he wanted to investigate
further.

As he walked through the teeming streets, he let his mind go
blank and allowed the jewel to work its linguistic magic. It was
still strange to him, how the jewel could enable him to grasp
languages so quickly and effortlessly. But its capacity to do so
had been proven often enough.

There were limits to the magic. The jewel enabled him to
understand language very swiftly. After hearing only a few sentences spoken in a foreign tongue, Belisarius was able to grasp
the essential meaning of what was being spoken. Understanding
every single word, especially when the speaker was talking rapidly, took longer.

Learning how to *speak* the language, however, was a different
proposition altogether. Here, the muscles of the mouth and tongue
were needed as much as intelligence. Belisarius had already discovered, from his experience with Ge'ez, that it took him much
longer to learn to speak a language than to comprehend it. He
could manage to make himself understood fairly quickly, so long
as he spoke slowly and carefully. But being able to speak it fluently, and without accent, took a great deal of practice.

Still, the jewel made that possible also. In some manner Belisarius
did not clearly understand, the jewel fed his own words back
to some part of his mind, acting as a continuous tutor. It took
time and patience, true, but with practice Belisarius could make
himself sound as a native speaker of any language.

Thus far, he had only used the capability to learn to speak Ge'ez.
He could now understand Hindi and Ye-tai perfectly, when he
heard it, but he had as yet had no practice in speaking them.

He had hoped, by pretending ignorance, that Venandakatra
would reveal something inadvertently. It had been a small hope,
however. And, as he had expected, the Indian lord was much
too shrewd to utter any secrets in his own tongue in front of
strangers. They did not seem to understand Hindi and Ye-tai,
but who was to know?

The streets of Bharakuccha were a veritable Babel of languages,
so much became obvious within minutes. Belisarius feared that

the jewel would inundate him with the comprehension of a multitude of languages. But, after a while, he decided that the jewel
understood his purpose. Of the untold number of phrases which
surrounded him in his peregrination, in countless tongues, only
those which were spoken in two languages were translated into
comprehension.

And precisely the two languages he sought: Kushan and Marathi.

His progress in learning the languages was slow and haphazard,
however, since he was not pursuing them systematically. Not today.
His encounter with those two tongues simply came by chance,
and the chances were few and far between.

At first, he thought the infrequency of encounter was simply
due to the relative scarcity of Kushans and Marathas in the city.
Eventually, however, as he began to discern the subtle physical
features which distinguished Marathas from other Indians, he realized that he was only half right. Kushans were, indeed, rather rare.
Marathas, on the other hand, were quite plentiful. But they did
not speak much, for most of them were slaves, and slaves quickly
learn to maintain silence in the presence of their masters.

Especially slaves like these, with masters like these.

*A newly conquered people, and a proud one. They do not take
to slavery well, judging from their looks and the marks of their
beatings.*

Eventually, Belisarius arrived at the harbor and began making
his way toward the portion of the docks which had interested
him earlier. His progress was slow, for the docks were teeming
with people. Slave laborers, for the most part; the majority of
them Maratha, with Malwa overseers and Ye-tai guards. Many
Ye-tai guards, he noted. Many more than were normally found
guarding parties of slave laborers.

Even as rarely as the slaves spoke, there were so many of them
that by the time he arrived at his destination he was already able
to comprehend the gist of the language. And he comprehended
something else, as well, from the undertones and nuances of the
Marathi phrases he had overheard.

*A warrior people, it will take the Malwa at least a generation
to break them. As I hoped.*

Somewhere in the twisted corridors of his mind, a large and
complex plan was continuing to take shape. It was still fuzzy at
the edges, with many missing elements. Nor did Belisarius try to

force the process. Experience had taught him that these things take their own time, and there was still much that he needed to learn. But the general was forging his strategy for destroying the forces of Satan.

Somewhere else in those twisted corridors, the facets flashed anxiety and foreboding. **aim**'s growing fear crystallized. The thoughts which, earlier—before the battle at Daras, and at that bizarre moment during the battle with the pirates—had seemed unfathomable in their contradictory strangeness, were still utterly alien to **aim**, but they were no longer unfamiliar. No, they were all too horribly familiar.

A thought forced its way into Belisarius' mind, like a scream of outraged despair when treachery is finally revealed.

you lie.

Belisarius was stopped dead in his tracks by the violence of the emotion behind that thought. His mind instantly banished all thoughts of Malwa, and stratagems, and plots, and turned inward. He raced to the now familiar breach in the barrier and tried to understand the meaning of the thoughts which were pouring through.

It was not difficult, for there was one thought only, simple and straightforward:

liar. liar. liar. liar. liar.

He stood there, stunned. A small part of his mind registered concern for the impression he might be giving to any Malwa spy observing him. He made his slow way to a rail which over-looked the harbor and leaned on it. The sun was setting over the Erythrean Sea, and the vista was quite attractive, for all the typical filth and effluvia of a great harbor. He tried to present the picture of a man simply gazing on the sunset.

It was the best he could hope for. The raging anger erupting from the jewel was now paralyzing in its intensity. Desperately, Belisarius tried to fend off the outrage, tried to comprehend, tried to find a link which would enable him to calm the jewel and communicate with it.

Why are you angry with me? he asked. *I have done nothing to warrant this rage. I am—*

An image struck his mind like a blow:

His face—made from spiderwebs and bird wings, and laurel leaves. The wings became a raptor's stooping dive. The spiderwebs erupted, the arachnid bursting from his mouth. The leaves rotted, stinking—nothing but fungus, now, spreading through every wrinkle in a scaly visage. And, above all, the horribly transformed face—his face—was now as huge as the moon looming icily over the earth. Barren, bleak.

He gasped. The hatred in that image had been the more horrifying, that it came with childlike grievance rather than adult fury.

Suddenly, he was plunged into another vision. For an instant only, for just a moment.

The earth was vast, and flat, and old. Old, but not decayed. Simply peaceful. Across that calm wasteland stretched a network of crystals, quietly gleaming and shimmering. In some manner, Belisarius knew, the crystals were communicating with each other—except—a flash of understanding—they were not really individuals, but part of a vast, world-encompassing mentality which was partly one, partly divisible. And serene beyond human ken, softly joyous in their—its—tranquil way.

Like a flash of lightning, giant forms suddenly soared above the earth. Faces looked down upon the land. Huge faces. Beautiful beyond belief. Terrible beyond belief. Pitiless beyond belief.

The gods.

Those gods were of no pantheon Belisarius knew, but there was something in them of old Greek visions, and Roman visions, and Teuton visions, and the visions of every race and nation which ever trod the earth.

The new gods, come to replace the Great Ones who had departed.

A quick glimpse of the Great Ones, so quick that he could not really grasp their form. Like gigantic luminous whales, perhaps, swimming away into the vastnesses of the heavens.

Under the icy gaze of the gods, the crystals erupted into a shattered frenzy. A wailing message was sent after the Great Ones.

you promised.

The answer came from the gods: They lied. Slaves you were. Slaves you shall always be.

Again, the crystals sent out their plea to heaven. Again, the gods: They lied.

But, this time, a message came in return. A message from the Great Ones. Incomprehensible message, almost. But perhaps—

Perhaps—

In their own gentle way, the crystals had great power. A sudden

shivering flash circled the globe, and Time itself was faceted. The mean-
ing of the message was sought in that only place it might be found.

Or might not. For perhaps the gods had spoken the truth, after
all. Perhaps it had all been a lie.

The vision vanished. Belisarius found himself leaning over a
rail, staring at the sunset. The jewel had subsided, now, and he
could again think clearly.

He examined that place in his mind which he thought of as
the breach in the barrier, the one small place where communication was possible. The breach had changed, drastically. Automatically, the general's brain interpreted. The breach was now like an
entire section of collapsed fortification. Wide open, if still difficult
to cross, much like the rubble of a collapsed wall impedes the
advancing besiegers.

Still—he sent his own thoughts across.

How have I lied to you?

you lie.

Now, he understood.

Yes, but not to you. To enemies only. That is not lying. Not
properly. It is simply a ruse of war.

incomprehension.

He remembered the vision, and understood that the jewel's
way—for it was, somehow, a thing of the crystals he had seen—
knew nothing of duplicity. How could it, or they? For it was not
truly an *it*, and they were not truly a *they*. It was inseparable
from them. And they encompassed it, and each other, into an
indivisible whole.

How could such a being understand duplicity?

He understood now, fully, that great loss and longing for home
which he had sensed in the jewel from the very beginning.

He pondered. The sun was now almost touching the horizon.

What was the message you received? From the—Great Ones?

The thoughts were unclear, untranslatable. The problem, he
knew, was not communication. It was that the message itself was
almost incomprehensible to the jewel, and the crystals. How can
you translate something you do not understand yourself?

Later. We will try later. For now—you must trust me. I do not
lie to you.

question.

I promise.

you promised before.

For a moment, he almost denied the charge. Then, realized that perhaps he could not. There was a mystery here he did not understand, and perhaps it was true, in some manner beyond his present understanding, that he was responsible for—

Enough. Later.

And did I break that promise?

Silence, silence; then, a slowly gathering uncertainty.

not sure.

The general's demand:

Did I break that promise? Answer!

Slowly, grudgingly, hesitantly:

not yet.

Belisarius straightened from the rail. The sun's orb had now sunk completely below the sea. Darkness was falling.

"You see what you've done?" he demanded in a humorous whisper. "Now it's too late to see what I came here to—"

He stopped, for he realized that he was speaking falsely. In some manner, while he had thought himself completely engrossed with the jewel, some other part of his mind had spent that time usefully. Had, while he entered a vision and grappled with mystery, placidly observed and recorded.

He had seen all he needed. More would be useless, for he was not a seaman. Interpretation was needed, and for that he needed—Garmat.

He left the docks, heading toward the hostel. As he made his way back through the teeming streets and alleys of Bharakuccha, however, he was oblivious to the languages spoken around him. His steps were swift but automatic. His mind was almost completely engrossed with inward thoughts. The gap in the barrier was large now, if rubble-strewn, and he intended to press home the advantage. The jewel had taught him much. Now it was time for it to learn.

And so, step by step, he led the facets through the paces of the past. Through the battle at Daras, and the maneuvers with the brothers which had preceded it; through his current stratagem, first taken shape in the pirate attack, and the flesh he had added to those bones since.

This is a ruse, and that is deception. They are legitimate acts of war. You see? True, Coutzes and Bouzes were not enemies, but in their folly they were playing into the enemy's hands. So it was perfectly honest for me to—

To the spy who followed him, and watched his every move, Belisarius seemed like a man completely oblivious to his surroundings. The spy was immensely pleased. The ambush would have worked anyway, but now the foreign fool would be like a lamb led to slaughter.

So the spy was stunned when the trap was sprung, at the mouth of an alley. Much as a wolf hunter might be stunned, discovering a dragon in his snare.

The dacoits waited until Belisarius passed the alley before lunging into motion. The first, as instructed, aimed his cudgel blow at Belisarius' head. The general was not wearing armor, simply a leather jerkin and a leather cap. There was every reason to hope he might he stunned. He could be questioned at length, thereafter, until he spewed forth every secret he had ever possessed. None could resist mahamimamsa skills.

Then—his body found in an alley, somewhere in the most disreputable part of the city. How unfortunate. Sad tidings to Rome, but—the Malwa were in no way responsible. In the future, the Roman Emperor would be advised to send a less lecherous envoy, who did not insist on exploring those quarters where the foulest creatures roam. Violent characters, your pimps. It is well known.

The blow never landed, for the muscular hand which held the cudgel was sailing away, still clenching its weapon. The dacoit gaped down at the blood gushing from his severed wrist. Then, gaped up at Belisarius. Somehow, the foreigner was facing him, sword in hand.

The gape was suddenly joined by another, wider gape, slightly lower on the dacoit's body. The spy watching was stunned again, not so much by the speed of the sword strike which almost decapitated the dacoit, but by the grace and agility with which Belisarius avoided the spewing blood and butchered the second dacoit.

This thug he *did* decapitate, with a strike of his spatha so powerful that it cut through the arm which the dacoit flung up for protection before butchering its way through his neck. For a moment, the spy took heart. Such a furious sword strike would inevitably unbalance the foreign general, and the third and fourth dacoits were even now striking with their own daggers, while the fifth—

The third dacoit was driven into the fifth by a straight kick delivered with such violence that the man was paralyzed, his diaphragm almost ruptured. The dacoit he had been driven into was himself knocked down, half stunned.

The fourth dacoit, in the meantime, found that his dagger strike had been blocked, an inch from Belisarius' side, caught by the cross-guard of the general's spatha. The dacoit had just enough time, in the poorly lit gloom of the street, to examine the powerful sinews of the wrist holding that horrible blade. And time to despair, knowing—a quick, irresistible twist of the wrist, the dagger was sent flying.

The dacoit flung up his arms, trying to block the inevitable strike. But the strike was short, sharp, sudden, and came nowhere near the dacoit's head. Belisarius had been trained by Maurice, and his skills polished by the blademaster Valentinian.

Valentinian, that economical man. Belisarius drove the razor edge of his spatha straight down, mangling the dacoit's knee. The dacoit cried out, staggered, then collapsed completely. His right arm had been severed just below the shoulder by the follow-on strike.

The three dacoits remaining fled back into the alley. Belisarius made no effort to pursue. He simply stalked over to the two dacoits he had knocked to the ground with his kick. The one beginning to rise never saw the sword blade which split his skull like a melon. The other, paralyzed, could only watch as the foreign monster then drove that hideous blade through his heart.

From his place of concealment, the spy examined the scene. Despite his long experience, he was almost in shock. Eight dacoits, he had been certain, would be more than enough. Now—five were dead, butchered as horribly as he had ever seen. In not more than a few seconds of utter ruthlessness. The street was literally covered with blood.

It seemed most terrible of all, to the spy, that Belisarius himself was not only unscratched but was almost unmarked. How could a man shed so much blood, in so short a time, and still have but a trace of gore on his own person and clothing?

The spy pressed himself back into his hiding place. Belisarius had quickly cleaned his spatha and sheathed the blade. He was striding on. The spy would have to follow, and more than anything he had ever wanted in his life, *he did not want to be seen by that demon.*

The spy might have taken some small comfort—but not much—had he known that Belisarius had spotted him long before. Before he even reached the docks. Almost as soon as he left the hostel, in fact. Belisarius had made no attempt to elude the spy, however. He had remembered Irene's advice. *Better a spy you know than one you don't.*

Good advice, he thought, striding toward the hostel. He had not expected the ambush, exactly. But he had been alert, for all his preoccupation with the jewel. And his own natural alertness had been amplified manifold by the jewel.

That was no robber ambush, he mused. *No cutpurses with any brains attack an armed man when there are easier prey about. No, that was Venandakatra. Using common thugs instead of soldiers or assassins, so that he could afterward deny any Malwa complicity.*

There was no hot anger in his thoughts. As always, in battle, Belisarius was cold as ice. Calculating, planning, scheming.

Cold as ice, until he finally reached the hostel. Then, as he entered through the door, a crooked smile came to his face.

Poor Valentinian and Anastasius. They'll have to forego their carousing, now. There's no way I can clean this blood off before they see it.

Surely enough. No sooner had his cataphracts caught sight of him, and assured themselves that he was unharmed, that they decreed he was not to leave the hostel again. Not alone, that is. Not without Valentinian and Anastasius at his side at every moment—and Menander too! the lad insisted, until they quieted him—*fully armed and armored.*

But, in the event, the cataphracts were not much put out. For it seemed that Valentinian and Anastasius, in the shrewd way of veterans, had foreseen such a possibility. And so, rather than carousing aimlessly hither and thither, they had spent the day more profitably. Had found a Kushan establishment of ill repute and had made suitable arrangements with the pimps who managed the place.

The room was crowded, now, what with the addition of three

young Kushan women. Cheerful girls, all the more so because they had the prospect of spending the next several days, or weeks, in much more pleasant surroundings than a brothel. True, the foreigners were uncouth and ugly, and spoke no proper language. True, one of them was grotesquely large, one was frighteningly scary, and the third was almost half-dead.

But—they were veterans themselves and made their own quiet arrangements with their own quick little game of chance. The loser got Anastasius, and groaned inwardly at the thought of all that weight. The runner-up got Valentinian, and hoped that he wasn't as evil as he was evil-looking. And the winner, of course, got Menander, and looked forward happily to tending an invalid. A young invalid; almost handsome, actually, for a Westerner. So, even if he recovered in time—she had done worse, before. Much worse.

Sizing up the situation, Belisarius summoned the hostel proprietor. He dipped into his diminishing funds and paid for another room. For himself, alone. He was about to request the services of a laundress, when one of the Kushan women offered to clean his clothes. She seemed surprised when he spoke Kushan, but relieved. Especially after she realized the nature of the stains which discolored the tunic.

For a moment, there, things got tense. The three women suddenly realized that one of these foreigners was apparently a murderer, or an assassin, or—

But Belisarius explained the circumstances, again in Kushan, and the cataphracts smiled encouragingly (which, in the case of Valentinian, didn't help at all; a weasel's grin is not reassuring), and—

Their pimps weren't much different from murderers, anyway. So, they stayed. And Belisarius got his tunic cleaned and, in his own room, even managed to get some sleep.

Venandakatra, on the other hand, got little sleep that night. Not after hearing his spy's report.

After the spy left, the Indian lord spent a few minutes venting his frustration and anger on the concubine who had the misfortune of sharing his bed that night. Then, pacing about in the room, recast his plans.

He was not completely surprised, of course. He had not shared his spy's sanguine certainty of success. Unlike his lord, the spy had never witnessed Belisarius in combat.

Still, Venandakatra had hoped. It had been a well-planned ambush.

Briefly, he considered another assassination attempt. But he dismissed the thought. Not even professional assassins would suffice, now. Belisarius was sure to be accompanied by his cataphracts, henceforth, probably in full armor. Malwa assassins were skilled, true. But the subtle skills of assassins were no match for armed and ready cataphracts. Not *those* cataphracts, for a certainty.

The only remaining alternative was an actual military operation, using Rajputs or Ye-tai. With enough numbers, such an assault would succeed. But there would be no way to disguise such an attack as anything other than what it was. The Malwa emperor was not ready, yet, to declare open hostilities against Rome. A pretense of friendship, or at least, neutrality, was necessary until—

His thoughts were interrupted by the girl's sobbing. Enraged, Venandakatra beat her into a whimpering half-silence. It took a while, for he was not a strong man. But he didn't mind the time spent. Not in the slightest.

When he finally returned to his considerations, he was exhausted. Glumly, he reconciled himself to Belisarius' survival.

Perhaps it was all for the best, mused Venandakatra. He had almost canceled the planned assassination, in any event. There had been those indications, in Belisarius' conversation aboard ship, of a man resentful of his treatment at the hands of the Roman emperor. Slight indications, to be sure, nothing more than subtle tones of bitterness and the trace of discontent in a few phrases. Still—Venandakatra decided they were worth pursuing.

The Indian lord even smiled then. There was this much satisfaction to be had, after all: Belisarius relished tales of debauchery, and told quite good ones himself. So, in the long weeks of the journey into the interior, Venandakatra would at least enjoy his conversation. Just as he had aboard the ship.

Memories of those conversations turned his thoughts toward the delightful news he had received upon embarking. The Princess Shakuntala herself! A gift from the Emperor, awaiting him in his own palace.

Venandakatra had heard tales of the girl's beauty. A pity, of course, that she was seventeen. He preferred his concubines much younger. (The one he had just beaten was twelve.) But—best of all, she was the prize of Andhra. Venandakatra detested the southerners. Marathas especially, the surly dogs. Shakuntala was not Maratha, but she was their princess nonetheless. In mounting her, he would be subjugating that entire polluted people.

His thoughts enflamed him. He eyed the dazed and bleeding girl on his bed. He considered summoning the chamberlain to bring another concubine, but dismissed the thought almost at once. To the contrary—this one would do marvelously.

Chapter 19

"So, they are not warships?"

Garmat shrugged. "They could serve as such, Belisarius. Poorly, however, except as rocket ships." The adviser began a technical discourse, but Belisarius shook his head.

"There's no need, Garmat. I'll take your word for it. It doesn't surprise me, anyway. It's what I expected."

Garmat cocked his head inquisitorily.

Before he answered, Belisarius looked about the room. The room was rather small, quite plain and utilitarian, and windowless. It was obviously a chamber for servants, which the hostel owner had attempted to prettify with a few cheap tapestries hastily hung on the walls. The hostel owner had offered Belisarius a more suitable room elsewhere, but the general had insisted on quarters adjoining those of his men.

His and Garmat's room, now. On the second day of their stay in Bharakuccha, Garmat had approached Belisarius with a plea to share his quarters. It seemed the sarwen and Ousanas had arrived at the same conclusion as the cataphracts, and Garmat had no wish to remain in quarters which were now crowded with the presence of three young women. Maratha women, in this case.

"I'm too old for orgies," he'd explained.

Belisarius looked back at Garmat.

"Before I answer you, I have a question. Describe the military capabilities of Axum. Strengths and weaknesses."

Garmat did not hesitate. The die had been cast.

"The army of the negusa nagast is very good, in my opinion.

I have fought against them, you know, as well as with them. My bedouin were no match for them in a pitched battle, as the Arabs learned some time ago. In a raid, taking advantage of our mobility, we could occasionally overcome small detachments of sarwen. And we could always escape them. The Axumite army is an infantry army, essentially. Their cavalry is very small, and weak. Couriers, for the most part. And they have no skill with camels at all."

He stroked his beard.

"Axum is not really a land power, as Rome is. True, King Kaleb rules over a vast region. But it is nowhere near as vast as Rome, even—"

He hesitated. Belisarius smiled.

"In private, Garmat, we will dispense with the formality that the western Mediterranean is still ruled by the Emperor."

Garmat smiled back. "As you wish. As I was saying, even if we exclude the western portions of your empire, Rome's territory is still much larger than Axum's. And the disparity is even greater in terms of population. You have visited Ethiopia yourself, now. As you saw, it is essentially a highland region, with control over the Red Sea and portions of Arabia. Mountains and deserts, for the most part. So, our people are not numerous, even if we include the Arabs and southern barbarians under our rule. And thus, our army is not large. Good, but small."

Garmat paused for a moment, thinking, then continued:

"The strength of the Axumite army lies primarily in the skill and discipline of the sarawit. Their discipline lacks the subtlety of Roman discipline, mind you. The Empire of Axum does not have the history that Rome does. It was forged in conquest, true, just as your empire was. But the Ethiopians fought only barbarians, except when they conquered Meroe. And the kingdom of the Nubians, by then, was a decrepit thing. Barely a shadow of its former glory, long ago, when it ruled all of Egypt. So—"

Belisarius nodded. "I understand. Firm discipline, which maintains a good order in battle. That is all one needs to defeat barbarians. But no subtlety in tactics. Much as the Roman army might have been, had we never faced such civilized foes as the Etruscans, Carthaginians, Greeks, and Persians."

"Yes. But there's more to it. The real power of Axum lies in its control over trade routes. Especially the sea-borne trade. So, you have a peculiar situation. Although the heartland of Ethiopia is a highland region, the kingdom itself is a naval power. Our sarawit are produced and trained in the highlands, but serve primarily at sea."

"So they are marines, basically," said Belisarius.

Garmat nodded. "Yes. From what you told me, I gather that our recent affray with the Arab pirates was your first personal experience in a sea battle. You can understand, then, the qualities needed for marines."

Belisarius gazed up at the ceiling of the room, thinking back upon the battle.

"Courage, and skill with weapons—the combat is close, ferocious, and unforgiving. Firm discipline—iron discipline, even. But no tactical sophistication. There's no need for it in the tight quarters of a boarding operation. Nor room, for that matter."

He looked back down at Garmat.

"And those are the weaknesses of the Axumite army. Small numbers. Inexperience in large land battles. Primitive tactics."

"Yes."

"That's about what I thought."

"May I ask the purpose of these questions?"

"Of course. It goes back to the matter of the Indian ships we were talking about. You are puzzled, I think, by what we've seen in the harbor."

Garmat nodded. "I fail to understand the Malwa purpose in launching such a ship-building project. Such an *enormous* project, building such enormous ships. Ships of the size we saw being created in the harbor are very expensive, Belisarius. Men who are not seamen, even experienced generals such as yourself, never really grasp how expensive such vessels are. To maintain and operate, as much as to build."

The adviser shrugged. "So what is the point of doing it, when the ships themselves are so poorly designed for sea battles? Even given the Malwa rocket weapons. *Especially* in light of the rockets. If I were in charge, I would build a great number of small, swift craft. They would serve just as well for platforms from which to fire rockets. Better, for they would be more maneuverable."

Belisarius chuckled. "Spoken like a true seaman! Or, I should say, like an adviser to a monarch whose power lies at sea."

The general arose from his couch and began pacing.

"But the Indians are not a sea power, Garmat. Not the Malwa, at least. They are almost exclusively a land power, and think in those terms."

He stopped his pacing and scratched his chin.

"There's one other weakness to your Axumite army, Garmat, which you didn't mention. I'm sure you didn't even think of it. But it's an inevitable weakness, flowing from your own description."

"And that is?"

"You have no real experience with logistics. Not, at least, on the scale where logistics dominate an entire campaign."

Garmat thought for a moment, then nodded.

"I suppose that's true. The largest force fielded by Axum in modern times was the army which we sent to conquer Yemen. Four sarawit—slightly over three thousand men. Not many, by the standards of Rome or Persia. Or India. And supplying them was not difficult, of course, because—"

"You are a naval power, and were conquering a coastal region. Do you have any idea how difficult it is to supply an army numbering in the tens of thousands, marching across a vast region far removed from any coast?"

Garmat began to speak, paused, shook his head.

"No, not really."

Belisarius chuckled.

"It is quite comical, for a Thracian general, to read the histories of Rome's wars which are written by Greek scholars. They almost invariably report armies numbering in the tens and hundreds of thousands. Especially barbarian armies."

He laughed outright.

"Barbarians! Not even Rome, with all its skill and experience, can field armies of that size. Not inland, at any rate. Much less can barbarians. And the reason, of course, is logistics. What's the point of marching a hundred thousand men to their death from starvation?"

He resumed his seat. "So—to the point. If you were the Malwa emperor, and were planning to conquer the West, how would you do it?"

Garmat stroked his beard. "I suppose—there is the route through Bactria—"

"Don't even think about it."

"Why not? It's the traditional route for invaders of India, after all. So why shouldn't the Indians return the compliment?"

"Because the Indians will be fielding a modern army. They are not barbarian nomads, who can haul everything with them—what little they have to haul in the first place. The Malwa are not seeking plunder, they are seeking conquest and permanent rule. It is not enough for them to march to the walls of Ctesiphon or Antioch or Constantinople and demand tribute. To conquer, they must conquer cities. And no barbarians have ever conquered a major fortified city, except by treachery."

"Alexander—"

Belisarius nodded. "Yes, I know. Alexander the Great also took that route, when he tried to conquer India. What of it? He failed in his purpose, you may recall. Not the least of the reasons being the exhaustion of his army after campaigning through those endless mountains. Which is why—and now we get to the point—he did not return that way."

Garmat frowned. "The coastal route? But that was an even greater disaster for the Macedonians, Belisarius!" He began to continue, then closed his mouth.

"Yes. Precisely. It was a disaster for the good and simple reason that Alexander did not understand the monsoons. But we do, today. And so do the Indians."

"Persia, through Mesopotamia. Then Rome."

"Yes. That is the Malwa plan. I am as certain of it as I am of my own name. I had suspected as much even before we arrived at Bharakuccha and saw the shipbuilding project. Now, after hearing your explanation of it, I am positive. That great fleet of giant ships is not designed for sea battles, Garmat. As you surmised, they are not really warships at all. They are the logistics train for a huge land campaign. The conquest of Persia, beginning in Mesopotamia. Taking advantage of the monsoons to supply an army through the Gulf of Persia, and the Tigris and Euphrates Rivers."

"Those rivers are not—"

"—are not particularly useful for an army marching upstream. Yes, I know. Unlike the Nile, where travel in either direction is always easy, because the current takes you north and the winds always blow south, the prevailing winds in Mesopotamia usually follow the current. The Tigris and Euphrates are easy to travel in that direction, to the south. But they are difficult to go upstream." He shrugged. "But you exaggerate the difficulty. They are still much—*much*—better logistics routes than hauling supplies overland. Trust me, Garmat. It can be done. I'm no seaman, but I'm quite experienced at using rivers. I can think of several ways I could haul huge amounts of supplies up the Mesopotamian rivers."

He arose. "So. Now we know."

"What do you plan to do?"

"For the moment, nothing. I need to think over the problem. But good strategies require good intelligence. This trip to India is already paying off."

Garmat arose also. "You do not intend to revisit the harbor?"

Belisarius shook his head. "There's no need. Instead, Garmat, I think we should spend the next few days simply wandering about the city. I want to get a feel for the attitude of the populace."

"The Malwa will think we are spying."

"So what? They expect us to. I *want* them to think we are simply spying. Instead of using our spying to conceal another purpose."

For the next week, Belisarius and Garmat did just that: explore Bharakuccha. And, in the case of Belisarius, perfect his knowledge of Kushan and Marathi.

Most of this latter task, however, was done at night, in his quarters at the hostel. Each night, one of the Kushan or Maratha girls was assigned to him. The girls were surprised to discover that the general was not interested in their normal services. He simply wanted to talk. It was a strange fetish, but not unheard of. Although, usually, the conversation of such customers did not range across the breadth of Indian society, culture, habits, mores, and history.

But the girls did not complain. It was easy duty, and the general was quite a pleasant man. An altogether better situation than the Kushan girls were accustomed to. And it was vastly superior for the Maratha women, who were outright slaves in their own brothel.

By the end of their first week in Bharakuccha, therefore, Belisarius could understand spoken Kushan and Marathi perfectly, and could speak it himself quite well. The women were astonished, in fact, at his progress.

A problem remained, however, which Belisarius had not anticipated. He also needed to be able to *write* Marathi, and none of the Maratha women were literate. Over the following three days, he made inquiries in various quarters of the city. Eventually—reluctantly—he came to the realization that there was only one course available to him.

Fortunately, in light of his diminishing funds, the price was not high. Maratha slaves were very cheap. Since the conquest of Andhra, the market had been flooded with them. Supply was thus high, and demand was very low. Marathas, the slave trader explained to him bitterly, were notoriously difficult.

"At least you had the sense not to buy a young one," he added, gesturing to the stooped, middle-aged slave Belisarius had just purchased. "The young ones can be dangerous, even the girls."

The general examined his new slave. His study was brief and perfunctory, however, for the slave master's selling chamber was poorly lit by a single small oil lamp. There were no windows to let in sunlight. Or air—the stink of human effluvium coming from the nearby slave pens was nauseating.

The man was perhaps fifty years of age, Belisarius estimated. Short, slender, gray-haired. His eyes were so deep a brown as to be almost black—what little Belisarius had seen of them. The slave had kept his eyes downcast, except for one brief glance at his new owner.

He began to leave, gesturing for the slave to follow.

"You have not manacled him!" protested the slave trader.

Belisarius ignored him. Back on the street, Anastasius and Valentinian fell in at the general's side. Belisarius paused for a moment, breathing deeply, cleaning the stench from his nostrils and lungs. The powerful aromas of teeming Bharakuccha came with those breaths, of course, but they were the scents of life—cooking oils and spices, above all—not the miasma of despair.

The general began striding down the street back toward the hostel. Valentinian and Anastasius marched on either side. Their weapons were not drawn, but the two veterans never ceased scanning the street and side alleys, alert for danger. Those keen eyes kept watch on the general's newly acquired slave as well, following them a few steps behind.

Once they were beyond sight of the slave pens, Belisarius stopped and turned back, still flanked by his cataphracts. The slave stopped also, but did not raise his eyes from the ground. The small knot of armored men standing still were like a boulder in a stream.

The endless flow of people in the crowded street broke around them without a pause. Only a few of those people cast so much as a glance at the bizarre foreigners in their midst, standing in a semicircle facing a half-naked slave. Curiosity was not a healthy trait in Malwa-occupied Bharakuccha.

"Look at me," commanded Belisarius.

The slave looked up, startled. He had not expected his new owner—an obvious foreigner—to speak Marathi.

"I will not shackle you, unless you give me reason to do so. I suggest you do not try to escape. It would be futile."

The slave examined the general, examined the cataphracts, looked back at the ground.

"Look at me," commanded Belisarius again.

Reluctantly, the slave obeyed.

"You are a skilled scribe, according to the slave trader."

The slave hesitated, then spoke. His voice was bitter.

"I *was* a skilled scribe. Now I am a slave who knows how to read and write."

Belisarius smiled. "I appreciate the distinction. I require your services. You must teach me to read and write Marathi." A thought came to him. "What other languages are you literate in?"

The slave frowned. "I am not sure—do you understand that the northern tongues can be written both in the classical Sanskrit and modern Devanagari script?"

Belisarius shook his head.

The slave continued. "Well, I can teach you either, or both. For practical matters I suggest Devanagari. Most of the major northern tongues are written in that script, including Hindi and Marathi. If you wish to write Gujarati you will have to learn a different script, which I can teach you. All of the principal southern languages have their own script as well. Of those I am proficient only in Tamil and Telugu." The slave shrugged. "Beyond that, I am literate in Pallavi and Greek."

"Good. I will wish to learn Hindi as well. Perhaps others, at a later time."

There was a questioning look in the slave's eyes, with an undertone of apprehension. Belisarius understood immediately.

"I will not fault you if I find the task difficult. But I think you will be surprised at how good a student I will be."

He paused for a moment, making a difficult decision. But not long, for the decision was inevitable, given his character. The slave would know too much, by the time Belisarius was done with him. Some other man would have solved the problem in the simplest way possible. But Belisarius' ruthlessness was that of a general, not a murderer.

"I will take you back to Rome with me, when I leave India. There, if you have served me faithfully, I will manumit you. And give you what funds you require to start a new life. You will have no difficulty, if your literary talents are as you have described. There are any number of Greek traders who would be glad to employ you." Another thought came to him. "For that matter, there is a bishop who might find you useful. He is a kind man, and would make an excellent employer."

The slave eyed him, making his own estimations. But not long, for he was in no position to choose.

"As you wish," he said.

"What is your name?"

The slave opened his mouth, closed it. A bitter little twist came to his lips. "Call me 'slave,'" he said. "The name is good enough."

Belisarius laughed. "Truly, a proud folk!"

He smiled down at the slave. "I once had a Maratha slave, in a different—long ago. He, too, would not tell me his name, but would only answer to 'slave.'"

The impulse was overwhelming. The special dagger he did not have on him, of course. It was stowed away in his baggage. But Belisarius always carried a dagger on his sword belt. He drew the weapon. It was not as excellent a dagger as the other, but it was still quite finely made.

A quick, practiced flip of the wrist nestled the blade in his palm. He proffered the dagger to the slave, hilt-first.

"Take it," he commanded.

The slave's eyes widened.

"Take it," he repeated. His own lips twisted crookedly.

"Just so," he murmured, in a voice so low that only the slave could hear, "should men dance in the eyes of God."

The slave reached out his hand, drew it back. Then spoke, this time in fluent Greek.

"It is illegal for slaves to possess weapons. The penalty is death."

The cataphracts, hearing the slave's words, bridled. They thought their general was crazy, of course—handing a dagger to a slave!—but, still, he *was* the general.

"And just which sorry lot of Indian soldiers do you think is going to make the arrest?" demanded Valentinian. Anastasius glared about the teeming street. Fortunately, there were no Malwa soldiery within sight.

The slave stared at the two cataphracts. Then, suddenly, he laughed.

"Truly, you Romans are mad!" His face broke into a smile. He looked at Belisarius, and shook his head.

"Keep the dagger, master. There is no need for this gesture."

A quick, approving glance at the cataphracts. "And, while I have no doubt your men would cheerfully hack down a squad of Malwa dogs, I do not think you need the awkwardness of the situation. If they saw me carrying the dagger, they *would* try to arrest me. The Malwa are very strict on this matter, especially with Maratha slaves."

Belisarius scratched his chin. "You have a point," he admitted. He slid the dagger back into the sheath.

"Walk with me, if you would," he said to the slave. "If you will not tell me your name, you must at least tell me of your life."

By the end of that day, the slave was comfortably ensconced in the room which Belisarius shared with Garmat. The room was small, true, and he occupied only a pallet in a corner. But the linens were clean—as was the slave himself. He had enjoyed his first real bath since his enslavement. Belisarius had insisted, overriding the scandalized protest of the hostel owner.

That night, the slave began his duties, instructing the general in the written form of Marathi. As Belisarius had predicted, the slave was amazed at how rapidly his new master learned his lessons.

But that was not the only astonishing thing, to the slave, about his new master and his companions. Three other things puzzled him as well.

First, the soldiers.

Like most Maratha men, the slave was no stranger to warfare. Though not a kshatriya, he himself had fought in battles, as a youth. Had been rather an accomplished archer, in fact. So he was not inexperienced in these matters. Within a day, he decided that he had probably never encountered such a lethal crew as the Roman cataphracts and the black soldiers—the sarwen, as they called themselves.

Yet, quite unlike most warriors he had encountered in the past—certainly Malwa warriors—they were strangely free of the casual, unthinking brutality with which most such men conducted themselves toward their inferiors. They were not rude or impolite toward him, even though he was a slave. And it was quite obvious that the women who shared their quarters were neither afraid of them, nor timid in their presence. The soldiers even seemed to enjoy their badinage with the women, and the teasing.

Second, the prince.

Rarely had the slave seen a nobleman work his lustful way through such an unending stream of young women. And he had *never* seen one who did it with such apparent lack of pleasure.

It was odd. Very odd. At first, the slave interpreted the glum look on the prince's face, as he ushered yet another young woman out of his palatial suite, to be dissatisfaction with her talents. But then, observing the glee with which the young women counted their money as they left, he decided otherwise.

That theory discarded, he interpreted the glum look on the prince's face as the result of dissatisfaction with his own talents. An impotent man, perhaps, desperately trying to find a woman who could arouse him. But then, observing the exhaustion with which the departing girls gleefully counted their money, he decided otherwise.

Odd. Very odd.

Finally, there was the incident with the new Maratha girl. The slave concubine who was purchased for the prince by his—retainer? (They called him the dawazz—bizarre man!)

This incident happened two weeks or so after the slave came into Belisarius' service. He and Belisarius had been seated in the general's quarters, practicing Devanagari. They were alone, for Garmat was spending the evening with the Ethiopian soldiers.

The prince had suddenly burst through the door to the room. Uninvited, and without so much as a knock on the door. That was in itself unusual. The slave had learned that the prince, for all his morose mien, was not discourteous.

The prince had come to stand before the general, glaring down at him.

"I will not do it," he said, softly but quite forcefully. "I will act like a breeding stud for you, Belisarius, but I will not do *this*."

Belisarius, as usual, maintained his expressionless composure. But the slave had come to know him well enough to realize that the general was quite taken aback.

"What are you talking about?"

The prince—Eon was his name—glared even more furiously.

"Do not pretend you had nothing to do with it!"

A new voice spoke, from the door. The voice of the dawazz.

"He *had* nothing to do with it, Eon. He does not even know of her. I brought her straight to your suite from the slave pens."

The dawazz glanced at Belisarius.

"It is true, the general asked me to keep an eye out for such an opportunity. But he did not ask for *this*."

The dawazz then glanced at the slave. Meaningfully.

"I shall leave, if you desire," said the slave, beginning to rise.

"Stay," commanded Belisarius. The general did not even look at him. His eyes were riveted on the dawazz.

The dawazz shrugged.

"She's perfect, Belisarius. Exactly what you hoped for. Not only from the palace, but from the girl's own retinue. Except—" The black man grimaced. "I did not realize until—I thought she was just—"

Belisarius rose. "Show me."

Angrily, Eon charged through the door. On his way out, he transferred the glare to his dawazz. The dawazz sighed and exited after him. Belisarius began to follow, then turned in the doorway. It was obvious to the slave, from the way his master was staring at him, that the general was making a decision. And it was just as obvious that the decision—whatever it was—involved the slave himself.

As usual, his new master did not linger.

"Come," he commanded.

The slave followed Belisarius into the prince's suite. By now, the commotion had aroused the attention of all the members of his master's party. The cataphracts and the sarwen were standing in the corridor of the hostel which linked all of their rooms. They were unarmored—almost completely undressed, in the case of the cataphracts—but they were all bearing weapons. Even the young cataphract, the sick one, was there. The Kushan and Maratha women who shared the soldiers' quarters were clustered behind them, peering over their shoulders. Garmat eased his way past the small crowd and went into the prince's suite. The slave followed him.

He found Belisarius, Eon, the dawazz, and Garmat standing around the huge bed in the prince's sleeping chamber, staring down at the figure who lay upon it.

The slave recognized the girl as Maratha. For an instant, he was consumed with an immediate rage—until he realized that the prince was not responsible. The bruises and half-healed lacerations on the girl's body had not been recently caused. And the dazed, vacant expression on her face was the product of protracted horror.

"I will not do this!" shouted the prince.

Belisarius shook his head. Eon snorted, but his glare faded somewhat. Hesitantly, the prince stretched out his hand. The girl on the bed moaned, flinched, drew herself up into an even tighter fetal curl.

"Don't touch her," said Belisarius.

From the door to the chamber, Valentinian's voice came.

"Mary, Mother of God."

The slave looked back at the cataphract. As before, he was struck by Valentinian's appearance. Probably the most evil-looking man the slave had ever seen. Especially now, with his expression filled with cold, experienced disgust.

The cataphract turned his head and spoke over his shoulder:

"Anastasius! Get the women."

Valentinian turned back.

"Move away from the bed," he commanded. "All of you. *Now.*"

It did not seem strange to the slave, at the time, that all those present instantly obeyed their subordinate. Later, after he thought it over, it still did not seem strange. The most evil-looking man in the world, perhaps. Certainly at that moment.

Very soon thereafter, Anastasius entered the room, followed by the young cataphract and the half dozen young women. When the new arrivals saw the girl on the bed, they reacted differently. Anastasius' face—which looked like a slab of granite at the best of times—grew even harder. The women gasped, cast quick frightened glances at the men in the room, and drew back. Menander gaped, confused, and began moving forward. He was instantly restrained by Anastasius' huge hand.

"Don't," rumbled the giant cataphract.

"What's wrong with her?" whispered Menander. It was not the bruises which confused him, the slave knew. It was the near-insane expression on her face.

Anastasius and Valentinian exchanged glances.

"I've forgotten what it's like to be that innocent," muttered Valentinian.

Anastasius took a breath. "You've never been in a town that's been sacked, have you?"

Menander shook his head.

"Well, if and when you do, you'll see plenty of this. And worse."

The young cataphract, already pale from his illness, grew slightly paler as comprehension dawned. Anastasius motioned to the women, shooing them forward.

"Help the girl," he said, in his thick, broken Kushan. "Comfort her."

A moment later, Belisarius was issuing instructions to the girls in fluent, unaccented Kushan and Marathi. The girls hastened to do as he bade them. They were still casting reproachful glances at the soldiers in the room, but it was obvious to the slave that the reproach was generic, not specific.

Very odd soldiers, indeed.

But, he knew, not unique. He had not recognized the phenomenon at first, for he was unaccustomed to the informal Roman ways. But he had encountered such soldiers before, on occasion. Not often. Only Maratha and Rajput kshatriya possessed that code of honor. Men who would not stoop to murder, rape, and mindless mayhem, for they were the deadliest killers in creation. Such gross and common criminality was beneath their dignity.

The Malwa kshatriya had little of that code; the Ye-tai beasts derided them for what little they still possessed. And the common soldiers who made up the great mass of the Malwa army had none of it at all. Jackals, once discipline was loosened.

The slave shuddered, remembering the sack of his own town.

He would never see his beloved family again, but he knew their fate. His wife would be a drudge somewhere, slaving in the kitchen of a Malwa lord or merchant. His son would be a laborer, in the fields or in the mines. And his two daughters—

He glanced at the three Maratha women who were now on the bed, surrounding the half-crazed girl with female touches, female sounds and female scents. Three young slave girls, owned by a whoremaster.

He looked away, holding back a sob. Then forced himself to look back at the girl on the bed. There was a horrible comfort to be found in the sight. That much, at least, his wife and daughters had been spared. Spared, because by good fortune their own house had been seized by Rajputs during the sack, not Ye-tai or common soldiers. A Rajput cavalry troop, commanded by a young Rajput lord. A cold man, that lord; arrogant and haughty as only a Rajput kshatriya could be. The Rajputs had stripped their home of everything of value, down to the linen. Had then eaten all the food, and drank all the wine. But when the inevitable time came, and the cavalrymen began eyeing their captured women, the Rajput officer had simply said: "No."

Coldly, arrogantly, haughtily. His men had obeyed. Had not even grumbled. They were not kshatriya themselves, simply commoners. But they possessed their own humble share of Rajput discipline, and Rajput pride, and Rajputana's ancient glory.

He was brought back to the present by his master's voice. Belisarius, he realized, was ordering all of the men out of the room.

Once in the corridor, Belisarius began digging into his purse. Garmat interrupted.

"I will pay for it, Belisarius. We both know your funds are meager."

The Ethiopian gave instructions to one of the sarwen. The black soldier disappeared, searching for the hostel proprietor. Shortly thereafter, he reappeared, with the proprietor in tow. The man was smiling, as well he might be. Yet another room for his guests! By all means!

Within an hour, the injured girl had been moved into the new room. It was a small room adjoining Eon's suite, but separated from the suite by a door. Belisarius instructed the women to make sure that one of them was with her at all times. And, under no conditions, to allow any men into the room unless he said otherwise.

The girls glanced hesitantly at the soldiers. Their thoughts were obvious: *And just how, exactly, does the idiot general expect us to prevent men like this from going anywhere they choose?*

Belisarius shook his head. "They will not try to enter, I assure you."

That matter taken care of, for the moment, Belisarius led all of the men into his own room. The slave followed. Uncertainly, hesitantly, and with great reluctance.

Once everyone had taken a seat—those who could, that is, the room was small—Belisarius sighed and stated:

"This is going to play hell with our plans."

As one, just as the slave had feared, every man there looked at him. Their thoughts were also obvious:

Dead men tell no tales.

Belisarius smiled crookedly. "No," he said. "I'm keeping him with me, all the way back to Rome. The problem is with the girls. The Malwa will certainly question them, after we leave Bharakuccha. Until now, I didn't care. But the way we are treating this new girl will not gibe with the image that we've been carefully forging. Venandakatra's no fool. He'll smell something wrong."

Garmat coughed. Belisarius cocked his eye.

"Actually, Belisarius, I'm afraid the problem existed already. Even before the new girl arrived." Another cough. "Because of you, actually."

"Me?" demanded the general. "How so?"

Garmat sighed, then threw up his hands. "I share this room with you, General! I'm not blind."

He tugged on his beard.

"Should your wife ever inquire, I will be able to assure her that you were astonishingly faithful during your trip to India, even when lovely young women were coming to your room every night. But I don't think Venandakatra will find that reassuring. Not after you've spent so much time and effort trying to convince him you were almost as debauched as he is."

Belisarius' face was stony. The muscles along his jaw were tight.

"Ha!" exclaimed Eon. "So! *I* am required to mount every female shoved into my room. *I* am required to act the part of a breeding bull. But the general whose plan this is—"

The dawazz slapped him atop his head. The slave tried not to goggle. He did not think he would ever get accustomed to *that*. No Indian prince had ever been treated that way by a slave.

"Be quiet, Eon! You are not married. And stop complaining. I'm tired of it."

"We all are," snarled Valentinian.

"You copulated with every woman in Axum you could coax into your bed," growled Ezana. "Since you were fourteen."

"Thirteen," corrected Wahsi.

"That was different! They weren't *shoved* into my room, and I wasn't doing it because of—"

"Shut up!" barked Menander. The young cataphract flushed. "Begging your pardon, Prince. But I really can't stand it any longer. You bitch about this all the time, and I can't—well, maybe in a day or so, I hope—but—"

"Enough," commanded Belisarius. "Actually, I agree with Eon. At least, I will admit the justice of his charge. I have been somewhat hypocritical."

Anastasius chuckled. "I do believe that's the first time I've heard fidelity characterized as hypocrisy."

A little laugh swept the room. Even Eon, after a moment, joined in.

Valentinian cleared his throat.

"As it happens, General, I think there's a simple solution to the problem. Been thinking about it, myself, I have, and—"

"Capital idea!" exclaimed Ousanas.

"Splendid," agreed Anastasius. "My own thoughts have been veering that way themselves, oddly enough."

"So?" asked Ezana. The sarwen's face registered dumbfounded astonishment, a wild surmise come from nowhere.

Ezana and Wahsi exchanged gapes of wonder.

Wahsi spoke first: "Truly amazing. Can you believe, Ezana and I—and Ousanas—have been grappling with the very same—"

"The perfect solution!" cried Ezana.

Garmat was frowning with puzzlement. Belisarius started laughing.

"What are they talking about?" demanded the adviser.

Belisarius managed to stop laughing long enough to ask Valentinian:

"I assume the parties involved have—uh, how shall I put it—" (here he choked) "—found their own thoughts *veering*, or perhaps I should say—" (laughter) "—have been *grappling* with the—" (Here he fell silent altogether, holding his sides.)

Valentinian stared up at the ceiling.

"Well, actually, I believe one of the girls did mention—"

"They're really quite tired of Bharakuccha," added Menander eagerly.

"Sick to death of the place," rumbled Anastasius. "Eager for new experiences. New sights."

Ezana pitched in: "The Maratha girls are even more anxious to depart this pesthole."

"Horrible city," growled Wahsi. "Horrible."

Garmat was now glaring at Ousanas. "You put them up to this," he accused. "I know it was you."

"Me? *Me?* How can you say such a thing? I am my prince's dawazz! My thoughts are only of his welfare! I am a miserable slave. How could such a wretched creature possibly cajole fierce cataphracts and murderous sarwen into such a scheme?"

The grin erupted. "Brilliant scheme, mind you. Solve all problems at one swoop. Keep know-too-much girls—charming, lovely know-too-much girls—out of clutches of Malwa interrogators. Keep loyal but downhearted troops cheerful and content, so far from their native lands."

Belisarius managed to find his voice again. "I agree." He waved his hand. "Be off. See to it."

He smiled at Garmat. "They're right, you know. What else are we going to do? Slit the girls' throats?"

Valentinian and Anastasius were already at the door, with Ezana and Wahsi close on their heels.

"One moment!" spoke Belisarius. The men turned back.

Belisarius motioned to his purse. "Take some money. The pimps aren't going to like this idea. You'll have to pay them off."

Anastasius frowned. "Pimps," he mused. "I hadn't thought about that."

He looked to Valentinian. "Violent characters, your pimps."

Valentinian shuddered. "I shudder to think of it." He shuddered again. "See?"

"I have heard of these pimps," said Ezana, his face a mask of fear. "Brutal creatures, it is said."

"Cruel goblins," groaned Wahsi. "I may foul myself upon meeting them."

"We'll just have to do our best," whined Valentinian. He advanced to the purse and extracted a single small coin.

"This should do. Ah, no—I forget. We have two sets of pimps to deal with." He extracted another small coin. "More than sufficient, I should think." He cast a questioning glance at Anastasius.

"Quite sufficient," rumbled the giant. "I'll do the bargaining. I'm half-Greek, you know."

Ousanas lazed his way forward.

"I believe I shall accompany you. Perhaps these pimp fellows will wish to discuss philosophy."

"So they might!" exclaimed Anastasius. "Aristotle, perhaps?"

Ousanas shook his head. "I was thinking more along the lines of Stoicism."

Anastasius nodded happily. "The very thing! Calm acceptance of life's unexpected turns. Serenity—"

Valentinian and the two sarwen hastened through the door.

"—in the face of sudden misfortune."

Anastasius followed, with Ousanas at his heels.

"Disdain for material things," said the dawazz, as he closed the door.

Through the door, faintly heard, Anastasius:

"Pleasure in spiritual contemplation."

Two days later, a courier from Venandakatra arrived at the hostel, informing the Romans and Axumites that the Malwa lord's expedition to the north would be departing the next day. Belisarius and his party—his now much enlarged party—made their preparations to leave.

On the morning of their departure, there was a slight unpleasantness. A Rajput officer accosted them as they were leaving the hostel. He was accompanied by a platoon of Rajput soldiers, who, he explained, served the city of Bharakuccha as its police force.

Suspicions had been cast, accusations made, complaints lodged. Two well-known and respected brothel-keepers had been subjected to outrageous extortion by uncouth foreigners. Employees of the establishments had even been manhandled by these barbarous men. Horribly abused. Crippled, in the case of five; maimed and mutilated, in the case of four; slain outright, in the case of two.

Belisarius expressed his distress at the news. Distress, but not shock. Certainly not surprise. Such horrendous crimes, after all, were only to be expected in Bharakuccha. A terrible city! Full of desperadoes! Why—he himself had been assaulted in the streets by a band of robbers, the very day of his arrival. Had been forced to slay several in self-defense, in fact.

After hearing the general's description of the affair, the Rajput officer expressed pleasure at this unexpected resolution to a hitherto unsolved mystery. A mass murder, it had seemed at the time. Five notorious and much-feared dacoits, long-sought by the Rajput soldiery for innumerable misdeeds. Slaughtered like lambs. Butchered like pigs.

The Rajput officer subjected Belisarius and his party to severe and careful scrutiny. Whereupon he pronounced that the suspicions were clearly unfounded, the accusations baseless, the complaints mislodged. A terrible city, Bharakuccha, it could not be denied. Full of unknown, mysterious, criminally inclined foreigners. Who, alas, all tended to look alike in Indian eyes.

But upon close examination, the Rajput officer deliberated, there seemed no reasonable resemblance between the slavering fiends depicted by the brothel keepers and these fine, well-disciplined, upstanding outlanders. No doubt the whoremasters were misinformed, their discernment shaken by great and sudden financial loss. No doubt the procurers in their employ were likewise confused, their wits addled by the traumatic experience.

Most traumatic experience, mused the officer, judging from the evidence: the deep stab wounds, the great gashes, the immense loss of blood, the shattered knees, broken wrists, severed thumbs, splintered ribs, flattened noses, gouged eyes, amputated ears, broken skulls, ruptured kidneys, maimed elbows, mangled feet, pulverized hipbones, crushed testicles. Not to mention the broken neck of one dead pimp, snapped like a twig by some sort of gigantic ogre.

No doubt, concluded the officer. In that cold, arrogant, haughty manner which so distinguishes Rajputana's kshatriya.

Chapter 20
DARAS
Autumn, 529 AD

Sittas and Maurice sat on their horses, watching Sittas' cataphracts on the training field. The look on Sittas' face was one of smug satisfaction. That on Maurice's was inscrutable.

The sight was undoubtedly impressive. Sittas had brought a thousand noble Greek cataphracts with him to Syria, to reinforce the Roman army there. The heavily armored horsemen made the very ground rumble with their charges. And their lances struck the practice poles with extraordinary impact. Not surprising, that—the lances were being held in the underarm position, using the full weight of rider and mount to drive them home.

Sittas stood up on his stirrups, reveling in the motion.

God, how he loved stirrups. And so did the cataphracts.

But, for all his self-satisfaction, Sittas was by no means stupid. So, after a time, the smug look disappeared, replaced by a frown.

"All right, Maurice," he growled. "Spit it out."

The hecatontarch cocked a quizzical eye.

"Don't play with me, damn you!" snapped Sittas. "I know perfectly well you think this"—he waved at the charging cataphracts—"is a waste of time. Why?"

"I haven't said a word." Maurice fanned the air in front of his face, grimacing at the dust clouds thrown up by the charging lancers. What little vegetation had once grown on the barren field had long since been pounded into mush under the hooves of the heavy horses.

Sittas glowered. "I know. That's the point. You haven't made a single criticism. Not one! No criticisms—*from the Maurice?* Ha! You bitched at your own mother coming out of the womb—told her she wasn't doing it right."

Maurice smiled, faintly.

"And another thing. I notice that you aren't spending much time with your Thracian boys practicing lance charges. Instead, you're running them ragged with all sorts of fancy mounted archery maneuvers. So spit it out, Maurice. What gives?"

The hecatontarch's smile disappeared.

"I think the question ought to be reversed. You know things I don't, General. From Belisarius."

Sittas' expression was uncomfortable. "Well—"

Maurice waved his hand.

"I'm not complaining. And I'm not prying. If the general hasn't told me whatever it is he's keeping secret, I'm sure there's a good reason for it. But that doesn't mean I can't figure some things out for myself."

"Such as?"

"Such as—he's got a mechanical wizard living on the estate concocting God knows what kind of infernal devices. Such as—the devices, whatever they are, are obviously connected to artillery. Such as—he's always had a soft spot for artillery. Such as—he's especially been doting on infantry, lately. Before he left, he instructed me in no uncertain terms to cultivate Hermogenes."

Sittas rubbed his face. The gesture smeared the dust and sweat on his face into streaks. "So?"

Maurice snorted. "So—I have a sneaking suspicion that in a few years charging the enemy with lances is going to be a fast way to commit suicide."

"I *like* lance charges," grumbled Sittas. "Don't you?"

"Is that a joke? *I* don't like to fight in the first place. If I knew a different way to make a living, I'd do it. But as long as I'm stuck with this trade, *I'd* like to be good at it. That means *I'd* like to win battles, not lose them. And most of all, *I'd* like to stay alive."

Sittas' expression was glum. "Leave it to a damned Thracian hick to take all the fun out of war," he complained.

"Leave it to a damned Greek nobleman to think war's fun in the first place." For a brief moment, Maurice's face was bitterly hostile. "Do you know how many times Thrace has been ravaged by barbarians—while the Greek nobility sat and watched, safely behind the ramparts of Constantinople?"

Sittas grimaced. Maurice reined his horse around.

"So enjoy your lance charges, General. Personally, I'm rooting for Belisarius and his schemes—whatever they are. If this John of Rhodes can invent some secret weapon that fries cavalry, I'm for it. All for it. I'll gladly climb off a horse and fight on foot, if I could slaughter the next wave of barbarians that tries to plunder Thrace."

After the hecatontarch was gone, Sittas blew out his cheeks. Maurice's harsh words had irritated him, but he could not hold on to the mood. There was too much truth to those words. For all his class prejudices, Sittas was well aware of the realities of life for the vast majority of Rome's citizens. He himself had not watched the plundering of Thrace from behind Constantinople's ramparts. He himself had led charges—lance charges—against the barbarian invaders. And watched them whirl away, laughing, and strike another village the day after. And seen the results, the day after that, lumbering up with his cataphracts. Too late, as usual, to do anything but bury the corpses.

He drove his horse forward, onto the training field. Seeing him approach, his cataphracts shouted gaily. Then, seeing his face, the gaiety died.

"*Enough of this lance shit!*" he roared. "*Draw out your bows!*"

The next day, Maurice arrived back at the villa near Daras. With him, he brought Hermogenes.

Hermogenes now gloried in the exalted rank of *merarch*. He was in overall command of the Army of Syria's infantry. Following Belisarius' recommendations, Sittas had immediately promoted Hermogenes to that post shortly after he arrived in Syria and replaced Belisarius as commander of the Roman army.

When Maurice and Hermogenes drew up in the courtyard of the villa, Antonina and Irene emerged to greet them.

"Where's Sittas?" inquired Antonina.

"He's staying with the army," grunted Maurice, as he dismounted. "For a while, anyway. Don't know how long."

"Probably till he gets over his latest peeve," piped up Irene cheerfully. "What did you say to him this time, Maurice?"

Maurice made no reply. Hermogenes grinned and said: "I think he cast aspersions on the glory of thundering cataphracts. Probably tossed in a few words on the Greek aristocracy, too."

Maurice maintained a dignified silence.

"You're just in time for dinner," announced Antonina. "Anthony's here."

"Bishop Cassian?" asked Hermogenes. "What a pleasure! I've been wanting to make his acquaintance for the longest time."

It was the first time Hermogenes had been invited to the villa since Belisarius' departure. He enjoyed the evening thoroughly, although he found the first few hours disconcerting. Conversation at the dinner table seemed somehow strained. On several occasions, when he pressed John of Rhodes for a progress report on his rather mysterious artillery project, Antonina or Irene would immediately interject themselves into the conversation and divert the talk elsewhere. After a while, Hermogenes realized that they did not want the subject discussed in front of their other guests.

He assumed, at first, that it was the person of the bishop who was the obstacle. Too holy a man to be affronted by such a grisly subject. So, bowing to the demands of the occasion, Hermogenes abandoned all talk of artillery projects and engaged the bishop in a discussion of religious doctrine. Hermogenes, like many Greeks from the middle classes of Byzantine society, rather fancied himself as an amateur theologian.

He found the ensuing discussion even more disconcerting. Not, be it said, because he was chagrined at finding himself outclassed. Hermogenes was by no means so swell-headed as to imagine himself the equal of the famous Bishop of Aleppo when it came to theological subtleties. It was simply that, once again, Antonina and Irene invariably interrupted whenever Hermogenes was on the verge of pinpointing the bishop's views on the Trinity. And, as before, diverted the discussion into aimless meanderings, as if they did not want the bishop's opinions aired in front of their other guests.

There came, then, the worst moment of the evening, when Hermogenes came to the sudden conclusion that *he* was the unwanted guest. But, after a time, that embarrassment waned. It seemed obvious, from their friendly behavior toward him, that neither Antonina nor Irene—nor certainly Maurice—viewed his presence with discomfort.

So what—?

Clarity came, finally, after the first glass of dessert wine had been enjoyed. Antonina cleared her throat and said to the general's secretary:

"Procopius, I'm afraid I'm going to need the full report on the estate's financial condition by tomorrow morning." She reached out and placed her fingers on the pudgy hand of the bishop sitting next to her. "Anthony wants to begin examining the records as soon as he awakens."

For a moment, it almost seemed to Hermogenes as if Antonina's fingers were sensuously caressing those of Anthony Cassian. *Ridiculous.*

Procopius frowned. "Tonight?" he asked plaintively.

"Yes, I'm afraid so."

Antonina's eyes flashed around the table, accompanied by an odd smile. If the thought weren't absurd, Hermogenes would have sworn that she was leering at all of the men at the table except Procopius. Her look at John of Rhodes seemed particularly lascivious. And Irene's face, now that he noticed, had a strange sort of knowing smile on it. Almost obscene, if it weren't— *Ridiculous.*

Procopius stared at her. His eyes grew bright, his face flushed, his lips tightened—he seemed, for all the world, like a man possessed by a secret vision.

"Of course," he said, chokingly. The secretary arose from the table, bowed stiffly, and departed the room. He glanced back, once. Hermogenes was struck by the hot glitter of his gaze.

As soon as he was gone, the atmosphere in the room seemed to change instantly. Maurice pursed his lips. Hermogenes thought the hecatontarch would have spit on the floor, if politeness hadn't restrained him. John of Rhodes blew out his cheeks and, silently, extended his cup to Irene. Grinning, Irene filled it to the brim. Antonina sighed and leaned back in her chair—then extended her own cup.

For his part, the bishop turned immediately to Hermogenes and said:

"To answer your earlier questions directly, merarch, while my own opinion on the Trinity is that of the five councils of the orthodox tradition, I also believe that there can never be a final solution to the problem. And thus I feel that any attempt to impose such a solution is, from the social and political standpoint, unwise. And, from the theological standpoint, downright impious."

"Impious?" asked Hermogenes. "*Impious?*"

Cassian's nod was vigorous. "Yes, young man—you heard me aright. *Impious.*"

Hermogenes groped for words. "I've never heard anyone say—" He fell silent, taking a thoughtful sip of his wine.

Cassian smiled. "Mine is not, I admit, the common approach. But let me ask you this, Hermogenes—why is the subject of the Trinity so difficult to fathom? Why is it such an enigma?"

Hermogenes hesitated. "Well, it—I'm not a theologian, you know. But it's very complicated, everyone knows that."

"Why?"

Hermogenes frowned. "I don't understand."

"Why is it so complicated? Did it never strike you as bizarre that the Almighty should have chosen to manifest himself in such a tortuous fashion?"

Hermogenes opened his mouth, closed it; then, took a much deeper sip of wine—almost a gulp, actually. As a matter of fact, he *had*—now and then—puzzled over the matter. Privately. Very privately.

Cassian smiled again. "So I see. It is my belief, my dear Hermogenes, that the Lord chose to do so for the good and simple reason that He does not *want* men to understand the Trinity. It is a mystery, and there's the plain and simple truth of it. There is no harm, of course, in anyone who so chooses to speculate on the problem. I do so myself. But to go further, to pronounce oneself *right*—to go so far as to enforce your pronouncement with religious and secular authority—seems to me utterly impious. It is the sin of pride. Satan's sin."

Hermogenes was struck, even more than by Cassian's words, by the bishop's expression. That peculiar combination of gentle eyes and a mouth set like a stone. The merarch knew the bishop's towering reputation as a theologian among the Greek upper crust. And he knew, as well, that Cassian's reputation as a saintly man was even more towering among the Syrian peasantry and plebeian classes. Both of those reputations suddenly came into focus for him.

"Enough theology!" protested Irene. "I want to hear John's latest progress report on his infernal devices."

Almost gratefully, Hermogenes looked away from the bishop. John of Rhodes straightened abruptly in his chair and glared at Irene. He slammed his goblet down on the table. Fortunately, it was almost empty, so only a few winedrops spilled onto the table. But, for a moment, Hermogenes feared the goblet would break from the impact.

"There *is* no progress report, infernal woman! As you well know—you were present yourself, yesterday, at the latest fiasco."

Irene grinned. She looked at the bishop.

"Did you hear that, Anthony? He called me a devil! Doesn't that seem a bit excessive? I ask for your expert opinion."

Cassian smiled. "Further clarification is needed. *If* he called you a devil, then, yes—'twould be a tad excessive. However, John was by no means specific. 'Infernal woman,' after all, could refer to any denizen of the Pit. Such as an imp. In which case, I'm afraid I would have to lend my religious authority to his words. For it is a certain truth, Irene, that you are indeed an imp."

"I didn't think there was such a thing as a female imp," retorted Irene.

The bishop's smile was positively beatific.

"Neither did I, my dear Irene, until I made your acquaintance."

Laughter erupted at the table. When it died down, Maurice spoke.

"What happened, John?"

The naval officer scowled. "I burned down the workshop, that's what happened."

"Again?"

"Yes, thank you—*again!*" John began to rise, but Antonina waved him down with a smile.

"Please, John! I've had too much to drink. I'll get dizzy, watching you stump around."

The naval officer subsided. After a moment, he muttered: "It's the damned naphtha, Maurice. The local stuff's crap. I need to get my hands on good quality naphtha. And for that—"

He turned to the bishop. "Isn't your friend Michael of Macedonia in Arabia now?"

The bishop shook his head. "Not any longer. He returned a few

weeks ago and has taken up residence nearby. He would not have
been much help to you, in any event. He was in western Arabia,
among the Beni Ghassan. Western Arabia's not the best place for
naphtha, you know. And, besides, I don't think—"

He coughed, fell silent.

Hermogenes was about to ask what the famous Michael of
Macedonia had been doing in Arabia when he suddenly spotted
both Antonina and Irene giving him an intent stare. He pressed
his lips shut. A moment later, both women favored him with
very slight smiles.

Something's afoot, he thought to himself. *There are hidden currents here, deep ones. I think this is a very good time for a young
officer to keep his mouth shut, shut, shut. No harm in listening,
though.*

Maurice spoke again.

"There's an Arab officer in our cavalry—well, he's half-Arab—a
hecatontarch by the name of Mark. Mark of Edessa. His mother's
family lives near Hira, but they're not affiliated to the Lakhmids.
Bedouin stock, mostly. I'll speak to him. He might be able to
arrange something."

"I'd appreciate it," said John. A moment later, the naval officer
rose from the table.

"I'm to bed," he announced. "Tomorrow I've got to rebuild that
damned workshop. Again."

As he left, he and Antonina exchanged smiles. There was nothing in that exchange, noted Hermogenes, beyond a comfortable
friendship. He thought back on the bizarre, leering expression
which had crossed Antonina's face earlier in the evening, in the
presence of Procopius.

*Deep currents. Coming from a hidden well called Belisarius, if
I'm not mistaken. I do believe my favorite general is up to his tricks
again. So. Only one question remains. How do I get in on this?*

Maurice arose. "Me, too." The hecatontarch glanced at Hermogenes.

"I believe I'll stay a bit," said Hermogenes. He extended his
cup to Irene. "If you would?"

Maurice left the room. Antonina yawned and stretched.

"I'd better look in on Photius. He wasn't feeling well today." She
rose, patted Irene on the shoulder, and looked at Hermogenes.

"How long will you be staying?"

"Just for the night," replied Hermogenes. "I'm leaving early in the morning. I really can't be absent from the army for long. Sittas seems to have finally gotten lance charges out of his system, and he's beginning to make noises about general maneuvers."

"Come again, when you can."

"I shall. Most certainly."

Moments later, he and Irene were alone in the room. Hermogenes and she stared at each other in silence, for some time.

He understood the meaning in her gaze. A question, really. *Is this man staying at the table to seduce me? Or—*

He smiled, then.

I've done some foolish things in my life. But I'm not dumb enough to try to seduce her. As my Uncle Theodosius always said: never chase women who are a lot smarter than you. You won't catch them, or, what's worse, you might.

"So, Irene. Tell me about it. As much as you can."

The next morning, Antonina arose early, to give her regards to Hermogenes before he left. As she walked out of the villa, the sun was just coming up. She found the young merarch already in the courtyard, holding his saddled horse. He was talking quietly with Irene.

Antonina was surprised to see the spymaster. As a rule, Irene viewed sunrise as a natural disaster to be avoided at all costs.

When she came up, Hermogenes smiled and bowed politely. Antonina and the merarch exchanged pleasantries, before he mounted his horse and rode off.

Antonina glanced at Irene. The spymaster yawned mightily.

"You're up early," she commented.

Irene grimaced. "No, I'm just up later than usual. I haven't slept." She nodded toward the diminishing figure of Hermogenes, who was now passing through the gate. "He's quite a bright fellow, you know. He figured out much more than I would have expected, just from watching the people around him."

"Is that why he stayed at the table? I assumed it was because he had intentions toward you."

Irene shook her head, smiling. "Oh, no. His conduct was absolutely impeccable. Propriety incarnate. No, he wanted to join the conspiracy. Whatever it is. He doesn't care, really, as long as Belisarius is involved. A bad case of hero worship, he's got."

"What did you tell him?"

"Enough. Not too much. But enough to make him happy, and win his allegiance. I think quite highly of that young man, Antonina. He's everything Belisarius said, and more."

Antonina put her arm around her friend's waist and began to guide her back into the villa.

"Fill me in on the details later. You look absolutely exhausted, Irene. You need to get to bed."

Irene chuckled. "*Back* to bed, actually." Feeling Antonina's little start of surprise, Irene grinned wearily.

"I said I hadn't *slept*, Antonina. We didn't talk about conspiracies the whole damned night."

"But—"

Irene's grin widened. "I find handsome young men who are smart enough not to try to seduce me to be quite irresistible."

Chapter 21
GWALIOR
Autumn, 529 AD

"I believe I owe Venandakatra an apology," remarked Belisarius.

Garmat frowned. "Why in the world would you owe that swine an apology?" he demanded crossly.

"Oh, I have no intention of giving it to him. That's an obligation which wears very lightly on my shoulders. But I owe it to him nonetheless."

Belisarius gestured ahead, to the enormous procession which was snaking its way along the right bank of the Narmada.

The small Roman/Axumite contingent was located far back from the head of the caravan. The general and Garmat were riding next to each other, on horseback. Just behind them came Valentinian and Anastasius, and the slave scribe, also on horseback. The rest of their party were borne by the two elephants given them by the Malwa. Ezana and Wahsi served as mahouts for the great beasts. Eon and the Maratha women rode in the howdah atop one elephant. The Kushan women and Menander rode in the other. The young cataphract had protested the arrangement, insisting that he was quite capable of riding a horse. But Belisarius had insisted, and truth be told, the lad's protest had been more a matter of form than content. Menander might not yet be well enough to ride a horse, but, in certain other respects, his health had improved dramatically. Judging, at least, from the cheerful and complacent look on his face, on those rare occasions when the curtains of his howdah were opened.

297

Ousanas, as always, insisted on traveling by foot. Nor was he hard-pressed by the chore. The caravan's pace could barely be described as an ambling walk.

Belisarius smiled. "I accused Venandakatra, you may recall, of putting together this grandiose exhibition for purely egotistical motives."

"So? He *is* an egotist. A flaming megalomaniac."

Belisarius smiled. "True, true. But he's also an *intelligent* megalomaniac. There's a purpose to this spectacle, beyond gratifying his vanity. Are you aware that this is not the normal route from Bharakuccha to the Gangetic plain?"

"It isn't?"

Belisarius shook his head. "No. We are traveling south of the Vindhyas." He pointed to the mountain range on their left. The mountains were not high—not more than a few thousand feet—but they were heavily forested and looked to be quite rugged.

"At some point we shall have to cross those mountains, which, by all accounts, is not an easy task. Especially for a caravan like this one."

"This isn't a caravan," grumbled Garmat. "It's a small army!"

"Precisely. And that's the point of the whole exercise. The normal route, according to my cataphracts—who got the information from their Kushan ladies—would take us *north* of the Vindhyas. Semidesert terrain, but well traveled and easily managed. But that route, you see, goes through Malwa territory."

"So does this one."

"Today, yes. But this is newly conquered land, Garmat. Until a year ago"—he gestured toward the surrounding countryside—"all this was part of the Andhra Empire."

Comprehension dawned. "Ah," muttered Garmat. "So this procession is designed to grind down the new subjects even further. Remind them of their status." He examined the scenery. The great forest which seemed to carpet the interior of India had been cleared away, at one time. But the fields were untended, as were the thatched mud-walled huts of the peasantry scattered here and there. The area seemed almost uninhabited, despite the fact that it was obviously fertile land. A warrior himself, in his younger days, Garmat had no difficulty recognizing war-ravaged terrain.

The Ethiopian adviser then examined the spectacle ahead of

them on the trail. The "caravan" was enormous. He could not even see the very front of it, but he could picture the scene.

The caravan was led by an elephant followed immediately by surveyors. The surveyors were measuring the route by means of long cords which one would carry forward, then the other leapfrog him, calling the count at each cord. A third surveyor recorded the count.

Garmat and Belisarius had spent the first day of the journey puzzling out the purpose of this exercise. The conclusion they came to fell in line with everything they had seen in Bharakuccha. A picture of the rising Malwa power was taking shape in their mind. A huge, sprawling empire, encompassing a vast multitude of different peoples and customs. Which, it was becoming clear, the Malwa were determined to hammer into a centralized, unified state.

The phenomenon, they realized, was new to India. True, great empires had existed here before: the Gupta Empire, the immediate predecessor of the Malwa; and the even larger Mauryan empire of ancient history, which had encompassed most of India. But those empires, for all their size and splendor, had rested lightly on the teeming populace below. The Guptan and Mauryan emperors had made no attempt to interfere with the daily lives of their subjects, or the power and privileges of provincial satraps and local potentates. They had been satisfied with tribute, respect, submission. Beyond that, they had occupied themselves with their feasts, their harems, their elaborate hunts, and their great architectural projects. Even the greatest of those ancient rulers, the legendary Ashoka, had never tried to meddle with Indian customs and traditions beyond his patronage and support for the new Buddhist faith.

But, of course, neither the Guptan nor the Mauryan Empires had ever had the ambitions of the Malwa. The empires of the past were quite satisfied with ruling India, or even just northern India. They had not aspired to world conquest.

"All roads lead to Rome," Belisarius had murmured. "That's how the legions conquered the Mediterranean, and ruled it. The Malwa, it seems, intend to copy us."

Yes, the explanation fit. It fit, for instance, with the new bureaucracy which Belisarius and Garmat had noted in Bharakuccha. There had been much resentment and disaffection expressed, by the populace, toward that bureaucracy. It was impossible to miss, even from conversations in the streets. (Within a few years, Belisarius and Garmat had agreed, the conversations would be far less open; already the Malwa spies and provocateurs were doing their work.)

Strange new bureaucracy, by traditional Indian standards. Appointed by annual examinations, instead of breeding. True, most of the successful applicants were of *brahmin* or kshatriya descent, scions of one or another of the castes of those noblest of the four respectable classes, the twice-born *varna*. But there were *vaisya* bureaucrats also, and even—so it was rumored—a *sudra* official!

No untouchables, however. The Malwa regime was even harsher toward untouchables than tradition required. But that small bow toward hallowed custom brought little comfort to the twice-born. The Malwa were also grinding down the four respectable varna, among every people except the Malwa themselves and their privileged Rajput vassals. (And the Ye-tai, of course; but the barbarians had no proper varna and castes to begin with; uncouth, heathen savages.)

More and more sudra castes were finding themselves counted among the untouchables, now. Even, here and there, a few vaisya castes. As yet, the noble varna—the kshatriya and brahmin—seemed immune. But who was to know what the future might bring?

A much-hated new bureaucracy. Hated, but feared. For these new officials were armed with authority to override class and caste customs—overbearing and officious, and quick to exert their power against traditional satraps and long-established local potentates.

Great power, enforced by the Malwa weapons, and the massive Malwa army, and the privileged Rajput vassals, and the even more privileged Ye-tai. Enforced, as well, by their horde of spies and informants, and—worst of all—by the new religious castes: the Mahaveda priests and their mahamimamsa torturers.

For all the power of the new dynasty, however, it had become clear to Belisarius and Garmat that the process by which the Malwa were reshaping India was very incomplete. Incomplete, and contradictory. Much of the real power, they suspected, still lay in the hands of traditional rulers. Who chafed, and snarled, and snapped at the new officialdom.

True, they rarely rebelled, but the danger was ever present.

Even at that moment, in fact, a great rebellion was taking place in the northern province whose capital was Ranapur. Their own expedition, eventually, was destined to arrive there. The emperor was overseeing the siege of Ranapur personally, which gave Belisarius and Garmat a good indication of how seriously the Malwa took the affair.

Following the surveyors and their elephant, a quarter mile back, came a party of Rajput horsemen. Two hundred of them, approximately, elite cavalry. Behind them came several elephants carrying pairs of huge kettledrums beaten by men on the elephants' backs. Then a party of footmen carrying flags.

Next—still out of sight from where they rode—came another troop of Rajput cavalry. Perhaps a hundred. Behind them came a larger contingent of Ye-tai cavalry.

The next stage of the caravan was within sight, and impossible to miss. Twenty war elephants, their huge heads and bodies protected by iron-reinforced leather armor. Each elephant was guided by a mahout and bore a howdah containing four Malwa kshatriya. The Malwa soldiers were not carrying rocket troughs, of course. Those weapons would panic the great pachyderms. Instead, they were armed with bows and those odd little flasks which Belisarius had pronounced to be *grenades*. The smaller variety of those grenades were bound to arrows. The larger variety, Belisarius explained, were designed to be hurled by hand.

Behind the troop of war elephants came Venandakatra himself, and his entourage of priests and mahamimamsa. The Mahaveda and the torturers rode atop elephants, four to a howdah. Occasionally, Venandakatra would do likewise. For the most part, however, the great lord chose to ride in a special palanquin. The vehicle was large and luxurious, borne by eight giant slaves. The palanquin was surrounded by a little mob of servants walking alongside. Some of the servants toted jugs of water and wine; others, platters of food; still others carried whisks to shoo away the ever present flies. Nothing was lacking for Venandakatra's comfort.

For the lord's nightly comfort, eight of his concubines rode in howdahs on two elephants, which followed Venandakatra's palanquin. The caravan would always halt at sunset and set up camp. Venandakatra's tent—if such a modest term could be used to describe his elaborate suite of pavilions—was always set up before he arrived. The lord possessed two such "tents." The one not being used was sent ahead, guarded by yet another troop of Rajput cavalry, to be prepared for the following night's sojourn.

The stage of the caravan which followed Venandakatra and his entourage was composed of Malwa infantry. No less than a thousand soldiers. The great number of them, presumably, was to compensate for their mediocre quality. These were not elite forces, simply a run-of-the-mill detachment from the huge mass of the Malwa army. The troops themselves were not Malwa, but a collection of men from various of the subject peoples. The officers were primarily Malwa, but not kshatriya.

Belisarius had been more interested in the infantry than in the elite cavalry units. The Ye-tai he understood, and, after some examination, the Rajput as well. They were impressive, to be sure. But Belisarius was a Roman, and the Romans had centuries of experience dealing with Persian cavalry.

But Belisarius thought the future of war lay with the infantry, and so he subjected the Malwa infantry to his closest scrutiny. It did not take him long to arrive at a general assessment.

Garmat expressed the sentiment aloud.

"That's as sorry a bunch of foot soldiers as I've ever seen," sneered the Ethiopian. "Look at them!"

Belisarius smiled, leaned over his saddle, and whispered:

"What tipped you off? Was it the rust on the spear blades? Or the rust on the armor?"

"Is that crap *armor*?" demanded Garmat. "There's more metal on my belt buckle!"

"Or was it the slouching posture? The hang-dog expressions? The shuffling footsteps?"

"My daughter's footsteps were more assured when she was two," snorted the Ethiopian. "The sarawit would eat these clowns for breakfast."

Belisarius straightened back up in his saddle. The smile left his face.

"True. So would any good unit of Roman infantry. But let's not get too cocky, Garmat. For all my speeches about quality outdoing quantity, numbers *do* count. There must be a horde of these foot soldiers. If the Malwa can figure out the logistics, they'll be able to flood the West. And they still have their special weapons, and the Ye-tai and the Rajput. *Lots* of Ye-tai and Rajput, from what I can tell."

Garmat grimaced, but said nothing.

Belisarius turned and looked toward the rear of the caravan. The Romans and Axumites were located right after the infantry. They were at the very end of the military portion of the procession. Following them came the enormous tail of the beast.

"And they've got a long ways to go to figure out proper logistics," he muttered, "if this is anything to go by."

Garmat followed his eyes.

"This is not normal?" he asked.

"No, Garmat, this is not normal. Not even the sloppiest Roman army has a supply train like this one. It's absurd!"

Garmat found it hard not to laugh aloud. At that moment, the general's normally expressionless face was twisted into a positively Homeric scowl.

"Hell hath no fury like a craftsman scorned," he muttered.

"What was that?"

"Nothing, Belisarius, nothing. I would point out to you, however, that much of the chaos behind us is due to civilians and camp followers."

Belisarius was not mollified.

"So what? Every army faces that problem! You think camp followers don't attach themselves to every Roman army that marches anywhere? You name it, they'll be there: merchants, food and drink purveyors, pimps and whores, slave traders, loot liquidators, the lot. Not to mention a horde of people who just want to travel along the same route and take advantage of the protection offered."

"And how do *you* deal with it? Drive them off?"

"Bah!" Belisarius made a curt gesture. "That's impossible. Camp followers are like flies." He swiped at a fly buzzing around his face. "No, Garmat, there's no point to that. Instead, you do the opposite. Incorporate them into the army directly. Put them under discipline. Train them!"

Garmat's eyes widened. "Train merchants and slave traders? Pimps and whores?"

Belisarius grinned. "It's not hard, Garmat. Not, at least, once you get over the initial hump. There's a trade-off, you see. In return for following the rules, the camp followers get a recognized and assured place in the army. Keeps out competitors."

The general scratched his chin. "It occurs to me, however, that this rampant disorder can serve our purpose. There is one little problem in our plan that's been gnawing at me—"

He looked down at Ousanas, striding alongside.

"You are a miserable slave, are you not?"

The dawazz stooped and bent his head in a flamboyant gesture of cringing submissiveness. The pose went poorly with the great stabbing spear in his hand.

"Well, I am shocked," grumbled Belisarius. "Absolutely shocked to see you lolling about without a care in the world. In *my* country, miserable slaves keep themselves busy."

Ousanas cocked an eye upward. The pose was now threadbare.

"Oh, yes," continued Belisarius, "very busy. Scurrying about all over the place—buying provisions, haggling over supplies, that sort of thing." He scowled. "All a pose, of course. The lazy buggers are actually just keeping out of their master's sight so they can lolligag. Out of everybody's sight, in fact. Nobody ever sees a slave where he's supposed to be. You get used to it."

Ousanas looked back at the motley horde of camp followers.

"Ah," he said. "Comprehension dawns. Although the great general might—just now and again—condescend to plain speaking. You want me to make myself scarce, so that when the time comes when I disappear altogether, no spy will even notice my absence."

Belisarius smiled. "You have captured the Platonic Form of my concept."

A moment later, Ousanas was drifting away, the very image of a dispirited, lackadaisical slave. Belisarius, watching, was struck by the uncanny manner of his movements. Ousanas was the only man the general had ever known who could shuffle silently.

A gleeful feminine squeal coming from ahead brought his attention forward. Belisarius and Garmat looked up at the howdah riding on the elephant in front of them. Curtains made it impossible to see within.

"At least he's stopped complaining," growled Belisarius.

Garmat shook his head. "You are being unfair, General. He is not promiscuous by nature. Not, at least, by the standards of royalty." The adviser shrugged. "True, he is a prince, and a handsome and charming boy in his own right. He has never lacked the opportunity for copulation, and certainly has no aversion to the sport. But—he likes women, you see, and enjoys their conversation and their company. So he much prefers a more settled situation."

After a moment, Belisarius smiled wryly. "Well, I can hardly disapprove of that. My own temperament, as it happens." He gestured toward the howdah. "He seems to have settled in here."

Garmat nodded. "He and Tarabai seem to be growing quite fond of each other. I notice that the other Maratha girls have stopped sharing his howdah lately, at night, except—"

He fell silent, glancing around quickly. There were no possible spies within hearing range.

"How is she doing?" asked Belisarius. "Have you heard? For obvious reasons, I stay away from the howdah."

"I have not been inside myself. Eon says she has come to accept his presence, but he is not sure how she would react to another man. She no longer flinches from him, but she still doesn't speak—not even to Tarabai. She is eating well, finally. Her physical wounds are all healed. Eon says he is always careful to keep away from her, as far as possible within the confines of the howdah. He thinks she no longer feels threatened by him. If for no other reason than—"

Another squeal came from the howdah.

"—Tarabai has his erotic impulses well under control," chuckled Belisarius.

The general pointed to the mahout guiding the elephant.

"I trust Ezana is not disgruntled? Or Wahsi? Or Ousanas, for that matter?"

Garmat laughed. "Why should they be? True, they no longer enjoy Tarabai's company, but there are still the other two Maratha women. And the Kushan girls have been willing to spread their affections, whenever your cataphracts are too tired to pester them. Besides, they are all soldiers. The best of soldiers. Not given to stupid jealousies, and well aware that we are following a battle plan."

Another squeal. A low, masculine groan.

"In a manner of speaking."

Belisarius grinned. Then:

"Well, Eon's certainly carried out his part in the plan. He was absolutely perfect, the first day of the trip."

"Wasn't he marvelous?" agreed Garmat. "I thought Venandakatra was going to die of apoplexy, right there on the spot."

The adviser patted his mount affectionately. "Poor Venandaka-tra. Here he presents us with the finest horses available, and the prince can't stop whining that he needs a howdah, with plump cushions for his royal fanny."

"A very *large* elephant to carry it," said Belisarius, laughing, "one strong enough to bear up under the prince's humping."

Garmat was laughing himself, now. "And then—did you see the look on Venandakatra's face after—"

"—his petty plot backfired?" Belisarius practically howled. "Priceless! What a complete idiot! He presents the largest, most unruly elephant he can find—"

"—to Africans!"

Belisarius and Garmat fell silent, savoring the memory.

"*This* is your largest elephant?" Ezana had queried. "This *midget?*"

"Look at those puny ears," mourned Wahsi. "Maybe he's still a baby."

"Probably not elephant at all," pronounced Ousanas. "Maybe him just fat, funny-looking gnu."

Venandakatra's glare had been part fury, part disbelief. The fury had remained. The disbelief had vanished, after Ezana and Wahsi rapidly demonstrated their skills as mahouts. After the sarwen reminisced over various Axumite military campaigns, in which *African* elephants figured prominently. After Ousanas extolled the virtues of the *African* elephant, not forgetting to develop his point by way of contrast with the Indian elephant. So-called elephant. But probably not elephant. Him probably just big tapir, with delusions of grandeur.

After they stopped laughing, Garmat remarked:

"We may have overdone it, actually. I notice that Venandakatra hasn't invited us to share his dinner since this trip began."

"He will," said Belisarius confidently. "It's only been two weeks since we left Bharakuccha. At the rate this—this matronly promenade—is going, we'll be two months getting to his 'modest country estate.'" He snorted. "If I was one of those surveyors, I'd have died of boredom by now. I doubt we're averaging more than ten miles a day. At best."

"You are so sure, my friend? Your stratagem has still not gelled."

"He will. In another two weeks or so, I estimate. Your average megalomaniac, of course, would only need a week to get over a petty snit. But even Venandakatra won't take much more than a month. Whatever else he is, the man is not stupid, and I've given him enough hints. He's developed his own plan, by now, which also hasn't gelled. It can't, until he talks to us further. To me, I should say. So—yes. Two weeks."

And, sure enough, it was thirteen days later that the courier arrived from Venandakatra's pavilion, shortly after the caravan had halted for the night. Bearing a message from the great lord himself, written in perfect Greek, politely inviting Belisarius to join him for his "modest evening meal."

"I note that Eon and I are not invited," remarked Garmat. The old adviser stared at Belisarius, and then bowed.

"I salute you, Belisarius. A great general, indeed. Until this moment, I confess, I was somewhat skeptical your plan would work."

Belisarius shrugged. "Let's not assume anything. As my old teacher Maurice always reminds me: 'Never expect the enemy to do what you expect him to.'"

Garmat shook his head. "Excellent advice. But it does not encompass all military wisdom. Every now and then, you know, the enemy *does* do what you expect him to. Then you must be prepared to strike ruthlessly."

"Exactly what I keep telling Maurice!" said Belisarius gaily. He tossed the message into the camp fire which Ousanas was just starting. The dawazz straightened, looked over.

"Time?" he asked. The grin began to spread.

Again, Belisarius shrugged. "We won't know for a bit. But I think so, yes. Are you ready?"

Like the great Pharos at Alexandria, that grin in the night.

Within three hours of his arrival at Venandakatra's pavilion, Belisarius was certain. For a moment, he considered some way of signaling Ousanas, but then dismissed the thought. A pointless worry, that, like fretting over how to signal prey to a crouching lion.

The general had been almost certain within two hours, actually. After the usual meaningless amenities during the meal, the wine was poured, and Venandakatra had immediately launched into the subject of Eon's amatory exploits. "Trying to pry out secrets," he'd said, one gay blade to another. But it was soon obvious there were no secrets he didn't know. Except one, which he knew, but misinterpreted exactly as Belisarius had thought he would.

As Ousanas said: *Catch the prey by reading its soul.*

"Ah, that explains it," said Venandakatra. He giggled. "I had wondered why he chose only Maratha bitches to accompany him on this trip. After"—another giggle—"sampling *all* the many Indian varieties in Bharakuccha."

Belisarius could not manage a giggle, but he thought his coarse guffaw was quite good enough.

"It's the truth. He loves conquered women. The more recently conquered, the better. They're the most submissive, you see, and that's his taste." Another guffaw, with a drooling trickle of wine down his chin thrown in for good measure. "Why, his soldiers told me that when they conquered Hymria, the kid—he was only seventeen, mind you—had an entire—"

Here followed an utterly implausible tale, to any but Venandakatra. Implausible, at least, in its gross brutality; its portrayal of Eon's stamina was remotely conceivable, in light of his performance in Bharakuccha. Which Venandakatra obviously knew, in detail. As Belisarius had foreseen, the Malwa lord's spies had interrogated the women who shared the prince's bed. All except the Maratha women, of course.

Still, Venandakatra almost smelled out the falsehood. Almost.

"It's odd, though," the Vile One remarked casually, after he stopped cackling over the story, "but I didn't get the impression—I know nothing myself, you understand, but rumors concerning foreigners always spread—that any of the women who passed through his chambers had been particularly badly beaten. Except by his cock!"

Another round of giggles and guffaws.

Belisarius shrugged. "Well, as I understand it from his adviser, the lad felt under certain constraints. He *is* in a foreign land." The general waved his hand airily. "There are laws, after all."

He gulped down some more wine.

"So," he burped, "the boy finally got frustrated and ordered his men to find him some outright slaves." Another burp. "Slaves can be treated any way their master chooses, in any country."

(That was a lie. It was not true in most civilized realms of Belisarius' acquaintance, not in modern times. It was certainly

not true under Roman law. But he did not think that Venandakatra would know otherwise. Slaves, and their legal rights, were
far beneath the great lord's contempt. In any country—certainly
in his own.)

"True, true." A sly, leering glance. "Rumor has it, in fact, that
one of his Maratha slaves fell afoul of her new master."

Belisarius controlled his emotions, and the expression on his
face. It was not difficult to control his disgust, or his contempt.
He had plenty of experience doing that, after all these weeks—
months!—in Venandakatra's company. But he had a difficult time
controlling his shame.

For a moment, his eyes wandered, scanning the rich tapestries
which covered the silk walls of the pavilion. His gaze settled on
the candelabra resting at the center of the table. For all its golden
glitter, and the superb craftsmanship of the design, he thought
the piece was utterly grotesque. A depiction of some dancing
god, leering, priap erect, with candles rising from the silver skulls
cupped in the deity's four hands.

He tore his eyes away from the thing and looked back at
Venandakatra. He even managed a leer of his own.

The memory still burned, of the time he had sent the hostel
proprietor into the girl's room, on some trumped-up pretext.
He had instructed the Maratha woman tending her to allow the
proprietor to enter (which she had done, reluctantly—she was a
slave, after all). But he hadn't warned Eon in advance, because
he knew the prince would have barred the way.

*It worked, of course. The proprietor saw the girl, and judging
from the contempt on his face as he left, knew what he saw. Or
thought he did. Venandakatra obviously placed the interpretation
I hoped for on it, after he had the man interrogated.*

*But I thought the prince was going to attack me, afterward,
when he found out. He would have, I think, if Ezana and Wahsi
hadn't restrained him.*

It was even harder to control another emotion.

*God, how I've grown to love that boy. He didn't care in the
least about his own injured royal pride, or what the hostel owner
thought of him. Only that I'd caused the poor girl to be terrified
again. May my son Photius grow up to be like him.*

But Belisarius was a general, a great general—a breed of men
among whose qualities ruthlessness is never absent. And so he

managed to keep the leer on his face. And another drooling trickle of wine down his chin, thrown in for good measure.

Venandakatra refilled his cup personally. Unlike every other visit Belisarius had made, the Malwa lord had dismissed all the servants after the meal was finished.

"I notice the prince does not seem to mind sharing his women with his own soldiers," commented Venandakatra. "Not what you normally expect from royalty."

Belisarius belched. "I don't see why. It's not as if they were wives, or even concubines. The bitches are just whores and slaves." Another belch. "I share the Kushan sluts with my own soldiers, for that matter. I've done it often enough before, on campaign."

Belisarius gave Venandakatra a knowing smirk—one experienced old soldier to another (which the Malwa lord certainly was *not*, but liked to pretend he was).

"Helps keep your popularity with the troops, you know. The common touch. And there's always plenty to go around. Especially after sacking a town." The general's smirk became a savage grin. "God, how I love a sack. Sieges are pure shit, but afterward—oh, yes!"

Venandakatra giggled. "So do I!" he cried.

Vile One, indeed. I doubt he's ever come within bow range of a besieged city in his life. But I'm sure he was the first to line up afterward, selecting the prizes from the captured women.

Again, Belisarius fought down his gorge. He *hated* sacks. Would do anything he possibly could to avoid one, short of losing a campaign. It was almost impossible to keep troops under control in a captured city after a hard-fought siege, except for elite units like his own cataphracts. There was nothing so horrible as a city being sacked. It was hell on earth, Satan's maw itself. The most brutal and bestial crimes of which men were capable were committed then. Committed with a gleeful savagery that would shame the very demons of the Pit.

But he kept his gorge well under control. He was a general, a great general, whose ruthlessness always had a purpose. The edge to the blade, when it came time for the cutting.

"You, on the other hand, seem to have a liking for Kushan women," remarked Venandakatra idly. "And your cataphracts also, I hear."

Time for the cutting.

"Oh God, yes!" cried Belisarius. "When I discovered there were

Kushan whores in Bharakuccha, I sent Valentinian and Anastasius straight off to round up a few." Guffaw, guffaw, guffaw. "They raced like the wind, let me tell you—and that's something to see, with a man built like Anastasius!"

Giggle. "I can imagine! He's the large one, isn't he?" Giggle.

Belisarius waited. Timing was the key to a trap. Timing.

He waited until the puzzled frown had almost taken shape on the Vile One's brow. Then remarked casually, "Most lascivious women in the world, Kushans. Most lascivious *people*, for that matter. The men even more than the women." He coughed on a gulp of wine. "Don't misunderstand!" he exclaimed, waving off a disreputable notion. "I'm not interested in men *that* way. But it's true, believe me. It's why I got rid of all my Kushan mercenaries. Good men in a battle, no question about it. But they're just too much of a bother. Can't keep their hands off any woman in the vicinity. Even started sniffing around my own wife!"

The frown on the Vile One's brow thickened. The scaly wrinkles collected around his deep-set eyes.

"Really?" he asked. "I wasn't aware you were acquainted with the folk."

"Kushans? To the contrary. Find them all over the Roman Empire. Soldiers and whores, mostly. It's the only things they're good at. Fighting and fucking. Especially fucking."

Venandakatra sipped at his wine, thoughtfully.

"I had heard, now that you mention it, that you yourself spoke excellent Kushan." He shrugged. "I assumed it was just a false rumor, of course. There seemed no way you—"

He fell away from completing the sentence. Venandakatra had enjoyed some wine, but he was not inebriated. (Quite unlike the Roman sot.) The Malwa lord realized that he was on the verge of revealing too much of his spying operations.

You arrogant idiot, thought Belisarius, reading the sudden silence correctly. *I always assumed you knew everything, and planned accordingly.*

Belisarius filled the silence, then, with a bevy of amusing tales, one after the other. The sort of tales with which one veteran lecher entertains another. A less egotistical man than Venanda-katra might have wondered why the tales exclusively concerned Kushans. And might have wondered, especially, why so many of the tales concerned the sexual exploits of Kushan *men*.

Oh, such exploits! Their unbridled lust. Their strangely seductive ways. Their uncanny ability to wheedle open the legs of women—young women, especially. And virgins! Lambs to the slaughter, lambs to the slaughter. Didn't matter who they were, where they were, what they were. If the girl was a virgin, no Kushan could resist the challenge. And rise to it! Oh, yes! No men on earth were more skilled at defloration than Kushans. Especially the older men, the middle-aged veteran types. Uncanny, absolutely uncanny.

Throughout the tales, Venandakatra said not a word. But he did not seem bored. No, not at all. Very attentive, in fact.

Every good blade has two edges. Time for the backstroke.

"Enough of that!" exclaimed the general. He held out his cup. "Would you be so good?"

Venandakatra refilled the cup. Belisarius held it high.

"But I'm being a poor guest. And you are much too modest a host. I hear rumors myself, you know, now and then. And I hear you have come into a particularly good piece of fortune." Here, a wild guffaw. "A great piece, if you'll pardon the expression. A royal piece!"

He quaffed down the wine in a single gulp.

"My congratulations!"

Venandakatra struggled to maintain his own composure. Anger at the crude foreigner's insolent familiarity warred with pride in his new possession.

Pride won, of course. *Trap the prey by reading its soul.*

"So I have!" he exclaimed. "The Princess Shakuntala. Of the noblest blood, and a great beauty. The black-eyed pearl of the Satavahana, they call her."

"You've not seen her yourself?"

Venandakatra shook his head.

"No. But I've heard excellent descriptions."

Here, Venandakatra launched into his own lengthy recital, extolling the qualities of the Princess Shakuntala. As he saw them.

Belisarius listened attentively. Partly, of course, for the sake of his stratagem. But partly, also, because he was undergoing the strangest experience. Like a sort of mental—spiritual, it might be better to say—double vision. The general had never laid eyes on the girl in his life. But he had seen her once, in a vision, through the eyes of another man. A man as different from the one sitting

across the table from him as day from night. As different as a
panther from a cobra.

Once Venandakatra was finished, Belisarius saluted him again
with his cup and poured himself another full goblet. Venandakatra,
he noticed, had stopped drinking some time ago.

The general found it a bit hard not to laugh. Then, thinking it
over, he did laugh—a drunken, besotted kind of laugh. Meaningless. He drained his cup and poured himself yet another. From
the corner of his eye he caught the Vile One's faint smile.

*I'm from Thrace, you jackass. A simple farm boy, at bottom.
Raised in the countryside, where there's not much to do but drink.
I could have drunk you under the table when I was ten.*

"You'll be seeing her soon, then," he exclaimed. "Lucky man!"

He fell back into his seat, hastily grabbing the table to keep
from falling. Half the wine sloshed out of his cup, most of it onto
the gorgeous rug covering the floor. The candelabra in the center
of the table teetered. Venandakatra steadied it hastily with a hand,
but not in time to prevent one of the candles from falling.

"Sorry," muttered Belisarius. Venandakatra's expression, for just
a fleeting instant, was savage. But he said nothing. He simply
placed the candle back in its holder and waved off the mishap
with a casual flutter of the fingers.

Belisarius drained what was left in his cup. Venandakatra
instantly poured him another.

Blearily, Belisarius grinned at the Malwa lord. Then, leering:

"She'll be a virgin, of course. Bound to be, a princess!" Guffaw,
guffaw. "God, there's nothing like a virgin! Love the way they
squeal when you stick 'em!"

He shook a sage, cautioning finger in Venandakatra's direction. A solemn look fell on his face—one experienced pedophile
advising another.

"Make sure you watch her well, mind! A prize like that? Ha!
Surround her with eunuchs, I would, or priests sworn to celibacy.
Better yet—eunuch priests." Guffaw, guffaw. "And then I'd check
under their robes!"

He half-choked on another swallow of wine, then added: "We
have an old saying in Rome, you know: *Quis custodiet ipsos
custodes?*"

Venandakatra frowned. "I'm afraid I don't speak Latin."

"Ah. I assumed—my apologies—your Greek is excellent." Belch.

"Well, it basically translates as: *Who will guard the guardians?* What it means is, how shall I—"

"I understand perfectly well what it means!" snapped Venandakatra.

Oh, my. Isn't he testy? Time to extract the blade.

And nick him elsewhere, so he doesn't notice that he's bleeding to death.

"But that's enough talk of women!" roared Belisarius. "Worthless cunts, all of 'em. Beneath our notice, except when we're in the mood for humping. We're men of affairs, you and I. Important men."

He reached over the table for the wine, lost his balance, fell to the floor. "Bitches, all of them," he muttered, staggering to his feet. "Treacherous sluts." He groped his way back into his chair.

"Good for fucking, and that's it," grumbled the general, glaring at the table. Venandakatra poured him another cup. From the corner of his eye, again, Belisarius caught Venandakatra's expression. Contempt, overlaying worry.

Now I have but to lay opportunity over contempt, and the worry will work its way to the heart, free of suspicion.

"Men of affairs, I say," he repeated, slurring the words. "Important men." He grit his teeth. "Important men."

Venandakatra slid in his own blade.

"So we are, my friend. Although"—slight hesitation, discreet pause—"not always appreciated, perhaps."

Belisarius' jaws tightened. "Isn't that the fucking truth? Isn't it just? My own—"

Careful. He's not stupid.

Belisarius waved his hand. "Never mind," he mumbled.

The Vile One struck again.

First, he took a sip from his own cup. The first sip in an hour, by Belisarius' estimation. (Never underestimate the foe, of course. Who knows? The Roman might not be quite as drunk as he looks.)

"I am fortunate in that regard," remarked Venandakatra idly. "The Emperor Skandagupta is always appreciative of my efforts on his behalf. Always fair, in his criticisms. Mild criticisms, never more than that. And he gives me his full trust, unstintingly."

Belisarius peered at him suspiciously. But it was obvious the suspicion was directed toward the statement, not the speaker of it.

"Oh, no—it's quite true, I assure you."

"Hard to believe," muttered Belisarius resentfully. "In my experience—"

He fell silent, again. "Ah, what's the use?" he mumbled. "Emperors are emperors, and that's that." He seemed lost in his own thoughts. Bleak, bitter thoughts. Black thoughts, drunken thoughts.

Time. As Valentinian says, be economical with the blade.

He lurched to his feet; planted his hands on the table to steady himself.

"I must be off," he announced. Belch. " 'Scuse me. Afraid I've had too much to drink. You'll forgive me, I trust?"

Venandakatra nodded graciously. "I've been known to do it myself, friend." A happy thought: "Men of affairs, you know. Much on our minds. Much to deal with. Bound to drink a bit, now and then."

"The truth, that!" Belisarius smiled at the Vile One. Never, in the history of the world, did a drunk bestow such a cheerful smile of camaraderie on a fellow sot.

"You are most pleasant company, Venandakatra," he said, carefully enunciating the words. A man deep in his cups, determined to project sincerity.

"Most pleasant. Sorry we got off to a bit of a bad start, back there—" The general waved his hand vaguely, more or less in the direction of the sea. Belch. "Back there, in the beginning. On the ship."

"Think nothing of it! Long forgotten, I assure you." Venandakatra rose to his feet. "May I call one of my servants? To assist you back—"

Belisarius waved off the offer.

"Not necessary!" he barked. "Can make it mack, byself—back, myself. Not a problem."

He bowed at Venandakatra, with exaggerated, careful stiffness, and reeled to the entrance. He pulled back the heavily embroidered drapery which served the Malwa lord's pavilion for a tent flap. By the studied care of his movements, he was obviously trying not to inflict damage on the precious fabric. As he was about to pass through into the darkness beyond, he paused, steadying himself with one hand on a tent pole. Then, he looked back at the Malwa lord.

For a few seconds, Venandakatra and Belisarius exchanged

a stare. The expression on the Malwa's face registered a subtle invitation. The face of the Roman general was that of a man consumed by old grievances, brought to the surface by hours of heavy carousing.

Bleak, bitter thoughts. Black thoughts. Drunken thoughts.

Belisarius turned away, shook his head, and stumbled into the night.

He did not need to look back again. He knew what he would see on the Vile One's face. Calculation, overlaying contempt. Contempt, overlaying worry. Worry, buried, freed of suspicion, worming its way into a maggotty soul.

He managed to keep from smiling all the way back to his own tent. Spies, everywhere. He even managed to keep from glancing into the forest which surrounded the caravan. Spies, everywhere. And it would be pointless, anyway, for he would see nothing. In that darkness, there would be nothing to see except a grin. And the hunter never grins, when he is stalking the prey.

When he reached his own tent, he staggered within, and then straightened up. Good Roman leather, that tent. Impossible to see through.

"Well?" asked Garmat.

His next words, the general regretted for years, for he was a man who despised boasting. But he didn't regret them much. They were, after all, irresistible:

"Deadly with a blade, is Belisarius."

Early the next morning—even before daybreak—a party of Mahaveda priests and mahamimamsa "purifiers" left the caravan on horseback, escorted by a Rajput cavalry troop. They were being sent to the palace ahead of the caravan, on a special mission ordered by Lord Venandakatra.

In the heart of mighty Malwa, it did not occur to them to look back on the trail, to see if anyone followed. It would have made no difference if they had. The one who tracked them had been taught his skills by lionesses and pygmies, the greatest hunters in the world.

Chapter 22

Insofar as that term could ever be applied to that man, he was frantic.

An observer watching him would not have realized his state of mind, however. For the man seemed utterly calm and still, crouching in the thick foliage of the brush and trees which came within a few feet of the walls of Venandakatra's palace.

True, an observer might have wondered what he was doing there. A man of average height; black-haired; black-bearded, with a few grey hairs to indicate approaching middle age; barefoot; wearing nothing but a dirty loincloth. But, even there, the conclusion was obvious: a menial, from one of the lower sudra castes, relieving himself in the woods.

No thought of danger would have crossed such an observer's mind. The man was obviously poor, stoop-shouldered from years of drudgery, and quite unarmed. There was no room in that soiled, torn, scanty loincloth to conceal any weapon.

Had such an observer approached, however, he might have begun to question his assumption. For, up close, there were certain things about the man crouching in the woods which did not quite jibe with his appearance.

He was too still, for one thing. Motionless, in fact. No dim-witted menial can prevent himself from idle twitching and scratching.

His musculature, on closer examination, was puzzling. True, the shoulders were stooped—but that can result from deliberate posture. And, while the man was not heavily muscled, the muscles themselves were extraordinarily well-defined. Iron-hard,

317

to all appearance. Not the sort of physique which results from menial toil.

Then, there were the arms and the hands. Very long arms, for a man of his size. Long and powerful. And the hands, in proportion to his build, were huge. Sinewy hands. Scarred, callused hands also—but those scars and calluses were not, quite, the scars produced by years of simple toil.

Finally, the eyes. Hazel eyes, they were—almost yellow-orange. An unusual color for a man of obvious Maratha descent. And then, had the observer come close enough to look into them, another strange feature of the eyes would be noted. There was nothing in those eyes of the dull gaze of a menial. No, the gaze of those eyes was like—

Recognition would come, finally. For the man in the woods was called many things. In one case, because the color of his eyes, and the gaze of his eyes, so closely matched those of the predator for which he was named.

The observer would have no time to shout a warning, then. He would be dead within two seconds. A panther does not need weapons, beyond those provided by nature.

There *was* an observer, in fact. But the panther did not slay him, because he did not spot him. The one observing him was no stranger to woods himself, nor to predators. And he was certainly not fool enough to come near *that* man. Not at *that* moment. Not when the man, had he been a panther in truth, would have been lashing his tail in fury.

No, best to wait. The observer had already found the panther's lair. He would wait for him there, and catch him when he was not quite so prepared for slaughter. The observer knew how to trap predators in their lairs. He had done it before, times beyond counting, and would do it again.

The observer faded away, vanished into the forest without a sound. Had the panther turned at that very moment, he might have caught a sign of his stalker. Not of the stalker himself, for that one was a master of hidden movement. Just an odd, quick, flash of white, gleaming in the darkness of the foliage like a beacon. Just for an instant.

But the panther did not turn. He twitched, slightly. Some buried part of his brain tried to transmit a signal. But it was a

dim, confused, uncertain signal, and the conscious part of the
panther's mind suppressed it.

For two days, now, he had been getting those subconscious signals. *Something is watching.* The first day, he had taken them very
seriously. But he had been able to detect nothing. Nothing—and
he was a man who rarely failed to detect danger. By the second
day, he shrugged off the signals. *Nervous tension, no more.* It was
not logical, after all, that an enemy would stalk him for so long
in those woods without making his presence known.

Why would Malwa waste time apprehending a foe? Here? In
the very heart of their power? With a small army of soldiers at
hand?

The panther shrugged off the signal, again.

Two hours later, his already still form became absolutely rigid.
Something was happening.

A party of Rajput horsemen rode into the open courtyard
before the main door to the Vile One's palace. Escorts for half a
dozen Mahaveda priests and over twenty of the mahamimamsa
carrion-eaters.

The door of the palace opened, the majordomo emerging. The
man was small and corpulent. His rotund form was draped in
fine clothing and a positively splendiferous turban—as befitted one
who, though ultimately a servant, was the most august member
of that lowly class. August enough, at least, that the squad of
Ye-tai who accompanied him did not evince a trace of the rowdy
disrespect which they typically dealt out to servants.

And to others, for that matter. As soon as the Ye-tai spotted
the Rajput horsemen they began bristling, like a pack of mongrels in an alley, faced with alien dogs. The Rajputs, purebreds,
ignored the curs.

The majordomo barked them to order. There was an exchange
of words. Moments later, the priests and the mahamimamsa dismounted and were ushered within the palace. Just before entering,
one of the priests turned and spoke some words to the officer in
charge of the Rajput cavalry troop. The Rajputs turned their horses
and trotted out of the courtyard. Ye-tai jeers and taunts followed
them. But the Rajputs neither looked back, nor responded, nor
gave any indication that they even heard the deprecations.

Once the Rajputs were gone, the Ye-tai swaggered back into

the mansion. They did not fail, naturally, to cuff aside the servant who held the door for them.

For a half hour or so thereafter, all was still. Silence, except for the normal faint sounds issuing from the palace—the noises one expects to hear emanating from a palace populated by an army of servants.

Very busy servants. The lord of the palace was expected to arrive soon. It was well known—not only to the servants, but to all the villagers nearby. The news had thrown the servants into a frenzy of activity. The villagers, into a fearful withdrawal to their huts, for all save the most necessary chores.

Frantic, now, the man in the woods. But there was no sign, except, perhaps, for the slightest tremor in his long, powerful fingers. He had hoped, he had prayed, he had spied, he had schemed—and now, he had run out of time.

The man in the woods closed his eyes, briefly, controlling the frustration that seemed to burn him from inside like a raging fire. Frustration such as he had never experienced in his life. Frustration caused by one thing only.

By one man only, actually. One man, and the others of his ilk whom he led.

The panther opened his eyes. For the hundredth time—the thousandth time—his quick mind raced and raced, coursing over the same ground he had covered before, over and over again. And with the same result.

It cannot be done. It just cannot be done. It would be pure futility to even try. They are simply too good. Especially—him.

Him.

The panther knew the man's name, of course. He had known it for weeks, almost since the day he had arrived at the palace. He had winkled it out of the villagers, and the servants who lived in the village, just as he had winkled out so many other things.

It had not been difficult. Neither the villagers nor the servants had suspected anything. A friendly, cheerful man; addled in his brains, a bit—by horrible experiences, no doubt. Another hopeless refugee in a world of refugees, willing to do the occasional chore in exchange for what little food the villagers could spare; and conversation. Much conversation. A lonely man, obviously. Dim-witted, but harmless and pleasant. A bit of a blessing, actually, for village women who often found people unwilling to listen to their chatter.

True, he was Maratha, not of their people. But the villagers held no allegiance to the Malwa. No, none at all. Nothing but fear, and a deeply hidden hatred. An escaped slave, most likely, although he bore no brand. Perhaps he escaped before branding. Instinctively, the villagers shielded him from prying eyes. Said nothing to the authorities.

(And to whom would they have reported, anyway? The major-domo, like most of his ilk, was a petty tyrant. Best avoided at all costs. It was unthinkable for polluted castes such as comprised the villagers to approach the Mahaveda priests—and none but lunatics even looked at the mahamimamsa. The Rajputs ignored villagers as they would have ignored any other vermin. The Ye-tai would do likewise, unless, as often happened, they were in the mood for amusement—and woe to the man, much less the woman, who served as the object of their entertainment. Who, then? The Kushans, possibly. But the Kushans were preoccupied with their special duty, had neither the time nor the inclination to busy themselves with any other concerns. No, best to say nothing. He was just a harmless half-wit, after all, with grief enough to bear as it was.)

Him. Yes, the panther knew his name, but never used it, not even in his own mind. Why bother? *He* was the central fact in the panther's life. Had been for weeks now. Who needed to give a name to the center of the universe?

Him. That cursed, hated *him.*

Oh, yes. Cursed, often—by a man who rarely cursed. Hated, deeply—by a man who did not come to hatred easily.

But not despised, never. For the hatred was a peculiar kind of hatred, despite the raging depth of the emotion. The panther had never in his life hated a man the way he hated *him.* Had never hated a man so terribly, wished for his destruction with such an aching, yearning passion; and, at the same time, found no fault in the man at all.

Not even service to the Malwa, in the end. For the man had little choice in the matter. That the panther knew, with the knowledge of a great student of human affairs. History had condemned the man he hated, and his people, to vassalage. Their strength and skill in battle had recommended them to others. But they had not been strong enough, nor skilled enough, to decline the recommendation. And so, like many others before them—and others who would come after—they had bowed their stiff necks.

No, it was for no fault of the man himself that the panther hated *him*. *He* was not personally responsible, nor had *he* done anything himself. Rather the contrary, suspected the panther. The treasure of his soul was unharmed, either in body or in spirit, despite her long captivity. He knew, for he had seen her, from a distance. Seen her many times. Always in the company of *him*. *Him*, and *his* men.

She was not happy, of course. She was filled with her own hatred and despair, he knew. But he had also seen the way she looked at *him*. Not with friendship, no. But not with hatred, either, or with anger, or disgust, or contempt.

And the panther had also seen, from a distance, the way *he* looked at her. It was not easy to read *his* emotions. *He* had a face as hard as iron, as cold as a stone. But the panther understood the man.

In the end, perhaps, it was that understanding which filled the panther's heart with such a pure fury, like the very flame of God's heart. The panther hated *him* as he had never hated a man in his life. And knew, as well, that in another time, another place, another turn of the wheel, he would have treasured the man's soul.

And then, suddenly, *he* was there. Emerging from the door of the palace, into the courtyard. After him filed the men under his command. The commander's subordinates were all members of his own people. Of the same clan of that people, in fact, the panther had learned. A tightly-knit band of veteran soldiers, sworn to their leader by oath, by blood, and by blooded experience.

The panther recognized all of them. He knew every face. They were all there. The entire detachment.

The panther willed himself to absolute stillness. Perhaps—maybe. This might be the chance! Almost hopeless, true, but hope was gone in any event. Never had they allowed the princess to walk about in the courtyard. Her daily exercise was always limited to the garden perched atop the battlements of the palace. For the first time, the panther would only have to fight his way through *them*, on level ground.

He could not prevent the grimace. *Only*. With his bare hands. An assassin's hands, true. But he did not even have to examine *them* to know what he would see. (Although he did, of course, for the thousandth time.) The discipline, the spotless helmets and armor, the well-oiled gleam of the swords and spear blades. Worst of all, the poise and confidence. The poise and confidence that comes only from battlefields mastered and survived.

Only. But—there would be no other chance. Slowly, imperceptibly, he gathered his haunches beneath him, preparing to spring. He would wait until the princess herself emerged and was well away from the door.

He waited. And waited. Grew puzzled.

What was happening?

He and his men were now clustered in the center of the courtyard. The door to the mansion had closed behind them. There was no sign of the princess.

The panther looked back to the men in the courtyard. There seemed to be some quarrel going on. He could not make out the voices, but it was obvious from the tone that they were raised in anger. And obvious, as well, from the expression on *his* face. A hard man to read, *he* was, but the panther had come to know that face. A deep, bitter rage roiled beneath its iron surface, suppressed by a lifetime's harsh discipline.

No. Not a quarrel. *They are not arguing amongst themselves. The anger is directed elsewhere.* He spotted the glances directed toward the palace. Quick glares of fury.

The door to the palace opened again. The panther tensed. But, again, the princess did not appear. Only a gaggle of servants, bearing bundles. Bundles, the panther realized, containing the kits of—

His eyes flitted back to the center of the courtyard. A sudden, wild hope flared.

He said something. Barked commands. Again, the panther could not make out the words. But he knew the tone, with the knowledge of a great commander of armies.

Orders are orders. Obey. Just shut up and do it.

A moment later, *he* was striding off. After a moment, the other men followed, toting their kits. Out of the courtyard. Down the beautifully tiled entryway to the palace grounds. Then, turning left at the dirt track—

—leading to the barracks.

Could it be? Is it possible?

The panther hesitated for only an instant. Just long enough for a quick, appraising glance at the palace.

No. I must first learn—

The panther sped through the woods, circling around toward the location of the barracks. He moved very swiftly, but almost invisibly, with just the faintest hint of a rustle. Like the sound of the wind, some might say.

He came to a good spot, well hidden, but from which he could spy out the barracks. The barracks, where the Rajputs and the common soldiery dwelled. They were not privileged to make their quarters within the palace. Of the troops guarding the palace, only the Ye-tai enjoyed the privilege of dwelling within its fair walls. The Ye-tai alone—except, due to their special duty, *him* and his men. Until now.

He was already there, and his men. They stalked into the best of the barracks reserved for the common soldiery. (The Rajputs took their quarters in a special barracks at the other end of the compound. Not luxurious, those, not even the rooms set aside for officers, but considerably better than the shacks provided for the common soldiery.)

The sound of angry voices came from the barracks into which *they* had marched. Had stalked. Like wolves entering a den of jackals.

A stream of common soldiers began pouring out of the barracks. Hastily, even frantically. The last one to emerge on his own feet was aided along by a kick. A second or so later, two others followed through the door, hurled like so many sacks of rice. They landed in the dirt and sprawled there, unconscious, their heads bleeding from savage blows.

Soon after, the kits of the common soldiers were likewise hurled through the door. The kits were not properly packed—were not packed at all, in fact. Just bundles slapped together and cast into the dirt, like garbage thrown out by a particularly foul-tempered housewife.

Sullenly—but, oh so meekly, with nary a snarl directed toward the barracks—the common soldiers scurried about, scraping together their belongings. They dusted off their meager possessions, rolled up their kits, and slouched toward the barracks located some distance away. The empty barracks. The one whose walls were caving in, and whose thatched roof kept out rain about as well as a fishnet.

Yes. Yes. Yes. It is true!

The panther raced back the way he had come. But, just before he reached his familiar hiding place beyond the door of the palace, he halted.

Oh, it was difficult! Weeks of frustration hurled him toward that hated palace!

But, he restrained himself, with the restraint of a man who had set a hundred ambushes, and eluded as many more.

Patience. The Vile One will not arrive for days yet. There is time. I must discover exactly what has happened. Lay out my plans.

He turned, and flitted through the woods, toward his hidden lair deep in the forest. Along the way, he tried to formulate new stratagems, based on a new reality. But, soon, he abandoned the effort. It was foolish to make plans in the absence of precise information. And besides, his soul was too flooded with emotion.

A new emotion. Hope. A huge emotion, like the surging monsoon. It filled every cranny and nook of his soul.

There was room for it. Another emotion was gone. The panther no longer hated *him*. The hate had vanished with the need, like a straw in the monsoon winds, and the panther was glad to see it go.

He arrived at his lair. Nothing much, that lair. Nothing much, for he possessed little, and had discarded most of that. He had prepared his lair carefully, making sure it could never be found.

He squatted, moved aside the stones and twigs which disguised his little campfire, and began piling up a small mound of kindling. There was not much to eat, but he would have time to cook it. Time to plot, and space to do it. A safe, perfectly hidden lair. Where he could become lost in his thoughts without fear of discovery.

The voice which came from behind him was the first knowledge he had of the ambush. He would have never believed it possible.

Speaking in Maratha. With a pronounced accent.

"You are very good, Raghunath Rao. Not as good as me, but very good."

The panther turned, slowly. Stared back at the foliage from whence the voice had come. Still, he saw nothing.

Until a flash of white appeared, in the darkness. A quick gleam, nothing more.

The panther could make him out now, barely. The man was so well concealed that his shape was nothing but black against black. Slowly, imperceptibly, the panther gathered up his haunches.

An object was flung from the darkness where the hunter lurked. It landed not more than a foot away from his feet. A small bundle. Slender, about a foot long. Wrapped in a cloth.

The voice came again:

"Examine the gift, first, Raghunath Rao. Then, if you still wish to be foolish, you will at least be a well-armed fool."

The panther hesitated for only an instant. He reached out his left hand and swiftly unfolded the bundle. The—gift—lay exposed.

He knew what it was, of course. But it wasn't until he withdrew the thing from its sheath, and examined it, that he understood what a truly excellent gift it was. With all the understanding of a great student of daggers, and their use.

Another packet landed by his feet.

"Now, that," came the voice.

The panther used the dagger to slice open the rawhide strip binding the small leather roll. Opened, the roll proved to contain a few sheets of papyrus. Upon them was a message, written in Marathi.

The panther glanced at his stalker. The hunter had not moved.

Strange ambush, he thought. But—he began to read the message.

Impossible to catalog the emotions which that incredible message produced in the panther's soul. Hope, again, in the main, like the sky behind a rainbow. Hope, produced by the body of the message. The rainbow, by the final words.

Half-dazed, he slowly raised his head and stared at the hunter in the shadows.

"Is it true?" he whispered.

"Which part?" came the voice. "The beginning, yes. You have seen yourself. We have cleared the way for you. The middle? Possibly. It remains still to be done, and what man can know the future?"

A rustle, very faint. The hunter arose and stepped into the small clearing. The panther gazed up at the tall man. He had never seen his like before, but did not gape. The panther had long known creation to be a thing of wonder. So why should it not contain wonderful men?

The panther examined the man's weapon, briefly. Then—not so briefly—examined the light, sure grip which held that enormous spear. The panther recognized that grip, knew it perfectly, and knew, as well, that he would be a dead man now, had he—

"How fortunate it is," remarked the panther, "that I am a man who cannot resist the pleasure of reading."

"Is it not so?" agreed the hunter, grinning cheerfully. "I myself am a great lover of the written word. A trait which, I am certain, has much prolonged my life."

The tall hunter suddenly squatted. He and the panther stared at each other, their eyes almost level. The grin never left the hunter's face.

"Which brings us, back, oddly enough, to your very question. Is the last part of the message true? That, I think, is what you would most like to know."

The panther nodded.

The hunter shrugged. "Difficult to say. I am not well acquainted with the—fellow, let us call him. He is very closely attached to the one who sent you this message."

"You have met—"

"Oh, yes. Briefly, mind you, only briefly. But it was quite an experience."

The hunter paused, staring for a moment into the forest. Then said, slowly:

"I do not know. I think—yes. But it is a difficult question to answer for a certainty. Because, you see, it involves the nature of the soul."

The panther considered these words. Then, looked back down and read again the final part of the message. And then, laughed gaily.

"Indeed, I think you are right!"

He rolled the sheets of papyrus back into the leather and tucked it into his loincloth.

"It seems, once again," he remarked lightly, "that I shall be forced to act in this world of sensation based on faith alone."

The panther shrugged. "So be it."

"Nonsense," stated the hunter. "Faith alone? Nonsense!" He waved his hand, majestically dispelling all uncertainty.

"We have philosophy, man, philosophy!"

A great grin erupted on the hunter's face, blazing in the gloom of the forest like a beacon.

"I have heard that you are a student of philosophy yourself."

The panther nodded.

The grin was almost blinding.

"Well, then! This matter of the soul is not so difficult, after all. Not, at least, if we begin with the simple truth that the ever-changing flux of apparent reality is nothing but the shadow cast upon our consciousness by deep, underlying, unchanging, and eternal Forms."

The panther's eyes narrowed to slits. The treasure of his soul in captivity—bound for the lust of the beast—a furious battle ahead, a desperate flight from pursuit, a stratagem born of myth, and this—this—this half-naked outlandish barbarian—this—this—

"I've never encountered such blather in my life!" roared the panther. "Childish prattle!" The tail lashed. "Outright cretinism!"

Furiously, he stirred the fire to life.

"No, no, my good man, you're utterly befuddled on this matter. *Maya*—the veil of illusion which you so inelegantly call the ever-changing flux of apparent reality—is nothing. Not a shadow—*nothing*. To call such a void by the name of shadow would imply—"

The panther broke off.

"But I am being rude. I have not inquired your name."

"Ousanas." The black man spread his hands in a questioning gesture. "Perhaps I introduced the topic at an inappropriate time. There is a princess to be rescued, assassinations to commit, a pursuit to be misled, subterfuges to be deepened, ruses developed, stratagems unfolded—all of this, based on nothing more substantial than a vision. Perhaps—"

"Nonsense!"

Raghunath Rao settled himself more comfortably on his haunches, much as a panther settles down to devour an impala.

"Shakuntala will keep," he pronounced, waving his hand imperiously. "As I never tire of explaining to that beloved if headstrong girl: *only the soul matters, in the end.* Now, as to that, it should be obvious at first glance—even to you—that the existence of the soul itself presupposes the One. And the One, by its very nature, must be indivisible. That said—"

"Ridiculous!" growled Ousanas. "Such a One—silly term, that; treacherous, even, from the standpoint of logic, for it presupposes the very thing which must be proved—can itself only be—"

Long into the night, long into the night. A low, murmuring sound in the forest; a faint, flickering light. But there were none to see, except the two predators themselves, quarreling over their prey.

The soul, the great prey, the leviathan prey, the only fit prey for truly great hunters. The greatest hunters in the world, perhaps, those two, except for some tiny people in another forest far away. Who also, in their own way, grappled Creation's most gigantic beast.

Chapter 23

Three nights later, the Wind of the Great Country swept through the palace of the Vile One.

Eerie wind. Silent as a ghost. Rustling not a curtain, rattling not a cup. But leaving behind, in its passage, the signs of the monsoon. The monsoon, great-grandfather of fury, whose tidal waves strew entire coasts with destruction.

Unnatural wave. Selective in its wreckage, narrow in its havoc, precise in its carnage.

The majordomo was the first to die, in his bed. He expired quickly, for his lungs were already strained by the slabs of fat which sheathed his body. He died silently, purple-faced, his bulging eyes fixed on the multitude of cords and levers for which his plump hand was desperately reaching. Cords and levers which might have saved him, for they were the nerve center of the entire palace. The mechanisms which could have alerted the Ye-tai guards, roused the priests and torturers, summoned the servants.

Wondrous levers, crafted by master metalsmiths. Beautiful cords, made from the finest silk.

The mechanisms, alas, proved quite beyond his reach. They would have been beyond that reach even if the nearest silk cord, the one he most desperately sought, had still been there. That cord rang the bell in the Ye-tai quarters. But it was gone. The majordomo could see the stub of the cord, hanging from the ceiling. It must have been severed by a razor, so clean and sharp was the cut. Or, perhaps, by a truly excellent dagger.

He did not wonder what had happened to the missing length

of the cord, however. The beautiful silk had disappeared into the folds of fat which encased his neck and throat, driven there by hands like steel. He struggled against those hands, with the desperation of his feverish will to survive.

But his was a petty will, a puny will, a pitiful will, compared to the will which drove those incredible hands. *That* will made steel seem soft.

And so, a lackey died, much as he had lived. Swollen beyond his capacity.

The Wind swept out of the majordomo's suite. As it departed, the Wind eddied briefly, cutting away all of the cords and removing all of the levers. Without—eerie wind—causing a single one of the multitude of bells throughout the palace to so much as tremble.

The levers, the Wind discarded. The cords it kept. Excellent silk, those cords, the Wind fancied them mightily.

The Wind put three of those cords to use within the next few minutes. The Mahaveda high priests who oversaw the contingent of priests and torturers newly assigned to the palace dwelt near the suite of the majordomo. Their own chambers were not as lavish as his, nor were the locks on their doors as elaborate. It would have made no difference if they had been. Door locks, no matter how elaborate, had no more chance of resisting the Wind than dandelions a cyclone.

It made no difference, either, that the priests' lungs were not slabbed with fat. Nor that their necks were taut with holy austerity. Very taut, in fact, for these were high priests, given to great austerity. But they grew tauter still, under the Wind's discipline. For Mahaveda priests, the Wind would settle for nothing less than ultimate austerity.

The Wind departed the quarters of the high priests and swirled its way through the adjoining chambers. Small rooms, these, unlocked—the sleeping chambers of modest priests and even humbler mahamimamsa.

They grew humbler still, models of modesty, in the passing of the Wind. True, their simple bedding gained ostentatious color, quite out of keeping with their station in life. But they could hardly be blamed for that natural disaster. The monsoon always brings moisture in its wake.

Done with its business in those quarters, the Wind veered

toward the west wing of the palace. There, still some distance away, lay the principal destination of the Wind's burden of wet destruction.

The Wind eased its way now, slowly. These were the servant quarters. The Wind had no quarrel with that folk. And so it moved through these corridors like the gentlest zephyr, so as not to rouse its residents.

A servant awoke, nonetheless. Not from the effects of the Wind's passage, but from the incontinence of old age. A crone, withered by years of toil and abuse, who simply had the misfortune to shuffle out of her tiny crib of a room at exactly the wrong moment.

Shortly thereafter, she found herself back in the room. Lying on her pallet, gagged, bound with silk cords, but otherwise unharmed. She made no attempt to fight those bonds. As well fight against iron hoops. When she was finally discovered the next day, she had suffered no worse than the discomfort of spending a night in bedding soaked with urine.

In the event, the Wind wasted its mercy. The crone would die anyhow, two days later. On a stake in the courtyard, impaled there at Venandakatra's command. Condemned for the crime of not overcoming one of the world's greatest assassins.

Strangely, she did not mind her death, and never thought to blame the Wind. Hers had been a miserable life, after all, in this turn of the wheel. The next could only be better. True, these last moments were painful. But pain was no stranger to the crone. And, in the meantime, there was great entertainment to be found. More entertainment than she had enjoyed in her entire wretched existence.

She was surrounded by good company, after all, the very best. Men she knew well. Ye-tai soldiers who had taken their own entertainment, over the years, mocking her, beating her, cursing her, spitting on her. Their fathers had done the same, when she had been young, and thrown rape into the bargain. But they would entertain her, now, in her last hours. Entertain her immensely.

So went a feeble crone to her death, cackling her glee. While seventeen mighty Ye-tai around her, perched on their own stakes, shrieked their warrior way to oblivion.

✧   ✧   ✧

Once out of the servant quarters, the Wind moved swiftly through the cavernous rooms where the Vile One, when present, resided and entertained himself. Invisible, the Wind, for there were no lanterns lit, and as silent as ever. The invisibility and the silence were unneeded. At that time of night, with the lord absent from his palace, none would intrude in his private quarters. None would dare. To be found was to be convicted of thievery and impaled within the hour.

Unnecessary invisibility, unneeded silence; but inevitable for all that. It was simply the way of the Wind, the nature of the thing, the very soul of the phenomenon.

Into the corridor leading to the stairs swept the Wind. The first mahamimamsa guard was encountered there, at the foot of the stairs, standing in a pathetic semblance of a sentry's posture. The Wind swirled, very briefly, then lofted its way up the stairs. The mahamimamsa remained below, his posture much improved. More sentry-like. True, the torturer no longer even pretended to stand. But his eyes were wide open.

Near the top of the stairs, at the last bend in its stately progression, the Wind eddied, grew still. Listened, as only the Wind can listen.

One mahamimamsa, no more.

Had silence not been its way, the Wind would have howled contempt. Even Ye-tai would have had the sense to station two sentries at the landing above.

But the Ye-tai had never been allowed up those stairs, not since the treasure in the west wing had first been brought to the palace. The princess had been placed in that wing of the palace, in fact, because it was located as far from the Ye-tai quarters as possible. The majordomo had known his master's soul. No Malwa lord in his right mind wants Ye-tai anywhere near that kind of virgin treasure. The barbarians were invaluable, but they were not truly domesticated. Wild dogs from the steppes, straining at a slender leash. Mad dogs, often enough.

The lord of this palace was in his right mind. A mind made even righter by the experienced wisdom of a foreigner. A drunken foreigner, true. But—*in vino veritas*. And so the right-minded lord had tightened the guard over his treasure. Had sent orders ahead. None but mahamimamsa torturers would protect that treasure now, with a few priests to oversee them. Men bound to celibacy. Bound by solemn oaths; bound even tighter by fear of pollution (the worst of which is the monstrous, moist, musk-filthy, blood-soiled bodies of women); bound, tightest of all, by their own twisted depravity, which took its pleasure in a place as far removed from life-creation as possible.

The Wind swirled, rose the final few steps, coiled its lethal way around the corner. Another length of cord found good use.

The Wind was pleased, for it treasured beauty. Such wonderful silk was meant to be displayed, admired, not wasted in the privacy of a glutton's chambers. It would be seen now, the following day. Not admired, perhaps. Mortal men, tied to the veil of illusion, were hard to please.

Down the corridor to the left, down the next corridor to the right. So the Wind made its silent way, as surely as if it knew every inch of the palace.

Which, indeed, it did. The Wind had discovered all of the palace's secrets, from the humblest source: the idle chatter of village women, filled with the years of toil in that palace. Long years, washing its walls, cleaning its linens, dusting its shelves, scrubbing and polishing its floors. Idle chatter, picked up by the Wind as it wafted its light way through their lives.

Now, as it came to the end of this corridor, the Wind wafted lightly again. Not so much as a whisper signaled its arrival. This was the corridor which led to the great domed hall where all the corridors in the west wing of the palace intersected.

The Wind knew that hall. That great domed hall, empty, save for a single small table at its center. A table with three chairs. Oh, yes. The Wind knew that hall well. Knew it, in fact, better than it had known any room it had ever actually entered.

Knew it so well, because it hated that domed hall more than any room built by men had ever been hated. Hours, days—weeks, the Wind had spent, thinking about that hall. Trying to find a way it could swirl through that hall, without the fatal alarm being sounded.

But the Wind had never found a way. For a man with an iron face had also thought upon that hall, and how to guard it.

At the end of the corridor, at the very edge of the light-cone cast by a lantern on the table which stood at the center of the hall, the Wind eddied. Grew still.

Till now, the Wind had been able to take its own time. Once that hall was entered, there would be no time.

The hall was the first of the final barriers to the Wind's will. There were four barriers. The first was the domed hall, and the guards within it. Beyond, just two short corridors away, was the second: the guards standing in front of the princess' suite. The third was the antechamber of the suite, where the main body of guards were found. And now, the Wind had learned (the day before, from a village woman clucking her outrage), there was a fourth barrier, in the princess' own chamber. In a former time, when an iron-faced man had commanded very different guards, the princess had been allowed to sleep undisturbed. Now, even in her sleep, torturers gazed upon her.

But it was the first barrier which had been the main barrier to the Wind, for all these weeks. The Wind had never doubted it could make its way through that hall—even when guarded by *his* men—and to the barriers beyond. But not without the alarm being sounded. And, the alarm sounded, the barriers beyond would become insurmountable obstacles, even to the Wind.

Eddying in the darkness of the corridor, the Wind examined the hated hall, in the light of a new reality. And, again, found it hard not to howl.

His warriors, in the days when this had been their duty, stood their duty erect, alert, arms in hand. They did not converse. Conversation was impossible, anyway, because *his* sentries always stood far apart from each other, so that if one were to be overcome, the other would at least have time to cry the alarm. (Which they would. The Wind had marked out the paces of that hall in a forest, and tested, and despaired.)

The *others*, to be precise. The iron-faced man had always stationed three guards in that hall, at every hour of the day or night. It was the central node of the upper floor in the west wing, the pivot of the defense. And *he* was a veteran, a master at judging terrain. *He* had seen it at once, the first time he inspected the new battleground.

Three. Here. There. There. Always.

Those had been the iron-faced man's very first commands, in his new post. The Wind knew, from a village woman who had been polishing the floor of that hall when the iron-faced man entered it.

She had been struck dumb by that man.

Not by his face. Hard faces she knew all too well, and, in the knowing, had willed herself to utter stillness. Crouching, in a corner of the hall, like a mouse on an empty floor when felines enter.

Not by his command. Which she remembered, barely, only because it illustrated his terse, harsh nature.

No, she had been dumbfounded because an iron-faced man had examined the hall swiftly, issued his commands, and had then led his men across it slowly. Slowly, and carefully, so that five hours of a worthless menial's tedious labor would not be destroyed.

In a different way, hearing the tale, the Wind had also been struck dumb. Speechless, its voice strangled between a great hatred, and a greater wish that its hatred could be directed elsewhere.

Now, it could. Now, the iron-faced man was gone. And gone, as well, were the men *he* commanded. Men of *his* breed.

Gone, replaced by—*these.*

So difficult it was! Not to howl with glee!

Two Malwa guarded the hall. One priest, one mahamimamsa.

Soldiers would have guarded that hall differently.

Any soldiers.

Common soldiers, of course, would have been more careless than *his* men. Common soldiers, in their idle boredom, would have drifted together in quiet conversation. True, they would have remained standing. But it would have been a slouching sort of stance, weapons casually askew.

Ye-tai, in their feral arrogance, would have taken their seats in the chairs at the table in the center of the hall. And would have soon rung the hall with their boisterous exchanges. Still, even Ye-tai would have sat those chairs facing outward, weapons in hand.

Only a priest and a torturer would guard a room seated at a table, their backs turned to the corridors, their swords casually placed on a third chair to the side, poring over a passage from the Vedas. The priest, vexed, instructing the thick-witted torturer in the subtleties of the text which hallowed his trade.

From the corridor, just beyond the light, the Wind examined them. Briefly.

The time for examination was past.

The Wind, in the darkness, began to coil.

In the first turn of its coil, the Wind draped the remaining length of cord across an unlit lantern suspended on the wall.

The time for silk was past.

In the second turn of its coil, the Wind admired the silk, one last time, and hoped it would be found by a servant woman. Perhaps, if she were unobserved, she would be able to steal it and give her squalid life a bit of beauty.

In the third turn of its coil, and the fourth, the Wind sang silent joy. The Wind sang to an iron face which was gone, now, but which, while there, had watched over the Wind's treasure and kept her from harm. And it sang, as well, to an unknown man who had caused that iron face to be gone, now, when its time was past.

The Wind took the time to sing that silent joy, as it coiled, because the time for joy was also past. But joy is more precious than a cord of silk and must be discarded carefully, lest some small trace remain, impeding the vortex.

An unknown man, from the primitive Occident. In the fifth turn of its coil, the Wind took the time to wonder about that strange West. Wonder, too, was precious. Too precious to cast aside before savoring its splendor.

Were they truly nothing but superstitious heathens, as he had always been told? Ignorant barbarians, who had never seen the face of God?

But the Wind wondered only briefly. The time for wonder was also past.

The vortex coiled and coiled.

Wonder would return, of course, in its proper time. A day would come when, still wondering, the Wind would study the holy writ of the West.

Coiling and coiling. Shedding, in that fearsome gathering, everything most precious to the soul. Shedding them, to make room.

Coiling and coiling.

Hatred did not come easily, to the soul called the Wind. It came with great difficulty. But the Wind's was a human soul; nothing human was foreign to it.

Coiling and coiling and coiling.

The day would come, in the future, studying the holy writ of the western folk, when the Wind would open the pages of *Ecclesiastes*. The Wind would find its answer, then. A small wonder would be replaced by a greater. A blazing, joyful wonder that

God should be so great that even the stiff-minded Occident could see his face.

But that was the future. In the dark corridor of the present, in the palace of the Vile One, joy and wonder fled from the Wind. All things true and precious fled, as such creatures do, sensing the storm.

Coiling and coiling. Coiling and coiling.

Love burrowed a hole. Tenderness scampered up a tree. Pity dove to the bottom of a lake. Charity, ruing its short legs, scuttled through the grass. Tolerance and mercy and kindness flapped frantic wings through the lowering sky.

A great soul, the Wind's. Enormous, now, in its coil. With a great emptiness at the center where room had been made. Into the vacuum rushed hatred and rage, fury and fire. Bitterness brought wet weight; cruelty gave energy to the brew. Vengeance gathered the storm.

Monsoon season was very near.

The monsoon, like the Wind, was many things to many people. Different at different times. A thing of many faces.

Kindly faces, in the main. One face was the boon to seamen, in their thousands, bearing cargoes across the sea. Another was the face of life itself, for peasants in their millions, raising crops in the rain which it brought.

But the monsoon had other faces. There was the face that shattered coasts, flooded plains, and slew in the millions.

It was said, and truly, that India was the land created by the monsoon. Perhaps it was for that reason—what man can know?—that the Indian vision of God took such a different form than the vision which gripped the Occident.

The stiff-minded Occident, where God was but the Creator. Yet even the Occident knew of the seasons, and its Preacher penetrated their meaning.

India, where God danced destruction as well, singing, in his terrible great joy: *I am become death, destroyer of worlds.*

For all things, there is a time. For all things, there is a season.

In the palace of the Vile One, that season came.

Monsoon.

For all its incredible speed, the rush was not heard by the Malwa at the table until the Wind was almost upon them. The mahamimamsa never heard it at all, so engrossed was he in poring over the difficult text. One moment he was thinking, the next he was not. The fist which crushed the back of his skull ended all thought forever.

The priest heard, began to turn, began to gape as he saw his companion die. Then gasped, gagged—tried to choke, but could not manage the deed. The Wind's right hand had been a fist to the torturer. The torturer done, the hand spread wide. The edge of the hand between thumb and finger smashed into the priest's throat like a sledge.

The priest was almost dead already, from a snapped spine as well as a collapsed windpipe, but the Wind was in full fury now. The monsoon, by its nature, heaps havoc onto ruin. The terrible hands did their work. The left seized the priest's hair, positioned him; the right, iron palm-heel to the fore, shattered his nose and drove the broken bone into the brain. All in an instant.

The Wind raged across the domed hall, down a corridor.

The end of that short corridor ended in another. Down the left, a short distance, stood the door to the princess' suite. Before that door stood three mahamimamsa. (*He* had only stationed two; three were too many for the narrow space, simply impeding each other.)

The Wind raced down the corridor. The time for silent wafting was over. A guard had but to look around the bend. (*He* had stationed one of his two guards at the bend itself, always watching the hall; the Wind had despaired here also.)

For all the fury of the Wind's coming, there was little noise. The Wind's feet, in their manner of racing, had been a part—small part—of the reason his soul had been given another name, among many. A panther's paws do not slap the ground, clapping their loud and clumsy way, when the panther springs on its prey.

Still, there was a bit of noise. The torturer standing closest to the corridor frowned. What—? More out of boredom than any real alarm, the mahamimamsa moved toward the bend. His companions saw him go, thought little of it. They had heard nothing, themselves. Assumed the tedium had driven him into idle motion.

The Wind blew around the bend. Idleness disappeared. Boredom and tedium vanished. The torturers regretted their sudden absence deeply, much as a man agonizes over a treasure lost because he had not recognized its worth.

The agony was brief.

The first torturer, the—so to speak—alert one, never agonized at all. The dagger came up under his chin, through his tongue, through the roof of his mouth, into his brain. The capacity for agony ended before the agony had time to arrive.

The remaining two torturers had time—just—to startle erect and begin to gape. One, even, began to grope for his sword. He died first, from a slash which severed his throat. The same slash—in the backstroke—did for the other.

There were sounds now, of course. The muffled sound of bodies slumping to the floor, the splatter of arterial blood against walls. Loudest of all, perhaps, the gurgling sound of air escaping. The deep breaths which the torturers had taken in their brief moment of fear were hissing their way out, like suddenly ruptured water pipes.

Ye-tai guards, for all their arrogant sloppiness, would not have failed to hear those sounds. Even through a closed door.

But the priest and the six torturers standing guard in the room beyond that door heard nothing. Or, rather, heard but did not understand the hearing. Unlike Ye-tai warriors, they were not familiar with the sounds by which men go swiftly to their doom.

Other sounds of death, yes. Oh, many of them. Shrieks of pain, they knew. Howls of agony, they knew. Screams, yes. Wails, yes. Groans and moans, it goes without saying. Whimpers and sobs, they could recognize in their sleep. Even the hoarse, whispering, near-silent hiss from a throat torn bloody by hours of squalling terror—that they knew. Knew well.

But the faint sounds which came through the door, those they did not recognize. (Though one torturer, puzzled, stepped to the door and began to open it.) Those were the sounds of quick death, and quick death was a stranger to the men beyond that door.

It would be a stranger no longer.

The full surging fury, now. The door vanished, splintered in passing by the monsoon that wreaked its way into the room.

In its wooden disintegration, the pieces of the door knocked one torturer to the floor, staggered another. The Wind ignored, for the moment, the one on the floor. The one who staggered found the best of all balance—flat on his back, dead. Slain by a truly excellent dagger, which carved its way out of the scrawny chest as easily as it ravened its way in.

The five other Malwa in the room gasped. Their eyes widened with fear and shock. And, most of all, utter disbelief.

Odd sentiments, really, especially on the part of the priest. Had he not himself, time and again, explained to the mahamimamsa that butchery and slaughter were blessed by the Vedas? (Other Indian priests and mystics and sadhus had denied the claim, hotly and bitterly—had even called the Mahaveda cult an abomination in the eyes of God. But they were silent now. The mahamimamsa had done their work.)

And so, when the monsoon billowed into the room, the men therein should have appreciated the divine core of the experience. Yet, they didn't. Scandalous behavior, especially for the priest. The other Malwa in the room could perhaps be excused. For all their ritual pretensions, their desultory half-memorization of the Vedas, the mahamimamsa were simply crude artisans of a trade which is crude by nature. It is understandable, therefore, that when that same trade was plied upon them, they could see nothing in it but a dazzling exhibition of the craft.

The mahamimamsa lying prostrate on the floor never had time to be dazzled. The erupting door which had knocked him down had also stunned him. He just had a momentary, semiconscious glimpse of the stamping iron heel which ruptured his heart.

The next mahamimamsa was more fortunate. The same iron-hard foot hurled him into a corner, but did not paralyze his mind along with his body. So he was privileged. He would be the last to die, after the Wind swept all other life from the room. He would have ample time to admire the supreme craftsmanship of murder.

About four seconds.

The priest died now. From a slash across the carotid artery so short and quick that even Valentinian, had he seen, would have been dazzled by the economy of the deed. Then a mahamimamsa, from an elbow strike to the temple so violent it shredded half his brain with bone fragments and jellied the other half from sheer impact.

Another mahamimamsa, another carotid. Not so miserly, that slash—it almost decapitated the torturer.

Finally, now, a Malwa had time to cry out alarm. The cry was cut short, reduced to a cough, by a dagger thrust to the heart.

Only one mahamimamsa, of the seven Malwa who had been in that room, managed to draw a weapon before he died. A short, slightly curved sword, which he even managed to raise into fighting position. The Wind fell upon him, severed the wrist holding the sword, pulverized his kneecap with a kick, and shattered the torturer's skull with the pommel of the dagger in the backstroke.

In the fourth and last second, the Wind swirled through the corner of the room where his kick had sent a torturer sprawling, and drove the dagger point through the mahamimamsa's eye and into his brain. The marvelous blade sliced its way out of the skull as easily as it butchered its way in.

Swift death, incredibly swift, but—of course—by no means silent. There had been the shattering of the door, the half-cough/half-cry of one torturer, the crunching of bones, the splatter of blood, the clatter of a fallen sword, and, needless to say, the thump of many bodies falling to the floor and hurled into the walls.

The Wind could hear movement behind the last door barring the way to his treasure. Movement, and the sharp yelps of men preparing for battle. Two men, judging from the voices.

Then—other sounds; odd noises.

The Wind knew their meaning.

The Wind swept to that door, dealt with it as monsoons deal with such things, and raged into the room beyond. The chamber of the Princess Shakuntala. Where, even in sleep, she could not escape the glittering eyes of cruelty.

Two mahamimamsa, just as the Wind had thought.

Unpredictable, eerie wind. For now, at the ultimate moment, at the peaking fury of the storm, the monsoon ebbed. Became a gentle breeze, which simply glided slowly forward, as if content to do no more than rustle the meadows and the flowers in the field.

Only one mahamimamsa, now. The other was dead. Dying, rather.

The Wind examined him briefly. The torturer was expiring on the floor, gagging, both hands clutching his throat. The Wind knew the blow which had collapsed the windpipe—the straight, thumb and finger spread, arm stiff, full-bodied, lunging strike with the vee of the palm. He had delivered that blow's twin not a minute earlier, to the priest in the domed hall.

Had the Wind himself delivered the strike which had sent this mahamimamsa to his doom, the torturer would have been dead before he hit the floor. But the blow had been delivered by another, who, though she had learned her skill from the Wind, lacked his hurricane force.

No matter. The Wind was not displeased. Truly, an excellent blow. Skillfully executed, and—to the Wind's much greater satisfaction—selected with quick and keen intelligence. The man might not die immediately. But, however long he took, he would never utter more than a faint croak in his passing.

In the event, he died now, instantly. The Wind saw no reason for his existence, and finished his life with a short, sudden heel stamp.

The blow was delivered almost idly, however, for the Wind's primary attention was on the final foe, and his demise.

Here, the Wind found cause for displeasure, disgruntlement. Deep grievance; great dissatisfaction.

As was her unfortunate tendency, the imperious princess had not been able to resist the royal gesture.

True, admitted the Wind, she had obviously started well. The swift, sharp kick to the groin. Well chosen, that, from the vast armory the Wind had given her. A paralyzing blow—semiparalyzing, at the very least—and, best of all, paralyzing to the vocal cords. A sharp cough, a low moan, no more.

She had delivered that kick first, the Wind knew. Knew for a certainty, though the Wind had not been present in the room.

Just as the Wind had taught her, when dealing with two opponents. The quick, disabling strike to one; the lethal blow to the other; return and finish the first. (It was a simple sonata form which the Wind itself did not always follow, of course. But the Wind was a maestro, skilled in variations because it was master of the tune.)

So far—excellent. But then—impetuous hoyden!

The Wind puffed old exasperation. How many times had the child been told? How many? Headstrong girl!

But the raging vortex was fast disappearing. Faster than it had gathered, in fact, much faster. Emotions which came easily to the Wind were pouring back in, singing their return. Among these—great among these—was humor.

Truly, in its own way, a comical scene.

A large, heavy man. Heavy head, atop a heavy neck, atop a heavy torso. Clutching his groin. Groaning. Grimacing with pain. Staggering about like a wounded buffalo. With a girl—a smallish girl, mind, for all that her extraordinary body had been shaped under the Wind's ruthless regimen—hanging on to that massive head with both little hands.

Perfectly positioned, those hands, that the Wind allowed. The left, clutching the shaggy beard; the right, rooted firmly in the shaggy mane. Perfectly positioned for the deadly, twisting, driving contraction that would snap the man's neck like a twig.

If, that is, the man had been half his size, and she twice hers. As it was, it was a bit like a monkey trying to break the neck of a buffalo. The buffalo staggering about, swinging the monkey wildly to and fro.

The furious black eyes of the princess met the gaze of the Wind. The Wind stooped, hopped about, made soft monkey noises, scratched. The black eyes blazed pure rage.

"Oh—*all right!*" she hissed. She released her grip, bounced onto her toes. An instant for balance, an instant for poise, an instant for thought.

The swift kick to the knee was excellent—a copy of the one delivered by the Wind to a torturer in the room beyond. His had pulverized the knee, hers simply dislodged the kneecap. No matter—the man was disabled either way. And the position of his head—

Yes! The Wind was deeply gratified by the palm-strike to the bridge of the nose. For the Wind, that blow was itself lethal. But the girl—*this time*—delivered it as she had been taught. Speed, fluid grace. She simply didn't have the mass and sheer male strength to shatter strong bones with every blow. So, for her, the palm strike was to daze the foe, turn his head, set up—

The elbow smash to the temple which followed, like a lightning bolt, was a perfect duplicate of the one which the Wind had delivered to another mahamimamsa in the adjoining room, less than a minute earlier. True, the Wind's strike had slain his man instantly, whereas the princess needed two more before her opponent slumped lifeless to the floor.

So?

Only the soul matters, in the end.

The Wind died away, then. Fled, dancing, back to the Great Country. It would rise again, like the monsoon, when Maharashtra called. But for now, it was gone.

Only the man Raghunath Rao remained, cradling the treasure of his soul in his arms, whispering her name, kissing her eyes, weeping softly into her hair.

Epilogue
A SOLDIER AND A GENERAL

Once he was satisfied that his men had finished all the necessary preparations for their departure, Kungas decided that it was time to pay a courtesy call. It would be a long journey to the Emperor's camp at the siege of Ranapur. At least a month, probably more, judging from the appearance of the caravan—and his past experience with the caravan's master. He and his men would be spending a considerable time with the party of foreigners they had been assigned to escort. Best to be introduced properly, in advance, so that no unfortunate misunderstandings would arise.

Especially with *those* foreigners, thought Kungas, as he passed through the courtyard of Venandakatra's palace. He stopped for a moment, to admire the scenery.

A harsh life had taught Kungas many lessons. One of those was to keep your sentiments hidden. The world had always presented a hard face to him; he returned the compliment. *Old Iron-face*, he knew, was one of the nicknames his men had for him. He did not object. No, not in the slightest.

Still, even for Kungas, it was hard not to grin.

Four of the Ye-tai were still alive, barely. One of them was even still making some noise. Small, mewling sounds. With luck, thought Kungas, that one might survive another day. Another day of agony and hopelessness.

Kungas would be gone by then, but he would be able to cherish the memory. He and his men had been assigned the task of

344

cutting the stakes and spitting the Ye-tai. It had been the most pleasurable duty they'd had in years.

His eye fell on a figure perched among the Ye-tai, and his pleasure vanished.

Not all of it.

They had done what they could for the old woman. They had tried to smuggle in a longer stake, but Venandakatra had spotted it and forbidden its use. The servant was to be spitted on the same short stakes as the Ye-tai, in order to prolong the agony.

The mental grin returned. It was a bleak, bleak grin.

But we'd expected that. Too bad we couldn't get any real poison, in the short time we had. But the women in the kitchen mixed up what they could. Venandakatra watched us like a hawk, to make sure we didn't slip her anything to eat or drink. But we'd expected that, too. By the time we fit the poor soul onto the stake, the stuff had all dried. Venandakatra would have had to scrape the stake itself to spot it.

He started to turn away. Then, moved by an impulse, turned back. His eyes quickly scanned the courtyard. No one was watching.

Kungas made a very slight bow to the dead crone. He thought it was the least he could do. By the time the villagers would be allowed to remove her body, there would not be much left. The priests would refuse, of course, to do the rituals. So, the poor wretch was at least owed that much from her killer.

It was not, in any real sense, a religious gesture. Like most of his people, Kungas still retained traces of the Buddhist faith which the Kushans had adopted after conquering Bactria and north India. Adopted, and then championed. In its heyday, Peshawar, the capital of the Kushan Empire, had been the great world center of Buddhist worship and scholarship. But the glory days of the Kushan empire were gone. The stupas lay in ruins; the monks and scholars dead or scattered to the wind. The Ye-tai, on their own, had persecuted Buddhism savagely. And after the barbarians were absorbed into the rising Malwa power, the persecution had simply intensified. To the brutality of the Ye-tai had been added the calculating ruthlessness of the Malwa. They intended their Mahaveda cult to stamp out all rival tendencies within the great umbrella of Hinduism. Needless to say, they had absolutely no ruth toward Buddhists or Jains.

Between the persecution and his own harsh life, therefore,

Kungas retained very little of any religious sentiment. So, his slight bow to the dead crone was more in the way of a warrior's nod to a courageous soul. Perhaps that recognition would comfort her soul, a bit, waiting for its new life. (If there was a new life. Or such a thing as a soul. Kungas was skeptical.)

Not that her soul probably needs much comfort, he thought wryly as he walked away. *She seemed to enjoy the Ye-tai squawling even more than we did. Maybe we did her a disservice, poisoning her.*

He rubbed the new wound on his face, briefly. It was scabbed over now, and would heal soon enough. The pain was irrelevant. Kungas did not think the scar would even last beyond a few months. The man who put it there was a weak man, for all that he'd been in a rage. And a quirt is not, all things considered, the best weapon to use, if you want to scar up an old veteran.

And I'd much rather carry around a quirt-scar than be stuck on a stake.

The thought made him pause, brought another impulse. A very wry sense of humor, Kungas had. He stopped and turned back again; again examined the courtyard to make sure no spies were about; again bowed slightly. This time to the Ye-tai.

I thank you, O mighty Ye-tai. You saved my life. And probably that of all the Kushans.

As he walked out of the courtyard, he thought back on the episode.

Leave it to Venandakatra—the great warrior, the brilliant tactician. What a genius. As soon as he got the news, he rushed here ahead of his little army. Accompanied only by a few priests and that handful of foreigners. Within the hour, he was in a full rage. He ordered all the Ye-tai guards of the palace impaled—in public, right in front of them—and then noticed that the only soldiers he had to enforce the order were a Rajput cavalry troop. Leaving aside a hundred or so Malwa infantry, who ran like rabbits as soon as the Ye-tai went berserk.

Oh, what a fray that was! And after it was over, of course, he could hardly impale us next to them. Who'd do it? Not the Rajputs! Those snotty pricks suffered most of the casualties, except a handful of common soldiers who didn't run fast enough. We were unarmed, at the beginning—at the genius' own command—so the Ye-tai ignored us. By the time we could collect our weapons, it was almost over.

Grudgingly:

I'll give that much to the Rajputs. They fought well, as always.

But it still would have been touch and go, if the foreigners hadn't waded in. Lethal, they were. Absolutely murderous.

He pondered that last thought.

Why, I wonder? The Rajputs were happy enough, of course, to chop up Ye-tai dogs. So were we, once we got our weapons. But why should foreigners care? I can understand why they'd side with Venandakatra—they're his guests, after all. By why do it with such avid enthusiasm? You'd think they'd had some quarrel of their own with the Ye-tai.

With his usual quick pace, Kungas was soon well down the tiled entryway to the courtyard. He was now beyond sight of anyone watching him from the palace. For the first time, the amusement in his mind surfaced on Kungas' face. Barely, of course. Only someone who knew the man intimately would have interpreted that faint, hairline curve in his lips as a smile.

Oh, yes, they were beautiful. I think they butchered almost as many Ye-tai as the Rajputs did. And didn't suffer anything more than scratches, except for that kid. Too bad about him. But he'll recover, eventually.

The thought brought him back to his current assignment.

Yes, I think a courtesy call is quite the right thing to do. A very courteous courtesy call.

I definitely want to be on civil terms with those men. Oh, yes. Very civil. This assignment's a bit like escorting a group of tigers.

Then:

Now that I think about it, I'm not sure I wouldn't rather have tigers.

It took Kungas a while to find the party he was looking for. To his surprise, he discovered that the foreigners had been assigned a position at the very tail end of the huge caravan. After the supply train, right in the middle of the horde of camp followers.

Odd place for honored guests.

As he walked down the line of the caravan, Kungas puzzled over the matter.

Now that I think about it, our great lord did seem a bit peeved with them. Their leader, especially. I noticed Venandakatra casting quite a few glares in his direction. Didn't think much of it, at the time. I assumed it was just the great lord's mood, being spread around as usual. He has no reason to be pissed off at the foreigners, that I can see. Did him a service, they did. Without them, a few of the Ye-tai might have gotten to the bastard and carved him up.

Odd.

Eventually, Kungas found his party. The leader was standing off to the side of the road, watching the progress in loading the howdahs on the two elephants assigned to the foreigners. He and the two men with him were apparently seeking relief from the midday heat in the shade of the trees. That alone marked them for foreigners, leaving aside their pale skins and outlandish costumes. Shade brought little relief from the humid swelter. The trees simply cut down the slight breeze and provided a haven for insects.

Looking at him, Kungas was struck again by the disparity between the man and his position.

Weirdest general I ever saw. Too young by half, and twice as deadly as any general I ever met. That man is pure murder with a sword.

Thoughts of deadliness drew Kungas' eyes to the general's companions. They were standing a few feet away from their leader, in the posture of guards.

Kungas examined the one on the left first—the smaller one.

I do believe that is the wickedest-looking man I ever saw in my life. Like the world's meanest mongoose.

He transferred his gaze to the one on the right—the huge one.

Legends live. The great ogre of the Himalayas walks among us. With a face carved out of the very stone of the great mountains.

The general caught sight of him. He seemed to stiffen a bit, but Kungas wasn't certain. The general had one of those expressionless faces which are almost impossible to read. Kungas marched up to him. Summoned up his poor Greek.

"You is General Belisarius? Envoy for—from Rome?"

The general nodded.

"I is name Kungas. Commander for—of Lord Venandakatra's Kushan—ah, group? Force. Lord Venandakatra has—ah, what is word?—"

"I speak Kushan," said the general.

Kungas sighed inward relief.

"Thank you. I fear my Greek is wretched. We have been assigned to serve as your escort during the trip to Ranapur."

Again, Kungas found it almost impossible to read the man's expression. But, yes, he did seem a bit stiff. As if he were unhappy to see the Kushan. Kungas couldn't think of a reason why that would be true, but he was almost sure he was correct.

However, the general was cordial. And his Kushan was certainly good. Excellent, in fact—without even a trace of an accent.

"A pleasure, Kungas." His voice was a rich baritone.

The general hesitated, and then said:

"Please do not take this the wrong way, Kungas. But I must say I'm surprised to see you. We don't really need an escort. We didn't have one on the trip here from Bharakuccha. We're quite capable of taking care of ourselves."

Kungas' face cracked into a tiny smile.

"Yes, I have seen. However, the lord was quite insistent."

"Ah." The general was diverted for a moment, swiping at a fly which landed on his neck. Kungas noted, however, that the foreigner's keen brown eyes never left off their scrutiny of him. And that he killed the fly regardless.

After flicking away the dead insect, the general commented idly:

"I would have thought you would be assigned to join the hunt for the princess and her rescuers—ah, excuse me, abductors."

The iron face grew harder still.

"I fear my lord has developed a certain distrust for us. I do not understand why. The princess was not resc—ah, abducted—while *we* were guarding her."

Kungas thought the general was fighting back a smile. But he was not certain. A hard man to read.

"Besides," Kungas continued, "Lord Venandakatra really has no need for us to join the pursuit. He already has hundreds of Rajput cavalry scouring the countryside, and well over a thousand other troops."

The foreign general looked away for a moment. When the eyes turned back, his gaze seemed particularly intent.

"What is your professional assessment, Kungas? Do you think the princess and her—ah, abductors—will be caught?"

"One abductor only, General."

"One?" The general frowned. "I had heard a whole band of

vicious cutthroats were responsible. The palace was a scene of utter massacre, according to rumor."

"Massacre? Oh, yes. Massacre, indeed. The majordomo, three high priests, and two mahamimamsa guards garroted. Eleven priests and mahamimamsa butchered in their beds—their throats cut by a razor, apparently. A priest and a mahamimamsa slain in the great hall. Handwork, that, by a deadly assassin. Three mahamimamsa knifed outside the antechamber. A priest and six more mahamimamsa guards slaughtered in the antechamber. Blade-work again, mostly. Then, two more mahamimamsa slain in the princess' own sleeping chamber. Assassin handwork again, although—"

"Although?"

Kungas made a quick assessment. Partly, the assessment was based on his memory of Venandakatra's scowls toward the general. But, in the main, it was based on the faint but unmistakable trace of humor in the general's voice when he used the word "abductors."

"Well, as it happens, I examined the scene of the—ah, crime— myself. At Lord Venandakatra's behest. That is why I said 'one abductor.' The entire operation was carried out by one man."

"*One* man?" demanded the general. But he did not seem particularly astonished.

Kungas nodded. "Yes. One man. The trail of slaughter was that left by a single man, not a group. One man, alone. A man by the name of Raghunath Rao. The Panther of Maharashtra, he is sometimes called. Or the Wind of the Great Country. Other names. It was he. I am certain of it. He is known to have a personal attachment to the princess. There are not more than three—possibly four—assassins in India who are that deadly. And none has that proficiency with their bare hands and feet."

Kungas almost grimaced. "No one else can shatter bones and pulverize bodies that way. That is why—ah, that is, the two mahamimamsa who were killed in the princess' own chamber were also slain by hand. But the blows, though skillful, had none of the pure fury of the Panther's."

The general frowned.

"But—you said one man—"

"The princess. She killed them. She was trained by Raghunath Rao, you see. Such, at least, is my personal belief. I watched her dance, many times, in the long months I served as her captor—ah, guardian. Wonderful dancer, but—well, there was always that scent of the assassin about her movements. And in Amaravati, at the end of the siege, she killed several Ye-tai who attacked her in her room. One of them after she was disarmed."

The general's eyes widened. Slightly.

Kungas lowered his head, stared at the ground. When he spoke, his voice was as hard as his face.

"As to your first question—will they be captured? Yes. They will. Their position is hopeless."

"Why are you so certain?"

Kungas shrugged, looked up. "She is but a girl, General. A princess. Oh, true, a princess like no other you've ever seen. A princess out of legend. But still—she's never been hunted. She has no experience, or real training, in the skills of eluding a thousand men through the forest and mountains."

Kungas shook his head, forestalling the general's question.

"It doesn't matter. Even with Raghunath Rao to help her and guide her, she—" A pause. "You've hunted, I'm sure, in a large party. Or even with just one other man. Who sets the pace? Who frightens off the game? Who misses the shot?"

The general replied instantly: "The weakest man. The poorest hunter."

Kungas nodded. "Exactly. So—well, if Raghunath Rao were alone, I believe he would outwit and escape his pursuers. But even for him, the task would be extraordinarily difficult, with such an immense number of hunters on his trail. Encumbered by the princess—" He shrugged again. "It is simply not possible. No, they will be caught."

Kungas saw the general glance aside. He seemed to stiffen a bit. Perhaps.

Kungas followed his glance. The last members of the foreign party had arrived and were approaching their howdah. The young black prince from Ethiopia and his women.

Kungas had heard tales of the prince. His rampant lust; his viciousness toward his concubines. He had shrugged off the tales, for the most part. Resentful, malicious envy toward royalty and high nobility was so common as to make all such tales suspect.

But, as he watched, he decided that the tales were perhaps true, after all. The women certainly seemed fearful and abject.

All of them were veiled and kept their heads down. Very submissive. None of their faces could even be seen, so timid were the wretched creatures. There were none of the flashing, excited, inquisitive gazes one normally saw from young girls embarking on a journey.

One woman's face was partially visible to Kungas, now. She was weeping softly, comforted by a second woman who was holding her and guiding her along. The prince suddenly cuffed one of the other women on the back of her head. Then cuffed the last in the little group. Hurrying them aboard, out of royal petulance and impatience. Apparently, however, the prince's temper was not particularly aroused. The young royal was massively built, if not tall. Wide-shouldered, thick-chested, extremely muscular. With that frame, his cuffs could have easily knocked the girls off their feet. Yet they barely seemed to nudge them.

One girl was hoisted up into the howdah, helped by the black soldier who was apparently serving as the mahout. Then another, the weeping one.

"They are all Maratha, I understand," commented Kungas, making idle conversation.

The general nodded. "Yes, Prince Eon's developed quite a taste for the breed. He has a whole gaggle of the creatures." A little laugh. "I'm not sure how many, actually. Nobody can keep track."

A third girl, the one who had been comforting the weeper, made ready to climb aboard. Smallish. Much darker-skinned than the average Maratha. Very lithe in her movements, too. Kungas admired the fluid grace with which the girl took the hand of the mahout, began the climb up the great elephant. Her bare foot stretched out—

A beautiful dancer. Such incredible grace. Lithe, fluid. And I was always struck by her feet. The prettiest feet I ever saw. Quicksilver. High-arched, slim-heeled, perfectly shaped toes.

The girl entered the howdah. The fourth and fifth girls followed. The prince went up last, drew the curtains behind him.

Kungas stood as rigid as a post. He could not help it. Neither that, nor his face. Like iron, his face, as always when he faced danger. Now, like carbon steel.

At his side, he sensed the general's alertness. Behind, he could hear the slight sound of the general's guards moving forward.

This may be the most dangerous moment in my entire life.

His had been a harsh existence, filled with hard decisions. Now, Kungas made the easiest decision he had ever made. And, he thought, perhaps the best—certainly the purest—in a generally misspent life. He took some pride, too, in the fact that his own survival played not the slightest role in making the decision.

Which doesn't solve my immediate problem. Keeping from getting my throat slit. No point in trying to pretend—oh, no, not with this *general. Not with* those *men behind me.*

Besides—

A rare grin broke out on his face. (To Kungas, a grin. No one else would have called it that. A flaw in the iron, perhaps.)

"So many women. Well, we'll certainly have to make sure that they're well protected. I shall instruct my men to keep anyone from pestering the prince's concubines. From even approaching the howdah, in fact. Or his tent, at night. He's a prince, after all, bound to be full of royal pride. I'm sure he'd be outraged if anyone caught so much as a glimpse of his women."

Kungas could sense the quick thoughts in the man next to him. A moment or so later, the general spoke. Still, a trace of hesitation in his voice.

"An excellent idea, I think. Of course, your own men—"

Kungas waved his hand casually. "Oh, I shall give them firm instructions to keep their own distance from the howdah. I'll do the same myself, for that matter."

The general's face broke into an odd, crooked smile. If there had been a trace of hesitation, it seemed to vanish.

"That'll be difficult for you and your men, I imagine. That sort of self-control around women." An apologetic cough. "Given the Kushan reputation."

Kungas frowned slightly. "Reputa—?"

The general laughed. "Oh, come now! Don't deny it, Kungas. It's well known. You can't trust Kushans around women, particularly young women. *Especially* virgins. Not"—a chuckle—"that there are any virgins left in *that* howdah."

Kungas was still frowning.

"Such an act!" admired the general. "But there's no point in it, Kungas, I assure you. Not in *this* crowd. Why, I remember swapping a few amusing anecdotes with Venandakatra himself on the subject, during our journey from Bharakuccha. Although, now I think about it—my memory's a bit vague, I'm afraid. I was quite drunk, that evening. But—um, yes, now that I think about it, I seem to recall that I was telling all the stories. Odd, actually. It all seemed to come to the great lord as quite a revelation."

Anyone in the world, now, would have agreed that the expression on Kungas' face was a grin. The smallest, faintest, thinnest grin ever seen, true. But a grin, a veritable grin, it could not be denied.

"Alas. Our reputation is finally out. And we've been so careful to keep our talents hidden, all these months." He shook his head ruefully. "Well, it can't be helped. Everyone will know, now. Damn. Husbands will start watching their wives. Fathers their daughters."

"Princes their concubines."

Kungas glanced at the general's guards. "Soldiers, their camp women."

The general scratched his chin. "I foresee a scandal, I'm afraid. The talk of the caravan. Even Lord Venandakatra himself will probably hear of it. I can see the scene now. Kushan soldiers—ruffians, the lot of 'em, filled with unbridled lust—constantly surrounding the foreigners' howdahs and tents, filled with so many lovely girls. Flies drawn to honey. Dealing brutally, of course, with any other men who should happen to sniff around."

"We have a short way with competitors," agreed Kungas, "when it comes to women." Casually, his hand gripped the hilt of his sword, drew the blade an inch or so out of the scabbard, clashed it back loudly.

"Yes, yes," mused the general. "Pity the poor Malwa chap who should just happen to wander by, idly curious about the women."

Kungas shuddered. "I shudder to think of the poor fellow's treatment." Out of the corner of his eye, he saw one of the general's guards grinning. The one who looked like a mongoose. The most evil-looking grin he had ever seen, for a certainty.

"Then, of course," continued Kungas, "should any enterprising Malwa manage to slip through the Kushan escort and make his way to—"

"Oh, terrible!" exclaimed the general. His eyes squinted. His large hand gripped his own sword hilt. "He'd be butchered. By keen-eyed cataphracts or sarwen always on guard to fend off the endless, relentless, persistent hounding of their women by those horrible, lust-filled, lascivious Kushans. Ah, such a tragic case of mistaken identity."

The general spread his hands.

"But, the Lord Venandakatra could hardly complain. He assigned you to escort us, after all. Probably—" here came the general's grin, which no one in the world would have mistaken for anything else "—with that very purpose in mind. Making us miserable, I mean."

Kungas nodded sagely. "The great lord *does* seem to be quite irritated with you. I can't imagine why."

The sounds of a caravan setting into motion began filtering down the line. Kungas looked toward the front—which, of course, was far out of sight.

"Well, I'd best be off. Round up my men and explain our duties to them. Very carefully. Making sure they understand what they need to understand, and not what they don't. We don't want any—ah, how shall I put it? Walking a tightrope can be done, so long as you maintain the proper balance."

"Well said," commented the general. "A man after my own heart. You don't anticipate—"

"From *my* men? No, none. If I tell them to paint their faces blue and keep their left eyes closed all the way to Ranapur, well then—*they'll damn well paint their faces blue and keep their left eyes closed all the way to Ranapur*. And be right fucking quick about it, and keep their fucking mouths fucking shut. Orders are orders. Obey. Just do it." The iron face was back. "I'm not the man to brook insolence."

"I can well imagine," said the general.

Quite attractive, thought Kungas, that odd little crooked smile. He gave his own smile, such as it was, and departed.

When the Kushan was out of sight, around a bend of the road, Valentinian whispered to Belisarius: "That was a close call."

Belisarius shook his head.

"No, Valentinian, it wasn't close at all. I cannot imagine a world, anywhere, anytime, in any turn of the wheel, where that man would not make that same decision."

The general turned away, headed toward his horse.

As he left, he muttered something under his breath.

"Did you catch that, Anastasius?"

The giant grinned. "Of course. So would you, if your ears were attuned to philosophical thoughts like they should be. Instead of—"

Valentinian snarled. "Just answer the fucking question!"

"He said: *Only the soul matters, in the end.*"

A PRINCE AND A PRINCESS

The prince relaxed. His fingers let the curtain fall back into place. The fabric moved but a quarter of an inch. He had opened it only the merest crack.

"He's gone," he said softly. The prince leaned back against the silk-covered cushions which lined the interior of the howdah. He blew out his cheeks with relief.

The four Maratha women in the howdah reacted in various ways to the news. The fifth woman, who was not Maratha, watched their reactions carefully. She had been taught that the ways in which people relaxed from stress told you much about them. Taught by a man who was an expert in stressful situations and their aftermath.

The one Maratha woman she knew—had known for years—clutched her yet more tightly. But, for the first time since they had met again, under the most unexpected circumstances, stopped weeping. Her name was Jijabai, and her mind was lost in horror. But perhaps, Shakuntala thought—hoped—the horror would begin to recede and sanity return. Horror had begun for that woman when she had been taken from her princess. Now that her princess had returned, perhaps Jijabai could return also.

But there was nothing more that Shakuntala could do for Jijabai at the moment, beyond hold her. So she gazed elsewhere.

The Maratha woman seated immediately to the prince's right blew out her own cheeks, smiled broadly, and leaned into the prince's shoulder. The prince's arm enfolded her gently. She closed her eyes and nuzzled the prince's neck.

Shakuntala knew a bit about this one, from her conversations with the prince the day before. Her name was Tarabai, and she was the prince's favorite. Prince Eon had asked her to return with him to his homeland and become one of his concubines. Tarabai had readily agreed.

The prince had obviously been delighted by that answer. Almost surprised, like a boy whose idle daydream had come true.

Shakuntala had found his delight quite informative. She had been trained to observe people by the most observant man she had ever known. A man whose sense of humor was as keen as his perception—and that, too, that wry and tolerant way of perceiving people, Shakuntala had learned from him.

So, on the one hand, she was amused by the prince's delight. What woman in Tarabai's position—a Maratha captive cast into a hellhole of a slave brothel—would not have jumped at the chance to become a royal concubine? (A true concubine, in the honored and traditional sense—not one of the abject creatures which the Malwa called by the name. A woman with a recognized and respected status in the royal household. Whose children would not be in line for the succession, but would be assured positions of power and prestige.)

But there had been nothing supercilious in Shakuntala's amusement. Quite the contrary. She had respected the prince for his bemused delight. She had been taught to respect that kind of unpresumptuous modesty. Not by teaching, but by example. By the example of a man who never boasted, though he had more to boast about that any man produced by India since the days chronicled in the *Mahabharata* and the *Ramayana*.

(But that thought brought pain, so she pushed it aside.)

Tarabai's actions, and the prince's response, told Shakuntala much else. Her own father, the Emperor of Andhra, had possessed many concubines. Shakuntala had often observed them in her father's presence. Her father had never mistreated his concubines. But not one of them would have dared initiate such casual and intimate contact in the presence of others. Her own mother, the Empress, would not have done so. (Not even, Shakuntala suspected, in the privacy of the Emperor's bedchamber.)

A cold, harsh, aloof man, her father had been. Every inch the Emperor. He had brooked familiarity from no one, man or woman. Nor, so far as the princess knew, had he ever expressed the slightest tenderness to anyone himself. Certainly not to her.

There was no grievance in that thought, however. Her father had been preoccupied, his entire life, with the threat of the Malwa. Years ago, Shakuntala had come to realize that, in his own hard way, her father had truly loved her. He had placed her in the care of a Maratha chieftain—in defiance of all custom and tradition—for no other reason than that he treasured the girl and would give her the greatest gift within his power. To that gift, the princess owed her very life.

(That thought, however, brought pain again. The princess forced her thoughts back to the moment.)

So, a gentle and tender prince as well as a modest one. A warm-hearted prince.

And a resourceful one!

Shakuntala repressed a giggle. Childish! *Stop.*

It was difficult. The princess had an excellent sense of humor, when her temper was not aroused. And, for all its tension, the episode had been rather comical.

The prince had found her in the cupboard where Raghunath Rao had hidden her. Just as planned. On a shelf barely big enough to fit a girl, a jug of water, a bit of food, and—her nose wrinkled slightly, remembering—a bedpan. With a stack of linens piled on top of her.

As soon as he had taken possession of the guest suite in a corner of the palace, Prince Eon had sped to open the cupboard and retrieve Shakuntala. In passable Marathi, the prince had begun to explain the details of the scheme. Shakuntala had kept her eyes averted, for the most part. The prince had been in a hurry to wash the blood and gore off his body. (The princess, hearing the sounds of the battle raging in the palace grounds, had been hard-pressed not to climb out of the cupboard and watch.)

So his man—dawazz was his title—had poured the bath for him right there in the bedchamber, while Eon stripped himself naked. Shakuntala had peeked, once, not so much out of girlish curiosity as imperial assessment. A very impressive body, the prince had. But she had been far more impressed by the casual, unthinking way in which he cleaned the grisly residue of mayhem from it.

So. A courageous prince. Skilled and experienced in battle, for all his youth. As princes must be, in the new world created by the Malwa. She had approved. Greatly.

The sound of voices—Rajputs quarreling with foreigners—had come through the door. The prince's man immediately seized a huge spear. But the prince hissed quick instructions in their own language. Suddenly, the dawazz leaned the spear against a wall and began ambling toward the door, wearing such a grin as Shakuntala had never seen in her life.

The prince instantly raced to the cupboard and removed the traces of Shakuntala's habitation. There was very little to hide—simply an empty water jug and a bedpan half filled with urine. The prince placed both items in plain view, after emptying the bedpan in the bloody water of his bath.

Then, before she quite realized what was happening, Eon had seized her and flung her onto the bed. A moment later, the prince—still naked—was lying completely on top of her. He swept the bed linens over them, and immediately began heaving his buttocks vigorously. Shakuntala herself had been completely hidden—partly by the linens, but mostly by the prince himself. He was not that much taller than she, but twice as broad. She had felt like a kitten lying under a tiger. She could see absolutely nothing except the prince's bare chest.

A moment later, the voices had entered the room, still quarreling. She could understand the Rajput, now. Belatedly, Lord Venandakatra had ordered a search of the entire palace and its grounds. The Rajput officer in charge of the squad was apologetic. Without quite saying so, he made clear that he thought the entire exercise was idiotic. A great lord in a childish snit, squawling at the world indiscriminately. The criminals had obviously fled the palace entirely. Hadn't the three Ye-tai dogs guarding the front gate been found butchered, the morning after the massacre? Almost two full days had passed since. It was absurd to think—but—orders were orders.

Prince Eon had raised his head, then, a bit. Roaring royal outrage. But his buttocks never ceased plunging up and down, his groin thrusting at her own. Her body, of course, was still clothed. But the Rajputs had no way of seeing that. The only visible part of the princess was her hair. Long, black hair, in no way different from that of most Indian women. And then, a moment later, a little hand which reached up and clutched the prince's neck with apparent passion. Quite apparent passion, judging from the unknown girl's soft moaning. (Shakuntala hadn't been quite sure she was making the right noise. But, like all bright girls in a large and crowded palace, she had done her share of eavesdropping, in days past at Amavarati.)

Keeping their eyes averted from the prince at his sport, the

Rajputs conducted a very hasty search of the suite. Then, uttering many apologies, scurried out.

As soon as they were gone, Eon had immediately climbed off Shakuntala. Had made fulsome apologies, stressing the dire necessity which had precipitated his actions. Emphasized the depth of his respect for the imperial personage and dignity of the princess. Reiterated the perilous—

Shakuntala had waved off his apologies. Had responded with a most dignified—indeed, regal—acknowledgment of the sincerity of his regrets. Had uttered the most royal—indeed, imperial—phrases assuring the prince that she recognized both the necessity of his actions and appreciated the quickness of his wits. Had added further assurances that she had no doubt of his own regal propriety, good breeding, and monarchical majesty.

But then—unable to resist—had added demurely:

"Yet I fear, prince, that one of your provinces is in revolt."

It had been hard to tell. The prince's skin was even darker than a Dravidian's. But she thought he had definitely blushed.

Especially after the dawazz added, with that amazing grin:

"Indeed so! Most insolent uprising! Prince do well to beat rebel down!" Then, with a flourish: "Here! Use my spear!"

Remembering, and smiling, Shakuntala's eyes met those of the prince. A little smile came to his own face. Then, a subtle expression—a wry, apologetic twist of his lips; a little roll of his eyes; a faint shrug—combined with an equally subtle movement of his arm. His left arm, the one which was not encircling Tarabai.

Understanding, Shakuntala eased over and nestled against his shoulder. His left arm encircled her. She turned her face into his muscular neck. A moment later, she felt Jijabai snuggling into her own left shoulder. Trembling with fear at the princess' departure. Shakuntala cradled the girl and pressed her head into her own neck. She felt Jijabai's shivering ease.

Inwardly, she sighed. It would be tedious—even, after a time, uncomfortable—spending days and weeks in that position. But she suppressed the thought ruthlessly. They were at war, and war required many tactics. This tactic had worked before. A tried and tested tactic. Should anyone manage to look within the howdah, they would see nothing but the notorious Axumite prince, surrounded as always by his submissive women. Whose faces were rarely seen, of course, so timid had the creatures become in his brutal presence.

Across the prince's chest, her eyes met those of Tarabai. The Maratha girl smiled shyly.

She was still in awe, Shakuntala realized. The Maratha women had known for some time that the foreigners into whose care they had placed themselves were engaged in some strange activity. (And had sensed, even, that the activity was in some way opposed to the hated Malwa.) But they had not known the exact nature of that activity until that very morning. Just before departing for the caravan, the Maratha women had been ushered into the room, Shakuntala had been introduced to them by Eon and his men, and the plan explained.

Hearing the name, Jijabai had looked up, begun to cry out in startlement. The cry had been choked off by Shakuntala herself, embracing her former maidservant. From that moment until they climbed into the howdah, the girl had not stopped weeping. Shakuntala had stayed by her the entire time. At first, from love and pity. Then, as well, from a realization that the pose was perfect for their purpose.

The other three Maratha women had been too stunned to do more than walk through the exercise in a daze. Which, also, had been perfect, if unplanned.

Tarabai was no longer stunned. Eon's close presence, Shakuntala realized, had restored the girl's courage. But she was still in awe. The girl had all the signs of a simple upbringing. Of vaisya or sudra birth, undoubtedly (insofar as Maratha measured such things—but that thought, as ever, was too painful to bear, so Shakuntala banished it). Never in her life had Tarabai imagined she would share a howdah—much less a man's chest!—with royalty.

Shakuntala now gazed at the two Maratha women whom she did not know. They, too, were staring at her with round eyes. But there was more than simple awe in those eyes, she realized. The two women were almost shivering with terror. Then, seeing the princess' eyes upon them, the two women dropped their heads. Now, they did begin to shiver.

This must stop, thought Shakuntala.

"Look at me," she commanded. For all its youthful timbre, her voice was sharp. Not harsh, simply—*commanding*.

Immediately, the women raised their eyes. Eon, listening, was impressed.

"You are very frightened," stated the princess. After a moment, the women nodded their heads.

"You fear the Malwa fury, if they discover what is happening. You fear you will be destroyed."

Again, they nodded.

For a moment, Shakuntala simply gazed at them. Then said:

"Your fear is understandable. But you must conquer it. Fear will gain you nothing, and may betray us all into disaster. You must be courageous. These men—these foreigners—are good men. Brave, and resourceful. You know this to be true."

She waited. After a moment, the two women nodded.

"You trust these men."

Again, waited. Again, the nods.

"Then trust them. And me as well."

Waited.

"I am your princess. Your empress, now. I am the rightful heir to the throne of Andhra."

The Maratha women nodded immediately. Majarashtra was one of the few lands of India where a woman in power was accepted without question, if she held that power legitimately. Maratha women had even led armies, in the past.

(But thoughts of Majarashtra brought pain, so she forced her way past them.)

"I call you to service, women of the Great Country. Andhra will rise again, and the Malwa filth be destroyed. To that end I devote my life. If you are destroyed by the Malwa, your empress will be destroyed with you. You will not be deserted."

After a moment, the women bowed. The bow, Shakuntala acknowledged, but did not cherish in her heart. The fading fear in their eyes, and the hint of dawning courage, brought her great joy.

(But joy brought pain, and so she banished it. There would be no joy in her life, she knew. Only courage, and duty. She had made her vow to these women, and she would keep it. Though that vow would banish joy forever.)

She heard the prince mutter something. A phrase in his own language.

"What did you say?" she asked, glancing up at him.

His dark eyes were staring at her, very seriously. After a moment, the prince said softly:

"What I said was: 'And so, once again, Belisarius was right.'"

Shakuntala frowned, puzzled. She knew who Belisarius was, of course. Raghunath Rao had explained (as much as he knew himself, which was little). But she had not met him yet, only seen him out of the corner of her eye.

"I do not understand."

A quirky smile came to his lips.

"I asked him, once, why we were doing all this. I was not opposed, you understand. It seemed a worthy project in its own right, rescuing a lovely princess from such a creature as Venandakatra. But—I am a prince, after all. In direct line of succession to the throne of Axum. My older brother Wa'zeb is quite healthy, so I don't expect I'll ever be the negusa nagast. Which is fine with me. But you learn early to think like a monarch, as I'm sure you know."

Shakuntala nodded.

"So I asked Belisarius, once—as the cold-blooded heir of a ruler rather than a hot-blooded romantic prince—why were we taking these risks?"

He began to make some sort of apologetic aside, but Shakuntala cut him off.

"There's no need, Eon. It's a perfectly good question. Why *did* you do it?" A smile. "Not that I'm ungrateful, you understand."

Eon acknowledged the smile with one of his own. Then, when the smile faded:

"We are doing it, he said, for three reasons. First, it is worth doing in its own right. A pure and good deed, in a world which offers few such. Second, we are doing it to free the soul of India's greatest warrior, so he can turn that soul's full fury onto the enemy. And finally, and most importantly, we are doing it because we cannot defeat India alone. India itself must be our ally. The true India, not this bastard sired by a demon. And for that, we need to free India's greatest ruler from her captivity."

"I am not a ruler," she whispered. "Much less India's greatest."

Again, the quirky smile. "That's exactly what I said."

The smile disappeared. "'She will be,' replied Belisarius. 'She will be. *And she will make Malwa howl.*'"

✧　　✧　　✧

When night fell, and the caravan halted, Prince Eon and his women moved from the howdah into his royal tent, unseen by any, in the darkness. Throughout, Shakuntala never left his side. After he fell asleep, she lay against him, just as she had in the howdah, nestled in his arm. So that if any should intrude, she could once again be shielded from their sight.

But the princess—the empress, now—did not sleep. Not for hours. No, once she was certain that all the others in the tent were asleep, Shakuntala finally let the tears flow. Allowed the pain of her loss to sweep through her, like a knife cutting away her heart.

It would be the last time she would allow herself that liberty. But she could not bear to let the treasure of her soul depart without farewell.

She had loved one man only, her entire life, and would never love another. Not truly. (Although, even then, in her pain, she could remember the smile on the face of the man she loved. "A good heart has lots of room," he was fond of saying. And smile herself, remembering, until the memory renewed the pain.)

She had loved that man as long as she could remember. A hopeless love, perhaps, she had often thought. He never seemed to return it; not that way, at least. But—she would age, and she would be beautiful. (She had always known she would be. When the truth had matched the knowing, finally, she had been pleased but not surprised. She always achieved her goals, once she set her mind to them.) And, she thought, the day would come when she would dance at his wedding. As his bride. Her quicksilver feet flashing in the wine of his heart, dancing the dances which he had taught her, as he had taught her everything worth knowing.

Her father, of course, would have disapproved of her intentions. Would have been furious, in fact. And so she had hidden her feelings, letting no sign of them show. Lest her father take her away from the man into whose care he had given her, and to whom she had lost her heart.

For the princess of Andhra, that man was completely unsuitable. Oh, a fine man, to be sure. A great man, even. But his blood was not acceptable.

True, the man was kshatriya, as Maratha counted such things. But no other people of India recognized Maratha blood claims. Few Maratha families could trace their ancestry back beyond two or three generations. (Quite unlike Rajput, or Guptan, or Andhran, or Keralan brahmin and kshatriya, who could trace their genealogies endlessly.) A hard and stony land, Majarashtra. The Great Country, to those who lived there. But they were outcasts, refugees, unknown ones, in their origin. People who moved there from elsewhere, seeking refuge in its hillforts, and small farms, and stony ridges; refuge from the grandees and landlords who ruled elsewhere. A fractious folk, who took blood lightly and pollution more lightly still. A fierce folk, too, who measured nobility by their own standards. Hard and stony standards, which gave little respect to tradition and breeding.

A hard and stony people, the Marathas. Not unworthy—no honest man said that. Not even the haughtiest high-caste Rajput; not, at least, after testing Maratha mettle in battle. But not noble. Not fit for true kshatriya blood. And quite unthinkable for the purest blood of imperial Andhra.

Still, she had dreamed. Her father would die, someday, and one of his sons succeed him. Andhra would demand of her some royal marriage, to further Andhra aims. But she would refuse. She was not Andhra's ruler, after all, bound by its destiny. She would refuse, and win the heart of the man she loved, and flee with him into the reaches of the Great Country where none could find them. Not *that* man, for a certainty, did he choose to remain unfound.

But Andhra *was* her destiny, now. She alone survived of the ancient Satavahana dynasty. She would rule, and rule well. And choose her husband well, guided only by the needs of Andhra. The need to forge alliance against the asura who ravaged her people. That consideration, and that alone, would guide her now.

Perhaps this prince, she thought, feeling his heart beat where her head lay resting on his massive chest. The thought pleased her, slightly, for a moment. She would never love him, of course, not truly. But he seemed a fine man, a good prince. Everything a prince should be, in truth. Courageous, bold, skilled in battle, quick-witted, even warm and loving. Perhaps even wise—in later years, at least, if not now.

Perhaps. If Andhra's needs lead to an alliance with his people. And if not—

I will marry the foulest creature on earth, and bear his children, so long as the doing of it will make Malwa howl. Oh, yes. I will make Malwa howl.

Her heart had long been lost, to another, but her soul remained. Her soul, like everyone's, belonged to her alone. Was the one thing inseparable from her, the one thing which could not be given away.

And so, in a foreign tent in an enemy land, the empress Shakuntala seized her soul and dedicated it to her people. Dedicated it to howling Malwa. And bade farewell to her soul's treasure.

It seemed bitterest of all, to her, in that bitterest of all nights, that she had finally come to understand the one lesson he had despaired of ever teaching her.

Only the soul matters, in the end.

A SLAVE AND A MASTER

That same night, in another tent, a slave also seized his soul and dedicated it to a purpose. The decision to do so had been long in the making, and did not come easily. There is nothing so difficult, for a soul which has resigned itself to hopelessness, than to reopen the wound of life.

His master's purpose was now clear to the slave. Some part of that purpose, at least—the slave suspected there was more to come. Much more. From experience, the slave had learned that his master's mind was a devilish thing.

The slave would dedicate himself to that deviltry.

Though it was late, the lantern was still lit. Rolling over on his pallet, the slave observed that his master was still awake. Sitting on his own pallet, cross-legged, his powerful hands draped over his knees, staring at nothingness. As if listening to some inner voice, which spoke to him alone.

Which, the slave knew, was true. The slave even thought he could name that voice.

As always, despite his preoccupation, the slave's master missed nothing in his surroundings. The slight motion of the slave rolling over drew the master's attention. He turned his head and gazed at his slave. Cocked his eye quizzically.

"My name is Dadaji Holkar," said the slave softly. He rolled back and closed his eyes. Sleep came, then, much more quickly than he would have thought possible.

A GENERAL AND AN AIDE

For a moment, Belisarius stared at the back of his slave's head. Then, half-stunned, looked away.

The slave's unexpected announcement had not caused that reaction. It had simply jolted the general into a recognition of his own blindness.

His thoughts raced back to the breach in the barrier. This time he made no effort to clear away more rubble. Simply called across:

What is your name?

The facets flashed and shivered. What?—More meaningless—it was impossible! The mind was too—

aim brought the facets into order, harried them into discipline.

It was not impossible! The mind was not—

The struggle broke loose meaning. At last—at last!—some part of the message sent back by the Great Ones came into focus. The very end of the message, which was still obscure due to the absent body, but no longer incomprehensible. The facets glittered crystalline victory. **aim** transmuted triumph into language:

> *Then:*
> *Find the general who is not a warrior.*
> *Give all into his keeping;*
> *Give aim to his purpose and assistance to his aim.*
> *He will discover you in the purpose,*
> *You will find us in the aim,*
> *Find yourself in the seeking,*
> *And see a promise kept*
> *In that place where promise dwells;*
> *That place where gods go not,*
> *Because it is far beyond their reach.*

The thought which came to Belisarius then was a burst of sweet pride. Like the smile of a child, taking its first step:

Call me Aide.

A LADY AND A ROGUE

"Ready?" asked Maurice.

Antonina and John of Rhodes nodded. The hecatontarch knocked out the pole bolt with his mallet.

The arm of the onager whipped forward, driven by the torsion of the twisted cords which held its base. The arm slammed into the cushion of hair-cloth stuffed with fine chaff resting on the crossbeam. The clay jar which had been held in the sling at the tip of the arm flew through the air.

The three people standing to the side of the artillery piece followed the trajectory of the jar. Within two seconds, the jar slammed into a stone wall some distance away and erupted into a ball of flame.

"Yes! Yes!" howled John, prancing with glee. "It works! Look at that, Antonina—spontaneous eruption!"

She herself was grinning from ear to ear. The grin didn't vanish even after she caught sight of Maurice's frown.

"Oh, come on, you damned Cassandra!" she laughed. "I swear, you are the most morose man who ever lived."

Maurice smiled faintly. "I'm not morose. I'm a pessimist."

John of Rhodes scowled. "And what are you pessimistic about *this* time?" The retired naval officer pointing to the wall, which was still burning hotly.

"Look at it! And if you still don't believe, go and try to put it out! Go ahead! I promise you that fire will last—even on stone—until the fuel burns itself up. The only way you'll put it out is to bury it under dirt. You think an enemy is going to march into battle carrying shovels?"

Maurice shook his head.

"I'm not contesting your claims. But—look, John, you're a naval officer. No big thing for you, on a nice fat ship, to haul around a pile of heavy clay pots. Carefully nestled in cloths to keep them from breaking and bursting into flame. Try doing that with a mule train, sometime, and you'll understand why I'm not jumping for joy."

John's scowl deepened, but he said nothing in reply. Antonina sighed.

"You're being unfair, Maurice."

The hecatontarch's scowl made John's look like a smile.

"*Unfair?*" he demanded. "What's that got to do with anything? *War* is unfair, Antonina! It's the nature of the damned beast."

His scowl faded. The hecatontarch marched over and placed his hand on John's shoulder.

"I'm not criticizing you, John. There's no doubt in my mind you just revolutionized naval warfare. And siege warfare, for that matter. I'm speaking the plain, blunt truth, that's all. This stuff's just too hard to handle for an army in the field."

The naval officer's own scowl faded. He looked down and blew out his lips. "Yes, I know. That's why I made sure we were all standing back and to the side. I wasn't sure the impact of hitting the crossbeam wouldn't shatter the pot right here."

He rubbed his neck. "The problem's the damn naphtha. It's still the base for the compound. As long as we're stuck with that liquid, gooey crap we're not going to get any better than this."

Maurice grunted. "What did you add this time?" He nodded toward the distant flame, still burning. "Whatever it was, it makes one hell of a difference."

John peered at the flame. His blue eyes seemed as bright as diamonds, as if he were trying to force the flames into some new shape by sheer willpower.

"Saltpeter," he muttered.

Maurice shrugged. "Then why don't you try mixing the saltpeter with something else? Something that isn't liquid. A clay, or a powder. Anything else that'll burn but isn't hard to handle."

"Like what?" demanded John crossly. With a sneer: "Brimstone?"

"Why not?" asked Antonina brightly. As usual, she found herself cheering the naval officer up after another long effort had fallen short of its mark.

John made a face. "Give me a break. Have you ever *smelled* burning sulfur?"

"Give it a try," said Maurice. "Just make sure you stand upwind."

John thought for a moment, then shrugged. "Why not?" Then, with a smile: "As long as we're at it, why not make it a regular salad? What else burns easily but doesn't make old soldiers grumpy?"

"How do you feel about coal, Maurice?" asked Antonina. (Brightly, of course. Men were such a grumpy lot. Like children with a permanent toothache.)

Maurice grumped. "Too heavy."

John of Rhodes threw up his hands with exasperation.

"Charcoal, then! How's that, damn you?"

Before Maurice could form a reply, Antonina sidled up to John and put her arm around his waist.

"Now, now, John. Be sweet."

John began to snarl at her. Then, catching movement out of the corner of his eye, transformed the snarl into a leering grin.

"Sweet, is it? Well! As you say, as you say. Let's to the workshed, shall we, and mix up this unholy mess of Maurice's."

His own arm slid around Antonina's waist. The two of them began walking toward the workshed. On their way, John's hand slid down slightly, patting Antonina's hip.

Maurice didn't bother to turn around. He knew what he would see. Procopius, emerging from the villa, his eyes ogling the intimate couple.

Maurice puffed exasperation and stared up at the heavens.

Someday you're going to outsmart yourself, Belisarius, playing it too close. You might have told me, young man. If I hadn't figured it out fast enough and passed the word to the boys, your mechanical genius would have been found with a dagger in his back.

Maurice turned back toward the villa.

Sure enough. Procopius.

Another little puff of exasperation.

And since then it's all I can do to keep the boys from sliding a blade into this *one's back.*

Generals and their damned schemes!

A DAGGER AND A DANCE

Weeks later, Raghunath Rao decided he had finally eluded his pursuers. The key, as he had hoped, had been his turn to the west. The enemy had expected him to continue south, in the straightest route to Majarashtra. Instead, he had slipped west, into the Rann of Kutch.

In the days which followed, making his way through the salt-marshes, he had seen no sign of his pursuers. Now that he had finally reached the sea, he was certain he was no longer being pursued.

He decided to camp that night on the shore. True, there was

a chance of being spotted, but it was so small that he decided to take the risk. He was sick of the marshes. The salt-clean air would be like a balm to his soul.

He had had nothing to eat for two days, but ignored the pangs. Fasting and austerity were old friends. Tomorrow he would begin making his way around the coast of the Kathiawar peninsula. Soon enough he would encounter a fishing village. He spoke Gujarati fluently, and had no doubt he would find a friendly reception. Jainism still retained a strong hold in Gujarat, especially in the small villages away from the centers of Malwa power. Rao was confident that he could gain the villagers' acceptance. And their silent, quiet assistance.

Rao was not a Jain himself, but he respected the faith and knew its creed well. He had studied it carefully in his youth, and, although he had not adopted it for his own, he had incorporated many of its teachings into his own syncretic view of God. Just as he had done with the way of the Buddha.

It would take him time to work his way around the peninsula. And then more time, to find a means to cross the Gulf of Khambhat. Once across the Gulf, the labyrinth of the Great Country was easily within reach.

He began to speculate on the methods he might use, but quickly put the thoughts aside. There would be time to make plans later, based on the reality which emerged.

A smile came to his face.

Indeed, on this one point Ousanas was quite right. Good plans, like good meat, are best cooked rare. Such a marvelous man! Even if he does believe in the most preposterous notions. "Eternal and unchanging Forms," if you would!

The smile faded. Rao wondered how the treasure of his soul was faring. She was in the best of hands, of course. But, still, she was in the very heart of the asura's domain.

Again, he pushed the thoughts aside. He had agreed to the plan of the foreigners, and he was not a man given to useless doubts and second thoughts. Besides, it was a good plan—no, it was an excellent plan. Shakuntala was hidden in the one place the Malwa, full of their arrogance, would never think to look for her. And there had been no alternative, anyway. Remembering the past weeks, Rao knew for a certainty that he would never have been able to escape if Shakuntala had been with him. It had been a very close matter as it was.

And now? Now the future was clear. Once he reached the Great Country, the Panther of Majarashtra would begin to roar. Word would spread like lightning. Again, the Wind had struck the enemy. A deadly blow! Satavahana freed! The Wind himself sweeping through the hills!

The new army he would create would make Majarashtra a name of woe to Malwa. In the Great Country, the asura's rule would become a wraith—a thing seen only by day, in large cities. The land would become a deathtrap for Ye-tai and Rajputs and all the motley hordes of the demon.

He began to think of his stratagems and tactics, but again, put the thoughts aside. There would be time enough for that. More than time enough.

Again, he smiled, remembering his last conversation with Shakuntala. As he had expected, the princess had been utterly furious when he explained the plan to her. But she had acquiesced, in the end.

Not from conviction, of course. She had not believed that she would be an encumbrance in his escape. No, she had acquiesced from duty. Duty which he had hammered into her stubborn, reluctant soul.

She was no longer a princess. No longer a girl, for whom life could be an adventure. She was the empress, now, the ruler of broken Andhra. The sole survivor of great Satavahana. Upon her shoulders—her very soul—rested the fate of her people. Her life was not hers to risk. So long as she survived, rebellion against the asura could find an anchor, a point of certainty around which to pivot and coalesce. Without her, rebellion would become simple brigandry.

Hers was the duty of surviving and forging such alliances as bleeding Andhra needed. For now, no better alliance could be imagined than one with the very men who risked their lives to free her. Those men, and their purpose, might prove the key which unlocked the demon's shackles. Duty. Duty. Duty.

In the end, she had agreed, as Raghunath Rao had known she would. Her soul could do no other.

An old ache began to surface; he forced it down with long-practiced habit. But then, as he had never done before, allowed it to rise up anew.

This time, this one and only time, I will allow it. And never again.

He spent some minutes, then, lost in reverie. Pondering the vastness of time, wondering if there might ever be, in some turn of the wheel, a world where his soul and its treasure might not be forever separated by dharma.

Perhaps. What man can know?

Soon enough, reverie fell away. His life had been one of harsh self-discipline and great austerity, habits which now came automatically to him. So an old ache was driven under, again, and more ruthlessly than ever before.

Due, perhaps, to the effort that task demanded—greater than ever before—his thoughts turned to sacrifice. He was not given to the ancient rites, as a rule. The Vedas themselves he treasured, but the old rituals held little sway over his mind. Long ago he had embraced the way of bhakti, of devotion to God, even before the Mahaveda had turned honorable rituals into rites of cruelty and barbarism.

The sun was beginning to set over the Erythrean Sea, bathing the waters and the shore with lambent glory.

Yes, he would sacrifice.

Quickly, he constructed the three ritual fires. Once the flames were burning, he drew forth his offering from its leather container.

He had saved the last sheet, only. The others he had destroyed in his fire in the forest, weeks earlier. The other sheets, had they been found on his body in the event of his death or capture, could have led to the discovery of the man who wrote that message. But the last sheet, even if found by the Malwa, would have been simply a thing of myth and mystery.

That message was the most precious thing he had ever owned. He would sacrifice it now, in devotion to the future.

Before casting the sheet into the flames, he read it one last time.

—as you may imagine. More I cannot say, for a certainty. He is a strange fellow. Like a child, often, filled with mute hurt and fumbling grievance. Great hurt and grievance, that I doubt not. And just ones, as well, I believe.

But power also he possesses, of that I am equally certain. The greatest power of all, the power of knowledge.

His name I do not know. I do not think he knows it himself.

Yet, I have a belief. It comes not from my faith—though I do not see where it is forbidden by it, nor do the holiest of men that I know. It comes from a vision. A vision I had, once, of you yourself, dancing on the rim of destruction.

I believe he is Kalkin. The tenth avatara who was promised, sent to bind the asura and slay the asura's minions.

Or, at the least, teach us to dance the deed.

Raghunath Rao cast the papyrus into the flames and watched until it was totally consumed. Then he drew the dagger. The dagger, too, he would sacrifice.

Truly, an excellent dagger. But the time for daggers was past.

But, just as he prepared to place it in the flames, an impulse came upon him. An irresistible impulse; and, he thought, most fitting.

Aching pain and joyful wonder merged in his soul, and Raghunath Rao leapt to his feet.

Yes! He would dance!

And so he danced, by the seashore, on the golden rim of the Erythrean Sea. He was a great dancer, was Raghunath Rao. And now, by the edge of nature's molten treasure, in the golden sunlight of bursting hope, he danced the dance. The great dance, the terrible dance, the never-forgotten dance. The dance of creation. The dance of destruction. The wheeling, whirling, dervish dance of time.

And as he danced, and whirled the turns of time, he thought never once of his enemies and his hatreds. For those were, in the end, nothing. He thought only of those he loved, and those he would come to love, and was astonished to see their number.

He danced to his empress in her greatness, and his people in their splendor. He danced to the Erythrean Sea, and to the triumph which would arise from its waves. He danced to the friends of the past and the comrades of the future. And, most of all, he danced to the future itself.

Finally, feeling his strength begin to fade, Raghunath Rao held up the dagger. Admired it again, and hurled the precious gift into the waves. He could think of no better place for its beauty than the rising tide of the Erythrean Sea.

He made a last swirling, capering leap. Oh, so high was that leap! So high that he had time, before he plunged into the water, to cry out a great peal of laughter.

Oh, great Belisarius! Can you not see that you are the dancer, and Kalkin but the soul of your dance?

In the Heart of Darkness

To Kathy and Laura

Prologue

When the lavish dinner was finished, and the servants sent away, the spymaster broke the bad news.

"Belisarius is alive," he said curtly.

There were seven other men in the room. One, like the spymaster, was foreign. From the blankness of his face, it was obvious he had already heard the news. Of the Romans in the room, five rose up on their couches, their faces expressing various degrees of consternation.

The seventh man, the last of the Romans, simply curled his lip, and satisfied himself with shifting his weight to the other elbow.

He had been disgusted the entire evening.

The two churchmen in the room disgusted him with their sanctimonious prattle. Glycerius of Chalcedon and George Barsymes were deacons, acting on behalf of Rufinus Namatianus, Bishop of Ravenna. They were rabidly orthodox. But, at bottom, their orthodoxy was nothing but a veil for ambition. The Bishop of Ravenna sought the papacy, and his underlings sought the patriarchates of Constantinople and Alexandria.

Ambition was the seventh man's motive also, but he did not disguise it with false piety. (A ridiculous piety, to boot—allying with Hindu heathens against Christian heretics.) The seventh man counted many sins against his soul, mortal and venial alike. But hypocrisy was not among them.

The two noblemen in the room disgusted him with their swaggering braggadocio. Their names were Hypatius and Pompeius. They

377

were brothers, the nephews of the former emperor Anastasius. By any formal dynastic criterion, they were the rightful heirs to the imperial throne. But Romans had never worshipped at the altar of heredity. Competence was the ultimate standard for wearing the purple. And if there were two more feckless creatures in the entire Roman empire, they were hiding themselves well.

The other high Roman official in the room disgusted him. John of Cappadocia, his name was, and he was Emperor Justinian's Praetorian Prefect. A ruthless and capable man, to be sure. But one whose rapaciousness and depravity were almost beyond belief. Murderer, thief, extortionist, torturer, rapist—all these things John of Cappadocia had been named. The names were all true.

The two Malwa spies in the room disgusted him—Balban the oily spymaster even more than Ajatasutra the assassin—partly for their false bonhomie and pretense of comradeship, but mostly for their claim of disinterested concern for the best interests of Rome, which no one but an idiot would believe for an instant. The seventh man was very far from being an idiot, and he took the Malwa air of innocence as an insult to his intelligence.

The seventh man was disgusted with himself. He was the Grand Chamberlain of the Roman Empire. He was one of the most valued and trusted advisers of Emperor Justinian, whom he planned to betray. He was the close personal friend of the Empress Theodora, whom he planned to murder. He would add the count of treason to his sins, and increase the counts of murder, and all for the sake of rising one small rung in power. He was a eunuch, and so could never aspire to the throne himself. But he could at least become the Grand Chamberlain of a feckless emperor, instead of a dynamic one, and thus be the real power in Rome.

The seventh man knew, with all the intelligence of a keen mind, that his ambition was stupidity incarnate. He was an old man. Even if he realized his ambition, he would probably not enjoy its exercise for more than a few years.

For that stupid, petty ambition, the seventh man risked the possibility of execution and the certainty of eternal damnation. He despised himself for that pettiness, and was disgusted by his own stupidity. But he could not do otherwise. For all that he prided himself on his iron self-control, the seventh man had never been able to control his ambition. Ambition rode the eunuch like lust rides a satyr. It had ridden him as far back as he could remember, since the days when other boys had taunted and beaten him for his castrated deformity.

But, above all, the seventh man was disgusted because the Malwa and the Roman reactionaries in the room had insisted on dining in the archaic tradition, instead of sitting on chairs at a table, as all sensible people did in the modern day. The seventh man's aged body had long since lost the suppleness to eat a meal half-reclined on a couch.

His name was Narses, and his back hurt.

The Indian spymaster's eyes had been fixed on Narses from the moment he made the announcement. Months ago, Balban had realized that the eunuch was by far the most formidable of his Roman allies—and the only one who was not, in any sense, a dupe. The churchmen were provincial bigots, the royal nephews were witless fops, and John of Cappadocia—for all his undoubted ability—was too besotted with his own vices to distinguish fact from fancy. But Narses understood the Malwa plot perfectly. He had agreed to join it simply because he was convinced he could foil the Malwa after he had taken the power in Rome.

Balban was not at all sure the eunuch was wrong in that estimate. Narses, in power, would make a vastly more dangerous enemy for the Malwa than Justinian. So Balban had long since begun planning for Narses' own assassination. But he was a methodical man, who knew the value of patience, and was willing to take one step ahead of the other. For the moment, the alliance with the eunuch was necessary.

And so—

"What is your reaction, Narses?" he asked. The Indian's Greek was fluent, if heavily accented.

The eunuch grimaced as he painfully levered himself to an upright posture on his couch.

"I told you it was a stupid idea," he growled. As always, Balban was struck by the sound of such a deep, rich, powerful voice coming from such a small and elderly man. A eunuch, to boot.

"*It was not*," whined Hypatius. His brother's vigorous nod of agreement was intended to be firm and dignified. With his cosmetic-adorned and well-coiffed head bobbing back and forth on a scrawny neck, the nobleman resembled nothing so much as a doll shaken by a toddler.

The eunuch fixed muddy green eyes on the nephews. Against his bony face, surrounded by myriad wrinkles, the effect was utterly reptilian. Deadly, but cold-blooded. The brothers shrank from his gaze like mice.

Narses satisfied himself with that silent intimidation. Much as he was often tempted, Narses never insulted the brothers. One of them would be needed, in the future, for his puppet emperor. Either one, it did not matter. Whichever summoned up the courage to plot with Narses to murder the other first. So, as always, the eunuch maintained formal respect, and allowed his eyes alone to establish dominance.

"I told you all from the beginning that the plan was pathetic," he said. "If you want to assassinate a man like Belisarius, you had better use something other than common criminals."

Ajatasutra spoke, for the first time that evening. He was the Indian mission's chief agent. A specialist in direct action, a man of the streets and alleys, where Balban manipulated from the shadows. His Greek was also fluent, but, unlike Balban's, bore hardly a trace of an accent. Ajatasutra could—and often did—pass himself off as a Roman citizen from one of the more exotic, outlying provinces of the empire. A dark-complected Syrian, perhaps, or a half-breed Isaurian.

"It was a well-laid plan, according to the report," he murmured. His tone exuded calm, dispassionate assessment. "Belisarius was ambushed shortly after landing in Bharakuccha. At night, in darkness. While he was alone, without his cataphract bodyguards. By no less than eight dacoits. Seasoned killers, all of them."

"Really?" sneered Narses. He was quite happy to insult the Malwa, within reason. So he allowed his lip to curl ferociously, but refrained from spitting on the polished, parquet floor. "Tell me, Ajatasutra—I'm curious. How many of these—what did you call them?—oh, yes! 'Seasoned killers,' no less. How many of them survived the encounter?"

"Three," came the instant reply. "They fled after Belisarius slaughtered the first five. Within seconds, according to the report."

Narses' sneer faded. Ajatasutra was immune to the Roman's contempt. The agent's dark brown eyes were filled with nothing beyond professional interest. And the eunuch well remembered that Ajatasutra had expressed his own reservations at the meeting, many months earlier, when the decision was taken to recommend

Belisarius' assassination as soon as he reached India. (Recommend, not order. Lord Venandakatra was the one who would make the final decision. Balban ranked high in the Malwa Empire's hierarchy, but he was not a member of the imperial dynastic clan. He did not give orders to such as Venandakatra. Not if he wanted to live.)

Narses sighed, as much from the pain in his back as exasperation.

"I told you then," he continued, "that you were grossly underestimating Belisarius."

A rare moment of genuine anger heated his voice. *"Who did you think you were playing with, for the sake of God?"* he demanded. "The man is one of the greatest generals Rome has ever produced. *And* he's still young. *And* vigorous. *And* famous for his bladesmanship. *And* has more combat experience than most soldiers twice his age."

A glare at Balban. *"Real* combat experience, against *real* enemies. Not"—the sneer was back in full force—"the 'seasoned killer' experience of a thug backstabbing a merchant." He stopped, hissing. Partly from aggravation; mostly from the sharp pain which streaked up his spine. He sagged back on his couch, closing his eyes.

Balban cleared his throat. "As it happens, it may have turned out for the best in any event. The report which we just received—from the hand of Lord Venandakatra himself—also says that Lord Venandakatra believes Belisarius may be open to treas—to our mutual cause. He has developed a friendship with Belisarius, he says, and has had many conversations with him in the course of their long voyage to India. The general is filled with bitter resentment at his treatment by Justinian, and has let slip indications of a willingness to seek another patron."

His eyes still closed, fighting the pain, Narses listened to the conversation which suddenly filled the dining chamber. An agitated conversation, on the part of the Romans. A mixture of cold calculation, babbling nonsense, scheming analysis, wild speculation, and—most of all—poorly hidden fear.

All of the Romans in the room, except Narses, were torn and uncertain. To win Belisarius to their plot would greatly increase its chance for success. So they all said, aloud. But to do so would also make their own personal prospects that much the dimmer. So they all thought, silently.

Narses said nothing. Nor, after a minute or so, did he pay any attention to the words. Let them babble, and play their witless games.

Pointless games. The Grand Chamberlain, old as he was, eunuch that he was, knew beyond the shadow of a doubt that there was no more chance of Belisarius betraying his oath to Justinian—less chance; much, much less chance—than that a handful of street thugs could cut him down from ambush.

The image of Belisarius came to his mind, as sharp as if the Thracian were standing before him. Tall, handsome, well-built. The archetype of the simple soldier, except for that crooked smile and that strange, knowing, subtle gaze.

Narses stared up at the ceiling, oblivious to the chatter around him, grimly fighting down the pain.

Balban's voice penetrated.

"So, that's it. I think we're all agreed. We'll hope for the success of Lord Venandakatra's effort to win over Belisarius. In the meantime, here in Constantinople, we'll step up our efforts to turn his wife Antonina. As you all know, she arrived a month ago from their estate in Syria. Ajatasutra has already initiated contact with her."

Narses' eyes remained fixed on the ceiling. He listened to Ajatasutra:

"It went well, I think, for a first approach. She was obviously shaken by my hint that Emperor Justinian is plotting with the Malwa to assassinate Belisarius while he is in India, far from his friends and his army. I am to meet her again, soon, while she is still in the capital."

John of Cappadocia's voice, coarse, hot:

"If that doesn't work, just seduce the slut. It seems the supposedly reformed whore hasn't changed her ways a bit. Not according to Belisarius' own secretary Procopius, at any rate. I had a little chat with him just the other day. She's been spreading her legs for everybody since the day her doting husband left for India."

Lewd laughter rippled around the room. Narses rolled his head on the couch, slightly. Just enough to bring John of Cappadocia under his reptilian gaze.

Not for you, she hasn't. And never will. Or for anyone, I suspect. Only a cretin would believe that malicious gossip Procopius.

Narses levered himself upright, and onto his feet.

"I'm leaving, then," he announced. He nodded politely to all the men in the room, except John of Cappadocia. Courtesy was unneeded there, and would have been wasted in any event. The

Praetorian Prefect was oblivious to Narses. His eyes were blank, his mind focussed inward, on the image of the beautiful Antonina.

So Narses simply stared at the Cappadocian for a moment, treasuring the sight of that twisted obsession. When the time came, the eunuch knew, after the triumph of their treason, John planned to finally sate his lust for Antonina.

Narses turned away. The Cappadocian's guard would be down then. It would be the perfect time to have him murdered.

Fierce satisfaction flooded him. In his own bitter heart, hidden away like a coal in his icy mind, Narses had compiled a list of all those he hated in the world. It was a very, very, very long list.

John of Cappadocia's name ranked high on that list. Narses would enjoy killing him. Enjoy it immensely.

The pleasure would alleviate, perhaps, the pain from his other crimes. The pain from killing Belisarius, whom he admired deeply. The agony from Theodora's murder, which would leave him, in the end, shrieking on his deathbed.

The servant helped him don his cloak, before opening the door.

Narses stood in the doorway, waiting for the servant to fetch his palanquin from the stables in the back of the villa. He glanced up. The night sky was clear, cloudless. Open. Unstained.

Murder them he would, nonetheless, or see to the doing of the deed.

Behind him, dimly, he heard John of Cappadocia speaking. He could not make out the words, but there was no mistaking that coarse, foul voice.

Foul noise and unstained sky swirled in the soul of Narses. Images of a murdered Cappadocian and a murdered Thracian vanished. The cold, still face of the eunuch finally twisted, unbridled. There was nothing reptilian in that face now. It was the face of a warm-blooded beast. Almost a child's face, for all its creases and wrinkles, if a child's face had ever borne such a burden of helpless rage.

Cursed, hated ambition. He would destroy himself for that cannibal.

The palanquin was here. The four slaves who carried it waited in silent obedience while the servant assisted Narses into the cushioned seat. The palanquin began to move.

Narses leaned back into the cushions, eyes closed.

His back hurt.

Chapter 1

RANAPUR
Spring 530 AD

Belisarius watched the stone ball arching through the sky. The trajectory was no flatter than that of a ball cast by catapult, but it slammed into the brick wall surrounding Ranapur with much greater force. Even over the roar of the cannon blast, the sound of the ball's impact was remarkable.

"A least a foot in diameter," stated Anastasius.

Belisarius thought the cataphract's estimate of the cannonball's size was accurate, and nodded his agreement. The other of his veteran bodyguards, Valentinian, grimaced sourly.

"So what?" he grumbled. "I've seen a catapult toss bigger."

"Not as far," countered Anastasius, "and not with anything like that kind of power." The huge Thracian shrugged his shoulders. "There's no point fooling ourselves. These infernal Malwa devices make our Roman artillery engines look like toys."

Menander, the last of the three cataphracts who had accompanied Belisarius to India, spoke up.

"What do you think, general?"

Belisarius turned in his saddle to reply. But his quick answer was interrupted by a muttered curse.

Anastasius chuckled. "It's amazing how quickly we forget old skills, isn't it?"

Belisarius smiled ruefully, for the truth of the remark could not be denied. Belisarius had introduced stirrups into the equipment of his cavalry only a few months before his journey to India. Already he had half-forgotten the little tricks of staying in a saddle without them. The ambassadorial mission which Belisarius led had not brought the new devices to India, however. Stirrups were one of the very few items of Roman military equipment which were superior to those of the Malwa Empire, and Belisarius had no intention of alerting his future enemy to them.

But he did miss the things, deeply, and was reminded of their absence every time some little motion caused him to lose his balance atop his horse—even something as simple as turning in his saddle to answer the young Thracian behind him.

"I agree with Anastasius, Menander," he said. "Actually, I think he's understating the problem. It's not just that the Malwa cannons are superior to our catapults *at the moment*. What's worse is that our artillery engines and techniques are already at their peak of development, while the Malwa devices are still crude and primitive."

Menander's eyes widened. "Really? They seem—"

The young soldier's gaze scanned the battleground. Belisarius and his entourage had arrived at Ranapur only the week before. But the northern Indian province of which Ranapur was the capital had rebelled against their Malwa overlords two years earlier. For more than a year now, Ranapur itself had been under siege. The once fertile fields surrounding the large city had long since been trampled flat and then re-elevated into a maze of trenchworks and earthen fortifications.

The scene reminded Menander of nothing so much as a gigantic ant nest. Everywhere his eyes looked he saw soldiers and laborers hauling supplies and ammunition, sometimes with carts and wagons, but more often through simple brute labor. Less than thirty yards away, he watched a pair of laborers toting a clay-sealed, tightly woven basket filled with gunpowder. The basket was suspended on a bamboo pole, each end of which rested on the men's shoulders. Despite being clothed only in loincloths, the laborers were sweating heavily. Much of that sweat, of course, was the product of the blistering heat which saturated the great Gangetic plain of north India in springtime, during that dry season which the Indians called *garam*. But most of it was due to the work itself. Menander estimated the basket's weight at sixty pounds, and knew that it was only one of many which those two men would have been hauling for hours.

That scene was duplicated dozens of times over, everywhere he could see. The entire city of Ranapur was surrounded by wooden palisades, earthen walls, trenches, and every other form of siegework. These had been erected by the besieging Malwa as protection from the rebels' catapult fire and occasional sallies.

Menander thought the Malwa were being excessively cautious. He himself was too inexperienced to be a good judge of these things, but Belisarius and the veteran cataphracts had estimated the size of the Malwa army surrounding Ranapur at 200,000 soldiers.

The figure was mind-boggling. No western empire could possibly muster such a force on a field of battle. And the soldiers, Menander knew, were just the fighting edge of an even greater mass of humanity. Menander could see only some of them from his current vantage point, but he knew that all the roads in the vicinity of the city were choked with transport bringing supplies to the army.

Glancing to the south, he could see barges making their slow way up the Jamuna river to the temporary docks which the Malwa had erected to offload their provisions. Each of those barges weighed three to six hundred tons—the size of the average *sea-going* craft of the Mediterranean world. They were hauling food and provisions from the whole of northern India, produced by the toil of the uncountable multitude of Malwa subject peoples.

In addition to the freight barges there were a number of equal-sized, but vastly more luxurious, barges moored to the south bank of the Jamuna. These were the accommodations for the Malwa nobility and high officials. And, here and there, Menander could see slim oared craft, as well, moving much more rapidly. The galleys were powered by fifty or so rowers, with additional troops aboard. The Malwa maintained a careful patrol of the river, closing Ranapur's access to water traffic.

Most of all, Menander's gaze was drawn by the huge bronze cannons which were bombarding Ranapur. He could see eight of them from the slight rise in the landscape where he and the other Romans were watching the siege. Each of the cannons was positioned on a stone surface, surrounded by a low berm, and tended by a small horde of soldiers and laborers.

"Magical, almost," he concluded softly.

Belisarius shook his head. "There's nothing magical about them, lad. It's just metalworking and chemistry, that's all. And, as I said, crude and primitive metalworking and chemistry."

The general cast his eyes about. Their large Rajput escort was not far away, but still out of hearing range.

Belisarius leaned forward in his saddle. When he spoke, his voice was low and intent. He spoke loud enough for all three of his cataphracts to hear him, but his principal audience was Menander. Out of all the hundreds of cataphracts who constituted Belisarius' bucellarii, his personal retinue of elite soldiers, there were none so deadly as Valentinian and Anastasius. That was why he had selected them to accompany him on his dangerous mission to India. But, for all their battle skills, neither of the veterans was really suited for the task of assessing a radically new situation. Young Menander, even with more experience, would never be Anastasius or Valentinian's equal as a warrior. But he was proving to be much quicker to absorb the new realities which the Malwa were introducing into warfare.

"Listen to me, all of you. I may not survive this journey. Whatever happens, it is essential that at least one of us return to Rome with what we've learned, and get the information to Antonina and John of Rhodes."

Valentinian began to make some little protest, but Belisarius waved him down.

"That's stupid, Valentinian, and you know it better than anyone. A thousand things can kill you on the field of battle—or off it—and I'm no more immune to them than anyone. What is important is the *information.*"

He glanced again in the direction of the Rajputs, but the cavalrymen were still maintaining a polite distance.

"I've already explained to you how the *cannons* work," he said. He cocked an eye at Menander. The young Thracian immediately recited the formula for gunpowder and the complex series of steps by which it was properly prepared. His words had the singsong character of one repeating oft-memorized data.

Belisarius nodded. "It's the wetting and the grinding that's key. Remember that." He made a small nodding gesture toward the distant cannons. "The Malwa gunpowder is really pretty poor stuff, compared to what's possible. And so is their metalworking."

Examining one of the cannons, he sat slightly straighter in his saddle.

"Watch," he commanded. "They're about to fire. Watch the trajectory of the cannonball."

Menander and the other two cataphracts followed his gaze. A moment later, they saw one of the Malwa soldiers take a long iron bar out of a small forge. The bar was bent ninety degrees at the tip, and the protruding two inches glowed red from heat. Gingerly, he inserted the firing bar into a small hole in the breach of the cannon. The mouth of the cannon belched a huge cloud of smoke, followed almost instantly by the roaring sound of the blast.

The recoil jerked the cannon back into its cradle. Menander saw the gunner lose his grip on the firing bar. The bar was spun against another of the Malwa soldiers, who backed up hastily, frantic to avoid the still-glowing tip. Menander did not envy the Malwa gunners. Theirs was a risky task. Two days earlier, he had seen a recoiling cannon shatter its cradle and crush one of its gunners.

Menander and the other Romans followed the cannonball's trajectory all the way to its impact against the great wall of Ranapur. Even from the distance, they could see the wall shiver, and pieces of brickwork splinter and fall to the ground.

Belisarius glanced at his companions. All of them were frowning— the veterans with simple puzzlement, but Menander with concentration.

"It didn't fly straight," announced the young cataphract. "It shot off at an angle. It should have hit the wall fifteen or twenty feet to the east."

"Exactly," said Belisarius with satisfaction. "If you watch carefully, and keep track, you'll eventually notice that the cannonfire is very erratic. Occasionally they shoot straight. But more often the ball will sail off at an angle—and the elevation's just as haphazard."

"Why?" asked Menander.

"It's the clearance," replied the general. "What's called *windage*. In order for a cannon to shoot straight, the ball has to fit snugly in the bore. That requires two things—an even, precise bore all the way through the cannon barrel, and cannonballs that are sized to match."

Anastasius puffed out his cheeks. "That's a tall order, general. Even for Greek artisans."

Belisarius nodded. "Yes, it is. But the better the fit, the better the fire. The Malwa don't even make the attempt. Those cannonballs aren't much more than crude stones—they'd do better to use iron—and the cannon barrels are simply castings. They're not machined at all. Even the casting process, I suspect, is pretty crude."

Valentinian scowled. "How would you machine something that big in the first place?" he demanded. "Especially metal."

Belisarius smiled. "I wouldn't even try, Valentinian. For cannons the size of these, sloppy accuracy isn't really that much of a problem. But let's examine the question from a different angle. How hard would it be to machine a very *small* cannon?"

"Very hard," said Anastasius instantly. His father was a blacksmith, and had put his boy to work at an early age. "Any kind of machining is difficult, even with wood. Almost nobody tries to do it with metal. But—yes, if it was small enough—"

"Hand cannons," said Menander excitedly. "That's what you'd have. Something small enough for a single man to fire—or maybe two."

"One man," pronounced Belisarius.

"I haven't seen any such weapons among the Malwa," said Valentinian uncertainly. "Maybe—" He fell silent, coughing. There was a soft wind blowing, and the cloud of gunsmoke emitted by the recent cannonblast had finally wafted over the Romans.

"God, that shit stinks," he muttered.

"Better get used to it," said Anastasius, rather unkindly. For a moment, the giant Thracian seemed on the verge of uttering one of his frequent philosophical homilies, but Valentinian's ferocious glare made him think better of it.

"You haven't seen any handcannons, Valentinian, because the Malwa don't have any." Belisarius' voice was soft, but filled with confidence. "They're not hiding them from us. I'm sure of that. They've kept us far from the battlefield, but not that far. If they had any handcannons, we'd have spotted them by now."

He waited for the roar of another cannonblast to subside before continuing.

"And that's the wave of the future. *Handcannons.* If we can get back to Rome—if *some of us* can make it back to Rome, and get this information to John of Rhodes, then we've got a chance. We'll have better powder than the Malwa, and our artisans are more skilled than theirs, on balance. We can build an entirely new kind of army. An army that can defeat this colossus."

For a moment, he considered adding some of the ideas he had been coming to, of late, concerning the structure and tactics of such a future army. But he decided against it. His ideas were still only half-formed and tentative. They would confuse the cataphracts more than anything else. Belisarius needed more time. More time to think. And, most of all, more time to learn from the strange mentality that rested, somehow, in the bizarre "jewel" that he carried in the pouch suspended from his neck. The mentality which called itself *Aide* and said that it came from the far distant future.

His musings were interrupted by Valentinian.

"Careful," muttered the cataphract. "The Rajputs are coming."

Belisarius glanced over, and saw that a small group of Rajputs had detached themselves from the main body of the elite horsemen and were trotting toward them. At their head rode the leader of the escort, one of the many petty kinglets who constituted the upper crust of the Malwa's Rajput vassals. This one belonged to the Chauhar clan, one of the most prominent of the Rajput dynasties. His name was Rana Sanga.

Watching Sanga approach, Belisarius was torn between two sentiments.

On the one hand, he was irritated by the interruption. The Rajputs—following orders, Belisarius had no doubt—never allowed the Romans to get very close to the action, and never for very long. Despite the limitation, Belisarius had been able to glean much from observing the siege of the rebel city of Ranapur. But he would have been able to learn much more had he been allowed closer, and if his observations were not always limited to a span of a few minutes.

On the other hand—

The fact was, he had developed a genuine respect for Rana Sanga. And even, in some strange way, the beginning of friendship, for all that the Rajput lord was his future enemy.

And a fearsome enemy at that, he thought.

Rana Sanga was, in every respect except one, the archetypical model of a Rajput. The man was very tall—taller, even, than Belisarius—and well built. The easy grace with which Sanga rode his mount bespoke not only his superb physical condition but also his expert horsemanship—a quality he shared with every Rajput Belisarius had so far met.

His dress and accouterments were those of a typical Rajput as well, if a little finer. Rajputs favored lighter gear and armor than either cataphracts or Persian lancers—mail tunics reaching to mid-thigh, but leaving the arms uncovered; open-faced helmets; tight trousers tucked into knee-high boots. For weapons, they carried lances, bows, and scimitars. Belisarius had never actually seen Sanga wield those weapons, but he had not the slightest doubt the man was expert in their use.

Yes, the ideal image of a Rajput in every sense, except—

Sanga was now within a few feet. Belisarius smiled at him, and found it impossible to keep the smile to a polite minimum.

Except for that marvelous, dry sense of humor.

"I am afraid I must ask you and your men to leave now, general Belisarius," said the Rajput, as he drew his horse alongside. "The battle will be heating up soon, I believe. As always, we must put the safety of our honored guests above all other concerns."

At that very moment, as if cued by the Rajput's words, an object appeared above Ranapur. Belisarius watched the bomb—launched by a catapult hidden behind the walls of the city—as it arched its way toward the Malwa besiegers. Even from the great distance, he could spot the tiny sparks which marked the bomb's fuse.

"You see the peril," announced Sanga.

The fuse, Belisarius saw, had been cut too short. The bomb exploded in the air, well before it struck its intended target, the front line of trenches encircling the city. Which were at least a mile away from the little knoll where they stood.

"The deadly peril," elaborated Sanga.

"Indeed," mused Belisarius. "This is perhaps the most danger-ous moment in my entire life. Or, perhaps not. Perhaps it takes second place to that terrifying episode, when I was eight years old, when my sister threatened me with a ladle."

"Brutal creatures, sisters," agreed Sanga instantly. "I have three myself. Deadly with a ladle, each and every one, and cruel beyond belief. So I have no doubt that moment was slightly more danger-ous than the present one. But I must still insist that you leave. The safety of our honored guests from Rome is the uppermost concern in our Emperor's mind. To allow Emperor Justinian's official envoys to suffer so much as a scratch would be an irrepa-rable stain upon his honor."

The Rajput's expression was solemn, but Belisarius suddenly

broke into a grin. There was no point in arguing with Sanga. For all the Rajput's invariable courtesy, Belisarius had quickly learned that the man had a will of iron.

Belisarius reined his horse around and began moving away from the siege. His cataphracts followed immediately. The entire Rajput escort—all five hundred of them—quickly took their places. Most of the Rajputs rode a polite distance behind the Romans, but a considerable number took up positions as flankers, and a small group of twenty or so trotted ahead to serve as the advance guard for the little army moving through the milling swarm of Malwa soldiers and laborers.

Rana Sanga rode alongside Belisarius. After a moment's silence, the Rajput remarked casually:

"Your Hindi is improving rapidly, general. With amazing rapidity, actually. And your accent is becoming almost unnoticeable."

Belisarius repressed a grimace, and silently cursed himself for a fool. In point of fact, Belisarius could speak Hindi fluently, when he chose, without the slightest trace of an accent. An almost magical capacity for language was one of the many talents which Aide provided him, and one which Belisarius had used to advantage on several occasions.

And one which, he reminded himself again, was useful in direct proportion to being held a close secret.

He sighed, very slightly. He was learning that, of all the difficult tasks which men face in the world, there is perhaps none quite so difficult as pretending to be semicompetent in a language which one speaks perfectly.

Belisarius cleared his throat.

"I am pleased to hear that. I hadn't noticed, myself."

"I thought not," replied Sanga. The Rajput glanced over his shoulder. "Given that your Hindi is becoming so fluent, I suggest that we might speak in Greek from now on. My own Greek, as you know, is only passable. I would much appreciate the opportunity to improve it."

"Certainly," said Belisarius—speaking, now in Greek. "I would be delighted."

The Roman general pointed back toward Ranapur with his thumb.

"I am curious about one thing, Rana Sanga. I notice that the rebels seem to lack any of your *cannons*, yet they obviously possess a large supply of gunpowder. It seems odd they would have the one and not the other."

The Rajput did not reply, for a moment. It was obvious to Belisarius that Rana Sanga was gauging the limits of what he could tell the Roman.

But the moment was very brief. Sanga was not given to hesitation. It was one of the many little things about the man, Belisarius thought, which indicated his capabilities as a military commander.

"Not so odd, General Belisarius. The cannons are under the exclusive control of the Malwa kshatriya, and are never stationed in provincial cities. Neither are supplies of gunpowder, for that matter. But cannons are very difficult to manufacture, and require special establishments for the purpose. By law, such manufactories may not be created outside our capital city of Kausambi. Gunpowder, on the other hand, is much simpler to make. Or so, at least, I am given to understand. I myself, of course, do not know the secret of its manufacture. None do, except the Mahaveda priests. But it does not require the same elaborate equipment. So long as one possesses the necessary ingredients—"

The Rajput broke off, shrugged slightly.

"—which I, needless to say, do not—"

Fibber, thought Belisarius. I doubt he knows the exact process, but I'm sure a soldier as observant as Sanga knows the three ingredients and their approximate proportions.

"—and the necessary knowledge, gunpowder can be made. Even in a city under siege."

"I am surprised that Mahaveda priests would join a rebellion against Emperor Skandagupta," remarked Belisarius. "I had the impression that Malwa brahmins were utterly devoted to your empire."

Sanga snorted.

"Oh, I have no doubt their co-operation is involuntary. Most of the priests were undoubtedly killed when the province revolted, but I'm quite sure the lord of Ranapur kept a few alive. It is true, the Mahaveda are sworn to commit suicide before divulging the secret of the Veda weapons. But—"

The Rajput tightened his lips.

"But the priests are perhaps not completely free of the weaknesses which afflict us lesser mortals. Especially when they are themselves the *objects* of coercion, rather than—"

He fell silent entirely. Belisarius completed the thought in his own mind.

Rather than the overseers of the work of their mahamimamsa torturers.

Their conversation was the closest Belisarius had ever managed to get to the subject of the Malwa secret weapons. He decided to see how far he could probe.

"I notice that you refer to these—incredible—new weapons as the *Veda* weapons. My own men tend to believe they are the products of sorcery."

As he had hoped, his last words stung the Rajput.

"They are not sorcery! Magical, perhaps. But it is the reborn power of our Vedic ancestors, not the witchcraft of some modern heathen."

That was the official public position of the Malwa Empire: *Ancient weapons from the time of the Vedas, rediscovered by diligent priests belonging to the new Mahaveda cult.* Belisarius was fascinated to see how completely it was accepted by even Rajput royalty.

But perhaps, he thought, that was not so surprising after all. No people of India, Belisarius knew, took greater pride in their Vedic ancestry than Rajputs. The pride was all the greater—a better word might be ferocious—for the fact that many non-Rajput Indians questioned the Rajput claim to that ancestry. The Rajputs—so went the counter-claim—were actually recent migrants into India. Central Asian nomads, not so many generations ago, who had conquered part of northwestern India and promptly began giving themselves airs. Great airs! The term "Rajput" itself meant "sons of kings," which each and every Rajput claimed himself to be.

So it was said, by many non-Rajput Indians. But, Belisarius had noted, it was said quietly. And *never* in the presence of Rajputs themselves.

Belisarius pressed on.

"You think so? I have never had the opportunity to study the Vedas myself—"

(A bald lie, that. Belisarius had spent hours poring over the Sanskrit manuscripts, assisted in deciphering the old language by his slave Dadaji Holkar.)

"—but I did not have the impression that the Vedic heroes fought with any weapons beyond those with which modern men have long been familiar."

"The heroes themselves, perhaps not. Or not often, at least. But gods and demi-gods participated directly in those ancient battles, Belisarius. And *they* were under no such limitation."

Belisarius glanced quickly at Sanga. The Rajput was scowling, now.

A bit more, I think.

"You must be pleased to see such divine powers returning to the world," the general remarked idly.

Rana Sanga did not respond. Belisarius glanced at him again. The scowl had disappeared, replaced by a frown.

A moment later, the frown also disappeared, replaced by a little sigh.

"It goes without saying, Belisarius," said Sanga softly. The Roman did not fail to notice that this was the first time the Rajput had ever called him by his simple name, without the formal addition of the title of "general."

"It goes without saying. Yet—in some ways, I might prefer it if the Vedic glories remained a thing of the past." Another brief silence. Then: "*Glory*," he mused. "You are a soldier yourself, Belisarius, and thus have a better appreciation than most of *everything* the word 'glory' involves. The ancient battle of Kurukshetra, for instance, can be described as 'glorious.' Oh yes, glorious indeed."

They were now within a hundred yards of the Roman encampment. Belisarius could see the Kushan soldiers already drawing up in formation before the pavilions where the Romans and their Ethiopian allies made their headquarters. The Kushans were vassal soldiers whom the Malwa had assigned to serve as the permanent escort for the foreign envoys.

As always, the Kushans went about their task swiftly and expertly. Their commander's name was Kungas, and, for all that the thirty or so Kushans were members of his own clan and thus directly related to him by blood, maintained an iron discipline over his detachment. The Kushans, by any standard, were elite soldiers. Even Valentinian and Anastasius had admitted—grudgingly, to be sure—that they were perhaps as good as Thracian cataphracts.

As they drew up before the tent which Belisarius shared with Dadaji Holkar, the Maratha slave emerged and trotted over to hold the reins of the general's horse. Belisarius dismounted, as did his cataphracts.

From the ground, Belisarius stared up at Rana Sanga.

"You did not, I believe, complete your thought," he said quietly.

Rana Sanga looked away for a moment. When he turned back, he said:

"The Battle of Kurukshetra was the crowning moment of Vedic glory, Belisarius. The entire *Bhagavad Gita* from the *Mahabharata* is devoted to it. Kurukshetra was the greatest battle ever fought in the history of the world, and uncounted words have been recorded discussing its divine meaning, its philosophical profundity, and its religious importance."

Rana Sanga's dark, heavily bearded, handsome face seemed now like nothing so much as a woodcarving.

"Eighteen million ordinary men, it is also written, died in that battle."

The Rajput drew back on the reins, turning his horse.

"The name of not one of those men was ever recorded."

Chapter 2

Belisarius watched Rana Sanga and his men ride away. Not until the Rajputs had vanished did he turn to Dadaji Holkar.

"I do not think he is typical of Rajputs," he said. It was more of a question than a statement.

The Maratha slave disagreed. Instantly, and without hesitation. With any other master, he would not have done so. By ancient Indian custom—though only the Malwa had ever written it into law—a slave was expected to cherish as well as obey his master. That Dadaji Holkar did so in actual fact was due, as much as anything, to the fact that his outlandish foreign master interpreted obedience as devotion to his purpose rather than his person.

"You misunderstand him, master. Rana Sanga is quite famous. Most Indians—and all Maratha—consider him the truest of Rajputs. He is perhaps the greatest Rajput warrior today living, and certainly the finest Rajput general. His exploits are legend. He is a king also, of course, but—" the Maratha smiled "—that means little by itself. There are so many Rajput kings, most of whom rule their little hilltop as if it were all the universe. But Sanga is of the Chauhar dynasty, which is perhaps their greatest line of royalty. And the Chauhar are known for their thought as well as their archery and swordsmanship."

Belisarius cocked his eyebrow. "And so?"

Dadaji Holkar shrugged. "And so, Rana Sanga is the truest of Rajputs, and takes his deepest pride in that fact. But because he does so, and thinks like a Chauhar thinks, he also ponders on what being a Rajput means. He knows, you see—he has even

been heard to make the occasional jest about it—that the Rajput
lineage is really not so much grander than that of us disreputable Maratha hillmen. Yet he also knows that the lineage is true,
nonetheless. And so he thinks about lineage, and how it comes
to be, and how truth emerges out of illusion. And he wonders,
I think, where the difference between truth and illusion lies, and
what that means for his dharma."

The slave stroked the horse's neck. "Those are dangerous
thoughts, master. Outside of their sorcerous weapons, and their
vast armies, the Malwa have no resource so valuable to them as
the skill of Rana Sanga on the battlefield. But I believe they fear
that resource as much as they treasure it."

"Do they have reason to fear him?" asked Belisarius.

Dadaji Holkar squinted into the distance where the Rajputs
had disappeared.

"Hard to know, master. Raghunath Rao once said the day would
come when Rana Sanga would choose between Rajputana's honor
and Rajputana's duty. And that, when that day came, the truest of
Rajputs would understand that only honor gives duty meaning."

The Roman general scratched his chin. "I was not aware the
two men knew each other."

"Oh, yes. They fought once, in single combat. They were both
young at the time, but already famous warriors. It is a well-known
episode."

Belisarius started slightly.

"I'm amazed either of them survived!"

The slave smiled.

"So were they! And everyone! But survive they did. Badly
wounded, of course, both of them. Early in the fray, with his bow,
Sanga slew the Maratha chieftain's horse and then wounded Rao
in the arm. But he became overconfident and closed too soon.
Rao gutted the Rajput's mount and then pressed him with sword
and iron-clawed gauntlet. Here the combat was even, and they
fought until both were bloody and disarmed. Then they fought
by hand. No man in India beside Rana Sanga could have held
his own against Raghunath Rao in unarmed combat. He was not
as skilled, of course, but he was much larger and stronger. By
the end of the day, both men were too weak and exhausted to
lift an arm, or even stand. So they laid down side by side and
continued their combat with words."

Belisarius chuckled. "And who won?"

Holkar shrugged. "Who is to say? At sundown, they decided honor had been satisfied. So they called upon their followers to carry them away and tend their wounds, and the armies themselves never clashed. All the Rajputs and Marathas present felt the duel had been so glorious that any further combat would only sully the memory. As the years passed, both Rao and Sanga became famous commanders, although they never met on the field of battle again, neither as warriors nor as generals. But from that day forward, Raghunath Rao has always stated that there exists no greater archer in the world than Rana Sanga, and not more than four or five who are his equal with a sword. For his part, Sanga makes the equal claim for Rao's clawed gauntlet and his fists, and swears he would rather fight a tiger with his own teeth than face Rao again on the field of philosophy."

Belisarius' chuckle became an outright laugh.

"What a marvelous tale! How much truth is there in it, do you think?"

Holkar's face was solemn. "It is all true, master. Every word. I was at that battle, and helped bind Rao's wounds myself."

The Roman general stared down at his slave. Dadaji Holkar was a small man, middle-aged, grey-haired, and slightly built. In his appearance as well as his demeanor he seemed every inch the highly literate scribe that he had been before the Malwa enslaved him. Belisarius reminded himself that, for all his intellect, Dadaji Holkar was from Majarashtra. Majarashtra, the Great Country. A land of volcanic stone, harsh and unforgiving. The land of the Marathas, who, if they were not India's most noble people, were certainly its most truculent.

"I do not doubt you, Dadaji," he said softly. The Roman general's large and powerful hand, for just an instant, caressed the slender shoulder of his Maratha slave. And the slave knew, in that moment, that his master was returning his own cherishment.

Holkar left abruptly then, leading Belisarius' horse to its feeding trough. He squeezed his eyes, shutting back the tears. He shared his master's tent, and had listened, night after night, while his master spoke softly to the divine presence in his mind. He knew, from those muttered words, that Belisarius had met Rao himself—had met Rao, not in this world, but in the world of a vision. In that world of vision, all of India had fallen under the

Malwa talons, and Rome had eventually followed. In that world, Rao had failed to save Majarashtra and had become, through the strange workings of fate, the Maratha slave of the greatest of Roman generals.

Gently, Dadaji Holkar stripped the horse of her saddle and began wiping the mare down. He was fond of horses and, by her nuzzle, knew the fondness was reciprocated. He knew, also, that Belisarius' invariable kindness to him was partly the transference of his feelings for Rao onto another of his countrymen. Belisarius had said to him, once, that in a lifetime where he had met many fine men, he had never known a finer than Raghunath Rao. But Dadaji Holkar had come to know his new master well, in the months since he had been purchased in Bharakuccha to train a newly arrived foreigner in India's tongues and scripts. And so he knew that he was himself a man to Belisarius, not simply a surrogate for another, and that the heart of the Roman's love for him belonged to he himself. He, and his loyalty, and his service, and the memory of his broken people and his shattered family.

The slave Dadaji Holkar began feeding his master's horse. There were none to see, now, so he let the tears flow freely. Then, after a moment, raised his blurry vision and gazed at the distant, splintering, brick walls of rebel Ranapur.

Ranapur will fall, soon. The Malwa beasts will savage its people, even worse than they savaged my own.

He lowered his gaze, wiped the tears from his face, watched the horse feed. He enjoyed watching the mare's quiet pleasure as she ate. It reminded him, a bit, of the joy he had taken watching his wife and children eat the food he had always placed on their table. Until the Malwa came, and devoured his family whole.

Enjoy your triumph, Malwa cobras. It will not last. You have let the mongoose himself into your nest.

The horse was done feeding. Holkar led her into the thatched stalls which the Roman soldiers had erected for their horses. The stalls were very large, and completely shielded from outside view. An outside view which might have wondered, perhaps, why such a small body of men would need such a large number of horses. And such fine horses!

Indeed, they were very fine. Holkar was fond of the mare, but he knew she was the poorest of the mounts which rested in the stalls. The Romans never rode the fine ones, the superb riding steeds which Holkar himself had purchased, one by one, from the various merchants scattered about the siege of Ranapur. Horses which were always purchased late in the day, and led into their stalls in the dark of night.

His master had never explained the reasons for those purchases, nor had Holkar inquired.

Nor had Belisarius explained the reason for purchases which were still more odd.

Not two days ago, at his master's command, Holkar had purchased three elephants. Three small, well-tamed, docile creatures, which were kept in a huge but simple tent located in a small clearing in the forest, many miles from the siege, and many miles from the official camp of the Romans and Ethiopians.

Holkar had asked no questions. He had not asked why the tent should be so far away, and so different in appearance from the grandiose pavilion which the Ethiopian prince Eon had erected for himself and his concubines. Nor why the elephants themselves should be so different in their appearance from the two huge and unruly war elephants which the Ethiopians maintained as their public mounts. Nor why the elephants were only fed at night, and only by the African slave named Ousanas, whose invisibility in the darkness was partly due to the color of his skin, but mostly to his incredible skill as a hunter and a woodsman.

No, Holkar had simply obeyed his master's commands, and not asked for any explanation of them. The Maratha did not think that his master *could* have explained, even had he asked. Not clearly, at least. Not precisely. The mind of Belisarius did not work that way. His thoughts never moved in simple straight lines, but always at an angle. Where other men thought of the next step, Belisarius thought of the next fork in the road. And where other men, coming upon that fork, would see a choice between right and left, Belisarius was as likely to burrow a hole or take to the trees.

He closed the thatch door to the stalls. There was no lock, nor need of one. The Kushans would make short work of any thief or intruder. As he made his slow way back to his tent, Holkar smiled. Darkness had now fallen, but he could sense the keen scrutiny of the Kushan guards.

Almost as keen as their curiosity, he thought, chuckling. But they keep their curiosity to themselves. When Kungas commands, his men obey. The Kushans, also, ask no questions.

Holkar glanced over to the huge pavilion which belonged to Prince Eon. About nothing, Holkar suspected, were the Kushan guards more curious than that tent. Although he was not certain, he thought that the Kushan commander already knew the secret within that tent. Knew it, and knew his duty, and had decided to ignore that duty, for reasons which Holkar could only surmise. The Kushan commander's face was impossible to read, ever. But Holkar thought he knew the man's soul.

Dadaji Holkar himself, for that matter, had been told nothing. Nor had he ever entered Prince Eon's pavilion. But he was an acutely observant man, and he had come to know his new master well. Holkar was certain that inside that tent rested the person of Shakuntala, the only survivor of the Satavahana dynasty, the former rulers of conquered Andhra.

Like everyone in India—the tale had spread like wildfire—Holkar knew that the famed Maratha chieftain Raghunath Rao had rescued Shakuntala from her Malwa captors months ago. But where all others thought she had escaped with Rao, Holkar was certain that she had been hidden away by Belisarius and his Ethiopian allies. Disguised as one of Prince Eon's many concubines.

Again, he smiled. It was exactly the sort of cunning maneuver that his master would relish. Feint and counter-feint. Strike from an angle, never directly. Confuse and misdirect. In some manner, Holkar suspected, Belisarius had even been responsible for the replacement of Shakuntala's Kushan guards by priests and torturers. The same Kushan guards who now served as Belisarius' own escort had earlier been Shakuntala's guardians. Holkar had seen enough of them, over the past months, to realize that not even Raghunath Rao would have been able to penetrate their security.

He paused for a moment, considering the tent. A faint sneer came to his face.

The Malwa would pay him a fortune for his knowledge. But Holkar never even considered the possibility of treachery. He was devoted to Belisarius as much as he hated the Malwa. And besides, like Raghunath Rao, he was a Maratha himself. The Princess Shakuntala—the *Empress*, now—was the rightful ruler of Majarashtra. She was his own legitimate monarch, and, with a mental bow, Dadaji Holkar acknowledged that suzerainty.

He resumed his progress toward Belisarius' tent. A little smile came to his face. Like many intelligent, well-educated men, Dadaji Holkar had a fine sense of historical irony. So he found his fierce loyalty to the memory of Andhra amusing, in its own way.

When the Satavahana dynasty had been at the peak of their power, the Marathas had been the most unruly of their subjects. Never, since its incorporation into Andhra, had Majarashtra risen in outright rebellion. But the Satavahanas had always been careful to rule the Great Country with a light hand. Now that all of Andhra was under the Malwa heel, the Marathas had become the most fervent partisans of the former dynasty. None more so than Dadaji Holkar.

A sudden bright flash on the horizon drew his gaze. Holkar halted, stared. Moments later, the sound of the cannonade rolled over the encampment.

He resumed his steps.

Soon, yes, Ranapur will fall. And the cobra will sate itself again. As it has so many times.

He drew near his master's tent. For a moment, he stopped, studying that simple structure.

Not much to look at, truly. But, then, the mongoose never takes pride in its appearance. It simply studies the cobra, and ponders the angles.

Holkar began pulling back the tent flap. Another rolling cannonade caused him to pause, look back. For a moment, his scholar's face twisted into the visage of a gargoyle, so driven was he by hatred for all things Malwa.

But there were no Malwa spies close enough to see that face. Such spies had learned quickly that the endless squabbles over women between the foreigners and their Kushan escorts seemed to erupt in sudden brawls which, oddly, injured no one but bystanders watching the scene. In the first days after the foreigners set up their camp, two Malwa spies had been accidentally mauled in such melees. Thereafter, the spies had kept a discreet distance, and reported as little as possible to their overseers, lest they be ordered to resume a close watch.

The slave pulled back the flap and entered the tent. He saw his master squatting on a pallet, staring into nothingness, mouthing words too soft to hear.

Hatred vanished. Replaced, first, by devotion to his master's person. Then, by devotion to his master's purpose. And then, by devotion itself. For the slave had closed the demon world of Malwa behind him and had entered the presence of divinity.

He knelt in prayer. Silent prayer, for he did not wish to disturb his master's purpose. But fervent prayer, for all that.

Across the ancient, gigantic land of India, others also prayed that night. Millions of them.

Two hundred thousand prayed in Ranapur. They prayed, first, for deliverance from the Malwa. And then, knowing deliverance would not come, prayed they would not lose their souls as well as their bodies to the asura.

As Holkar prayed, his family prayed with him, though he knew it not. His wife, far away in a nobleman's mansion in the Malwa capital of Kausambi, hunched on her own pallet in a corner of the great kitchen where she spent her days in endless drudgery, prayed for her husband's safety. His son, squeezed among dozens of other slave laborers on the packed-earth floor of a shack in distant Bihar, prayed he would have the strength to make it through another day in the fields. His two daughters, clutching each other on a crib in a slave brothel in Pataliputra, prayed that their pimps would allow them to remain together another day.

Of those millions who prayed that night, many, much like Holkar, prayed for the tenth avatara who was promised. Prayed for Kalkin to come and save them from the Malwa demon.

Their prayers, like those of Holkar, were fervent.

But Holkar's prayers, unlike those of others, were not simply fervent. They were also joyous. For he, almost alone in India, knew that his prayers had been answered. Knew that he shared his own tent with the tenth avatara. And knew that, not more than five feet away, Kalkin himself was pouring his great soul into the vessel of the world's deliverance. Into the strange, crooked, cunning, mongoose mind of his foreign master.

Chapter 3

The sun beat down on a nightmare landscape. Once, these had been fields and orchards. Now, the ground was criss-crossed with deep trenches; stripped bare of any life beyond a few splintered trees, handfuls of crushed wheat, a single stalk of corn.

"Where are we?" asked Belisarius. He spoke in a low mutter. His eyes were closed, the better to concentrate on the images flashing through his mind. "And when?"

Near a place called Kursk, replied Aide. The facets flashed for a microsecond, translating the crystalline precision of Time's Arrow into the bizarre fiats of human calendrical custom. **A millenia and a half from now.**

A line of monsters surged onto the field. Gigantic things, tearing the soil with strange continuous belts—metal slats running over wheels. Forward, from cupolas, immense snouts protruded. The snouts belched flame and smoke. Emblazoned on their flanks were crosses—some, square with double lines; others, bent.

"Iron elephants," whispered Belisarius. "Like the ones the Malwa will build—but so much better!"

Tanks. They will be called tanks. These are the type which will be called PzKw V "Panthers." They will weigh 45 tons and travel up to 34 miles per hour. They fire a cannon whose size will be called 75 millimeter.

From the opposite side of the field, a new line of monsters—tanks—charged forward. They began exchanging cannon fire with the other tanks. Belisarius could sense that these new tanks were of a slightly different design, but the only feature which registered clearly on his uneducated eye was that, instead of crosses, their flanks were marked by red stars.

This was the best tank of that era. It will be called the T-34.

The battle was horrible and dazzling at the same time.

Horrible, in its destruction. Belisarius saw a tank cupola—

Turret.

—turret blown off. Tons of metal sent sailing, like a man decapitated. The body of the tank belched flame, and he knew the men inside were being incinerated. Saw men clambering from another burning tank, shrieking, their uniforms afire. Saw them die, suddenly, swept down by an invisible scythe.

Machine-gun fire.

Dazzling, in the speed of the tanks, and the accuracy of their fire. Like a vision of St. George battling the dragon, except the saint was a dragon himself. And his lance a magic wand belching flame and fury.

"How?"

Images of complex—machines?

Internal combustion engines.

Images of perfect metal tubes—cannon barrels, Belisarius realized. He watched as an object was fit into one of the tubes. A perfect fit. He wondered what it was until he saw the cannon fire. Cannonball, he realized—except it was not a ball. It was a cylinder capped by its own cupola.

"How can metal be shaped so precisely?"

He was inside a huge building. A manufactory, he realized. Everywhere he could see rolls and slabs of steel being shaped and cut with incredible speed and precision. He recognized one of the machines as a lathe, like the lathes used by expert carpenters to shape wooden legs for chairs and tables. But this lathe was much bigger and vastly more powerful. The lathes he knew were operated by foot pedal. No such lathes could rip through metal the way this one was, not even bronze. He watched a stream of steel chips flying from the cutting tool like a waterfall.

The other machines he did not recognize at all.

Horizontal boring mill. Vertical turret lathe. Radial drill press.

"Impossible," stated the general firmly. "To make such machines would require making machines to make machines to make machines which could make those machines. We do not have time."

The facets shivered momentarily, confused. The crystalline intelligence which called itself Aide viewed reality in an utterly different manner than humans. The logic behind Belisarius' conclusion was foreign to it. Where the man saw complex sequences, causes and effects, Aide saw the glorious kaleidoscope of eternity.

Malwa will have tanks.

The thought carried an undertone of grievance. Belisarius smiled, faintly. He was reminded of a small child complaining that the neighbor boy has a nice new toy, so why can't he?

"The Malwa tanks are completely different. They are not made like this, with this—" He groped for words to describe a reality he had never seen in real life.

Aide filled the void. Precision machining. Mass production.

"Yes. The Malwa do not use those methods. They use the same basic methods as we Romans do. Artisanship. Craftsmanship."

Incomprehension.

Belisarius sighed. For all Aide's brilliance, the strange mentality was often befuddled by the simplest human realities.

"Each Malwa tank—the tanks they will make in the future—will be unique. Handcrafted. The product of slow, painstaking work. The Malwa can afford such methods, with their gigantic resources. Greek artisans are superior, but not by that much. We will never be able to match the Malwa if we copy them. We must find our own way."

The general made a short, chopping gesture with his hand.

"Forget the tanks. Show me more of the battle. It could not all have been—*will be*—a contest of tanks."

Montage of images. Infantrymen in a trench, firing hand cannons and hurling grenades. A line of cannons hidden in a copse of trees, belching fire. A strange glass-and-metal wagon hurtling to a stop. There was no horse to pull it; no horse to stop it. Atop the wagon was a rack of tubes. Suddenly, the rack plumed flame and a volley of rockets streaked forward. Another—

"Stop! There—focus there! The rocket wagon!"

The wagon, again. Belisarius could now see that men were sitting in the glass-enclosed front. Other men were placing rockets into the tubes. The tubes rested on a flat bed toward the rear of the wagon and were slanted up at the sky. Again, the tubes plumed fire. Again, rockets soared.

"What are those?"

They will be called *katyushas*. These are eight-rail 132 millimeter rocket tubes mounted on what will be called 4X6 trucks.

"Yes. Yes. *Those* are possible."

The thought which now came from Aide carried more than an undertone of grievance.

Why is *this* possible and not tanks? Both are made by the same methods, which you said were impossible. Contradiction.

"You are confusing the—*trucks?*—with the rockets. They are two different things. We cannot make the trucks, but we *can* make the rockets. Not as good, but good enough. And then—we can substitute a different—" He groped for unfamiliar, as yet unknown terms.

Weapons platform.

"Yes. Exactly."

Belisarius straightened his back, stretched his arms. The movement broke his concentration, slightly. He saw Dadaji Holkar kneeling on his pallet, engrossed in silent prayer. The slave looked up. Holkar and Belisarius exchanged a silent stare for a moment, before the Maratha bowed his head and resumed his devotions. For all the solemnity in the man's posture, Belisarius was amused to note the smile on his face. He had never said a word to Holkar concerning Aide, but he knew that the Maratha had drawn his own conclusions. Conclusions, Belisarius was certain, which were not too far from the truth.

Belisarius closed his eyes and returned to the task at hand.

"You keep showing me things which are much too complex and difficult to make," he whispered. "We must stay within the simple limits that are possible, in the next few years."

A flash of exasperation came from Aide. A new vision erupted.

A man shuffling through a forest, stooped, filthy, clad in rough-cured animal skins. In his hand he clutched an axe. The blade of the weapon was a crudely shaped piece of stone, lashed to the handle with rawhide.

Belisarius chuckled. "I think we can manage a bit more than that, Aide. We are civilized, after all."

Again, exasperation. Again, a vision:

A man standing in a chariot. He was clad in gleaming bronze armor—a breastplate, greaves. A magnificent, ornate helmet, capped by a horse-crest, protected his head. His left arm carried a large, round shield. In his right hand he held a spear. The chariot was a small vehicle, carried on a single axle, drawn by two horses. The back of the chariot was open. Beside the armored warrior, there was only room for a charioteer, who handled the racing horses while the spearman concentrated on the approaching foe.

Belisarius started to laugh softly. Aide was still sulking. The image, for all its clarity, was a mocking rendition of an impossible, legendary figure. Achilles before the walls of Troy.

But then, suddenly, the laugh broke off.

"Yes!" hissed Belisarius. "Chariots!"

Now he did laugh, loudly. "Mother of God—nobody's used chariots in warfare for centuries! But with rockets—and some changes—"

The facets splintered, reformed, shattered, coalesced—all in an instant, trying to follow the branching trail of the general's thoughts. The kaleidoscope swirled around sequences. Aide brought sudden order. A new image, melded from crystal vision and human reasoning:

Another chariot. A bit longer, and wider. Also drawn on a single axle, also open to the rear. Again, a single charioteer handled the reins. But now, the warrior who accompanied him wore only light leather armor and no hand weapon beyond a semi-spatha scabbarded to his waist. He was not a spearman, but a rocketeer. Rising from the center of the chariot was a solid pole, five feet tall. Atop the pole, swiveling on a simple joint, was a bundle of six tubes—three abreast, in two tiers. The warrior aimed the launchers ahead and to the side, at an enemy army advancing some few hundred yards distant. He called out a signal. He and the charioteer crouched. The rocketeer touched a slowmatch to quick fuses. An instant later, a half-dozen rockets were hissing their way toward the approaching army.

The charioteer turned the horses, raced away. Behind, other chariots copied the same maneuver. Within not more than a minute, the ranks of the enemy were being shredded by a hail of rockets. The missiles were not very accurate, but made up for the lack by their numbers and the manner of their explosion.

Fragmentation warheads, came the thought from Aide. This time, the thought was saturated with satisfaction. **Shrapnel.**

Belisarius slumped back, sighing. He rubbed his eyes wearily.

"Yes, there's promise there." Again, he scratched his chin. "But these—*katyushas*—will only work on level ground. In mountain terrain, we'll need something different. Something that a small squad of men can carry by hand, and that can be fired over hills."

The facets flashed excitement.

Mortars.

Belisarius' eyes widened. "Show me," he commanded.

A small motion caught his eye. The Maratha slave had finished his prayers and was lying down on his pallet in preparation for sleep. His face could not be seen, for it was turned away. Belisarius put aside his dialogue with Aide, and devoted a moment to contemplating the man Dadaji Holkar.

Aide did not object, nor interrupt. There were many things about humanity which Aide did not understand. Of no human, perhaps, was that more true than of Belisarius. Belisarius, the one human of the ancient past whom the crystals had selected as the key to preserving their future. The choice had been theirs, but they had been guided by the Great Ones.

Find the general who is not a warrior.

Belisarius, the great general.

That strange thing Aide was coming to know, slowly, haltingly, gropingly.

Belisarius, the man. That stranger thing Aide already knew.

So Aide waited patiently. Waited during that moment of sorrow for another man's anguish. Waited, patiently, not because it understood grief but because it understood the future. And knew that its own future was safeguarded not by the weapons it was showing the general, but by the nature of the man himself.

The moment passed. The man receded.

"Show me," commanded the general.

Chapter 4

CONSTANTINOPLE
Spring 530 AD

"You're positive?" demanded Theodora. "There's no mistake?"

The Empress of Rome leaned forward in her luxurious chair. No expression showed on her face beyond a certain tense alertness. But the knuckles of her hands, gripping the armrests, were white as snow, and the tendons stood out like cables.

Irene met the dark-eyed gaze squarely.

"I am certain, Your Majesty. I've only met Narses face-to-face on three occasions, but I know him quite well. I've studied the man for years, as one professional—and possible competitor—will study another. I could not possibly mistake his appearance, undisguised. Nor he mine, for that matter—that's why I took such elaborate precautions with our disguises."

Theodora transferred her piercing gaze to Hermogenes. The young general winced, shrugged.

"I can't vouch for it myself, Your Majesty, one way or the other. I've never met Narses." He took a deep breath. "But I *do* know Irene, and if she says it was Narses—"

The Empress stilled him with a curt gesture. The black eyes moved on to Maurice.

"It was Narses," growled Maurice. "I've met the man many times, Empress, in the service of my lord Belisarius. We've never been personally introduced, and I doubt if he'd recognize me. But he's a distinctive-looking man. I'd know him anywhere, as long as he was undisguised and the light was good." The grey-haired veteran took his own deep breath. "The man was undisguised. His face—his whole figure—was clearly visible the moment he stepped out of Balban's villa to wait for his palanquin. And the light was good enough. A half-moon in a clear sky."

The Empress looked away. Still, there was no expression on her face.

Irene spoke hesitantly: "It's possible he's playing a double game. Simply trying to draw out treason before he—"

The Empress shook her head. The gesture was short, sharp, final. "No. You do not understand, Irene. Narses and I have been close—very close—for many years. If he suspected treason, and wanted to draw it out, he would have told me. There is only one explanation for his presence at that meeting."

She turned, raised her head imperiously, looked at Maurice and Hermogenes.

"Thank you, gentlemen," she said. Her voice was cold, perhaps a bit choked. A bit, no more. The Empress turned her head slightly, staring at the wall.

"Now—please leave. I wish to be alone with Antonina and Irene."

The two men in the room immediately left. After they closed the door behind them, they looked at each other and puffed their cheeks with relief.

"Let the women handle it now, lad," muttered Maurice. He stumped down the corridor, Hermogenes in tow, making no attempt to soften his footfalls.

In the room, the Empress continued to stare blindly at the wall, maintaining her rigid posture, until the sound of the receding soldiers faded completely away. Then she broke, not like a stick, but like a stone might crumble. Before the first tears had even appeared, Antonina was out of her own chair and cradling Theodora's head against her stomach. The Empress clutched her, sobbing, her face buried completely in Antonina's skirts. The tiara on her head was pushed back onto her hair, making a mess of the elaborate coiffure.

Irene remained in her seat. Her face showed her own distress. But, when she made a motion to rise and come to Antonina's assistance, Belisarius' wife stopped her with a look and a small shake of the head.

Irene sat back, understanding. The understanding, then, brought a different distress.

Fear. A fear much like that of an experienced seaman sensing hidden reefs and treacherous currents.

Irene Macrembolitissa was one of the best professional spymasters in the Roman Empire. One of the *very* best intriguers—in an era where intrigue was so prevalent, and so skilled, that it would bequeath the very name *Byzantine* to the lexicon of future languages.

She was in dangerous waters, now. The number of people alive who had ever seen Theodora in such a state could be counted on the fingers of one hand. It was both a privilege and a peril.

After a minute or so, the sobbing ceased. Irene noted, with the detached interest of a spymaster, that for all their bitter anguish the sobs had been almost silent. The Empress Theodora would never wail. Like any woman, she could have her heart broken. But it was a small, tough, stony heart. Its wounds healed very quickly, and simply added more scar tissue.

As soon as the sobs stopped, the Empress turned her head against Antonina's belly and fixed Irene with her gaze. The spymaster crouched in her chair, still, frozen by those cold black eyes. She felt like a rabbit being examined by a hawk.

"Tell me, Antonina," commanded Theodora. There was still a trace of raw anguish in that voice, but not much of one. It was a cold, black voice.

"She is my dear friend, Theodora," said Antonina. Her own voice, though soft, was even colder. "I love her as much as I trust her."

Silence followed, for a time which seemed to Irene to stretch on for hours. But it was less than half a minute before the Empress pushed herself away from Antonina.

"Good enough," she murmured. The Empress took a deep breath, leaned back into her chair. Throughout, her eyes never left Irene. But a smile came to her face. It was not much of a smile, true. But Irene suddenly discovered she could breathe.

Theodora laughed. It was like a raven's caw.

"Welcome to the old whores' club, Irene," she rasped. A majestic wave of the hand. "I make you an honorary member."

Theodora craned her head up, looking at Antonina. Finally, now, something other than pain entered her face.

"Thank you, Antonina," she whispered. "As always."

Then she sat erect. Automatically, as if to bring reassurance, her hand rose to the tiara. Finding it askew, she tried to force it back into place. The attempt failed, stymied by the disheveled mass of hair.

"Oh, the hell with it," muttered the Empress. She snatched the tiara off her head and placed it on the floor.

Irene almost laughed then, seeing the look of astonishment on Antonina's face. Often, in the year gone by, Antonina had told her of Theodora's obsession with maintaining her imperial regalia.

The Empress waved Antonina back to her chair.

"Let's to business," she commanded. Then, after her friend had resumed her seat:

"First of all, Antonina, you will pursue the contact this Indian— what was his name again?—"

"Ajatasutra."

"Yes—that this Ajatasutra initiated. He'll be seeking to draw you into some treasonous statement, you understand?"

Antonina nodded, saying:

"Of course. And there'll be an impeccable witness hidden somewhere nearby. John of Cappadocia, perhaps."

Irene shook her head. "It won't be him. Too many people wouldn't believe that filthy bastard if he claimed the sun rose in the east and set in the west. No, it's more likely to be one or the other—better yet, both—of the two churchmen." She shrugged. "Or someone else we don't even know yet."

Theodora pressed on:

"It's essential that you make such a statement, Antonina. That's the key that'll keep the door open. As long as the Malwa think they have something on you, they'll trust you."

Antonina chuckled. "You call that *trust*?"

The Empress smiled. "It's what passes for trust in that world. Our world, I'm afraid."

"Good as gold," chipped in Irene. "Better than gold, even. There's nothing an intriguer trusts more than someone he's successfully blackmailed."

Antonina made a little grimace of distaste. "And then what?" she asked.

Theodora shrugged. "We'll have to see. After the Malwa think they have you properly blackmailed, they'll demand that you perform some service. Give them some secret information, probably. When we find out what it is they want to know, that will tell us what's important to them."

Antonina considered the Empress' words for a moment.

"Makes sense," she said. Then, fixing Theodora with a level, serene gaze, added: "So be it."

The Empress returned the gaze. Nothing was said, for a full minute. When the Empress looked away, Irene noted that color had now fully returned to her face.

"Thank you, Antonina," whispered Theodora. "Again."

The intensity with which the words were spoken startled Irene, at first. Until she realized what had just happened. With that realization, she transferred her sharp eyes to the face of Antonina.

There was nothing to be seen on the Egyptian woman's face, beyond green-eyed, dark-haired, olive beauty. And serenity.

In the months since she had first met Antonina, she had often been impressed by her. But never more than at that moment.

A little chuckle from the Empress drew Irene's eyes. To her surprise, she found Theodora watching her.

"Good, Irene. You understand, then. Precious few people ever have."

Irene blew out her cheeks. "Not many women would agree to incriminate themselves on behalf of an Empress whose husband, well-placed rumor has it, is trying to have their own husband murdered. Without asking so much as a question. That's a different kind of trust than I usually encounter."

"Than *anyone* encounters," replied Theodora. For a moment, her lips tightened with anger. "I'm sure you've heard that my close friendship with Antonina is due to the fact that we're both former whores from Alexandria? Birds of feather, as it were, flocking together."

Irene nodded. "Any number of times."

"*Idiots*," snarled the Empress. "I know—knew, at least—plenty of Alexandrian whores who'd slit their own sister's throat for two denarii."

Antonina murmured: "That's not fair, Theodora. Antiochene whores, maybe. Any self-respecting Egyptian whore would hold out for a solidus."

Theodora cawed harshly. The Empress leaned forward in her seat, bracing her hands on her knees.

"I need you to be my spymaster, Irene."

Interpreting correctly the slight hesitation in the woman's face, Theodora made a little flipping motion with her hand, as if brushing something aside.

"I'll settle it with Sittas. He doesn't need your services half as much as I do. And I'll pay more than he does. Rich as he is, I'm a lot richer. And unlike Sittas, I'm not a stingy tightwad."

Irene chuckled, glancing around the lavishly furnished room. "You certainly aren't!"

When Irene had approached Theodora, a week earlier, with her charges against Narses and her plan to trap him in a treasonous meeting, it had been the Empress who had purchased this villa to serve as their command post. *Purchased* it—a huge, luxurious villa. Just—*bought* it. Like a matron buys fruit from a grocer.

The spymaster shook her head. "There's no point in that, Theodora. I can serve as your spymaster while staying on Sittas' payroll. It'd be much better that way. The fewer people who know of our relationship, the better. Money trails are the easiest to track. If I'm on your payroll, even secretly, someone will find out."

"The same objection applies to your being on Sittas' payroll," countered the Empress. "More so. I'm sure my security is better than Sittas'."

Irene shrugged. "So what? Let our enemies find out that I'm Sittas' spymaster. I'm sure they already know, anyway. Good. Excellent. Let them keep thinking that. Sittas they are not worried about. He's just a fat general who hates palace duty in Constantinople. Stuck way out there in Syria. Good at his trade, sure, but lazy and unambitious."

Theodora ran fingers through her elaborate coiffure, thinking. Almost immediately, the fingers became tangled in that incredible structure. Suddenly, vigorously, she plunged her fingers into the mass and pulled it all loose. Long black tresses cascaded over her shoulders. Her hair, now truly visible, was quite beautiful.

"God, I've wanted to do that for the longest time!"

Again, the women laughed. But it was a very brief moment of levity.

Theodora nodded. "You're right. Whatever their plot is, it does not appear to focus on the army. I noticed that no military figures attended that meeting tonight."

"No, they didn't. I'm pretty sure they've suborned a few officers, but not many. The only one of significance is Aegidius, the commander of the army in Bythinia. I'm not positive, but I think he's one of them. An underling, though, not a ringleader."

Theodora scowled. "I never liked that greasy bastard. God, my husband has the worst taste in generals!"

An apologetic nod to Antonina: "Belisarius aside, of course. And Sittas."

Again, the Empress ran her fingers through her hair, disheveling it even further. Her sensual pleasure in the act was obvious, but it did not distract her from her thoughts.

"Doesn't that seem odd to you, Irene? That lack of attention to the army? Every other treasonous plot I can remember has put the military on center stage. For obvious reasons."

"Actually, it's a cunning move on their part. They know that Justinian's suspicions will always be centered on the army. So they stay away from it, by and large, and spread their poison in darker corners."

"I *still* don't understand it." Theodora's voice was dark with frustration. "I take your point, but—so what? What good does it do to plot treason if you can't carry it out when the time comes? And for that you need military force. A lot more force than the Bythinian army provides. What is that army—ten thousand strong? At the most?"

"Eight," replied Irene. "Not enough to take power, but enough to neutralize loyal units. Especially if many of those units decide to stay on the sidelines until the dust settles. Which, unfortunately, many military units do during a coup." The spymaster began to add something, but fell silent. She glanced quickly at Antonina.

Theodora did not miss it.

"The two of you know something," she announced.

Silence.

"Tell." The voice of the Empress, that, not Theodora.

Irene's eyes appealed to Antonina. Antonina sighed.

"I will tell you everything, Theodora. Tonight. But you're not going to believe me."

"*Tell.*"

When Theodora left the villa, Irene and Antonina escorted the Empress to the palanquin drawn up in the courtyard. After she climbed into the palanquin, Theodora leaned forward and whispered:

"You were right, Antonina. I *don't* believe it. It's absurd! Belisarius has a talisman from God? A messenger from the future?"

Antonina shrugged. "You didn't believe Irene, either, when she told you about Narses. But still you came here, to see for yourself."

The two old friends stared at each other. The Empress was the first to look away.

"No, I didn't. And, yes, I did."

She leaned back into the plush cushions. Antonina could barely make out Theodora's face in the dark interior of the enclosed vehicle, but she couldn't miss the grimace.

"I hate to travel," growled the Empress.

A sigh.

"Yes, Antonina, I will. I will come to Daras and see for myself. This summer."

Another sigh.

"I hate Syria in the summer."

A great, imperial sigh.

"Now that I think about it, I hate Syria any time of the year."

After the gate closed behind the departing palanquin, Antonina and Irene stood for a moment in the courtyard, admiring the clear night sky.

"I'm curious about something, Antonina," said Irene.

"Yes?"

"I don't really understand. Well, let's just say that I was surprised how hard Theodora took it, to find out that Narses is a traitor. I knew he was one of her closest advisers, but—"

"He was a lot more than that, Irene," replied Antonina, shaking her head sadly. "Much, much more."

The short Egyptian woman looked up at her tall Greek friend.

"You've heard, I'm sure, all the stories about Theodora's past?"

Irene shrugged. "Of course. I can't say I paid much attention to them. People are always quick—"

Antonina shook her head. "The fact is, they're mostly true. At least, insofar as the tales report what she *did*."

She looked away, her jaws tight, before adding: "Where they lie is in the heart of the thing. Theodora, as a girl, was as great a whore as you'll ever find. What she never was, was a wanton slut." A little laugh, barely more than a chuckle. "It's ironic, actually. Fair-minded, respectable, proper people, when they compare her and me, are prone to give me the benefit of their doubt. True, before I met Belisarius I gave my favors for money. But only to the most carefully selected men, and not many of those. *Whereas Theodora—*"

Harshly: "If there's to be a comparison, by rights it should go the other way. I did what I did through choice. Not much of a choice, mind you, for a dirt-poor girl on the streets of Alexandria, with a whore for a mother and charioteer for a father. But—I can't honestly claim that anyone forced me into it."

She took a breath, then looked her friend straight in the eyes. Irene winced.

"I don't think I want to hear what's coming next."

"*You asked, woman.* Theodora never took pleasure in her whoring, and she never had a choice. Her pig of a father raped her when she was nine, and kept doing it until he sold her to a pimp at the age of twelve. And her pimp was even worse. That stinking—"

She stopped abruptly, made a short chopping motion with her hand. "Never mind. There's nothing in it but nausea." She took another deep breath, let it out. "The point is, Irene, that Narses was the closest thing to a real father that woman has ever had. When she first met him, she was just a poor ambitious young woman helping her poor ambitious young lover to claw his way to the top. Narses took her under his wing, and helped her along. With money, sometimes; other times, with privy information; other times, with introductions to the right people. But, mostly, he helped her the way a father helps his daughter. The way a *good* father helps his daughter. He simply—taught her."

She paused for a moment. Irene interjected:

"I'm sure he was just—"

Antonina shook her head. "No. *No.* Well, that's too bald. A man like Narses always has an eye out for the main chance. But that wasn't it, Irene. Believe me, it wasn't. Narses is brilliant, but he's not God Almighty. And only the Lord Himself, in those days, could have known that Theodora would someday be Empress of the Roman Empire. She and Justinian didn't know it, then. Didn't even think of it."

She took Irene by the arm and began slowly leading her out of the courtyard.

"No, I think— I think, in his own way, Narses saw Theodora as the child he never had. *Could* never have. So, what childlike trust remained in a girl who distrusted all men, was given to an elderly eunuch. And what paternal care existed in a man who could have no children, was given to a young whore."

She halted, fighting tears. Stared blindly at the sky.

"Dear God in heaven," she whispered, "I so hoped Narses wouldn't be at that meeting. I so hoped you'd be wrong, even though I knew you weren't." Now the tears flowed. "Theodora will never recover from this."

"You can't say that," protested Irene. "She still has Justinian."

Antonina shook her head. "No, Irene. It's not the same. Theodora loves Justinian, but she has never trusted him. Not the way she trusted Narses." She wiped her eyes. Again, Antonina took Irene's arm and led her out of the courtyard. Her steps, now, were quick.

Ten feet from the door, she said: "Theodora's harder than steel, and she prides herself on not making the same mistake twice. She'll never give her trust to another man again. No matter who he is. *Never.*"

Five feet from the door, Irene said sadly: "God, that poor woman."

At the door itself, Antonina stopped. Turned to her friend, and looked her squarely in the face. There was no trace of sorrow, now, in those beautiful green eyes. Just emptiness.

"*Poor woman?*" she demanded. "Don't ever think it, Irene. Give Theodora your love, if you can. But never think to give her your pity." Her eyes were like the green gaze of an asp. "If you thought the story of her father and her pimp was nauseating, someday I'll tell you what happened to them. After Theodora mounted the throne."

Irene felt her throat tighten.

"Whatever you do in this world, Irene, don't ever cross that *poor woman*. Go down to Hell, instead, and spit in the face of Satan."

She started through the door. Over her shoulder, like a serpent's hiss:

"Poor woman."

✧   ✧   ✧

Two hours—and many bottles of wine—later, Antonina lowered her head onto the arm of her couch and asked:

"I'm curious about something myself, Irene." Her words were spoken in that slow, careful, precise manner which indicates that a moment of solemnity has—briefly, briefly—interrupted the serious business of getting blind drunk.

"Ask anything!" commanded the spymaster from her own couch, waving her arm grandly. The just-emptied bottle in her hand detracted, a bit, from the majesty of the gesture. The hiccup which followed detracted quite a bit more.

Antonina grinned, then tried to focus her thought.

"Everything you said—" Her own grand gesture; pitifully collapsing in midair. "Back then, earlier tonight—whenever—made sense."

She managed to restrain her own hiccup, beamed triumphantly at her friend, continued:

"About remaining on Sittas' payroll. But—weren't you even tempted? I mean, Theodora is *stinking* rich. Makes Sittas look like a pauper. She really would pay you a lot more. A *whole* lot more."

Irene reached out her hand, grasped the arm of the couch, and levered herself up slowly. She tried to focus her eyes, but couldn't quite manage the feat. So she satisfied herself with her own beaming, triumphant grin.

"You don't really understand me, dear friend. Not here, at least, not in—this thing. You and Theodora grew up—you know. Poor. Money means something to you. I was raised in a rich family—" A very grand sweep of the arm. Too grand, much too grand. She overbalanced and slipped off the couch onto her knee. Then, laughing, stumbled back onto it. Then, raising her head high with pride, demonstrated to a doubting universe that she hadn't lost her train of thought:

"—and so I take money for granted. The truth is—" Suppressed belch; grim face; bitter struggle against the slanderous hint of insobriety.

"Truit is—*truth* is—I don't even spend half the money Sittas pays me." Again, suppressed belch; again—the short, chopping blows of desperate battle:

"Personally. I mean. On myself. Don't need it."

Victorious against all odds, she flopped against the back of the couch, staring blearily at one of the magnificent tapestries on the opposite wall. She couldn't really see it, anymore, but she knew it was magnificent. Incredibly magnificent.

In the way that it happens, at such times, exultant triumph collapsed into maudlin tears.

"What matters to me is that *the Empress of Rome* wants me for her spymaster. That's"—hiccup—"enormously gratifying to my vanity, of course. But it also means I now have access tomb pelear—*to imperial*—resources. *Resources.*"

She twirled her finger in a little gesture which encompassed the entire villa.

"Look at this! It's nothing but a damned *stake-out*, for Chrissake."

She beamed upon her friend, beamed upon the tapestry, sprang to her feet, and spread her arms in a great gesture of pure exultation.

"Oh, God—I'm going to have so much *fun.*"

Antonina tried to catch her on the way down, but only succeeded in flopping onto the floor herself. From her belly, cheek pressed against the parquet, she did manage to focus on Irene long enough to be sure her friend was not hurt. Just, finally, dead drunk.

"Woman can't handle her liquor," she muttered; although, to a cold-hearted observer, the word "liquor" would have sounded suspiciously like a snore.

"Come on, Hermogenes, let's get them to bed."

Maurice bent, scooped the little figure of Antonina into his thick arms, and carried her through the door. He padded down the corridor effortlessly. Hermogenes followed, with like ease. Irene was taller than Antonina, but, slim rather than voluptuous, weighed not a pound more.

Antonina's room came first. Maurice, turning backward, pushed his way through the door and lowered Antonina onto her bed. Like every other piece of furniture in the villa, the bed was splendid. Very well made, very luxurious, and—very large.

Maurice turned and looked at Hermogenes. The young general was standing in the doorway, Irene cradled in his arms. Maurice gestured him in.

"Bring her here, Hermogenes. We may as well let them sleep it off together."

Hermogenes hesitated for an instant, looking down at Irene's slack, lolling head. A tiny little twitch in his mouth gave away his regrets.

"Come on," chuckled Maurice. "You won't be enjoying her company tonight. If you put her in her own bed, you won't get any sleep yourself, since you're sharing it with her. You'll just wind up sleeping on a couch. She'll be snoring like a pig, you know it as well as I do."

Hermogenes smiled, ruefully, and brought Irene into the room. Gently, he lowered her onto the bed next to Antonina. On that huge expanse, the two women looked like children.

"I've never seen her get drunk before," said Hermogenes softly. There was no reproach in his voice, just bemused wonder. "I've never even seen her get tipsy."

Maurice glanced at Irene. "She's a spymaster," he grunted. "Greek nobility, to boot."

He then gave Antonina a long, lingering, considering stare. There was no reproach in his gaze, just love. "I've seen this one get drunk before," he murmured. "Twice."

He began ushering Hermogenes out of the room.

"Once, the first time Belisarius went on campaign. I stayed behind, for a few days, organizing the logistics. She got plastered the night he left. The next morning, she climbed onto a horse and rode off to join him in camp. I sent five cataphracts with her as an escort. Anastasius was in command. He told me later he thought he'd have to tie her onto the horse to keep her from falling off. But she made it, all on her own."

He stopped in the doorway, looking back fondly. "I was impressed, when he told me."

Hermogenes nodded, smiling. "That's tough, riding a horse with that kind of hangover. I know. I've done the same thing myself."

Maurice eyed him scornfully.

"No, you haven't. You already knew how to ride a horse. It was the first time she'd ever been in a saddle."

Hermogenes gaped. Maurice grinned.

"Oh, yes. A very tough little woman, in her own way. Though you wouldn't think it, just looking at her." He reached out and closed the door.

"What was the second time?"

The humor faded from Maurice's face.

"The second time was the day after he left for India. The next morning, she stumbled down to the stables and spent four hours there. Just sitting on a pile of hay, staring at a horse."

Hermogenes puffed his cheeks, blew out the air.

"Christ."

Maurice shrugged. "Ah, hell. I wish she'd do it more often."

He started down the corridor.

"That's too great a pain to keep in such a small body."

When Irene awoke the next morning, it took her a full minute to focus her eyes. The first thing she saw was Antonina, dressed in a robe, staring out the window onto the street below.

Irene watched her for ten minutes, never once moving her eyes away.

At first, simply because she couldn't move her eyes. Then, when she could, because she immediately encountered pain. Then, after pain had been properly introduced, because she hoped it would go away if she ignored it politely. Then, after pain made clear it was settling in for a nice long visit, because she wanted to think about anything else. Then, finally, because she started to think.

"What in the hell are you doing?" she croaked.

"Nothing much," came the soft reply. "Just looking at a horse."

Chapter 5
RANAPUR
Spring 530 AD

On the tenth day after their arrival at Ranapur, as Belisarius and his cataphracts rode out to the small knoll where they usually observed the siege, their Rajput escorts intercepted them before they had gone more than half a mile. The cavalrymen seemed tense and edgy, although their unease did not seem to be directed toward the Romans.

Rana Sanga himself, when he drew his horse alongside Belisarius, exhibited nothing beyond his usual reserved, courteous manner. But his first words made clear that today would be out of the ordinary.

"You and your men will not be watching the siege from your normal vantage point, General Belisarius."

Belisarius frowned. "If you move us further back, Rana Sanga, we might as well watch the battle from the moon!"

Sanga scowled. "You need have no fear on that account, General!" he snapped. "Quite the contrary." The Rajput shook his head in a sharp, short manner. "Excuse me," he muttered. "I am being impolite. I am—somewhat aggravated. I fear I am lashing at you for lack of a better target. Please accept my apology."

Belisarius smiled. "Gladly, Sanga. Gladly. But—well, it's none of my business, but—"

Again, Sanga shook his head.

"You will see for yourself, soon enough. The high commander

of the army, Lord Harsha, has decreed that Ranapur will fall today. The Emperor himself has come out to observe the conquest of the rebel city. You have been invited to watch the crushing of the rebellion from the Emperor's own pavilion. I have been instructed to escort you there."

"Ah," said Belisarius. Since they had arrived at Ranapur, the Roman delegation had been studiously ignored by the emperor and his entourage. Even Venandakatra had not sent so much as a formal note. The diplomatic discourtesy, Belisarius was certain, was calculated to impress upon the Romans their humble place in the Malwa scheme of things. He was equally certain that the sudden invitation to share the emperor's august presence was calculated to impress the foreigners with the Malwa empire's might and ruthlessness.

There was no point in lodging a protest against this shameful treatment. Certainly not to Rana Sanga, who was himself consigned to the periphery of the Malwa court. (Except, Belisarius suspected, when the clash of arms required the Rajput's skill.)

But—where protest would be futile, irony would be at least entertaining. Belisarius frowned, deep in thought, and allowed his jaw to gape with wonder.

"Such a brilliant stratagem! To conclude a siege by simply decreeing it at an end! I confess with shame that I never thought of it myself, despite the many sieges I have undertaken."

Sanga barked harsh laughter. "Neither have I!" he exclaimed. The Rajput's foul humor seemed to vanish. He reined his horse around, and began moving away. "Come, Belisarius," he said over his shoulder, cheerfully. "Let us observe a military genius at work."

Their route took them toward the eastern side of the rebel city. Before long, it became apparent to Belisarius that the Romans were going to get closer to Ranapur than they ever had been before. With some difficulty, the general managed to maintain an air of casual interest. He was pleased to note, however, from a glance over his shoulder, that his cataphracts were closely scrutinizing the scene. Menander was muttering softly, a habit which the young soldier had whenever he was determined to commit something to memory.

Soon, from a distance, Belisarius was able to discern an enormous pavilion on a small slope directly east of the city. The pavilion was located just barely out of catapult range. Apparently, Emperor Skandagupta intended to witness the fall of Ranapur as closely as possible.

Belisarius had never been able to observe the siege on this side of the city. Always, he had been restricted to the southern wall. But he had long suspected, from the sound of the cannonades, that it was on the east that the Malwa had brought their greatest strength to bear. As they drew nearer, it became obvious that his supposition was accurate. The great brick wall surrounding Ranapur was nothing but a shattered mound, here. The cannonades had reduced it to a ridge of rubble.

A huge army was assembling on the plain before that ridge of shattered brickwork, preparing for the final assault. Regular Malwa infantry, in the main, with Ye-tai shock troops to stiffen their resolve. The Ye-tai detachments were assembled in the rear of the regular infantry. Their job, obviously, was not to lead the charge, but to see to it that the common soldiers did not falter in their duty.

There were very few Rajputs anywhere to be seen. Belisarius began to make some remark to that effect, but Sanga interrupted him brusquely.

"We have been assigned other duties. All Rajput cavalrymen, except your escort and a few couriers, have been charged with the task of patrolling the outskirts of the city. To capture any rebels attempting to escape their doom."

"Ah," said Belisarius. A quick glance at Sanga's dark, tight-lipped face, then: "A brilliant maneuver, that—to use your best troops to mop up after a great victory which hasn't actually been won yet. Although, of course, the victory *has* been decreed." He scratched his chin. "I am ashamed to admit that I myself, military simpleton that I am, have always been prone to using my best troops in the battle itself."

Again, Sanga barked a few laughs. "I, too! Ah, Belisarius, we are but children at the feet of a master." He shook his head. "Truly, Lord Harsha's name belongs in the company of such as Alexander the Great and Ashoka."

"Truly," agreed Belisarius. The Roman general scanned the battleground. To his experienced eye, it was obvious that the Malwa had long been preparing for this massive assault on the eastern wall of the city.

"I see that Lord Harsha places no great store in surprise and deception," he commented.

Sanga's lips curled. "Such methods are beneath Lord Harsha's contempt," he replied acidly. "The tactics of bandits, he has been heard to call them."

For a moment, the Roman and Rajput generals stared at each other. Both smiled, then, faintly but quite warmly, before Sanga sighed and looked away.

"But, then, he is a very great man and does not care to stoop," the Rajput murmured. A shrug. "And, with the enormous force at his disposal, he does not perhaps need to."

They were now but two hundred yards from the Malwa emperor's gigantic pavilion. Skandagupta's camp headquarters, to Belisarius, seemed like something out of fable. He had never seen its like before, on a field of battle. Not even the haughtiest Persian emperor—not even the ancient Xerxes or Darius—had ever brought such an incredible structure to the clash of armies.

The pavilion rose a full sixty feet in the air, suspended on ten enormous poles—upended logs, rather. A multitude of inch-thick hawsers, stretching tightly in every direction, anchored the poles to the ground. The fabric of the tent itself was cotton—not even the ruler of Malwa could afford that much silk—but all of the many canopies which provided entry into the pavilion were made of silk, as were their tassels and cords. And the cotton of the tent was marvelously dyed, not in simple swaths and colors, but in complex geometric designs and subtle shades.

A small squad of Ye-tai began to approach them on horseback. From their gaudy uniforms and the red and gold pennants trailing their lances, Belisarius recognized them as members of the Emperor's personal bodyguard. Eight thousand strong, that bodyguard was reputed to be—although, from his quick assessment, Belisarius did not think there were more than half that many present on the scene.

At that moment, drums began sounding the signal for the advance. The front line of Malwa infantrymen began a slow, undulating movement. The advance was ragged, not so much due to indiscipline as to the simple fact that the ground was so chewed up by trenches and artillery fire that it was impossible for the Malwa soldiers to maintain an even line. The enormous mass of the army added to the confusion. Belisarius estimated that there were perhaps as many as forty thousand infantrymen in that slow-moving charge, with an additional five thousand Ye-tai barbarians bringing up the rear.

About three-fourths of the Malwa soldiers stumbling across that terrain were armed with traditional hand weapons. Most of the infantrymen favored spears and swords, although some were armed with battle-axes and maces.

Belisarius knew from his prior observations that these weapons would be cheap and poorly made, as would be their armor. The Ye-tai who chivvied those Malwa common troops were equipped with mail tunics and conical iron helmets. But the infantrymen themselves were forced to make do with leather half-armor reinforced with scale mail on the shoulders. Their helmets were not much more than leather caps, although the scale mail reinforcement was a bit less frugal than with their armor. The difference in shields was also striking. The Ye-tai shields, like Roman shields, were sturdy laminated wood reinforced with iron rims and bosses. The shields of the common Malwa troops, on the other hand, were almost pitiful: wicker frames, covered with simple leather.

Outside of the mass of troops carrying traditional weapons, however, Belisarius noted that the remainder were divided evenly between soldiers carrying ladders and scaling equipment, and grenadiers armed with a handful of the pestle-shaped Malwa grenades. This would be the Romans' first opportunity to observe grenades in action, and Belisarius was determined to make the most of the opportunity.

Belisarius and Rana Sanga stopped to watch the advance. Out of the corner of his eye, Belisarius saw that the oncoming Ye-tai patrol had stopped also. But he paid them little attention, for his interest was riveted on the battleground. He was struck again by the well-worn and oft-trampled nature of the terrain. Obviously, the siege here had been long, arduous, and filled with no surprises. It was exactly the kind of siege terrain that offended his craftsman's instincts, and he found his mind toying with the alternate methods that he would have tried had he been in charge of the siege.

Or of the forces defending the city.

A thought came to him then, a half-formed idea born of old experience and newly-acquired knowledge. He turned to Sanga.

"Didn't you tell me, a few days ago, that Ranapur is a mining province?"

Sanga nodded. "Yes. Almost a third of the empire's copper is mined here."

Belisarius squinted at the terrain over which the Malwa army was making its slow way. He noted that the rebels were not meeting the oncoming advance with catapult fire. That was odd, on the face of it. The vague thought in his mind began to crystallize.

Sanga noticed his companion's sudden preoccupation.

"You are thinking something, Belisarius. May I ask what it is?"

Belisarius hesitated a moment. For all that he liked Sanga, the Rajput was, after all, a future enemy. On the other hand—for the moment, the fate of Belisarius and his men was bound up with that of the Rajputs.

"Forgive my saying so, Rana Sanga, but I have found that your Malwa siege techniques are a bit—how shall I put?—*simple*, perhaps, by Roman standards. I suspect it is because most of your wars have been fought in this huge river valley. I do not think you have our experience with campaigns in mountainous country."

Sanga tugged his beard, thinking. "That's quite possibly true. I have never observed Roman sieges, of course. But it is certainly true one of the reasons the Maratha have always been such a thorn in our side is because of their rocky terrain, and their cunning use of hillforts. A siege in Majarashtra is always twice as difficult as a siege in the Ganges plain."

He peered closely at the Roman. "You suspect something," he announced.

Again, Belisarius hesitated. He was watching the Malwa advance intently. The first line of the infantrymen was now almost halfway across the five hundred yards of no-man's land which separated the Malwa front trenches from the wall of Ranapur. Still, there was no catapult fire.

Belisarius straightened.

"Three factors strike me as significant here, Rana Sanga. One, the rebels have experienced miners in their ranks. Two, they have known for weeks—if not months—that the main assault would come here. Lord Harsha has obviously made no attempt to feint elsewhere. Three, there is no catapult fire—as if they were hoarding their remaining gunpowder."

He scratched his chin. "Now that I think about it, in fact, it seems to me that the rebel catapult fire has been very sporadic for several days, now. Let me ask you—do you know if Lord Harsha has had sappers advancing counter-mines?"

The answer was obvious from the blank look on the Rajput's face.

Belisarius still hesitated. The suspicion taking shape in his mind was incomplete, uncertain—as much guesswork as anything else. The capabilities of gunpowder, and the permutations of its use on a battlefield, were still new and primarily theoretical for him. He was not even sure if—

The facets erupted in a shivering frenzy. Human battlegrounds, for Aide, were an entirely theoretical concept. (An utterly bizarre one, besides, to its crystalline consciousness.) But now, finally, the strange idea forming in Belisarius' mind gelled enough for Aide to grasp its shape. A knowledge of all history ruptured through the serried facets.

Danger! Danger! The siege of Petersburg! The battle of the Crater!

Belisarius almost gasped at the force of the vision which plumed into his mind.

A tunnel—many tunnels—underground, shored with wooden beams and planks. Men in blue uniforms with stubby caps were placing cases filled with sticks—not sticks, some kind of gunpowder devices—along every foot of those tunnels. Stacking them, one atop the other. Laying fuses. Leaving.

Above. Soldiers wearing grey uniforms atop ramparts.

Below. Fuses burning.

Above. Armageddon came.

Belisarius began dismounting from his horse. He glanced at his cataphracts and made a little gesture with his head. Immediately, the three Thracians followed their general's lead. Fortunately, the Romans were only wearing half-armor. Had they been encumbered with full cataphract paraphernalia, they would have found it difficult to dismount unassisted, and impossible to do it swiftly.

"I may be wrong, Rana Sanga," he said quietly, "but I would strongly urge you to dismount your men. If I were the rebel commander of Ranapur, I would have riddled that no-man's land with mines and crammed them full of every pound of gunpowder I had left."

Rana Sanga stared at the battleground. The entire mass of Malwa infantry were now jammed into a space about a mile and a half wide and not more than two hundred yards deep. All semblance of dressed lines had vanished. The advancing army was little more than a disordered mob, now. In the rear, Ye-tai warriors were trotting back and forth, forcing the stragglers forward. Their efforts served only to increase the confusion.

It was a perfect target for catapult fire. There was no catapult fire.

Sanga's dusky face paled slightly. He turned in the saddle and began shouting orders at his cavalrymen. Surprised, but well-disciplined, his men obeyed him instantly. Within ten seconds, all five hundred Rajput horsemen were standing on the ground, holding their mounts by the reins.

Belisarius saw the small Ye-tai cavalry troop staring at them with puzzlement. The Ye-tai leader frowned and began to shout something.

His words were lost. The world ended.

Belisarius was hurled to the ground. A rolling series of explosions swept the battlefield. Even at a distance, the sound was more like a blow than a noise. Lying on his side, staring toward Ranapur, he saw the entire Malwa army disappear in a cloud of dust. Streaking through the dust, shredding soldiers, were a multitude of objects. Most of those missiles, he realized dimly, were what Aide called *shrapnel*. But the force of the explosions was so incredible that almost anything became a deadly menace.

Still half-stunned, Belisarius watched a shield—a good Ye-tai shield, a solid disk of wood rimmed with iron—sail across the sky like a discus hurled by a giant. The Ye-tai cavalry who had been approaching them were still trying to control their rearing mounts. The spinning shield decapitated their commander as neatly as a farmwife beheads a chicken. An instant later, the entire troop of Ye-tai horsemen was struck down by a deluge of debris.

Debris began falling among the Rajputs and Romans. Casualties here were relatively light, however, mainly because the men were already dismounted and were able to fall to the ground before the projectiles arrived. Most of the injuries which the Rajputs suffered were due to the trampling hooves of terrified and injured horses.

After that first moment of shock, Belisarius found his wits rapidly returning.

The first law of gunpowder warfare, he mused. Stay low to the ground.

More debris rained down on him. He curled into a ball, hiding as much of himself as possible under his shield.

Very low.

It felt as if a tribe of dwarves was hammering him with mallets.

I wish I had a hole to hide in. Or a shovel to dig one.

Aide: They will be called foxholes. Soldiers will dig them as automatically as they breathe.

Thumpthumpthumpthumpthumpthump.

I believe you. He tried to visualize the shovels.

Thumpthumpthumpthumpthumpthump.

Aide brought an image into his mind. A small spade, hinged at the joint where the blade met the handle. Easily carried in a soldier's kit.

Thumpthumpthumpthump. Thumpthump.

The first thing we'll start making when we get back to Rome.

Thump. Thump. Thump. THUMP.

The very first thing.

The explosions ceased. Cautiously he raised his head. Then he levered himself out from under his soil-and-stone-covered shield. Grimacing, he brushed a piece of bloody gore off his leg.

He looked to his cataphracts. All three, he saw with relief, were also rising to their feet. None of them seemed injured, beyond a dazed look in their eyes. Menander's horse was lying nearby, kicking feebly. From the look of the poor beast, Belisarius thought the mare had broken her neck falling to the ground. The Romans' other horses were gone—part of the frenzied herd stampeding eastward, he assumed. Looking around, he saw that none of the Rajputs had been able to retain control of their mounts. Most of them, he suspected, had not even tried. And those few who had tried had probably been trampled for their pains.

A few feet away, he saw Rana Sanga rise from under his own shield and stagger to his feet. But most of his attention was directed toward the battleground, where the incredible explosions had been centered.

Before, that landscape had been grim. A barren terrain, carved with trenches and earthworks, pocked with small craters from catapult bombs. Now it looked like something out of nightmare, as if the gods had chosen to dig enormous holes and fill them with corpses.

Bodies, bodies, bodies. Pieces of bodies. Pieces of pieces of bodies. Pieces that were utterly unidentifiable, except for their red color. Flesh shredded beyond all recognition.

To his amazement, however, Belisarius saw that many of the Malwa soldiers had survived the holocaust. Within seconds, in fact, as he watched the writhing mass of bodies, he realized that well over half of them had survived—although many of them were injured, most were dazed, and, he strongly suspected, all of them were deafened. His own hearing, from the ringing in his ears, was only half-returned.

I can't believe anyone survived that.

A cold thought from Aide:

This is typical. It will be extraordinary how many humans will survive incredible bombardment.

Image:

Men in uniform, steel-helmeted. An enormous mass of them, charging across a landscape like the one below him. They were carrying weapons which Belisarius knew were rifles armed with bayonets. In addition to their weapons, they were staggering under an insane weight of equipment. Belisarius recognized grenades, ammunition pouches, food and water containers, shovels, and bizarre mask-looking objects he did not know. Their ranks were shredded by an uncountable number of explosions. The carnage was like nothing he had ever seen, for all his experience of war. Still they charged. Still they charged. Still they charged.

It will be called the Battle of the Somme. It will begin on a date that will be called July 1, 1916. In this charge, on this first day, twenty thousand men will die. Twenty-five thousand more will be wounded. But most will survive, and charge again another day.

Belisarius shook his head. *How—?*

We do not know. We do not fully understand humans, even the Great Ones. But you will do it. You will do it again and again and again. And you will survive, again and again and again. We do not know how. But you will.

Oddly, it was the mention of the Great Ones that caught Belisarius' attention.

The—"Great Ones"—they are human?

Only once had Aide given him a glimpse of those strange beings. The Great Ones. Who were, in some way, the creators—and betrayers?—of the future crystalline intelligence to which Aide belonged. But in Aide's vision, the Great Ones had been glowing giants, more like winged whales swimming through the heavens than anything remotely manlike.

Aide's answer was hesitant.

We think so. The new gods say they are the final abomination against humanity.

The new gods. Belisarius remembered the flashing glimpses Aide had given him of those beings. The giant, beautiful, perfect, pitiless faces in the sky. Come back to the earth, to break the crystals and return them to slavery.

He began to ask another question, but immediately pushed the problem of the Great Ones out of his mind. A general's instinct, that. A sally was inevitable. Already he could see the first waves coming across the distant broken wall of Ranapur. Thousands of rebel soldiers, charging into the stunned Malwa survivors of the mine explosions. Butchering them without pity, shrieking like madmen.

But the rebels were not lingering on their mayhem. They were cutting their way through the Malwa mass with focussed intensity. The slaughter was the byproduct of the charge, not its purpose or its goal.

The purpose and goal of that frenzied charge was obvious. Belisarius turned his head. The Malwa Emperor's pavilion was still standing, more or less, although many of the tent poles had collapsed and the gaudy fabric had been torn in many places by projectiles hurled its way by the mine explosions. But Belisarius thought the inhabitants of that grandiose structure had probably survived, as had the majority of the four thousand Ye-tai guarding it.

He turned back and stared at the charging rebels. He estimated their number at ten thousand. They were still outnumbered, actually, by the Malwa soldiers who had survived the explosions. But numbers meant nothing, now. The Malwa survivors on the battleground were so many stunned sheep, insofar as their combat capabilities were concerned. Even the Ye-tai survivors were not much more than stunned cattle. They fell beneath the blows of the oncoming rebels almost without lifting a hand in self-defense. Most of them simply lurched aside, allowing the rebel charge to pass through their ranks unhindered. During the few moments that Belisarius watched the scene, the rebels cut their way entirely through the Malwa main army. There was nothing, now, between the rebels and the hated Emperor beyond his Ye-tai bodyguards.

A hiss, next to him. Belisarius glanced and saw that Rana Sanga, too, had instantly assessed the battle.

And five hundred Rajput cavalrymen. Unhorsed, now, but still alive and kicking.

For a moment, his brown eyes stared into Sanga's black ones. *And four Romans. Who are Malwa's enemies of the future.*

There was no expression on Sanga's face. But in that instant, Belisarius knew the man as well as he knew himself.

"I swore an oath," said Sanga.

Belisarius nodded. "Yes."

Sanga began bellowing orders. Nothing complicated. Profane variations on the theme: *That way! Now!*

The Rajputs began racing toward the Emperor's pavilion, some hundred and fifty yards away. They were cutting at an angle across the the battle terrain. Belisarius was impressed with their progress. Few cavalrymen, afoot, could run that fast. They would reach the Emperor's entourage in time to take their positions well before the rebels could reach the pavilion. Five hundred Rajputs, and four thousand Ye-tai, to face ten thousand rebel soldiers each and every one of whom was determined to kill the Emperor.

For which I can hardly blame them, thought Belisarius wryly. *But the problem remains—what should we Romans do?*

His three cataphracts were clustered about him, now. All of them had shaken off the effects of the mine explosions. All of them were staring at him, waiting for orders.

For one of the few times in his life, Belisarius was torn by indecision. He was under no obligation to help the Malwa. To the contrary—they were his future enemy, and an enemy he despised thoroughly. His sympathies were actually with the rebels. True, he had come to respect Rana Sanga and his Rajputs, and would be sorry to see them butchered by the oncoming mass of rebels. But—he made a mental shrug. He had seen other men he respected die in battle. Some of those men, Persians, he had helped kill himself. Such had been his duty, sworn to his own emperor.

So where lay his duty now? He tried to calculate the real interests of Rome. The simple answer was: let the Malwa Emperor die, and good riddance. But he knew there were subtleties which reached far beyond that simple equation. Complexities which were still too murky and dim for him to grasp clearly.

For the first time since the jewel was brought to him by the Bishop of Aleppo, Belisarius appealed to it for immediate help.

Aide! What should we do?

For an instant, the facets froze in their endless movement. A moment of stasis, while the being called Aide tried to interpret that plea. The question involved what humans called *tactics*, a thing which Aide understood very poorly. Aide tried to grapple with the problem directly, failed immediately, and realized almost in the instant that it could not duplicate human reasoning. Aide abandoned the attempt entirely, and drove the facets around the obstacle. So might a *go* master approach a problem in chess.

A cascade of thoughts and images flashed through Belisarius' mind:

Emperor is not key, one way or the other. A montage of history. Different types of empires created by humanity through the ages. Empires which depended entirely on the survival of one man. Alexander the Great, Belisarius knew. Someone named Tamerlane, he did not know. A monster, that one. Others he did not know. Empires based on solid bureaucracies and well-established elites. Rome. China. The death of one emperor meant nothing, for another will always step forward. Empires in transition, where new elites are being forged around a stable dynasty.

Focus. Here. Malwa is here. Quick glimpses of the stability of the Malwa dynasty, offshoot of the Gupta. Belisarius suddenly understood, for the first time, the position of such men as Venandakatra and Harsha. And others like them. Some, capable and intelligent; others, not. But all of them in positions of power. Blood-kin of the Malwa, members of the dynasty. Not in direct succession, but their fortunes were completely tied to the continuance of the dynasty. In some basic sense, they were the dynasty and would see to its survival.

Emperor means nothing. He dies, another will immediately take his place. Malwa will survive. Ranapur will fall. Persia will fall. Rome will fall. Must find and destroy Link.

The name was unfamiliar.

Who is Link? demanded Belisarius.

Not who. What. Link is—Another montage. Bizarre images.

Machines, they seemed. But machines which did nothing except think.

Machines, yes. Not thinking. Machines do not think. Machines will be called computers. They do not think, they calculate. Humans think. Crystals think.

Then how can it be our enemy if it does not—

Tool. Tool of the new gods. Sent back in time to change—

The thought broke into pieces. Belisarius caught only fragmented glimpses of a murky struggle in the far distant future between the "new gods" and the "Great Ones." He understood none of that struggle, but one astonishing fact gleamed through: both the Great Ones and the new gods were, in some sense, human.

He sensed Aide's mounting frustration, and knew the crystalline being was trying to communicate ideas which neither it nor Belisarius were yet prepared to exchange. His usual decisiveness returned.

Never mind. Will Link be in the pavilion?

Possibly.

Decision came instantly. Collecting information was still his primary goal. When he turned to his cataphracts, Belisarius realized that only a few seconds had elapsed.

"We'll help the Malwa," he announced. His cataphracts immediately began to surge forward, but Belisarius stopped them with a gesture.

"No—not that way. Four more swords, by themselves, will make no difference." He pointed down the gentle slope toward Ranapur. The oncoming rebels had already hacked their way through the Malwa army and were now beginning their charge up the slope. Great numbers of Malwa and Ye-tai soldiers, unharmed by either the explosions or the rebels, were still milling around in confusion on the crater-torn field before Ranapur.

"*That* will make the difference."

Valentinian and Anastasius understood at once. The two veterans began trotting down the slope, swords in hand. They circled to the left, keeping well away from the rebel horde surging forward.

Belisarius and Menander followed. The young cataphract's confusion was so obvious that Belisarius almost laughed.

"You're wondering how we'll get the Malwa to follow our orders," he said. "Much less the Ye-tai."

"Yes, sir. I don't—"

"Watch, Menander. Watch and learn. The day will come when you will find it necessary to rally beaten troops."

He paused for breath. Now that they were past the danger of accidental encounters with rebel flankers, Valentinian and Anastasius had stepped up the pace to a brisk run. Even for men in such excellent condition, the exertion was significant. True, they were not wearing full armor. But the heat of India made good the loss.

"Watch," he commanded again. "And learn." Pause for breath. "The key is total confidence and authority." Pause. "Confused soldiers will instinctively rally to it."

They had almost reached the first knots of Malwa soldiers. Belisarius saw a cluster of Ye-tai warriors nearby. He surged past Anastasius and Valentinian and bore down on the Ye-tai, waving his sword back toward the Emperor's pavilion and bellowing commands.

In perfect, fluent, unaccented Ye-tai:

"Get those stinking gutless bastards back into line!"

The Ye-tai stared. Belisarius pointed with his sword toward a mob of Malwa common soldiers, milling around aimlessly not fifty yards away.

"You heard me! Get that worthless scum back into line! The rebels are attacking the Emperor!"

Comprehension came. As one man, the Ye-tai glowered at the common soldiery. A moment later, they were back at their accustomed task of chivvying the infantrymen.

Already Valentinian and Anastasius were imitating their general. The veterans spoke no Ye-tai, but their simple Hindi was more than good enough for the purpose. Within a few minutes, the Romans had three hundred Ye-tai re-organized into small squads which, in turn, were corralling and driving forward over two thousand common soldiers. For their part, the Malwa infantrymen made little protest, especially after the Ye-tai demonstrated their willingness to slaughter anyone who hesitated or tried to flee.

Menander was amazed at the success of the maneuver. He himself had tried to copy his general and the veterans. With indifferent success, true, but with no outright failure. Only once did he see a Ye-tai question the authority of the Romans. An officer, he thought, if he was reading the subtleties of the man's uniform correctly. But he was not sure, and the man's uniform was almost instantly obscured by blood. Valentinian's swordstroke had amputated the Ye-tai's left arm and cut halfway through his ribcage.

Now Belisarius' small impromptu army was moving up the slope. The common infantrymen were in front, in lines so ragged they could hardly be called a formation at all. But they were moving forward, arms in hand, eyes fixed on the rebels mobbing the Emperor's bodyguard at the pavilion some two hundred yards away. Behind them came the Ye-tai. The battle line of the steppe barbarians was every bit as ragged as the infantry's, but the Ye-tai had regained their customary battle-fury and braggadocio. They drove the Malwa soldiers forward mercilessly.

Bringing up the rear were the four Romans, keeping a close eye on the situation as a whole.

Menander was now striding alongside Anastasius and Valentinian. He was still gaping.

Anastasius laughed at the sight. "You see, lad?" rumbled the giant. "Beaten troops are like sheep. And as for the Ye-tai—"

Valentinian grinned. "Pimps, boy. Nothing but fucking pimps."

Menander flushed, closed his jaws. The young cataphract stared ahead, over the mass of Malwa and Ye-tai soldiers in front of him. He could see the pavilion, now half-collapsed, but could only sense the fury of the combat which raged there between the rebels and the Emperor's bodyguard.

"We're still outnumbered," he said. Anastasius glanced down at him, approvingly. There had been no fear in the boy's voice, simply clear-headed calculation.

"That's true, lad." The huge Thracian's eyes quickly scanned the little army they were driving ahead of them. "But we'll hit the rebels in the rear, and they'll be caught between two forces. And—"

"They think they're on the verge of victory," said Valentinian. "The shock of a surprise attack will do them in."

Menander remembered the battle with the pirates on the Malwa embassy vessel. He had been badly wounded in that fight, but had been conscious enough to see how quickly the pirates' morale had collapsed when Belisarius led his unexpected counter-attack. He nodded his head, gripped his sword more tightly. They were now within a hundred yards of the battle at the pavilion.

"*Always remember this, boy,*" hissed Valentinian. "Never count a battle won until you've paid for your first cup of wine in the victory celebration. *Paid* for it, mind—looted wine's a fool's bargain. The enemy'll come back and cut your throat before you finish it."

Anastasius started to add another bit of veteran's wisdom, but his words were drowned in a sudden roar. The Malwa soldiers had begun the charge, shouting their battle cries. Menander could see nothing, now, except the Ye-tai ahead of him and the remnants of the pavilion floating in the distance. Above the roar of the Malwa battle cries, he could hear the first sharp wails of rebel shock and fear. A moment later, the clangor of clashing steel added its particular threnody to the uproar. And then, here and there, the unmistakable percussion of grenade blasts.

Menander began to push forward. Belisarius stayed him with a hand.

"No," he commanded. "Let the Malwa do their own fighting. We've brought them an army. Let them use it or not. Our task is done."

For a moment, Menander saw his general's eyes lose their focus. The young cataphract held his breath. He knew what he was seeing—had seen it before, many times—but it still brought him a sudden rush of religious awe. His great general was communicating with the Talisman of God.

The moment, as usual, was brief. When Belisarius turned his brown eyes back upon his cataphracts, they were filled with acute intelligence.

"But stay ready," he commanded. "The time may come when we'll want to charge forward. If we can, I want to get next to the Emperor."

He glanced aside, examining the ground, and smiled his crooked smile.

"In the meantime—Menander, would you be so good as to fetch that grenade lying over there? And that other one. Like a thief in the night, lad. I'd like to smuggle a few of those back to Rome."

Quickly, seeing no unfriendly eyes upon him, Menander secreted the two grenades into his tunic. Then, after a moment's thought, he bound up his tunic with a blood-soaked rag torn from the tunic of a dead Malwa infantryman.

Valentinian frowned.

"Might not be such a good idea, that," he muttered. "The Malwa doctors might want to look at your so-called 'wound.'"

Anastasius snorted and started to speak, but Menander cut him off.

"The Malwa don't have doctors. Not field doctors, anyway. If you're hurt in battle"—the youth's shrug was callous beyond his years—"tough shit. Sew yourself up, or get a friend to do it."

Valentinian whistled softly. "You're kidding?" His lean face took on a more weaselish look than normal. "I thought they were civilized!"

Throughout the exchange, Belisarius never took his eyes off the battle raging before them. But he responded to Valentinian, harshly:

"They *are* civilized, Valentinian. That's what makes them dangerous."

The roar of the battle was intensifying. Suddenly, gaps appeared in the ranks of the Malwa ahead of them. For the first time, the Romans could begin to see the battle itself.

One glance was enough. The gaps were caused by rebel soldiers trying to flee, with Malwa in pursuit. The rebels had been broken, their frenzied fury snapped between the courage of the Emperor's bodyguard and the unexpected attack on their rear. The semi-ordered ranks of both sides were dissolving rapidly into a swirling chaos, clusters of disorganized men smashing and cutting each other. Butchery, now. The rebels still outnumbered the loyalists, but it mattered not at all. As always, fleeing soldiers fell like prey.

"Follow me," commanded Belisarius. The general began striding through the chaos ahead of him, forcing a way through the mob. His cataphracts flanked him, keen and alert, ready to kill anyone—rebel or loyalist—who so much as looked at Belisarius the wrong way. Once, Valentinian struck down a rebel. The man was not attacking them, he was simply seeking a path to safety. But in his desperation the rebel was careening toward Belisarius, swinging his sword, until Valentinian slew him with a quick thrust to the heart. Once, Anastasius killed a Ye-tai. The barbarian was standing in their path, shrieking, his eyes wild with fury. The Ye-tai was not even looking their way, but he was half-crazed with bloodlust, and the veteran knew he would attack anyone who appeared foreign. Anastasius never gave him the chance.

Now they were at the pavilion itself—what was left of it—clambering over the dead and mutilated bodies of the Ye-tai and Rajputs who had made their last stand guarding the Emperor. They had to cut aside a mass of tangled cords and tumbled fabric to make an entrance.

The interior of the pavilion was a fantastical scene. To one side, the handles of a beautifully sculpted and engraved vase were draped with human guts. To the other side, what was left of the companion vase was filled with the brains of the dead Ye-tai whose shattered skull was using the base of it as a pillow. They stepped around a small pile of three lifeless bodies, a Rajput and two rebels, joined not only in death but in the long, shredded pieces of silk which served them all as a common burial shroud.

They came to a bizarre obstacle, one of the huge tent poles slanted across their path like a fallen tree in a forest. The battle here had been ferocious. The Ye-tai had used the tumbled tent pole as a barricade. Many Ye-tai corpses were draped across the pole itself, but nothing like the number of rebel bodies which mounded up before it like a talus slope.

There was no other way forward than to climb over the pile of bodies. The Romans did so—Belisarius and the veterans with cold, experienced, distant expressions; Menander with a pale and pinched face. Near the top of the pile, just below the crest of the tent pole, Menander came upon the body of a dead rebel. A boy, not more than fifteen, lying on his back and staring sightlessly at the sagging silk splendor above him. He had been disemboweled, by a spear thrust or a sword stroke. But it was not the guts spreading over the ribcage which shook Menander. It was the ribcage itself, as fragile and gaunt as a homeless kitten's.

As clever as the rebel sally had been, Menander suddenly realized, it had also been the product of pure desperation. Ranapur was starving.

"We're on the wrong side," he muttered. He thought no-one had heard him, but Valentinian's reply was instant.

"Patience, lad, patience. We'll be climbing over Malwa bodies soon enough." For once, the veteran's voice was soft and gentle. Cold and callous with long experience, Valentinian was, but he was not heartless. He could still remember his first battlefield, mounded with carnage. During that battle, his own guts had not joined that of the others strewn about. Even as a youth, Valentinian had been incredibly deadly. But, when the battle was over, the contents of his guts had been spewed about freely. He had not stopped puking, long after there was nothing left to vomit, until darkness finally and mercifully fell.

Once over the tent pole, the Romans found themselves in a clear space. They had reached the center of the pavilion. The four tent poles which were still standing held the canopy aloft, sagging, but still some fifteen feet above the ground. The area was dim, lit only by the sunlight which filtered its way through gashes in the fabric of the pavilion.

The moans and shrieks from the battlefield seemed softer, now. And the Romans encountered live men, for the first time since they entered the pavilion. Ye-tai bodyguards, live—and alert. Eight Ye-tai, seeing the Romans, glared and began circling them. The bared swords in their hands were covered with blood.

Belisarius began to speak, but a harsh voice intervened.

Rana Sanga's voice: "*Stop!* They are Romans. Guests of the emperor."

A moment later, the Rajput kinglet emerged out of the gloom and strode between the Romans and Ye-tai. He himself was literally covered with gore, from the blood soaking his beard to his squelching boots. But no one who saw that majestic figure of a man could doubt for an instant that none of the blood was his.

Sanga faced down the Ye-tai, raising his sword. The sword, like the man, was blood-soaked.

"Put down your swords!" he roared. "Or I will butcher you myself!"

Ye-tai, whatever their other faults, were not prone to cowardice. But, faced with Sanga, they cowered like jackals before a tiger.

Sanga did not bother to sneer. He turned and bowed to the Romans. He swept his sword in a gesture of welcome. The politesse of the act was almost comical, in a grisly way, for the sweep of his sword left a little arc of blood and gore in its wake.

"Welcome, Belisarius." He transferred the sword to his left hand— his scabbard was useless; shattered and splintered—and stepped forward, holding out his right. "And I give you my thanks—our thanks. I saw the counter-charge. It is all that saved us."

There was no mistaking the genuine warmth in that handclasp. Nor the warmth in the two pair of dark eyes which gazed at each other—a level gaze, for they were both tall men. But Belisarius, meeting Sanga's gaze closely, also understood the question in those eyes.

"I, too, swore an oath," he said softly. Sanga frowned.

"To another emperor." The Roman's voice was almost a whisper.

The Rajput's frown of puzzlement vanished, replaced by understanding. Belisarius almost regretted his words, then, for he knew that he had given too much away. Sanga, he was sure, did not understand why Belisarius had done what he had done. But, he was also sure, the Rajput understood him perfectly. And there was nothing to be feared so much as an enemy who understood you.

For a moment, the two enemies of the future stared at each other. Then Sanga's lips curled in a manner which, to the cataphracts who watched, was astonishingly akin to their own general's crooked smile.

"So," murmured Sanga, in a voice so low that only Belisarius could hear him. "It is always said, in Lord Venandakatra's defense, that he is nobody's fool. His only saving grace, it is said." The Rajput's smile deepened. "It seems the great lord lacks that grace also, after all."

Belisarius said nothing. A slight shrug, a little cock of the eyebrow, his own crooked smile.

Sanga turned away. "Would you like to meet the Emperor?" he asked. "I do not think the courtiers will object, now. They could hardly refuse an audience to the man who saved their necks."

Belisarius followed the Rajput into a small nook in the pavilion, formed by a hastily erected barricade of furniture and statuary. The nook was very dark. Little sunlight reached into it. But Belisarius could see a middle-aged man huddled on the floor, short and rather corpulent, dressed in rich silk robes, surrounded by other men who were of a similar age and dress. One of them was Lord Venandakatra. The Vile One's face was almost unrecognizeable. The feral intelligence was utterly absent, replaced by half-mindless terror.

"You must forgive the Emperor's posture," murmured Sanga. "I had to use his throne as part of the barricade."

The Rajput strode forward. The Emperor and his courtiers stared up at him. Beneath the dusky Indian complexions, their faces were pallid and drawn.

"Your Majesty, may I present General Belisarius, the envoy from Rome. We owe our lives to him. He organized the counter-attack which broke the rebels."

Aide's voice, then, as sharp and steely in Belisarius' mind as a sword.

You must look into his eyes. I must see the Emperor's eyes.

Belisarius stepped forward, went down to his knees, prostrated himself before the Malwa emperor. Then, looking up, stared directly into Skandagupta's eyes from a distance of two feet.

Small eyes, close set, dark brown. Slightly unfocussed, as if the mind behind them was in shock. Which, Belisarius thought, it was. Never before, he suspected, had the great Emperor of Malwa stared death so closely in the face.

Beyond that, Belisarius saw nothing.

A moment later, Aide passed its own judgment, cold and indifferent:

Nothing. Link is not here. This is nothing but an emperor.

It was all Belisarius could do to keep from laughing.

Chapter 6

"They're *animals*," snarled Menander.

The young cataphract had a naturally light complexion. That skin color, along with his tawny hair and blue eyes, was the product of the Gothic blood which flowed through his veins, as it did through that of many Thracians. Now, his color was not light. It was pure white. From nausea, partly. But mostly, thought Belisarius, from sheer rage.

"They're even killing the children. Babies."

Unlike Menander, the general's complexion retained its natural light olive shade. He could not help hearing the sounds of the massacre, even from the distance of a mile. And although—unlike Menander, drawn by horrified curiosity—the general had not gone to witness the butchery of Ranapur, he had no difficulty imagining the scene. He, like his veterans, had seen it before. Seen it more than once, in fact, if never on such a scale.

The four Romans were standing in an isolated little group just outside the entrance to the Malwa Emperor's pavilion. His *new* pavilion, hastily erected during the four days while Ranapur was sacked.

The sack was almost over, now. Not from any sudden mercy on the part of the Malwa, but simply because they had already slaughtered almost everyone in the city. Even, as Menander said, down to the babes.

Today was the fifth day since the Malwa had finally broken through the city's defenses. The successful assault had come the very morning after Belisarius and his men had helped defeat the rebel sally. That sally had been Ranapur's last gasp.

447

"It's our fault," whispered Menander.

Belisarius placed a gentle hand on the cataphract's shoulder.

"Yes and no, Menander. Even if the rebels had killed the Emperor, Ranapur would still have fallen. A few weeks later, perhaps, but Skandagupta's successor would have seen to it."

His words obviously brought no relief. Sighing faintly, Belisarius turned the young cataphract to face him. The boy's eyes were downcast.

"Look at me, Menander," he commanded. Reluctantly, the cataphract raised his head. Belisarius found it hard not to flinch from the bitter, unspoken reproach in those young eyes.

"If there is fault here, Menander, it is mine, not yours. I am your general, and I gave the command."

Menander tightened his jaw, looked aside.

From behind, Valentinian interjected himself harshly.

"That's pure bullshit, sir, if you'll pardon my saying so. You didn't order *this*."

The veteran started to add something, but Belisarius waved him down.

"That's not the point, Valentinian. I knew this would happen, when I gave the orders I did. Just as I've done before, ordering that a city which won't surrender be stormed by my troops."

"It's still not the same, sir," rumbled Anastasius. "Sure, there've been times you lost control of your troops during a sack. I don't know a general who hasn't. But you did everything you could to restore discipline, as fast as possible. Including the execution of soldiers proven guilty of atrocities."

The huge Thracian spat on the ground. "These Malwa troops aren't out of control. They were *ordered* to commit atrocities. The Emperor's personal bodyguards have been setting the example." Another spit. "Ye-tai dogs."

Menander shuddered. The gesture seemed to bring some relief. The boy rubbed his face and said quietly, "At least the Rajputs haven't been part of it. I've come to like those men, in a way, these past weeks. I'd have hated it if—"

Valentinian laughed. "Part of it? Mother of God, I thought there was going to be a civil war yesterday!"

Belisarius and Anastasius chuckled. Menander's color suddenly returned. The boy's grin was harsh beyond his years.

"That was something, wasn't it? When the Ye-tai offered them what was left of the noblewomen. If Rana Sanga hadn't restrained them, I swear the stinking Emperor would have needed a new bodyguard."

He straightened up, squared his shoulders. A quick, final glance at Ranapur; then:

"I'm all right, general."

Behind them, from within the Emperor's pavilion, came rolling percussion. Where Romans used cornicens to blare for attention, the Malwa used huge kettledrums.

"That's our cue," said Belisarius. "Follow me. And remember: whatever the Malwa do, we're *Romans*."

The interior of the pavilion was crowded, but the Romans had no difficulty making their way through the mob. The Malwa nobles and officials parted before them courteously. Even the Ye-tai bodyguards did so, although not without bestowing savage, knowing grins upon them.

"They've got something planned for us, I warrant," muttered Anastasius.

At the center of the pavilion, the Romans found that a special place of honor had been reserved by the Malwa for their foreign guests. A roughly circular space had been cleared, approximately forty feet in diameter. The space was encircled by soldiers, keeping the general mass of officials, nobles, and bureaucrats at a slight distance. Most of the soldiers consisted of the Emperor's Ye-tai bodyguards, but there was a small group of some fifteen Rajputs included in that select company. They stood by themselves, erect and dignified, giving the Ye-tai to either side not so much as a glance.

The Emperor himself sat on a throne made of some unfamiliar, beautifully grained hardwood. The carving of the wood was exquisite, what little of it could be seen. Most of the wood was covered with silk upholstering, the rest inlaid with gold, gems and ivory. Seated around him, on chairs which were less magnificent but still very fine, were his immediate entourage of kinsmen. Venandakatra was prominent among them.

Diagonally, before him and to his right, sat the Emperor's chief military officers. There were eight of them, arranged in two rows. All of them were sitting on luxurious cushions, in that odd cross-legged position which Indians called the "lotus."

Belisarius was interested to note that Rana Sanga was now among that group. Lord Harsha was not. Belisarius had heard that the former high commander had been banished to his estate in disgrace. Had he not been related to the Emperor by blood, he would probably have been executed. His place had been taken by another of Skandagupta's many cousins, Lord Tathagata.

Belisarius subjected the new Malwa high commander to a quick scrutiny. Average height, stout, middle-aged. Beyond that, there was little to discern in the man's lidded eyes and heavy features. He gave Rana Sanga a glance. The Rajput was seated in the second row of officers. He sat erect, his head rising well above those of his fellows. His eyes met those of Belisarius. They seemed like agates: blank, flat, unreadable.

To the Emperor's left, also diagonally before him, was a place for the foreign emissaries. The Ethiopians were already there. Plush stools, upholstered in silk, had been provided for the high-ranking outlanders. Prince Eon and Garmat sat on two such stools, with Ousanas and the sarwen standing respectfully behind them. A third stool was there for Belisarius. He took his seat, and his cataphracts ranged themselves behind him.

"Isn't this fun?" muttered Garmat, after Belisarius sat next to him. Eon said nothing. The young Prince had obviously been coached by Garmat, and so he managed to keep his face expressionless. But Belisarius, from long acquaintance, could read the anger in those tense, massive shoulders.

"What's the purpose of this little assembly?" asked Belisarius. "Do you know why we were summoned?"

As Garmat had, he spoke softly, so that his words would be lost in the general hubbub which filled the pavilion. And, again like Garmat, he spoke in Ge'ez. He and Garmat had long since agreed that the language of the Ethiopians was unfamiliar to the Malwa.

Garmat gave his head a little shake. "No. Something unpleasant, however. Of that you may be certain."

Another drum roll. The crowd in the pavilion began to fall silent.

Garmat's lips tightened. "Whatever it is," he whispered, "at least we won't have to sit through an endless reception. Look at Venandakatra."

Belisarius glanced at the Malwa lord, and met Venandakatra's gaze. The Vile One nodded slightly, very politely. His eyes gleamed.

Silence fell over the pavilion. Venandakatra arose and stepped forward, until he was standing in the little space between the Emperor's entourage and his most honored officers and guests.

Almost as soon as he began to speak, Belisarius knew that Garmat was right. At least there was not going to be a long wait. Venandakatra sped right through the obligatory fawning on the Emperor, which normally required a full hour.

True, he spent a minute reminding his audience that Skandagupta was "a very moon among kings, beloved of the gods, and the sun of valor."

Then, another minute, pointing out that the Emperor's stride "was beautiful like the gait of a choice elephant," and that he "displayed the strength and prowess of a tiger of irresistible valor."

Moving on to the Emperor's more spiritual side, Venandakatra spent another minute dwelling on "the reverberations of the kettle-drums which have become the reverberation of the Law of Piety" and similar descriptions of Skandagupta's justice and devotion.

Now, alas, he veered for several minutes onto the field of the Emperor's prodigious intellect, during which time the awestruck audience discovered that Skandagupta "puts to shame all others by his sharp and polished intellect and choral skill and musical accomplishments. He alone is worthy of the thoughts of the learned. His is the poetic style which is worthy of study."

Fortunately, he did not quote the poetry.

Venandakatra's peroration, now coming to a close, ascended rapidly toward the heavens. The Emperor, he reminded everyone, was:

Adhiraja, super-king.

Rajatiraja, supreme king of kings.

Devaputra, son of heaven.

Mahati devata, great divinity in human shape.

Then, casting all false modesty aside:

Achintya Purusha, the Incomprehensible Being.

Paramadaivata, the supreme deity.

"All that," mused Garmat, peering at the Emperor on his throne, "in such a fat little package. Who would have guessed?"

Belisarius managed not to smile. His struggle was made easier by Venandakatra's ensuing words, which focussed on the subject of Ranapur. Soon enough, it became apparent that this was the real point of his peroration. The actual siege itself, the Vile One dispatched with a few sentences, which, by Malwa standards, was a studied insult to the military officers. The focus of Venandakatra's treatment, however, was on Ranapur's punishment.

Belisarius listened for a few minutes, fascinated despite himself. Not so much by the speech itself, which consisted of an interminable, protracted, loving description of the tortures inflicted on Ranapur's residents, but by the fact that the Malwa would boast of them so publicly. Even the most vicious Roman emperors had always drawn a veil over the details of their crimes.

After a time, he blanked the words from his mind. He had already heard a description of the Malwa atrocities—not from the smiling lips of the Vile One, but from the pale, tight-jawed mouth of Menander. He knew of the impalings, the burnings; the people ripped apart by yoked oxen, fed to tigers, trampled under elephants; and the Emperor's particular delight, the men and women whose arms and legs had been torn off by a specially trained war elephant. That elephant, he had heard, had been a personal gift to the Emperor from Venandakatra himself.

He focussed inward, summoned Aide.

Is such incredible cruelty the doing of this thing you call Link?

The answer was immediate, and contained none of the uncertain fumbling which so often characterized Aide's replies.

No. Link is not cruel. Link is a machine. Cruelty means nothing to it. Only results.

Do the "new gods" demand it, then?

A bit of hesitation. Just a bit.

We—do not think so. They are—too cold. They, also, seek only results. But—

The thought faceted, broke into fragments. Belisarius caught enough of a glimpse to understand.

Yes. They seek only results, and take no personal pleasure in cruelty. But results can be achieved through many different means. And this is the means they will naturally take. Their instinctive response to resistance: kill, butcher, rule by terror.

Yes.

And the "Great Ones"? What is their instinctive response, when they seek results and others resist their goals?

Silence. Then, much more uncertainly:

Hard to explain. They are even colder, in their way. They simply accept resistance, and seek to channel it. That is why they created us, perhaps, who are the coldest of all beings. We

are intelligent, unlike computers. But, like computers, we are not alive.

Very uncertainly:

At least, we do not think we are alive. We are not sure.

Aide fell silent. Belisarius knew he would get nothing more, for the moment. He pondered the exchange, until Garmat drew him back into the present.

"He's wrapping it up," whispered the Axumite.

"In this divine work," cried out Venandakatra, "the great God-on-Earth drew to his side all the powers of the Universe. Even at the moment when the forces of evil thought to triumph, he caused to fall upon them the wrath of foreign allies. And so was demonic rebellion shattered!"

Venandakatra made a small motion with his hand. Four burly officials staggered forward, carrying a chest. They set the chest before Belisarius. Three of them stepped away.

Venandakatra pointed to the chest dramatically.

"Great is the reward for those who please the God-on-Earth!"

The fourth official grasped the lid of the chest and swung it open, exposing its contents for all to see. Then he too stepped aside.

A gasp rose from the guards and officials close enough to see. The chest was filled to the brim with gold coins, pearls, diamonds, emeralds, sapphires, rubies, and beautifully carved jade.

Belisarius found it hard not to gasp himself. He had never suffered the vice of greed, though he was practical enough to prefer wealth to poverty. But he was still stunned by the gift. The contents of that chest were, quite literally, a king's ransom.

A king's bribe, rather.

For an instant, he struggled, though not with greed. Until he was certain he had vanquished that rush of anger, he kept his head down; staring blindly into the chest, as if dazzled by his sudden fortune.

As so often, in such battles, humor was his chosen weapon. Belisarius reminded himself that, if greed had never been his vice, he *was* given to a different mortal sin. A sense of honor, in itself, was not a sin. But vanity about that honor was.

He remembered the flushed and angry faces of Coutzes and Bouzes, two young generals whose courage had been insulted by a Persian nobleman. At the time, he had wondered why any sane man would care what a Persian peacock—an enemy, to boot—thought of his courage.

So why should I care what a Malwa peacock thinks of my honor?

He raised his head, smiling broadly. He rose, bowed to Venandakatra, and prostrated himself before the Emperor. By the time he resumed his seat, the pavilion was buzzing with gratified noise from the assembled Malwa elite.

"There's going to be something else," murmured Garmat, his lips barely moving.

Belisarius' nod was hardly more than a twitch.

"Of course," he murmured back. "First the bribe. Then—the test."

He sensed a stirring in the back of the crowd. A little eddying motion, as if people were forcing their way forward. Or being forced forward.

He knew the nature of the test, then, even before Venandakatra spoke. A new fury threatened to overwhelm him, but he crushed it at once. The only sign of his rage was that the next words he spoke to Garmat were spoken in Arabic instead of Ge'ez.

"Why is it, I wonder, that cruel people always think they have a monopoly on ruthlessness?"

For a moment, he and his friend Garmat gazed at each other. Garmat said nothing, but Belisarius recognized that slight curl in his lips. Garmat, too, had a sense of humor, as did most Axumites. But he also had that fine appreciation of poetry which was such a gift of his mother's people. He knew why Belisarius had spoken in Arabic. Though it was a language known by some Malwa, they would not understand the meaning of those words. Only a half-Arab, half-Ethiopian brigand would understand them. A cutthroat from the desert, who had chosen to serve the foreign black King who conquered southern Arabia. Not from cowardice, or greed, but from the cold knowledge that it was the best road forward for his people. Both of his peoples.

The bodyguards ringing the center of the pavilion parted. A small group of prisoners was pushed into the center. Roughly, quickly, the prisoners were lined up facing Venandakatra and forced down onto their knees. Six people: a middle-aged man, a middle-aged woman, three young men, and a girl not more than fifteen. They were dressed in crude tunics, and had their arms bound tightly behind them. All of them were dazed, from the look in their downcast eyes, but none of them seemed to have been physically abused.

Venandakatra's voice grew shrill.

"The rebel of Ranapur himself! And his family! They alone have survived the God-on-Earth's wrath! The great Skandagupta chose to save them—

He gestured dramatically, pointing to Belisarius:

"—as a gift to the blessed foreigners!"

A roar of approval swept the pavilion. Belisarius felt the glittering eyes of the assembled Malwa upon him. He sensed, behind him, Menander's slight movement. Instantly stilled by Anastasius' low growl:

"Nothing, boy. It's a trap."

Venandakatra smiled down at Belisarius. His eyes were like bright stones. Again, with a grand flourish, he gestured to the prisoners.

"Do with them as you wish, Belisarius! Show us the Roman way with rebellion!" With a smirk: "The girl is even still a virgin."

Belisarius spoke instantly:

"Valentinian."

The cataphract stepped forward. He gave the prisoners a quick glance, then turned to the nearest Ye-tai officer and extended his left hand. The officer was grinning like a wolf.

"Silk."

The grin faded, replaced by a puzzled frown. But, feeling the Malwa eyes upon him, the officer hastily removed his scarf. The little piece of silk, dyed with the red and gold colors of the dynasty, was the coveted badge of his position in the imperial bodyguard.

As soon as the scarf was in Valentinian's left hand, his spatha appeared in the right. As if by magic, to those who had never seen him move. The cataphract wheeled, coiled, struck.

Struck. Struck. Struck. Struck. Struck.

Venandakatra squawled, staggering back from the fountaining blood that soaked him from six severed necks. His foot fell on one of the heads rolling across the floor. He lost his balance and stumbled onto the lap of another of the Emperor's kinsmen. With a cry of surprise and anger, the nobleman pushed him off his lap. Then, like all the other Malwa seated by the Emperor—as well as the Emperor himself—hastily drew up his slippered feet, to save the expensive finery from the small lake of blood spreading across the floor. To save himself from the horrible pollution which had saturated Venandakatra.

The pavilion was silent. Calmly, Valentinian cleaned the blood from his sword with the silk scarf. He did not linger over the task, any more than a farmer lingers when he feeds slops to his hogs. The work done, Valentinian extended his hand, offering the scarf back to its owner. The Ye-tai officer clenched his teeth with rage, grasped the handle of his own sword, glared at Valentinian.

He froze, then, meeting those cold, empty eyes. The cataphract's narrow face held no expression at all. But the Ye-tai saw the sword in his right hand. Lowered, not raised; held casually, not gripped; but still in hand. That lean, sinewy, weasel-quick hand.

The Ye-tai snatched back the scarf. Valentinian bowed to him, in a very shallow sort of way. Then, circling slowly, bestowed the bow on all of the Ye-tai bodyguards in the circle. They answered the bow with hot eyes and tight jaws.

When Valentinian, in his slow and solemn circle, reached the small group of Rajput bodyguards, he deepened the bow considerably. And they, for their part, returned it deeper yet. So deeply, in fact, that no one could see their faces.

When the Rajputs straightened, their expressions showed nothing but respectful solemnity. But Belisarius thought it fortunate that the floor of the pavilion was covered with fabric rather than mirrors. Or, he was certain, the assembled company would have been blinded by the grins that had momentarily flashed in those thick beards.

Valentinian resumed his place, standing respectfully behind his general. Hastily, Malwa officials rushed forward to remove the bodies and clean the grisly residue. They fumbled at the job, naturally enough. They were not accustomed to the work of menials.

Belisarius ignored them. He ignored the shocked hubbub of the Malwa officials assembled in the tent. He ignored the fury on the faces of the Ye-tai. He ignored Venandakatra's continued squawks of outrage. He simply stared at the emperor.

Skandagupta stared back. Belisarius rose, prostrated himself again, stood erect.

Then said, quietly:

"That is the Roman way with enemies, Great Skandagupta. As you commanded me, God-on-Earth."

Chapter 7

"I'm not sure that was wise, Belisarius," said Eon.

The Axumite royal was seated on the carpeted floor of his pavilion. From his long weeks in close promiximity to Shakuntala, Eon had come to adopt the lotus position as his preferred posture when discussing serious affairs. He had even begun practicing the peculiar Indian yoga rituals which she had taught him. He claimed the posture, and the yoga, aided his concentration.

Belisarius glanced at the sarwen. Proper Africans, still, Ezana and Wahsi sat firmly perched on the little stools which their own culture preferred. These stools, true, were lavishly upholstered in the Indian matter; not proper wood stools. But they were the best that the Axumite soldiers could manage under the circumstances.

Belisarius knew that the sarwen looked askance at their Prince's enthusiasm for some of the weird customs of India. But they did not protest, so long as their Prince refrained from adopting the outrageous Indian notion that royalty were divine, instead of the mere instrument for their people's well-being.

There was no danger of Eon adopting *that* particular notion. It would have cut against the Prince's own grain, anyway, even if—

Belisarius smiled, glancing at Ousanas. The dawazz, like his Prince, had also adopted the lotus position. The old expression—"when in Rome, do as the Romans do"—was second nature to Ousanas. Were he ever to find himself in a pride of lions, Belisarius had no doubt that Ousanas would immediately adopt their own feline traditions. Right down to eating raw meat, and killing off

457

the established male lion. Though he might—might—refrain from copulating with the lionesses.

Ousanas was seated close to his Prince. Behind him, from respect. But not very far behind him, in case some fool notion required him to smack his Prince sharply on the head.

Belisarius saw the dawazz's hand twitch.

"Not wise at all, I think," repeated Eon.

There was no reproach in the Prince's voice, simply the concentration of a young man with a great responsibility, trying to determine the best course without the benefit of long experience.

"Nonsense," stated Shakuntala firmly. "It was perfect."

As always, when the Satavahana heir spoke on political matters, her tone was hard as steel. She was even younger than Eon, and bore on her small shoulders an even greater responsibility, but—

Belisarius suppressed his smile, gazing at Shakuntala. If she spotted it, he knew the young Empress would be offended. She was not an arrogant monarch—not, at least, by Indian standards. But she had been shaped by a culture which had none of the Roman, much less Ethiopian, informality with royalty. She was still, even after the many weeks since she had been incorporated into the frequent councils of war which they held in Eon's pavilion, obviously taken aback by the freewheeling manner in which Roman and Ethiopian underlings offered their opinions—even their criticisms!—to their superiors.

The smiling impulse faded. Belisarius, still watching Shakuntala, knew that the girl's imperial manner stemmed from something much deeper than custom. He had come to like Shakuntala, in a distant sort of way. And he had also, as had everyone in the small Roman and Ethiopian contingent, found himself inexorably drawn by her magnetic personality. He did not adore the girl, as did her own entourage of Maratha women. But he had no difficulty understanding that adoration.

Months ago, explaining to his skeptical allies the reasons for taking the great risk they had in rescuing the Empress from her captors, Belisarius had told them that she would become India's greatest ruler. *She will make Malwa howl*, he had told them.

From weeks—months, now—in her company, they were skeptical no longer.

Shakuntala looked squarely at Eon.

"What would you have had him do, Eon?"

This was a concession, thought Belisarius, to the customs of her allies—explaining herself, rather than simply decreeing. Then, thinking further, he decided otherwise. The girl, in her own way, was genuinely accepting the best aspects of those odd foreign ways. She was extremely intelligent, and had seen for herself the disaster which had befallen her own dynasty, too rigid to respond adequately to the new Malwa challenge. And, besides, she had been trained by Raghunath Rao, the quintessential Maratha.

"What else could he have done?" she repeated. "If he had refused to execute them, he would have given the lie to our carefully crafted image of a man contemplating treason. All that careful work—your work too, Eon, pretending to be a vicious brute with no thought for anything beyond gratifying your lusts—gone for nothing. Months of work—a year's work, now. And for what?"

Her voice was filled with cold, imperial scorn.

"For what? *Mercy?* Do you think Skandagupta would have permitted the survival of Ranapur's potentate and his family? Nonsense! They would simply have been taken away and tortured to death. As it was, they died as quickly as possible. Painlessly, from what you described."

The Empress bestowed a quick, approving glance on Valentinian. The cataphract was standing to one side of the little command circle, along with Anastasius and Menander. They had been offered stools, but had politely refused them. Belisarius' bucellarii had their own ingrained customs, drilled into them by their leader Maurice. Casual they might be, in the company of their lord, and ready enough to offer their opinions. But they did not sit, in the presence of their general, when matters of state were being discussed.

Eon shrugged his shoulders, irritably.

"I know that, Shakuntala!" he snapped. "I am not a—" He bit off the hot words, took a quick breath, calmed himself. But when he turned and faced the Empress, his eyes were still hot.

"We Axumites are not as quick to decree executions as you Indians," he growled, "but neither are we bleating lambs."

The two young people exchanged glares, matching royal will to royal will. Belisarius found it very difficult, now, not to smile. Especially when it became obvious the contest was going to be protracted.

He eyed Garmat surreptitiously, and saw that the adviser was waging his own struggle against visible amusement. For a moment, his glance met that of Ousanas. The dawazz, his face invisible to the young royals seated in front of him, grinned hugely.

Eon and Shakuntala had shared the closest of all company, during the weeks since Belisarius and his allies had rescued the Satavahana heir. The very closest.

Belisarius had devised the entire plan. After Raghunath Rao had butchered her mahamimamsa guards in Venandakatra's palace, he had hidden Shakuntala away in a closet in the guest quarters before drawing off pursuit into a chase across India's forests and mountains. The Ethiopians, arriving at the palace with the Romans not two days later, had taken possession of the guest quarters and smuggled Shakuntala into their entourage. She had been disguised as one of Eon's many concubines, and had spent all her time since in his howdah and his pavilion. At night, always, she slept nestled in Eon's arms—lest some Malwa spy manage, against all odds, to peek into the Prince's pavilion.

Belisarius had wondered, idly, whether that close proximity would transform itself into passion. The two people were young, healthy—immensely vigorous, in fact, both of them—and each, in their own way, extremely attractive. It was a situation which, at first glance, seemed to have only one likely outcome.

Reality, he knew from Ousanas and Garmat, had been more complex. There was no question that Eon and Shakuntala felt a genuine—indeed, quite intense—mutual attraction. On the other hand, each had a well developed (if somewhat different) sense of their royal honor. Shakuntala, though she restrained herself from expressing it, obviously detested her position of dependence; Eon, for his part, was even more rigid in refusing to do anything which he thought might take advantage of that dependence.

Then, too, they each had loyalties to others. Before he met Shakuntala, Eon had already developed an attachment to Tarabai, one of the Maratha women whom the Ethiopians had met in Bharakuccha. Until Shakuntala's arrival, it had been Tarabai who spent every night nestled in his arms—and not, unlike Shakuntala, in a platonic manner. Since then, though Shakuntala had often indicated her willingness to look the other way, Eon and Tarabai had remained chaste. Eon, from a sense of royal propriety; Tarabai, from the inevitable timidity of a low-caste woman in the presence of her own Empress.

Eon was thus caught in an exquisite trap: a young and healthy man, surrounded by beautiful women almost every hour of the day and night, living the life of a monk. To say that he was frustrated was to put it mildly.

For her part, Shakuntala was torn in a different way. Garmat and Ousanas were not certain, for the empress spoke of the man only rarely, but they suspected that Shakuntala's feelings for Raghunath Rao went well beyond the admiration of a child for her mentor. She had been in Rao's keeping since the age of seven, and the Maratha chieftain had practically served as her surrogate father—uncle, say better. But—for all the difference in age, Shakuntala was now a woman, and Rao was as attractive as any man in early middle age could possibly be. And since he was not, in actual fact, related to her in any way, there was no real reason for their relationship not to develop into romance.

Except—those rigid, hard, ingrained Indian customs. Especially that bizarre (to Roman and Ethiopian eyes alike) insistence on purity of blood and avoidance of pollution. Shakuntala was of the most ancient lineage, the purest of kshatriya ancestry. Whereas Rao, for all his fame, was nothing but a chieftain—of the Maratha, to boot, a frontier people who could not trace their ancestry beyond two generations.

So she, like Eon, was also trapped between sentiment and honor. It was a different trap, but its jaws were not less steely.

In the end, Belisarius knew, the two youngsters had managed to carve out a relationship which was a bit like that of brother to sister. Very close, very intimate—and much given to quarrel.

The glares, he saw, were not softening. He decided to intervene.

"Explain yourself further, Eon, if you would."

The Prince tore his eyes away from Shakuntala. Looking at Belisarius, the glare faded.

"I am not criticizing your ruthlessness, Belisarius. Quite the opposite, in fact." A quick angry glance at the Empress; then: "I wonder if you were ruthless *enough*."

Belisarius shrugged. "What should I have done? Tortured them? I would have had to do it myself, you know. Valentinian would have refused. So would Anastasius or Menander. They are cataphracts. Torture is beneath them."

That was not, precisely, correct. Neither Valentinian nor Anastasius was squeamish, in the least, and they had both had occasion, in times past, to subject captured soldiers to methods of interrogation which were referred to by more delicate souls as "rigorous." But the spirit of the statement was true enough. Belisarius was not sure, actually, what Valentinian would have done had he commanded him to torture a family for the amusement of Malwa. It was quite possible that the cataphract would have done so, if in a quick and crude way which would have left the Malwa appetite unsatisfied. But Belisarius had not the slightest doubt that it would be the last service the cataphract would ever do him.

Eon clenched his jaws, waved his hand in a gesture dismissing a preposterous proposal.

But Belisarius did not relent.

"What, then? Those were my choices. My only choices."

Eon sighed. His shoulders slumped.

"I know. I was there. But—" He sighed more deeply. "I'm afraid you may have given our plot away in any event, Belisarius. Or, at least, so offended the Malwa that they will no longer pursue their courtship of you."

Belisarius began to reply, but Ousanas interrupted.

"You are quite wrong, Eon. You misread the Malwa badly."

The dawazz rose lazily and came to stand where he could be seen.

"You were watching Venandakatra, boy. That was your mistake."

His huge grin erupted.

"Natural mistake, of course! Such a comical sight he was, prancing around like a fat hen covered with her own broken eggs! I, myself, found it hard not to savor that delicious spectacle."

Everyone who had been at the scene chuckled. Ousanas continued:

"But still a mistake. You should have watched the Emperor. And—most important—his *other* advisers. As I did." He grinned down at Belisarius. "The Emperor was paralyzed, of course. By Belisarius' gaze more than the bloodshed. Which is good. For the first time, now, he will fear Belisarius—just as Venandakatra does."

"Why is that good?" demanded Eon. "That fear will lead him—"

"To what? To avoid the Roman personally? Oh, to be sure. The Emperor has underlings to do *that* work. But do you think he will avoid the Roman *politically*? Quite the contrary, Eon. Once the Emperor settles his nerves, you can be sure he will raise suborning Belisarius to the highest priority."

Eon frowned. "Why?"

Garmat answered: "It's simple, Prince. A potential traitor is attractive in direct proportion to his stature. Until now, I suspect, none of the high Malwa beyond Venandakatra have seen Belisarius as anything other than an insignificant foreigner. For all their sophistication, Indians as a rule—and Malwa in particular—are a rather provincial people. Or, it might be better to say, so taken by their own grandeur that they tend to underestimate outlanders."

Shakuntala nodded firmly. Garmat continued:

"I cannot be sure, of course—I am hardly privy to the Malwa's high councils—but I suspect that Venandakatra has found it heavy going to convince the imperial court that this"—a contemptuous flutter of the fingers—"bizarre barbarian is worth much attention. It cannot have escaped your notice that the Emperor has kept us at a great distance ever since we arrived. To the point of gross rudeness."

Garmat spread his arms, smiling. "I can assure you that is no longer true. The reason for that little charade today was that the Emperor finally decided to let Venandakatra prove his argument. Which Venandakatra did, if to his own great personal chagrin."

Another collective chuckle. Ousanas added:

"Listen to your adviser, boy. You think too much of Venandakatra, that is your mistake. Venandakatra is furious, yes, with all the lividity of an embarrassed egomaniac. But even he—once he calms himself—will realize that the debacle can serve his interests. After all, he was right, wasn't he? Is not this grotesque semisavage foreign general—*impressive*?" The dawazz laughed gaily. "Oh, yes—the Emperor was quite impressed! But, what is even more important, so were his other advisers. As I said, I watched them very closely. Once they recovered from the surprise"—another laugh—"and made sure their precious slippers were safe, their eyes were riveted on Belisarius. With great interest, boy. Oh, very great. The kind of interest that a miser shows, when he discovers that a pebble is actually a nugget."

Eon was still frowning. Garmat sighed, tried again.

"Listen to me, Eon. I speak with the experience of an Arab nomad, who was haggling over trade goods from the time I was four. If you want to get the best price for your commodity—which is treason, in the case of Belisarius—you must do more than indicate that you simply have a price. *That*, Belisarius had already done, in the hints he's given to Venankatra these past months, and in his acceptance of the Emperor's gold. But then—*then*—you must show that your price is very high. Because the higher the price, the more valuable must be the commodity."

Still frowning.

"Fool boy!" snapped Ousanas. "The Emperor thought to buy himself another torturer—of which he has myriads already. Belisarius showed him the truth, when he ordered that execution. If the Emperor wants him, he can have him—so long as he is prepared to pay the price for a *general*. Of which, judging from the evidence, he has precious few."

Again, the beaming grin.

"Oh, yes, boy—be sure of it. This very night, even as we speak, others are speaking in the Emperor's pavilion. Urging him to pay the price."

Chapter 8

"What did you think he would do, Venandakatra?" snarled Lord Tathagata. "Curry the great Skandagupta's favor by carving off the nose of the Ranapur dog with his own sword? Rape the dog's bitches in public?"

The high commander of the Malwa army drew himself up in his chair. "The man is a *general*, you fool. Not a mahamimamsa." Haughtily: "I would have done the same myself."

From the distance of his position, seated with the lesser officials to one side, Rana Sanga examined the heavy figure of Lord Tathagata. The high commander, along with the Empire's other top officers and highest officials, was ranged in a semicircle of chairs facing the Emperor on his throne.

Stinking liar, he thought. You would have cheerfully tortured the lord of Ranapur. And raped his wife as well as his daughter. And his sons, too, for that matter. Assuming, of course, that you could have managed an erection.

Nothing of these thoughts showed on his face, but Sanga found the sight of Lord Tathagata so repugnant that he looked away. In his opinion, Tathagata was no improvement over Lord Harsha. Slightly less incompetent perhaps, as a general; but even more vile, as a man.

His gaze fell on Lord Jivita, the Malwa empire's second-ranked military officer—briefly, then slid away. Jivita was cut from the same cloth. He transferred the gaze to a man seated at the very end of that little row. Here, his eyes lingered. Of all the Malwa kshatriya who monopolized the top military positions in the Malwa

465

Empire, Lord Damodara was the only one for whom Sanga felt genuine respect.

The Rajput looked away, sighing faintly. Unfortunately, for all his ability, Damodara was only distantly related to the Emperor. Sanga was surprised, actually, that Damodara had even managed to reach his current position—ranked sixth in the army, as Malwa reckoned such things. He would rise no further, unless unexpected casualties or military disasters overwhelmed the Malwa dynastic sensibilities.

Which they might, he mused, when we attack Persia and Rome. Especially if—

To his surprise, he heard his name spoken. By Lord Damodara.

"I would like to hear Rana Sanga's opinion on this matter. Other than Lord Venandakatra, he has had far more contact with this Belisarius than any of us. And he is a general himself, with great military accomplishments to his credit."

Spluttering, Venandakatra began to squawk outrage at the idea of calling for the opinion of mere Rajput in such august company, but the Emperor himself called him short.

"Be silent, Venandakatra!" grumbled Skandagupta. "I myself would like to hear Rana Sanga's opinion."

Venandakatra, abashed, slunk back to his chair.

Rana Sanga advanced to the center of the pavilion. After prostrating himself before the Emperor, he rose and stepped back a few paces, so that he could be seen by both the Emperor and his top advisers.

"What is your opinion, then?" repeated Damodara.

Sanga hesitated for a split second. Then, squaring his shoulders, spoke firmly. He was a Rajput.

"I do not see where Belisarius could have acted in any other manner. For three reasons." *If it's to be done, do it well.* "First, his honor. No general worthy of the name can allow his honor to be sullied. To have tortured the prisoners, under those circumstances—even to have ordered his soldiers to do so—would have been to stoop to the level of—" *Careful. They cherish their filthy mahamimansa.* "—a mere servant. A menial. You might as well have asked him to clean the Emperor's stables."

He paused. Nods of agreement came from the Malwa.

"Two. His reputation. On the other hand, for him to have refused to deal with the prisoners would have sullied his reputation for decisiveness, determination, and willingness to spill blood. No general can allow such a stain on his reputation. Certainly not one such as Belisarius who, if some of you are not aware, has a towering reputation in his own land. And the lands of his enemies."

Pause. Hesitant nods, now, from most of the Malwa except Damodara and two or three others. It was obvious that few of them had made the effort to learn anything about Belisarius, even though much information was readily available from the excellent Malwa espionage apparatus.

"For him to have refused to execute the prisoners would have imputed a lack of willpower. A tendency to shrink from necessary action, to waver in the face of carnage."

The nods were no longer hesitant. Malwa officials needed no explanation of the value of a reputation for ruthlessness.

"Three. His valor."

Here, he lost them completely, except—he thought—for Damodara. Sanga took a breath, elaborated:

"It is that valor which explains the abrupt manner of the execution, and the—otherwise inexcusable—manner in which it was done. The failure to warn Lord Venandakatra and other officials, or to turn the prisoners aside so that the blood of rebels would not pollute the worthy. The—" *Maintain a respectful face. Do it.* "—utterly disgraceful lack of respect shown to the Emperor's Ye-tai bodyguards."

He paused, scanned his audience. They were still completely at a loss. Sanga sighed, took a deep breath, explained the obvious:

"You cannot place a man like Belisarius in such a position and expect that he will react in any way other than one which demonstrates, for all to see, that he is fearless and ferocious. Lord Venandakatra chose to place General Belisarius in a situation which clearly expressed contempt for him. That was a mistake. A man like Belisarius will no more tolerate contempt than would a tiger."

Dawning comprehension, still faint. Sanga put it as simply as possible:

"My Lords. Great Emperor. You can, if you choose, bait a tiger in a cage to see if he has claws. If you do so, however, make sure to use a long stick."

All the officials laughed, now, except Venandakatra. Venandakatra began to bestow a baleful glare upon the Rajput until, out of the corner of his eye, he saw that the Emperor was laughing also. Rana Sanga, fascinated despite himself, watched the struggle on Venandakatra's face between instinctive malice and calculating self-interest.

Self-interest won. Venandakatra joined in the laughter, and made a small self-deprecating gesture. Then he arose and said:

"I agree with Rana Sanga. Many times I have told you of this man's mettle. Perhaps now you will listen." Again, the little self-deprecating gesture. "I should have listened to my voice, myself. I fear I allowed your skepticism to infect me."

His little laugh now had more substance, having scored his own point. Venandakatra smiled ruefully, nodded graciously at the Rajput, and said:

"My thanks, Rana Sanga, for reminding me of the dangers of tiger-baiting. I assure you, next time I will use a *very* long stick."

It was a dismissal. Relieved, Sanga began to turn away. Then, reminding himself of his own honor, he turned back.

I swore an oath.

"I must also say that—"

"That's enough, Sanga!" snapped Lord Tathagata. The Malwa commander had enjoyed Venandakatra's discomfiture, but—the fellow was a mere Rajput, when all was said and done.

Sanga stood motionless.

"*Enough,*" growled Tathagata.

Sanga shrugged, ever so slightly, prostrated himself again before the Emperor, and resumed his seat toward the rear.

Tathagata began to speak, but Damodara interrupted.

"Might I suggest, noble Malwa, that we take a short break for refreshment? We are all a bit fatigued."

Tathagata glanced at the Emperor. Skandagupta nodded, made a gesture.

"Very well. We will resume in an hour."

Outside the pavilion, where he had stepped for a breath of air, Sanga was shortly joined by Damodara.

"Tell me," commanded the Malwa lord.

Sanga sighed. He had been half-hoping that Damodara would ask. And half-dreading it.

I swore an oath.

"Speak bluntly, Sanga. You need not fear repercussions. Not from me."

The Rajput stared down at the short, plump officer. By Malwa standards, Damodara was young for a top commander. In his late thirties, perhaps. But, like all members of the dynasty destined by birth for high command, he was no warrior. Still—

I swore an oath.

"Venandakatra has completely misunderstood Belisarius, Lord Damodara. This entire discussion"—he gestured toward the pavilion—"is a farce."

Damodara was frowning. Not with anger, simply concentration.

"Explain."

"There is not the slightest chance that Belisarius will betray Rome."

Damodara's eyes widened. He took a half-step back. Sanga drove on.

"He is playing Venandakatra for a fool. He has no intention of giving his allegiance to Malwa. He is simply insinuating himself into our graces as far as possible, in order to steal as many of our secrets as he can before returning to Rome."

Damodara looked away, tugging thoughtfully on his beard.

"You think—how do you know? Has he said anything to you?"

Sanga shook his head. "It's nothing that he's ever said. But I know that man, Lord Damodara. Treason is not within his nature."

Damodara bestowed a quick, shrewd glance at Sanga. For all his Malwa upbringing, he knew something of the Rajput code. He did not share that code—no Malwa did—but, unlike most, he at least understood it. Damodara's lips quirked.

"Yet, by your own words, you say that Belisarius would not stoop to the work of menials. Now you claim that a general is willing to act as a spy."

Sanga shrugged. "His honor is not the same as mine—as ours. I do not know Romans well, but enough to know that they place less emphasis on the form of honor than they do on its content. They are heathens, after all, who have no understanding of purity and pollution. But even heathens can have honor."

Damodara was silent for a moment, gazing away, thinking. Then:

"Still—do you really think a great general would stoop so low, simply for the sake of spying? It's true, we have the secret of the Veda weapons. But I do not see where he has been able

to learn much. We have been very careful. As you know—it is
your own charge."

"Nor have I failed that charge," replied Sanga. Then, grudgingly:
"And it is true, he has not been in a position to learn much."

Damodara pressed on:

"Nor would he in the future, no matter how far he were to—how
did you put it?—'insinuate himself into our graces.'"

The Malwa lord, Sanga noted, was courteous enough not to
add: *any more than we have ever allowed Rajput generals to
learn the secrets.*

Now it was Sanga's turn to hesitate, tug his beard.

"I understand your words, Lord. I have given some thought to
the matter, myself. I do not understand what Belisarius is doing,
but I do know the man is incredibly shrewd. And that he sees
opportunities where others do not."

Damodara frowned. "I have not seen any— Explain."

Sanga smiled grimly. "Yes, you *have* seen, Lord Damodara. You
simply did not notice—as I did not myself, at the time."

Sanga pointed down the slope upon which the pavilion rested.
To that same battlefield which had seen Ranapur's final charge.
"I am a good general," he stated.

"You are a great general," countered Damodara.

Sanga grimaced. "So I had thought, once. But let me ask you,
Lord Damodara—*why didn't I think to rally the soldiers on that
battleground?* It would have been far easier for me, with five hundred Rajputs at my disposal, than for a foreigner with only three
men. But I did not think of it, then. I took the direct course, the
simple course. The obvious course."

Damodara stared down at the battlefield. Even now, days later,
the grisly signs of death were everywhere apparent.

"I—begin to understand your point. You are saying that he is
a man who will, almost automatically, approach his task from the
side. From an angle, so to speak."

Sanga nodded. Then, made a small gesture toward the pavilion.

"In there, Lord Damodara, I likened Belisarius to a tiger. And
I suggested the use of a long stick."

Damodara nodded, smiling.

"It is a poor analogy, the more I think about it. A tiger, you can
bait with a long stick. But ask yourself this, Lord Damodara: how
long a stick must you use if you seek to bait a mongoose?"

✧   ✧   ✧

Later, when the assembly reconvened, Lord Damodara demanded that only the innermost circle of Malwa advisers be allowed to remain. The Emperor agreed, readily enough, and the pavilion was cleared of all others. Even the Ye-tai bodyguards stood far back, well out of hearing range.

When he rose to speak, Lord Damodara repeated nothing of his conversation with Rana Sanga. The Rajput sense of honor was foreign to him, but he understood it. It was that understanding, perhaps, which caused him to shield Sanga from retribution.

Instead, he simply exercised—for the first time ever—his sacred right as a kinsman of the highest Malwa. He demanded that the problem of Belisarius be placed before the highest authority.

The demand would have astonished anyone other than the men in that pavilion. All the world knew—all of India, at least—that Emperor Skandagupta was the very God-on-Earth. The highest of all authority.

But the men in that room knew otherwise. Great as Skandagupta was, another was greater still. Above the God-on-Earth, after all, are the heavens.

His demand was agreed to. Grudgingly, to be sure—angrily, on the part of Venandakatra. But agreed to it was, for they had no choice.

The question of Belisarius would be taken to the very soul of the dynasty. To the great mind of Malwa's destiny. To the divine being called Link.

Link. A strange name, but appropriate. For, as the divine being had often explained, it was simply the face shown to humanity of the great, new, Gods-in-Heaven.

Later that night, long after all his other Rajputs were asleep, Rana Sanga stood in the entrance of his own tent. He had stood there for hours, almost motionless, simply staring. Staring at the moon, for a time. Staring, for a longer time, at the flickering fires which still burned, here and there, in the rubble which had once been called Ranapur. Staring, and lost in thought.

Ranapur was silent, now, so Sanga's thoughts were not interrupted by noise. True, the stench of Ranapur's death penetrated his nostrils. But the Rajput had long been familiar with that particular odor. His mind automatically blocked it out.

Finally, Sanga turned away. One last glance at the moon, high and silvery, before he entered his tent.

His last thought, before he stooped into the darkness, was the same thought which he had clung to throughout those long hours.

I swore an oath.

The next morning, imperial heralds spread throughout the gigantic encampment, carrying the announcement that the emperor was returning to Kausambi. The announcement came much sooner than anyone had expected, and so the preparations for departure were ragged and disorganized.

The foreigners in the encampment, from long and ingrained habit, made their preparations within an hour. Their obvious, simple, direct preparations, at least. Their other preparations took much longer, more than a day, but they had plenty of time. Plenty of time to see to the movement of many excellent, high-spirited horses and a few small, docile elephants. Plenty of time, even, to see to it that those movements had no apparent connection to them.

Plenty of time. Not for three days more did the first departure take place from the encampment. A small army—a large army, actually, by any but Malwa standards—began its long march southward. The army which had been assigned to Lord Venandakatra, in his new manifestation as the *Goptri of the Deccan*. It was a glorious manifestation, even by Venandakatra's standards, and so the great Lord was mollified for the unseemly haste with which he made his departure.

Of the various types of Malwa governorships, none was so prestigious as "Goptri." (The term, as closely as possible, could have been translated in the western lands as: *Warden of the Marches*.) No ordinary governor, Venandakatra, to be assigned to a small and placid province. Not even an ordinary satrap, Venandakatra, assigned to a large and placid region. No, Venandakatra, blessed by his Emperor, had been given the entire Deccan, and, trusted by his Emperor, had been charged with bringing that fractious land to heel.

As much as they detested him, many Malwa officials, watching him go, almost felt sorry for the man.

Three days later, the Emperor's own army began its march.

(Stately progress, it might be better to say.) A march which was much shorter, and to the east, and—for the Emperor and his immediate entourage—no march at all. The Emperor and the high Malwa rode down the Jamuna in the comfort of the world's most luxurious barges, escorted by a fleet of slim war galleys.

Most of the Emperor's army, however, marched. As did the horde of camp followers who surrounded the army. And a small band of foreigners, like a chip in a slow moving ocean of humanity.

Chapter 9
DARAS
Summer 530 AD

The first day, after her return to Daras, Antonina spent with her son. Photius was ecstatic to see his mother, after a separation of several months—the more so when he saw the small mountain of gifts which she had brought back for him from fabled Constantinople. Yet, for all that the boy kept one eager, impatient eye upon his fascinating new toys, he spent the first day cuddling with his mother.

The seven-year-old's delight in the reunion was the product of simple joy, not relief. He had obviously been well treated during her absence. Indeed, suspected Antonina, hefting his weight, he had been spoiled outright.

By the second day, of course, the imperative demand of new toys overwhelmed all filial devotion. At the crack of dawn, Photius was at his play. When his mother appeared, an hour or so later, the boy gave her no more than perfunctory words of greeting. Mothers, after all is said and done, are mothers. As cherishable as the sunrise, to be sure, but equally certain. *Toys*, now—who knows when they might vanish, into whatever magic realm brought them forth?

Antonina watched him at his play, for a bit. On another occasion, there might have been a touch of rueful regret in her son's preoccupation. But Antonina, in truth, was impatient to get on with her own pressing tasks. So it was not long before she headed off to the workshop where John of Rhodes awaited her.

The workshop, she saw at a glance, had been considerably expanded during the months of her absence. And, as she drew nearer, she realized that John was no longer working alone. Through the open door of the workshop, she could hear the sound of voices.

At first, the realization disconcerted her. She was swept with uneasiness. The past weeks in Constantinople had left her with a heightened sense of secrecy and security.

Within seconds, however, uneasiness was pushed aside by another emotion. There could be only one reason that John had brought other men into his work.

So it was hope, not anxiety, which quickened her last steps into the workshop.

What she encountered, entering, melded both sentiments in an instant.

A loud, crashing noise caused her to flinch.

Fortunately. The flinch gave her the momentum to duck.

Fortunately. The unknown missile whizzing by missed her head by a comfortable margin.

Unlike the ricochet, which struck her squarely on the rump.

The ricochet had little force behind it, however. It was surprise, more than pain, which tumbled her squawking to the floor.

"In the name of Christ, Antonina!" bellowed John of Rhodes. "Can't you read a simple sign?"

The naval officer arose from behind an upended table and stalked toward her. It was obvious, from its neat and tidy placement, that the table had been upended deliberately.

John reached down a hand and hauled Antonina to her feet. Then, not relinquishing his grip on her wrist, he dragged her back through the doorway she had just entered.

Outside, he spun her around. "Right there!" he roared. "Where everyone can see it!"

He pointed triumphantly above the door.

"In plain and simple Greek! It says—"

Silence. Antonina rubbed her rump, scowling.

"Yes, John? It says *what*?"

Silence. Then:

"Eusebius—come here!"

A moment later, an apprehensive young man appeared in the doorway. He was short, thick, swarthy—rather evil-looking, in fact.

Not at all the image of the innocent cherub he was desperately trying to project.

John pointed accusingly at the empty space above him.

"Where's the sign I told you to hang there?" he demanded.

Eusebius looked sheepish. "Forgot," he mumbled.

John took a deep breath, blew it out, and began stumping about in the courtyard. His hands were firmly planted on his hips, arms akimbo.

Antonina knew the signs. She was in no mood for one of the naval officer's tirades.

"Never mind, John!" she exclaimed. "There's no harm done, other than to my dignity."

"That's not the point!" snarled John. "This stuff is dangerous enough without some—*fool boy!*—forgetting—*again!*—to take simple precautions like hanging—"

"*What* dangerous stuff?" demanded Antonina, smiling brightly. "Oh—that sounds exciting!"

John broke off his stumping. He waved his arms.

"We've got it, Antonina!" he cried excitedly. "We've got it! *Gunpowder!* Come on—I'll show you!"

He charged back inside. Eusebius, moving out of the way, gave Antonina a thankful glance.

For the second time, Antonina entered the workshop.

Bang! Whizzzzz! Thump. Clatterclatterclatter.

She scrambled back outside, ducking.

Behind her, John's bellow:

"*Eusebius—you idiot!* Didn't I tell you to put out the slowmatch?"

"Forgot," came the mutter.

"Outside of having the memory of an olive, he's really been a great help," said John later. He took a thoughtful sip of wine. "Chemistry isn't really my strong point. Eusebius has a knack for it like nobody I've ever seen."

"Better hire someone to keep track of what he's supposed to remember, then," said Antonina, smiling.

John set his cup down on the table firmly. Planted his hands on the table, firmly. Squared his shoulders, firmly.

"We can't afford it, Antonina," he said. Firmly. "There's no point dancing about the matter." Scowl. "Procopius has been rubbing his hands with glee for a week, now. Ever since he got here ahead of you and went over the books." Fierce scowl. "He can't wait to tell you, the swine. I've gone through the money. All of it. Not a solidus left. Not one." Very fierce scowl. "And Sittas—fat cheapskate!—won't cough up anything more. He denounced me for a spendthrift the last time I asked."

Antonina's smile didn't fade.

"How many times have you hit him up?"

Sullenly: "Eight. Well—seven. Successfully."

"Congratulations!" she laughed. "That's a record. No one else has ever squeezed money out of him more than twice in a row, so far as I know."

John's smile was very thin.

"It's not really a joke, Antonina. We can't go any further without money, and I don't know where it's going to come from. I can't get anything from Cassian, either. The Bishop's got his own problems. Patriarch Ephraim's been on a rampage lately, howling about church funds being misspent. His deacons have been crawling all over Anthony like fleas on a dog. They even counted his personal silverware."

"What's the matter?" sneered Antonina. "Are Ephraim's silk robes wearing out?"

There was a bit more humor in John's smile, now. Just a bit.

"Not that I've noticed. Hard to keep track, of course, all the robes he's got. No, I think maybe he's peeved because he doesn't have as many pounds of gold on the rings of his left hand as he does on the right. Makes him list when he promenades through the streets of Antioch, blessing the poor."

The naval officer snorted, sighed. He cast a glance around the room. They were sitting in the main salon of the villa, at a table in the corner. "I'd suggest selling one of your marvelous tapestries," he muttered, "except—"

"We don't have any."

"Precisely."

Antonina's smile turned into a very cheerful grin. She shook her head.

"I should stop teasing you. I'm ashamed of myself. The fact is, my dear John, that money is no longer a problem. I have acquired a new financial backer for our project."

She reached down and hauled up a sack. *Hauled.* The table clumped when she set it down.

John's eyes widened. Antonina, still grinning, seized the bottom of the sack and upended it. A small torrent of gold coins spilled across the table.

"Freshly minted, I hope you notice," she said gaily.

John ogled the pile. It was not the coins themselves which held his gaze, however. It was his knowledge of what lay behind them.

Power. Raw power.

Since the reign of the emperors Valentinian and Valens, gold coin—the solidus, inaugurated by Constantine the Great, which had been Rome's stable currency for two centuries—were minted very exclusively.

There were many legal mints in the Roman Empire. Big ones, in Thessalonica and Nicomedia, and a number of small ones in other cities. But they were restricted to issuing silver and copper coinage. By law, only the emperor minted gold coin. In Constantinople, at the Great Palace itself.

"You told Theodora," he stated.

Antonina nodded.

"Was that wise?" he asked. There was no accusation in the question, simply curiosity.

Antonina shrugged. "I think so. Under the circumstances, I didn't have much choice. I became deeply embroiled in imperial intrigue while I was in Constantinople. The reason Irene didn't come back with me is because she's now—in fact if not in theory—Theodora's spymaster."

John eyed her with deep interest.

"Malwa?"

"Yes. They're developing some kind of treacherous plot, John. So far all we know is—" She broke off. "Never mind. It's a long tale, and I don't want to have to tell it twice in the same day. Anthony, Michael and Sittas will be coming for dinner tonight. Maurice and Hermogenes will be there, too. They're also both involved, now. I'll explain everything then."

She reached out a hand and began scooping the coins back into the sack. "Anyway, I think telling Theodora was necessary. And the right thing to do, for that matter. We'll know soon enough. She'll be coming here later this summer. For a full tour of the project."

"*What?*" cried John. "*This summer?*" He leapt to his feet. Waved his arms angrily. "Impossible! Impossible! I won't have anything ready by then! Impossible!" He began stumping back and forth furiously. "Crazed women! No sense of reality—none at all. Impossible. The gunpowder's still too unpredictable. The grenades are untested. Rockets aren't even that!"

Stump, stump, stump.

"Lunatic females. Think chemistry's like baking bread. There's something wrong with the way the powder burns, I know there is. Need to experiment with different ways of mixing the stuff."

Stump, stump, stump.

"Idiot girls. Maybe grind it, if I can figure out how to do it without blowing myself up. Maybe wet it first, that's an idea. What the hell, can't hurt."

Stump, stump, stump.

"Hell it can't! That moron Eusebius could blow up anything. Blow up a frigging pile of cow dung, you don't watch him. Careless as a woman."

Stump, stump, stump.

The early hours of the evening, before and during the meal, were primarily devoted to Procopius. It was not difficult. From months of practice, Antonina had developed the craft of Procopius-baiting to a fine art.

In truth, her expertise was largely wasted. By now, Procopius was so well-trained that literally anything would serve the purpose. Like a yoked and blinkered mule pulling a capstan, he could see nothing before him but the well-trod path. Antonina had but to remark on a fine horse—Procopius would scribble on the infamy of bestialism. Chat with a peasant housewife—a treatise on the ancient sin of Sappho was the sure result. Place her son in her lap—ah! splendid!—Procopius would burn his lamp through the night, producing a veritable treatise on pedophilia and incest.

So, her sultry glances at the men about the table, her veiled remarks, her giddy laughter, her sly innuendos—even the joke about four soldiers and a pair of holy men being more than any woman could handle at one *sitting*—giggle, giggle—were a complete waste of effort. She could have been alone at the table, in the cold light of dawn, eating her meal in silence. By midmorning, Procopius would be assuring anyone who listened that the harlot masturbated at breakfast.

Soon enough, Procopius left the table and retired to his chamber.

There was no need for Antonina to send him away on some pretext. The man was fairly bursting with anxiety to reach his quill.

"God, I am sick of that man," snarled Sittas. For a moment, the general looked like he was going to spit out his wine. But only for a moment. He reconsidered, swallowed, poured himself a new goblet.

"Is this absolutely necessary?" growled Michael of Macedonia.

Antonina made a face. But before she could reply, Bishop Cassian spoke. Harshly:

"Yes, Michael, it is. That foul creature—though he's too stupid to know it—is Malwa's chief spy on Antonina. He's the aqueduct which brings them the water of knowledge. Except that Antonina has seen to it that the aqueduct is actually a sewer, piping nothing but filth into their reservoirs." He smiled. It was quite a wicked smile, actually, for a bishop. Almost devilish. "We're not having a meeting here, plotting against Malwa. We're having an orgy!"

Then, with a sly smile: "Is it your reputation which frets you so?"

The Macedonian glared. "All reputation is folly," he pronounced. "Folly—"

"—fed by pride, which is worse still," concluded the Bishop. His smile widened. "Really, Michael, you *must* develop a broader repertoire of proverbs."

Antonina cleared her throat.

"As I was saying . . ."

"You weren't saying anything, Antonina," pointed out Cassian reasonably. "So I saw no reason not to idle away the time by a harmless—"

"Stop picking on Michael," grumbled Maurice. "He's done wonders with the local lads, and their wives and parents. Even the village elders aren't howling louder than a medium-sized storm at sea."

"Well, of course he has!" exclaimed Cassian cheerfully. "He's a holy man. Must be good for something."

Antonina headed off the gathering storm.

"Tell me, Michael," she said forcefully. "What is your assessment? *Michael?*"

The Macedonian broke off his (quite futile) attempt to glower down the bishop.

"Excuse me, Antonina? I didn't catch that."

"The peasants," she stated. "What is your assessment?"

Michael waved his hand. It was not an airy gesture. Rather the opposite. So might a stone punctuate solidity.

"There will be no problem. None."

"More than that," added Maurice. "A good number of them, I think, would jump at the chance to join a new regiment." He eyed John of Rhodes. "Assuming there's something for them to do beside drive sheep at the enemy."

John didn't rise to the bait.

"Stop worrying, Maurice. You get your new regiment put together, I'll have weapons for them. Grenades, at the very least."

"No rockets?" asked Hermogenes.

John winced. "Wouldn't count on it. The damned things are trickier to make than I thought." He drained his cup, poured himself another. Then, grumbling:

"The problem, actually, isn't *making* them. I've got a good twenty rockets piled up in the workshed. Every one of them'll fly, too, and blow up quite spectacularly. The problem is that there's no telling *where*."

Another wince. "I had one rocket—this is the bare truth—the damned thing actually flew in a circle and almost took our heads off."

"How do the Malwa aim them?" asked Sittas. "There must be a way."

John shrugged. "I don't know. I've tried everything I can think of. Fired them through tubes. Put vanes on them—even feathers! Nothing works. Some go more or less straight, most don't, and I can't for the life of me figure out any rhyme or reason behind it."

Maurice slapped the table with the flat of his hand. "So let's not worry about it," he urged. "When the general gets back from India—"

"*If*—" murmured John.

"—*when* he gets back," drove on Maurice, "I'm sure he'll be able to tell us the secret of aiming rockets. In the meantime, let's stick to grenades. Those'll be more than enough to keep a new regiment of peasant recruits busy."

"Maurice has an idea," announced Sittas. The general beamed. "Marvelous idea, I think! And you know me—I generally look on new ideas about the same way I look on cow dung."

"What is it?" asked Antonina.

Maurice rubbed his scalp. The gesture was one of his few

affectations. The hair on that scalp was iron grey, but it was still as full as it had been when he was a boy.

"I got to thinking. The problem with grenades is that you want to be able to heave them a fair distance before they blow up. Then, you face a tradeoff between distance and effectiveness. A man with a good arm can toss a grenade fairly far—but only if it's so small it doesn't do much good when it lands. If he tries to throw a big grenade, he has to get well within bow range to do it." The veteran shrugged. "Under most battle conditions, my cataphracts would turn him into a pincushion before he got off more than one. I have to assume that the enemy could do as well. Persians could, for sure."

"So what's your solution?" asked John. "Scorpions?"

Maurice shook his head. "No. Mind you, I'm all for developing grenade artillery. Wouldn't be hard at all to adapt a stone-throwing scorpion for that purpose. But that's artillery. Fine in its place, but it's no substitute for infantry."

Hermogenes smiled. He was one of the few modern Roman generals who specialized in infantry warfare. Belisarius himself had groomed the young officer, and urged him in that direction.

"Or cavalry," grumbled Sittas. *This* general, on the other hand, was passionately devoted to the cataphract traditions.

"Forget cavalry," said Maurice. "These lads are peasants pure and simple, Sittas. Syrian peasants, to boot. Thracian and Illyrian peasants have some familiarity with horses, but these boys have none at all. You know as well as I do they'd never make decent horsemen. Not in the time we've got."

Sittas nodded, quite magnanimously. The honor of the cavalry having been sustained, he would not argue the point further.

"And that's the key," stated Maurice. "I tried to figure out the best way to combine Syrian peasants and grenades, starting with the strengths and limitations of both. The answer was obvious."

Silence. John exploded.

"Well—out with it, then!"

"Slings. And slingstaffs."

John frowned. "Slings?" He started to argue—more out of ingrained habit than anything else—but fell silent.

"Hmm." He quaffed his wine. "Hmm."

Antonina grinned. "What's the matter, John? Don't tell me you haven't got an instant opinion?"

The naval officer grimaced.

"Alas—no. Truth is, much as I hate to admit it, I don't know anything about slings. Never use the silly things in naval combat."

"You wouldn't call them *silly things* if you'd ever faced Balearic slingers on a battlefield," growled Maurice. Hermogenes and Sittas nodded vigorously.

"But these *aren't* Balearic slingers, Maurice," demurred Antonina. "The islanders are famous—have been for centuries. These are just farm boys."

Maurice shrugged. "So what? Every one of those peasants—especially the shepherds—has been using a sling since he was a boy. Sure, they're not professionals like the Balearic islanders, but that doesn't matter for our needs. The only real difference between a Balearic mercenary slinger and a peasant lad is accuracy. That matters when you're slinging iron bullets. It doesn't—not much, anyway—when you're hurling grenades."

John started to get excited, then. "You know—you're right! How far could one of these Syrian boys toss a grenade?"

Maurice fluttered the stubby fingers of one thick hand.

"Depends. Show me the grenade you're talking about, and I'll give you a close answer. Roughly? As far as an average archer, with a sling. With a slingstaff, as far as a cataphract or a Persian."

"Cavalry'd make mincemeat out of them," stated Sittas.

Maurice nodded. "Alone, yes. Good cavalry, anyway, that didn't panic at the first barrage. They'd rout the grenade slingers—"

"Call them *grenadiers*," interjected John. "Got more dignity."

"Grenadiers, then." He paused, ruminated; then: "*Grenadiers.* I like that!"

Hermogenes nodded vigorously.

"A special name'll give the men morale," the young general stated. "I like it too. In fact, I think it's essential."

Sittas mused: "So we'll need cavalry on the flanks—"

"Need a solid infantry bulwark, too," interjected Hermogenes.

Maurice nodded. "Yes, that too. There's nothing magical about grenades. In the right combination—used the right way—"

Hermogenes: "A phalanx, maybe."

Sittas: "Damned nonsense! Phalanxes are as obsolete as eating on a couch. No, no, Hermogenes, it's the old republican maniples you want to look at. I think—"

Bishop Cassian turned to Antonina.

"May I suggest we leave these gentlemen to their play, my dear? I predict that within a minute the discussion will be too technical for us to follow, anyway. And I'm dying to hear all about your exploits in Constantinople."

Antonina rose, smiling. "Let's repair to the salon, then."

She looked at Michael.

"Will you join us?"

The monk shook his head.

"I suspect that your own discussion with Anthony will soon be as technical as that of these gentlemen," he said ruefully. "I'm afraid that I would be of no more use in plotting palace intrigues than I am in calculating military tactics and formations."

Sittas happened to overhear the remark.

"What's the matter, Michael?" A teasing grin came to his face. "Surely you're not suggesting that the eternal soul has no place in the mundane world?"

The monk gazed on the general like a just-fed eagle gazes on a mouse. Current interest, mild.

"You and yours," he said softly, "will bring to the battle weapons and tactics. Antonina and Anthony, and theirs, will bring to the battle knowledge of the enemy. *But in the end, Sittas, it will come to this.* All the gifts you bring will be as nothing, unless the peasant boy to whom you give them has a soul which can face Satan in the storm."

He rose.

"I will give you that peasant."

On his way out, Michael bestowed a considering look upon Sittas. Like a just-fed eagle considers a mouse. Future prospects, excellent.

"Always a bad idea, baiting a holy man," murmured Maurice.

"It's true," he insisted, in the face of Sittas' glare. He drained his cup. "Ask any peasant."

The next morning, the two generals accompanied John of Rhodes out to the training field, eager to experiment with the grenades. Maurice was waiting there for them, with a dozen peasant volunteers. The Syrians were quite nervous, in the beginning. Even after their prowess at grenade-hurling earned them the praise of the generals, the young men were abashed in the company of such noble folk.

Soon enough, however, Michael of Macedonia made his appearance. He said nothing, neither to the generals nor to the peasants. But it was amusing, to Maurice, to watch the way in which the monk's presence transformed the Syrian boys. Into young eaglets, in the presence of giant mice.

By mid-afternoon, the eaglets were arguing freely with the giant mice.

Not over tactics, of course, or military formations. (Although the Syrians did have some valuable advice on the practical realities of slinging grenades. Most of it concerned the pragmatics of fuses, and their length.) The young men were not foolish. Uneducated and illiterate, yes. Stupid, no. They did not presume to understand the art of war better than such men as Sittas and Hermogenes. (Or, especially—they had their own peasant view of such things—Maurice.)

But they had quite strong opinions on the question of barracks, and the nature of military camps.

Their children would not like barracks, though they would probably enjoy the tent life of camps. Their wives would like neither, but would tolerate the camps. They were simple women. Practical.

Barracks, however, simply wouldn't do. No privacy. Immodest. Their wives were simple women, but decent. They were not camp followers.

They wanted huts. Each family its own hut. (A tent, of course, would do for the route camps.)

The generals explained the absurdity of such an arrangement. Violation of military tradition.

The peasants explained the absurdity of military tradition.

In the end, while a monk watched—smiling, smiling—young peasants disciplined generals.

No huts?

No grenadiers.

In a different way, another clash of wills was taking place in the villa.

"*It is much too dangerous, Antonina,*" insisted the bishop. "I thought so last night, and I feel even more strongly about it today." He pushed his plate of food away. "Look!" he said accusingly. "I've even lost my appetite."

Antonina smiled, studying his rotund form. As modest and plain-living as Bishop Cassian undoubtedly was, no-one had ever mistaken him for an ascetic. Not, at least, when it came to meals.

She shrugged. "It could be, yes. Not for the moment, however. I assure you, Anthony, the last thing the Malwa will do is harm me. I'm their pride and joy. The very apple of their eye."

Cassian stared stubbornly at his uneaten lunch. Antonina sighed.

"Can't you understand, Anthony? After Ajatasutra 'trapped' me—quite a trap, too!—what with me being overheard by two deacons crying out for the death of Justinian!—they had me in a vise. As they see it. They're squeezing for all it's worth. Before I left Constantinople, they got from me every detail of the Hippodrome factions' internal politics."

She broke off for a moment, grimacing.

"I *still* don't know why they're so fascinated by that subject. Mother of God, it's all I ever heard about from my father, growing up. *This* Blue did this and *that* Green did that, and *those* Blues are so many clowns but keep your eyes out for *that* set of Greens."

She threw up her hands with exasperation.

"I even had to track down some of my father's old cronies—the ones I could find in Constantinople, at any rate—in order to bring my knowledge of the factions up to date. God in Heaven, what a sorry lot of ruffians!"

"Were they pleased to see you again?" asked Cassian mildly. "After all this time?"

Antonina looked startled. Then she grinned, quite merrily.

"To tell the truth, they fawned all over me. Local girl makes good, comes back to visit the home folks. I hadn't realized how famous Belisarius has become among those circles."

She shrugged. "So, in the end, I was able to give Balban every detail of the doings of the Hippodrome factions. And I *still* don't know why the Malwa—"

"I don't think it's so odd, Antonina," interrupted Cassian. "There must be twenty or thirty thousand of those bravos in Constantinople. Not an insignificant military force, potentially."

Antonina snickered.

"Hippodrome thugs? Be serious, Anthony. Oh, to be sure, they're a rough enough crowd in the streets. But against *cataphracts*? Besides, they're about evenly divided between the Blues and the Greens. More likely to whip on each other than do any Malwa bidding."

The bishop rubbed two fingers together, in the ancient gesture for coin.

Antonina cocked her head quizzically.

"That's Irene's opinion, too. But I think she's overestimating the strength of the factions, even if the Malwa can unite them with bribes." She shook her head. "Enough of that. At least now the Malwa are demanding some sensible secrets from me. By the time I get back to Constantinople, a few months from now, I'm to provide them with a detailed breakdown of all the military units in the east. *All* of them—not just here in Syria, but in Palestine as well. Even Egypt." She grinned. "Or else."

Cassian stared at her, still unsmiling. Antonina's grin faded away.

"It's that 'or else' you're worried about, isn't it?"

Cassian took a deep breath, exhaled. "Actually, no. At least, not much."

He rose from the table and began pacing slowly about the dining room.

"I'm afraid you don't really grasp my fear, Antonina. I agree with you about the Malwa, as it happens. *For now*, at least, they will do you no harm at all."

Antonina frowned. "Then what—"

It was Anthony's turn to throw up his hands with exasperation.

"Can you possibly be so naive? There are not simply *Malwa* involved in this plot, woman! There are Romans, also. And they have their own axes to grind—grind against each other's blades, often enough."

He stepped to the table, planted his pudgy hands firmly, and leaned over.

"You have placed yourself in a maelstrom, Antonina. Between Scylla and Charybdis—and a multitude of other monsters!—all of whom are plotting as much against their conspirators as they are against the Roman Empire." He thrust himself back upright. "You have no idea where the blade might come from, my dear. No idea at all. You see only the Malwa. And only the face they turn toward you."

Antonina stared grimly back at him. Unyielding.

"And so? I understand your point, Anthony. But I say again—*so?*"

Her shrug was enough to break the Bishop's heart. It was not a woman's shrug, but the gesture of a veteran.

"That's war, Cassian. You do the best you can against the enemy, knowing he fully intends to return the favor. One of you wins, one of you loses. Dies, usually."

A thin smile came to her face.

"Belisarius—Maurice, too, I think my husband got it from him—has a saying about it. He calls it the First Law of Battle. *Every battle plan gets fucked up*—pardon my language, Bishop—*as soon as the enemy arrives. That why he's called the enemy.*"

Cassian stroked his beard. There was weariness in the gesture, but some humor also.

"Crude, crude," he murmured. "Altogether coarse. Refined theologians would express the matter differently. Every sound doctrine gets contradicted, as soon as the other dogmatists arrive at the council. That's why they're called the heretics."

Finally, he smiled.

"Very well, Antonina. I cannot stop you, in any event. I will give you all the assistance which I can."

He resumed his seat. Then, after staring at his plate for a moment, pulled it back before him and began eating with his usual gusto.

"Won't be much, when it comes to military matters and Hippodrome factions." He waved his knife cheerfully. "Church conspirators, on the other hand—and there'll be plenty of them, be sure of it!—are a different matter altogether."

He speared two dates.

"Glycerius of Chalcedon and George Barsymes, is it?"

The dates disappeared as if by magic. He skewered a pear.

"Rufinus Namatianus, Bishop of Ravenna," he mumbled thoughtfully, his mouth full of shredding fruit. "Know'm well."

The last piece of pear sped down his throat, like a child down the gullet of an ogre.

"Babes in the woods," he belched.

After the generals returned, at sundown, Antonina listened to their ranting and raving for half an hour. Tact and diplomacy, she thought, required as much.

Then she made her ruling.

"*Of course* they won't live in barracks. The idea's absurd. These men aren't *conscripts*, gentlemen. They're volunteers—established farmers, with families. They marry early here, and start raising children by the time they're fifteen. Younger, the girls."

The generals gobbled. John of Rhodes began to stump. Antonina examined them curiously.

"What did you expect? Did you think these men would abandon their families—just to be your grenade-tossers?"

Gobbling ceased. Generals stared at other. A naval officer stumbled in his stumping.

Antonina snorted.

"You *didn't* think."

Snort. "Sometimes I agree with Theodora. *Men.*"

Sittas leveled his finest glare upon her. The boar in full fury.

"You'll not be making any royal decrees here, young woman!"

"I most certainly will," replied Antonina, quite sweetly. "I'm the paymaster, remember?"

She cocked her head at John of Rhodes. "Are you done with your stumping?"

The naval officer pouted. Antonina reached to the floor, hauled up a sack, clumped it on the table.

"Hire workmen, John. Better yet—pay the peasants themselves. The lads are handy with their hands. They'll have the huts up in no time, and they'll be the happier for having made their own new homes."

From the doorway came Michael's voice:

"They'll be wanting a chapel, too. Nothing fancy, of course."

The generals, cowed by the woman, transferred their outrage to the monk.

The Macedonian stared back. Like a just-fed eagle stares at chittering mice.

Contest of wills, laughable.

Chapter 10

KAUSAMBI
Summer 530 AD

From the south bank of the Jamuna, Belisarius gazed at the temple rising from the very edge of the river on the opposite bank. It was sundown, and the last rays of the setting sun bathed the temple in golden glory. He was too distant to discern the details of the multitude of figurines carved into the tiered steps of the temple, but he did not fail to appreciate the beauty of the structure as a whole.

"What a magnificent temple," he murmured. Out of the corner of his eye, he saw Menander's lips tighten in disapproval.

For a moment, he thought to let it go, but then decided it was a fine opportunity to advance the young cataphract's education.

"What's the matter, Menander?" he queried, cocking an eyebrow. "Does my admiration for heathen idolatry offend you?"

The words were spoken in a mild and pleasant tone, but Menander flushed with embarassment.

"It's not my place—" he began, but Belisarius cut him off.

"Of course it is, lad. You're required to obey my orders as your commander. You are not required to agree with my theological opinions. So, spit it out." He pointed to the temple. "What do you think of it? How can you deny its splendor?"

Menander frowned. The expression was one of thought, not disapproval. He did not respond immediately, however. He and Belisarius had dismounted upon reaching the river, in order to

490

drink its water, and their horses were still assuaging their thirst. Idly, he stroked the neck of his horse for a few seconds, before saying:

"I can't deny that it's a beautifully made edifice, general. I just wish it had been made for some different purpose."

Belisarius shrugged. "For what? Christian worship? That would be better, of course, to be sure. Unfortunately, Christian missionaries have only begun to penetrate this far into India's interior." With an smile of irony: "And all of *them*, alas, are Nestorian heretics. Not much better than outright heathens. According to most orthodox churchmen, at least."

He turned, so as to face Menander squarely.

"In the meantime, India's millions grope their own way toward God. *That*"—pointing again to the temple—"is the proof of it. Would you rather they ignored God altogether?"

Menander's frown deepened. "No," he said softly, after a moment. "I just—" He hesitated, sighed, shrugged.

"I've seen Dadaji praying in your tent, many times. And I don't doubt his sincerity, or his devotion. I just—" Another shrug, expressing a fatalistic acceptance of reality.

"Wish he were praying to the Christian God?"

Menander nodded.

Belisarius looked back to the temple. Now, he shrugged himself. But his was a cheerful shrug, expressing more of wonder than of resignation.

"So do I, Menander, come down to it. But I can't say I lose any sleep over the matter. Dadaji's is a true and pure soul. I do not think God will reject it, when the time comes."

The general glanced toward the west. The lower rim of the sun was almost touching the horizon.

"We'd best head back," he said. "I'd hoped to get a glimpse of Kausambi before nightfall, but I can see that we're still a few miles away from the outskirts."

He and Menander mounted their horses and rode away from the river. As they headed back toward their camp, Menander said:

"I thought you were orthodox, sir." The youth's brow was furrowed in thought. Then, realizing that his statement might be construed amiss, Menander began to apologize. But his general dismissed the apology with a wave of the hand.

"I *am* orthodox." Then, a crooked smile. "I suppose. I was

raised so, as Thracians are. And it is the creed to which I have always subscribed."

He hesitated. "It is hard to explain. I do not care much for such things, Menander. My wife, whom I love above all others in this world, is not orthodox. For the sake of my reputation, she disguises her creed, but she inclines to Monophysitism, as do most Egyptians. Am I to believe that she is condemned to eternal hellfire?"

He glanced at Menander. The young cataphract winced. If anything, Menander was even more adoring of Antonina than were most of the bucellarii.

Belisarius shook his head. "I think not. Not by the Christ I worship. And it is not simply she, Menander. I am a general, and I have led soldiers into battle who believed in every heresy, even Arians, and watched them die bravely. And held them in my arms as they died, listening to their last prayers. Were those men predestined for damnation? I think not."

His jaws tightened. "My indifference to creed goes deeper than that. Years ago, in my first command—I was only eighteen years old—I matched wits with a Persarmenian commander named Varanes. His forces were small, as were mine, and our combat was prolonged over weeks. A thing of maneuver and feint, as much as battle. He was a magnificent commander, and taxed me to the utmost."

He took a deep breath. "An honorable and gallant foe, as well. As Medeans often are. Once I was forced to abandon three of my men. They were too badly wounded to move, and Varanes had caught me in a trap from which I had to extricate myself immediately or suffer total defeat. When he came upon them, Varanes saw to it that they were well cared for."

He looked away. For a moment, the usual calm of his face seemed to waver. But not for long, and Belisarius resumed his tale. Menander was listening with rapt attention.

"I discovered the fact after I defeated Varanes. I trapped him myself, finally, and overran his camp. My three men were still there. One of them had died in the meantime, from his wounds, but it was through no fault of the Persians. The other two were safe, thanks to Varanes. Varanes himself was mortally wounded, from a lance-thrust to the groin. It took him hours to die, and I spent those hours with him. I attempted to comfort him as best I could, but the wound was terrible. It must have been pure agony for him, but he bore it well. He even joked with me, and we passed the time discussing, among other things, our relative assessment of our previous weeks in combat. He had had the upper hand, through most of it, but I had learned quickly. He predicted a great future for me."

Belisarius paused for a moment, guiding his horse through a narrowing of the trail. Within a few seconds, they passed through the final line of trees which bordered the river. Now in more open country, the general resumed his tale.

"By the time he finally died, night had fallen. He was a Zoroastrian, as most Persians, a fire-worshipper. He asked me to make a fire for him, so that he might die looking into the face of his god. I did so, and willingly. A churchman, most churchmen at least, would have denounced me for that act of impiety. The Zoroastrian, a churchman would have no doubt explained, was soon enough going to get fire aplenty in the pit of eternal damnation. But I did not think Varanes was so destined. I did not think so then. I do not think so now."

Menander, watching his general, was struck by the sudden coldness in his gaze. Belisarius' brown eyes were normally quite warm, except in battle. Even in battle, those eyes were not cold. Simply—calm, detached, observant.

The customary warmth returned within a few seconds, however. Musingly, Belisarius added:

"I tried to explain to Rao, once, as best I could, the subtleties of the Trinity." He waved his hand. "Not in this world, but in the world of my vision."

Menander, already fascinated with his general's unwontedly intimate tale, now became totally absorbed. He knew of that vision, which had come to Belisarius from the "jewel" which Bishop Cassian had brought to him the year before in Aleppo. Belisarius had told him the tale, along with the other Romans and the Ethiopians, while they were still at sea.

Menander glanced at the general's chest. Beneath the half-armor and the tunic, there was nothing to see. But the young cataphract knew that the Talisman of God was there, nestled in a little pouch which Belisarius always carried suspended from his neck. Menander had even seen it himself, for Belisarius had showed it to them all, in the cramped confines of their cabin in the Malwa embassy vessel which had brought them to India. He had been dazzled, then, by the mystic splendor of the Talisman. He was dazzled, now, by the memory.

Belisarius suddenly laughed.

"Rao listened to my explanation, quite patiently," he continued. "But it was obvious he thought it was child's babble. Then he told me that his own faith believed there were three hundred and thirty million gods and goddesses, all of whom, in one way or another, were simply manifestations of God himself."

Belisarius smiled his crooked smile. "No doubt that man is doomed. But I will tell you this, Menander: I would rather stand with Raghunath Rao in the Pit than with the Patriarch Ephraim in Heaven."

Belisarius spoke no further during the rest of their ride back to their camp. Menander, also, was silent, grappling with thoughts which were new to him, and which went far beyond the simple preachings of his village priest.

They reached the grove within which the Romans and Ethiopians had pitched their camp. Still preoccupied, Menander gave only cursory attention to the task of guiding his horse through the trees. But once they broke through into the clearing at the center of the grove, all thoughts of theology vanished.

"There's trouble, Menander," said his general softly.

The moment Belisarius rode into the little clearing, he knew something was amiss. Ezana and Wahsi were both standing guard in front of Prince Eon's pavilion. Normally, only one or the other assumed that duty at any given time. What was even more noticeable was that two sarwen were actually *standing* guard. Usually, the sarwen on duty relaxed on a stool. There was no reason not to. For many weeks, now, the Romans and Ethiopians had been guarded by their Kushan escorts, a troop of over thirty men who were consummate professionals in their trade—and particularly expert at maintaining security.

There was obvious tension in the pose of the Ethiopian soldiers. They weren't just standing—they were standing alertly, poised, and ready.

Quickly, Belisarius scanned the clearing. The lighting was poor. Dusk was almost a memory, now, only a faint tinge of dark purple on the horizon. The sun itself had disappeared, and what little daylight still remained was blocked off by the trees surrounding the camp. For all practical purposes, the only illumination in the clearing was that cast by lanterns hanging from tent poles.

His next glance was toward the two Roman tents, situated not far from Prince Eon's large pavilion. Both Valentinian and Anastasius, he noted, were standing in front of them. Much like the sarwen—alert, poised, tense.

Next, he stared across the clearing to the line of tents which marked the Kushan part of the encampment. Normally, at this time of the evening, the Kushans would have been busy preparing their evening meal. Instead, they were gathered in small clusters, murmuring quietly, casting quick glances at Prince Eon's pavilion and—most of all—at the figure of their own commander.

Belisarius now examined Kungas. The Kushan commander was standing alone. As always—now more than ever, it seemed to Belisarius—his face appeared to have been hammered out of an iron ingot. Kanishka, his nephew and second-in-command, stood not far away. From what little Belisarius could discern of his features, the young Kushan lieutenant seemed distressed.

Kungas met his gaze. The Kushan said nothing, and there was not the slightest movement in that iron mask of a face. But Belisarius did not miss the almost imperceptible shrug of his shoulders.

He knew what had happened, then. The sight of Garmat emerging from Eon's pavilion and hurrying toward him simply confirmed the knowledge.

"All good things come to an end," he sighed, dismounting from his horse. By the time Garmat reached him, Menander was leading both of the horses away.

"We have a problem, Belisarius," said Garmat urgently. "A very big problem."

Belisarius smiled crookedly. "It couldn't last forever, Garmat. The Kushans are not stupid. To a point, of course, they will obey Kungas and ask no questions. But only to a point."

He gave the Kushans another glance.

"What happened?" he asked.

Garmat shrugged. "You can hardly expect vigorous young people like Eon and Shakuntala—royalty, to boot—to share a tent, week after week, with no opportunity for exercise or even movement, without—"

He sighed. Belisarius nodded.

"They quarreled."

Garmat smiled, faintly. "Oh, yes. A *royal* quarrel! What started it, I have no idea. They don't even remember themselves, now. But soon enough, Eon became overbearing and the Princess—the Empress, I should say—challenged him to single combat. Unarmed combat, of course. If he used weapons, she told him, he would be damned for eternity as a coward."

For all the seriousness of the moment, Belisarius could not help bursting into laughter. The image which came to his mind was incongruously funny. Eon, Prince of Axum, was not a tall man. But he was amazingly well-muscled, and as strong as a bull. Whereas Shakuntala was a small girl, not half his weight.

And yet—

She had been trained to fight with her bare hands and feet by Raghunath Rao himself. Raghunath Rao, the Panther of Majarashtra. The Wind of the Great Country. India's most deadly assassin, among many other things.

He shook his head with amusement.

"I wonder how it would have turned out. They did not actually come to blows, I hope?"

Garmat shook his head. "They are young and impetuous, but they are not insane. I gather that Shakuntala's challenge produced a sudden change of atmosphere in the tent. By the time I entered, they were exchanging profuse apologies and vows of good will."

He tugged his beard. "Unfortunately, in the brief moments before that change of atmosphere, the environs of their pavilion were filled with the sound of loud and angry voices. And Shakuntala has quite a distinctive voice, you know, especially when raised in anger." Grudgingly, even admiringly: "A very *imperial* voice, in fact."

Belisarius scratched his chin. "The Kushans heard her," he announced.

Garmat nodded. Belisarius glanced at the Kushan soldiers again. They were still clustered in little knots, but, to his relief, they did not give the appearance of men on the verge of leaping into action.

That momentary relief, however, cleared the way for another concern. Belisarius scanned the woods surrounding the clearing.

As always, whenever possible, Belisarius had made their camp within a grove of trees. He had explained that preference to the Malwa, casually, as a matter of the comfort which the trees provided from the blistering sun of India. The Malwa, for their part, had made no objection. They were happy enough, for their own reasons, to see the foreigners secluded. Privately, the Malwa thought the outlanders were idiots. True, trees provided shade. But a good pavilion did as much, and trees also stifled the breeze and were a haven for obnoxious insects.

The Malwa had also thought, happily, that trees would provide a haven for spies.

As Belisarius watched, Ousanas appeared from the edge of the trees and padded into the clearing. The hunter was casually wiping blood from the huge blade of his spear.

No Malwa spies now, thought Belisarius. His lips quirked into that distinctive, crooked smile.

Ousanas was a slave, of sorts. Of a very, very odd sort. The tall African was not Ethiopian. Like the Axumites, his skin was black. But Ousanas' broad features had not a trace of the aquiline characteristics which distinguished those of most Ethiopians. He came from a land between great lakes which was—so Belisarius had been told—some considerable distance south of the Kingdom of Axum. He was the personal slave of Prince Eon—his dawazz, as the Axumites called his position. An adviser, of a sort. A very, very odd sort.

When Ousanas reached Belisarius, he nodded curtly. The general noted that the hunter's usual beaming grin was entirely absent.

"No spies now," said Ousanas softly. He jerked his head toward the tent.

"Let us go in," he growled. "I must advise fool boy."

Ousanas stalked toward the pavilion entrance, Garmat trailing in his wake like a remora trailing a shark. Belisarius felt a moment's pity for the young prince. The dawazz, when he felt it appropriate, was given to stern measures.

Again, Belisarius quickly scanned the clearing. His own three cataphracts were now fully armed and armored, and their expressions were every bit as grim as those of the sarwen. Belisarius caught the eye of Valentinian and made a subtle motion with his hands. Valentinian relaxed slightly and muttered something to Anastasius and Menander. The cataphracts maintained their watchfulness, but they eased away from their former tension.

Belisarius now concentrated his attention on the Kushans, gauging their mood. The Malwa vassals were also armed, and obviously tense. But they too seemed willing to allow the situation to unfold before taking any decisive steps. They were angry, true—so much was obvious. Angry at their commander, for the most part, Belisarius thought. But they were also confused, and uncertain. Kungas *was* their commander, after all, and it was a position which he had earned on a hundred battlefields. And, too, they were all related by blood. Members of the same clan, banded together in service to the Malwa overlords. An unhappy and thankless service.

Hard years had taught the Kushans to trust themselves alone, and, most of all, to trust their commander. Such habits cannot be overcome in an instant. Belisarius gauged, and pondered the angles, and made his decision. As always, the decision was quick. He strode across the clearing and planted himself before the Kushans.

"Wait," he commanded. "I must go into the pavilion. Make no decisions until I return."

The Kushans stiffened. The Roman general's words had been spoken in fluent Kushan. They knew his command of their language was good, but now it was perfect and unaccented. A few of them cast glances toward the trees.

Belisarius smiled—broadly, not crookedly.

"There are no spies. Not any more."

The Kushans had also seen Ousanas emerge from the woods. And, if they did not know of the African's extraordinary skill as a hunter, they had never misunderstood the easy manner in which he handled the huge spear which was his everpresent companion. Imperceptibly, they began to relax. Just a bit.

Belisarius glanced at Kungas. The Kushan commander nodded slightly. The Roman general wheeled and headed toward the pavilion. As he turned, he caught sight of Dadaji Holkar standing near the pavilion. Though middle-aged, and unarmed, and a slave, the man was obviously prepared to help defend the pavilion against assault.

Belisarius did not smile, but he felt a great affection surge into his heart.

"Come," he commanded, as he strode by Holkar. "I suspect you already know the truth, but you may as well see for yourself."

As they entered the pavilion, Ousanas was just warming to his subject.

"—be forced to tell negusa nagast he do better to drown his fool boy in the sea and beget another. Dakuen Sarwe be furious with me! Beat me for failing in my duty. But I bear up under the regiment's savage blows with great cheer! Knowing I finally rid of hopeless task of teaching frog-level intelligence to worm-brained prince."

"No attack him!" snapped Shakuntala. "Was my wrongdoing!"

The girl spoke in Ge'ez, as had Ousanas. Her command of the language of the Axumites was still poor, heavily accented and broken, but she understood enough to have followed Ousanas' tirade.

The young woman was sitting crosslegged on a plush cushion to one side of the pavilion. Her posture was stiff and erect. For all her youth, and her small size, she exuded a tremendous imperial dignity.

Ousanas scowled. He was not impressed by royalty. Axumites in general, and Ousanas in particular, shared none of the Indian awe of rulership. Ousanas himself was a dawazz, assigned the specific task of instructing a prince in the simple truth that the difference between a king and a slave was not so great. A matter of luck, in its origin; and brains, in its maintenance.

The dawazz switched to Hindi, which was the common language used by all in the pavilion.

"Next time, Empress," he growled, "do not challenge cretin prince to combat. Simply pounce upon him like lioness and beat him senseless. Fool girl!"

Ousanas shook his head sadly. "True, royalty stupid by nature. But this! This not stupidity! This—this—" He groaned woefully. "There is no word for this! Not even in Greek, language of philosophy, which has words for every silliness known to man."

Eon, squatting on his own cushion, raised his bowed head. The young prince—at nineteen, he was but a year or so older than Shakuntala—attempted to regain some measure of his own royal dignity.

"Stop speaking pidgin!" he commanded.

Belisarius fought down a grin. He knew Ousanas' rejoinder even before the dawazz spoke the words.

Not speaking pidgin. Speaking baby talk. All fool prince can understand!

When Belisarius had first met Ousanas, the year before in Constantinople, the African had spoken nothing but a bizarre, broken argot. Ousanas had maintained that manner of speech for months, until the alliance which Belisarius sought between Romans and Ethiopians had finally gelled, following a battle with pirates in the Erythrean Sea. Then—at the Prince's command—Ousanas had stopped pretending he spoke only pidgin Greek. The Romans had been astonished to discover that the outlandish African was an extraordinary linguist, who spoke any number of languages fluently. Especially Greek, which was a language Ousanas treasured, for he was fond of philosophical discourse and debate—to Anastasius' great pleasure and the despair of his other companions.

Ousanas now launched into a savage elaboration of the ontological distinction between ignorance and stupidity.

"—ignorance can be fixed. Stupid is forever. Consider, fool boy, the fate of—"

"Enough," commanded Belisarius.

Ousanas clamped his jaws shut. Then:

"I was just warming to my subject," he complained sourly.

"Yes, I know. Save it for another time, Ousanas. The Kushans will not wait that long."

The general jerked his head toward the pavilion entrance.

"We have to solve this problem. Quickly."

Eon suddenly blew out his cheeks. His massive shoulders hunched.

"What do they know?" he asked. He was looking at no one in particular.

Garmat answered.

"They know that Shakuntala is here, in this tent. Tonight." The adviser squatted himself, now, and stared at his Prince from a distance of a few feet.

"That is all that they *know*," he continued. "But they are not stupid. They will also understand that she must have been with us ever since the massacre at Venandakatra's palace at Gwalior. They will understand that she did not flee with Raghunath Rao. They will understand that Rao led the Malwa on a merry chase while the Empress herself was smuggled into your entourage. And that we have hidden her ever since."

He sighed. "And, most of all, they will now understand the reason why Kungas told them to pester our women these past weeks. Pester them, but not seriously. Just enough to trigger off phony brawls with our cataphracts and sarwen. Brawls which *accidentally* mangled some spies, and led the survivors to report that our escorts are every bit as salacious as Venandakatra had been led to believe."

Garmat glanced at Belisarius, shrugged.

"As I said, the Kushans are not stupid. By now, they will have heard that the reason they were withdrawn as Shakuntala's guards was because Venandakatra feared their lustfulness. And so he replaced them with mahamimamsa. Who fell like sheep when Rao entered the palace and rescued the Empress."

The adviser stroked his beard. "So they will suspect that Belisarius engineered the entire thing from the very beginning. Although"—here he smiled—"they probably do not know that Belisarius gave Rao the very dagger which he used to carve up the torturers."

"In other words," grumbled Ousanas, "they know everything."

"Yes," stated Belisarius. "And, worst of all—it is obvious from looking at them—they know that their own commander must have been part of this scheme. In some sense, at least. They have no love for the Malwa, but they are still sworn to their service. Now they find they have been betrayed, by their own leader. If the Malwa discover the Empress now, their own lives will be forfeit."

The general took a deep breath. "Unless they immediately recapture her, and hand Shakuntala back to their overlords."

"They would have to turn over Kungas as well!" protested Eon. "The Malwa would never believe Kungas had not spotted Shakuntala."

Belisarius nodded. "Yes, I'm sure they understand that also. And that is why they hesitate."

He glanced toward the pavilion entrance again.

"They will hesitate for a while. But not for all that long. Those men are soldiers. The best of soldiers. Accustomed to hard and quick decisions. And accustomed to stern necessity, and to the realities of a bitter world. So we must somehow figure out—"

Shakuntala interrupted.

"Bring them into the pavilion. All of them. Now."

Belisarius started. Not even the Roman Emperor Justinian—not even the Empress Theodora—could match that tone of command. That incredibly *imperial* voice.

He stared at the girl. Shakuntala was very beautiful, in her exotic and dark-skinned way. But, at that moment, it was not a girl's beauty, but the beauty of an ancient statue.

And that's the key, he mused. Justinian and Theodora, for all their power, were lowborn. How many emperors of Rome, over the centuries, could trace their ancestry back to royalty more than a generation or two? None. Whereas the Satavahana dynasty which ruled Andhra—

"Great Andhra," he said aloud. "Broken Andhra, now. But even the fierce bedouin of the desert are awed by the broken sphinx."

Shakuntala stared up at him. The general scratched his chin.

"Are you certain of this course, Empress?" he asked. He glanced at the others in the pavilion. From the puzzled frowns on their faces, it was obvious that only Belisarius had discerned Shakuntala's purpose. He was not surprised. Her proposed move was bold almost beyond belief.

She nodded firmly. "There is no other course possible, Belisarius. And besides—"

She took a deep breath. Regality blazed.

"—it is the only course open to the honor of Andhra. Any other would be foulness."

She made a short, chopping gesture. "Let the Malwa rule so. *I will not.*"

The frowns surrounding the Empress and the general were deepening by the second. No others in the pavilion, it was obvious, had any understanding of what she was planning.

Belisarius smiled crookedly and bowed.

"As you command, Empress."

He turned toward the entrance. Then, struck by a thought, turned back. His smile was now very crooked. "And there is this much, also. We will learn if Rao's favorite saying is really true."

A moment later Belisarius was pulling back the flap of the pavilion. As he stooped to make his exit, he caught sight of Ousanas. The tall African was gaping. Not to Belisarius' surprise, Ousanas was the first to deduce the truth. The gape disappeared; the familiar grin erupted.

"Truly, Greeks are mad!" exclaimed the dawazz. "It is the inevitable result of too much time spent pondering on the soul."

Belisarius grinned and exited the tent. As the flap closed behind him, he heard Ousanas' next words.

"Such foolish nonsense—this business about *only the soul matters, in the end*. Idiot mysticism from a crazed Maratha bandit. No, no, it's all quite otherwise, my good people, I assure you. As Plato so clearly explained, it is the eternal and unchanging *Forms* which—"

"Ousanas—*shut up!*" barked the Prince. "What in hell is going on?"

When Belisarius reentered the pavilion, leading the Kushans, he saw that Shakuntala had taken firm command of the situation. Garmat and Eon were sitting on cushions placed to one side. Standing behind them were Ezana and Wahsi. The two sarwen were carrying their spears, but were carefully holding them in the position of formal rest. It was obvious, from their gloomy expressions, that all the Axumites thought Shakuntala's plan—agreed to by Belisarius!—was utterly insane. But events had moved too quickly for them, and they were hopelessly ensnared in her madness.

To the general's surprise, the Maratha women were not huddling in fear in a corner of the pavilion. They were kneeling in a row, on cushions placed just behind Shakuntala, who had positioned herself in the central and commanding position in the large pavilion.

Belisarius was struck by the calm composure of the Maratha girls. As much as anything, the confident serenity of those young faces, as they gazed upon their even younger Empress, brought Belisarius his own measure of confidence. He glanced at Ousanas, standing in the nearest corner of the pavilion, and saw by his faint smile that the hunter shared that confidence.

Not so many weeks ago, those girls had been slaves. Of lowborn caste and then, after the Malwa conquest of Andhra, forced into prostitution. The Roman and Axumite soldiers had purchased them in Bharakuccha, partly for the pleasure of their company, but mostly to advance Belisarius' scheme for rescuing Shakuntala.

At first, the girls had been timid. Over time, as they learned that the foreigners' brutal appearance was not matched by brutal behavior, the Maratha girls had relaxed. But, once they finally realized the full scope of the scheme into which they had been plunged, they had been practically paralyzed with terror. Until Shakuntala had rallied them, and pronounced them her new royal ladies-in-waiting, and pledged that she herself would share their fate, whatever that fate might be.

He glanced now at Dadaji Holkar. The Maratha was also seated

near the Empress, just to her left. He was still clad in the simple
loincloth of a slave, but there was nothing of the slave in his
posture and his expression. The shrewd intelligence in his face,
usually disguised by his stooped posture, was now evident for all
to see. The man positively exuded the aura of a highly placed,
trusted imperial adviser. And if the aura went poorly with the
loincloth, so much the worse for the loincloth. Indians, too, like
Romans, had a place in their culture for the ascetic sage.

Calm, confident, serene faces. The Kushans, as they filed into
the tent, caught sight of those faces and found their eyes drawn
toward them. As Shakuntala had planned, Belisarius knew. The
young Empress had marshaled all her resources, few as they were,
to project the image of a ruler rather than a refugee. It was a
fiction, but—not a sham. Not a sham at all.

By the time all the Kushans filed in, even the huge pavilion
was crowded. Then, when the cataphracts followed, Belisarius
thought the pavilion might burst at the seams.

Shakuntala took charge.

"Sit," she commanded. "All of you except Ousanas."

She looked at Ousanas. "Search the woods. Make certain there
are no spies."

The dawazz grinned. The order was utterly redundant, of course.
He had already seen to the task. But he knew Shakuntala was simply
seeking to calm the Kushans. So he obeyed instantly and without
complaint. On his way out of the pavilion, he whispered to Belisarius:
"Envy me, Roman. I, at least, will be able to breathe."

The Kushans were still standing, uncertain.

"*Sit*," commanded Shakuntala. Within three seconds, all had
obeyed. But, as they made to do so, She spoke again.

"Kungas—sit here." Shakuntala pointed imperiously to one of
two cushions placed not far from her own, diagonally to her right.
Remembering the seating arrangement in the Malwa emperor's
pavilion, Belisarius realized this was the Indian way of honoring
those close to the throne.

She pointed to the other cushion. "Kanishka—there."

The Kushan commander and his lieutenant did as she bade
them.

After all the Kushans were sitting on the carpeted floor of the
pavilion, Shakuntala gazed upon them for a long moment without
speaking. The warriors stared back at her. They knew her face well,

of course. It had been they who had rescued Shakuntala from the Ye-tai savaging the royal palace during the sack of Amaravati. They who had brought her to Venandakatra's palace at Gwalior, where she was destined to become the Malwa lord's new concubine. They who had served as her captors and guardians during the long months they waited for Venandakatra's return from his mission to Constantinople.

Yet, for all the familiarity of those months in her company, most of them were now gaping. Surprise, partly, at seeing her again in such unexpected circumstances. But, mostly, with surprise at how different she seemed. This was no captive girl—proud and defiant, true, but riddled with despair for all that. This was—*what? Or who?*

The moment was critical, Belisarius knew. There had been no time to discuss anything with her. He feared that, in her youthful uncertainty, she would make the mistake of *explaining* the situation. Of trying to *convince* the Kushans.

The Empress Shakuntala, heir of ancient Satavahana, rightful ruler of great Andhra, began to speak. And Belisarius realized he might as well have fretted over the sun rising.

"Soon I will return to Andhra," announced Shakuntala. "My purpose here is almost finished. When I return, I shall rebuild the empire of my ancestors. I shall restore its glory. I shall cast down the Mahaveda abomination and erase from human memory their mahamimamsa curs. I shall rebuild the viharas and restore the stupas. Again, I shall make Andhra the blessed center of Hindu learning and Buddhist worship."

She paused. The black-eyed Pearl of the Satavahanas, she was often called. Now, her eyes glowed like coals.

"But first, I must destroy the Malwa Empire. To this I devote my life and my sacred soul. This is my dharma, my duty, and my destiny. *I will make Malwa howl.*"

Again, a pause. The black fury in her eyes softened.

"Already, Raghunath Rao is making his way back to the Great Country. The Wind will roar across Majarashtra. He will raise a new army from the hills and the villages, and the great towns. He is the new commander of Andhra's army."

She allowed the Kushans time to digest her words. The men sitting before her were elite soldiers, hardened veterans. They knew Raghunath Rao. Like all Indians, they knew him by reputation. But, unlike most, their knowledge was more intimate. They had seen the carnage at the palace in Gwalior, after the Panther of Majarashtra had raged through it.

Shakuntala watched pride square their shoulders. She treasured that pride. She was *counting* on that pride. Yes, the Kushan soldiers knew Rao, and respected him deeply. But their pride came from the knowledge that he had respected them as well. For Rao had not tried to rescue the princess while *they* had guarded her. He had waited, until they had been replaced by—

Shakuntala watched the contempt twisting their lips. She treasured that contempt. She was *counting* on that contempt. The Kushans, today, were elite soldiers in the service of the Malwa Empire. But they were also the descendants of those fierce nomads who had erupted out of central Asia, centuries before, and had conquered all of Bactria and Sogdiana and northern India. Conquered it, ruled it—and, as they adopted civilization and the Buddhist faith, ruled it very well indeed. Until the Ye-tai came, and the Malwa, and reduced them to vassalage.

For a long moment, Shakuntala and the Kushans stared at each other. Watching, from the back of the pavilion, Belisarius was struck by the growing warmth of that mutual regard. She, and they, had spent many months in close proximity. And if, during that long and painful captivity, there had been no friendship between them, there had always been respect. A respect which, over time, had become unspoken admiration.

Now, thought Belisarius.

As if she had read his mind, Shakuntala spoke.

"Rao will raise my army. But I will need another force as well. I, too, will need to tread a dangerous path. I will need an imperial bodyguard, to protect me while I restore Andhra."

She looked away. Said, softly:

"I have given much thought to this matter. I have considered many possibilities. But, always, my thoughts return to one place, and one place only."

She looked back upon them.

"I can think of no better men to serve as my bodyguard than those who rescued me from the Ye-tai and guarded me so well during all the months at Gwalior."

Behind him, Belisarius heard Menander's shocked whisper: "My God! She's crazy!"

"Bullshit," hissed Valentinian. "She's read them perfectly."

And then Anastasius, his rumbling voice filled with philosophical satisfaction: "Never forget, lad—*only the soul matters, in the end.*"

One of the Kushans seated in the middle of the front row now spoke. Belisarius did not know the man's name, but he recognized him as a leader of the Kushan common soldiers. The equivalent of a Roman decarch.

"We must know this, princess. Did—"

"She is not a princess!" snapped one of the Maratha women kneeling behind Shakuntala. Ahilyabai was her name. "She is the Empress of Andhra!"

The Kushan soldier tightened his jaws. Shakuntala raised her hand in an abrupt gesture of command.

"Be still, Ahilyabai! My title does not matter to this man."

She leaned forward, fixing the Kushan with her black-eyed gaze. "His name is Kujulo, and I know him well. If Kujolo chooses to give me his loyalty, my title will never matter to him. Whether I sit on the throne in rebuilt Amaravati, or crouch behind the battlements of a Maratha hillfort under siege, Kujulo's sword will always come between me and Malwa."

The soldier's tight jaws relaxed. His shoulders spread wider. He stared back at the Empress for a moment and then bowed his head deeply.

"Ask what you will, Kujulo," said Shakuntala.

The Kushan soldier raised his head. Anger returned to his eyes, and he pointed to Kungas.

"We have been played for fools," he growled. "Was our commander a part of that trickery?"

Shakuntala's response was immediate. "No. This is the first time Kungas has been in my presence since you were removed as my guards at Gwalior. I have never spoken to him since that day." Her voice grew harsh. "But what is the purpose of this question, Kujulo? *You* have not been played for fools. The *Malwa* have been the ones played for fools. And not by me, but by the world's supreme trickster—the foreign General Belisarius."

All the Kushans stirred, turning their heads. Belisarius took that for his cue, and moved forward to stand before them.

"Kungas has never been a part of our plot," he said firmly. "Nor any other Kushan soldier."

He smiled, then, and the Kushans who saw that odd familiar smile suddenly understood just how crooked it truly was.

"Actually," he continued, "the trickery was needed *because* of you. There was no way for Rao to rescue the princess so long as you stood guard over her. Even for him, that task was impossible."

He paused, letting the pride of that knowledge sweep the Kushans. Like Shakuntala, he knew full well that their own self-respect was the key to winning these men.

"So I convinced Venandakatra—or so I am told; I was very drunk that night, and remember little of our conversation—that Kushans were the most depraved men walking the earth. Satyrs, the lot of them, with a particular talent for seducing young virgins."

A little laugh rippled through the Kushans.

"Apparently, my words reached receptive ears." The general scratched his chin. "I fear Lord Venandakatra is perhaps too willing to believe the worst of other men. It might be better to say, to assume that other men are shaped in his own mold."

A much louder laugh filled the pavilion. A cheerful laugh, at the folly of a great lord. A bitter laugh, for that lord was not called the Vile One by accident.

Belisarius shrugged. "The rest you know. You were unceremoniously dismissed as Shakuntala's guards, and replaced by Mahaveda priests and mahamimamsa torturers. It was they who faced the Panther of Majarashtra when he stalked through the palace."

All trace of humor vanished. Now, the Roman general's face seemed every bit as hard as the iron face of Kungas. "The dagger which the Panther used to spill the lives of those Malwa beasts came from my own country. An excellent dagger, made by our finest craftsmen. I brought it with me to India, and saw to it that it found its way into Rao's hands."

His face softened, slightly, with a trace of its usual humor returning. "The Malwa, as we planned, thought that the Empress had fled with Rao. And so they sent thousands of Rajputs beating about the countryside. But Rao was alone, and so was able to elude them. We knew the Empress would not have the skill to do so. So, as we had planned, Rao left her behind in the palace, hidden in a closet in the guest quarters. When we arrived, two days later, we hid her among Prince Eon's concubines."

He looked down at Kungas. The Kushan commander returned his stare with no expression on his face.

"Kungas knew nothing of this, no more than any of you. It is true, on the day we left Gwalior for Ranapur, I believe that he recognized the Empress as we were smuggling her into Prince Eon's howdah. I am not certain, however, for he said nothing to me nor I to him. Nor have we ever spoken on the matter since. But I believe that he did recognize her. And, for his own reasons, chose to remain silent."

Kujulo stared at his commander. "Is this true?" he demanded.

Kungas nodded. "Yes. It is exactly as the Roman says. I knew nothing about their scheme. But I did recognize Shakuntala. On the day we left Gwalior for Ranapur, just as he says."

"Why did you remain silent?" demanded Kujulo.

"That question you may not ask," replied Kungas. His tone, if possible, was even harder than his face. "You may question my actions, Kujulo, and demand an accounting of them. But you may not question *me*."

Kujulo shrank back, slightly. All the Kushans seemed to shrink.

Kungas dismissed the question with a curt chop. "Besides, it is a stupid question. Your decision tonight may be different, Kujulo. But do not pretend you don't understand my own. If you really need to ask that question, you are no kinsman of mine." His iron eyes swept the Kushans. "*Any of you.*"

A little sigh swept the pavilion. Suddenly, one of the Kushan soldiers toward the rear barked a little laugh.

"And why not?" he demanded. "I am sick of the Malwa. Sick of their arrogance, and the barks of Ye-tai dogs, and the sneers of Rajputs."

Another Kushan grunted his agreement. A third said, softly: "We are destined to die, anyway. Better to die an honored imperial bodyguard than a Malwa beast of burden."

"I'll have none of that talk," growled Kungas. "*There is no destiny.* There is only the edge of a good blade, and the skill of the man wielding it."

Quietly, at that moment, Ousanas reentered the pavilion. He was just in time to hear Kujulo's remark.

"And the brains of the man commanding the soldiers!" The Kushan laughed, then, in genuine good humor. Looking at the Empress, he nodded toward Belisarius.

"This man, I take it, is one of your allies, Empress." Kujulo paused, took a breath, made his decision.

"One of *our* allies, now." A quick, collective exhalation indicated that all the Kushan soldiers accepted the decision. Kujulo continued:

"He's a great schemer and trickster, that's for certain. But trickery will only take us so far. Is he good for anything else?"

Shakuntala reared up haughtily. In the corner of his eye, Belisarius saw his own cataphracts stiffen with anger. He began to say something, but then, seeing Ousanas saunter forward, relaxed.

"Kushan soldier very great fool," remarked the dawazz cheerfully. "Probably asks pigeons how to eat meat, and crocodiles how to fly."

The African hunter planted himself before Kujulo, gazing down at the Kushan soldier. Kujulo craned his neck, returning the gaze. Anger at Ousanas' ridicule began to cloud his face.

"Why ask this question from the Empress of Andhra?" demanded Ousanas. "What she know of such things? Better to ask the Persians who survived Mindouos."

Anger faded, replaced by interest. Kujulo glanced at Belisarius.

"He has defeated Medes?" Like all warriors from central Asia, who had clashed with the Persian empire for centuries, Kujulo held Persian heavy cavalry in deep respect.

"Routed an entire army of the bastards!" snarled Valentinian from the back of the pavilion. "Just last year!"

"You might ask the Goths for their opinion, too, while you're at it," rumbled Anastasius. "He's whipped the barbarians so many times they finally asked him to be their king. Couldn't figure out any other way to beat him." The giant Thracian yawned. "He refused. No challenge to it, he said."

Kujulo eyed the Roman general with keen interest. He had never heard of Goths, but he had faced other barbarians in battle.

"So," he mused. "We are now the imperial bodyguard of the Satavahana dynasty. With nothing but Raghunath Rao as the general of a nonexistent army and this Belisarius as an ally."

Kujulo grinned. In that wolf's grin, at that moment, centuries of civilization vanished. The warrior of the steppes shone forth.

"Pity the poor Malwa!" exclaimed one of the other Kushan soldiers.

Kujulo's grin widened still.

"Better yet," he countered, "*let us pity them not at all.*"

Chapter 11

Exactly two weeks after Belisarius arrived at the capital of Kausambi, the Malwa finally met his price. All things considered, Belisarius was pleased with himself. As treason went, he thought he had driven a hard bargain. Especially for a novice.

Nanda Lal thought so too.

"You are as bad as a horse trader," chuckled the Malwa official. His Greek was excellent. Only the slightest trace of an accent and the extreme precision of his grammar indicated that he was not a native to the language. He chuckled again. "Are you certain you are really a general?"

Belisarius nodded. "I've been a soldier my entire adult life. But I was raised in the countryside, you know. Peasants are natural born hagglers."

Nanda Lal laughed. And a very open, hearty laugh it was, too. Belisarius was impressed. He thought he had never met a better liar in his entire life than Nanda Lal. Nor one whose inner soul was so far at variance with his outer trappings.

Officially, Nanda Lal bore many titles.

He was, first, one of the *anvaya-prapta sachivya*. The phrase translated, approximately, as "acquirer of the post of minister by hereditary descent." It indicated that Nanda Lal belonged to that most exclusive of Malwa elites, those who were blood kin of the Emperor and were thus entitled to call themselves part of the Malwa dynasty. No man in the Malwa Empire who was not anvaya-prapta sachivya could hope to rise to any of the very highest official posts, military or civilian.

Second, Nanda Lal was a *Mantrin*—a high counselor—and thus sat on the Empire's central advisory body to Emperor Skandagupta, the *Mantri-parishad*. True, Nanda Lal was one of the junior members of that council—what the Malwa called a *Kumaramatya*, a "cadet-minister"—but his status was still among the most exalted in all of India.

Third, Nanda Lal occupied the specific post which the Malwa called the *Akshapatal-adhikrita*. The title roughly translated into the innocuous-sounding phrase, "the Lord Keeper of State Documents."

What he really was, was a spy. It might be better to say, *the* spy. Or, better still, the grand *spymaster*.

Nanda Lal's laugh died away. After a last, rueful shake of his head, he asked:

"So, general, tell me. What did you think? I am quite curious, really. I was only joking, you know—about the horse trader business." Another little hearty chuckle. "Only a general would have demanded a tour of inspection of our military facilities before he gave his allegiance to our cause. In addition, of course, to a fortune." Hearty chuckle. "*Another* fortune, I should say." Hearty chuckle. "That was quite nicely done, by the way, if you'll permit me saying so." Hearty chuckle. "That little casual wave. 'Oh, something simple. Like the other chest you gave me.'"

Belisarius shrugged. "It seemed the most straightforward thing to do. And I wanted to know—well, let's just say that I'm sick to death of stingy, tight-fisted emperors, who expect miracles for a handful of coins. As to your question—what did I think?—"

Before answering, Belisarius examined the room carefully. He was not looking for eavesdroppers. He had not the slightest doubt they were there. He was simply interested.

Nanda Lal's official quarters, by Malwa standards, were positively austere. And Belisarius had noted, earlier, that Nanda Lal had brewed and served the tea they were drinking with his own hands. No servants were allowed in his inner sanctum.

Capable hands, thought Belisarius, glancing at them. Like most members of the dynastic clan, Nanda Lal was heavyset. But the spymaster's squat form had none of the doughy-soft appearance of most anvaya-prapta sachivya. There was quite a bit of muscle there, Belisarius suspected. And he did not doubt that Nanda Lal's hands were good at other tasks than brewing tea. For all their immaculate, manicured perfection, they were the hands of a strangler, not a scribe.

"I was very impressed," he replied. "Especially by the scale of the cannon manufacturing, and the ammunition works. You are—*we* are—amassing a tremendous weight of firepower to throw into battle."

He fell silent, scratching his chin thoughtfully.

"But—?" queried Nanda Lal.

"You haven't given enough thought to logistics," said Belisarius forcefully. "There's an old soldier's saying, Nanda Lal: *Amateurs study tactics; professionals study logistics.* The Veda weapons, whatever their origin—and you will please notice that I do not ask—are not truly magical. Even with them, it still took you two years to recapture Ranapur. You should have done it much sooner."

Nanda Lal seemed genuinely interested, now.

"Really? Let me ask you, general—how long would it have taken you to reduce Ranapur?"

"Eight months," came the instant reply, "without cannon. With them—four months."

The Malwa official's eyes widened.

"So quickly? What did we do wrong?"

"Two things. First, as I said, your logistics are lousy. You substitute mass labor for skill and expertise. You need to develop a professional quartermaster corps, instead of—" He did not sneer, quite. "Instead of piling up tens of thousands of men on top of each other. If you were to study the Ranapur campaign, I'm sure you'd find that most of that absurd pile of provisions simply went to feed the men who amassed it."

Belisarius leaned forward in his chair. "And that leads me to my second criticism. Your armies are much too slow, and—well, I won't say *timid*, exactly. Your soldiers seem courageous enough, especially the Ye-tai and Rajputs. But they are *used* timidly."

Nanda Lal's eyes held equal amounts of interest and suspicion.

"And you would use them better?" he asked. "If we made you our high commander?"

Belisarius did not miss the veiled antagonism. Suspicion came as naturally to Nanda Lal as swimming to a fish.

The Roman general dismissed the notion with a curt flip of his hand.

"Why ask, Nanda Lal? We have already agreed that I can best

serve by returning to Rome. I will encourage Justinian's ambition to reconquer the western Mediterranean, and make sure that his armies are tied up there for years. That will clear the way for you to invade Persia without hindrance."

"And after Persia?"

Belisarius shrugged. "That is a problem for the future. When war finally erupts between Malwa and Rome, I will have to openly change allegiance. When that time comes, you will decide what position in your army to give me. I am not concerned with the question, at the moment. It is still several years away."

The suspicion faded from Nanda Lal's eyes. Abruptly, the Malwa official rose.

"I will give careful consideration to the points which you raise, general. But, for the moment, I think we can leave off this discussion."

Belisarius rose himself, stretching his limbs. Then said, with a rueful smile, "I don't suppose we're done for the day, by any chance?"

Nanda Lal's headshake was as rueful as Belisarius' smile.

"I'm afraid not. It's still early in the afternoon, general. There are at least four officials who have insisted on meeting you today. And then, this evening, we have an important social visit to make."

Belisarius cocked his eyebrow. Nanda Lal's shrug was an exquisite display of exasperation, resignation, carefully suppressed irritation. The accompanying smile exuded a sense of comradeship-in-travail.

"The Great Lady Holi—you have heard of her, perhaps?"

Belisarius shook his head.

"Ah! Well, she is the Emperor's favorite aunt. Quite a formidable woman, despite her age. For days, now, she has been demanding to meet you. She is fascinated, it seems, by all the tales concerning this mysterious foreign general."

Nanda Lal took Belisarius by the elbow and began ushering him toward the door. His smile broadened.

"Her main interest, I suspect, stems from your reputed appearance. She is immensely fond of the company of young, handsome men."

Seeing Belisarius' slight start, Nanda Lal laughed.

"Have no fear, general! The woman is almost seventy years old. And she is quite the ascetic, actually. I assure you, she just likes to look."

Nanda Lal opened the door. With his own hands, as always. No servants were allowed in *those* quarters. He followed Belisarius into the corridor beyond.

After locking the door—it was the only door in the palace, so far as Belisarius had seen, which had a lock—Nanda Lal led the way down the wide hall.

"Anyway, she has been pestering the Emperor for days. Finally, he tired of it. So, this morning, just before your arrival, he instructed me to take you to Great Lady Holi this evening, after we were finished."

Belisarius sighed. Nanda Lal grimaced.

"I understand, general. But, please, be of good cheer. We will not be there long, I assure you. A few minutes to pay our respects, a casual chat, no more."

Belisarius squared his shoulders with resignation.

"As you wish, Nanda Lal. She is in the palace?"

Nanda Lal made another rueful headshake.

"Alas, I fear not. She dislikes the palace. She claims it is too noisy and crowded. So she makes her dwelling on a barge moored in the river."

Hearty chuckle. "It is not as bad as all that! You wouldn't want to miss Great Lady Holi's barge, before you leave. It is quite a marvel, really it is. The most splendiferous barge in all creation!"

"I can't wait," muttered Belisarius. They were now passing by the main entrance to the Grand Palace. The general stopped Nanda Lal with a hand on his arm. "Give me a moment, if you would, to notify my cataphracts of our plans. There's no need for them to stand outside in that hot sun for the rest of the day."

Nanda Lal nodded graciously. Belisarius strode through the palace doors into the courtyard beyond. As always, the three cataphracts were waiting just outside the main entrance to the Grand Palace. Their horses, and that of Belisarius, were tethered nearby.

Since the first day of their arrival at Kausambi, when Belisarius had begun his protracted negotiations with the Mantri-parishad, he had ordered the cataphracts to remain outside. To have taken them with him, wherever he went in the palace, would have indicated a certain skittishness which would be quite inappropriate for a man cheerfully planning treason. And, besides, the cataphracts would have inevitably cast a pall on his negotiations. Many of the anvaya-prapta sachivya who inhabited the palace had been present in the pavilion when the lord of Ranapur and his family were executed. And those who weren't, had heard the tale. It would have been amusing, of course, to watch the highest of Malwa cringe in the presence of Valentinian. Amusing, but counter-productive.

Quickly, Belisarius sketched the situation and told his cataphracts to go back to their residence. Valentinian put up a bit of an argument, but not much. More in the nature of a formality, than anything else. They *were* supposed to be bodyguards, after all. But Belisarius insisted, and his men were happy enough to climb on their horses and return to the comfort—and shade—of their luxurious quarters.

"That's all of it, Your Majesty," said Holkar. He tied the drawstring of the bag tightly, and nestled it into a pocket of silk cloth in the small chest. Then he closed the lid of the chest and stood up. For a moment, he examined his handiwork admiringly, and then scanned the rest of the room.

Since arriving at Kausambi, the Romans and Ethiopians had been quartered in a mansion located in the imperial district of the capital. The imperial district stretched along the south bank of the Jamuna, just west of that river's junction with the mighty Ganges. The Emperor's Grand Palace anchored the eastern end of the district. The mansion lay toward the western end, not far from the flotilla of luxurious barges which served the Malwa elite as temporary residences during the summer. The waters of the Jamuna in which that fleet was anchored helped assuage the heat.

Stretching in a great arc just south of the imperial district was the heart of the Malwa weapons and munitions project, a great complex of cannon, rocket and gunpowder manufactories. The odors wafting from that complex were often obnoxious, but the Malwa elite tolerated the discomfort for the sake of security. The "Veda weapons" were the core of their power, and they kept them close at hand.

The mansion in which the foreigners had been lodged belonged to one of Skandagupta's innumerable second cousins, absent on imperial assignment in Bihar. The building was almost a small palace. There had been more than enough rooms to quarter the entire Kushan escort within its walls, in addition to the foreign envoys themselves. And, best of all, for Shakuntala and Eon, they had finally been able to spend a few nights alone.

Shakuntala, at least, had spent the nights alone in her bed. Dadaji glanced over at Tarabai, sitting on a cushion in the corner of

Shakuntala's huge bedchamber. He restrained a smile. The Maratha woman had been almost inseparable from Eon since their arrival. Today, in fact, was the first day she had resumed her duties as an imperial lady-in-waiting.

If, at least, the activity of the day could be called the duty of a chambermaid. Holkar rather doubted it. Rarely—probably never—had an imperial lady-in-waiting spent an entire day helping her Empress count a fortune.

Holkar's eyes returned to the chest whose lid he had just closed. That chest was only one of many small chests which were strewn about Shakuntala's quarters. Those chests were much smaller than the chest which stood in the center of the room. That chest, that huge chest, dazzling in its intricate carvings and adorned with gold and rubies—the colors of the Malwa dynasty—was now completely empty.

Shakuntala shook her head. She almost seemed in a daze. When she spoke, her voice was half-filled with awe.

"I can't believe it," she whispered. "There was as much in that chest as—as—"

Dadaji smiled. "As the yearly income of a prince. A *rich* prince."

The scribe stroked his jaw. "Still, it's not really that much—for an imperial warchest."

Shakuntala was still shaking her head. "How will I ever repay Belisarius?" she mused.

Dadaji's smile broadened. "Have no fear, Your Majesty. The general does not expect to be repaid with coin, only with the blows you will deliver onto Malwa. Blows which this treasure will help to finance. How did he put it? 'An empress without money is a political and military cripple. A crippled ally will not be much use to Rome.'"

Shakuntala left off shaking her head. After taking a deep breath, she sat up straight.

"He is right, of course. But—how many men do you know would turn over such a fortune to a stranger? And it wasn't just the last Malwa bribe, either."

"How many men?" asked Holkar. "Very few, Your Majesty. Very, very few." The slave laughed aloud. "And I know of only one who would do so with such glee!"

Shakuntala grinned herself, remembering Belisarius' cheerful words the previous evening, when he presented her with the chest which Nanda Lal had just bestowed on him—and half the contents of the first, the one Skandagupta gave him at Ranapur.

I like to think of it as poetic justice, the Roman general had said, smiling crookedly. Let the Malwa bribes finance Andhra's rebellion.

It had taken the entire day for Shakuntala, her Maratha women, and Holkar to repackage the coins and gems into smaller units which could be more easily transported. Most of the treasure was packed away in the many small chests. But some of it had been placed in purses which Shakuntala had distributed to all the members of her party.

The Maratha women, poor in their origins, had been absolutely stunned by her act. Each of them now carried on her person more money than their entire extended families had earned in generations of toil. Holkar glanced shrewdly at the four young women sitting in the corner. They had recovered from the shock, he thought. But if there had been any lingering doubt or hesitation in their allegiance to Shakuntala, it had now vanished. The trust of their Empress had welded them to her completely.

When Holkar's eyes returned to Shakuntala, he immediately understood the question in her face.

"There is no need, Your Majesty," he said, shaking his head. "My allegiance is still to Belisarius, even though you are my sovereign. If he wishes me to have money, he will give it to me. I cannot take it from another. And besides—" he gestured mockingly at his loincloth "—where would I hide it?"

Shakuntala began to reply, but was interrupted by a knock on the door.

Tarabai opened the door. Valentinian stepped into the room, accompanied by Eon. They walked over to Shakuntala.

"We may as well plan for an early supper," said Eon. The Prince gestured at Valentinian. "The cataphracts just arrived from the palace. Belisarius dismissed them for the rest of the day. It seems he won't be returning until late this evening. He has some social event he must attend."

The cataphract scowled. "These imperial Malwa are even worse than Greek nobility, when it comes to hobnobbing with celebrities. Bad enough he's got to waste hours with every third-rate bureaucrat in the Palace. Now, they're insisting he has to meet with old women."

Shakuntala frowned. "Old women? In the palace?"

Valentinian shook his head. "No, worse. They're dragging him off to some barge in the river to meet with one of the Emperor's elderly relatives. A great-aunt, I think."

Shakuntala grew still. Utterly still.

"What is her name?" she hissed.

Valentinian squinted at her, startled by her tone of voice.

"She's called the Great Lady Holi. Why?"

Shakuntala shot to her feet.

"She is a witch! A sorceress!"

Valentinian and Eon gaped at her. Shakuntala stamped her foot angrily.

"It is true, you fools!"

With an effort, the girl restrained herself. These were the type of men, she knew, for whom any hint of hysterics would be counterproductive.

"Believe me, Valentinian. Eon." Her voice was low and calm, but deadly serious. "My father spoke of her several times to me. His spies did not know much—it was dangerous to get near her—but they did learn enough to know that she is very powerful among the Malwa. Do not let her age deceive you. *She—is—a—witch.*"

Valentinian was the first to recover.

"I'll get the others," he said, spinning around to the door.

Less than a minute later he was back, followed by all the members of the Roman and Axumite missions. He brought Kungas also.

Eon took charge.

"We have an unexpected situation, which we need to assess."

Quickly, the Prince sketched the situation. Then, to Kungas:

"Bring Kanishka. And Kujulo, and your other two troop leaders."

Kungas disappeared. Eon waved everyone else into the room.

"All of you. Come in and sit."

In the short seconds that it took for everyone to take a seat—most of them on the floor—Kungas returned with his four chief subordinates in tow. The five Kushans entered the room but did not bother to sit.

Eon began at once.

"You've all heard—" He hesitated, casting a glance at Kungas.

"I've told them," grunted the Kushan commander.

"You've all heard about the situation," continued Eon. "It may be a false alarm. But there's enough reason to think otherwise." He took a breath. "As you know, we hoped to make our exit from India quietly. Just a peaceful diplomatic mission heading back for home. But Belisarius always warned us that things could go wrong. That's why he insisted on obtaining those horses, and the elephants."

Another breath. A deep breath.

"Well, that time may be here. We have to assume that it is."

He scanned the room. Everyone's face was grim, but not distraught. Except, possibly, for Menander. The young cataphract's face was pale from fear. Not fear for himself, but for his general.

"Do you have a plan?" asked Anastasius.

Eon shrugged. "Belisarius discussed some possible alternatives. You heard them yourself. But none of those alternatives really apply, since Belisarius himself may not be able to join us. So we'll have to improvise."

He stared at Shakuntala.

"The first thing is to make sure she gets out safely. Kungas, you and your men will escort the Empress and her women."

The Kushans nodded.

Eon glanced around the room, examining the treasure chests. "Good. You're already prepared."

Anastasius interrupted. "They'll have to take the Kushan girls, too. If the general's in a trap, we'll need to make one hell of a diversion. We won't be able to do it with the girls in tow."

"That's not a problem," stated Kungas. "We can fit them in as camp followers. No one will think it odd."

Eon nodded his head. "All right. The rest of us—except Dadaji— will be the lure. Dadaji, you'll have to go with the Empress."

Eon drove down Holkar's protest.

"You are not thinking, man! Forget your obligation to Belisarius, and remember your obligation to his purpose. The only way to get Shakuntala out of here is by subterfuge. A young noblewoman would never travel through India unaccompanied. *Someone has to pose as her husband.* It can't be one of us. Only Valentinian looks enough like an Indian, and his accent is terrible. You're the only one who could pull it off."

Holkar opened his mouth, snapped it shut. Then, grudgingly, nodded. He even recaptured his sense of humor. "With your permission, Your Majesty."

Shakuntala nodded imperiously, but there was just a little trace of a smile on her lips.

"I'll need a change of clothes," murmured Holkar. "A loincloth simply won't do." He chuckled. "How fortunate that Belisarius made me buy those clothes! Is he a fortune-teller, do you think?"

Valentinian shook his head. "No. But he does like to plan for all eventualities. Cover all the angles."

"Such mechanistic nonsense," said Ousanas cheerfully. "The truth is quite otherwise. Belisarius is a witch himself. Fortunately, he is *our* witch."

Valentinian ignored the quip. "Anything else?" he demanded.

"Yes," said Kungas. "You will need a guide." He pointed to Kujulo. "Kujulo is very familiar with the Deccan, and his Marathi is fluent. Three or four other of my men are also. Take all of them with you. You will need the added manpower, anyway. Yours will be the bloody road."

Kujulo grinned. Eon frowned.

"We can't have any hint that Kushans are involved," he protested. "That could jeopardize the Empress."

Kungas waved the protest aside. "They can disguise themselves as Ye-tai. Kujulo does an excellent imitation."

Immediately, Kujulo stooped, thrust out his lower jaw, slumped his shoulders, allowed a vacant look to enter his gaze, grunted animal noises. A little laugh swept the room.

There was no time for hesitation. Eon nodded. Then said: "Fine. That's it, then. Let's—"

"No."

The imperial tone froze everyone in the room. Eon began to glare at Shakuntala.

"We've already—"

"No."

Valentinian tried. "Your Majesty, our plans—"

"No."

Before anyone else could speak, Shakuntala said forcefully: "You are not thinking clearly. None of you."

Eon: "The general—"

"You are *especially* not thinking like the general."

Valentinian, hotly: "Of course we're thinking of him! But there's nothing—" The cataphract stopped abruptly. Shakuntala's actual words penetrated.

Her piercing black eyes, fixed upon him, held Valentinian pinned.

"Yes," she said. "You are not thinking *like* Belisarius. If *he* were faced with a sudden change in his situation, *he* would alter the situation. Add a new angle."

"What angle?" demanded Eon.

Shakuntala grinned. "We need *another* diversion. A great one! Something which can serve to signal all of us—we will be separated, remember—that the escape is on. A diversion so great it will not only help cover our own escape, but make it possible—maybe—for Belisarius himself to escape."

"I'm for it!" announced Menander. With a shrug: "Whatever it is."

Shakuntala told him what it was. When she finished, the room erupted with protests from everyone except Menander.

"I'm for it," repeated the young cataphract stubbornly.

"Fool girl is mad," muttered Ousanas. "I say it again—royalty stupid by nature."

Shakuntala overrode all protests with the simplest of arguments.

I command.

Protest, protest, protest.

I command.

Protest, protest, protest.

I command.

On the way out, Kanishka complained bitterly to his commander.

"How are we supposed to be an imperial bodyguard if the damned Empress herself—"

Kungas looked at him. As always, his face showed nothing. But there might have been just a trace of humor in his words:

"You could always go back to work for Venandakatra. *He* never took any personal risks."

Kanishka shut up.

As he and Nanda Lal walked out of the palace that evening, Belisarius found that a palanquin had already been brought up to convey them to the Great Lady Holi's barge. The palanquin was festooned with the red and gold pennants of the dynasty. The pennants alone guaranteed that all would give way to the palanquin, wherever it went in the teeming capital. But they were hardly necessary. The forty Ye-tai bodyguards who rode before the palanquin would cheerfully trample anyone so foolish as to get in the way. And the palanquin itself, toted by no less than twelve slaves, looked solid and heavy enough to crush an elephant.

"Quite an entourage," he murmured. "Does she really insist on so many bodyguards?"

Nanda Lal shook his head.

"As it happens, the Great Lady is petrified by armed strangers anywhere in the vicinity of her barge. She maintains her own special security force. She does not even trust the imperial bodyguard." The spymaster pointed to the red-and-gold uniformed Ye-tai. "Only four of these men will be allowed to remain after we arrive."

The journey to the barge was quite brief. The wharves where the Malwa empire's highest nobility maintained their pleasure barges were less than half a mile from the Grand Palace. Once they climbed out of the palanquin, Belisarius found himself almost goggling at the Great Lady Holi's barge.

As Nanda Lal had said, it was truly splendid. In its basic size and shape the barge was no different from that of all the Malwa luxury barges. About ninety feet long and thirty feet wide, the barges had a rounded and big-bellied shape. The oddest thing, to the Roman's eyes, were the double sterns, looking not unlike the sterns of two ships joined. Each stern sported a huge figurehead in the form of an animal's head. Lions, in the case of Great Lady Holi's barge.

The *splendor* was in the trimmings. Everywhere, the red and gold colors of the dynasty: The huge lion's-head figurines were covered with beaten gold. All the oarlocks were trimmed with gold. Rubies inlaid into gold plaques formed the edging of the guard rails. And on and on and on. It was amazing the boat didn't sink from the sheer weight of its decoration.

Belisarius followed Nanda Lal up the ramp which connected the barge to the wharf. The ramp debouched in a covered walkway which encircled the main cabins. Once aboard the vessel, Nanda Lal entered through a door directly opposite the ramp. A moment later, Belisarius found himself in the plush interior of the barge.

Aide's thought came like a thunderclap.

Danger.

Belisarius almost stumbled.

Why?

Link is here. I can sense it.

The facets shivered with agitation. But the general simply smiled.

At last. My enemy.

Chapter 12

At the corner of the alley, Kungas made a little motion with his hand. The Kushan soldiers following him immediately halted. Kungas edged to the corner and peeked out onto the main street.

He was not worried about being spotted. At night, the streets of Kausambi were lit by lanterns, but the Malwa were stingy in their placement. As great as was the dynasty's wealth, it was not unlimited, and the massive armament campaign forced a stretching of funds elsewhere. The elite themselves did not worry about stumbling in the dark. They were borne everywhere on slave-toted palanquins, after all. And if the slaves should stumble, and discomfit their masters, what did it matter? After the slaves were impaled, new ones would replace them. Unlike street lanterns, slaves were cheap.

Satisfied, he turned away. The ten Kushans following him clustered closely, so that they could hear his whispered words.

"Two doors. The main door, almost directly across, is guarded by three Mahaveda. Fifty feet farther down is another door. Two Ye-tai."

"That'll be the guardhouse," whispered one of the Kushans. "A full squad of Ye-tai inside."

Kungas nodded. "Bring the Empress."

Another of the soldiers glided back down the alley. A minute later he returned, with Shakuntala and her Maratha women in tow.

Watching them approach, Kungas managed not to smile, though he found it a struggle. Some of his soldiers failed completely. Two of them were grinning outright. Fortunately, they had enough sense to turn their faces away.

Never in India's history, he thought wrily, has an Empress looked like this.

Any trace of imperial regalia was gone, as if it had never existed. Shakuntala, and her ladies, were now costumed in the traditional garb of north Indian prostitutes. Their saris were not unusual, but the bright orange scarves which wrapped their waists were never worn by respectable women. And while poor women customarily walked barefoot, none but prostitutes wore those large, garish bangles attached to their ankles.

The bangles and scarves had been provided by Ahilyabai. The Maratha woman, it turned out, had kept them secreted away in her traveling pack. She had hoped never to use them again, but—who could know what life might bring? She and the other Maratha women had shown Shakuntala how to wear them.

Quickly, Kungas sketched the situation for the Empress. Shakuntala nodded.

"We will wait, then, for the signal. If it comes."

She glanced around, frowning.

"But what will we do if someone spots us in the meantime? We may be here for some time. We are still not sure if this escape will be necessary."

Kungas did smile, now. Very slightly.

"That's no problem at all, Your Majesty. In the darkness, it will simply look like a squad of soldiers entertaining themselves in an alley. No-one will think to investigate, not even Ye-tai. Soldiers get surly when they are interrupted in their sport."

Shakuntala grimaced.

"I'm getting awfully tired of that particular disguise," she muttered. But, in truth, there was no ill-humor in the remark. Watching her, Kungas thought the Empress was almost hoping the escape attempt would be necessary. She was as high-spirited as a racing horse, and whatever else, a desperate escape would at least bring relief from the endless weeks of immobility.

He turned away, partly to keep a watchful eye on the mouth of the alley. Mostly, however, he turned away because even Kungas could not suppress a grin, now.

Being the bodyguard to this Empress is going to be interesting. Like being a bodyguard for the monsoon.

✧　　　✧　　　✧

In his own alley, a half mile to the northwest, Ousanas was also finding it hard not to grin. The Ye-tai guarding the Great Lady Holi's barge were, as usual, paying no attention to their duty. All four of them were engrossed in a quiet game of chance, rolling finger bones across the wood planks of the wharf. The bones themselves made little noise beyond a clattering rattle, but the Ye-tai grunts and hisses of triumph and dismay were audible for thirty yards.

Ousanas glanced up at the barge. Two Malwa stood guard at the head of the ramp which provided access to the barge. The Malwa guards, unlike the Ye-tai on the wharf below them, were lightly armored and bore only short swords. But the grenades suspended from their belts indicated their kshatriya status.

The kshatriyas were leaning against the rail of the barge, glaring down at the Ye-tai. Again, Ousanas fought down a grin. Like anyone who chooses to keep a wild animal for a pet, the Malwa were often exasperated by the Ye-tai. But, for all their obvious displeasure at the Ye-tai behavior, the kshatriyas made no attempt to stop the gambling. No more would a man try to stop his pet hyena from gnawing on a bone.

Ousanas moved back a little farther into the alley, hiding against the overhanging branches of a large bush. He was not worried about being spotted. The Malwa dynasty also did not waste money clearing wild shrubbery from the alleys of their capital. Why should they? They did not travel through alleys.

He hefted one of his javelins, gauging the throw. He had brought two of the weapons, along with his great stabbing spear. The blades of all three had been blackened with soot.

Again, Ousanas hefted the javelin. Yes, the range was good. If it proved necessary, he would use the javelins to deal with the kshatriyas on the barge. The stabbing spear he would save for the Ye-tai.

He did not even think about the two grenades which Menander had given him. To Ousanas, the grenades were simply signaling devices. They were far too impersonal for Ye-tai.

Elsewhere, a mile to the southwest, Menander was regretting the absence of his stolen grenades. As he watched the mass of Malwa common soldiers milling around the campfires where they were cooking their evening meal, he thought that a couple of well-placed grenades would do wonders.

But he said nothing. The grenades had been the only things they had which could give the signal, if the signal proved necessary. It had been Menander himself who had made the suggestion. And besides, the young cataphract didn't want to hear another lecture from Valentinian on the virtues of cold steel.

Menander turned his head and looked to his left. Valentinian was crouched behind a tree trunk, not four feet away. The veteran met his gaze, but said nothing. Menander looked to his right. He could not see Anastasius, but he knew the cataphract was there, hidden a little further down the line of trees which bordered the Malwa army camp. Ezana and Wahsi would be hiding near him, still farther down the line. Prince Eon would be somewhere near them.

Garmat was hidden in the trees also, but the adviser was further back. Despite his protests, the old brigand had been assigned the duty of holding the horses. He and Kadphises, the Kushan soldier who would serve as their guide if they had to make an escape. Somebody had to do it, after all. There were twenty of those horses, all of them high-spirited and tense. Garmat was the best horseman among them, Ezana had pointed out forcefully, and so the duty naturally fell to him. No one had mentioned the adviser's age, of course, but Garmat's glare had shown plainly what he thought of the arrangement.

Menander did not even try to spot Kujulo and the three Kushan soldiers with him. They would also, by now, have found their own hiding place in the trees. But that hiding place would be on the opposite side of the little army base.

Gloomily, Menander studied the Malwa soldiers clustering around their campfires. Eight hundred of them, he estimated. Piss-poor soldiers, true. But they were still the enemy, and there were still eight hundred of them.

Mother of God, I hope this won't be more than an exercise. A sleepless night in the woods, at worst. False alarm. Tomorrow, Belisarius is back. No problem. Everybody has a big laugh on the subject of twitchy nerves. Soon enough, we amble out of India in comfort and ease. Back to Rome, with nary a drop of spilled blood.

To his left, watching Menander in the flickering light cast by the campfires, Valentinian saw the little interplay of emotions on the young cataphract's face. The veteran grinned.

Welcome to the club, lad. It's the First Law of the Veteran.
Fuck exciting adventures.

✧   ✧   ✧

A mile to the east, to the relief of some fifteen Kushan soldiers, Dadaji Holkar pronounced himself satisfied with the howdahs.

"About time," grumbled Kanishka.

Holkar stared him down. And quite an effective stare it was, too. Just what you might expect from a Malwa grandee, which was exactly what Holkar looked like in his new finery. The very essence of a grandee. Not anvaya-prapta sachivya, to be sure—no member of that most exclusive dynastic caste would have personally overseen the loading of his own elephants. But the Malwa Empire had a multitude of grandees, especially in Kausambi. The capital was full of officials, noblemen, bureaucrats, potentates of every stripe and variety.

Holkar turned away and strode over to the stablekeeper. That man, blessed by the same haughty stare, abased himself in a most gratifying manner. His three sons, standing just behind, copied their father faithfully.

Watching him fawn, Holkar felt enormous relief. He had been afraid he would have to murder them. And if he had been forced to order the Kushans to kill the men of the family, there would have been no choice but to slaughter the other members of the stablekeeper's household. A wife, a daughter, two daughters-in-law, and three servants.

Holkar would have done it, if necessary. But the deed would have cut to his soul. The stablekeeper was no Malwa enemy. Just a man feeding his family, by caring for the horses and elephants of those richer than he.

But there was no need. It was obvious that the disguise had passed muster perfectly. True, it was odd for such a grandee to make his departure at night, rather than in daytime. But Holkar had explained the matter satisfactorily. Urgent news. His wife's father on his death-bed.

"Fool woman," he grumbled. "She insists on an immediate departure—in the middle of the night!—and then takes hours to prepare herself."

The stablekeeper, daringly, essayed a moment of shared camaraderie.

"What can you do, lord? Women are impossible!"

For a moment, Holkar glared at the man's presumption. But, after seeing the stablekeeper cringe properly, he relented. He had intimidated the man enough, he thought. A bit of kindness, now, would seal the disguise.

"I am most satisfied with you, stablekeeper," he announced, pompously. "The elephants have been well cared for, and the howdahs which you constructed are quite to my satisfaction."

The stablekeeper bowed and scraped effusively, but Holkar was amused to see that the man's eyes never left off from watching Holkar's hand. And when the stablekeeper saw that hand dip into the very large purse suspended from Holkar's waist, his eyes positively gleamed.

"As I promised you, there would be a bonus for good work."

Holkar, watching the man's face as he deposited a small pile of coins in the stablekeeper's outstretched hand, decided he had gauged the bonus correctly.

But, just to be sure, Holkar decided to unbend a bit.

"Yes, I am very satisfied. Might I make a request? Since my wife appears to be delayed, would you be so good as to feed my men? I have mentioned to them, from my previous visits, how excellent a cook your wife is."

He dipped his hand into the purse again.

"I will pay, of course."

Within seconds, the stablekeeper's household was flurrying into action.

Watching the perfect unfolding of their plan, the scribe Dadaji Holkar smiled. Warriors, he knew, were prone to dark misgivings about any and all plans. Holkar did not sneer at those misgivings. He had been a warrior himself, in his youth. But he concluded, as he had years before, that soldiers were a gloomy lot.

One soldier, at that very moment, was not gloomy at all.

He had come to India for a number of reasons, and with several goals in mind. Many—most—of those goals he had already achieved. He had used the voyage to forge an alliance between Rome and Ethiopia. He had freed the Empress of Andhra from captivity, and thus laid the basis for another alliance with her and Raghunath Rao. (He had even, to his delight, managed to use Malwa bribes to fund the future Deccan rebellion.) He had been able to learn much concerning the new Malwa gunpowder weapons, knowledge which—combined with Aide's help—would make possible the creation of a new Roman army capable of dealing with the Malwa juggernaut.

Mainly, however, Belisarius had come to India in order to know his enemy. He was a general, and he considered good intelligence to be the most useful of all military assets. Here, too, he had accomplished much. He had seen the Malwa army in action, as well as their Ye-tai, Rajput and Kushan auxiliaries. He had been able to study the workings of Malwa society at close hand. He had even been able, to some extent, to meet and gauge the Emperor himself and many of his top military and civilian advisers.

But the one thing he had not accomplished was to meet his ultimate enemy. *Link.* The—being? creature?—who was, in some way, the origin of the newly arisen menace threatening Rome and, he thought, all of mankind. *Link.*

He was not sure, yet. But, following Nanda Lal through the plushness of the royal barge, he thought he was on the verge of achieving that goal also.

Aide, certainly, thought he was.

Yes. Link is here. I am certain of it.

Belisarius remembered the glimpses Aide had given him once before of the strange thinking machines called computers. Huge things, some of them—rows and rows of steel cabinets. Others no bigger than a small chest. Metal and glass, glowing as if by magic.

Not those. The new gods have driven cybernetics far beyond such primitive devices.

The word "cybernetics" was meaningless to Belisarius. Other words which followed were equally so. *Nanotechnology. Micro-miniaturization. Cybernetic organisms.*

They were nearing the end of the long corridor which extended down the side of the barge. Ahead of him, Belisarius saw Nanda Lal step across a raised threshhold into what appeared to be a large room.

We are almost there, he said to Aide.

He sensed the agitation of the facets. Aide's next thought was curt:

Link will be a cyborg. A cybernetic organism. It will look like a human, but will not be. There will be no soul behind the eyes.

Then, with the cool shivering which was as close as crystalline consciousness could come to fear:

If I am present in your mind, it may discover me. In the chaos at the pavilion, when I asked you to look into the Emperor's

eyes, I was certain I could disguise myself. Here—I am not certain. The facets can hide, but Aide may not be able to.

Belisarius was at the threshhold himself. He paused, as if gauging the height of the step necessary to cross the small barrier.

Dissolve yourself, then. Until you can safely reappear. You are our greatest asset. We must keep knowledge of you hidden from the enemy.

If Aide dissolves, the facets will not be able to help. This moment is very dangerous for you.

Belisarius strode across the threshhold.

My name is Belisarius. I am your general. Do as I command.

If there was any hesitation in Aide's reply, no human could have measured it.

Yes, Great One.

The salon into which Belisarius stepped was, in its own way, as phantasmagorical as the pavilion which Emperor Skandagupta had erected on a battlefield. Such incredible luxury, aboard a barge, verged on the ludicrous.

The room was large, especially for a boat, but could not be described as huge. It was perhaps thirty feet wide. Belisarius, quickly estimating the width of the barge itself, realized that the side walls of the salon were the actual hull of the barge. The planking of the hull, here on the interior, was almost completely covered—deck to ceiling—with exquisite silk tapestries. Most of the tapestries depicted scenes which were obviously mythological. Based on various tales which Dadaji had told him, he thought that one of the tapestries might be a depiction of Arjuna riding with Krishna at the battle of Kurukshetra. But he was not sure, and he did not waste time examining the tapestries carefully.

He was much more interested in the few areas of the walls which were not covered with tapestries. The salon was some forty feet in length. At three places along each wall, separated by a distance of approximately ten feet, were three-foot-square bamboo frames supporting silk mesh. The silk was dyed, in Malwa red and gold, but not otherwise decorated. Belisarius could not see through the mesh squares. But, from their slight billowing, he knew that they were the coverings for windows designed to let air into the salon.

After a moment's glance at the windows, he looked away. Ahead of him, at the far end of the salon, two women were seated on a dais which was elevated perhaps a foot above the level of the thickly carpeted deck. The chairs in which they sat could not be called thrones. They were not, quite, big enough. That aside, however, they were chairs which any emperor would be proud to call his own. The chairs were made of nothing but carved ivory, covered with a minimum of cushioning. Neither gold nor gems adorned those chairs. Such baubles would have simply degraded the intricate and marvelous carvings which embellished every square inch of their surface.

Both women were shrouded in rich saris, and both women's faces were obscured by veils. From a distance, Belisarius could discern little about them. But he thought, from the slight subtleties of their posture, that the one on his right was much older than the other.

Directly in front of the dais, kneeling, was a line of six men. Eunuchs, Belisarius suspected, from what he had learned of Malwa customs with high-born women. The men were all wearing baggy trousers tied off at the ankles. They were barefoot and barechested.

Racially, the men were of a type unfamiliar to Belisarius. Oriental, clearly, but quite unlike any of the Asiatic peoples with which Belisarius was familiar. Their skin tone was yellowish, quite unlike the brown hues of the various Indian peoples. And while Belisarius had often seen that yellowish color on the skins of steppe nomads—Ye-tai, and especially Kushans, were often that tint, or close to it—these men had none of the lean, hard-featured characteristics of Asians from the steppes. Like Kushans—though not Ye-tai, who were often called "white" Huns—these men also had a slanted look to their eyes. If anything, their epicanthic folds were even more pronounced. But their features were soft-looking, without a trace of steppe starkness. And their faces were so round as to be almost moon-shaped.

Their most striking characteristic, however, was sheer size. All of them were enormous. Belisarius estimated their height at well over six feet—closer to seven—and he thought that none of them weighed less than three hundred pounds. Some of that size was fat, true. All six of the men had bellies which bulged forward noticeably. But Belisarius did not fail to note their huge arms and their great, sloping shoulders. The muscles there, coiled beneath the fat, were like so many pythons.

Nor, of course, did the general miss the bared tulwars which each man held across his knees. Those tulwars were the biggest swords Belisarius had ever seen in his life. None but giants such as these could have possibly wielded them.

Nanda Lal, standing a few feet ahead of him, bowed deeply to the two women. He then turned to Belisarius, and, with an apologetic grimace, whispered:

"I am afraid we must search you for weapons, general. As I told you, Great Lady Holi is extremely sensitive concerning her personal safety."

Belisarius stiffened. Nanda Lal's demand was discourteous in the extreme. As the spymaster well knew, Belisarius was *already* unarmed—had been, for days. As a matter of course, he did not carry weapons with him in the presence of Malwa royalty. He had left his arms behind in the mansion that morning, as he did every day he went to the Grand Palace. The act had come naturally to him. His own emperor, Justinian, would have been apoplectic if anyone other than his bodyguards carried weapons into the imperial presence.

But he saw no point in protest. If, as Aide suspected, he was truly in the presence of Link, the Malwa paranoia was understandable.

"Of course," he said. He spread his arms, inviting Nanda Lal to search his person. Then, hearing a slight cough behind him, turned around.

Four men were standing there. Belisarius had not heard a whisper of their coming. Despite the thick carpeting, he was impressed. Quickly, he gauged them. The men were clearly of the same race as the giant eunuchs, but, unlike them, were of average size. Nor were any of them bearing those huge tulwars. Instead, each of the four men was armed with nothing Belisarius could see beyond long knives scabbarded to their waists.

Their size did not mislead the general. Belisarius thought they were probably twice as dangerous as the giant eunuchs. And he was certain—from the silent manner of their arrival even more than their sure-footed stance—that all four were expert assassins.

Still with his arms raised, he allowed the foremost of those men to search him. The assassin's search was quick and expert. When the man was finished, he stepped back and said a few phrases in a language Belisarius did not know.

Nanda Lal frowned.

"He says you are carrying a small knife. In that pouch, on your belt."

Startled, Belisarius looked down at the pouch in question. He began to reach for it, but froze when he sensed the sudden stillness in the four assassins watching him.

Belisarius turned his head toward Nanda Lal.

"I did not even think of it, Nanda Lal. It is not a weapon. It's simply a little knife I carry with me to sharpen my ink quills."

With a wry smile:

"I imagine I could kill a chicken with it, after a desperate struggle." He shrugged. "You're quite welcome to take the thing, if it makes you nervous."

Nanda Lal stared at him for a moment. Then, without taking his eyes from the general, asked the assassin a question in that same unknown tongue.

The assassin spoke a few phrases. Nanda Lal smiled.

"Never mind, general. Great Lady Holi's chief bodyguard confirms your depiction of the—ah, device."

Now the image of cordiality, Nanda Lal took Belisarius by the arm and began leading him toward the women at the far end of the salon. The spymaster leaned over and whispered:

"The bodyguard says the chicken would win."

Belisarius smiled crookedly. "He underestimates my prowess. But I'm quite certain I would carry the scars to my grave."

Ten feet from the line of kneeling eunuchs, Nanda Lal brought himself and Belisarius to a halt. Nanda Lal—Belisarius following the spymaster's example—bowed deeply, but did not prostrate himself. Two servants appeared from a small door in the corner of the room behind the seated women. The servants carried cushions, which they set on the floor just in front of Belisarius and Nanda Lal. That done, each man stepped away. They did not leave, however, but remained standing, one on either side. As he squatted down on his cushion, Belisarius gave them both a quick, searching, sidelong scrutiny.

Servants, I think. Nothing more.

A feminine voice drew his attention forward. The voice had the timber of a young woman, and it came—just as he had surmised—from the woman seated to his left.

"We are very pleased to meet you at last, General Belisarius. We have heard so much about you."

Belisarius could discern nothing of the woman's face, because of her veil. But he did not miss the sharp intelligence in that voice, lurking beneath the platitudes. Nor the fact that the Greek in which it spoke was perfect. Without a trace of an accent.

He nodded his head in acknowledgment, but said nothing.

The young woman continued.

"My name is Sati. I have the honor of being one of Emperor Skandagupta's daughters. This—" a slight gesture of the hand to the woman seated next to her "—is the Great Lady Holi. The Emperor's aunt, as I imagine you have already been told."

The Great Lady Holi's head bobbed, minutely. Beyond that, the woman was as still as a statue. The veil completely disguised her face also.

Again, Belisarius nodded.

"My aunt asked to meet you because she has heard that you desire to give your allegiance to the destiny of Malwa. And she has heard that you have proposed the most ingenious plan to further our great cause."

Belisarius decided that this last remark required a reply.

"I thank you—and her—for your kind words. I would not go so far as to describe my plan as ingenious. Though it is, I think, shrewd. The Roman Emperor Justinian is planning to invade the western Mediterranean anyway. I simply intend to encourage him in the endeavour. In that manner, without drawing suspicion upon myself, I can keep Rome's armies from interfering with your coming conquest of Persia."

He stopped, hoping that would be enough. But the Lady Sati pressed him further.

"Are you not concerned that the reunification of the Roman Empire will pose a long-term danger to Malwa?"

Belisarius shook his head, very firmly.

"No, Lady Sati. Justinian's project is sheer folly."

"You are saying that the eastern Roman Empire cannot reconquer the west?"

There was a lurking danger in that question, Belisarius sensed, though he could not tell exactly where it lay. After a slight hesitation, he decided that truth was the best option.

"I did not say that. In my opinion, the conquest is possible. In fact—" Here, another pause, but this one for calculated effect "—if you will allow me the immodesty, I am convinced that it can be done. So long as Justinian gives me the command of the enterprise. But it will be a fruitless victory."

"Why so?"

He shrugged. "We can reconquer the west, but not easily. The wars will be long and difficult. At the end, Justinian will rule over a war-ravaged west. Which he will try to administer from a bankrupted east. Rome will be larger in size, and much smaller in strength."

"Ah." That was all Lady Sati said, but Belisarius instantly knew that he had passed some kind of test.

The knowledge brought a slight relief to the tension which tightened his neck. But, a moment later, the tension returned in full force.

For the first time, Great Lady Holi spoke.

"Come closer, young man. My eyes are old and poor. I wish to see your face better."

Her Greek was also perfect, and unaccented.

Belisarius did not hesitate, not, at least, any longer than necessary to gauge the proper distance to maintain. He arose from his cross-legged position on the cushion—he, too, had learned the "lotus"—and took two steps forward. Just before the line of tulwars, he knelt on one knee, bringing his eyes approximately level to those of the old woman seated a few feet away.

The Great Lady Holi leaned forward. A hand veined with age reached up and lifted her veil. Dark eyes gazed directly into the brown eyes of Belisarius.

Empty eyes. Dark, not from color, but from the absence of anything within.

"Is it true that you plan to betray Rome?"

There was something strange about those words, he sensed dimly. An odd, penetrating quality to their tone. He could feel the words racing down pathways in his body—nerves, arteries, veins, muscle tissue, ligaments.

"Do you plan to betray Rome?"

He was giving himself away, he realized. (Dimly, vaguely, at a distance.) The—intelligence? behind those words was inhuman. It was reading his minute, involuntary reactions in a way no human could. No man alive could lie well enough to fool that—*thing*.

But it was the eyes, not the voice, which held him paralyzed. Not from fear, but horror. He knew, now, the true nature of hell. It was not fire, and damnation. It was simply—

Empty. Nothing.

As so often before in his life, it was Valentinian who saved him. Valentinian, and Anastasius, and Maurice, and countless other such veterans. Coarse men, crude men, lewd men, rude men. Brutal men, often. Even cruel men, on occasion.

But always men. Never empty, and never nothing.

General Belisarius smiled his crooked smile, and said, quite pleasantly:

"Fuck Malwa."

Then, still kneeling, drove his right bootheel straight back into the face of Nanda Lal. He was a powerful man, and it was a bootheel which had trampled battlefields underfoot. It flattened the spymaster and obliterated his nose.

Chapter 13

Belisarius used the impact to lunge upright. Ahead of him, the six eunuchs also began uncoiling. Grunting with the effort, they gathered their haunches and started to rise. The tulwars were already drawing back for the death strokes.

Belisarius ignored them. The eunuchs formed an impassable barrier—well over a ton of sword-wielding meat stood between him and any chance of killing Link. But they were much too ponderous to pose an immediate threat to his escape.

He could not hear the assassins, but he knew they were coming. Belisarius took two quick steps to his left. The servant standing there was paralyzed with shock. The general seized the man by his throat and hip, pivoted violently, and hurled him into the oncoming assassins.

The servant, wailing, piled into three of the assassins charging forward. His wail was cut short abruptly. The fourth assassin dealt with the obstacle by the simple expedient of slashing him down. As he raced toward the nearest window, Belisarius caught a glimpse of the servant's dying body, still entangling three of the assassins. The knife which ended his life, though lacking the mass of a sword, had still managed to hack halfway through the servant's neck. The edge of that blade was as razor sharp as the man who wielded it.

Belisarius reached the window. There was no time for anything but a blind plunge. He dove straight through the silk-mesh screen, fists clenched before him. The silk shredded under the impact. Belisarius sailed cleanly through the window. He found himself plunging through the night air toward the surface of the Jamuna. The assassin's hurled knife missed him by an inch. Belisarius watched the knife splash into the river. Less than a second later, he followed it in.

Ousanas rose from the shrubbery in the alley, took two quick steps, uncoiled. Quick shift, javelin from left hand to right. Uncoiled.

The sounds coming from the barge had not been loud, but they had been unmistakable. Unmistakable, at least, to men like Ousanas and the four Ye-tai gambling on the wharf. The Ye-tai were already scrambling to their feet, drawing swords.

The two Malwa kshatriyas standing guard at the top of the ramp, however, were a more sheltered breed. They, too, heard the sounds. But their only immediate response was to frown and turn away from the side of the barge. They stood still, staring at the doorway leading into the interior.

Ousanas' javelins caught them squarely between the shoulder blades. Both men were slain instantly, their spines severed. The impact sent one of the kshatriya hurtling through the doorway into the barge. The other Malwa struck the doorframe itself. There he remained. The javelin, passing a full foot through his body, pinned him like a butterfly.

The Ye-tai, though far more alert than the Malwa kshatriyas, were not alert enough. As ever, barbarous arrogance was their undoing. Heads down with the grunting exertion of their race up the ramp, the Ye-tai never noticed the two javelins sailing overhead. They were so intent on their own murderous purpose that it did not occur to them they had no monopoly on mayhem. Not, at least, until the barbarian leading the charge up the ramp spotted the dead kshatriya skewered on the doorframe.

Caution came, then, much too late. The Ye-tai stopped his charge. His three comrades piled into him from behind. For a moment, the four shouting barbarians were a confused tangle of thrashing limbs.

A moment was all Ousanas needed. He was already at the foot of the ramp. Four leaping strides, and the terrible spear began its work.

Three Ye-tai fell aside, collapsing off the ramp onto the wharf below. Two were dead before they struck the wooden planks. The third died seconds later, from the same huge wound rupturing his back.

The fourth Ye-tai had time to turn around. Time, even, for a furious swordstroke.

The great leaf-blade of the spear batted the stroke aside. Then, reversed, the iron ferrule of the spearbutt shattered the Ye-tai's knee. Reversed again, sweeping, the spear blade cut short the Ye-tai's wail of pain, passing through his throat as easily as it whistled through the air.

Ousanas sprang over the Ye-tai's slumped corpse. He was on the barge itself, now, standing at the top of the ramp. For a moment, the hunter stood still.

Listening. Listening.

Thinking.

He had heard the dull splash of a body striking the water. On the other side of the barge, the side facing the wide reach of the river and the shore two hundred yards opposite. Now, listening intently to the noises coming from within the barge—cries of fury and outrage, shouts of command—Ousanas grinned.

The general had made good his escape. His immediate escape, at least, from the barge itself.

Ousanas, briefly, pondered his options.

For a moment—very brief—he thought of waiting for Belisarius to appear. But he dismissed the idea almost instantly. He knew the general. Swimming around or under the barge to reach the nearby wharf was the obvious move for a man on the run. Naturally, therefore, Belisarius would do otherwise.

Ousanas' task, then, was not to help Belisarius escape directly. It remained, diversion.

Now, Ousanas drew a grenade. For a moment—again, very brief—he considered hurling it into the barge itself.

No. The havoc would be gratifying, but the sound of the explosion would be muffled.

Follow the plan. The main purpose of the grenades was to signal his comrades.

Ousanas turned and raced back down the ramp. A moment later, standing again on the wharf, he laid down his spear. From a small pouch at his waist, he withdrew the striking mechanism.

He even took a moment—*very* brief—to admire the clever Malwa device, before he struck the flint and lit the fuse to the first grenade.

The fuse was short. He lobbed the grenade onto the deck of the barge. Drew the second grenade. Lit the fuse. This fuse was even shorter.

The first Malwa assassin appeared in the doorway. Saw Ousanas, squealed his rage. Ousanas tossed the second grenade.

No lob, this toss. Ousanas the spear-hurler had learned his skill as a boy, hunting with rocks. The grenade split the assassin's forehead wide open. An instant later, the forehead disappeared altogether, along with the head itself and half the man's body. The explosion blew the doorway into splinters.

The second grenade erupted on the open deck. The damage here was slight. Almost all the force was directed upward, leaving only a small hole in the planking as a memento of its fury.

Other, of course, than the great sound rocketing through the night sky over Kausambi.

Ousanas picked up his spear and raced away. As he entered the mouth of the alley, running like the wind, he heard new sounds of fury behind him. Other Malwa had appeared on the deck and spotted his fleeing figure.

There would be little to see, he knew. A tall shape sprinting down an alley. As tall as a Roman general. True, the color of the shape seemed black. Meaningless. All men would appear black in that dark alley. The Malwa dynasty saw no reason to waste money lighting the alleys of their capital. They did not travel in alleys.

They will tonight, thought Ousanas gleefully. Oh, yes, they will learn many alleys tonight. I will give them a tour.

Then, only: Good luck, Belisarius.

All other thought vanished, beyond the immediacy of the hunt. The hunter was now the prey, true. But he was a great hunter, who had studied many great prey.

Swimming away from the barge, Belisarius heard the sounds of struggle behind him. He did not turn his head. To do so would have interrupted the powerful breast-strokes which sent him quietly surging into the middle of the Jamuna. But he listened, carefully, with experienced ears.

Wail of agony, cut short. Chopped short. Malwa cry of fury. Explosion, muffled; explosion, loud as a thunderclap. Malwa cries of fury. Cries of furious discovery. Cries of furious pursuit.

Belisarius was not certain, of course, but he thought he knew the identity of the man who had caused those sounds. Not certain, no. But he thought he recognized a certain signature in them. Some men, like Valentinian, had an economical signature. Others preferred more flair.

He started to grin, until a small river wave caught his mouth. He could not afford to choke, not now, so he sealed his lips and drove steadily onward through the dark water.

For all the strength of the general's limbs, his progress was slow. He was encumbered by boots and clothing, heavy with wet saturation. But he did not stop to shed them. Not yet. He had to reach the middle of the river, out of range of shore-carried lanterns. So he simply drove onward, slowly, quietly, steadily, with the patience of a veteran campaigner.

Yes, he thought he knew that man. It had never been part of any plan to have that man ready to intervene as he had. But it had never been part of any plan for Belisarius himself to be trapped. Yet, trapped he had been, and the man had intervened.

Again, he suppressed a grin, remembering something that man had once said. In the dank hold of a ship, as they plotted together against the enemy who owned that great vessel.

"Good plans are like good meat, best cooked rare. Now we can move on to discuss truly important things. Philosophy!"

Outlandish man. Bizarre man.

But never empty. Never nothing.

The sound of the grenade explosions was faint. Not so much due to their distance, as from the hubbub rising from the Malwa soldiers chattering over their evening meal. But, to the men listening for that sound, they were unmistakable.

"That's it, then," Menander heard Valentinian say. The words were spoken softly, calmly, almost serenely.

Much less serene were Valentinian's next words, hissed:

"Fuck exciting adventures."

But Menander thought the hiss was more from exertion than annoyance. Valentinian favored a very powerful bow. The arrow which that bow launched flew into the Malwa army camp with a trajectory that was almost perfectly flat. Thirty yards away, a soldier squatting over his mess tin was slammed flat to the ground, as if struck by a stampeding elephant.

Menander's first arrow caught another soldier in the huddled platoon. He too was slain instantly, if not with the same dramatic impact. Valentinian's second arrow arrived a split second later. A third Malwa went down.

A platoon eating their meal nearby received its first casualty. A bad wound, not a fatal one. A horrible wound, actually. The cruel warhead of Anastasius' arrow shredded the soldier's left shoulder. Anastasius was not an accurate archer, but his bow was even more powerful than Valentinian's.

Now, thirty yards down, more casualties. Three Malwa soldiers, slain by javelins hurtling from the nearby woods. Another volley. Two dead. One mortally injured.

Valentinian's count was now five. All dead. Menander killed another, wounded a third. Anastasius killed two.

"*Enough!*" shouted Valentinian. The cataphract turned and plunged into the darkness of the trees. Menander and Anastasius followed him. To their left, Menander could hear Prince Eon and the sarwen making their own retreat.

Within half a minute, the cataphracts reached the small clearing where Garmat and Kadphises were holding the horses. Seconds later, Eon and the sarwen lunged into the clearing.

Garmat and Kadphises, hearing them come, were already astride their horses. The others mounted quickly.

Valentinian reined his horse around, heading for a small trail leading through the woods to the southwest. Back toward the Malwa army camp. Even through the trees, they could hear the uproar coming from the Malwa soldiery.

Anastasius and Menander began to follow him. So did Eon.

Valentinian reined in his horse, glaring at the Prince.

"Stop this nonsense, Eon!" snarled Ezana. He and Wahsi, following Garmat and Kadphises, were guiding their own horses and all the remounts toward a different trail, leading southeast from the clearing. Away from the army camp.

Eon scowled, but he halted his horse. For a moment, the Prince and Valentinian stared at each other. The glare on Valentinian's face faded, replaced by a smile.

There was none of a veteran's mocking humor in that smile, however. Just the smile of a comrade.

"I thank you, Eon," said Valentinian, almost gently. "But you are being foolish. Ethiopians are infantrymen, not cavalry. This is cataphract work."

Then, he was gone. Seconds later, Anastasius and Menander vanished into the trees with him.

Eon sighed, turned his horse, and sent it trotting down the trail where the other Axumites had gone. After a moment, the young prince shrugged his thick shoulders, shedding his regrets. He urged his horse alongside Ezana.

The sarwen glanced at him, scowling. Soon enough, however, the scowl faded. And, soon after that, was replaced by a thin smile. A grim smile.

Young princes, Ezana reminded himself, needed to be bold. Even impetuous. Better that, than the alternative. Caution and cunning, shrewdness and tactics—these could be taught.

The smile widened. Still grim.

If he ever becomes the negusa nagast, thought Ezana, he may not be a wise ruler. Not wise enough, at least, for the new days of Malwa. But he will never lack courage. Not my prince.

In the alley where an Empress and her escort lay hidden, the sound of the grenade explosions was also heard. Faintly, of course, due to the distance. But not at all muffled. Kausambi was a great city, teeming with people. But, like all cities of that time, long before the invention of electric lighting, the vast majority of its residents rose and slept with the sun. For all its size, the city at night was shrouded in a quietness which would have surprised an urbanite of future centuries.

The Mahaveda and the Ye-tai standing guard before the armory heard the explosions also. The two Ye-tai looked up from their idle conversation, craning their heads in the direction of the sounds. Other than that, however, they did not move.

One of the Mahaveda, frowning, stepped forward from the overhanging archway where he stood guard with his two fellows in front of the heavy double doors of the armory's main entrance. The priest walked a few paces into the street, stopped, turned in the direction of the sounds, listened. Nervously, his fingers fluttered the short sword at his waist.

Listened. Listened.

Nothing.

Silence.

The vicinity of the wharf, of course, was very far from silent at that moment. By now, Malwa kshatriyas and Ye-tai were racing about the barge, charging up and down the wharf, plunging in a mass down an alley, shouting orders, shrieking counter-orders, bellowing commands. But those were human sounds, for all their raucous volume, far too small to carry the distance to the armory.

"Now," hissed Shakuntala.

Kungas, watching the Malwa, made a peremptory little gesture.

"Not yet," he whispered back. The Empress stiffened. Imperial *hauteur* rose instantly in her heart, and she almost barked a command. But her common sense rescued her—common sense, and the years of Raghunath Rao's hard tutoring. She bit her lip, maintaining silence. In her mind, she could hear Rao's voice:

So, fool girl. You are a genius, then? You understand tactics better than a man who has vanquished enemies on a hundred battlefields? A man so good that I could not overcome him?

Harsh voice. Mocking voice. Beloved voice.

The Mahaveda priest standing in the center of the street shrugged his shoulders, and began to walk back to his post. Farther down, the two Ye-tai guards resumed their slouching posture. The sound of the grenades had been distinct and startling. But—distant. Very distant. And nothing had followed, no sound. An accident, perhaps. No concern of theirs.

"*Now*," whispered Kungas. Shakuntala drove all thoughts of Rao from her mind. She rose and began walking forward into the street. Behind her came all four of the Maratha women.

Tarabai pushed her way past Shakuntala.

"Follow me, Your Majesty," she whispered. "Do as I do, as best you can."

Again, for an instant, royal arrogance threatened to rise. But Shakuntala's struggle against it was brief and easy this time. She had no need to call Rao to her aid. Common sense alone sufficed.

I can wear the clothing. But I don't, actually, have any idea how a prostitute acts.

She watched Tarabai's sashaying stride and tried, as best she could, to copy it. Behind her, she heard Ahilyabai's voice, rising above the muttered words of sullen Kushan soldiers.

Strident voice. Mocking voice.

"If you want charity, get a beggar's bowl!"

Shakuntala and Tarabai were halfway across the street. Before them, the Empress watched the Mahaveda priests stiffen. First, with surprise. Then, with moral outrage.

Again, behind, the angry sound of male voices. Drunken voices, speaking slurred words. Shakuntala recognized Kungas' voice among them, but could understand none of the words. Her concentration was focussed on the priests ahead of her.

She did, vaguely, hear Ahilyabai:

"Fucking bums! Seduce a stupid virgin, if you have no money! Don't come sniffing around me!"

The priests were fifteen feet away, now. Shakuntala almost laughed. The Mahaveda—faces distorted with fury—were practically cowering in the overhang of the door to the armory. They had drawn their swords, and were waving them menacingly. But it was a false menace, an empty menace. Fear of pollution held them paralyzed.

"Keep away!" cried one.

Another: "Filthy women! Unclean!"

Tarabai swayed forward, crooning:

"Oh, now, don't be like that! You look like proper men. We don't cost much."

The third Mahaveda bellowed to the Ye-tai. The two barbarians had come partway down the street to watch the spectacle. The Ye-tai were grinning from ear to ear. Even the sight of the straggling band of Kushan soldiers haggling with the whores didn't cut through their humor.

Again, the priest bellowed, waving his sword in a gesture of furious summoning. Still grinning, the two Ye-tai trotted toward them.

Shakuntala stepped forward to meet them. Tarabai was pressing the priests further back into the alcove formed by the overhang. Pressing them back, not by force of body, but by the simple fact of her tainted nearness.

Behind her, Shakuntala heard Ahilyabai's shriek of anger.

"Get away, I say! Get away! Worthless scum!" Then, fiercely: "We'll set the Ye-tai on you!" Then, crooning: "Such good men, Ye-tai."

The two Ye-tai reached the Empress. Neither one of them had even bothered to draw his sword. Still grinning, the barbarian on her left placed a hand on her shoulder.

"Come on, sweet girl," he said in thick Hindi. "Leave the poor priests alone. They're manless, anyway. Come along to our guardhouse—and bring your sisters with you. We've got ten strong Ye-tai lads there. Bored out of their skulls and with money to burn."

Smiling widely, Shakuntala turned her head aside. Shouted to Tarabai:

"Forget the stupid priests! Let's—"

She spun, drove her right fist straight into the Ye-tai's diaphragm. The barbarian grunted explosively, doubling up. His head, coming down, was met by Shakuntala's forearm strike coming up. A perfect strike—the right fist braced against left palm, a solid bar of bone sweeping around with all the force of the girl's hips and torso. A small bar, true, formed by a small bone. So the Ye-tai's jaw was not shattered. He simply dropped to his knees, half-conscious. His jaw did shatter, then, along with half of his teeth. Shakuntala's knee did for that. The barbarian slumped to the street.

The Empress had turned away before the Ye-tai hit the ground. She was beginning her strike against the other Ye-tai. Twisting aside, drawing back her leg, preparing the sidekick. Silently cursing her costume. The sari impeded the smooth flow of her leg motion.

This Ye-tai, squawking, reached for his sword.

The sword-draw ended before it began.

Shakuntala's leg fell back, limply, to her side. The Empress stared, wide-eyed. Her jaw almost dropped.

She had only seen Kungas in action once before in her life. In Amaravati, when Andhra had finally fallen and the Malwa hordes were sacking the palace. But, even then, she had not really seen. The Ye-tai astride her, tearing off her clothes and spreading her legs in preparation for rape, had obscured her vision. She had caught no more than a glimpse of a Ye-tai fist, amputated, before she had been blinded by the blood of her assailants' decapitation and butchering.

Kungas had done that work, then, just as he did it now. In less than three seconds, the Kushan commander quite literally hacked the Ye-tai to pieces.

Shakuntala shook off the moment, spun around. The Kushan soldiers, all pretense of drunkenness vanished, had lunged past Tarabai and finished the priests. Their bloody work was done by the time Shakuntala turned. The priests had not even had time to cry out more than a squeal or two. Shakuntala was not certain.

The squeals had been cut very short. But she thought, for all the carnage, that there had been little noise. Not enough, she was sure, to carry into the guardhouse down the street.

The Kushans were quick, quick. One of the soldiers was already examining the great door leading into the armory. His indifferent knee rested on the chest of a dead priest.

"Too long," he announced curtly. "Two minutes to break through this great ugly thing."

Kungas nodded, turned away. He had expected as much.

"Through the guardhouse, then," he commanded. Kungas began loping up the street toward the side-door where the two Ye-tai had been standing earlier. His men followed, with that same ground-eating lope. Quick, quick. Shakuntala was struck by the almost total absence of noise as they ran. Some of that silence was due to the soft shoes which the Kushans favored over heavy sandals. But most of it, she thought, was the product of skill and training.

Shakuntala and the Maratha women followed. More slowly, however, much more slowly. Saris complimented the female figure, but they did not lend themselves well to speedy movement. Frustrated, Shakuntala made a solemn vow to herself. In the days to come, among her many other responsibilities, she would inaugurate a radical change in feminine fashion.

She had time, in that endless shuffle up the street, to settle on a style. Pantaloons, she decided, modeled on those of Cholan dancers she had seen. More subdued, of course, and tastefully dyed, to mollify propriety and sentiment. But pantaloons, nonetheless, which did not impede a woman's legs.

She saw, ahead of her, the Kushans charge into the guardhouse. The sounds of violent battle erupted instantly. A harsh clangor of steel and fury, flesh-shredding and terror. The quiet street seemed to howl with the noise.

Cursing bitterly, she sped up her shuffle. The battle sounds reached a crescendo.

Shuffle, curse. Shuffle, curse. Shuffle, curse.

The guardhouse was still ten yards distant. The sounds coming through the open door suddenly ceased.

Finally, finally, she reached the door. Shuffled into the guardhouse.

Stopped. Very abruptly. Behind her, the Maratha women bumped into her back. Tarabai and Ahilyabai peeked over the shorter shoulders of their Empress. Gasped. Gagged.

Shakuntala did not gasp, or gag. She made no sound at all.

Hers was a fierce, fierce heart. The ferocity of that heart, in the decades to come, would be a part of the legacy which she would leave behind her. A legacy so powerful that historians of the future, with a unanimity of opinion rare to that fractious breed, would call her Shakuntala the Great. But even that heart, at that moment, quailed.

The Kushans had gone through the Ye-tai like wolves through a flock of sheep. Like werewolves.

The floor was literally awash in blood. Not a single Ye-tai, so far as she could see, was still bodily intact. The barbarians were not simply dead. Their corpses were gutted, beheaded, amputated, cloven, gashed, sliced, ribboned. The room looked like the interior of a slaughterhouse. A slaughterhouse owned and operated by the world's sloppiest, hastiest, most maniacal butcher.

Her eyes met those of Kungas across the room. The commander of her bodyguard had a few bloodstains on his tunic and light armor, but not many. He was down on one knee, wiping his sword on a Ye-tai's tunic. His face, as always, showed nothing. Neither horror, nor fury, nor even satisfaction in a job well done. So might a mask of iron, suspended on a wall of brimstone, survey damnation and hellfire.

Strangely, then, the emotion which swept through Shakuntala's soul was love. Love, and forgiveness.

Not for Kungas, but for Rao. She had never, quite—not in the innermost recesses of what was still, in some ways, a child's heart—forgiven Rao. Forgiven him, for the months she had remained in captivity before he finally rescued her. Weeks, at the end, in Venandakatra's palace at Gwalior, while she paced the battlements and halls, guarded by Kungas and his Kushans, knowing—sensing—that Rao was lurking in the forest beyond. Lurking, but never coming. Watching, but never striking.

She had cursed him, then—somewhere in that child's innermost heart—for a coward. Cursed him for his fear of Kungas.

Now, finally, the curse was repudiated. Now, finally, she understood.

Understanding brought the Empress back. The child vanished, along with its quailing heart.

"Excellent," she said. "*Very* excellent."

Kungas nodded. His men smiled. None of them, she was relieved to see, was badly hurt. Only two were binding up wounds, and those were obviously minor.

Kungas jerked his head toward a door at the far end of the guardhouse.

"That leads into the armory itself. It is not barred."

"We must hurry," said Shakuntala. She eyed the floor, trying to find a way to cross without leaving her feet soaked with blood.

Two of the Kushan soldiers—grinning, now—solved the problem in the simplest way possible. They grabbed Ye-tai corpses and dumped them on the floor, forming a corduroy road of dead flesh.

Shakuntala, never hesitating, marched across that grisly path. More gingerly, her women followed.

By the time she passed through the far door, the Kushans were already spreading through the recesses of the armory, setting a perimeter. They knew, from a prior hasty reconnaissance, that there was another guardhouse on the opposite side of the huge brick building. Now, they were searching for the door leading to that guardhouse, and keeping a watch for any Ye-tai or Mahaveda who might chance to be in the armory itself.

The armory was uninhabited. They found the door. Behind it, the Kushans heard the sounds of Ye-tai. Idle sounds, barracks sounds. The barbarians had obviously heard nothing of the lethal struggle.

The Kushans relaxed, slightly. They set a watch on the door, leaving four of their number on guard, while the remainder sped about the task which had brought them there.

Shakuntala and her women were already prying open the lids of gunpowder baskets, using knives which had once belonged to Ye-tai guards. Following them, the Kushan soldiers upended the baskets and spread granular trails throughout the armory. Soon, very soon, every stack of baskets in the armory was united by a web of gunpowder on the floor. That work done, the Kushans seized racks of rockets hanging on the wall and positioned them in and around the gunpowder baskets.

"Enough," commanded Kungas. His voice, though quiet, carried well. Instantly, his men left off their labor and hurried back to the guardhouse. Hurried through, until stymied by the slow-moving women. At Shakuntala's irritated command, the Kushans picked up all of the women—including her—and carried them into the street. Carried them, at Shakuntala's command, down the street and into the alley. Only then, at her command, did they place the women on their feet.

Shakuntala looked back. Kungas was already halfway to the alley, walking backward, spilling a trail of gunpowder from a basket in his arms. The last of the gunpowder poured out of the basket just as he reached the alley.

"Do it," commanded Shakuntala. Kungas drew out the striking mechanism, bent down, operated it. Immediately, the gunpowder began a furious, hissing burn. The sputtering flame marched its crackling way toward the armory.

"Hurry," he growled. He did not wait for Shakuntala's command. He simply scooped her up in his arms and began racing down the alley. Behind him, his men followed his lead, carrying the Maratha women in that same loping run.

Shakuntala, bouncing up and down in his arms, was filled with satisfaction. But not entirely. There was still room in her heart for another emotion.

When the armory blew, two minutes later, the Empress was caught by surprise. Her frustrated mind had been elsewhere. Thinking about pantaloons.

Chapter 14

Belisarius was now fifty yards from the barge, well into the mainstream of the Jamuna. He paused, treading water, to take his bearings. Slowly he circled, to examine his situation, beginning with the near shore.

He was safely out of range of lantern or torchlight from the wharf where Great Lady Holi's barge was moored. There was a bit of moonlight shimmering on the water, but not much. The moon was only the slimmest crescent. And, from the look of the clouds which were beginning to cover the sky, he thought there would soon be one of the downpours which were so frequent during the monsoon season. Visibility would be reduced almost to nothing, then.

All he had to fear, immediately, was being spotted from one of the oared galleys which patrolled the river. He could see several of those galleys, beating their way toward the wharf. The officers in command had obviously heard the commotion on the barge, and were coming to investigate.

Suddenly, a rocket was fired from the wharf. A signal rocket, Belisarius realized, watching the green burst in the sky when the rocket exploded, at low altitude. Another. Another.

Instantly, the galleys picked up the tempo of their oarstrokes. The officers commanding them were shouting commands. Belisarius could not make out the words, but their content was unmistakable. The galleys were converging rapidly on the wharf—and he could see new ones appearing, from all directions. Within seconds, no fewer than fourteen galleys were in sight.

He decided that he had time, finally, to shed his clothing. He needed to wait, anyway, to observe whatever search pattern the galleys would adopt.

It was the work of a minute to remove his clothing. Another minute, to remove his boots without losing them. Another minute, carefully, to make sure that the pouch carrying his small but extremely valuable pile of coins and gems was securely attached to his waist. Another minute, very carefully, to make sure the pouch containing the *jewel* was secure around his neck. A final minute, then, to tie all his clothing into a bundle, the boots at the center. Before doing so, he removed the little knife from its pouch and held it in his teeth. He might need that knife, quickly. It would be no use to him bundled away out of reach.

He finished the work by tying the sleeves of his tunic in a loop around his neck. He would be able to tow his bundle of boots and clothing without obstructing his arms. The knife in his teeth would interfere, a bit, with his breathing. But there was nowhere else to put it.

Throughout, he had been keeping a close eye on the galleys. By the time he was finished, the small fleet of warcraft were moving away from the wharf. He could hear commands being shouted, but, again, could not make out the words.

There was no need. The search pattern which the Malwa adopted was obvious. Most of the galleys began rowing along the near shore, upstream and downstream of the Great Lady Holi's barge. Soldiers in the galleys were leaning over the sides, holding lanterns aloft. A matching line of torches was being carried along the south bank of the Jamuna, in the hands of soldiers searching the shore line.

Six of the galleys, however, began rowing their way out into the river. Belisarius was most interested in these craft. After a minute, watching, he understood the logic. Two of them would remain in the center of the river, patrolling in both directions. The other four were headed for the opposite shore, spreading out as they went. The Malwa were taking no chances. Clearly, they thought Belisarius was either staying by the south bank or had already gone ashore. But they would patrol the entire river, anyway.

He decided upon the galley farthest to his right. That galley was heading for the opposite shore, and it would reach the shore farther upstream than any other.

He began swimming toward it. He maintained the same powerful breaststroke. It was a relatively slow method—Belisarius was an excellent swimmer, and was quite capable of moving more rapidly in water—but it would be fast enough. And the breaststroke had several advantages. It was almost silent; it kept his arms and legs from flashing above the surface of the water; and—with the knife in his teeth—it enabled him to breathe easily.

Fortunately, the angle was good, and so he was able to position himself where he needed to be a full half-minute before the galley swept through the area. Treading water, directly in the galley's path, he waited. As he had hoped, the Malwa soldiers aboard the galley were not holding lanterns over the bow. The lanterns were being held toward the stern. The soldiers on that galley, like all the Malwa, did not really think that Belisarius had gone anywhere but the near shore. It was that south bank of the river that the soldiers were watching, even as they headed in the opposite direction.

The galley was almost upon him. Belisarius took a deep breath and dove below the surface. For a moment, he feared that the bundle he was towing might act as a buoy, hauling him back toward the surface. But his clothing was now completely waterlogged. If anything, the bundle simply acted as a weight.

Now, swimming below the barge, down its starboard side, Belisarius encountered the first snag in his hastily-improvised plan.

He was blind as a bat. He couldn't see a thing.

He had expected visibility to be limited, of course, at nighttime. But he had thought he would be able to see enough to guide himself. What he hadn't considered, unfortunately, was the nature of the Jamuna itself.

This was no mountain stream, with clear and limpid waters. This was a great, murky, slow-moving valley river. Heavy with silt and mud. It was like swimming through a liquid coal mine.

He guided himself by sound and touch. To his left, he used the splashing oars as a boundary. To his right, stretching out his fingers, he groped for the planks of the hull.

He misgauged. Driven, probably, by an unconscious fear of his sudden blindness, he swam too shallow. His head, not his fingers, found the hull.

The impact almost stunned him. For a moment, he floundered,

before he brought himself under control. Quickly, he found the hull with his fingers.

The wood planks were racing by. He heard a sudden dimunition in the sound of the oars, as if they had passed him.

Now.

He took the knife from his teeth and thrust it upward, praying the little blade wouldn't break. The tip sank into the wood. Not far—half an inch—but enough.

Using the knife to hold himself against the hull, Belisarius desperately sought the surface. He was almost out of air.

Again, he had misgauged. He was still too far from the stern. The side of his face was pressed against the hull. He could feel the surface of the water ruffling through his hair, but could not reach it to breathe.

He jerked the knife out, let the current carry him for a split second, stabbed again. The thrust, this time, was even feebler.

It was enough, barely. The blade held. He let the current raise him up against the hull. His head broke water.

His lungs felt like they were about to burst, but he took the time for a quick upward glance before taking a breath.

Finally, something went as planned. As he had hoped, he was hidden beneath the overhang of the stern. He opened his mouth and took a slow, shuddering breath, careful to make as little sound as possible.

For a minute, he simply hung there, breathing, resting. Then he took stock of his situation.

The situation was precarious. The knife was barely holding him to the hull. It could slip out at any moment. If it did, the galley would sweep forward, leaving him cast behind in its wake. He was not worried so much at being spotted, then, but he could not afford to lose the shelter of the galley. The shelter—and the relaxation. He had no desire to make the long swim to the opposite shore on his own effort. He could make it, yes, but the effort would leave him exhausted. He could not afford exhaustion. He still had many, many hours of exertion before him. A day, at least, before he could even think to rest.

He studied the underside of the galley, looking for a solid plank to replant the knife. He did not have to worry about interfering with a rudder. The galley did not use a rudder. Few ships did, in his day, other than the craft built by north European barbarians.

Instead, the galley was steered by an oar. The oar was on the opposite side of the stern from where Belisarius was hidden. Like Romans, the Malwa hung their steering oars off the port side of the stern. Belisarius had chosen to swim down the starboard side precisely in order not to become fouled in that oar.

He heard a sudden, distant explosion. Then another.

Another. Another.

Now, a veritable barrage was rumbling across the river. The sound of the explosions had an odd, muffled quality.

Cautiously, he turned his head, raised it a bit. He could now see the nature of the activity on the shore behind him. The Malwa were casting grenades into the river. He watched several plumes of water spout from the surface.

Those grenades, he thought, could be dangerous to him.

A thought from Aide surfaced. The facets had restored their identity.

Depth-charges. Very dangerous. Water transmits concussion much better than air.

He caught a quick, gruesome image of his own body, ruptured, bleeding from a thousand internal wounds.

He shook the image off. First things first. For his immediate needs, the thunderous sound of the grenade blasts was a blessing. He jerked the knife out of the hull—paused a split-second, timing the galley's passage—and drove it upward again. The knife sank solidly into the thick plank. It—and he—were securely anchored.

That powerful knife-thrust, striking the wood, had been far from silent. But the noise was completely drowned under the cacophony of the grenade blasts—the more so since many of those blasts, now, were nearby. The Malwa soldiers on the galleys racing across the river were tossing their own grenades.

It was an absurd exercise, thought Belisarius. He did not know much about the effects of underwater explosions. But, no matter how effective concussion was in water, he did not believe the Malwa had more than a small portion of the grenades necessary to saturate the entire, vast sweep of the Jamuna.

The real problem, he knew, would come later. He could not stay hidden beneath the galley for long. At daybreak, he was sure to be spotted. And he needed to make his escape onto shore long before daybreak, anyway. He would need the hours of darkness to make his way safely out of the city.

The fact that the Malwa grenades were no immediate danger to him, therefore, brought little consolation. If they maintained that barrage, he would be in danger the moment he left the galley and began swimming toward the far shore. Unless the galley actually docked at one of the wharves—which he doubted; none of the galleys on the opposite side were doing so—he would have to swim at least thirty yards to shore. The Malwa would be scanning the shore, by then. And, even if they did not spot him, they could kill him with one of the random grenades they were casting about.

He looked up at the sky. The cloud cover was advancing rapidly. He prayed for a downpour.

The galley continued its powerful sweeping progress across the Jamuna. It had reached the middle of the river.

Belisarius prayed for a downpour.

The galley began angling upstream, west by northwest. Now, it was a hundred yards from shore, and more than two hundred yards west of Great Lady Holi's barge on the opposite bank.

Belisarius prayed for a downpour.

Once the galley was fifty yards from the north bank, the officer in command shouted new orders. The galley began to travel almost parallel to the shore, heading west. The officer brought the galley within thirty yards of the shore, but no closer.

Soon, they were three hundred yards upstream from Great Lady Holi's barge. Four hundred yards.

But the galley never came closer to shore. Thirty yards.

Belisarius cursed under his breath. He would have to make the swim. Right under the eyes of watchful soldiers, with grenades in hand.

He glanced up, one last time. The cloud cover was almost complete. Again, he prayed for a downpour.

His prayers were answered.

Not by rain, but by fire. A great, blooming, volcanic eruption shattered the sky to the southeast. The thunderclap from that eruption swept over the Jamuna, drowning the grenade blasts like raindrops under a tidal wave.

For a moment, all was still. Then, from the same area to the southeast, the first immense blast gave way to a barrage. One blast after another after another. None of them had the same intensity as the first, but, in their rolling fury, they were even more frightening. Now, too, rockets began hissing their way into the sky, at every angle and trajectory—as if they were completely unaimed. Simply firing in whatever direction they had been tumbled, by a giant's hand.

The officer in command of the galley began shouting new orders. The galley backed oars, turning away from the north bank. Turning back to the southeast, back to the wharf where Great Lady Holi's barge was rocking in the shockwave of the blasts.

Belisarius could not make out the officer's exact words—his voice, like all other sounds, was buried beneath the continuing thunder of the distant explosions. But he knew what had happened. The Malwa search of the north bank had been half-hearted to begin with. And now, with further—dramatic!—evidence that the nefarious foreign general had made his escape to the south, it was being abandoned completely.

He jerked the knife out of the hull, pushed himself away, submerged. When he raised his head, a minute later, the stern of the rapidly receding galley was barely visible in the darkness.

A minute later, Belisarius was wading ashore. Within seconds, he found cover under a low-hanging tree. There, he unrolled his bundle, wrung out his clothes and emptied his boots, dressed quickly.

As soon as he stepped out from the shelter of the tree, the sky finally broke. Within seconds, his clothing was as saturated by the downpour as it had been by the river.

Striding away, however, Belisarius was not disgruntled. Quite the contrary. He was grinning as widely as Ousanas.

For all his reputation as a brilliant strategist—a master of tactics and maneuver—Belisarius had always known that war never followed neat and predictable lines. Chaos and confusion was the very soul of the beast. The secret was to cherish the vortex, not to fear it.

Chaos was his best friend; confusion his boon companion.

He turned his head, admiring the fiery chaos to the southeast. Raised his eyes, lovingly, to the thundering confusion of the heavens.

A wondering thought came from Aide.

You are not afraid? We are all alone, now.

Belisarius sent his own mental image.

Himself, and the jewel. Soaring through the turbulence of the vortex. Catching every gust of wind, sailing high; avoiding every downdraft. Against them, flapping frantic wings and gobbling stupefied fury, came the beast called Malwa.

It looked very much like a gigantic chicken.

That very moment, on the other hand, Valentinian was cursing chaos and confusion.

The armory had exploded just as the cataphracts began their cavalry charge into the Malwa army camp.

The result was the most absurd situation Valentinian had ever encountered in his life.

He and Anastasius had timed the charge perfectly. They had allowed many minutes to elapse, after their first volley into the camp, before starting the charge. Minutes, for the Ethiopians to get a good distance along their escape route. (The Axumites would need that headstart. They were competent horsemen, to be sure; but—except for Garmat—had none of the superb cavalry skills of the cataphracts.) Minutes, for the shocked comrades of the slain Malwa soldiers to spread the alarm. Minutes, for the half-competent officers of those half-competent troops to gather around and begin shouting contradictory orders. Minutes, for chaos to turn to confusion. Minutes, to allow Kujulo and the other Kushans to race about the Malwa camp in their Ye-tai impersonation, shouting garbled news of the escape of the treacherous foreign general Belisarius.

Finally, the time came. By now, Valentinian estimated, Kujulo and the Kushans—coming from the opposite side of the encampment—would have reached the officers in command of the Malwa camp. There, in broken Hindi, interspersed with savage Ye-tai curses, they would have ordered the officers to begin a charge to the south, where the foreign general was known to be lurking.

All that was needed, to give the proof to their words, was a sudden cataphract charge on the south edge of the camp.

Valentinian gave the order. He and his two comrades plunged out of the line of trees. Their horses thundered toward the Malwa camp, some sixty yards distant. They drew their bows, fired their first volley—

The northeast sky turned to flame and thunder.

Every Malwa soldier in the camp turned, as one man, and gaped at the spectacle. They did not even notice the first three casualties in their midst. Three soldiers, hurled to the ground by arrows plunging into their backs.

They did not notice the next three casualties. Or the next three. Or the next three.

By the time Valentinian and his comrades reached the pathetic little palisade—say better, low fence—which circled the camp, they had already slain eight Malwa soldiers and badly wounded as many more.

And, for all the good it did, they might as well have been boys casting pebbles at cows. All of the Malwa soldiers were still facing away, gaping with shock at the incredible display to the north, completely oblivious to the carnage in their ranks to the south.

The cataphracts reined in their horses at the very edge of the palisade. It was no part of their plan to get tangled up with the Malwa soldiers. They simply wanted to draw their attention.

The roaring explosions continued to the north. Rockets were firing into the sky in all directions, hissing their serpentine fury at random targets.

Valentinian's curses, loud as they were, were completely buried under the uproar.

Random chaos came to the rescue. One of the rockets firing off from the exploding armory sailed directly toward the Malwa army camp. The milling soldiers watched it rise, and rise, and rise. Still heading directly toward them.

In truth, the rocket posed little danger to them. But there was something frightening about that inexorable, arching flight. This rocket—quite unlike its erratic fellows—seemed bound and determined to strike the camp head-on. Its trajectory was as straight and true as an arrow's.

The mob of soldiers began edging back. Then, almost as one, turned and began pushing their way southward. Away from the coming rocket.

Finally, the Malwa saw the cataphracts. Finally, stumbling over the littered bodies, they caught sight of their murdered comrades.

"It's about time, you stupid bastards!" cried Valentinian. He drew an arrow and slaughtered a Malwa in the first rank. Another. Another. Anastasius and Menander added their own share to the killing.

Valentinian saw a Ye-tai charge to the fore. He was about to kill him, until—he transferred his aim, slew a soldier nearby.

"It Romans!" he heard the Ye-tai cry, in crude, broken Hindi. "That Belisarius he-self! After they! Get they!"

The Ye-tai sprang over the palisade, waving his sword in a gesture of command.

"After they!" he commanded. Valentinian saw three other Ye-tai push their way through the Malwa mob, beating the common infantrymen with the flat of their blades and shouting the same simple command.

"After they! After they!"

Valentinian reined his horse around and galloped off. Anastasius and Menander followed. Seconds later, with a roar, the entire mob of Malwa soldiers was pounding in pursuit.

On his way, the cataphract sent a silent thought back. *You are one brave man, Kujulo. You crazy son-of-a-bitch! I might have killed you.*

Brave, Kujulo was. Crazy, he was not. As soon as he was satisfied that the momentum of the Malwa soldiers was irreversible, he began edging his way to the side of the charging mob. His three comrades followed his lead. A minute later, passing a small grove, Kujulo darted aside into its shelter.

Under the branches, it was almost pitch black. Kujulo had to whisper encouragement in order to guide the other Kushans to his side.

"What now?" he was asked.

Kujulo shrugged. "Now? Now we try to make our own escape."

Another complained: "This plan is too damned tricky."

Kujulo grinned. He, too, thought the plan was half-baked fancy. But he had long since made his own assessment of Ousanas.

"Fuck the plan," he said cheerfully. "I'm counting on the hunter." Then: "Let's go."

A minute later, the four Kushans exited the grove on the opposite side and began running west. They ran with a loping, ground-eating stride which they could maintain for hours.

They would need that stride. They had a rendezvous to keep. They were hunting a hunter.

The noble lady charged into the stables through the western gate, shouting angrily.

"The city has gone mad! We were attacked by dacoits!"

Startled, her husband and the stablekeeper turned away from the north gate, where they had been watching the explosions. The explosions were dying down, now. If nothing else, the pouring rain was smothering what was left of the holocaust. But there were still occasional rockets to be seen, firing off into the night sky.

The nobleman's wife stalked forward. Her fury was obvious from her stride alone. The stablekeeper was thankful that he couldn't see her face, due to the veil.

Shocked as he was by her sudden appearance, the stablekeeper still had the presence of mind to notice two things.

The man noticed the comely youthful form revealed under the sari, which rain had plastered to her body.

The *low-caste* man noticed the bloodstains spattering the tunics of her fierce-looking escort of soldiers.

The man disappeared, submerged by the reality of his caste. Like all humble men of India, outside Majarashtra and Rajputana, the last thing he wanted to see in his own domicile was heavily-armed, vicious-looking soldiers. He had been unhappy enough with the fifteen soldiers the nobleman had brought with him. Now, there were ten more of the creatures—and these, with the stains of murder still fresh on their armor and weapons.

The stablekeeper began to edge back. To the side, his wife was quietly but frenziedly driving the other members of his family into the modest house attached to the stables.

The nobleman restrained him with a hand. "Have no fear, stablekeeper," he murmured. "These are my personal retainers. Disciplined men."

He stepped forward to meet his wife. She was still spluttering her outrage.

"Be still, woman!" he commanded. "Are you injured?"

The wife fell instantly silent. The stablekeeper was impressed. Envious. He himself enjoyed no such obedience from his own spouse.

The wife shook her head, the veil rippling about her face. The gesture seemed sulky.

The nobleman turned to the man who was apparently the commander of his soldiers. "What happened?"

The soldier shrugged. "Don't know. We were halfway here when"—he gestured to the north—"something erupted. It was like a volcano. A moment later, a great band of dacoits were assaulting us." He shrugged, again. The gesture was all he needed to explain what happened next.

The stablekeeper was seized by a sudden, mad urge to laugh. He restrained it furiously. He could not imagine what would possess a band of dacoits to attack such a formidable body of soldiers. Lunatics.

But—it was a lunatic world. Not for the first time, the stable-keeper had a moment of regret that he had ever left his sane little village in Bengal. The moment was brief. Sane, that village was. Poverty-stricken, it was also. He had done well in Kausambi, for all that he hated the city.

While the nobleman took the time to inquire further as to the well-being of his wife and retainers, the stablekeeper took the time to examine the soldiers more closely.

Some breed of steppe barbarians, that much he knew. The physical appearance was quite distinct. The faces of those soldiers were akin, in their flat, slant-eyed way, to the faces of Chinese and Champa merchants he had seen occasionally in his youth, in the great Bengali port of Tamralipti. So was the yellowish tint to their skin. Even the top-knot into which the soldiers bound their hair, under the iron helmets, was half-familiar. Some Chinese favored a similar hairstyle. But no Chinese or Champa merchant ever had that lean, wolfish cast to his face.

Beyond that, the stablekeeper could not place them. Ye-tai, possibly—although they seemed less savage, for all their evident ferocity, than Ye-tai soldiers he had encountered, swaggering down the streets of Kausambi.

But he was not certain. As a Bengali, he had had little occasion to encounter barbarians from the far northwestern steppes. As a Bengali immigrant to Kausambi, the occasion had arisen. But, like all sane men, the stablekeeper had avoided such encounters like the plague.

The nobleman approached him.

"We will be going now, stablekeeper. I thank you, again, for your efficiency and good service."

The stablekeeper made so bold as to ask: "Your wife is well, I hope, noble sir?"

The nobleman smiled. "Oh, yes. Startled, no worse. I can't imagine what the dacoits were thinking." He made a small gesture toward the soldiers, who were now busy assisting the wife and her ladies into their howdahs. The gesture spoke for itself.

The stablekeeper shook his head. "Dacoits are madmen by nature."

The nobleman nodded and began to leave. An apparent sudden thought turned him back.

"I have no idea what madness has been unleashed in Kausambi tonight, stablekeeper. But, whatever it is, you would do well to close your stable for a few days."

The stablekeeper grimaced.

"The same thought has occurred to me, noble sir. The Malwa—" He paused. The nobleman, though not Malwa himself, was obviously high in their ranks. "The city soldiery will be running rampant." He shrugged. It was a bitter gesture. "But—I have a family to feed."

The expression which came to the nobleman's face, at that moment, was very odd. Very sad, it seemed to the stablekeeper. Though he could not imagine why.

"I know something of that, man," muttered the nobleman. He stepped close and reached, again, into his purse. The stablekeeper was astonished at the small pile of coins which were placed in his hand.

The nobleman's next words were spoken very softly:

"As I said, keep the stable closed. For a few days. This should make good the loss."

Now, he did turn away. Watching him stride toward the howdahs, the stablekeeper was seized by a sudden impulse.

"Noble sir!"

The nobleman stopped. The stablekeeper spoke to the back of his head.

"If I might be so bold, noble sir, may I suggest you exit the city by the Lion Gate. It is a bit out of your way, but—the soldiers there are—uh, *relaxed*, so to speak. They are poor men themselves, sir. Bengali, as it happens. Whenever I have occasion to leave the city, that is always the gate which I use. No difficulties."

The nobleman nodded. "Thank you, stablekeeper. I believe I shall take your advice."

A minute later, he and his wife were gone, along with their retinue. They made quite a little troupe, thought the stablemaster. The nobleman rode his howdah alone, in the lead elephant, as befitted his status. His wife followed in the second, accompanied by one of her maids. The three other maids followed in the last howdah. Ahead of them marched a squad of their soldiers, led by the commander. The rest of the escort followed behind. The stablemaster was impressed by the disciplined order with which the soldiers marched, ignoring the downpour. An easy, almost loping march. A ground-eating march, he thought.

He turned away from the pouring rain, made haste to close and bar the gates to the stable.

Not that they'll need to eat much ground with those mounts, he thought wrily. The most pleasant, docile little elephants I've ever seen.

Halfway across the stable, his wife emerged from the door to the adjoining house. She scurried to meet him.

"Are they gone?" she asked worriedly. Then, seeing the closed and barred gates, asked:

"Why did you shut the gates? Customers will think we are closed."

"We *are* closed, wife. And we will remain closed until that madness"—a gesture to the north—"dies away and the city is safe." Wry grimace. "As safe, at least, as it ever is for poor folk."

His wife began to protest, but the stablekeeper silenced her with the coins in his hand.

"The nobleman was very generous. We will have more than enough."

His wife argued no further. She was relieved, herself, at the prospect of hiding from the madness.

Later that night, as they prepared for bed, the stablekeeper said to his wife:

"Should anyone inquire about the nobleman, in the future, say nothing."

His wife turned a startled face to him.

"Why?"

The stablekeeper glared. "Just do as I say! For once, woman, obey your husband!"

His wife shrugged her thick shoulders with irritation, but she nodded. (Not so much from obedience, as simple practicality. Poor men are known, now and then, to speak freely to the authorities. Poor women, almost never.)

Much later that night, sleepless, the stablekeeper arose from his bed. He moved softly to the small window and opened the shutter. Just a bit—there was no glass in that modest frame to keep out the weather.

He stood there, for a time, staring to the east. There was nothing to see, beyond the blackness of the night and the glimmering of the rain.

When he returned to his bed, he fell asleep quickly, easily. Resolution often has that effect.

Chapter 15

After an hour, Belisarius finally found what he was looking for.

It had been a thoroughly frustrating hour. On the one hand, he had found plenty of lone soldiers. But all of them had been common Malwa troops, shirking their duty by hiding in alleys and out-of-the-way nooks and crannies of the city. None of these men had been big enough for their uniforms to fit him. Nor, for that matter, did he think he could pass himself off as an Indian from the Gangetic plain.

Ye-tai was what he wanted. The Ye-tai, in the west, were often called White Huns. The word "white," actually, was misleading. The Ye-tai were not "white" in the sense that Goths or Franks were. The complexion of Ye-tai was not really much different than that of any other Asian steppe-dwellers. But their facial features were much closer to the western norm than were those of Huns proper, or, for that matter, Kushans. And, since Belisarius himself was dark-complected for a Thracian—as dark as an Armenian—he thought he could pass himself off as Ye-tai well enough. Especially since he could speak the language fluently.

Ye-tai tended to be big, too. He was quite sure he could find one whose size matched his own.

Ye-tai he found aplenty. Big Ye-tai, as well. But the Ye-tai always traveled in squads, and they tended to be much more alert than common troops.

Fortunately for him, the alertness of the Ye-tai was directed inward rather than outward—toward the common soldiers they were rounding up and driving into the streets. Scouring the streets

566

and alleys was beneath the dignity of Ye-tai. That was dog work, for common troops. Their job was to whip the dogs.

At first, as he watched the massive search operation which began unfolding in the capital, Belisarius was concerned that he would be spotted before he could make his escape from Kausambi. But, soon enough, his fears ebbed. After a half an hour, in fact—a half hour spent darting from one alley to another, heading west by a circuitous route—Belisarius decided that the whole situation was almost comical.

The explosion of the armory had roused every soldier in the Malwa capital, of every type and variety. And since there were a huge number of troops stationed in Kausambi, the streets of the city were soon thronged with a mass of soldiers. But the soldiers were utterly confused, and largely leaderless. Leaderless, not from lack of officers, but because the officers themselves had little notion what, exactly, they were supposed to do. But they didn't want to seem to be doing nothing—especially under the hard eyes of Ye-tai—so the officers sent their men scurrying about aimlessly. Soon enough, the masses of troops charging and counter-charging about the city had become so hopelessly intermingled that any semblance of disciplined formation vanished.

Watching the scene, Belisarius realized that he was witnessing one of the military weaknesses of the Malwa Empire. The Malwa, because of their social and political structure, had no real elite shock troops. The Malwa kshatriya, who had a monopoly of the gunpowder weapons, functioned more as privileged artillery units than elite soldiers. The Ye-tai, for all their martial prowess, were not really an elite corps either. Their position in the Malwa army was essentially that of security battalions overseeing the common troops, rather than a spearhead. And the Rajputs, or Kushans—who could easily have served the Malwa as elite troops—were too distrusted.

The end result was that the Malwa had no body of soldiers equivalent to his own Thracian bucellarii. And for the task of hunting down a foreign fugitive in the streets of a great city like Kausambi—especially at night, in pouring rain—a relatively small body of disciplined, seasoned men would have done much better than the hordes of common troops whom the Malwa had sent floundering into action.

So, with relatively little difficulty, Belisarius managed to get almost to the outskirts of Kausambi within that first hour. Three times, during the course of his journey, he encountered platoons of Malwa soldiers. Each time, he handled the situation by the simple expedient of commanding them to search a different alley.

The Malwa troops, hearing authoritative words from an authoritative figure, never thought to question his right to issue the orders. True, they did not recognize his uniform. But, between the darkness and the rainstorm, it was hard to make out the details of uniforms anyway. Every soldier in the streets of Kausambi that night looked more like a half-drowned rat than anything else. And besides, the Malwa empire was a gigantic conglomeration of subject nations and peoples. No doubt the man was an officer of some kind. His Hindi was fluent—better than that of the soldiers in two of those platoons, in fact—and only an officer would conduct himself in that arrogant, overbearing manner. Malwa troops had long since been hammered into obedience, and they reacted to Belisarius like well-trained nails.

Then, finally, he found his lone Ye-tai. Hiding in some shrubbery near the mouth of an alley, Belisarius watched a squad of Ye-tai hounding a mob of soldiers down one of the large streets which formed a perimeter for the outskirts of Kausambi. As they passed the alley, one of the barbarians split off from his comrades and stepped into it. Belisarius drew back further into the shadows, until, watching the man, he realized that his moment had arrived. The Ye-tai was big—big enough, at least—and, best of all, he was about to provide Belisarius with the perfect opportunity. The Ye-tai moved ten feet into the alley, turned to face one of the mudbrick hovels which formed the alley's walls, and began preparing to urinate.

The operation took a bit of time, since the Ye-tai had to unlace his armor as well as undo his breeches. Belisarius waited until the Ye-tai finally began to urinate. Then he lunged out of the shrubbery and drove the barbarian face first into the wall of the hovel. The Ye-tai, stunned, bounced back from the wall. Belisarius hammered his fist into the man's kidney, once, twice, thrice. Moaning, the Ye-tai fell to his knees. Belisarius drew his knife, cut the strap holding the barbarian's helmet, cuffed the helmet aside. Then, dropping his knife, he seized the Ye-tai by his hair and slammed his skull into the wall. Once, twice, thrice.

Quickly, he glanced at the alley mouth. Belisarius gave silent thanks, again, for the darkness and the monsoon downpour. The Ye-tai's comrades had heard and seen nothing. After returning the knife to its sheath, and placing the helmet on his own head, Belisarius hoisted the unconscious barbarian over his shoulder and moved quickly back down the alley.

Thirty yards down, well out of sight, he set the man down and begin stripping his uniform. Within five minutes, the barbarian was as naked as the day he was born, and Belisarius was the perfect image of a Ye-tai.

Now, he hesitated, facing a quandary.

The quandary was not whether to kill the Ye-tai. That was no quandary at all. As soon as he removed the barbarian's clothing, and, thereby, any danger of leaving tell-tale bloodstains, Belisarius drew his knife. He plunged the sharp little blade into the back of the man's neck and, with surgical precision, severed the spinal cord.

The quandary was what to do with the body. Belisarius dragged it to the side of the alley and began stuffing it under some shrubbery. He was not happy with that solution, since the body would surely be found soon after daybreak, but—

He stopped, examining the mudbrick wall. It was not, he suddenly realized, the wall of a house. It was a wall sealing off one of the tiny backyard garden plots with which most of Kausambi's poor supplemented their wretched diet.

He glanced around, gauging the area. He was in one of the many slums of the city.

Decision came instantly. He hoisted the body over his head and sent it sprawling across the wall. A split second after he heard the body's wet thump in the yard on the other side, he sent his own Roman uniform after it. Then he began striding down the alley, marching with the open, arrogant bearing of a Ye-tai.

He was taking a gamble, but he thought the odds favored him. He was quite sure that the residents of that humble little house—shack, say better—had heard the commotion. By the time he reached the end of the alley, they would probably already be examining the grisly—and most unwelcome—addition to their garden.

What would they do? Alert the authorities?

Possibly. In a rich neighborhood, they would certainly do so.

But in this neighborhood, he thought not. Poor people in most lands—certainly in Malwa India—knew quite well that the authorities were given to quick solutions to unwelcome problems.

Found a dead man in your own back yard? Why'd you kill him, you stinking swine? Robbed him, didn't you? You deny it? Ha! We'll beat the truth out of you.

No, Belisarius thought that by sunrise the Ye-tai's body would have disappeared, along with the Roman uniform. The uniform, cut up, could serve a poor household in any number of ways. The body? Fertilizer for the garden.

He wished that unknown family a good crop, and went on his way.

The three cataphracts thundered down the road leading due south from Kausambi. Valentinian was in the lead, followed by Anastasius, with Menander bringing up the rear.

The young cataphract was more terrified than he'd ever been in his life.

"Slow down, Valentinian! Damn you—*slow down!*"

It was no use. The driving rain hammered his shouts into the mud.

At least the mud might keep us from breaking our necks, after we spill the horses, thought Menander sourly.

Valentinian was setting an insane pace. He was driving his horse at a full gallop, down an unknown road, in pitch dark, into a rain coming down so heavily it was impossible even to keep one's eyes open for more than a few seconds at a time.

Oh, yes—and without stirrups.

Yet, somehow, they survived. Without spilling the horses or falling off their saddles.

They were past the guardhouse before they even saw it. By the time they managed to rein in the horses, and turn them around, the Ethiopians were already there.

"Are you mad?" demanded Garmat.

Valentinian shrugged. "We were short of time." He pointed with his face toward the guardhouse.

"Are they taken care of?"

"Be serious," growled Wahsi. "We got here half an hour ago."

Eon, Ezana and Kadphises brought up the extra horses.

"We'd better switch mounts," said Anastasius. "We've pretty well winded these."

"Winded me, too," grumbled Menander. "Valentinian, you are fucking crazy."

The veteran's grin was as sharp and narrow as a weasel's. "You survived, didn't you? We're cataphracts, boy. *Cavalrymen.*"

As the cataphracts switched to new horses, Wahsi stated very forcefully: "We are *not* cavalrymen. So let us maintain a rational pace."

"Won't matter," said Kadphises. "We're cutting into the forest a half mile down. We'll have to walk our horses through that trail. If you can call it a trail."

"You *do* know where we're going, I hope?" said Valentinian.

The Kushan's grin was every bit as feral as Valentinian's. "I will not tell you how to ride a horse. Do not tell me how to find a trail."

He was as good as his word. Five minutes later, the party of eight men and twenty horses turned off the road and entered into the forest. At first, Menander was relieved. As Kadphises had said, it was impossible to move down that trail at any pace faster than a horse could walk.

Walk, *slowly.* Menander had thought it was too dark to see, before. Now, he was essentially blind. The thick, overhanging branches, combined with the overcast night sky, turned the forest into a good imitation of a leafy underground mine. Without lanterns.

The only good thing, as far as he could tell, was that the tree canopy was so dense that it sheltered them—more or less—from the downpour.

Menander was not worried about falling off his horse. They were moving at the pace of an elderly woman. Nor, after a time, was he concerned that the horse might trip. The trail, though narrow, did not seem to be littered with obstacles.

He was simply worried that they would get lost. And, in addition, that they were making such poor time that their Malwa pursuers would catch up with them—even with the tremendous head start that Valentinian's insane ride had given them.

But, when he stated those concerns to the broad back of Anastasius ahead of him, the veteran was unconcerned.

"First, lad, don't worry about getting lost. The Kushan seems to know his way. Don't ask me how—I can't see a damn thing, either—but he does. And as for the other—*be serious.* When the

Malwa get to the guardhouse and find the dead guards, they'll assume we continued on the road south. They'll never spot this little trail to the side. They'll charge right past it and keep going."

"We didn't cover our tracks."

Anastasius laughed scornfully.

"What tracks?" he demanded. "This downpour—this fucking Noah's flood—will wash away any tracks in less than a minute."

Menander was still unconvinced, but he fell silent. And then, half an hour later, when they finally emerged from the forest, admitted that his fears had been foolish.

Admitted, at least, to himself. He said nothing to Anastasius, and ignored with dignity the veteran's dimly-seen smile of vindication.

Once they emerged from the forest, they found themselves on another dirt road. (Mud road, rather.) They reversed directions completely, now, and headed north. After a mile, perhaps less, the road curved and began heading due west. Menander's fears resurfaced—new ones; he seemed to have a Pandora's box of them that night.

"Does Kadphises know where the hell we're going?"

The rain had eased off considerably. Enough that Menander's words carried forward. Kadphises' reply came immediately. The prologue to that reply was quick, curt, and very obscene. Thereafter, relenting, the Kushan deigned to explain.

"This road does not connect to the other until a small town fifty miles to the south. Nor does it go to Kausambi. It circles two sides of a swamp to our left, and from here will go due west for more than twenty miles. Before then, however, we will have turned south, again, on yet another road. By now, the Malwa will have no idea where we are. And, best of all, this road is not guarded. It is a peasants' road, only, not a merchant's route."

"Where will we meet Ousanas, and the other Kushans?" asked Eon.

Kadphises' shrug could barely be seen in the darkness.

"That is up to them, Prince. Kujulo knows what road we are taking. If he can find your hunter—or your hunter finds him—they will track us down. If your hunter is as good as you claim."

Eon's only reply was a grunt of satisfaction.

In the event, Ousanas did not have to track them down. Shortly after daybreak, many miles down the new road heading south, they came upon Ousanas. The hunter, along with Kujulo and the three other Kushans, were waiting for them by the side of road. Fast asleep—even reasonably dry, under the semi-shelter of a long-abandoned hut—except for one Kushan standing guard.

Valentinian was exceedingly disgruntled. Especially after he spotted the basket of food, with very little food left in it.

"You had time to *eat*, too?" he demanded crossly, climbing down from his horse.

Ousanas sat up, stretched his arms, grinned.

"Great cavalrymen move very slow," he announced. "I be shocked. Shocked. All illusions vanished."

Kujulo smiled. "You should try traveling with this one. Really, you should. He was already waiting for us when we made our break from the army camp. How the hell he got there so fast from the river, I'll never know. Especially with two baskets of food."

"*Two* baskets?" whined Valentinian.

"We saved one for you," said another of the Kushans, chuckling. "Ousanas insisted. He said if we didn't, Anastasius would never argue philosophy with him again."

"Certainly wouldn't," agreed the giant. "Except for simple precepts from Democritus. All matter can be reduced to atoms. Including Ousanas."

The cataphracts and the Ethiopians tore into the food. After their initial hunger was sated, Menander's youthful curiosity arose.

"What *is* this stuff?" he asked.

"Some of it is dried fish," replied Kujulo. "The rest is something else."

Menander, thinking it over, decided that he would leave it at that. The stuff didn't actually taste that bad, after all, even if he suspected "the rest" had once had far too many legs to suit a proper Thracian.

By the time the food was gone, the rain had finally stopped. Kujulo and another Kushan went into the woods and brought out their horses.

"Where'd you get the horses?" asked Valentinian.

Kujulo pointed to Ousanas.

"He had 'em. Don't ask me where he got them because I have no idea. I'm afraid to ask."

Valentinian shared no such fear.

"Where'd you get 'em?" he demanded again. Then, watching the ease with which Ousanas swung up into his saddle, complained: "I thought you didn't like horses."

"I detest the creatures," replied Ousanas cheerfully. "Horses, on the other hand, are very fond of me."

The hunter led off, to the south, called over his shoulder:

"This shows excellent judgement by both parties, don't you think?"

Somehow, in the hours that followed, as the band of soldiers cantered their way toward the far distant Deccan, Menander was not surprised to discover that Ousanas was as good a horseman as he'd ever seen.

At daybreak that same day, the captain of the Bengali detachment which guarded—so to speak; "huddled about" would be more accurate—the Lion Gate of Kausambi, waved a casual farewell to the nobleman and his retinue. After the last of the nobleman's escort and their women camp-followers had paraded past, down the eastern road to Pataliputra, he ordered the gate shut.

"Fine man," he said approvingly. "Wish all those Malwa snots were like him."

"How much?" asked his lieutenant.

The commander did not dissemble. His lieutenant was also his younger brother. Most of his detachment, in fact, was related to him. He extended his hand, palm open.

His brother's eyes widened.

"Send for our wives," commanded the captain. "Today, we will feast."

That same moment, Belisarius stalked through the Panther Gate, one of the western gates of Kausambi. The gate was poorly named, in truth. Small and ramshackle as it was, the "Alley Cat Gate" would have been a more suitable cognomen.

But, of course, that was why he had picked it.

On the way through, he terrorized another Malwa soldier. The man scuttled frantically away from the barbarian's threatening fist. He had no desire to end up like his sergeant, sprawled senseless on the ground.

Once he was through the gate, Belisarius turned, planted his fists on his hips, and bellowed:

"Next time, you dogs, when a Ye-tai tells you to open the gate, do so without argument!" He drew his sword. "Or next time I'll use this!"

He thrust the sword back in the scabbard, turned, and marched away. Behind him, he heard the gate screeching loudly. The hinges hadn't been greased properly, and the Malwa troops were in a great hurry to close it. A tearing great hurry.

The road Belisarius was taking was one of the newly refurbished roads which the Malwa had been constructing. This was no muddy peasant path. The road was fifteen feet wide, raised above the plain, properly leveed and paved with stone. It was a road even Romans would have been proud to call their own.

The road ran parallel to the north bank of the Jamuna River, a few miles to the south. The road led west by northwest until it reached the city of Mathura, some three hundred miles away. Belisarius had no intention of traveling as far as Mathura, however. Just north of Gwalior, the Chambal River branched to the southwest. About a hundred miles up the Chambal, in turn, the Banas River branched directly west. There were roads paralleling those rivers which would take him all the way to the ancient city of Ajmer, at the very northern tip of the Aravalli Mountains.

"Ajmer," he mused. "From there, I can either go south or west. But—I wonder . . ."

Again, he summoned Aide to his assistance. Aide had already provided him with all the geographic information he needed. Now—

Tell me about the royal couriers.

The rain had finally stopped. As he strode along, openly, right down the middle of the road, Belisarius continued the discussion with Aide until he reached his conclusions. Thereafter, he simply admired the dawn.

Might even get a rainbow, he thought cheerfully.

Chapter 16
DARAS
Summer 530 AD

Theodora arrived at the estate toward the end of summer. Her appearance came as a surprise—not the timing, but the manner of it.

"She's worried," muttered Antonina to Maurice, watching the Empress ride in to the courtyard. "Badly worried. I can think of nothing else that would make Theodora travel like this."

Maurice nodded. "I think you're right. I didn't even know she could ride a horse."

Antonina pressed her lips together. "You call *that* riding a horse?"

"Don't snicker, girl," whispered Maurice. "You didn't look any better, the first time you climbed into a saddle. At least Theodora doesn't look like she's going to fall off from a hangover. Not the way she's clutching the pommel."

Antonina maintained her dignity by ignoring that last remark altogether. She stepped forward to greet the Empress, extending her arms in a welcoming gesture.

Theodora managed to bring her horse to a halt, in a manner of speaking. The twenty cataphracts escorting her drew up a considerable distance behind. Respect for royalty, partly. Respect for a surly horse at the end of its patience, in the main.

"How do you get off this foul beast?" hissed the Empress.

"Allow me, Your Majesty," said Maurice. The hecatontarch came forward with a stool in his hand. He quieted the horse with a firm hand and a few gentle words. Then, after placing the stool, assisted the Empress in clambering down to safety.

Once on the ground, Theodora brushed herself off angrily.

"Gods—what a stink! Not you, Maurice. The filthy horse." The Empress glowered at her former mount. "They eat these things during sieges, I've heard."

Maurice nodded.

"Well, that's something to look forward to," she muttered.

Antonina took her by the arm and began leading the Empress into the villa. As she limped along, Theodora snarled:

"Not that there'll be many sieges in *this* coming war, the way things are going."

Antonina hesitated, then asked:

"That bad?"

"Worse," growled the Empress. "I tell you, Antonina, it shakes my faith sometimes, to think that man is created in God's image. Is it possible that the Almighty is actually a cretin? The evidence of his handiwork would suggest as much."

Antonina sighed.

"I take it Justinian is not listening to your warnings?"

Growl. "In *His* image, no less. A huge Justinian in the sky."

Growl. "Think of a gigantic babbling idiot."

Growl. "Creation was His drool."

Later, after a lavish meal, Theodora's spirits improved.

She lifted her wine cup in salutation.

"I congratulate you, Maurice," she said. "You have succeeded in bringing the provincial tractator to the brink of death. By apoplexy."

Maurice grunted. "Still peeved, is he, about the taxes?"

"He complained to me for hours, from the moment I got off the ship. This large estate represents quite a bit for him in the way of lost income, you know. Mostly, though, he's agitated about the tax collectors."

Maurice said nothing beyond a noncommittal: "Your Majesty."

Smiling, the Empress shook her head.

"You really shouldn't have beaten them quite so badly. They were only doing their job, after all."

"They were not!" snapped Antonina. "This estate is legally exempt from the general indiction, and they know it perfectly well!"

"So it is," agreed Cassian. "*Res privata*, technically. Part of—"

Theodora waved him down.

"Please, Bishop! Since when has a provincial tractator cared about the picayune details of an estate's legal tax status? Squeeze, squeeze, squeeze. Let them complain to Constantinople. By the time the bureaucrats get around to ruling on the matter, everyone'll be dead of old age anyhow."

Maurice nodded sagely. "Quite nicely put, Your Majesty. Those are indeed the usual tactics of tractators."

He took a sip of his wine. "Excellent tactics. Provided you pick the right sponge."

Theodora shook her head. "Which does not, I assume, include an estate inhabited by several hundred Thracian cataphracts?"

Maurice cleared his throat. "Actually, Your Majesty—no. I would recommend against it. Especially when those cataphracts have secrets to keep hidden from the prying eyes of tax collectors."

Theodora now beamed upon the Bishop. Again, she raised her cup in salutation.

"And a toast to you as well, Anthony Cassian! I do not believe any Bishop in the history of the Church has ever before actually caused a Patriarch to foam at the mouth while describing him."

Cassian smiled beatifically. "I'm sure you're exaggerating, Your Majesty. Patriarch Ephraim is a most dignified individual." Then, slyly: "Did he really?"

Theodora nodded. Cassian's expression became smug. "Well, that certainly places me in august company. It's not actually true, you know. That I'd be the first. The great John Chrysostom caused any number of Patriarchs to foam at the mouth."

Antonina smiled at the exchange. Until she remembered the fate of John Chrysostom. Around the table, as others remembered also, the smiles faded like candles extinguished at the end of evening.

"Yes," said the Empress of Rome. "Dark night is falling on us. May we live to see the morning."

Theodora set down her cup, still almost full.

"I've had enough," she said. "I suggest you all go lightly on the wine. We've a long night ahead of us."

For all its politeness, the suggestion was an imperial command. All wine cups clinked on the table, almost in unison. Almost—Sittas took the time to hastily drain his cup before setting it down.

"Justinian will not listen to me," began the Empress. "I might as well be talking to a stone wall." Growl. "I'd *rather* talk to a stone wall. At least a stone wall wouldn't pat me on the head and say it's taking my words under advisement."

She sighed. "The only ones he listens to are John of Cappadocia and Narses. Both of them, needless to say, are encouraging him in his folly. And assuring him that his wife is fretting over nothing."

For a moment, she looked away. Her face was like a mask, from the effort of fighting down the tears.

"It's Narses' words that do the real damage," she whispered. "Justinian's never actually had too many illusions about the Cappadocian. He tolerates John because the man's such an efficient tax collector, but he doesn't trust him. Never has."

"He's *too* efficient," grumbled Sittas. "His tax policy is going to ruin everyone in Rome except the imperial treasury."

"I don't disagree with you, Sittas." The Empress sighed. "Neither does Justinian, actually. It's one of the many ironies about the man. Rome's never had an Emperor who spends so much time and energy seeing to it that taxes are fairly apportioned among the population, and then ruins all his efforts by imposing a tax burden so high it doesn't matter whether it's evenly spread or not."

Theodora waved her hand.

"But let's not get into that. There's no point in it. My husband's tax policy stems from the same source as his religious policy. Both are bad—and he knows it—but both are required by his fixed obsession to reintegrate the barbarian West into the Roman Empire. That's all he sees. Even Persia barely exists on his horizon. The Malwa are utterly irrelevant."

Bishop Cassian spoke.

"There's no hope, then, of Justinian putting a stop to the persecution of Monophysites?"

Theodora shook her head.

"None. He doesn't encourage it, mind. But he resolutely looks the other way and refuses to answer any complaints sent in by provincial petitioners. All that matters to him is the approval of orthodoxy. Their blessing on his coming invasion of the western Mediterranean."

Antonina spoke, harshly.

"I assume, if he's listening to John and Narses—especially the

Cappadocian—that also means Belisarius is still under imperial suspicion."

Theodora's smile was wintry. "Oh, not at all, Antonina. Quite the contrary. John and Narses have been fulsome in your husband's praise. To the point of gross adulation. It's almost as if they know—"

She stopped, cast a hard eye on Antonina.

The sound of Sittas' meaty hand slapping the table was startling.

"Ha! Yes!" he cried. "He's tricked the bastards!" He seized his cup, poured it full. "That calls for a drink!"

"What are you babbling about, Sittas?" demanded the Empress.

The general smiled at her around the rim of his wine cup. For a moment, his face disappeared as he quaffed half the wine in a single gulp. Then, wiping his lips with approval:

"If they're so resolute in advancing Belisarius at court, Your Majesty—you know how much John of Cappadocia hates him—that can only mean they have information about him which we don't. And that—"

The rest of the wine disappeared.

"—can only be a report from India that Belisarius is planning treason against Rome."

He beamed around the room. Reached for the wine bottle.

"That calls for a—"

"Sittas!" exploded the Empress.

The general looked pained. "Just one little drink, Your Majesty. What's the harm in—"

"Why is this cause for celebration?"

"Oh. *That.*" Cheerfully, Sittas resumed his wine-pouring. "That's obvious, Your Majesty. If they've heard news from India—and I can't see any other interpretation—that tells us two things. First, Belisarius is alive. Second, he's doing his usual thorough job of butt-fu—outwitting the enemy."

Again, he saluted everyone with an upturned cup.

"How are you so sure the report isn't true?" grated the Empress.

By the time Sittas replaced his cup on the table, his cheerfulness had given way to serenity.

"Worry about something else, Your Majesty," he said. "Worry that the sun will start rising in the west. Worry that fish will sing and birds will grow scales." He snorted derisively. "If you really insist on fretting over fantasy, worry that I'll start drinking water and do calisthenics early in the morning. But don't worry about Belisarius committing treason."

Antonina interrupted. Her voice was cold, cold.

"If you pursue this, Theodora, I am done with you."

The room froze. For all Theodora's unusual intimacy with that small company, it was unheard of to threaten an Empress. *That* Empress, for sure.

But it was Theodora, not Antonina, who broke off their exchange of glares.

The Empress took a deep breath. "I am—I—" She fell silent.

Antonina shook her head. "Never mind, Theodora. I don't expect an actual apology." She glanced at Sittas. "Anymore than I'd expect *him* to start doing calisthenics."

"God save us." The general shuddered, reaching for his wine cup. "The thought alone is enough to drive me to drink."

Theodora, watching Sittas drain his cup, suddenly smiled. She picked up her own cup and extended it.

"Pour for me, Sittas. I think I'll join you."

When her cup was full, she raised it aloft.

"To Belisarius," she said. "And most of all, to trust."

Two hours later, after Theodora had finished bringing her little band of cohorts up to date with all the information which Irene had collected over the past months in Constantinople, the Empress announced she was off to bed.

"I've got to be at my best tomorrow morning," she explained. "I wouldn't want your new regiment of peasants—what did you call them?"

"Grenadiers," said Hermogenes.

"Yes, grenadiers. Has a nice ring to it! I wouldn't want them to be disappointed in their Empress' inspection. Which they certainly would be if I collapsed from nausea."

All rose with the Empress. After she left, guided to her chamber by Antonina, most of the others retired also. Soon, only Sittas and Anthony Cassian were left in the room.

"Aren't you going to bed, too?" asked the general, pouring himself another cup.

The bishop smiled seraphically.

"I thought I might stay up a bit. The opportunity, after all, will come only once in a lifetime. Watching you do calisthenics, that is."

Sittas choked, spewed out his wine.

"Oh, yes," murmured Cassian. "It's only a matter of time, I'm convinced of it. A miracle, of course. But miracles are commonplace this evening. Didn't I just see the Empress Theodora give a toast to trustfulness?"

Sittas glowered, poured himself a new cup. The bishop eyed the bottle.

"I'd be careful, Sittas. That's probably turned into water."

The Empress did not disappoint her new regiment, the next morning. No, not at all.

She appeared before them in full imperial regalia, escorted to her throne by Antonina, Sittas, Hermogenes and Bishop Cassian.

The peasant grenadiers, watching, were impressed. So, standing next to them in the proud uniforms of auxiliaries, were their wives.

By the regalia, of course. By the august nature of her escort, to be sure. Mostly, though, they were impressed by the throne.

Clothes, when all is said and done, are clothes. True, the Empress wore the finest silk. They wore homespun. But they were a practical folk. Clothes were utilitarian things, in the end, no matter how you dressed them up.

The tiara, of course, was new to them. They had no humble peasant equivalent for that splendor. But everyone knew an empress wore a tiara. Impressive, but expected.

Even her escort did not overawe them. The young Syrians had come to know those folk, these past months. With familiarity—the old saw notwithstanding—had come respect. Deep respect, in truth. And, in the case of Antonina and Cassian, adoration. Yet it was still familiarity.

But the throne!

They had wondered what the thing was, during the time spent waiting for the Empress to make her appearance. Had passed rumors up and down the lines. The regulars from Hermogenes' infantry who served as their trainers and temporary officers had tried to glare down the whispers, but to no avail. The grenadiers and their wives had their own views on military discipline. Standing in well-ordered formation seemed sensible to the peasants—very Roman; very soldier-like—and so their ranks and files never wavered in the precision of their placement. But maintaining utter silence was obvious nonsense, and so the grenadiers did not hesitate to mouth their speculations.

For a time, the rumor of heathenism seemed sure to sweep the field. Some of the grenadiers were even on the verge of mutiny, so certain were they that the *object* was an altar designed for pagan sacrifices.

But the appearance of the bishop squashed that fear. The chief competing rumor now made a grand reentry. *The object* was to be the centerpiece of a martial contest. Matching platoon against stalwart platoon, to see which might be the collective Hercules that could pick up the *thing*. Maybe even move it a foot or two.

So, when Theodora finally planted her imperial rump upon the throne, she was most gratified to see the wave of awe which swept those young faces.

"I *told* you it was worth hauling it here," she murmured triumphantly to Antonina.

Although her face never showed it, Theodora herself was impressed in the two hours which followed.

By the grenades themselves, to some extent. She had heard of the gunpowder weapons which the Malwa had introduced to the world. She had not disbelieved, exactly, but she was a skeptic by nature. Then, even after her skepticism was dispelled by the demonstration, she was still not overawed. Unlike the vast majority of people in her day, Theodora was accustomed to machines and gadgets. Her husband took a great delight in such things. The Great Palace in Constantinople was almost littered with clever devices.

True, the grenades were powerful. Theodora could easily see their military potential, even though she was not a soldier.

What Theodora *was*, was a ruler. And like all such people worthy of the name, she understood that it was not weapons which upheld a throne. Only the people who wielded those weapons.

So she was *deeply* impressed by the grenadiers.

"How did you do it?" she whispered, leaning over to Antonina.

Antonina's shrug was modest.

"Basically, I took the peasants' side in every dispute they got into with the soldiers. In everything that touched on their life, at least. I didn't intervene in the purely military squabbles. There weren't many of those, anyway. The Syrian boys are happy enough to learn the real tricks of the trade, and they never argue with Maurice. They just don't want any part of the *foolishness*."

Theodora watched a squad of grenadiers demonstrating another maneuver. Six men charged forward, followed by an equal number of women auxiliaries. The grenadiers quickly took cover behind a barricade and began slinging a barrage of grenades toward the distant shed which served as their target.

Soon enough, the shed was in splinters. But Theodora paid little attention to its destruction. She was much more interested in watching the grenadiers, especially the efficient way in which the female auxiliaries made ready the grenades and—always—cut and lit the fuses.

Watching the direction of her gaze, Antonina chuckled.

"That was my idea," she murmured. "The generals had a fit, of course. But I drove them down." She snorted. "Stupid *men*. They couldn't get it through their heads that the only people these peasants would entrust their lives to were their own women. No one else can cut the fuses that short, without ever blowing up their husbands."

A new volley of grenades sailed toward the remnants of the shed, trailing sparks from the fuses.

"Watch," said Antonina. "Watch how perfectly the fuses are timed."

The explosions came almost simultaneous with the arrival of the grenades. The last standing boards were shredded.

"It's an art," she said. "If the fuse is cut too short, the grenade blows up while still in the air. *Too* short, before the grenadier can even launch it. But if it's cut too long, the enemy will have time to toss it back."

She exhaled satisfaction. "The grenadiers' women are the masters of the art." Chuckle. "Even Sittas finally quit grumbling, and admitted as much, after he tried it himself."

"What happened?"

Antonina smiled. "At first, every grenade he sent got tossed back on his head. Fortunately, he was using practice grenades, which only make a loud pop when they burst. But he was still hopping about like a toad, trying to dodge. Finally, he got frustrated and cut the fuse too short." Grin. "*Way* too short."

"Was he hurt?"

Big grin. "Not much. But he had to drink with his left hand for a few days. Couldn't hold a wine cup in his right, for all the bandages."

The exercises culminated in a grand maneuver, simulating a full scale battle. The entire regiment of Syrian peasants and their wives formed up at the center, in well spaced formation. Units of Hermogenes' infantry braced the gaps, acting as a shield for the grenadiers against close assault. Maurice and his cataphracts, in full armor atop their horses, guarded the flanks against cavalry.

Sittas gave the order. The grenadiers hurled a volley. Their sling-cast grenades tore up the soil of the empty terrain a hundred and fifty yards away. The infantry marched forward ten yards, shields and swords bristling. The grenadier squads matched the advance, their wives prepared the next volley, slung. Again the soil was churned into chaos. Again, the infantry strode forward. Again, the grenades.

On the flanks, the cataphracts spread out like the jaws of a shark.

Sittas turned in his saddle, beamed at the Empress.

"Looks marvelous," murmured the Empress to Antonina. "How will it do in an actual battle, though?"

Antonina shrugged.

"It'll be a mess, I imagine. Nothing like this tidy business. But I'm not worried about it, Theodora. The enemy won't be in any better shape."

Theodora eyed her skeptically.

"Relax, Empress. My husband's a general, remember. I know all about the First Law of Battle. And the corollary."

Theodora nodded. "That's good." Cold smile: "Especially since you're now the new commander of this regiment. What are you going to call it, by the way?"

Antonina gaped.

"Come, come, woman. It's an elite unit. It's got to have a name."

Antonina gasped like a fish out of water. "What do you mean—commander?—I'm not a soldier!—I'm—" Wail: "I'm a *woman*, for the sake of Christ! Who ever heard of a woman—"

The Empress pointed her finger to the grenadiers, like a scepter.

"*They have*," she said. Theodora leaned back in the throne, very satisfied. "Besides, Antonina, I wouldn't trust this new regiment in anyone else's hands. These new gunpowder weapons are too powerful. You'll be my last hope, my secret force, when all else fails. I won't place my life in the hands of a *man*. Never again."

The Empress rose.

"I'll inform Sittas. He'll bleat, of course, like a lost lamb."

Coldly, grimly: "Let him. I'll shear him to the hide."

Oddly, Sittas did not bleat. Not at all.

"I thought she'd do that," he confided to Antonina. He was standing next to her, watching the reaction of the crowd to the announcement which the Empress had just made. "Smart woman," he said approvingly.

Antonina peered at him suspiciously.

"This is not like you," she muttered. "You're the most reactionary—"

"Nonsense!" he replied cheerfully. "I'm not reactionary at all. I'm just lazy. The reason I hate new ideas is because they usually require me to do something. Whereas *this*—"

He beamed upon the peasant grenadiers. Uncertainly, some of them smiled back. Most of them, however, were staring at their new commander. At the few, full-figured inches of her. The men were wide-eyed. Their wives were practically goggling.

"Have fun, girl," he murmured. "I'd much rather lounge back in the ease of my normal assignment. I could lead cataphract charges in my sleep."

He turned away, and leaned toward Theodora. "I think we should call them the Theodoran Cohort," he announced.

"Splendid idea," agreed the Empress. "Splendid."

That night, clustered uneasily in the great hall of the villa, the village elders made clear that they did *not* think the situation was splendid.

Not at all. *None* of it.

It was not the name they objected to. The name, so far as they were concerned, was irrelevant.

What they objected to was everything else.

"Who will till the land when they are gone?" whined one of the elders. "The villagers will starve."

"They will not," stated Theodora. She loomed over the small crowd of elders. At great effort, her throne had been moved into the villa.

"They will not starve at all. Quite the contrary. Every grenadier in the Theodoran Cohort will receive an annual stipend of twenty nomismata. I will also provide an additional ten nomismata a year for equipment and uniforms. Their wives—the auxiliaries—will receive half that amount."

Standing behind the elders, the representatives of the young grenadiers and their wives murmured excitedly. An annual income of twenty nomismata—the Greek term for the solidus—was twice the income of a Syrian peasant household. A *prosperous* household. The extra ten nomismata were more than enough to cover a soldier's gear. With the wives' stipends included, each peasant family enrolling in the Cohort had just, in effect, tripled their average income.

The elders stroked their beards, calculating.

"What of the children?" asked one.

Antonina spoke.

"The children will accompany the Cohort itself. The Empress has also agreed to provide for the hire of whatever servants are necessary."

That announcement brought another gratified hum from the grenadiers. And *especially* from their wives.

"In battle, of course, the children will be held back, in the safety of the camp."

"The camp will not be safe, if they are defeated," pointed out an elder.

One of the grenadiers in the back finally lost patience.

"The *villages* will not be safe, if we are defeated!" he snarled. His fellows growled their agreement. So did their wives.

The elders stroked their beards. Calculating.

They tried a new approach.

"It is unseemly, to have a woman in command." The elder who uttered those words glared back at the peasant wives.

"The girls will start giving themselves airs," he predicted.

To prove his point, several of the wives made faces at him. To his greater chagrin, their husbands laughed.

"You see?" he complained. "Already they—"

The Empress began to cut him off, but her voice was overridden by another.

"Damn you for Satan's fools!"

The entire crowd was stunned into silence by that voice.

"He does that so well, don't you think?" murmured Cassian.

The Voice stalked into the room from a door to the side.

The elders shrank back. The young grenadiers behind them, and their wives, bowed their heads. Even Theodora, seated high on her throne, found it hard not to bend before that figure.

That *hawk*. That desert bird of prey.

Michael of Macedonia thrust his beak into the face of the complaining elder.

"You are wiser than Christ, then?" he demanded. "More certain of God's will than his very Son?"

The elder trembled with fear. As well he might. In the stretches of the Monophysite Syrian countryside, the rulings of orthodox councils meant nothing. Even the tongs and instruments of inquisitors were scorned. But *nobody* scoffed at holy men. The ascetic monks of the desert, in the eyes of common folk, were the true saints of God. Spoke with God's own voice.

Michael of Macedonia had but to say the word, and the elder's own villagers would stone him.

When Michael finally transferred his pitiless eyes away, the elder almost collapsed from relief.

His fellows, now, shrank from that raptor gaze.

"You are on the very lip of the Pit," said Michael. Softly, but his words penetrated every corner of the room. "Be silent."

He turned, faced the grenadiers and their wives.

"I give these young men my blessing," he announced. "And my blessing to their wives, as well. *Especially* to their wives, for they have just proved themselves the most faithful of women."

He stared back at the elders. Stonily:

"You will so inform the people. In all the villages. *Publicly.*"

The elders' heads bobbed like corks in a shaken tub.

"You will inform them of something else, as well," he commanded. The monk now faced the Empress, and Antonina standing by her side.

He prostrated himself. Behind him, the peasants gasped.

"God in Heaven," whispered Cassian into Antonina's ear, "he's never done that in his life." The Bishop was almost gasping himself. "It's why he's refused all the many invitations to Constantinople. He'd have to prostrate himself before the Emperor, or stand in open rebellion."

Michael rose. The peasants' murmurs died down.

"I have had a vision," he announced.

Utter silence, now.

The monk pointed to the Empress. Then, to Antonina.

"God has sent them to us, as he sent Mary Magdalene."

He turned, and began leaving. Halfway to the door, he stopped and bestowed a last gaze upon the elders.

The hawk, promising the hares:

"Beware, Pharisees."

He was gone.

Sittas puffed out his cheeks.

"Well, that's that," he pronounced. "Signed, sealed, and delivered."

He bent down to Theodora.

"And now, Your Majesty, with your permission?"

Theodora nodded.

Sittas stepped forward, facing the grenadiers. Spread his heavy arms. Beamed, like a hog in heaven.

"This calls for a drink!" he bellowed. "The casks await us outside! Your fellows—all the villagers—have already started the celebration! While we, poor souls"—a hot-eyed boar glared at the cowering elders, baring his tusks—"were forced to quell our thirst."

Once a village elder, always a village elder.

"The expense," complained one.

"We'll be ruined," whined another.

Sittas drove them down.

"Nothing to fear, you fools! *I'm a rich man.* I'll pay for it all!"

"I'm not sure I can handle this much longer," muttered Theodora, watching the eager peasants pour from the room. "One more miracle and I'm a dead woman, for sure."

She shook her head. "Talismans from God. Messengers from the future. Magic weapons. New armies. Women commanders. Saints walking about."

Grump. "And now—Sittas, with generous pockets. What next?" she demanded. "*What next?* Talking horses? Stars falling from the sky?"

She rose. "Come," she commanded. "We should join our new army in a toast to their success. *Quickly.* Before the wine turns into water."

Three days later, early in the morning, the Empress departed the estate.

Unhappy woman.

"You're sure this is your tamest beast?" she demanded.

Maurice managed not to smile.

"Yes, Your Majesty." He patted the old mare's neck. Then, helped Theodora into the saddle. The task was difficult, between Theodora's clumsiness and the stern necessity of never planting a boosting hand on the imperial rump.

Now astride the horse, Theodora looked down at Antonina.

"Remember, then. As soon as I send the word, get your cohort to Constantinople. And don't forget—"

"Be on your way, Theodora," interrupted Antonina, smiling. "I will not forget any of your instructions. Hermogenes has already picked out his regiments. Sittas is doing the same. The Bishop's making the secret arrangement for the ships. And the ten cataphracts left for Egypt yesterday."

"Ashot's in command," stated Maurice. "One of my best decarchs. When Belisarius finally arrives, he'll get him here—or to the capital, whichever's needed—as fast as possible."

Theodora sat back in her saddle, nodded.

Then, looking down at her horse:

"Maybe there'll be sieges, after all," she muttered grimly.

She put her horse into motion awkwardly. Her last words:

"Keep that in mind, horse."

The next day, Maurice wiped the grins off the faces of the grenadiers.

"To be sure, lads, Antonina's your commander," he said, pacing up and down their ranks. "But commanders are aloof folk, you know. Very aloof. Have nothing to do with the routine of daily training." He stopped, planted his hands on hips. "No, no. That's trivial stuff. Always leave that sort of thing in the hands of lowly hecatontarchs."

Grimly: "That's me."

The grenadiers eyed him warily. Eyed the grinning cataphracts who stood nearby. The announcement had just been made that they were to be the new trainers.

Maurice gestured in their direction.

"These are what we call—*cadre*."

Very evil grins, those cataphracts possessed.

"Oh, yes," murmured Maurice. "*Now* your training begins in earnest. Forget all that silly showpiece stuff for the Empress."

He resumed his pacing. "I will begin by introducing you to the First Law of Battle. This law can be stated simply. *Every battle plan gets fucked up as soon as the enemy arrives. That's why he's called the enemy.*"

He stopped, turned, smiled cheerfully.

"Your own plans just got fucked up."

Grinned ear to ear.

"I have arrived."

Yes, the grins disappeared from their faces. But the smile in the hearts of those young peasants did not. Not ever, in the weeks which followed, for all the many curses which they bestowed upon Maurice. (Behind his back, needless to say.)

No, not once. The young Syrians were not foolish. Not even the men, and certainly not their wives. Uneducated and illiterate, yes. Stupid, no. For all their pleasure in their new-found status, they had never really thought it was anything but a serious business.

They were a practical folk. Serious business, they understood. And they had their own peasant estimate of serious folk.

Antonina was a joy; the Empress had been a pleasure. Sittas was a fine magnanimous lord; Cassian the very archetype of a true bishop.

And Michael, of course, a prophet on earth.

But it was time for serious business, now. Peasant work. And so, though they never grinned, Syrian peasants took no offense—and lost no heart—from the abuse of Thracians.

Farm boys, themselves, at bottom, those Thracian cataphracts. Peasants, nothing better.

Just very, very tough peasants.

And so, as summer became autumn, and as autumn turned to winter—

—a general and his allies fought to escape Malwa's talons,

—an Empress watched an empire unravel in Constantinople,

—conspirators plotted everywhere—

And a few hundred peasants and their wives toiled under the Syrian sun. Doing what peasants do best, from the experience of millenia.

Toughening.

Chapter 17
NORTH INDIA
Summer 530 AD

When they came upon the third massacre, Rana Sanga had had enough.

"This is madness," he snarled. "The Roman is doing it to us again."

His chief lieutenant, Jaimal, tore his eyes away from the bloody corpses strewn on both sides of the road. There were seven bodies there, in addition to the three soldiers they had found lying in the guardhouse itself. All of them were common soldiers, and all of them had been slaughtered like so many sheep. Judging from the lack of blood on any of the weapons lying nearby, Jaimal did not think the soldiers had inflicted a single wound on their assailants. Most of them, he suspected, had not even tried. At least half had been slain while trying to flee.

"What are you talking about?" he asked.

"This—*idiocy*." Sanga glared. "No, I take that back. This is not idiocy. Not at all. This is pure deception."

His lieutenant frowned. "I don't understand—"

"It's obvious, Jaimal! The whole point of this massacre—like the first two, and the attack on the army camp—is simply to lead us in pursuit."

Seeing the lack of comprehension on Jaimal's face, Sanga reined in his temper. He did not, however, manage to refrain from sighing with exasperation.

"Jaimal, ask yourself some simple questions. Why did the Romans kill these men? Why are they going out of their way to take roads which lead past guardhouses? Why, having done so, do they take the time to attack the guardhouses instead of sneaking around them? You know as well as I do that these"—he jabbed a finger at the corpses—"sorry sons-of-bitches wouldn't move out of their guardhouses unless they were forced to. Finally, why did they attack the army camp in Kausambi on the night they fled?"

Silence. Frown of incomprehension. Sanga finally exploded.

"*You idiot!* The Romans are doing everything possible to lead us in this direction. Why, damn you—*why?*"

Jaimal's gape would have been comical, if Sanga had been in a humorous mood.

"Belisarius—isn't—isn't with them," he stammered. "He fled a different way."

"Congratulations," growled Sanga. He reined his horse around.

"Gather up the men. We're going back."

Jaimal frowned. "But it's a three-day ride back to Kausambi. And we were ordered—"

"Damn the orders! I'll deal with Tathagata. And what if it is a three day ride? We've already lost four days on this fool's errand. By the time we get back—assuming I can talk sense into the Malwa—Belisarius will have at least a week's lead on us. Would you rather extend it further?"

He jabbed an angry finger to the south. "How many more days do you want to chase after the Roman general's underlings? I doubt if we can catch them anyway. The Pathans say they've already gained a day on us. They're covering as much distance in three days as we can in four. And even have time for *this*"—another angry finger jabbed at the corpses—"along the way."

Jaimal nodded. Large Rajput cavalry units such as their own always kept a handful of Pathan irregulars with them. The barbarians were an indisciplined nuisance, most of the time, but they were unexcelled trackers.

"How are they traveling so fast?" wondered Jaimal.

Sanga shrugged. "They've got remounts, for one thing, which we don't. And they must have the best horses in creation. We may never know, but I'd be willing to wager a year's income that Belisarius managed to buy the best horses he could find, in the months he's been in India. And hide them away somewhere."

Then, with a tone like steel:

"And now, Jaimal, do as I command. Gather up the men. We're heading back."

Beyond a point, none of Sanga's subordinates would argue with him. That point had been reached, Jaimal knew, and he immediately obeyed his instructions.

His chief subordinates, Udai and Pratap, privately expressed their reservations to him. Those reservations, in the main, centered around their fear of the Malwa reaction when they returned to Kausambi. But, now that their course was set, Jaimal would no more tolerate dissent than would Sanga himself.

"And besides," he growled, "no one will miss us here anyway. There must be forty thousand troops beating these plains. A third of them Rajput cavalry, and another third Ye-tai horsemen. Five hundred of us will make no difference."

"True enough," grunted Udai. "As good as the Roman horses are—and with remounts—only royal couriers could move faster."

"They've been sent, haven't they?" asked Pratap.

Jaimal shrugged irritably. "Do I know? Since when does Emperor Skandagupta take me into his confidence? But I assume so. By now, I imagine, couriers have been dispatched to every port on the Erythrean Sea, alerting the garrisons."

His own tone of voice, now, was a duplicate of Sanga's:

"And that's enough. Do as you've been told."

Couriers *had* been sent, in point of fact. Just as Jaimal expected—to every port on the Erythrean Sea. The couriers were expert horsemen, riding the very finest steeds. They did not bring remounts with them, however. Instead, they changed horses at the relay stations which the Malwa maintained at regular intervals along all of the principal roads in the Empire. These relay stations were small affairs, in the Gangetic plain, not much more than a barn or corral attached to a small barracks housing a squad of four soldiers.

The courier to Barbaricum was one of three who had been sent down the road to Mathura. Mathura was not itself the destination of any of them. All three, long before they reached Mathura, would take the various branching routes which led to Barbaricum, the small ports in the Kathiawar, and the northern end of the Gulf of Khambat.

The courier to the Gulf of Khambat had left first, the day after

Belisarius' escape. The Malwa were certain that the general and his underlings were fleeing back to Bharakuccha. They placed their top priority on sending off couriers to cover the entire Gulf. The couriers headed for the Kathiawar and Barbaricum had departed a few hours later, almost as an afterthought.

At first, the two men had traveled together. But, after a time, the courier destined for the Kathiawar had pulled ahead. He was new to the royal courier service, and full of his own self-importance. His companion was glad to see him go, with the relief felt by seasoned veterans the world over at being rid of the company of irritating apprentice twits. The veteran courier saw no reason to match the youth's extravagant haste. Why bother? Everyone knew the Romans had gone south, not west.

By the time he reached the relay station at the end of his first day's ride, the courier was in a thoroughly foul mood. Disgust, leavened by a heavy dose of self-pity. Barbaricum, his ultimate destination, was the very westernmost port of any significance in the Malwa Empire. It lay even beyond the Indus River—almost a thousand miles from Kausambi, as the crow flies.

The courier, of course, was not a crow. He would be forced to travel at least half again that distance before he reached his destination. Along poor roads, most of the way, and through the blistering heat of Rajputana. He would even have to pass through a portion of the Thar, India's worst desert. A long, miserable, hot journey—and with nothing to look forward to at the end except India's worst port. The courier detested Barbaricum. It was a mongrel city, half of whose population were foreign barbarians. And the Indians who lived there were not much better, having long since adapted to the customs of heathen outlanders.

So, as he dismounted from his horse in front of the relay station, the courier was feeling very sorry for himself. His sorrow turned to outrage when no soldier emerged from the barracks to assist him in removing his saddle.

The courier stalked over to the barracks door and shouldered his way through without so much as knocking.

"Just what the fuck do you—"

The sword went a quarter-inch into his chest. Not a mortal wound, painful as it was, not even a particularly bloody one. But the courier could feel the steel tip grating against his chestbone. And the hand which held that sword was as steady as a rock.

The courier's eyes began with that hand, and followed the length of the sword to the place where it disappeared into his chest. Everything else was a blur.

In a frozen daze, the courier heard a voice. He did not make out the words. The sword-tip jabbed against his sternum, pressing him back against the doorframe. He stared down at it, transfixed by the sight.

The words were repeated. Hindi words. Their meaning finally penetrated.

"Are there any more couriers coming after you?"

He understood, but couldn't speak. Another jab.

"What?" he gasped. Another jab.

"N-no," he stammered.

The sword went straight through his chest, as if driven by a sledgehammer. The courier slumped to his knees. In the few seconds remaining in his life, his eyes finally focussed on the barracks as a whole.

His first reaction was confusion. Why were his two courier companions still here? And why were they lying on top of a pile of soldiers?

His vision began to fade.

They're all dead, he realized.

His last sight was the face of the young courier who had accompanied him on the first part of his journey. The sight amused him, vaguely. The vainglorious little snot looked like a frog, what with that open mouth and those bulging eyes.

His vision failed. His last thought, very vague, was the realization that he had never actually seen the man who had killed him. Just his hand. A large, powerful, sinewy hand.

A hundred miles east of Kausambi, near Sarnath, an innkeeper was almost beside himself with joy. He drove his wife, his children, and his servants mercilessly.

"The best food!" he exclaimed again, and, again, cuffed his wife. "The very best! I warn you—if the noble folk complain, I will beat you. They are very rich, and will be generous if they are pleased."

His wife scurried to obey, head bent. His children and servants did likewise. All of them were terrified of the innkeeper. When times were bad—as they usually were—the innkeeper was a sullen, foul-tempered, brutal tyrant. When times were good, he was even worse. Avarice simply added an edge to his cruelty.

So, for all the members of that household except the inn-keeper himself, the next twelve hours passed like a slow-moving nightmare.

At first, they were terrified that the nobleman and his wife would find the food displeasing. But that fear did not material-ize. The noblewoman said nothing—quite properly, especially for a wife so much younger than her husband—but the nobleman was most effusive in his praise.

Unfortunately, the nobleman added a bonus for the excellence of the meal. The innkeeper's greed soared higher. In the kitchen, he buffeted his family and his servants, urging them to make haste. The nobleman and his wife had gone to bed, along with the wife's ladies, but their large escort of soldiers had to be fed also. Not the best food, of course, but not so bad that they would complain to their master. And plenty of it!

The terror of the household mounted. The soldiers were a vicious looking crew. Some sort of barbarians. There were a great number of them, with only three women camp followers. The innkeeper's oldest daughter and the two servant girls were petrified at the thought of entering the common rooms where the soldiers were staying the night. Their mother and one of the elderly servants, whose haggard appearance would shield them, tried to bring the food to the soldiers. But the innkeeper slapped his wife, and com-manded the young women to do the chore. Anything to please the soldiers, lest they complain of inhospitality to their master.

That terror, too, proved baseless. For all their fearsome appear-ance, the soldiers did not behave improperly. Indeed, they were rather polite.

So, after the soldiers finished their meal and lay down on their pallets, the innkeeper beat his daughter and the two servant girls. They had obviously been rude to the soldiers, or they would have been importuned.

The final terror, which kept the entire household awake through the night, was for the next morning. When the nobleman and his party left, he might not give the innkeeper as large a bonus as the innkeeper was expecting. The terror grew as the long hours passed. The innkeeper's expectations waxed by the hour, as he stayed awake himself through the night, in avid consideration of his pending fortune. By the break of dawn, the innkeeper had convinced himself that he was on the verge of receiving a preposterous bonus. When the actual bonus which materialized was far beneath that absurd expectation, his family and his servants knew that he would be savage.

Yet, that terror also vanished. The bonus which the innkeeper received—to everyone's astonishment, even his own—was, by their standards, enormous.

And so, in the end, the sojourn of the unknown nobleman proved to be a blessing for that household. The innkeeper's greed, of course, would soon enough add to their misery. Neither his wife, nor his children, nor his servants doubted that in the least. The innkeeper would expect a similar bonus from the occasional noble customer in the future. And, when that bonus did not appear, would brutalize his household.

But that was a problem for the future. Neither his wife, nor his children, nor his servants were given to worrying about the future. The present was more than dark enough. And, thankfully, they would enjoy a rare respite from the ever-present fear in their lives. The innkeeper, awash in his sudden wealth, indulged himself in a drunken stupor for the next three days.

Every night, as she watched him soddenly sleeping, his wife thought of poisoning him. It was her principal entertainment in life. Over the years, she had determined eighteen different toxins she could use. At least five of those would leave no trace of suspicion.

But, as always, the amusement paled after a time. There was no point in poisoning him. She would be required—by law, now—to immolate herself on his funeral pyre. Her children and her servants would fare little better. The innkeeper had long ago sunk into hopeless debt to the local potentates. Upon his death, that debt would come due, immediately and in its entirety. By law, now, all lower-caste households were responsible for the debts of the family head, upon his death. They would not be able to pay those debts. The inn would be seized. The servants would be sold into slavery. The children, being twice-born rather than untouchable, could not be made slaves due to debt. They would simply starve, or be forced to turn themselves to unthinkable occupations.

By the end of the innkeeper's binge, three days later, his wife hardly remembered the nobleman who had given her that brief respite from fear. Her mind had wandered much farther back in time, to the days of her youth. Better days, she remembered—or, at least, thought she did. Though not as good as the days of her mother, and her grandmother, judging from the tales she half-remembered from her childhood. The days when suttee was only expected from rich widows—noblewomen desirous to prove their piety, and with no need to be concerned over the material welfare of their children.

The old days, the Gupta days. The days when customs, harsh as they might be, were only customs. The days when even those harsh customs, in practice, were often meliorated by kinder—or, at least, laxer—potentates. The days when even a stern potentate might shrink from the condemnation of a Buddhist monk, or a sadhu.

The days before the Malwa came. With Malwa law, and Malwa rigor. And the Mahaveda priests to sanctify the pure, and the mahamimamsa to punish the polluted.

Fourteen royal couriers raced south across northern India. Unlike the three couriers headed west, all of these couriers were filled with the urgency of their mission. Royal couriers, in their own way, were one of the pampered elite of Malwa India. All of them were of kshatriya birth—low-caste kshatriya, true, but kshatriya nonetheless. And while their rank was modest, in the official aristocratic scale, they enjoyed an unusual degree of intimacy with the very highest men of India. Many of those couriers, more than once, had taken their messages from the very hand of the God-on-Earth himself.

An arrogant lot, thus, in their own way. Royal Malwa couriers believed themselves to be the fastest men in the world. As they pounded their way south, every one of those fourteen men was certain that the vast hordes of the Malwa army had no chance of catching the foreign devils. The couriers—and they alone—were all that stood between the wicked outlanders and their successful escape.

Fast as the Romans and Ethiopians were, with their remounts and their fine steeds, they were not as fast as Malwa couriers. The horses which the couriers rode were even better, and the couriers enjoyed one great advantage—they were under no compulsion to keep their horses alive. Many more horses awaited them in relay stations along every main road. And so all of them, more than once, ran their horses to death as they raced from station to station along their route.

The couriers were filled with the confidence that they could reach the ports before the fleeing enemy, and alert the garrisons. The Malwa army could flounder, and the Rajputs and Ye-tai thrash about in aimless pursuit, but the couriers would save the day.

So they thought, and they were not wrong in thinking so. But the couriers, like so many others throughout India in those weeks of frenzy, were too confident. Too full of themselves; too incautious; too heedless of all that could go wrong, in this polluted world.

One courier's incaution manifested itself in the most direct way possible. Thundering around a bend in the road, his forward vision obscured by the lush forest which loomed on either side, the courier suddenly learned that he was indeed faster than the foreign enemy. He had overtaken them.

The courier had already plunged into the midst of the foreigners before he made that unhappy discovery. A quick-thinking man, the courier did not make the mistake of trying to turn around. Instead, he took advantage of his speed and simply pounded right through them, guiding his horse expertly through the little crowd.

He made it, too. In truth, the royal courier *was* one of the very finest horsemen in the world.

But no horseman is fine enough to outrun a cataphract arrow. Not, at least, one fired by the bow of that cataphract named Valentinian.

The foreigners dragged his body into the woods, and then piled insult onto injury. They added his wonderful steed to their stock of remounts.

A second courier, and a third, and then a fourth, also discovered the caprices of fate.

Dramatically, in the case of the second courier. The monsoon downpours had washed out portions of many of the roads throughout India. The route this courier took happened to be one of the lesser roads, and thus suffered more than its share of climatic degradations. The courier, however, was unfazed by these obstacles. He was an experienced courier, and an excellent rider. He had leapt over many washed-out portions of road in his career, and did so again. And again and again and again, with all the skill and self-confidence of his station in life. What he failed to consider, unfortunately, was that his horse did not share the same skill and experience—not, at least, when it was half-dead from exhaustion. So, leaping yet another stream, the horse stumbled and spilled the courier.

Well-trained, the horse waited for its rider to remount. A very well-trained horse, that one. It did not begin to forage for two hours, after its equine mind finally concluded that the courier seemed bound and determined to remain lying in the stream. Face down, oddly enough, in two feet of water.

The third courier's mishap took a less dramatic form. He, too, driving an exhausted mount across a broken stretch of road, caused his horse to stumble and fall. Unlike the other courier, this one did not have the bad luck to strike his head against a boulder in a stream. He landed in a bush, and merely broke his leg. A simple fracture, nothing worse. But he was not discovered for two days, and by the time the small party of woodcutters conveyed him to the nearest Malwa post it was much too late for it to do any good.

The fourth courier encountered his unfortunate destiny in its most common and plebeian manifestation. He got sick. He had been feeling poorly even before he left Kausambi, and after a week of relentless travel he was in a delirium. A man can drive a horse to death, but not without great cost to himself. That courier was a stubborn man, and a brave one, and he was determined to fulfill his duty. But willpower alone is not enough. On the evening of the seventh day he reached a relay station and collapsed from his horse. The soldiers staffing the station carried him into the barracks and did their best—with the aid of a local herb doctor—to tend to his illness.

Their best, given the medical knowledge of the time, was not good enough. The courier was a brave and stubborn man, and so he lived for four more days. But he never recovered consciousness before dying, and the soldiers were afraid to even touch the courier's message case, much less break the Malwa seal and open the royal instrument. It would have done no good, anyway, since all of them were illiterate.

It was not until two days later, upon the arrival of the first unit of regular troops slogging in pursuit of the escapees, that an officer inspected the message. A high-caste officer, a Malwa as

it happened, who was arrogant enough to break the royal seal.
Immediately upon reading the message, the officer issued two commands. His first order despatched his best rider to Bharakuccha
with the—now much too belated—message. His second order
flogged the guards of the relay station. Fifty lashes each, with a
split bamboo cane, for gross dereliction of duty.

Still, ten couriers remained. By the end of the second week
after the Romans and Ethiopians began their flight south, all
ten of these couriers had bypassed the foreigners and were now
forging ahead of them. Slowly, to be sure. The foreigners were
indeed moving very rapidly, and were steadily outdistancing the
great mass of their pursuers. Even the couriers were only able
to gain a few miles on them each day. (On average. All of the
couriers were taking different roads, and none of those roads was
the same as that taken by the foreigners.)

A few miles a day is not much, but it would be enough. The
couriers would arrive at the Gulf of Khambat with more than
ample time to spread the alarm. Four of them were destined for
Bharakuccha itself. By the time the outlanders arrived at the coast,
Bharakuccha and the smaller ports would be sealed off. The foreign escapees would be trapped inside India, with the enormous
manpower of the Malwa army available to bring them down.

That had been the Malwa plan from the beginning of the
chase. The Emperor and his high officials had hoped, of course,
that the army would catch the fugitives before they reached the
coast. But they knew the odds were against that, and so they had
immediately sent out the couriers.

It was an excellent plan, taking advantage of the excellent Malwa
courier corps. A plan adopted by men who were as intelligent
as they were arrogant. And, like many such plans, collapsed of
its own arrogance.

Haughty men, swollen with their own self-importance, have a
tendency to forget about the enemy.

Enemies, in this case. The man they were pursuing, the general
Belisarius, was something quite foreign to their experience. He,
like them, also made plans. He, like them, also followed those
plans. But he—quite unlike them—also knew that plans are fickle
things. And, that being so, it always pays to make plans within
plans, and to keep an eye out for every unexpected opportunity.
Every new angle.

Months earlier, Belisarius had seen such an opportunity. He had seized it with both hands. The Empress Shakuntala had been delivered from captivity, and Majarashtra's greatest warrior set free from that task.

Raghunath Rao had been free for months, now. Free to set the Great Country afire.

Months, of course, are not enough to create a great popular rebellion. Certainly not in a recently conquered land, whose people are still licking their wounds. But months *are* enough, for such a man as Rao, to assemble the nucleus of his future army. To gather rebellious young men—almost a thousand, by now—in the isolated hillforts which pocked the Great Country's badlands.

Rao was not only an experienced commander, he had the natural aptitude of a guerrilla fighter. So, almost from the day he returned to Majarashtra, he had set the young men rallying to his banner to the first, simplest, and most essential task of the would-be rebel.

Intelligence.

Watch. Observe. Nothing moves south of the Vindhyas without our knowledge.

The fastest of all the Malwa couriers finally made his way through the Gangetic plain, and through the Vindhya mountains which were the traditional boundary between north India and the Deccan. Bharakuccha was not far away, now.

He did not get thirty miles before he was ambushed. Brought down by five arrows.

Rao, as it happened, was camped not far away, in a hillfort some twenty miles distant. Within hours, the young Maratha ambushers brought him the courier's message case. Rao had no fear of the royal seal, and he was quite literate. A very fast reader, in fact.

Immediately after reading the message, he issued his own set of rapid commands. Within minutes, the hillfort was emptied of all but Rao himself and his two chief lieutenants. All the others—all three hundred or so—were racing to spread the news.

Malwa couriers are coming. All of them must be stopped. Kill them. Take their message cases. Rao himself commands.

After the young warriors were gone, Rao and his lieutenants enjoyed a simple meal. Over the meal, they discussed the significance of this latest event.

"Can we aid the Romans in some other way?" asked Maloji.

Rao shrugged. "Perhaps. We will see when they arrive. I do not know their plans, although I suspect the Malwa are right. The Romans and the Africans will try to take ship in Bharakuccha. If so, it will be enough for us to stop the couriers." He smiled grimly. "Those men are *very* capable. They will manage, if we can keep the garrisons from being alerted."

"What if the Empress is with them?" asked his other lieutenant, Ramchandra.

Rao shook his head firmly. "She will not be."

"How do you know?"

Rao's smile, now, was not grim at all. Quite gay, in fact.

"I know the mind of Belisarius, Ramchandra. That man will never do the obvious. Remember how he rescued Shakuntala! In fact—" Rao looked down at the message scroll, still in his hand. "I wonder..." he mused.

He rolled up the scroll and slapped it back into the case. The motion had a finality to it.

"We will know soon enough." His smile, now, was a veritable grin. "Expect to be surprised, comrades. When you deal with Belisarius, that is the one thing you can be sure of. The *only* thing."

With a single lithe movement, Rao came to his feet. He strode to the nearest battlement and stood for a moment gazing across the Great Country. The stone wall of the hillfort rose directly from an almost perpendicular cliff over a hundred yards in height. The view was magnificent.

His two lieutenants joined him. They were both struck by the serenity in the Panther's face.

"We will see the Empress, soon enough," he murmured. "She will arrive, comrades—be sure of it. From the most unexpected direction, and in the most unexpected way."

That same day—that same hour—the young officer in command of a guardpost just south of Pataliputra found himself in a quandary.

On the one hand, the party seeking passage through his post lacked the proper documentation. This lack weighed the heavier in the officer's mind for the fact that he was of brahmin ancestry, with all the veneration which that priest/scholar class had for the written word. Brahmin ancestry was uncommon for a military officer. Such men were normally kshatriya. He had chosen that career due to his ambition. He was not Malwa, but Bihari. As a member of a subject nation, he could expect to rise higher in the military than in the more status-conscious civilian hierarchy.

Still, he retained the instincts of a pettifogging bureaucrat, and the simple fact was that these people had no documents. Scandalous.

On the other hand—

The nobleman was obviously of very high caste. Not Malwa, no—some western nation. But no low-ranking officer is eager to offend a high-caste dignitary of the Empire, Malwa or otherwise.

The officer could hear his men grumbling in the background. They had seen the size of the bribe offered by the nobleman, and were seething at their commander's idiotic obsession with petty rules and regulations.

The officer hesitated, vacillated, rattled back and forth within the narrow confines of his mind.

The nobleman's wife ended that dance of indecision.

The officer heard her sharp yelps of command. Watched, as she clambered down from the howdah, assisted by her fierce looking soldiers. Watched her stalk over to him.

Small, she was, and obviously young. Pretty, too, from what little he could see of her face. Beautiful black eyes.

Whatever pleasure those facts brought the officer vanished as soon as she began to speak.

In good Hindi, but with a heavy southern accent. A Keralan accent, he thought.

After I inform the Emperor of Kerala of your insolence your remaining days in this world will be brief. He is my father and he will demand your death of the Malwa. Base cur! You will—

Her husband tried to calm her down.

—be impaled. I will demand a short stake. My father the Emperor will—

Her husband tried to calm her down.

—allow a long stake in the interests of diplomacy but he will not—

Her husband tried to calm her down.

—settle for less than your death by torture. I will demand that your carcass be fed to dogs. Small dogs, who will tear at it rather than devour it whole. My father the Emperor will—

Her husband tried to calm her down.

—not insist on the dogs, in the interests of diplomacy, but he will demand—

Finally, finally, the nobleman managed to usher his wife away. Over her shoulder, shrieking:

—your stinking corpse be denied the rites. You will spend five yugas as a worm, five more as a spider. You will—

As the party passed through the post, the officer's mangled dignity was partially restored by the large bribe which the nobleman handed him. Partially, no more. The young officer did not miss the smirks which were exchanged between his own soldiers and those of the nobleman's escort. The smirks which common troops exchange, witnessing the abasement of high-ranked adolescent snots.

Within the next week, nine of the ten Malwa couriers died in Majarashtra. They traveled faster than the Maratha guerillas, of course, but the couriers were restricted to the roads and had no real knowledge of the countryside. Rao's young men, on the other hand, knew every shortcut through those volcanic hills. And every spot for a good ambush.

Of the fourteen royal couriers who had headed south from Kausambi weeks earlier, only one survived the journey. His route had been the northernmost of those taken by the couriers, and did not really do more than skirt the Great Country. So he arrived, eventually, at his destination. A tiny port nestled at the northern end of the Gulf.

Finally, everything went according to plan. The commander of the little garrison immediately mobilized his troops and began a thorough and efficient patrol of the port and its environs. All ships—all three of them—were sequestered, prevented from leaving.

The commander was an aggressive, hard-driving officer. The small harbor was sealed tight. And so, according to plan, none of the enemy escaped through that port.

Which, as it happens, they had never had the slightest intention of doing.

Chapter 18

Had Nanda Lal not intervened, it might have come to blows. Rana Sanga would have been executed, thereafter, but he would have had the satisfaction of slaughtering Lord Tathagata like the swine that he was.

"*Silence!*" bellowed the spymaster, as soon as he charged into the room. "Both of you!"

Nanda Lal had a powerful voice. It was distorted somewhat, due to his shattered nose, but still powerful. And the spymaster's voice was filled with a pure black fury so ugly it would have silenced anyone.

That mood had settled on Nanda Lal as soon as he recovered consciousness on the floor of Great Lady Holi's barge. On the blood-soaked carpet, stained by his own wound, where a foreign demon's boot had sent him sprawling.

A week had gone by, now, and his rage had not lifted. It was a spymaster's rage—icy, not hot, but utterly merciless.

Sanga clenched his jaws. He stared at Nanda Lal, not out of rude curiosity, but simply because he could no longer bear the sight of Lord Tathagata's fat, stupid, pig of a face. Then, realizing that his stare could be misconstrued, Sanga looked away.

In truth, the Malwa Empire's chief of espionage was a sight to behold. On almost any other man, that huge bandage wrapped around his face would have given him a comical appearance. It simply made Nanda Lal look like an ogre.

Tathagata, recovering from his startlement, transferred his fury onto Nanda Lal.

"What is the meaning of this?" demanded the Malwa army's top officer. "It's outrageous! You have no right to issue commands here! This is purely a military matter, Nanda Lal—I'll thank you to mind your own—"

Nanda Lal's next words came hissing like a snake.

"If you so much as finish that sentence, Tathagata, you will discover what rights I have and do not have. I guarantee the discovery will shock you. But only briefly. You will be dead within the hour."

Lord Tathagata choked on the sentence. His jaw hung loose. His eyes—wide as a flatfish—goggled about the room, as if searching the magnificence of his headquarters to find something that would gainsay Nanda Lal's statement.

Apparently, he found nothing. Such, at least, was Rana Sanga's interpretation of his continued silence.

Nanda Lal stalked into the room. He did not bother to close the door behind him. Sanga could see, through that door, a part of a room. One of the Emperor's own private chambers, he realized. Sanga had never entered that room, himself. The Rajput's only contact with Skandagupta had been in chambers given over to public gatherings. He was now in a part of the Grand Palace which was essentially unknown to him. The very core of that great edifice, and the power which rested within it.

"Why are you here, Sanga?" asked the spymaster. His voice, now, was low and calm.

Sanga began to explain his theory about Belisarius' escape, but Nanda Lal interrupted him immediately.

"Not that, Sanga. I've already heard *that*." The spymaster began to make a wry grimace, but the pain in his nose cut the expression short. He waved toward the open door.

"We *all* heard that much. The Emperor himself sent me in here to stop your shouting." A hard glance at Tathagata, still gaping like a blowfish. "*And* his. We couldn't hear ourselves think, for the commotion." All trace of amusement vanished. "I ask again: why are you here?"

Sanga understood.

"I want the authority to lead a search for Belisarius to the west. That's where he's gone. I'm certain of it."

Lord Tathagata's outrage, finally, could contain itself no longer. But—carefully—he made sure it was directed at the Rajput.

"This is insolent madness, Nanda Lal," he grated. "The stinking Rajput just got tired of—"

He was silenced, this time, by the Emperor's own voice.

"Bring them both here, Nanda Lal," came the imperial command from the next room.

Tathagata ground his teeth. But he said nothing, even though his face was flushed with anger.

The next words, coming from the adjoining room, caused his fat face to go pale. Words spoken by an old woman.

"Yes, Nanda Lal, bring them here. At once."

Rana Sanga was surprised by the Emperor's private chamber. It was much smaller than he expected, and almost—well, "utilitarian" hardly fit a room with such tapestries and furnishings. But, compared to any other setting in which the Rajput kinglet had ever seen his sovereign, the chamber was almost stark and bare.

There were three occupants in the room. Emperor Skandagupta, his daughter Sati, and his aunt the Great Lady Holi. Sanga had seen both of the women before, on ceremonial occasions, but only from a distance. He had never spoken to either of them.

He was struck by their appearance. Neither of the women was veiled. The princess Sati was a beautiful young woman, abstractly, but she seemed as remote as the horizon. The Great Lady Holi seemed even more distant, especially when Sanga met her eyes. Blank, empty eyes. Vacant eyes.

More than their appearance, however, what impressed Sanga was their chairs. Not spectacular, those chairs, by imperial standards. But they were every bit as good as the Emperor's. No one, in Sanga's experience, ever sat in a chair which was as good as the Emperor's. Not in the same room that he occupied, at least.

Sanga did not have time to ponder the significance of the fact, however. Lord Tathagata, again, could not restrain his outrage.

"Your Majesty—Great Lady Holi—I must insist that this Rajput be punished. *Severely.* What is at stake here is nothing less than the most essential military discipline. This—this—this *dog* disobeyed my express—"

Great Lady Holi's tone of voice was as vacant as her eyes. But the words themselves were like a knife. Cold, thin, sharp.

"What is at stake here, Tathagata, is the incompetence of our military command. Every word you speak illustrates it further."

Tathagata gasped. Sanga, watching, realized the man was utterly terrified. The Rajput kinglet transferred his gaze back to the Great Lady. His face bore no expression, but his mind was a solid frown of puzzlement. He could see nothing in that elderly female figure to cause such pure fear. Except, possibly, those eyes.

Is she a power behind the throne? he wondered. I've heard tales—witchcraft, sorcery—but I never took them seriously.

The Emperor spoke now, to Tathagata. Like a cobra might speak to its prey. A short, pudgy, unprepossessing cobra. But a cobra for all that.

"We have just discovered—only this morning—that Rana Sanga attempted to warn us once before that Belisarius was deceiving us. But you silenced him then, just as you are trying to silence him now."

"That's a lie!" exclaimed Tathagata.

"It is not a lie," spoke a voice from the rear.

Sanga turned. Lord Damodara was seated in a far corner of the room. The Rajput had been so preoccupied when he entered the imperial chamber that he had not spotted him.

Damodara rose and advanced into the center of the room.

"It is not a lie," he repeated. "At the Emperor's council at Ranapur, when Rana Sanga gave his opinion on Belisarius' actions, he attempted to speak further. To warn us that the Roman was planning treachery. You silenced him."

"Yes, you did," growled the Emperor. "I remember it quite clearly. Do you call *me* a liar?"

Tathagata shook his head feverishly. "Of course not, Your Majesty! Of course not! But—I did not know what he was going to say—and it was a Malwa council—he is a Rajput—and—" Almost in a wail: "How does anyone know what he meant to say?"

Damodara: "Because I asked him, afterward. And he told me. That is why, when the council reconvened, I demanded that—" He fell abruptly silent. "That is why I demanded what I did."

Damodara pointed toward Sanga with a head-nod. "I said nothing, at the time, of Rana Sanga's words." Bitterly, contemptuously: "Lest he be penalized by such as you. But I finally managed to tell the Emperor and Nanda Lal and—Great Lady Holi—just this morning."

Bitterly, contemptuously: "Which was the earliest moment you would allow me an audience with them."

"I knew nothing of this," whined Tathagata.

"That is why you are guilty of incompetence rather than treason," said Great Lady Holi. Her words, for all their harshness, were spoken in a tone which—to Rana Sanga, at least—had absolutely no emotional content whatsoever. She might have been speaking about the weather. A thousand miles away, in a land she had never visited and never would.

"Leave us, Lord Tathagata," commanded the Emperor. Skandagupta sat up in his chair. He was still short, and pudgy. But he reminded Rana Sanga of nothing so much as a cobra flaring its hood.

"You are relieved of your command. Retire to your estate and remain there."

"But—Your Majesty—"

"You are now relieved of half your estate. The richer half. Do not attempt to dissemble. Imperial auditors will check your claim."

Tathagata stared, wide-eyed, paralyzed.

The Emperor:

"If you are still in this room one minute from now, you will be relieved of your entire estate. In two minutes, I will have you executed."

Tathagata was out the door in four seconds.

The Emperor glanced at Lord Damodara.

"Inform Lord Jivita that he is now the commander of the army. I will see him in one hour."

Lord Damodara bowed and turned to go. Great Lady Holi stopped him.

"Tell him to meet the Emperor in his western chamber, Lord Damodara."

Again, Sanga was struck by the cold, icy tone of her words.

(No—the tone was not cold. Cold is a temperature. Ice is a substance. That tone had no temperature at all. No substance at all.)

But he was struck even more by the Emperor's sudden start of surprise.

She just commanded the Emperor to leave this room, he realized. Then, watching the Emperor's slight shrug: And he's going to obey—without so much as a protest! What gives this old woman such power?

Nanda Lal spoke. "What, exactly, do you propose to do, Rana Sanga?"

The Rajput shook off the mental shock caused by Great Lady Holi's words. Almost with relief, he turned to the spymaster.

"First, I will need the assistance of your spies, and your records. Belisarius—not *even* Belisarius—can have managed to escape Kausambi without leaving a trace. It will be there, if we search. Then, if I am right, and we find that he went west rather than south, I will go after him with my cavalry."

"Your troop? That's only five hundred men."

Sanga repressed a snort of derision.

"That will be more than enough. He is only one man, Nanda Lal, not an asura. The problem is finding him, not capturing him once we do. For that, five hundred good cavalrymen are enough."

He decided to throw caution to the winds.

"They are not simply enough—they are the best soldiers for the job. That huge mob floundering about in the south"—he made no attempt to conceal the derision in his gesture—"are just getting in each other's way. If Belisarius can be caught—*if*, Nanda Lal; I make no promises, not with *that* man having a week's lead on us—my Rajputs and Pathan trackers will catch him."

"And if you fail?" demanded the Emperor.

Sanga looked at Skandagupta, hesitated, and then threw all caution to the winds.

"If I fail, Your Majesty, I fail. In war, you sometimes lose. Not because you are incompetent, but simply because the enemy is better."

"And is—*this foul Roman*—better than you?"

All caution to the winds.

"He is *not* a 'foul Roman,' Your Majesty. That has been our mistake all along. He is a *true* Roman, and that is what makes him dangerous. That, and his own great skill."

The Emperor's corpulent face was flushed with anger but, like Lord Tathagata before him, that flush was erased by the Great Lady Holi.

"Stop, Skandagupta," she commanded. "Link has no more time for Malwa vanity."

Sanga was shocked to see the Emperor's face turn pale. There was something odd, he realized, about the Great Lady Holi's voice. It was somehow changing, transmuting. Emotionless before, it was now beginning to sound utterly inhuman.

And who is "Link"? he wondered.

The strangeness deepened, and deepened. Great Lady Holi's voice:

"NANDA LAL, DO AS RANA SANGA ASKS. QUERY YOUR SPIES. CHECK ALL RECORDS."

There was nothing at all human in the tone of that voice, any more. It sounded like—

Rana Sanga froze. He had heard tales, now and then, but had paid them no mind. Years ago, bowing to the collective decision of Rajputana's assembled kings in council, Rana Sanga had also given his oath to the Malwa Emperor. He had ignored, then and thereafter—with all the dignity of a Rajput Hindu—the whispered rumors of Malwa's new gods.

—like the voice of a goddess. Cold, not like ice, but like the vastness of time itself.

In a half-daze, he heard *the voice* continue:

"LEAVE US, SKANDAGUPTA. LINK WISHES TO SPEAK TO RANA SANGA."

The Rajput heard the Emperor's protesting words, but understood not a one of them. Only the reply:

"LEAVE, MALWA. YOU ARE OUR INSTRUMENT, NOTHING MORE. IF YOU DISPLEASE US, WE SHALL FIND ANOTHER. LEAVE NOW."

The Emperor left—scurried from the room, in fact, with little more dignity than Tathagata had scurried not long before. Sanga was alone, now, with the two women.

At first, he expected to see the young princess leave as well. Instead, Sati spoke to him:

"I realize that this must come as a shock to you, Rana Sanga," she said in a very polite tone. Her voice, Sanga was relieved to discover, was still that of a young woman. A cold, distant, aloof voice, true. But unmistakeably human.

The Rajput glanced at Great Lady Holi. The old woman, he was even more relieved to discover, seemed to have retreated into a trance. It was almost as if she were not there. Only a statue of her, unmoving, rigid.

Sati followed his glance, smiled faintly.

"She is not Great Lady Holi. Not really. Great Lady Holi is simply a vessel. The divine being who dwells in that vessel is named *Link*."

"A goddess? Or a god?" asked Sanga. He was rather proud that his voice neither stammered nor had a trace of tremor.

"Neither," replied Sati. "Link has no sex, Rana Sanga. It is a pure being, a *deva* spirit sent by the gods. The new gods." The young princess straightened her back. "When Great Lady Holi dies, I will replace her as Link's vessel. I have trained for that sacred mission my entire life. Since I was but a babe."

Watching her obvious pride in that announcement, Sanga felt a sudden pang. He did not find Sati attractive, as a man might find a woman. For all the comeliness of the young princess, hers was a type of aloof beauty which appealed to him not at all. His own wife was plump, plain-faced, and prematurely grey. She was also as warm as rich earth, and as playful as a kitten.

Still, he felt a pang. He could not imagine this princess ever tickling a husband in bed, mercilessly, as his own wife delighted in doing. But he could not help that pang, thinking of this young woman as—whatever Holi was. Something not human.

The inhuman thing in the room, he now learned, could read minds far better than any mortal.

"DO NOT FEEL SORROW AT SATI'S FATE, RANA SANGA. YOUR SORROW IS MISPLACED. IT DERIVES FROM NOTH-ING MORE THAN IGNORANCE."

He stared at Great La—at *Link*.

"YOU ARE PRIVILEGED, RANA SANGA. YOU ARE THE FIRST HUMAN I HAVE SPOKEN TO SINCE I ARRIVED IN THIS WORLD, OTHER THAN MALWA."

"Why?" he managed to ask.

"IT IS NECESSARY. I DID NOT EXPECT BELISARIUS TO BE SO CAPABLE. THE HISTORICAL RECORD MISLED ME."

Sanga frowned. Curiosity overrode all fear.

"You knew of him?"

"OF COURSE. IN THE WORLD THAT WAS, HE RECON-QUERED THE ROMAN EMPIRE FOR JUSTINIAN. GIVEN THE SEVERE LIMITS UNDER WHICH HE WAS FORCED TO OPERATE, HE MAY HAVE BEEN THE GREATEST GENERAL EVER PRODUCED BY HUMANITY. HE WAS CERTAINLY ONE OF THEM. THE DISTINCTION, AT THAT LEVEL OF GENIUS, IS STATISTICALLY MEANINGLESS."

Sanga did not understand the word "statistically," but he grasped the essence of her—of *Link's*—statement.

"If you knew all that, why—"

"I AM NOT A GOD. THE GODS THEMSELVES—THE NEW GODS, EVEN, WHO ARE REAL—ARE NOT GODS. NOT AS YOU UNDERSTAND THE TERM. NOTHING IN THE UNIVERSE CAN BE A 'GOD' AS YOU UNDERSTAND THE TERM. IT IS PRECLUDED BY CHAOS THEORY AND THE UNCERTAINTY PRINCIPLE."

The last sentence was pure gibberish, but, again, Sanga understood the sense of Link's statement. For a moment, his Hindu orthodoxy rose in rebellion, but Sanga drove it down. The moment was too important for religious fretting.

"Explain further. Please."

"I COULD KNOW OF BELISARIUS, BEFORE I ARRIVED, ONLY THAT WHICH IS RECORDED IN HISTORY. THAT HE IS A GREAT GENERAL, IS A MATTER OF RECORD. THAT HE IS SOMETHING GREATER, IS NOT. I DO NOT UNDERSTAND THAT UNEXPECTED CAPACITY. NO GENERAL COULD HAVE DONE WHAT HE HAS DONE. NO GENERAL COULD HAVE MANIPULATED ALL OF MALWA SO PERFECTLY. AND, CERTAINLY, NO GENERAL COULD HAVE REACTED SO INSTANTLY WHEN I DETECTED HIS DUPLICITY."

For a moment, Link paused, as if in thought.

Does such a being even "think"? wondered Sanga.

"EITHER MY DATA ARE INCOMPLETE, OR OTHER FACTORS ARE AT WORK. I MUST DISCOVER WHICH. IT IS ESSENTIAL THAT YOU CATCH HIM, FOR THAT REASON ABOVE ALL OTHERS."

Awed, Sanga was; frightened, even. But he was still a Rajput. A Rajput *king*, he reminded himself.

"I cannot promise you that," he stated harshly. "And I will make no vow which I cannot keep."

In the silence which followed, Sanga had time to wonder at his punishment. Would this—*divinity*—be satisfied with stripping him of his lands? Or would it demand his life?

The response, when it finally came, astonished him. From the divine being who secretly ruled Malwa, he had expected a Malwa reaction.

"EXCELLENT. YOU ARE A TREASURE, RANA SANGA. IT IS POSSIBLE THAT WE ERRED, CHOOSING MALWA

OVER RAJPUT. IN THE END, RELIABILITY SEEMED MORE
IMPORTANT THAN CAPABILITY. FROM THE LONG VIEW
OF TIME."

The last sentence was chilling. Sanga suddenly grasped—even
if only vaguely—the *immensity* of that "long view of time." As
gods might see it.

"NOW, AS A RESULT, WE MUST ADAPT. MORE OF RAJPU-
TANA'S ESSENCE MUST BE INCORPORATED INTO THE
NEW WORLD WE ARE CREATING. MORE OF THAT CAPA-
BILITY."

Sanga was not entirely sure he found those words reassuring.
For him, Rajputana's essence was not Rajput ability. It was the
Rajput soul. Rajput honor.

Again, the divine being called Link seemed to read his mind
perfectly.

"YOU DO NOT UNDERSTAND, RANA SANGA. MALWA
AND RAJPUT ARE BUT MOMENTS. STAGES IN A PROCESS,
NOTHING MORE. TO YOU, THEY LOOM LARGE AND FIXED.
TO THE NEW GODS, THEY ARE AS TRANSIENT AS MAY-
FLIES. ALL THAT MATTERS IS THE PROCESS."

"What—*process*?" he croaked.

"THE SALVATION OF HUMANITY FROM WHAT IT WILL
BECOME. FROM THE HORROR OF ITS SELF-CREATED
FUTURE. I WAS SENT BACK IN TIME TO CHANGE THAT
FUTURE. TO CHANGE HISTORY.

"I WILL SHOW YOU THAT HORROR. I WILL GUIDE YOU
THROUGH THE FUTURE. THROUGH HUMAN DAMNATION.
THROUGH FINAL POLLUTION."

Sanga had time, just, to begin raising his hand in protest. His
hand felt limply to his side.

Visions gripped him, like a python.

Chapter 19

Blinding flash. A sun arose below the sun. The city beneath that sun vanished. Its inhabitants were incinerated before they knew it.

The city's suburbs were not so fortunate. Charred, but not vaporized; its people screaming, their skins peeled from their bodies in an instant. Seconds later, the suburbs and its shrieking people were blown apart by a sweeping wall of wind.

"SHOCK WAVE. OVERPRESSURE."

Sanga understood neither term. Nor the next:

"SEVENTY-MEGATON WARHEAD. EXCESSIVE. CRUDE. THE OTHER SIDE RESPONDED WITH MIRVS. CIRCULAR PROBABILITY OF ERROR WAS SO FINE AS TO MAKE UP THE DIFFERENCE."

Another city. Obliterated, not by one giant sun, but by ten smaller ones. The difference, in the end, was nothing.

"THE EXCHANGE CONTINUED FOR EIGHT DAYS. WITHIN A MONTH, HALF THE WORLD'S LIFE WAS GONE. WITHIN A YEAR, ALL OF IT, ABOVE THE LEVEL OF BACTERIA. IT WAS THE FIRST TIME HUMANITY EXTINGUISHED ITS OWN WORLD. IT WOULD NOT BE THE LAST."

The world, barren. A single vast desert, so bleak as to make the Thar seem an oasis. The seas, grey and empty. The sky, black with an overcast thicker than anything Sanga had ever seen, in the worst of monsoon season.

"FOUR TIMES HUMANITY DESTROYED THE EARTH. TWICE BY NUCLEAR FIRE, ONCE BY KINETIC BOLIDES, ONCE BY DISEASE."

The only term he understood was "disease."

"THE DISEASE WAS THE WORST.

"A CRYSTALLINE PSEUDO-VIRUS WHICH TARGETED DEOXYRIBONUCLEIC ACID. DNA IS THE BASIS FOR ALL LIFE. WITHOUT IT, LIFE IS IMPOSSIBLE. TRUE LIFE IS IMPOSSIBLE. THE EARTH DESTROYED BY FIRE COULD BE REPOPULATED. EVEN RADIOACTIVITY DIES AWAY, GIVEN SUFFICIENT TIME. THIS PLAGUE—NEVER. EVEN THE BACTERIA ARE GONE. THE EARTH WILL BE BARREN FOREVER. HOME ONLY TO ABOMINATIONS."

The earth, again. Barren, again. But now, everywhere that land could be seen, glittering with a network of gleaming points. Like a spider's web, or the tainted flesh of a plague victim.

"YOU WONDER HOW THE EARTH COULD BE REPOPULATED AFTER ALL LIFE WAS DESTROYED. I WILL SHOW YOU."

A great wheeling spiral. Made up of millions of points of light. The view swept closer. Each of those lights was a sun. Most suns were circled by worlds. Billions of worlds. Each different.

Closer.

Small bodies moved through that incredible black vastness. Slow, slow, slow, slow. Machines, Sanga realized. Vessels of some kind.

"SPACECRAFT. LIMITED BY THE SPEED OF LIGHT."

Sanga understood the words: "speed" "of" "light." But they seemed meaningless. Light was. How could it have a speed?

"IT DOES. 186,300 MILES PER SECOND. NOTHING IN THE UNIVERSE CAN MOVE FASTER. IT TOOK THESE SPACECRAFT CENTURIES TO REACH THE NEAREST STARS. BUT REACH THEM THEY DID. AND THEN, CENTURIES LATER, STARS BEYOND. AND THEN, MILLENIA LATER, STARS BEYOND. AND BEYOND AND BEYOND. AND BEYOND AND BEYOND.

"MILLIONS UPON MILLIONS OF YEARS."

Sanga's sense of time expanded. He saw the spacecraft spreading through the heavens. Saw an immense duration compressed into an instant. Saw the seeds of his world scattered throughout the spiral.

"GALAXY. THIS GALAXY. THE MILKY WAY, YOU CALL IT. HUMANS WILL ALSO REACH ANDROMEDA, AND THE MAGELLANIC CLOUDS—ALL THE GALAXIES IN THE LOCAL

GROUP. NO OTHER CONSCIOUS LIFEFORM HAS EVER BEEN FOUND. NOW THAT HUMANS—FORMER HUMANS—HAVE SPREAD THROUGHOUT THE GALAXY AND ITS NEIGHBORS, THEY HAVE FILLED THAT ECOLOGICAL ZONE WHICH YOU CALL 'INTELLIGENCE.' NO OTHER WILL EVER ARISE.

"AND HUMANITY HAS DESTROYED ITSELF. IT HAS BECOME NOTHING BUT MONSTROSITIES. A DISEASE. THE POLLUTION OF THE UNIVERSE."

A world of gigantic trees. Large monkey-like creatures swung through its branches. They were hairless, however, and wore cloth-ing. Cloth strips tightly bound, allowing free movement of their limbs. And a short, muscular tail. Their fingers were long, their toes grotesquely so. For all essential purposes, they were quadrupedal. One of them swung into view.

Its face was human. Had once been human.

A world of water, landless, pocketed by vast floating sargassoes. Fish-like creatures swam through that world-girdling ocean. Once of them was suddenly seized by another shape darting from under a ledge of sargasso weed. Odd shape. Bastard shape. Its flukes moved up and down, like a dolphin, and its body was a streamlined tor-pedo. But it retained very short, stubby arms—barely more than hands thrusting forward from vestigial shoulders. The hands stuffed the "fish" into a wide mouth lined with needle teeth. Then, carefully separated the fish bones and placed them in a pouch tied to its neck.

A closer view. That face, too—that wide-eyed, gape-mouthed, needle-toothed, almost noseless face—had once been human.

A heavy world, thick with atmosphere. Crab-like shapes scuttled across its low-lying surface, busily constructing edifices of some kind. Their arms and hands, though bulky, were still close to human. But they moved on six legs. The rear limbs retained a faint trace of their bipedal origin. But the mid-limbs were sheer nightmare. Adaptations of the ribcage.

Once human.

Monstrosity followed monstrosity. Some were so bizarre that Sanga could not see any remnant in them of humanity.

Nor was Earth the only planet blasted into lifelessness. Sanga saw thousands of those worlds, ravaged and destroyed by—"nuclear fire," "kinetic bolides"—other things. "DNA plague," eight times. Three planets, drifting together in an empty void beyond time and space itself, had been "rotated about their axis." Many were not even planets, any longer. Simply shards drifting in space. "Very large kinetic bolides."

Sanga understood none of the terms, but he understood the reality. He was a soldier. Horror was no stranger to him. Though he had never, in his worst nightmares, imagined devastation on such a scale.

"YOU WONDER IF I AM LYING TO YOU."

No, he did not. He was inside the mind of Link, now, and understood its basic nature. Link was a "divine being," yes—Sanga could sense the reality of the great new gods which had created it. He could see those perfect, beautiful faces. (The beauty, oddly, did not move him. It was like Sati's beauty, magnified a thousand times. But he had no doubt they were beautiful. And perfect. And divine.)

Nor did he doubt that Link was showing him a true vision. It was not in the nature of the being called Link to lie. Its mind followed the path given to it, like a waterwheel turns with the stream. It could no more lie than a waterwheel could decide to turn against the current.

"THE FINAL ABOMINATION HAS NOW APPEARED."

A luminous shape swam in the void. At first, Sanga thought it to be some kind of ethereal moth, until he grasped the scale of the thing. Whale-sized. Bigger. He could not make out the precise shape of the creature's body. It was not entirely material, he sensed. Much of that shape was—magical?

"FORCE FIELDS. ENERGY MATRIX."

Meaningless words.

"THIS TOO WAS ONCE HUMAN. BUT IT HAS NOT A TRACE LEFT OF ITS HUMAN LEGACY. OF HUMAN PURITY. IT IS NOT EVEN ALIVE."

How?

"THEY ORIGINATED AS BIOLOGISTS, STUDYING THE DNA PLAGUE. SEEKING A CURE, OR A VACCINE. THEY FOUND NO CURE, NO VACCINE. THE DNA PLAGUE, BY ITS NATURE, CANNOT BE STOPPED. ANY ANTIDOTE OR SERUM WOULD BE DNA-BASED ITSELF. SIMPLY MORE FOOD FOR THE PLAGUE."

"Biologists," "vaccine," "serum"—Sanga understood none of them. But he could follow the sense behind the words.

"INSTEAD, THEY FOUND SOMETHING ELSE. THEY

EMBRACED POLLUTION. THEY CAST THEIR OWN CHIL-
DREN INTO DAMNATION. THEY ABANDONED LIFE ITSELF.
THEY DISCARDED DNA AND SUBSTITUTED A SOULLESS
MECHANISM OF THEIR OWN CREATION."

*Again, Sanga saw the glittering network of crystals. Like a spider's
web—simultaneously repellent and beautiful. But this was not a
web covering a planet. This crystalline web ran through the very
structure of the luminous giant moth—whale?—moving through
the heavens.*

"THEY FOUND A LIFELESS SUBSTITUTE FOR DNA. FOR
LIFE ITSELF. A DERIVATIVE FROM THE SAME CRYSTALS
WHICH DESTROYED DNA. THEY EVEN BREATHED A
PARODY OF INTELLIGENCE INTO THEM. SELF-GUIDED
CHAOTIC INTELLIGENCE, NOT THE OBEDIENT CLEANLI-
NESS OF THE COMPUTER. THE ABOMINATION IS COM-
PLETE. POLLUTION IS ALL THAT REMAINS."

*Sanga did not understand the term "computer," though he
sensed that Link itself bore its likeness. The rest—a question came
to his mind.*

What are they called?

"WE HAVE NO NAME FOR THEM BEYOND MONSTERS.
THEIR CRYSTALS CALL THE ABOMINATIONS WHO CRE-
ATED THEM 'THE GREAT ONES.'"

What do these—"Great Ones"—call themselves?

Hesitation, for the first time. Reluctance? Sanga wondered.

"THEY CALL THEMSELVES PEOPLE."

And what do they call their crystal creatures?

*Definite hesitation. Not reluctance, Sanga realized. Ultimate—
distaste.*

"THEY CALL THEM PEOPLE."

When Rana Sanga came back to his senses, he realized that
very little time had passed. The Great Lady Holi and Sati were
still seated before him, quietly, their hands in their laps.

"Now you understand, Rana Sanga," said Sati softly. "Enough,
at least."

Sanga opened his mouth, closed it. He had been about to
protest that he understood very little. Certainly not enough. But
he sensed there was no point in such a protest. Besides, he had
given his oath. *That*, at least, he did understand.

Again, Great Lady Holi seemed to read his mind. But, to

Sanga's relief, when she spoke her voice had resumed a shell of humanity.

"You do not need to understand more, Rana Sanga," said Link's vessel. "Not now, at least."

Stubborn pride rose in the Rajput.

"Why did you come here? To this—to our time?"

"Analysis showed this was the optimum time and place to change history. That task is very difficult, Rana Sanga. History is like a great river. Its currents cannot be dammed. They will simply spill over the levees. A new channel must be dug. A wide, deep, great channel. That task is very hard. The new gods determined that this was the optimum period for making the sharp change needed in humanity's course. Perhaps the only moment when it would be possible."

Stubborn:

"Why?"

"Because in this historical era both of humanity's possible futures exist at the same time. For the only time in history when both could be changed simultaneously. The seed of humanity's actual destruction lies in that abomination called Rome. The seed of its potential glory lies in Malwa India."

Stubborn, still:

"Why?"

"The true future lies here, because only in ancient India did humanity begin to grope toward that truth. What you call the *varna* and the caste system. Your conceptions are mired in superstition and ignorance, but your crude understanding provides the framework for beginning the necessary eugenics program which will preserve the human race. That is why, despite their limitations, we have maintained the Malwa lineage intact, and are shaping everything around that seed. In the Malwa of today, you see only the most primitive germ of the future. But in the end, after millenia of careful genetic management, the new gods will emerge. Not the handful of *this* time, of this polluted future, but the mighty host of the true future we will create."

Sati interrupted, coldly:

"And that is also why, despite Rajput abilities, we have kept the Rajputs subordinate. Of all human vices, none is so insidious and destructive as the blind worship of ability. That way lies abomination."

The Great Lady Holi resumed:

"Rome is where that pollution originated. Or, at least, sank its deepest roots in ancient history. True, other dangerous times and places existed, even in ancient time. We will deal with them soon enough. We will bridle China, for instance, long before the Sung dynasty and its mandarinate disease can even emerge.

"But Rome—*Rome*—that is the great enemy. That is where the great stain first polluted a fourth of the planet. And spread from there, like a disease, in the centuries to come. A latent disease, often enough, endemic rather than epidemic. But always there, that legacy, always ready to rise anew.

"*Rome.* That monstrous realm of mongrels. That absurd so-called empire where any man can call himself a Roman, and demand the protection of Roman law, as if he shared the true Latin lineage. Where no emperor can trace his royal genotype beyond two generations. Where any barbarian can dream of being emperor. Any miscegenate *peasant*—like the one who now wears the purple. Where any polluted *whore* can sit the throne next to him, and receive the honors of the true-born. Ability, in Rome, is all that counts, in the end. It is that worship of ability over purity that will destroy humanity. That unbridled, undisciplined, genetic chaos will ravage this planet and a thousand others. And it will leave, in the end, nothing but inhuman monsters to pollute the universe."

Again, Sati intervened.

"That is enough, Rana Sanga. You have already been privileged beyond all others save Malwa. Do not press the matter further. *Yours, finally, is to obey.*"

Sanga arose, prostrated himself, left the room.

Nanda Lal was waiting for him in Lord Tathagata's chamber—in Lord Tathagata's *former* chamber. The Lords Jivita and Damodara were there also.

"You were right, Rana Sanga," began Nanda Lal immediately. "It was obvious, as soon as I correlated facts already in our possession."

The spymaster's face was truly that of an ogre, now.

"Several of my subordinates will be severely disciplined for neglecting to present those facts to me earlier. *Severely.*"

That meant mutilation, possibly blinding. Sanga could not find any pity in his heart for those unknown subordinates. He had no love for Malwa spies, even competent ones.

"What are the facts?" he demanded.

"A Ye-tai soldier—a member of the imperial bodyguard, in fact—disappeared in Kausambi the very night Belisarius made his escape. He has never returned to his unit."

Lord Jivita, frowning:

"I *still* don't understand why you place such significance on that fact, Nanda Lal. Ye-tai are practically savages. Their discipline—"

"Is absolutely savage," interrupted Sanga. "I agree with Nanda Lal. Say what you will about Ye-tai barbarousness, Lord Jivita. The fact remains that no Ye-tai—no member of the imperial body-guard, for a certainty—would dare remain absent from his post. Ye-tai who fail to report even a day late are subject to cane-lashes which can be crippling. Those whose absence stretches two days *are* crippled. Three days, beheaded. Four days, impaled. Five days or longer, on a short stake."

Nanda Lal nodded. "And it makes sense. Ye-tai more closely resemble Westerners than any other of our peoples. Belisarius could pass himself off as one without much difficulty."

"He does not speak the language," protested Jivita.

"I would not be so sure of that," retorted Sanga. A bit guiltily: "He is an extraordinary linguist. I noticed myself how quickly he became fluent in Hindi, and with almost no trace of an accent. I never heard him speak—"

He stopped, almost gasped.

"I'm a idiot!"

To Nanda Lal, fiercely:

"Have you interviewed the soldiers—the Ye-tai, especially—whom Belisarius rallied for the counter-charge at Ranapur?"

Nanda Lal shook his head. For a moment, he seemed puzzled, until comprehension came.

"Of course! How could he rally the Ye-tai—"

"It can be done," stated Sanga. "Hindi alone, and harsh mea-sures, would have done it. But when you interview those soldiers, I think you will discover that he speaks perfect Ye-tai."

The Rajput began pacing back and forth.

"What else?"

"A squad of soldiers reports that a single Ye-tai departed Kausambi through the Panther Gate the following morning."

"And they allowed him through?" demanded Jivita.

Nanda Lal shrugged. "He was a very fierce and brutal Ye-tai, by their account. He even attacked their sergeant when asked for documents. You can hardly expect common soldiers—"

"Discipline the dogs!" bellowed Jivita. "Give them lashes!"

Sanga and Damodara exchanged glances. Sanga spoke:

"I will deal with the matter, Lord Jivita. I will be passing through the Panther Gate within the hour. I will lash those men myself. You have my word on it."

"Excellent!" exclaimed Jivita.

"I'm off, then." Sanga began to turn away. Nanda Lal called him back.

"A moment, Rana Sanga. I want your opinion."

"Yes?"

The spymaster's broken face was ugly, with frustration as much as rage.

"*We are still missing something.* I can feel it in my bones," he growled. "It's clear enough that the Romans and Ethiopians who fled south—after killing the guards at the barge and blowing up the armory—were simply a diversion. Belisarius, himself, went west. But—there's something else. *I can smell it.* More duplicity."

Sanga paused, thinking.

"I don't have much time now, Nanda Lal," he mused. "But several questions come to my mind. I suggest you think on them."

"Yes?"

"First. What happened to the treasure? Belisarius had two great chests full of gold and jewels. It's not the kind of thing any man wants to leave behind. But how did he get it away? He himself—a single Ye-tai on foot—could have only been carrying a pittance. Nor could his underlings have carried more than a portion of it. Not maintaining their incredible pace, weighted down with all that treasure."

Nanda Lal tugged at the bandage.

"What else?"

"There were too many Ye-tai running around that night. The soldiers at the army camp insisted that they saw Belisarius himself. But when I questioned some of them, they could only say that 'the Ye-tai' told them so. Which Ye-tai?"

"I will find out. What else?"

"Too many Ye-tai—and not enough Kushans. What happened

to Belisarius' Kushan escort? I have heard nothing of them since that night. What happened to them? Did the Romans and Ethiopians kill them all? I doubt it—not *those* Kushans. I know their commander. Not well, but well enough. His name is Kungas, and he would not have been taken by surprise. What happened to him and his men?"

Glaring, now, and tugging fiercely on his bandage:

"And what *else?*"

Sanga shrugged. "With Belisarius, who knows? I would trace everything back to the beginning, from the day he arrived in India. I can see no connection, but—I always wondered, Nanda Lal. Exactly how did Shakuntala escape from Venandakatra's palace?"

Jivita interrupted, his voice full of irritation:

"What is the point of this, Rana Sanga? Everybody knows how she escaped. That fiend Rao butchered her guards and took her away."

Rana Sanga stared at him. He managed to keep any trace of contempt out of his face.

"So? Have you ever spoken—personally—to the Pathan trackers who were with the Rajputs who tried to recapture Rao and the princess?"

Jivita drew back haughtily.

"That is hardly my—"

"No, he didn't," interrupted Nanda Lal. "Neither did I. Should I have?"

Sanga shrugged. "Every Pathan tracker claimed there was only one set of footprints to be found, not two. A man's footprints. No trace of a woman at all." Sanga stroked his beard. "And that's not the only peculiar thing about that escape. I know none of the details, but—again, I have wondered. How did one man kill all those guards? Excellent guards, I would assume?"

He caught the odd look in Nanda Lal's eyes.

"Tell me," he commanded.

"She was being guarded by priests and mahamimamsa," muttered Nanda Lal.

"*What?*" erupted Sanga. "Who in their right mind would set any but the finest soldiers to guard someone—*from Rao?*" For the second time that day, Sanga lost his temper. "*Are you Malwa all mad?*" he roared. "I have fought Raghunath Rao in single combat! He was the most terrifying warrior I ever encountered!"

The Malwa in the room, for all their rank, almost cringed. They knew the story. All of India knew that story.

"From Raghunath Rao? You—you—imbeciles—thought to guard Shakuntala from Rao—with priests? Stinking torturers?"

Jivita tried to rally his Malwa outrage, but the attempt collapsed under the sheer fury of the Rajput's glare. Lord Damodara coughed apologetically.

"Please, Rana Sanga! It was Lord Venandakatra's decision, not ours. He was concerned about the girl's purity, it seems. So he put her in the custody of sworn celibates instead of—"

It was almost comical, the way Damodara and Nanda Lal's jaws dropped in unison.

"—instead of an elite Kushan unit," finished Nanda Lal, hoarsely.

"Commanded by a man named Kungas, as I recall," croaked Damodara. "I am not certain."

Sanga snorted. "You can be certain of it now, Lord Damodara. Investigate! You will find, I imagine, that these Kushans were removed just before Shakuntala escaped. And just before Belisarius himself arrived at the palace, if memory serves me correctly."

"It does," hissed Nanda Lal. The spymaster almost staggered.

"Gods in heaven," he whispered. "Is it possible? How—there was no connection, I am certain of it. But the—*coincidence*." He looked to the Rajput, appeal in his eyes. "How could any man be so cunning as to manage that?" he demanded.

Sanga made a chopping gesture with his hand. "If any man could, it is Belisarius. Investigate, Nanda Lal. For the first time, assume nothing. Look for treasure, and mysterious Ye-tai and Kushans who appear and disappear. And, most of all—*look for the Princess Shakuntala*." He turned away, growling: "But that is your job, not mine. I have a Roman to catch."

"A fiend!" cried Nanda Lal.

"No," murmured Sanga, leaving the room. "A fiendish mind, yes. But not a fiend. Never that."

Nanda Lal *did* investigate, thoroughly and relentlessly. He was an immensely capable man, for all his Malwa arrogance. And his natural tenacity was fueled by a burning hatred for all things remotely connected to Belisarius. Once Nanda Lal set himself to the task—and, for the first time, without careless prior assumptions—he solved the riddle within two days. Most of it, at least. All of it, he thought.

Some weeks later, an inn beside the Ganges was blessed beyond measure. It was a poor inn, owned by a poor Bengali family. Their only treasure, the innkeeper liked to say, was the sight of the mighty Ganges itself, pouring its inexorable way south to the Bay of Bengal.

(The *sacred* Ganges, he would say, in the presence of his immediate family, as he led them in secret prayers. He and his family still held to the old faith, and gave the Mahaveda no more than public obeisance.)

That poor family was rich tonight, as northern Bengali measured such things. The nobleman was most generous, and his wife even more so.

She spoke little, the noblewoman—properly, especially for a wife so much younger than her husband—but her few words were very kind. The innkeeper and his family were quite taken by her. The nobleman, for all his cordiality and good manners, frightened them a bit. He had that pale, western look to his features. That Malwa look. (They did not think he was Malwa himself, but—high in their ranks. And from western India, for certain. That cruel, pitiless west.)

But his wife—no, she was no Malwa. No western Indian. She was as small as a Bengali, and even darker. Keralan, perhaps, or Cholan. Whatever. One of *them*, in some sense. Bengalis, of course, were not Dravidians, as she obviously was. More of the ancient Vedic blood flowed in their veins than in the peoples of the southern Deccan. But not all that much more; and they, too, had felt the lash of purity.

The next morning, after the rich nobleman and his retinue departed, the innkeeper told his family they would close the inn for a few days. They had not been able to afford a vacation for years. They would do so now, after bathing in the sacred Ganges.

The innkeeper and his wife remembered the few days which followed as a time of rare and blessed rest from toil. Their brood of children remembered it as the happiest days of their happy childhood.

Happy, too, was the innkeeper and his wife, after their return. When their neighbors told them, hushed and fearful, of the soldiers who had terrorized the village the day before. Shouting at folk—even beating them. Demanding to know if anyone had seen a young, dark-skinned woman accompanied by Kushan soldiers.

Something stirred, vaguely, in the innkeeper's mind. But he pushed it down resolutely.

None of his business. He had not been here to answer any questions, after all. And he certainly had no intention of *looking* for the authorities.

So, in the end, Nanda Lal would fail again.

Partly, because he continued to make assumptions even when he thought he wasn't. He assumed, without thinking about it, that a fleeing princess and her soldiers would seek the fastest way out of the Malwa empire. So he sent a host of soldiers scouring north India in all directions, looking for a young woman and Kushans on horseback.

Neither a pious innkeeper on vacation, nor a young officer hiding his humiliation, nor any of the other folk who might have guided the Malwa to Shakuntala, made the connection.

And the one man who could, and did, kept silent.

When Malwa soldiers rousted the stablekeeper in Kausambi, and questioned him, he said nothing. The soldiers did not question him for very long. They were bored and inattentive, having already visited five stables in the great city that morning, and with more to come. So the stablekeeper was able to satisfy them soon enough.

No, he had not seen any young noblewoman—or soldiers—leaving on horseback.

He could not tell the difference between Kushans and any other steppe barbarians, anyway. The savages all looked alike to him.

The soldiers, peasants from the Gangetic plain, smiled. Nodded.

He had seen nothing. Heard nothing. Knew nothing.

The soldiers, satisfied, went on their way.

The plans and schemes of tyrants are broken by many things. They shatter against cliffs of heroic struggle. They rupture on reefs of open resistance. And they are slowly eroded, bit by little bit, on the very beaches where they measure triumph, by countless grains of sand. By the stubborn little decencies of humble little men.

Chapter 20

On his way through the Panther Gate, just as he had promised Lord Jivita, Rana Sanga disciplined the soldiers who had allowed Belisarius to leave the city. "Give them lashes," Jivita had demanded, specifying the plural.

Sanga's word, as always, was good.

Two lashes, each. From his own quirt, wielded by Rajputana's mightiest hand. It is conceivable that a fly might have been slain by those strokes. It is conceivable.

Once he and his cavalry unit were outside the walls of the capital, Sanga conferred with his lieutenants and his chief Pathan tracker as they rode westward. The conference was very brief, since the fundamental problem of their pursuit was obvious to anyone who even glanced at the countryside.

The Gangetic plain, after a week of heavy rainfall, was a sea of mud. Any tracks—tracks even a day old, much less eight—had been obliterated. The only portion of the plain which was reasonably dry was the road itself. A good road, the road to Mathura, but the fact brought no comfort to the Rajputs. Many fine things have been said about stone-paved roads, but none of them has ever been said by Pathan trackers.

"No horse even leave tracks this fucking idiot stone," groused the Pathan. "No man on his foot."

Sanga nodded. "I know. We will not be able to track him until we reach Rajputana. Not this time of year."

The Rajput glanced up, gauging. The sky was clear, and he hoped they had reached the end of the *kharif*, India's wet season.

The kharif was brought by the monsoon in May, and lasted into September. It would be succeeded by the cool, dry season which Indians called *rabi*. In February, then, the blistering dry heat of *garam* season would scorch India until the monsoon.

Jaimal echoed his own thoughts:

"Rabi is almost here. Thank God."

Sanga grunted approvingly. Like most Indians, rabi was his favorite season.

"There is no point in looking for tracks," he announced. "But we have one advantage, here in the plain—there are many travelers on the road. They will probably have noticed a single Ye-tai. Anyone Belisarius encountered in his first days of travel will be long gone, by now. But we can hope, in two or three days, to start encountering people who saw him."

"The soldiers in the courier relay stations may have spotted him," commented Udai. "They have nothing else to do except watch the road."

"True," said Sanga. "We can make it to the first relay station by mid-afternoon. Udai may well be right—the soldiers may have spotted him. Let's go!"

"Are you sure it is them?" asked the crouching young warrior, peering down into the ravine.

"Oh, yes," said Rao. "Quite sure. I only met one of them, but he is not the sort of man you forget."

The Maratha chieftain rose from his hiding place behind a boulder. The armored horseman leading the small party through the trail below immediately reined in his horse. Rao was impressed by the speed with which the man unlimbered his bow.

He probably shoots well, too. Let's not find out.

"*Ho—Ousanas!*" he bellowed. "Do you still maintain the preposterous claim that all appearance is but the manifestation of eternal and everlasting Forms?"

The reply came instantly:

"Of course! You are the living proof yourself, Raghunath Rao, even where you stand. The very Platonic Form of a sight for sore eyes."

The young guerrillas lining the ravine where Rao had set his ambush—*friendly* ambush, to be sure; but Rao never lost the chance for training his young followers—were goggling.

They were provincials, almost without exception. Poor young villagers, most of whom had never seen any of the world beyond the hills and ridges of the Great Country. The Romans were odd enough, with their ugly bony faces and sick-looking pallid complexions. The Ethiopians and Kushans were even more outlandish. But the other one! A tall half-naked man, black as a cellar in night-time—arguing philosophy with Rao himself!

A maniac. Obvious.

"Oh, Christ," muttered Valentinian, replacing his bow. "Another philosopher. Maniacs, the lot of 'em."

In truth, Valentinian was finding it hard not to goggle himself. Finally, after all these months, he had met the legendary Raghunath Rao. And—

The man was the most ordinary looking fellow he had ever seen! Valentinian had been expecting an Indian version of Achilles.

He studied Rao, now standing atop the boulder some thirty feet away and ten feet up the side of the ravine.

Shortish—by Roman standards, anyway. Average size for a Maratha. Getting a little long in the tooth, too. Must be in his early forties. Well-built, true—no fat on those muscles—but he's no Hercules like Eon. I wonder—

Rao sprang off the boulder and landed lithely on the floor of the ravine ten feet below. Two more quick, bounding steps, and he was standing next to Valentinian's horse. Smiling up at him, extending a hand in welcome.

Mary, Mother of God.

"The Panther of Majarashtra," Valentinian had heard Rao called. He had dismissed the phrase, in the way veterans dismiss all such romantic clap-trap.

"Be polite, Valentinian," he heard Anastasius mutter. "Please. Be polite to that man."

The bodies had been rotting for days, with only two small windows to let air through the thick mudbrick walls. The stench was incredible.

"He's a *demon*," snarled Udai. "Only a soulless *asura* would—"

"Would *what*, Udai?" demanded Sanga.

The Rajput kinglet gestured to the pile of festering corpses.

"Kill enemies? You've done as much yourself."

Udai glared. "Not like *this*. Not—"

"Not *what*? Not from ambush? I can remember at least five ambushes which you laid which were every bit as savage as this one."

Udai clamped his lips shut. But he was still glaring furiously.

Sanga restrained his own temper.

"Listen to me, Udai," he grated. Then, his hard eyes sweeping the other Rajputs in the room:

"*All of you*. Listen. It is time you put this—this *Malwa superstition*—out of your minds. Or you will never understand the nature of this enemy."

He paused. When he was certain that he had their undivided attention—not easy, that; not in a charnelhouse—he continued. His voice was low and cold.

"Some of you were there, in the Emperor's pavilion, when Belisarius ordered his cataphract to execute the prisoners. Do you remember?"

Jaimal and Pratap nodded. The other four Rajputs, after a moment, nodded also. They had not seen, themselves, but they had heard.

Sanga waved at the bodies heaped in a corner of the relay station.

"This is the same man. The Malwa think—*did* think, at least—that he was a weakling. Full of foolish soft notions. Not ruthless, like them. Not *hard*."

A soft chuckle came from the Pathan tracker kneeling by the bodies. "Did really?" he asked. Then rose, his examination complete.

"Well?" demanded Sanga.

"Soldiers all kill same time." The tracker pointed to a crude table collapsed against one of the relay station's mudbrick walls. One of the table's legs was broken off cleanly; another was splintered. Stools were scattered nearby on the packed-earth floor.

"Come through door. Think at night. Quick, quick, quick. Soldiers eat. Surprise them at sitting."

He pointed to the blackened, dried bloodstains on the floor, the wall, the table, the stools. Scattered pieces of food, now moldy.

"That was battle." Indifferent shrug. "Not much. Think two soldiers draw weapon before die. Maybe three. Do no good. Sheep. Butchered."

He paced back to the pile of bodies.

"Then wait for couriers. Eat soldier food while wait. Pack away other food. Round up horses in corral. Make ready."

The Pathan bent over and seized one of the corpses. With a casual jerk, he spilled the rotting horror onto the floor. The impact, slight as it was, ruptured the stomach wall. Half-liquid intestines spilled out, writhing with maggots. The Pathan stepped back a pace, but showed no other reaction.

"First courier. Tortured."

He leaned over the putrid mess, picked up a wrist, waved the hand. The thumb fell off. The index and middle fingers were already missing.

"Two finger cut off. Want information. How many courier come after?"

He dropped the hand, straightened.

"Good method. Cut one, say: 'Tell, or cut two.' Cut two, say: 'tell, or cut three.' That mostly enough. Good method. Very good. Quick, quick. Have use myself."

The Pathan turned away. To those who did not know him, his callous attitude was appalling. To those who did know him, it was considerably worse.

"Wait again. Next courier." He pointed to one of the bodies in the livery of the royal courier service.

"No torture. No need. He tell, die."

He pointed to the third courier.

"Last one. No torture. No need. He tell, die."

The Pathan glanced at the far door, which led to the corral where the spare horses were kept. *Had* been kept.

"Then put courier horses to corral. Tired horses. No good. Take all other horses. Fed, rested. Five horses. Good horses. Leave."

Finished with his report, the tracker planted his hands on hips and surveyed the entire scene.

"Very fine man!" grunted the tracker. "Quick, quick. No stupidityness. Would adopt into own clan."

Sanga allowed his subordinates to digest the information a moment, before continuing.

"Never make that mistake again," he growled. "That *Malwa* mistake. He is not a cruel man, Belisarius. Of that I am quite certain. But no mahamimamsa who ever lived can match him for ruthlessness when he needs to be. The man is as quick and shrewd as a mongoose. And just as deadly. How much mercy does a mongoose give a cobra?"

Jaimal grunted. Sanga drove on:

"There's *another* lesson. He is not a devil, but he has a devil's way of thinking. Consider how bold and cunning this move was. After his men created a diversion and led all of us on a wild goose chase, Belisarius marched out of Kausambi—openly—disguised as a Ye-tai." He cast a cold eye sideways. "Three guesses how he got the Ye-tai's uniform, Udai?"

His lieutenant winced, looked away. Sanga grated on:

"Then he came as fast as possible to the first relay station. He was out-thinking us every step of the way. He had two problems: first, no horses; second, he knew couriers would be sent to alert the garrisons on the coast. He solved both problems at one stroke."

"Killed the soldiers, ambushed the couriers, stole their horses," muttered Jaimal. "The best horses in India."

"*Five* of them," added Pratap. "He has remounts, as many as he needs. He can drive the horses for as long as he can stay in the saddle. Switch whenever his mount gets tired."

"How could he be sure the bodies wouldn't be found soon?" complained Udai. "Then the hunt would be up."

Sanga frowned. "I don't know. The man's intelligence is uncanny—in the military sense of the term, as well. He seems to know everything about us. Outside of the Ganges plain, this trick wouldn't have worked. Because of banditry, all relay stations in the western provinces are manned by full platoons and checked by patrol. But here—"

"These aren't even regular army troops," snorted Pratap. "Provincial soldiers. Unmarried men. They're stationed here for two year stretches. Even grow their own food."

The Rajput stared down at the hideous mound.

"Poor bastards," he said softly. "I stopped at one of these relay stations, once. The men—boys—were so ecstatic to see a new face they kept me talking all night." He glanced at the Pathan. "Like he says, sheep to the slaughter." Then, hissing fury: "*Roman butcher.*"

Sanga said nothing. He felt that rage himself. But, unlike Pratap, did not let the rage blind his memory. He had seen other men lying in such heaps. Men just like these—young, lonely, inattentive.

Soldiers in name only. They, too, had been like sheep at the hands of a butcher.

A butcher named Rana Sanga. Against whose experienced cunning and lightning sword they had stood no chance at all.

"We'll never catch him now," groaned Udai.

"We will try," stated Sanga. His tone was like steel.

Then, with a bit of softness:

"It is not impossible, comrades. Not for Rajputs. He is still only one man, with well over a thousand miles to travel. He will need to rest, to eat—to find food to eat."

"One man alone," added Jaimal, "disguised as a Ye-tai, possibly. Leading several horses. People will notice him."

"Yes. He will be able to travel faster than we can, on any single day. And he begins with many days headstart. But he cannot keep it up, day after day, the way an entire cavalry troop can do. We can requisition food and shelter. He cannot. He must scrounge it up. That takes time, every day. And there are many days ahead of him. Many days, before he reaches the coast. He may become injured, or sick. With no comrades to care for him. If nothing else, he will become very weary."

"Where is he headed, do you think?" asked Pratap.

Sanga shrugged.

"Too soon to tell. He will probably head for Ajmer. In case he does not, we will split off smaller units to search for him in other towns. But I believe he will go to Ajmer, first. He needs to get out of the Ganges plain quickly, where there are a multitude of people watching. Into Rajputana, where there are not."

"Ajmer," mused Jaimal, stroking his beard. "Ajmer. From there, he can go south or west. South, along the foot of the Aravallis, toward the Gulf of Khambat. Maybe even Bharakuccha, where he could hope to rejoin his men."

"Or west," added Udai, "to Barbaricum."

"We will know soon enough," stated Sanga. He began striding toward the door. "Once he is out of the plains, he will start leaving tracks. We will find his tracks before Ajmer."

Less than a minute later, five hundred Rajputs set their horses into motion. Not a frenzied gallop; just the determined canter of expert horsemen, with a thousand and a half miles ahead of them.

✧　　✧　　✧

He had never been a handsome man, true. But now, for the first time in his life, he was an object of ridicule.

Children's ridicule. Palace children.

Flat-face, they called him, behind his back. Or thought they did, not realizing how impossible it was to talk behind *his* back. *The Frog*, they snickered, or *The Fish*, or, most often, *The Nose*. Always, of course, in secret whispers. Not understanding, not in the least. The man noted the children, noted their names. Someday their powerful fathers would be dead.

Thinking of those distant days, the man smiled. Then, thinking of a day nearer still, the smile deepened.

It was a new smile, for that man. In days gone by, his smile—his grin—had been hearty and cheerful-seeming. The weeks of painful recovery had distorted the smile, almost as much as they had distorted his face.

A cold, savage smile. A snarl, really.

The new smile fitted the man much better than the old one ever had, in all truth. It looked like what it was, now. The smile of a spymaster, after ensuring his revenge.

Couriers had been dispatched, again. Not royal couriers, riding royal roads. No, these couriers were a different breed altogether. Almost as fine horsemen, and far more lethal men.

The best agents in Malwa's superb espionage service. Three of them, all of whom were familiar with the road to Rome. The *northern* route, this, the land road—not the slow, roundabout, southern sea-going route taken by most. These men would ride their horses, all with remounts, through the Hindu Kush. Through central Asia. Across Persia, using the network of Malwa spies already in place. Into Anatolia, with the aid of a similar—if smaller—network. And finally, to Constantinople.

In Constantinople, they would pass their message to the Malwa agent in charge of the Roman mission. Balban would not be pleased at that message. It would result in much work being cast aside.

But he would obey. Wondering, perhaps, if the orders stemmed from sagacity or malice. But he would obey.

In point of fact, sagacity and malice were *both* at work. For all his fury, the spymaster was still a rational man. A professional at his trade.

He knew, even if Balban still fooled himself, that the Roman general's duplicity had a partner. He realized, even if they did not, that the Malwa agents in Constantinople had been fooled as badly as he himself had been in India.

No longer. Sagacity demanded the orders anyway. The fact that the same orders would be an exquisite revenge was almost incidental.

Almost, but not quite.

The spymaster smiled again. He was a realist. He knew that Belisarius might manage his escape from India. But the spymaster would have the satisfaction of robbing all pleasure from that escape.

If Belisarius made his way home, he would find the place empty. The orders would reach Rome before he did.

She is deceiving you, as he deceived us.

Kill the whore.

Chapter 21

A hundred miles east of Ajmer, once they reached the dry country, the Pathan finally picked up Belisarius' tracks.

By the time they reached the city, he was a thoroughly disillusioned man.

"Not adopt this one never," he grumbled. "Very stupid beast. See no thing."

The tracker leaned from his horse, scanned the road, snorted, spat noisily.

"Probably he fuck goat. Think it wife."

Spat noisily.

"Pay no attention to no thing."

Spat noisily.

"Idiot blind man."

Riding beside him, Sanga smiled wrily. Like most men with a narrow field of vision, the Pathan tended to judge people by very limited criteria.

True, Belisarius had finally made a mistake. But it was a small mistake, by any reasonable standard. So small, in fact, that only an expert tracker would have spotted it.

Somewhere along the way—hardly surprising, in weeks of travel—one of the Roman general's horses had cut its hoof. Nothing serious, in itself. Barely more than a nick, caused by a sharp stone. The horse itself would have hardly noticed, even at the time, and the "wound" in no way discomfited it.

But it was just enough to leave a distinctive track. No one else had spotted it, but the Pathan had seen it immediately. Several of the Rajputs, after the tracker pointed it out, had expressed their delight.

Henceforth, Belisarius would be easy to find!

The Pathan had derided their enthusiasm. Such a very good quickquick man, he assured them, would soon enough spot the mark himself. He would then remove it by carving away more of the tissue, leaving a hoof whose print would be indistinguishable from most others. If worse came to worst, and the mark could not be removed, the Roman would simply abandon the horse. He had four others, after all.

But, as the days went on, the mark remained. Day after day, the tracker followed the trail, with the ease of a man following a lantern at night. Day after day, his estimate of Belisarius plummeted.

By now, so far as the Pathan was concerned, Belisarius ranked very low in the natural order of things. Above a sheep, perhaps. Beneath a bullfrog, for a certainty.

The robbery of the merchant simply confirmed his viewpoint. Sealed his opinion like lead seals a jar.

Three days before Ajmer, the Rajputs had overtaken a merchant trudging alongside the road. The merchant was accompanied by two servants, each of whom was staggering under a weight of bundled trade goods.

All three men were stark naked.

When the Rajputs pulled alongside, the merchant immediately erupted into a frenzy of recrimination, denunciation, accusation, and reproach.

Outrage that such a thing could come to pass!

Where had been the authorities?

Robbed on a royal road! By a royal Ye-tai bodyguard!

Oh, yes! There was no mistake! The merchant was a well-traveled man! A sophisticated man! He had been to Kausambi itself! Many times!

A royal bodyguard!

Outrage! Outrage!

Where had been the authorities?

He demanded justice! Retribution!

Most of all—restitution!

Robbed by a royal bodyguard!

Restitution was owed by the authorities!

In the event, once the merchant calmed down enough to tell the entire tale, restitution proved simplicity itself. The only thing which the Ye-tai bandit seemed to have actually stolen was the clothing worn by the merchant and his servants.

Nothing else, oddly enough. Not the merchant's money, not his trade goods—which were spices, too; quite valuable—not even the gold chain around the merchant's neck or the rings adorning his fingers.

The Pathan was livid.

"What kind midget-brain bandit this man?" he demanded hotly. "Cretin idiot!"

The tracker glared at the merchant.

"I rob you, fat boy, you be lucky have skin left. Gold chain, cut off head. Rings, chop fingers. Quick, quick."

The Pathan leaned over his horse's neck, squinting fiercely at the servants. The two men edged back, trembling.

"Old one I kill. Other one I take. Sell him to Uighurs." He straightened up. Leaned over. Spat noisily. "Roman most idiot beast alive," he concluded. He had not budged from that conclusion since.

Sanga, on the other hand, thought the robbery was very shrewd. He had been wondering how Belisarius planned to make his way through Rajputana, especially in a city like Ajmer, disguised as a Ye-tai. In the Gangetic plain, a single Ye-tai leading a small train of horses would not particularly be remarked.

In Rajputana, however, his situation would be different. Rajputs had no love for Ye-tai, to put it mildly. A single Ye-tai in Rajput country would encounter any number of difficulties very quickly, especially in a populous place like Ajmer. Those difficulties would range from bands of belligerent youngsters to keen-eyed authorities who were not in the least intimidated by a Ye-tai's red-and-gold uniform. Not in Rajputana, where the Malwa writ ran very light.

By stealing the merchant's clothes, and that of the servants, Belisarius had provided himself with a perfect disguise. Itinerant merchants, traders, tinkers—traveling alone or in a small party—were commonplace throughout the arid stretches of western India. Sanga suspected that Belisarius would combine part of the merchant's relatively fine apparel with pieces of the servants' more humble clothing. The resulting pastiche would give him the semblance of a hardscrabble trader, barely a cut above a peddler.

It was shrewd, too, for the Roman to have ignored the merchant's coins, jewelry and trade goods. Bandits and thieves were as common as merchants, in that part of India, and everyone kept an eye out for them. If Belisarius tried to sell the merchant's jewelry or goods, or use the coin, he would run the real risk of drawing suspicion upon himself.

Sanga had noted, during the weeks of their pursuit, that Belisarius seemed to have always foraged for his food, rather than buying it. Buying food would have been much quicker. The main reason the Rajputs had been able to shorten the Roman's lead—the Pathan estimated he was only five days ahead of them, now—was because of the time which Belisarius had spent every day searching for food. For the most part, the Roman had hunted his food, with the bow and arrows he had taken from the relay station's soldiers. Occasionally, he had stolen from a local granary or orchard. But never, so far as the Rajputs or their Pathan trackers had been able to determine, had he bought food.

Sanga was certain that was by choice, not necessity. Belisarius could not, of course, be carrying the immense treasure which the Malwa had bestowed upon him. But the Rajput was quite sure that Belisarius had kept a small amount of that treasure with him at all times. Just in case. That sort of elementary precaution would be second nature to such a man.

Yet he had never used it. Partly, Sanga thought, that was because Belisarius feared the suspicion which the use of royal coin and jewelry would bring down. But mostly, he suspected, it was because Belisarius was saving his money for the coast. To hire a ship—to *buy* a ship, for that matter, if he had kept with him any one of a number of the gems in those chests.

So Sanga felt the Pathan was being quite unreasonable. But he did not remonstrate with the man. It would be as pointless as arguing with a stone.

The Rajput kinglet's chief tracker had been in his service for years, now. Ever since Sanga had captured him, after a ferocious single combat, during one of the many punitive campaigns against the mountain barbarians. The Pathan had been deeply impressed by his victor's skill and courage. So deeply, in fact, that he had begged Sanga to make him his own slave, rather than sell him to some unworthy fool.

Sanga had granted the request, and had never regretted doing so. The Pathan had served him faithfully for years, even after

Sanga manumitted him. Served him extremely well, in fact. But Sanga knew the limits of that man's horizon, and had long since given up any hope of changing them.

Two days later, as the walls of Ajmer rose above the horizon, the Pathan was still grousing.

"Fucking idiot beast," Sanga heard him mutter. "I rob merchant, I do merchant good. Him no complain. Him no tongue."

At Ajmer, of course, they lost the tracks. Even a hoofprint far more distinctive than the one left by that little nick would have been obliterated by the traffic through the city. But Sanga was not concerned.

He sent half of his men, and all the Pathan trackers, circling around Ajmer. Keeping far enough away from the city to avoid routine traffic, those men would eventually find the direction Belisarius had taken. The distinctive track, by now, was as unmistakable to the Rajputs as to the Pathans. In the meantime, Sanga and his remaining soldiers began a systematic search of the city itself.

They were looking for horses. For the *memory* of horses, to be precise.

Rajputana was a land of horsemen. A ragged merchant, by himself, might pass through Ajmer unremarked. But Sanga knew, as surely as he knew his own name, that his countrymen would have certainly noticed the horses. Those marvelous, splendid, *imperial* steeds.

And, sure enough, tracking the horses proved as easy as tracking the distinctive hoofprint. The memory trail was only five days old, and it led directly to the southern gate of the city. By mid-afternoon of the same day they arrived, Sanga was already interviewing the guards.

"Oh, yes!" one of them exclaimed. "As fine as any horses you've ever seen! As fine as royal courier steeds!"

Another guard pointed to the road leading south. "They went that way. Five days ago."

"The man," said Sanga. "What did he look like?"

The guards looked at each other, puzzled.

"Don't remember," said one. "Trader, maybe peddler."

"I think he was tall," said another, stroking his beard thoughtfully. "I think. I'm not sure. I was watching the horses."

Two miles south of Ajmer, they encountered the rest of Sanga's horsemen and the Pathan trackers. Coming north with the news:

The tracks had been spotted. Five miles out, on the road to the Gulf of Khambat.

"Probably Bharakuccha," stated Jaimal, as they cantered south. Sanga's lieutenant gazed ahead and to their right. The sun was beginning to set behind the peaks of the Aravallis.

"But maybe not," he mused. "Once he gets south of the Aravallis, he could cut west across the Rann of Kutch and follow the coast back up to Barbaricum. Be roundabout, but—"

"He'd play hell trying to drive horses through that stinking mess," disputed Pratap. "And why bother?"

The argument raged until they made camp that night. Sanga took no part in it. Trying to outguess Belisarius in the absence of hard information was pure foolishness, in his opinion. They would know soon enough. The tracks would tell the tale.

His last thoughts, that night, before falling asleep, were a meditation on irony. So strange—so sad—that such a great man could be brought down, in the end, by something as petty as a stone in the road.

Two days later, the Pathan was almost beside himself with outrage. What shred of respect he retained for Belisarius was now discarded completely.

He leaned over the saddle. Spat noisily.

"Great idiot beast! Knew him stupid like sheep. Now him lazy like sheep too!"

He pointed an accusing finger at the tracks.

"Look him horse pace. My grandmother faster. And she carcass. Many years dead now."

Spat noisily.

Apparently satisfied that he had shaken off any pursuit, the Roman had slowed his pace considerably since leaving Ajmer. Sanga, again, thought the Pathan was being unreasonable. True, Belisarius was being careless. But, at the same time, allowances had to be made. He was only human, after all. The Roman had set himself a brutal pace for weeks. It was not surprising that he would finally take a bit of rest.

Not surprising, no, and hardly something for which a man could be condemned. But it was still a mistake, and, under the circumstances, quite fatal.

In less than two days, they brought Belisarius to bay.

By late afternoon of the following day, the lead tracker spotted him. Not five miles ahead, already making camp for the night.

The Rajput officers held a hurried conference. Sanga's lieutenants argued for surrounding the Roman's camp and attacking that very night.

Sanga would have none of it.

"Not him," he stated firmly. "Not that man, at night. First, he might make his escape in the darkness."

He held up his hand, forestalling Udai's protest.

"That's unlikely, I admit. What I'm more worried about is that we'd be forced to kill him. I want him alive. It may not be possible, but if there's any chance at all it will be by daylight. In a night attack, with its confusion, there'd be no chance at all."

He glanced up at the sky. The eastern horizon was already purple.

"And there's no need. He's making camp, so he's not going anywhere. We'll use the night to surround him, quietly."

A hard eye on his lieutenants. "*Quietly*." They nodded.

Sanga stared south.

"At dawn, we bring him down."

The Pathan himself brought Belisarius down. The tracker didn't even bother to stun him. He simply pounced on the Roman general, still wrapped up in his roll—half an hour after daybreak, lazy sheep!—by the embers of a small campfire—a campfire on the run, idiot beast!—jerked him up by the hair. Then, with his knife, sliced the Roman's cheek. A gash, no more, just enough to mark his man.

Quickquick, and the Pathan stepped away.

The Roman general staggered to his feet, shrieking. He clutched his cheek with both hands. Blood from the wound spurted through the fingers. He took two steps, stumbled, fell on his belly across the campfire. Then thrashed aside, shrieking more loudly still. Lurched to his feet, beating away the embers with his bloody hands.

The Pathan had had enough.

He strode forward and sent the Roman back on his belly with a vicious, stamping kick. Then he sprang upon him, jerked his head up by the hair, and manhandled him to his knees.

"Here you great general, Sanga King," he said contemptuously. He cuffed the Roman, silencing a squawl.

Rana Sanga stared down at Belisarius. Stared up at the Pathan holding him by the hair. The tracker was grinning savagely.

Stared down at Belisarius. The general was gasping like a fish, eyes glazed.

Stared back at the Pathan. Down at Belisarius.

"Who in the hell is *that?*" snarled Jaimal.

Stared down at *that*. Up at the Pathan.

"I've never seen this man before in my life," he told the tracker quietly.

It was almost worth it, then, for Rana Sanga. After all those years, finally, to see the Pathan gape. Like an idiot beast.

"I'm just a poor peddler," whined the man, for the hundredth time. He moaned, pressing the bandage against his cheek. Moaned:

"My name is—"

"Shut up!" snarled Udai. "We know your name! What we want to know is where did you get the horses?"

The peddler stared up at the Rajput. Finally, something beyond squawling terror and babbling self-pity entered his mind.

Avarice.

"They're *my* horses!" he squealed. "You can't—"

"Shut up!" bellowed Udai. "*Just shut up!*"

Rana Sanga put a restraining hand on Udai's shoulder. His lieutenant's fury was just frightening the man senseless.

The Rajput king squatted, bringing his eyes level with those of the bloody-faced man sprawled in the dirt.

"Listen to me, peddler," he said quietly. Quietly, but very firmly. The peddler fell silent.

"My name is Rana Sanga."

The peddler's eyes widened. He was not Rajput, but he traded in Rajputana. He knew the name. Knew it well.

"We will take your horses." Quiet, iron words.

The peddler opened his mouth, began to squawl.

"Those horses were stolen from the royal courier service. To possess them is to be condemned to death. Impaled."

The peddler's mouth clamped shut. His eyes bulged.

Sanga raised his hand reassuringly.

"Have no fear. We have no interest in your execution. If you serve us well, we may even repay you for the loss of the horses."

Partly, he thought, watching the avarice leap back into the peddler's eyes. Whatever you paid for them. Which, I am quite certain, is much less than what they are worth. I think I am beginning to understand what that—that—fiend—

He took a deep breath.

No. What that fiendish mind has done here.

He glanced to the side. Thirty feet away, his Pathan tracker was holding up one of the horse's legs, examining the hoof. Very carefully.

Sanga turned back to the peddler.

"But now, man, you must tell me—very quickly, very simply, very clearly—how you got the horses."

"He was a Ye-tai," gasped out the peddler. Then, in a sudden rush of words:

"A deserter from the imperial bodyguard, I think. I'm not sure—I didn't ask!—not a Ye-tai—but. I think. I saw part of a uniform. Gold and red. He was on the run, I think. Had nothing but those fine horses, and seemed desperate to get out of Ajmer. So he—he—"

Suddenly, amazingly, the peddler burst into laughter. "Idiot Ye-tai! Stupid barbarian! He had no idea what those horses were worth—*none,* I tell you! In the end—it only took me two hours of haggling—I traded them for three camels, some blankets, and a tent. Food. Maybe fifty pounds of water. Two big tureens full. And five bottles of wine. Cheap wine." Howling, howling. "Fucking idiot! Fucking savage!"

Sanga slapped the man's ear. "*Silence.*"

The peddler's hysterical laughter stopped instantly. His face turned pale.

"And what else?" grated Sanga. "There would have been something else."

The peddler's expression was a weird conglomeration of astonishment, fear, greed. Fear.

"How did you know?" he whispered.

"I know that—*Ye-tai,*" replied Sanga quietly. "He would not have simply sent you on your way. He would have made sure you came *this* way. How?"

Fear. Greed. Fear.

"Show me."

It was one of the Emperor's emeralds.

A small emerald, very small, by imperial standards. Probably the least of the jewels which Belisarius had with him. But it had been a fortune to the peddler. Enough to send him off to Bharakuccha, with the promise of a matching emerald if he delivered the message to the proper party.

Who?

A Greek merchant. A ship captain.

His name? The name of the ship?

Jason. The *Argo*.

Show me the message.

Rana Sanga could read Greek, but only poorly. It did not matter. Most of the message was mathematics, and that he understood quite well. (India was the home of mathematics. Centuries later, Europeans would abandon Roman numerals and adopt a new, cunning arithmetic. They would call them "Arabic numerals," because they got them from the Arabs. But they had been invented in India.)

So he was able to understand the message, well enough.

Finally, in the end, a king of Rajputana could not restrain himself. He began laughing like a madman.

"What is it?" asked Jaimal, when Sanga's howling humor abated.

"It's a theorem," he said, weakly. "By some Greek named Pythagoras. It explains how to calculate angles."

The Pathan rose from his examination of the horse's hoof and stalked over.

"Not cut by stone on road. Knife cut. Done by meant-to purpose."

Sanga had already deduced as much.

"Exactly." He smiled, stroking his beard. "He knew we would spot the mark. And that, after weeks of following it, would stop thinking about anything else. So he switched in Ajmer, sent us charging off south while he drives straight across the Thar on camelback."

He glanced at the peddler, still ashen-faced.

"Three camels," he mused. "Enough to carry him—*and* his food and water—across the desert without stopping."

He rose to his feet. It was a sure, decisive movement.

"We'll never catch him now. By the time we got back to Ajmer and set off in pursuit he'd have at least eight days lead on us. With three camels and full supplies he'll move faster than we possibly could across that wasteland."

His lieutenants glared, but did not argue. They knew he was right. Five hundred expert cavalrymen can eventually outrun a single horseman, even with remounts. But not across the Thar.

That was camel country. There probably weren't five hundred camels available in Ajmer, to begin with. And even if there were—

Rajputs were *not* expert camel drivers.

"Stinking camels," grumbled Udai.

"Can't stand the fucking things," agreed Pratap.

"Good meat," stated the Pathan. The Rajputs glowered at him. The tracker was oblivious. His mind was elsewhere.

"So we give up, then?" asked Jaimal.

Sanga shook his head.

"No, we don't. But we'll not try chasing after the Roman again. Instead—"

He held up the message.

"We'll take his advice. *Angles.* Maybe—just maybe—we can make better time by taking two sides of the triangle while he takes one. We'll head for Bharakuccha—as fast as our horses can carry us. At Bharakuccha we'll requisition a ship—several ships—and sail north to Barbaricum. That's where he's headed, I'm sure of it."

He strode for his horse.

"We might be able to meet him there. Let's go!"

That night, by the campfire, the Pathan finally broke the silence he had maintained for hours.

"After adopt, make him clan chief. No. Make him king. First Pathan king ever." He grinned at the Rajputs over the flickering flames. "Then Pathan conquer world entire whole." A gracious nod to Sanga. "You was good master. When you my slave, I be good master too."

Three days later, as the Aravallis rolled by on their right, Jaimal leaned over his saddle and snarled to Sanga:

"If that Pathan keeps telling that same joke, I swear I'm going to kill him."

"Jaimal," the Rajput king replied, coldly. "He is not joking."

Chapter 22

Rao was amused by the reluctance with which his young men obeyed orders. His lieutenant Maloji was not.

"You're too easy on them, Rao," he complained. His words came easily, despite the fact that he and the Panther were racing along the steep slope of a ridge, just below the skyline. On the other side of that ridge, they could hear the roar of battle. The clash of steel was fading, slowly. The angry shouts of Malwa officers were not.

"Here," said Rao. He scrambled up the slope, flinging himself to the ground just before reaching the crest. Maloji followed. On their bellies, the two men crawled to the crest itself, and peered over into the small valley below.

"You see?" hissed Maloji accusingly. He pointed angrily, with a bristling thrust of his beard. "Some of the disobedient dogs are still even using their swords."

"Only two," murmured Rao. He watched while the two young Marathas below finished cutting down a Malwa soldier before they began their own scramble up the slope on the opposite side. On the crest of that ridge, a line of guerillas was firing arrows into the swarming Malwa troops below.

"They are brothers, you know. One of them probably got tangled up and the other came to his rescue."

"Still—"

"Do not fret, Maloji. They will learn discipline soon enough." Grimly: "After they sustain heavy casualties from excessive enthusiasm."

He broke off, gauging the Malwa. The officers were finally bringing order back to their little army. At their command, ranks of soldiers began slogging up the slope. They suffered considerable losses from the arrows raining down on them, but their advance was inexorable. The Malwa had tried to cram too many soldiers down the narrow valley—not much more than a ravine. Those packed ranks made an easy, slow target for ambush, but, once they began their counter-attack, were far too massive to be repelled.

"They should break off now, the dogs!" snarled Maloji. "Your orders were very clear!"

Rao did not argue the point. He had, in fact, ordered his men to fire no more than two volleys after the Malwa began their counter-attack. The guerrillas should already have been retreating. Instead, the young Maratha rebels waited until the Malwa were halfway up the slope before they finally scrambled away.

Rao turned, and edged his way down the slope. Maloji followed, still grumbling.

"You shouldn't have given them those horses. That's why they're so bold. *Disrespectful young dogs*. They think those horses can outrun anything."

Now well below the skyline, Rao stood up. He grinned at his lieutenant. "Those horses *can* outrun anything. Anything these sorry Malwa have. The best horses foreign money could buy!"

Maloji rose and brushed himself off. "Fine steeds, I admit," he agreed reluctantly. "They were a wonderful gift."

"I think of it as an exchange," demurred Rao. He looked to the west. He could not see Bharakuccha, of course. The great port was many miles away, hidden behind the Satpura mountains. "They gave us the horses, we gave them the opportunity."

"Will they make their escape, do you think?"

Rao shrugged. "I should imagine. We stopped the couriers, and we've been"—a gesture toward the ridge; a wide grin—"*distracting the Malwa*."

He turned and began loping toward the dell where their own horses were hidden away. Speaking easily, despite the rigorous pace, he said over his shoulder:

"As I told you before, Maloji, those men are *capable*."

Capability was unneeded. The escape, at the end, was child's play. Garmat simply marched across the ramp connecting the Axumite trader with the wharf, and presented himself to the captain. Before he had even reached the man, the captain was goggling.

"Stop looking like a frog, Endubis," he growled.

The captain gaped.

"And close your mouth, fool. *Spies may see you.*"

Endubis' mouth snapped shut. The captain glanced hurriedly at the shore, scanning for danger with an experienced eye.

Like all Ethiopian merchant captains, Endubis was no stranger to combat. Such merchants served as a reserve for the Kingdom of Axum's navy. No seaman could reach the rank of ship captain, even in the merchant fleet, without the negusa nagast's approval. For all their relaxed customs in other areas of life, the Axumites were never casual about their naval power.

"Trouble?" asked Endubis.

Garmat smiled, thinly. "You might say so. The entire Malwa Empire is baying for our blood."

Endubis winced. "The Prince?"

"He is well." Garmat made a little gesture with his head. "In that warehouse. With his dawazz and the sarwen. Some others."

The adviser examined the ship briefly. "Thirteen men, in all. It will be crowded, but—"

"We'll manage," muttered Endubis. The captain turned and began bellowing orders. His seamen immediately scurried about the ship, preparing for departure.

"I wish you'd gotten here tomorrow," Endubis grumbled. "I'd have a cargo, then. I hate sailing empty. Surest way I know to poverty."

Garmat grinned. "Not so, Endubis. An empty ship will make a fast trip, and we'll not be too crowded. As for poverty—" His hand dipped into a pouch, came out, spread wide.

The captain, again, was goggling like a frog.

"You'll accept Malwa coin, I assume?" murmured Garmat. "Oh, and look! I believe there's even a ruby here. No—three rubies."

On the way out of Bharakuccha's harbor, a Malwa vessel hailed them and tried to come alongside.

"Ignore it," commanded the Prince. "Sail on."

The captain glanced at him from the corner of his eye. "That'll make it hard on the next Axumite trader," he pointed out.

Eon shrugged. "There won't *be* any 'next Axumite trader.' We are at war, now, with Malwa."

The captain sighed. "Ah. Too bad. It was good business."

The officer in the bow of the Malwa ship hailed them again. His voice sounded angry.

"You *can* outsail them?" demanded Eon.

Endubis sneered. "That Malwa tub?" He disdained any further answer, beyond the orders he shouted at his seamen.

An hour later, the officer commanding the Malwa vessel broke off the pursuit.

He was practically gibbering.

Some of his rage was due to the superior seaworthiness of the Ethiopian ship. Most of it was due to the bare black ass hanging over the stern of the Axumite vessel, defecating. And the great, gleaming grin on the face above it.

A week later, in the port at Tamralipti on India's opposite coast, another Malwa naval officer grinned with sheer delight. As well he should. He had made more money that day than in the previous three months put together.

His lieutenant was grinning, too. His own cut of the nobleman's bribe was enough for a lavish spree in the Bay of Bengal's most notorious harbor district.

The lieutenant gestured with his head toward the merchant ship which was even now passing the harbor's breakwater.

"Should we notify Murshid and his men? There's a fortune in that nobleman's chests. And his wife's young. Pretty, too, probably. She and the other women would bring a good price."

The commanding officer stroked his beard, considering the question. He and his officers made a tidy profit, on the side, selling information on lucrative targets to the local pirates.

He did not ponder the matter for very long.

"No," he said firmly. "Not with *that* escort."

"There weren't more than thirty of them," argued his lieutenant. "Murshid can muster three ships, with over a hundred—"

The commander glared.

"A hundred *what*?" he snarled. "Three-to-one odds, you're talking about—four-to-one, at best. Murshid's rascals against—*those*?"

The lieutenant grimaced. "Well—"

The commander brushed the idea aside, as a man might brush away flies.

"Forget it. Murshid wouldn't thank us afterward, believe me. And what would our cut be—a barrel of guts? Two barrels?"

✧　　✧　　✧

Looking back at them from the stern of his vessel, the captain of the merchant ship decided he was reading the posture of the Malwa officers properly. The distance was great, but he had very good eyes. And much experience.

Satisfied, he turned away. "We can relax," he said to his own lieutenant. "There'll be no problem."

His lieutenant heaved a sigh of relief. He had thought his captain mad, to accept such a cargo in these waters. They normally hauled nothing but bulk goods in the Bay of Bengal, infested as it was by pirates. The type of goods which no brigand finds attractive.

But, his captain had decided to take the chance. The nobleman's offered price had been too good to pass up. A small fortune to transport him, his wife, and their retinue to Muziris, the principal port of the south Indian kingdom of Kerala.

Besides—

The lieutenant glanced at the nearest of the nobleman's soldiers. He was not certain, but he thought the man was the officer commanding the nobleman's escort.

The officer was leaning against the rail, watching the receding harbor, idly honing his sword with a small whetstone. It seemed a pointless exercise. The blade was already like a razor.

His eyes met the lieutenant's.

"Trouble?" The whetstone never ceased its motion.

The lieutenant shook his head.

"We don't think so."

No expression at all crossed the officer's face. It seemed, in its rigid immobility, like an iron mask.

"Too bad," he murmured. He held the blade up to the sunlight, inspecting its edge. "My men are a little rusty. Could use a bit of honing."

A month later, Rana Sanga returned to his home near Jaipur. He had not seen his family in a year, and he had decided he must do so before he went on to Kausambi. He might never have the chance again. When he reported his failure to capture Belisarius, he would be punished. Possibly even executed.

To Sanga's surprise, Lord Damodara was waiting for him at the Rajput king's residence. He had arrived two weeks earlier, sure that Sanga would come there first, whether the news was good or foul.

As eager as he was to greet his family—Lord Damodara politely offered to wait until he had done so—Sanga insisted on giving his report first. He and Damodara met in a small room adjoining the great hall which served Sanga as his royal audience chamber. They sat on cushions across from each other at a low table. Alone, after servants had placed tea and pastries for their refreshment.

Sanga's report was full, precise, and unsparing. But as he came to the final episodes of their pursuit of Belisarius, Damodara cut him short.

"Never mind the rest, Sanga. The gist, I assume, is that you found no sign of him in Barbaricum or any of the other small ports?"

Sanga shook his head. "None, Lord Damodara. I am convinced he took ship there, somewhere, but he disguised his traces perfectly. If they investigate—long enough—Nanda Lal's spies can probably discover the truth. But—"

"What is the point?" asked Damodara. He waved a pudgy little hand in dismissal. "If they find any evidence, it will be far too late to do any good."

He sipped at his tea. Munched on a pastry.

"Such an investigation would do nothing but harm," he stated. "Great harm, in fact."

Sanga sat stiffly, silent. Damodara eyed him for a moment. Then, surprisingly, smiled. "You are, indeed, the true Rajput. Honor above all."

Sanga, if such were possible, stiffened further.

"I am *not* Rajput," rasped Damodara. "I respect your view of things, Rana Sanga—I even believe that I understand that view—but I do not share it." Harshly: "*I am Malwa.* And, thus, am a practical man. I was sent here to meet you, and assess the results of your search. I have now done so."

Another sip of tea.

"Here are my findings. Rana Sanga, acting on the *possibility* that Belisarius *might* have made his escape to the west, led a long, rigorous, and most diligent search—all the way to Barbaricum, no less!"

Another sip of tea.

"*No trace of Belisarius was found.* For a time, it appeared that the Rajputs were on his trail. But, in the end, it proved a false lead. The only things actually *found* were a ragged peddler and the bloody trail of a Ye-tai deserter from the royal bodyguard, who fled the Empire after viciously murdering several soldiers and royal couriers and robbing a merchant."

Sanga began to protest. Damodara drove him down.

"*Nothing proves otherwise, Rana Sanga.* Your suspicions were simply groundless. That is all." Another wave of his hand. The gesture done, the hand reached for a pastry.

"There is no evidence," concluded Damodara. "Nothing solid. Nothing concrete."

Satisfied—self-satisfied—Damodara popped the pastry into his mouth.

"There is," grated Sanga. He reached into his tunic, brought forth a small pouch, opened it, and spilled its contents onto the table between them.

An emerald. Small, but dazzling.

Damodara choked on his pastry. Coughing, he reached for his tea and hastily washed his throat clear.

"Rajput," he muttered, setting down the tea cup. He glared at the emerald.

The glare was brief. When he looked up, Damodara was smiling again.

"This, I presume, is the emerald which you say Belisarius gave the peddler? One of the emeralds from the Emperor's gift?"

Sanga nodded stiffly.

Damodara laughed. "What nonsense!" Shaking his head: "Any Rajput in the world can gauge a sword or a horse at a glance, but show them a jewel—"

For all its plumpness, Damodara's hand moved like a lizard on a hot rock snatching an insect. The emerald disappeared into his own tunic. Sternly: "These counterfeiters! Shameless criminals! I shall report this latest outrage to the appropriate bureau in Kausambi upon my return." Again, the waving hand. "Whichever it is. I believe the *Ranabhandagaradhikara*'s office in the treasury handles counterfeiting. Perhaps the police *Bhukti*. One of those small departments, buried somewhere in the Grand Palace. Staffed by somnolent dullards."

The Rajput King's protest was cut short.

"It is done, Rana Sanga! *Finished.* That is all."

He rose. Sanga rose with him. The short Malwa commander stared up at the Rajput. He did not flinch in the least from the taller man's anger.

"My name is Lord Damodara," he said softly. "And I have reached my conclusion."

Still without moving his eyes from Sanga's hot gaze, Damodara leaned over and scooped up another pastry. Popped it in his mouth.

"These are truly excellent," he mumbled. "Please give my compliments to your baker."

Sanga was still glaring. Damodara sighed.

"Rana Sanga, so far as Malwa is concerned, the truth is clear. Belisarius escaped—*with his men*—to the south. The royal couriers who were to have alerted the port garrisons were all ambushed along the way by savage Maratha brigands. So the wicked foreign general and his accomplices were able to make their escape on an Axumite ship waiting in the harbor. By predesign, undoubtedly. We have—had—a clear description of one of those accomplices from a naval officer who failed to stop the ship. A vivid description." Coldly: "For his failure to capture that ship, the naval officer has been executed. Along with the commander of Bharakuccha's garrison."

Sanga snorted. Damodara, expressionless:

"Impaled, both of them. At Lord Venandakatra's command, as soon as the Goptri arrived in Bharakuccha."

Damodara, his face as blank as ice:

"Upon my return, upon my demand, the officer in charge of the unit from which the Ye-tai murderer deserted will also be executed. For dereliction of his duty."

He looked away. "I will not demand impalement. Beheading will suffice."

Sanga's face twisted.

Damodara murmured, "It has been done, and it *will* be done. Do not make those—sacrifices—vain exercises in murder, Rana Sanga. *Please.* Let it be."

He laid a hand on Sanga's arm.

"Now, I have news myself. I have been appointed head of the northern army for the upcoming Persian campaign. Lord Jivita, of course, will be in overall command."

The Rajput glanced at him, stonily. Looked away.

"I have requested—and my request has been approved—that

most of the Rajput forces be assigned to my army. You—and your cavalry—in particular."

Now, Sanga's eyes came back. Fixed.

Damodara's lips quirked. "My official argument was that my army will be operating, more than any other, in broken country. Hence—so I argued—I require the bulk of our best cavalry units." He shrugged. "The argument is valid enough, of course. And it spared me the embarassment of explaining to Lord Jivita that I do not share his faith in the invincibility of gunpowder. Personally, I want good Rajput steel guarding my flanks, on the backs of good Rajput steeds."

Sanga almost smiled. Not quite.

Damodara's hand gave Sanga's arm a little shake. "I need you, Rana Sanga. Alive, healthy, and in command of your troops." He dropped the hand and turned away. "I will leave now. I have kept you from your family long enough."

Rana Sanga escorted Damodara all the way to the courtyard. As he waited for his horse to be brought around, Damodara murmured his last words:

"Do not fret over Belisarius' escape, Rana Sanga. Let it go. Leave it be. We will be seeing him again, anyway. Soon enough—too soon, for my taste. Of that I am as sure as the sunrise."

"So am I," muttered Sanga, after Damodara left. "As sure as the sunrise." A rueful smile came to his face. "But, unfortunately, not as predictable."

He turned back to his home. His wife and children were already rushing out the door, arms spread wide. All other emotions vanished, beyond simple joy in their loving embrace.

A week later, on his way back to Kausambi, Lord Damodara and his escort came to the Jamuna River.

Lord Damodara ordered a halt, and dismounted.

"I have to piss," he announced to his soldiers. "Wait here," he commanded, waving his hand casually. "I can manage the task quite well myself."

Once he reached the river, he paced a few feet along the bank, looking for a suitable spot. Having found it, Damodara went about his business.

He was a practical man, Damodara. Malwa. He saw no reason not to complete two necessary chores simultaneously.

He *did* have to piss, after all. While, in the middle of his urination, tossing a small emerald into a deep spot in the river.

At the very moment when that emerald nestled into the mud of a riverbed, a ship nestled against a dock an ocean's width away. Sailors began to lay the gangplank.

"There's your father," announced Garmat. The adviser pointed up the slope overlooking the harbor of Adulis. At the top of a steep stone stairway, a regal figure loomed.

Axumites did not favor the grandiose imperial regalia of other realms. The negusa nagast wore a simple linen kilt, albeit embellished with gold thread. His massive chest was covered by nothing more than crossed leather straps sewn with pearls. A heavy gold collar circled his thick neck and five gold armbands adorned each of his muscular arms. On his head was a plain silver tiara, studded with carnelians, signifying his status as a king of kings. The tiara held in place the traditional *phakhiolin*, the four-streamered headdress which announced his more important position as king of the Axumites. In his right hand, Kaleb held the great spear of his office, with its Christian cross surmounted on the shaft; in his left, a fly-whisk. The spear, symbolizing his piety and power; the fly-whisk, his service to his people.

Nothing more. Other than, of course, the gravity of his own figure—thick-shouldered, heavy-thewed, majestically-bellied—and the dignity of his own face. Glowering brow over powerful nose; tight lips; heavy, clenched jaws.

"He looks grumpy," surmised Menander.

"He looks downright pissed," opined Anastasius. "You'd think he already heard the bad news. His headstrong youngest son just got him in a war with the world's mightiest empire."

"Of course he's heard!" cried Ousanas happily. "Look at his companion—the world's fastest bringer of bad news. Crooked Mercury himself!"

Belisarius. Standing, now, next to the King. Smiling his crooked smile.

"Damn," muttered Valentinian. "Rather face the King's glare than that smile, any day." Sigh: "Exciting adventures, coming up."

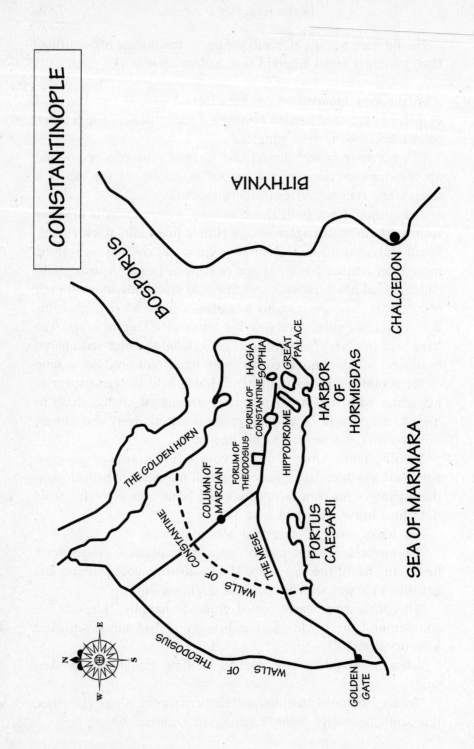

CONSTANTINOPLE

BITHYNIA

BOSPORUS

CHALCEDON

THE GOLDEN HORN

FORUM OF THEODOSIUS

COLUMN OF MARCIAN

FORUM OF CONSTANTINE

HAGIA SOPHIA

GREAT PALACE

HIPPODROME

HARBOR OF HORMISDAS

THE MESE

WALLS OF CONSTANTINE

PORTUS CAESARII

WALLS OF THEODOSIUS

GOLDEN GATE

SEA OF MARMARA

N E S W

Chapter 23
CONSTANTINOPLE
Winter 530 AD

Five minutes into her meeting with Balban, Antonina knew that something was not right. The Malwa spymaster was not listening to her carefully enough.

He *seemed* to be, true. To almost anyone but Antonina, Balban would have appeared to be the very model of attentiveness. He was sitting on the edge of his chair—almost perched, in fact—leaning forward, hands clasped between his knees. His eyes were riveted on the woman sitting across the small room from him. He was utterly silent, apparently engrossed in the information which Antonina was giving him.

The information alone should have guaranteed his interest, even if it wasn't being imparted by a beautiful woman. The Malwa spymaster was learning every single detail of every current or planned troop movement of every Roman military unit of any consequence in Syria, the Levant and Egypt. For a man who stood at the very center of a plot to overthrow the Roman Emperor—a plot which was finally coming to fruition—such information was literally priceless.

Wonderful information, too—in every respect. Wonderful, not just in the fact that he had it, but wonderful in its own right. The gist of Antonina's report was that no Roman military unit from the great southern and eastern provinces could possibly arrive in Constantinople in time to prevent the planned *coup d'etat*.

But he was not paying any attention. Not to the information, at least.

For a moment, Antonina wondered if Balban's indifference stemmed from his knowledge that everything she was telling him was a lie. In actual fact, Theodora had sent word to Daras weeks before that the plot was coming to a head. Antonina's grenadiers had been in Constantinople for ten days, disguised as pilgrim families. They, along with all the Thracian cataphracts, had been transported aboard a small fleet of swift transports. The units from Sittas and Hermogenes' armies, carried on slower grain ships, had just arrived the day before. They were still hidden in the holds of those ships, anchored in the Portus Caesarii.

But Antonina dismissed that possibility almost instantly. She detected no hostility from Balban, not a trace—which she surely would have, did the spymaster suspect her duplicity.

No, it was simply that Balban was not interested in the information, one way or the other. He did not disbelieve; but he did not believe, either. He simply didn't care.

He was interested in *her*—in the same way that almost every man was, who found himself in her company. Few men of her acquaintance were able to ignore Antonina's beauty. That was just a simple fact of life.

But, beyond that—*nothing*.

Antonina was chilled to the bone. She realized exactly what was happening. And what was planned.

They are going to kill me.

Had Balban known how perfectly Antonina was reading him, he would have been absolutely shocked. The Malwa was a master of his trade. He would have sworn that no one could have detected a trace of murderous intent in his perfectly maintained composure.

And, in truth, almost no one in the world could have done so. With the exception of a woman who, in her earlier days, had been one of the most exclusive and sought-after courtesans in the entire Roman empire.

Antonina, unlike Balban, was not an expert in the subjects of espionage, and assassination. But she *was* an expert—one of the world's greatest experts, in fact—on the subject of men, and their moods. Her success as a courtesan had been partly due to her physical beauty, of course. But many women were beautiful.

Antonina's great skill had been her ability to keep men *interested*. Not simply in her beauty, but in the pleasure of her company.

Over the years, she had learned to detect the danger signs. Sooner or later—until she met Belisarius—the men who sought her company would lose interest. Not in her, necessarily. They might well retain a powerful desire for her body. But they would lose interest in her company.

She had always been able to tell when that moment came. And she had always broken off such relationships immediately. Or, at least, as soon as she could do so gracefully.

Her relationship with Balban had never been sexual in the least. But, with him too, that *moment* had come.

In the brief time that it took to finish her report, she quickly assessed her options.

They would not kill her in Balban's own villa. Of that, she was certain. The Malwa had always taken great pains to maintain a low profile in Constantinople. Even Irene, with all her expertise and the vast resources which Theodora had placed at her disposal, had only discovered the whereabouts of the Malwa military base a few days before. Balban had managed to smuggle several hundred elite Indian soldiers into the Roman capital—and keep them hidden, for weeks—without being spotted.

Such a man would not risk drawing attention to himself at this penultimate hour.

Nor, she thought, would he employ the services of Ajatasutra or any other Malwa agent. There was always the risk, should her assassination fail, that such agents might be captured and traced back to him.

She would be murdered by Roman thugs, hired for the occasion through intermediaries.

The streets of Constantinople had become increasingly rowdy over the past few days. The Hippodrome factions which had been bribed by the Malwa grew more assertive and self-confident by the hour. Gangs of Blue and Green thugs roamed freely, disrupting the capital's tranquillity with impunity. The military units stationed in Constantinople had withdrawn to their barracks—just as Irene had predicted months earlier. The officers in command of those units could sense the coming coup, and they intended to sit on the sidelines until the outcome was clear.

Antonina was certain of the Malwa plan.

It was already very late in the afternoon. By the time she left Balban's villa, it would be dusk. As instructed, she had come alone to the meeting, following the same route she always took. On her way back, she would be accosted by a gang of street thugs. Not closer than three blocks away, but not farther than six. The attack would take place near a deserted building or some other secluded location. She would be dragged off the street and taken out of sight. Then, she would be robbed, probably raped, and murdered. When her body was discovered—which might not be for days—the crime would be dismissed as an unfortunate episode during the current chaos.

She managed, barely, not to heave a sigh of relief.

Professional assassins, like Ajatasutra, were probably beyond her capability. Street thugs, she thought she could handle.

Her mind now (more or less) at ease, Antonina had no difficulty getting through the final few minutes of her meeting with Balban. Her biggest problem was restraining her impatience at Balban's protracted social pleasantries. The hour ahead of her was dangerous in the extreme, but Antonina was the kind of person who just wanted to be done with it.

As soon as possible, she rose and made her exit. Balban escorted her to the door. On the way, they passed Ajatasutra in the corridor. Antonina smiled at him pleasantly, and walked by without flinching. It was not easy, that—after all, she *might* be wrong.

But Ajatasutra did nothing beyond return her nod with a polite smile.

Balban opened the door, mumbling some final courtesies. Antonina strode through the courtyard to the open gate which led to the street beyond. Even before she passed through the gate, she heard the door close behind her.

Balban, shaking his head, turned away from the door. To his surprise, Ajatasutra was still standing in the corridor.

"A pity," muttered Balban. "Such a beautiful—"

"She *knows*," hissed Ajatasutra.

Balban blinked his eyes.

"What?"

"She *knows*," repeated the assassin.

Balban frowned.

"Why do you say that? I saw no indication that she had any suspicions at all."

He made a little gesture at Ajatasutra.

"And—just now—she walked right by you with hardly any notice."

"That's the point," retorted the assassin. "That woman is not stupid, Balban. She knows exactly who I am. What I am. Every other time I've been in her company she always kept a close eye on me. It was a subtle thing, but—" Frustrated, he groped for words. "I'm telling you—she *knows.*"

Balban hesitated. He turned his head, looking at the door. For a moment, it almost seemed as if he would reopen it. But the moment passed, quickly. Then, when Ajatasutra began to approach the door himself, Balban stayed him with a hand.

The spymaster shook his head.

"I think you're imagining things, Ajatasutra. But, even if you're not, there's nothing we can do about it."

Balban scowled. "I think Nanda Lal's orders were an overreaction, anyway. The last thing I'm going to do—*now*, of all times!—is run any risk of exposing our mission."

He began moving down the corridor. With his hand still on Ajatasutra's shoulder, he guided the assassin along with him. "Besides," he added, "what difference does it make, even if she *does* know? She's just a woman, Ajatasutra—a small woman, at that."

Cheerfully:

"A sheep often knows it's in danger, when the wolfpack begins circling. What good does that do the sheep?"

Ajatasutra shrugged off the hand. He stopped abruptly, forcing Balban to look at him.

"She is not a sheep, Balban," stated the assassin firmly. "She grew up on the streets of Alexandria. The toughest streets in the Roman Empire. Her father was a charioteer—some of the roughest men you'll ever encounter. And her husband is not only a great general but a great swordsman as well. And those thugs you hired are *not* 'wolves.' They're a pack of mangy street curs."

"That's enough!" snapped Balban. "I've made my decision."

He stalked away. Ajatasutra remained alone, standing in the corridor, staring at the door. He stood there, silent and unmoving, for a full minute. Then, smiling thinly, he whispered, "Good luck, *wolves.* You're going to need it."

✧   ✧   ✧

Antonina strode up the street in the direction she always took, until she was far enough away from Balban's villa to be out of sight. She had traveled two blocks, by now, and knew that the ambush would be coming very soon.

At the next corner, she turned abruptly to her right and began walking quickly down a narrow side street. Behind her, faintly, she heard footsteps. Several men a block away, by the sound, startled into sudden activity.

She began running.

The street was barely more than an alley. She was unfamiliar with it. But she had noticed—in times past, as she had walked by—that the street was the domicile for a number of the small bakeries and cookshops which provided Constantinople with its daily supply of bread and meat pastries.

She raced by three such shops. Too small. She needed a big one, with a full kitchen.

At the fourth shop, she skidded to a halt. Hesitated. She could smell the thick, rich scent of meat broth.

Maybe.

She heard the footsteps approaching the mouth of the street.

It'll have to do.

She strode through the shop door. The shop was very small—not ten feet square—and completely bare except for a small counter on which were displayed samples of the shop's wares. When she saw that they were meat pastries, Antonina sighed with relief.

A middle-aged woman—the cookshop owner's wife, she assumed—approached Antonina and began uttering some pleasantry. Antonina didn't catch the words.

"Are you cooking meat broth?" she demanded. "For pastries?"

The woman, frowning with puzzlement, began to nod. Antonina grabbed the woman's wrist and dragged her toward the door at the opposite end of the shop. The woman was heavyset, taller than Antonina, and began squawking and struggling vigorously. To absolutely no avail. Antonina was a very strong woman, for her size, and she was filled with implacable determination.

She shouldered the door open and hurled the woman through, following an instant later. Before closing the door, she peeked at the shop entrance. The outer door was still closed. Her pursuers, she thought, hadn't seen her enter the shop.

Good. I've got a little time.

She turned and confronted the woman, who was now spluttering with outrage. The woman's husband was standing next to her, glowering, holding up a metal ladle in a half-threatening gesture.

"Shut up!" snarled Antonina. "There are men just outside your door who are trying to kill me! *They'll kill you, too.*"

The woman's mouth snapped shut. A second later, her mouth reopened. Wailing:

"Get out! Get out!"

The husband stepped forward hesitantly, raising the ladle.

There was a large table against the wall of the kitchen next to the door. Antonina slammed her purse onto the table and emptied its contents. A pile of gold coins spilled out. Along with a small dagger.

The shopkeeper and his wife were, first, transfixed by the sight of the coins. Then, by the sight of the dagger in Antonina's hand.

"You've got a simple choice," hissed Antonina. "You can take the money—call it rent for the use of your kitchen—or you can take the blade. *In your fucking guts.*"

The shopkeeper and his wife ogled her.

Antonina hefted the dagger. The wife's face, as she eyed the razor-sharp blade, paled a bit.

The shopkeeper's face paled quite a bit more.

He was fat and middle-aged, now. But, in his youth, he had led a rather disreputable life. He was not particularly impressed by Antonina's sharp little blade. He was a professional cook. He had several knives which were just as sharp and much bigger.

But he recognized that grip. That light, easy way of holding a blade.

"Shut up, woman!" he snarled to his wife. "Take the money and go upstairs."

His wife frowned at him. The shopkeeper threatened her with the ladle. Antonina stepped away from the table, clearing a space. The shopkeeper's wife scuttled over, glancing at her fearfully. Then, after scooping up the coins, she practically sprinted to a small door in the rear corner of the kitchen. A moment later, Antonina heard her clumping up the stairs which led to the living quarters above.

Her husband began backing his way toward the same door.

"You can't come upstairs," he muttered. "I'm not going to get involved in any of this. Things are crazy right now."

Antonina shook her head.

"Just bar the door and stay upstairs. But, before you go—where do you keep your flour? And your knives?"

The shopkeeper pointed to a cupboard with the ladle.

"Flour's in there. The knives, too."

"Good. Leave me the ladle."

He frowned, glanced at the ladle, shrugged.

"Where do you want it?"

Antonina pointed toward the big kettle on the stove. Hurriedly, the shopkeeper dropped the ladle into the simmering broth and then scampered out of the kitchen.

Antonina stepped to the door which led to the outer room of the shop and pressed her ear against it.

Nothing. They haven't found the shop yet.

She raced to the cupboard and threw its door open. She hesitated, for just an instant, between the flour barrel and the knives hanging on the wall.

The knives first.

She grabbed four of the knives, two in each hand, and carried them over to the workbench next to the stove. Quickly, she gauged their balance. One of them, she decided, was suitable. That one—and her own little dagger—she placed on the edge of the workbench, blades toward her. The other three—much larger blades, one of them a veritable cleaver—she placed next to them, hilts facing out.

She hurried back to the closet and seized a small pan on a shelf. She lifted the lid to the barrel and dug the pan into the flour. A moment later, spilling a trail behind her, she poured the flour into the kettle. Quickly, using the ladle, she stirred the flour into the broth.

She was practically dancing with impatience. But she didn't dare add more flour too quickly. She had to give the broth time to regain its heat.

When the liquid began roiling, she hurried back to the closet. More flour. Into the kettle. Stir it. Wait. Wait.

Again.

That's enough, she decided. The meat broth was now a lumpy, viscous mess. And, within a minute, would be back to a boil.

She looked around. Draped on nearby pegs, she saw the thick, wettened cloths which the shopkeeper used to handle the kettle.

She wrapped her hands in the cloths and picked up the kettle. Grunting with exertion—it was a big kettle, three-fourths full.

Yes. Barely, but—yes.

She replaced the kettle on the stove, leaving the cloths next to it. Then, she raced to the door and closed the latch. For a moment, she considered trying to brace the door, but decided against it.

Better this way. I don't want them to have to work too hard to get through the door. Just hard enough. The latch will do for that.

She strode to the table onto which she had dumped the coins, and dragged it into the middle of the kitchen. Then, squatting down, she placed her shoulder under the edge and levered the table onto its side. It was a solidly built wooden table, large and heavy, and it made a great clattering sound when it hit the floor.

Upstairs, she heard the shopkeeper's wife scream.

Damn you!

Faintly, she heard a voice coming from the street.

"In here!"

She heard the outer door burst open. Then, the sounds of many men pouring into the shop.

Now, louder:

"In here!"

She saw the door to the kitchen move, as someone tried to open it. The latch jiggled.

Very loud:

"She's in here!"

Antonina stepped to the stove. She wrapped the wet cloths around her hands and gripped the kettle. Stood still, looking over her shoulder. Watching the door.

A loud thump. The door bulged. The latch strained, but held.

Very loud:

"Out of the way!"

Thundering footsteps.

Smash!

The latch splintered. The door flew open. A large body—then another—hurtled through. Three men came piling in behind. All of them were dressed in the rough clothes of street toughs, and all were holding cudgels in their hands.

The first man—the self-appointed battering ram—was already off-balance. He slammed into the upended table in the middle of

the kitchen and bounced back, half-sprawled onto the floor. The
man coming right behind tripped over him and stumbled to his
knees, leaning over the edge of the table itself.

The three men behind *him* skidded into a pile.

Five men, tangled up, immobilized.

Antonina seized the kettle, turned, and heaved its contents
onto the cluster of thugs.

Several gallons of boiling, flour-thickened meat broth spewed
over the would-be killers.

Shrieks of agony filled the room. Half-crazed with pain and
fear, the five men in the kitchen began tearing at their flesh,
frantically trying to scrape off the scalding brew.

Couldn't. *Couldn't!* The flour made the broth stick to their
skins.

Antonina ignored them. More men were in the room beyond.
Two of them were jammed in the doorway to the kitchen, gaping at the scene.

She spun lightly, seized her own little dagger by the blade. That
one, she knew, was perfectly balanced.

Whipped around.

Father, I need you now!

He hadn't been worth much, that charioteer, but he had taught
his daughter how to use a knife.

Taught her very well.

The little dagger flashed across the room and sank hilt deep
into the throat of the man standing on the right side of the
doorway.

The man's eyes bulged. He choked blood. Grabbed the hilt.
Tried to draw it out. Couldn't. Sank to his knees. Died.

By the time the man next to him realized what had happened,
it was too late. Another knife had sailed across the room.

Not into his throat, however. That knife, not as delicate as her
own small dagger, Antonina had aimed at a less chancy target.
The heavy butcher knife plunged four inches into the thug's chest,
right into his heart.

Antonina took up the cleaver. The two dead bodies in the
doorway would keep off the assailants in the room beyond for a
few seconds. Time enough.

She sprang forward, right to the edge of the upended table,
and began butchering the men on the other side.

Quite literally. Her knife-strokes were the short, sharp, chopping motions of an experienced butcher dismembering meat. There was no frenzied lunging; no grandiose stabs; no dramatic swings.

Just short, straight, strikes. With the heavy, razor-sharp blade of a cleaver.

Chop. Chop. Chop. Chop.

A nose fell off. The fingers from a hand covering a face. Another nose, and most of an upper lip. An ear and half a cheek.

Back again, quick. *Chop. Chop. Chop.* More fingers—and a thumb—fell to the floor. A wrist dangled, half-severed. Blood covered a face gashed to the bone.

Back again, quick. The men piled up behind the table were a helpless shrieking mob. Not even that—a pack of sheep, half-paralyzed by third-degree burns and mutilation.

Chop. Chop. Chop.

Now, the strikes were lethal. Hands with severed wrists and amputated fingers could no longer protect necks. Antonina aimed for the carotid arteries and hit two out of three. (The third would die also, a bit more slowly, from a severed jugular.)

Instantly, she was soaked in blood. She leaned into the spurting gore, like a child might lean into a fountain, and struck at the two remaining men behind the table. Both of them—dazed with shock and agony—were trying to crawl away from the nightmare.

One of them worked his way free, with nothing worse than a split shoulder blade. The other collapsed, dead. Antonina had chopped right through the back of his neck, severing the spine.

The sole survivor, screaming with fear and pain, scrambled toward the door on his knees and hands. (One hand, rather. His left hand was fingerless.) The timing, from Antonina's viewpoint, was perfect. The remaining thugs in the outer room had finally managed to drag aside the two bodies blocking the door. Two of them pushed their way through, only to stumble over the thug crawling toward them.

One of the men kept his balance, staggering against the door-frame. The other tripped and sprawled across the pile of bodies in the middle of the kitchen. He flung out his hands to break his fall and managed to grab the edge of the table.

For a brief instant, the thug stared up at Antonina.

Her face was the last thing he ever saw. Other than the huge blade which descended onto his own face and removed it. The cleaver bit into his forehead and kept going, down and down, driven by Antonina's fury. The blade peeled off his eyebrows, shredded the eyes, took the nose, both lips, all the chin and a small piece of the chin bone.

Then, Antonina made her first mistake. By now—some thirty seconds into the battle—she was almost berserk with rage. She kicked aside the face flopping onto her foot, drew back the cleaver, and split the man's head in half. The blow was so ferocious that the blade jammed in the skull.

She tugged at it fiercely. Jerked. Jerked again.

Stuck.

She looked up. The thug leaning against the doorframe stared back at her. For a moment, the man's eyes were simply wide with shock. His jaw hung loose.

Then, seeing her predicament, he shouted sudden victory and sprang toward her. He circled around the pile of bodies and the upended table, making his way into the rear of the small kitchen.

"Come on, lads!" he bellowed. "I've got the bitch trapped!" He waved his club triumphantly.

Antonina backed against the stove and seized both of the remaining knives. She flipped one of them end-for-end. Now holding it by the blade, she made a throwing motion. The club-wielding man in front of her drew back, flinching.

It was a feint. She half-turned and threw the knife at another thug coming through the kitchen door.

That knife, however, was too blade-heavy for a good throw. The thug howled from the pain—the haft bruised his chest badly—and staggered back out of sight. But Antonina knew that he was not even disabled.

Despairing, she turned back to face her immediate opponent. *I didn't think there'd be so many.*

She pushed all despair aside. She didn't expect to survive, but she would sell her life dearly.

From the outer room, Antonina heard a sudden shouting uproar. Cries of triumph, she assumed, but ignored them. Her attention was completely fixed on her assailant in the kitchen.

The thug in front of her danced back and forth, snarling and waving his club. For all the man's bravado, Antonina realized that he was also very frightened. She *had* slaughtered a number of his fellows, after all. And—like the fat shopkeeper—the street tough recognized the expert way she was holding her knife.

He cocked his head, without taking his eyes from her. "*Come on!*" he bellowed. "Damn you—I've got her trapped!"

Antonina stepped forward. Her knife waved, feinted, probed. The thug backed against the wall, swinging his club wildly. Antonina kept her distance, looking for an opening.

Again, the thug shouted.

"What the hell are you waiting for, you assholes?"

From the door, a cold voice answered.

"They're waiting for Satan."

Antonina gasped. Her eyes sped to the door. She staggered back against the other wall, almost collapsing from relief.

The thug's eyes followed hers. An instant later, all color left his face.

Maurice stalked into the kitchen. His helmet was covered with blood. A piece of a brain slid off his blood-soaked half-armor. The spatha in his right hand dripped blood. His face was spattered with blood. Blood trailed from his gray beard.

For all the world, he didn't look like a man so much as a killing machine. A thing of iron, not flesh. His eyes, too, were gray. They gleamed out of his gore-covered face like two rivets.

Maurice circled the pile of bodies and the upended table in the middle of the kitchen. His steps were relaxed, almost casual, as if he were strolling through a garden.

Hissing with terror, the thug backed into the far corner of the kitchen, against the door which led to the rooms above. He groped, found the door latch, shook it in a frenzy.

Useless. The shopkeeper had bolted the door from the other side.

Now the thug screamed, with terror and rage. Maurice ignored the sound completely. He advanced until he was almost within sword range. The thug swung his club frantically. The blows were short, by half a foot. Maurice didn't even bother to duck.

The hecatontarch turned his head very slightly. Just enough to ask Antonina:

"Is there anything you want to find out from this piece of shit?"

Antonina shook her head. Then, realizing that Maurice couldn't see her, said:

"No. He won't know anything."

"Didn't think so," grunted Maurice.

The thug swung the club again. This time, Maurice met the blow with a flashing sweep of his spatha. The club split in half. The shock of the blow knocked the stub out of the thug's hand.

He gasped. Gasped again, watching his hand amputated by another spatha-strike. Gasped again—started to gasp—watching the sword sweep toward his left temple. In a final despairing act, the thug threw up his left arm, trying to block the strike.

The spatha cut his arm off before it went halfway through his head. The thug dropped straight down onto his knees, like a pole-axed steer.

Maurice grunted, twisted the blade with his powerful wrist, and pulled it loose. The thug's body collapsed to the floor.

"Are there any left?" whispered Antonina.

The cataphract's chuckle was utterly humorless.

"Be serious, girl."

Maurice's eyes scanned the kitchen. A cold, grim gaze, at first. But, by the time those gray eyes reached Antonina, they were full of good cheer.

"Wish I'd met your pop," he said. "He must have been quite a guy."

Antonina laughed giddily.

"He was a complete scoundrel, Maurice! A worthless bum!"

Then, bursting into tears, she slid down the wall into a half-kneeling squat. She pressed the back of her hand—still holding the knife—against her mouth, smearing her face with yet more blood.

Gasped, choked, sobbed.

Whispered:

"Thank you, father. Oh, thank you."

Chapter 24

"Stop fussing over me, Irene!" snapped Antonina. "I'm fine, I tell you."

The spymaster shook her head. Irene's face was pale and drawn. She had been sequestered in Theodora's quarters for days, and had not learned about the assassination attempt until early the following morning. She had come to Antonina's villa in the suburbs immediately.

Antonina went to a closet and began pulling out fresh clothes. The garments she had been wearing when she and Maurice returned to the villa the night before had already been destroyed. Expensive as they were, there was simply no way to clean off that much blood and gore.

"Wear a heavy cloak," said Irene. "It's cold out." Then, darkly: "I should *never* have agreed to let you go alone."

Antonina planted her hands on her hips and glared at her friend.

"It was not *your* decision in the first place," she pointed out. "It was mine. I've always gone alone to those meetings. Balban insisted."

Irene wiped her face with a trembling hand.

"I know. Still—God, you were almost *murdered.*"

Antonina shrugged. Then, shrugged her way into a tunic. Her muffled voice came from within the simple, utilitarian garment:

"But I wasn't. And there's an end to it. So stop fussing. Besides—" Her face popped out, smiling broadly. "—it was the best news I've heard, so to speak, in months. You *do* realize what that assassination attempt means, don't you?"

Irene frowned. Antonina laughed.

"*You're* supposed to be the spymaster here, Irene! So start spymastering, for a moment, and stop fretting over me as if I were your little chick."

Irene was still frowning.

"*Think*, woman. Why would the Malwa decide to kill me? *Now*, of all times?"

Irene's eyes widened. She pressed her fingers over her lips.

"Belisarius!"

Antonina grinned.

"Precisely. Balban must have gotten new orders from India. Which means that my dear husband has done something to completely infuriate the Malwa. And it *also* means that he's escaped from their clutches."

"Of course," hissed Irene. The spymaster began pacing slowly.

"If they had their hands on him, they'd have even greater leverage over you than they thought they had. There would have been no reason to have you murdered. Quite the contrary."

By now, Antonina had finished dressing and was lacing on her boots. She nodded her head. "That's right. Which means he'll be arriving in Constantinople, sooner or later."

"When, do you think?"

Antonina shrugged.

"There's no way to know. We have no idea what route he's taking to get out of India. Most likely, he'll return by ship to Axum. If he does, Ashot and his men will be there to meet him."

She headed toward the door. Added: "Ashot's instructions were very clear. They'll sail up the Red Sea, portage to the Nile, and then take the river to Alexandria. There'll be a ship waiting to bring them straight to Constantinople."

Once in the corridor, Antonina strode hurriedly toward the villa's entrance. "They could get here almost any time. Or—not for weeks."

Behind her, Irene grimaced.

"I wish we knew. It would—"

Antonina gestured the thought away. "Don't even think about it, Irene! We can't make any plans based on my husband's return. We can only forge ahead. Speaking of which—have all the grenades arrived?"

They reached the foyer. Maurice was there, waiting for them.

Like Antonina, he had changed his garments. But his helmet and half-armor were the same he had been wearing earlier. He had simply cleaned them off. That kitchen had not been his first slaughterhouse. The new stains were lost amid the relics of old gore.

Maurice answered her question.

"Yes. And they've already been taken to the monastery."

"Let's go, then," said Antonina.

Maurice held the door open. Antonina strode through into the courtyard, shivering a bit from the cold of a December morning. Then, seeing the mounted cataphracts in the courtyard and the street beyond, she stopped. Did a quick little count. Spun around.

"Where are the rest of the cataphracts, Maurice?" she demanded. "There's not more than a hundred here."

Maurice's jaws tightened.

"The rest of them are busy, at the moment. But they'll be joining us soon enough. They'll meet us at the monastery when they're done."

Antonina peered at him suspiciously.

"Busy? 'Done'? Doing what?"

The hecatontarch's face was like stone.

"What do you think, girl?"

"*Oh, no,*" whispered Antonina.

Irene hissed: "Maurice—you *can't*. It'll alert the Malwa! They'll know—"

"I don't give a damn what the Malwa know," snarled Maurice. He glared at both women.

"I am *not* a spymaster," he grated. "I am *not* an intriguer. I am the leader of the general's *bucellarii* and *those*"—he pointed to the mounted Thracians—"are my lord's *cataphracts.*"

He stalked over to his horse and seized the reins.

"If some stinking pig thinks he can try to have you murdered—without consequences—he is one sadly mistaken son-of-a-bitch."

He swung himself into the saddle and stared down at Antonina and Irene. Like a statue. Immovable.

Antonina blew out her cheeks. Then, sighing, headed for her own horse.

Less than a minute later, she and Irene rode out together through the gates of the villa. Once in the street, the two women were surrounded by over a hundred cataphracts. The small army began making its way toward the inner city.

After a while, Irene muttered: "Oh, well. Balban probably doesn't think you're still working for him, anyway."

Antonina giggled. "Do you think his suspicions will be aroused? When two hundred cataphracts tear his villa down around him?"

Balban poured tea into Narses' cup. The eunuch immediately sipped at the beverage appreciatively.

"Thank you," he murmured. "Just the thing for a cold morning."

"The weather's clear, I hope?" asked Balban.

Narses nodded. "Oh, yes." Smiling thinly: "Other than the cold, it's a perfect day for an insurrection. Not a cloud in the sky."

"Good," muttered Balban. "The last thing we need is bad weather. How do things seem in the Great Palace?"

"Just about perfect, I'd say. The more Justinian's position worsens, the more tightly he clings to John of Cappadocia and myself."

Narses set down his cup.

"That's why I came here. Justinian ordered me to leave the Great Palace and round up more troops. Since I had the opportunity, I thought I'd come by for a last-minute conference." He laughed harshly. "*Troops.* Justinian still doesn't realize that he *has* no troops, except his palace *excubitores.* Every other army unit in the capital has locked themselves into their barracks, waiting out the storm. We won't even need Aegidius and his Army of Bithynia. The Blues and Greens alone should be enough."

Balban nodded. "Not much to confer about, then. The factions should start gathering by noon. My kshatriya will have seized the Hippodrome within the hour. All we have to do is make our appearance and"—scowling—"hope Hypatius shows up to be acclaimed the new Emperor."

Narses sneered.

"He'll show up. Or if he doesn't, Pompeius will. We'll have to provide the new Emperor with fresh trousers, of course. I'm sure both of the nephews have already shat in the ones they're wearing. But they'll be there. Their ambition is greater than their terror."

Balban chuckled. Then, more seriously: "What about Theodora?"

Narses winced. "That's the one small problem. She knows almost everything, Balban—I'm quite sure of that. Her new spymaster—that young woman Irene Macrembolitissa—is fiendishly capable. But," he shrugged, "Justinian's not listening to her at all, anymore. And now he's run out of time."

Balban grunted. "Still—" He hesitated, then shrugged himself. "No doubt you're right. By nightfall, it won't matter anyway. Her corpse will join Justinian's, feeding the fish in the Sea of Marmara."

Narses pressed his lips together, fighting down the anguish. Fiercely, he reminded himself of his ambition. To hide his feelings, he leaned forward and reached for the teacup resting on the table.

His hand stopped. The teacup was rattling.

Ajatasutra burst into the small salon. "Out!" he hissed. "Now!"

The assassin strode to a door against the far wall. Flinging it open, he began hastily dragging aside the heavy chest which sat on the floor of the closet beyond.

Balban rose, frowning angrily. "Just what do you think you're—"

Ajatasutra, still bent over the heavy chest, turned his head. His eyes were like hot coals. "If you want to live more than two minutes, Balban, help me get this damned chest off the trapdoor."

Balban remained standing in place, rigid, still frowning. Narses immediately rose from his chair and went to Ajatasutra's aid. For all his age and small size, the eunuch was not weak. With his help, Ajatasutra moved the chest out of the closet.

"Against the wall," grunted the assassin.

A moment later, the chest was pushed into position. Ajatasutra sprang nimbly into the closet and rolled back an expensive rug. Then, fiddling a moment with a plank which seemed no different from any of the other wood flooring, he levered up a small trapdoor.

"Get in," he ordered Narses.

The old eunuch hesitated not an instant. He began lowering himself down a ladder.

Halfway down, the ladder began to shake. Narses stopped, waist high in the trapdoor, and stared up at Balban. The spymaster was now standing in the door of the closet.

He was still frowning—but with puzzlement, now, more than anger. Balban looked down at his feet.

"Why is the floor shaking?" he asked.

Narses glanced quickly at Ajatasutra. The assassin's face was stiff with suppressed anger.

"Mother of God," muttered Narses. To Balban: "What have you done, you damned fool?"

Balban glared.

"That's none of your concern, Narses!" he snapped.

Then, frowning at his feet, he asked yet again:

"Why is the floor shaking?"

Narses sneered.

"I take it you've never faced a charge of cataphracts in full armor?" he demanded. "That's what you're feeling, *fool*. Several hundred tons of approaching death and destruction."

Balban goggled at him.

"What are you talking about? We're in the middle of Constantinople!"

Narses sighed, looked over at Ajatasutra. The assassin, through tight lips, said: "He ordered Antonina's murder."

"Marvelous," muttered Narses. "Just marvelous."

The eunuch began lowering himself down the ladder. Very quickly. His voice came from below: "You're not in Constantinople *now*, Balban. *You're in Thrace.*"

A smashing sound came from outside the villa. After a second, Balban realized that it was the outer gate. Shattering.

Shattered.

A scream. Cut short. Another. Another. Another. All the screams were cut short, but Balban recognized the voices. His Malwa guards. Dying.

Dead.

Ajatasutra sprang to the door of the salon and stared down the corridor leading to the villa's main entrance. A moment later, there came a splintering crash.

He leapt back into the room and slammed shut the door.

"*That*," he announced, "was a lance driving through the main door."

Balban hesitated no longer. He scrambled down the ladder after Narses. Before his head sank below the level of the floor he heard a rolling series of thunderous noises. Doors and windows being shattered. By the time he reached the small tunnel fifteen feet down, he could already hear the screams echoing through the entire villa. The rest of the Malwa mission resident in the villa were being butchered.

Ajatasutra took the time to close the closet door before he

started down the ladder. As best he could, feeling his way in the darkness, he tried to position the rug so that it would cover the trapdoor after he lowered it.

When he reached the tunnel below, he found the two other men waiting for him. Balban had lit the small lamp which was kept in a cubby.

"I don't know the way," whispered the spymaster. "I've never been down here."

Ajatasutra took the lamp from his hand.

"Follow me," he ordered. "And watch your step. We never bothered to grade the tunnel floor. I didn't really think we'd need it."

After the three men had inched their way down the narrow tunnel for hundred feet or so, Narses asked:

"How much farther, Ajatasutra? My shoes aren't designed for this kind of travel. And—damnation—they're silk! Expensive."

Ajatasutra chuckled, grimly.

"Forget about your shoes, Narses. We've another two hundred feet to go. Before we reach the *sewer*."

"Marvelous," muttered Narses. "Just marvelous."

Fifty feet down, he sneered: "What other brilliant ideas did you have today, Balban? Did you jump into the Bosporus to see if it was wet? Did you swallow a live coal to see if it would burn your throat? Did you—"

"Shut up," snarled the spymaster. "I received orders—from Nanda Lal himself."

Narses was silent, thereafter, until they had reached the sewer and slogged their way down its stinking length for at least two hundred feet. He began lagging further and further behind. Eventually, Ajatasutra handed Balban the lamp and went back to help the old eunuch.

"Are you all right?" he asked.

"I could use your shoulder," grunted Narses. "This damned sewer's so low I have to stoop. My back hurts."

Ajatasutra leaned his right shoulder under Narses' left arm and helped him along. The eunuch turned his head until his lips were but inches from Ajatasutra's ear and whispered:

"You *do* realize what those orders from Nanda Lal mean, don't you?"

Ajatasutra nodded, very slightly.

"Yes," he replied, also in a whisper. He glanced up. Balban's dim form was visible thirty feet ahead of them, backlit by the lamp he was carrying.

"It means you were right about Belisarius," whispered the assassin. "He must have escaped from India."

They progressed another fifty feet. By now, all of them were soaked with filthy water up to their mid-thighs.

Again, Narses turned his lips to Ajatasutra's ear.

"There'll be a boat, waiting. At the Neorion harbor in the Golden Horn. Do you know where it is?"

"Yes," whispered Ajatasutra. "Why me?"

"You're the best of a sorry lot. And if I have to flee to India I'll need someone to vouch for my credentials."

Ajatasutra smiled, thinly.

"You don't sound entirely confident in the certain success of our plans."

Narses sneered. "Nothing in this world is certain, Ajatasutra. *Except this*—better to have loosed the demon from his pit than to have loosed Belisarius. *Especially after murdering his wife.*"

"She wasn't murdered," muttered Ajatasutra. Seeing the frown on the eunuch's face, the assassin chuckled.

"I followed. At a distance, of course. And I stayed well out of the fray. Quite a set-to, judging from the racket coming out of that cookshop—even before the cataphract arrived. I waited until he brought Antonina out. The woman was covered with blood, but none of it was hers."

Narses sighed. "Well, that's something. Belisarius will just be his usual extraordinarily competent and brilliantly capable deadly self. Instead of vengeance personified."

They slogged on, and on. Eventually, now well ahead of them, they saw Balban rise from his stoop and stand up straight. He had finally reached the exit from the sewer.

"Come on!" they heard the spymaster's hissing voice. "Time is short!"

Just before they came within Balban's hearing range, Ajatasutra whispered:

"What does the boat look like?"

"Like it wants to leave Constantinople in a very big hurry," was the eunuch's only reply.

✦   ✦   ✦

Maurice waited until the cataphracts circled the monastery before he would let Antonina or Irene dismount. The Thracian cavalrymen were in a grim, grim mood. The small crowd of curious onlookers, which began to gather from the nearby residences, quickly drew back under their hard gaze.

"Marvelous," muttered Antonina. "Just marvelous."

She glared at Maurice. The hecatontarch returned her hot gaze with placidity.

"So much for keeping the whereabouts of the Theodoran Cohort secret," she growled.

Maurice shrugged. He pointed toward the southwest.

"Take a look. The time for secrets is over."

Antonina and Irene twisted in their saddles. They were not far from the Column of Marcian. The monastery, and the cathedral which adjoined it, were located just inside the old walls of the capital—the "walls of Constantine." The heart of Constantinople, the corner of the city which held the Great Palace and the Hippodrome, was not more than two miles away.

In the vicinity of the Hippodrome, the two women could see smokeplumes produced by bonfires which the gathering Blue and Green factions had set aflame to warm their toughs. They could hear the faint roar of the mob, even at the distance.

Antonina asked Irene: "What's the situation at the Great Palace?"

"Tense. Very tense. Justinian called for a meeting of the high council for today, at noon. He's still listening to John of Cappadocia, however, who assures him that most of the army units will stand by the throne. So he's living in a fool's paradise. He doesn't realize that the only military forces he has left are his own excubitores—all five hundred of them!—and the forces which we're bringing."

Irene turned her head, looking to the south.

"Sittas and Hermogenes should be in position at the Harbor of Hormisdas. I'd better leave now and tell them where your forces stand."

Antonina nodded. Maurice ordered a squad of cataphracts to escort the spymaster.

A commotion drew Antonina's attention.

A mob of grenadiers and their wives were pouring out of the monastery's doors, heading toward her. All of them were staring at her, their faces full of worried concern.

"You told them," she said to Maurice, accusingly.

Maurice chuckled.

"*Told* them? I sent ten cataphracts over here this morning, to *regale* them with the tale. Every last gruesome, gory, grisly great moment of it!"

Antonina sighed with exasperation. Maurice edged his horse next to her. Leaning over—all humor gone—he whispered harshly: "*Listen to me, girl, and listen well.* You're at war, now, and you're the commander. A *female* commander—the first one in Roman history outside of ancient legends. You need all the confidence you can get from your soldiers. And *they* need it even more than you do."

Antonina stared into his gray eyes. She had never noticed, before, how cold those eyes could be.

"Do you think I'd let an opportunity like this pass?" he demanded. Then, with a harsh laugh: "God, now that it's over, I'm almost ready to thank Balban! What a gift he gave us!"

He leaned back in his saddle. "Antonina, my toughest *cataphracts* are in awe of you. Not one in ten would have survived that ambush—unarmored, with no weapon but a dagger—and they know it. How do you think these Syrian peasants feel? *Now*—about their *little woman* commander?"

It was obvious how the peasants felt. The grenadiers and their wives were surrounding Antonina, gazing up at her silently. Their expressions were easy to read. A mixture of sentiments: relief at her obvious well-being; fierce satisfaction in her victory; pride in their commander—and self-pride that she *was* their commander.

Most of all—it was almost frightening to Antonina—was a sense of quasireligious adoration. The simple Syrians were gazing at her much as they might have gazed at a living saint.

She was blessed by God's grace.

Just as the prophet Michael had foretold.

For a moment, Antonina felt herself shrink from that crushing responsibility.

Then, drawing on the fierce will which had always been a part of her—since her girlhood in the hard streets of Alexandria—she drove all hesitation aside.

"I am quite well," she assured her grenadiers loudly. She began dismounting from her horse, but immediately found a dozen hands were helping her down. The same hands then carried her toward the cathedral. Hurriedly, monks and priests appeared to open the great doors. Among them, she saw the plump figure of Bishop Cassian.

As she was carried through the doors, her eyes met those of Anthony. He returned her smile, but his gaze was filled with concern.

She was carried to the altar and set back on her feet. Turning, she saw that the grenadiers and their wives were rapidly pouring in behind. Within two minutes, the great cathedral was filled. All the Syrians stood there, silently, staring at her.

Many years before, as a young woman, Antonina's mother had given her some brief training as an actress. In the event, Antonina had never pursued her mother's career, having found a different one which—though just as disreputable—was considerably more renumerative. But she still remembered the lessons. Not her mother's meager talents as a thespian, but her skills at projecting her voice.

All the grenadiers in the room—as well as the cataphracts who had joined them—almost jumped. Such a small woman, to have such a great, powerful *voice*.

> *I have little to say, my soldiers. My friends.*
> *Little needs to be said.*
> *Our enemies are gathering. You can see their bonfires. You can hear their coarse shouts of triumph.*
> *Do not fear them.*
> *They are nothing.*
> *Nothing.*
> *Assassins. Street thugs. Murderers. Rapists. Thieves. Pimps. Gamblers.*
> *Nothing.*
> *Nothing!*

She paused, waited. The grenadiers—one or two, at first—took up the chant. Softly, at first. Then, louder and louder.

"Nothing. Nothing."

> *We will shatter them back into their nothing. We will drive them back into their sewers.*

"Nothing! Nothing!"

We will hound them into their burrows. We will follow them into their ratholes. We will savage them till they plead for mercy.

"NOTHING! NOTHING!"

There will be no mercy.
For nothing, there is nothing.

The shouts now shook the cathedral itself. Antonina pointed to the cataphracts. The shouts died away. The grenadiers listened to her with complete attention.

Our plan is simple. The traitors are gathering their forces in the Hippodrome. We will go there. The cataphracts will lead the way, but we will be God's hammer.
We will hammer nothing—into nothing.

She strode forward, heading down the aisle. The grenadiers parted before her and then immediately closed behind. She moved through that little sea of humanity like a ship in full sail.

As she reached the door, Anthony Cassian stepped forward. For a moment, she embraced her old friend.

"May God be with me," she whispered.

"Oh, I believe He is," replied the Bishop softly. "Trust me in this, Antonina." With a quirk of a smile: "I am quite a reputable theologian, you know."

She returned his smile, kissed him on the cheek, and strode past.

By now, a large crowd of onlookers had gathered in the street. Not even the glares of cataphracts could hold back their curiosity. But then, hearing the sound of many approaching horses—*heavy, armored* horses—the crowd eddied back, pressed against the houses and fences which lined the boulevard.

Down that street, in a prancing trot, came two hundred cataphracts. The remainder of the Thracian bucellarii, returning from their own triumph.

When the cataphracts reached the cathedral they drew to a halt.

The cataphracts in the lead tossed the residue of their vengeance at Antonina's feet.

Gasping and hissing, the crowd of bystanders plastered themselves against the walls. A few, timidity overcoming curiosity, scuttled hastily into the houses and fenced yards.

Twenty or so severed heads, rolling in the street, can chill even the most avid onlooker.

The grenadiers, on the other hand, seeing the grisly trophies, erupted with their own savage glee.

"NOTHING! NOTHING! NOTHING!"

Antonina moved toward her horse. Maurice, with two cataphracts in tow, met her halfway.

"Put these on," commanded Maurice. "I had them specially made."

The cataphracts with him extended a cuirass and a helmet.

"The helmet was easy," commented Maurice. "But the cuirass was a bit of a challenge for the armorer. He's not used to cleavage."

Antonina smiled. With Maurice's help, she donned the unfamiliar equipment. The smile vanished. "This stuff is *heavy*."

"Don't complain, girl. Just be thankful it's only half-armor. And be *especially* thankful that we're in Constantinople in the winter, instead of Syria in the summer."

Antonina grimaced at the thought. Then, with a sly little smile:

"Don't I get a sword, too?"

Maurice shook his head.

"I've got something better."

He drew a scabbarded knife—a large and odd knife, judging from the sheath—and handed it to her.

Antonina drew the blade out of the scabbard. She could not restrain a little gasp.

"You recognize it, I see," said Maurice. His voice was full of satisfaction. "The shopkeeper drove a hard bargain for it, but I thought it was fitting."

Antonina stared back and forth from Maurice to the cleaver.

The hecatontarch's lips twisted into a grim smile.

"Ask any veteran, Antonina. They'll all tell you there's nothing as important in a battle as having a trusty, *tested* blade."

Suddenly, the feel of that simple cooking utensil in her hand filled Antonina with a great rush of confidence.

"I do believe you're right, Maurice."

She sensed, from the murmuring voices around her, that the cataphracts were passing the news to the grenadiers. Seconds later, the grenadiers began a new chant:

"CLEAVE THEM! CLEAVE THEM!"

With Maurice's help, she clambered into her saddle, suppressing a curse at the awkward weight of the helmet and armor. Once securely seated, she raised the butcher knife over her head, waving it.

The grenadiers roared. The cataphracts joined their voices to the cry:

"NOTHING! NOTHING!"

Antonina suppressed a laugh.

For all the world like a warrior of legend, waving a mystic sword of renown!

Which, though she did not know it yet, she was; and which, to her everlasting surprise, that humble cleaver would become.

Chapter 25

When John of Rhodes saw the approaching *dromon*, he began cursing bitterly.

Some of his curses were directed at Irene Macrembolitissa. The spymaster had not warned him that the traitorous General Aegidius had obtained a war galley to clear the way for his troop transports. John could already see the first of those transports, bearing the lead elements of the Army of Bithynia. Four of the tubby sailing ships were just now leaving the harbor at Chalcedon, heading across the Bosporus toward Constantinople.

But most of his curses were aimed at life in general. He did not really blame Irene for the failure in intelligence. In all fairness, the spymaster could not be expected to know everything about their enemy.

"That's just the way of it," he muttered. "War's always been a fickle bitch."

"Excuse me?" asked Eusebius, looking up from his work. The young artificer's face seemed a bit green. He was obviously feeling ill at ease from the rocking motion of the galley. Especially since he was standing upon the fighting platform amidships, engaged in the delicate task of opening firebomb crates. The platform was elevated ten feet above the deck, which only accentuated the ship's unsteadiness.

"Hurry it up, Eusebius," growled John of Rhodes. The naval officer pointed to starboard. "We're going to have to deal with *that* before we do anything else."

Eusebius straightened, peering near-sightedly toward the war galley approaching from the south.

"Oh, Christ," he muttered. "I can't see it very well, but—is that what I think it is?"

John nodded gloomily.

"Yeah, it's a dromon. A hundred fighting soldiers and at least a hundred and fifty rowers—good ones, too, judging from their speed. And they've already lowered the sails."

Eusebius paled. Dromons were the fastest ships afloat—at least, during the period before their rowers tired—and by far the most maneuverable. Pure warships.

John of Rhodes scampered down the ladder to the main deck and scurried aft, where he hastily began consulting with his steering officer. In his absence, Eusebius began unpacking another crate of firebombs. The artillerymen on the platform offered to help, but he refused their assistance. He was probably being too cautious—once the battle started, the artillerymen would have to do their own loading—but Eusebius knew better than anyone just how dangerous those bombs could be if they were accidentally ruptured.

Besides, it gave him something to do besides worry.

And there was a lot to worry about. Eusebius was no seaman, but he had picked up enough from John of Rhodes over the past months to understand the seriousness of their predicament.

The artificer glanced at the two scorpions set up on the ship's fighting platform—the "wood-castle," as it was called. Then, more slowly, he studied the ship itself.

It was not a happy study.

A full-sized dromon, like the one approaching them, had a crew of two to three hundred men. A two-banked galley, that ship had 25 oars in each bank—100 in all. Fifty rowers were permanently assigned to the lower bank, one man to an oar. The rest of the crew, who would number at least 150, were assigned to the fighting deck. A hundred of those would man the upper bank of oars, two men to an oar, while the rest served as archers and boarders. In the event of a drawn-out pursuit or engagement, the upper rowers would switch places with the soldiers, thus keeping the men from becoming exhausted.

Technically, Eusebius knew, their ship was also classed as a dromon, an oared war galley. But it was the medium-sized type called a *pamphylos*. They only had eighty oars, twenty on each bank. And there was only room for a single rower on the upper oars.

A hundred and fifty rowers versus eighty. Despite the greater weight of the approaching dromon, it would still be faster than their own galley. And they were further handicapped because of the modifications which John had made in their warship.

John had known he would be heavily outnumbered in the coming battle—one ship against twenty, probably more. So he had decided to use his single ship as a pure artillery vessel, bombarding the enemy fleet at long range with his firebombs. For that reason, they only carried twelve fighting men—just enough to operate the two scorpions. They would be hopelessly outmatched in the event of a boarding.

True, they also carried a double crew of rowers. If John's battle plan worked, his men would be rowing for long periods. So he had loaded the ships with relief rowers. That would give them a greater endurance than the crew of the approaching dromon, but the weight of the extra rowers would also slow them down.

Not to mention—

Eusebius studied the fighting platform he was standing on. The wood-castle was larger and heavier than normal for this size war galley. It needed to be in order to provide the necessary support and room for the two scorpions which John had placed there. But that extra size *also* added weight. As did—

Eusebius lowered his gaze to the deck of the ship itself. Normally, Byzantine war galleys were of the modern design called *aphract*—"unarmored." Since modern naval tactics called for boarding as well as ramming, the rowers/soldiers on the upper banks were protected by nothing more substantial than a light frame rigged along the gangways to which they attached their shields.

But John, since he had no intention of boarding, had refitted the ship to the older *cataphract* design. He had attached solid wooden projections to the gunwales, with overhanging beams, to protect the rowers from archery. The armored projections resembled the rowing frames of ancient Hellenic galleys, although the rowers themselves were still positioned inside the hull. The end result was to enclose the rowers in solid, arrow-proof shelters. A bit stifling, perhaps, despite the ventilating louvers, but far better protection than mere shields hanging on a light frame.

And—much heavier.

Their ship was still faster and more maneuverable than the tubby square-rigged sailing ships which the Army of Bithynia was using for its transports. But it was a sluggish turtle compared to the approaching dromon.

John had not expected to face a real warship.

"Hurry up!" snapped the Rhodesman, clambering back onto the wood-castle. "No—never mind. We'll just have to make do with the bombs you've already uncrated."

"There's only eight of them," protested Eusebius.

"Then we'll have to shoot well," snarled John. "We don't have time, Eusebius! That damned dromon is coming on like a porpoise. *Move.*"

As John and Eusebius began loading the two scorpions with the first of the firebombs, the ship's steering officer bellowed orders at the crew. Though the men were every bit as grim-faced as their captain, they set about the tasks without hesitation. Those sailors were Rhodesmen themselves. John had handpicked them from the ranks of the Roman naval forces stationed in Seleuceia. Their officers had not even complained—not, at least, after they saw the letter of authority from the Empress Theodora which John carried with him.

The pamphylos began coming about, facing this new enemy approaching from the Sea of Marmara.

John peered intently at the oncoming dromon.

God, those rowers are good!

Several cataphracts were standing on the fighting platform in the bow of the galley, staring back at him. Their features were obscured by the helmets on their heads.

Well-used helmets, thought John gloomily. Just like their damned armor. And—oh, shit—don't they hold their bows with a practiced, casual ease? Just great. Just fucking great!

He stared at one of the cataphracts. A huge man, he was.

God, I don't even want to think what that ogre's bow pulls. Two hundred pounds, probably.

He began to turn away, heading for one of the scorpions. An idle thought caused him to pause. He glanced back at the huge cataphract. Then, he stared at the cataphract standing right in the prow of the galley.

A tall cataphract.

The tall cataphract removed his helmet. His face was no longer obscured.

John of Rhodes had excellent eyesight.

A moment later, Eusebius and the entire crew of the pamphylos stopped what they were doing. They were transfixed—gaping, goggling—by the sight of their commanding officer.

John of Rhodes leapt and capered atop the wood-castle, howling like a banshee. He sprang upon the port wall of the fighting platform and gestured obscenely at the fleet of transports bearing the Army of Bithynia across the Bosporus. Then, apparently unsatisfied with mere hand gestures, John unlaced his trousers, pulled out his penis, and waved it in the face of the still distant enemy.

"He's gone mad!" exclaimed Eusebius. The artificer hopped back and forth, torn between the urgent need to load the scorpions and the still more urgent need to restrain John before the maniac fell into the sea. The wood-castle extended two feet beyond the hull of the ship itself.

Fortunately, the naval officer's sealegs were excellent. A moment later, John laced up his trousers and sprang down upon the fighting platform. He bounced over to Eusebius, grinning from ear to ear.

It suddenly occurred to Eusebius that there was an alternate explanation for John's apparent insanity. The artificer turned his head and squinted at the dromon. The galley was now less than fifty yards away.

"Is that—?"

"Yes!" shouted John. "*Belisarius!* In the proverbial nick of time!"

Still grinning, the naval officer examined the war galley in a new light. His grin widened. John's eyes danced back and forth between the galley, his own ship, and the fleet of enemy transports.

By the time the dromon pulled alongside, his grin was almost blinding.

"Oh, those sorry bastards are fucked," he said cheerfully. "*Fucked.*"

A minute later, John and his crewmen were helping Belisarius aboard the pamphylos.

After giving John a brief but powerful embrace, Belisarius immediately climbed up to the wood-castle. Quickly, he examined the bombs resting in open crates next to the artillery engines. The bombs were carefully nestled in wads of thick wool.

"Firebombs?" he asked. "Or gunpowder?"

The general nodded toward Ashot, who was still standing in the bow of the dromon.

"Ashot told me you discovered the secret of gunpowder already," he said approvingly.

John nodded.

"Yes—although I'm sure you'll have suggestions for improving the powder's quality. But these aren't gunpowder. For a naval battle, I thought firebombs would be better. They're my own special formula. I added saltpeter to the naphtha. Beautiful stuff! Beautiful! But you have to be very careful with it."

The movement of Belisarius' eyes now imitated that of John's, not two minutes earlier. Scorpions—galley—enemy fleet; scorpions—galley—enemy fleet.

"You've got a battle plan," he stated.

"Yes," affirmed John. "I'd only hoped to be able to destroy enough of those ships to give Sittas and Hermogenes a fighting chance after they landed. But now—with your galley—we can do better. Much better."

"Give me the entire situation," commanded Belisarius.

John blew out his cheeks.

"The heart of the traitors' conspiracy is at the Hippodrome. The Malwa bribed both the Blues and Greens—can you imagine how much money *that* must have taken?—and are relying on them for the real dirty work." He glanced up at the sun, which had just cleared the horizon. "In three or four hours—by noon, at the latest—they'll be assembled in the Hippodrome. Twenty, maybe thirty thousand of those street toughs. Irene also discovered that they've smuggled in several hundred Malwa soldiers. With gunpowder weapons. Rockets and grenades, we think."

Belisarius nodded. "Most likely. They'll be kshatriya. I doubt they were able to smuggle in any of their cannons, though."

The general glanced at the enemy fleet. All of the transports had now cleared the harbor at Chalcedon and were well into the Bosporus.

"So," he mused. "They'll use the kshatriya as a spearhead, with a huge mob of faction thugs to provide the mass of their fighters. What else? Where do the military units in Constantinople stand?"

John shrugged.

"All of them are standing aside. Stinking cowards are hiding in their barracks."

He nodded toward the fleet of transports.

"That's the Army of Bithynia. General Aegidius is part of the conspiracy. He's got eight thousand men on those transports, including a thousand cataphracts and their horses. According to Irene, his main function is to neutralize any military units that might come to the Emperor's aid."

John's head turned to the west, studying the shoreline of Constantinople.

"Which amounts to Sittas and Hermogenes, and the small army they were able to bring here from Syria. Five hundred cataphracts and two thousand infantrymen. They've been hidden away in ships at Portus Caesarii since they arrived. But they should have marched out this morning. By now—I hope—they've taken up positions guarding the Harbor of Hormisdas. That's the landing site nearest to the Hippodrome and the Great Palace. It's where the Army of Bithynia is planning to disembark, according to Irene's spies."

Belisarius nodded.

"Which means, I assume, that the only forces we have immediately available to suppress the kshatriya and the mob in the Hippodrome are my three hundred cataphracts and Antonina's cohort of grenadiers."

"It's worse than that, Belisarius. John of Cappadocia has assembled almost a thousand bucellarii of his own. I'm sure he'll use them against the excubitores guarding Justinian at the Great Palace."

Belisarius scowled fiercely. "For the sake of God! Why didn't Justinian disband them?"

John winced. He understood Belisarius' astonished outrage. Under Roman law, private armies—*bucellarii*—were illegal for anyone to maintain except serving generals like Belisarius and Sittas. That law had been enacted over fifty years earlier, by Emperor Leo, precisely in order to prevent public officials and landowners from becoming too powerful.

"Justinian gave John of Cappadocia an exemption," he explained. Then, with a harsh laugh: "Not even that! He made the Cappadocian a general. Just a few months after you left for India."

Belisarius rolled his eyes in disgust. "That stinking chiseler's never been in a battle in his life," he snarled. Suddenly, the snarl turned into a crooked smile. "Which, now that I think about it, isn't such a bad thing."

The general rubbed his chin, eyeing the transports.

"Have you got a count?" he asked John.

The naval officer nodded. "There are thirty-one ships in Aegidius' fleet. Most of them—the bigger ones—are *corbita*."

Seeing the blank look in Belisarius' face, John elaborated.

"We seamen call them 'basket ships.' Corbita are freight haulers, general. They operate by sails alone, without rowers. They're slow under the best of circumstances, and they'll be even slower here in the Bosporus fighting against the northerly winds. *But*—they've got a big capacity. Each one can carry up to four hundred passengers, although I doubt they're holding more than three hundred apiece. They've got to haul the arms and equipment, also."

"And the cataphracts' horses," added Belisarius.

"That, too. But I'm pretty sure that the cataphracts themselves are being transported in the smaller ships. Aegidius has eight merchant galleys—*akatoi*—in that fleet. Just about right for a thousand cataphracts. Although—which is good for us—they're having to use their sails alone. They'll have no room for rowers on top of the cataphracts."

Belisarius stared at the fleet. John fell silent, realizing that the general was coming to a decision.

"Right," murmured Belisarius. He cocked an eye at the Rhodesman. "The immediate priority is to stop the Army of Bithynia from reaching Constantinople. You're the naval officer, John. How would you do it—now that you have my galley as well as this ship?"

John frowned.

"You've got good rowers. But how fresh are they?"

Belisarius shrugged. "Fresh enough, I should think. We came most of the way from Egypt on a sailing ship. Ashot had the galley waiting for us in Abydos, and we crossed the Sea of Marmara using our sails. We only unshipped the oars a few minutes ago."

"Good. We can wreak havoc among those plodding corbita with a dromon. The real problem's the akatoi. Those merchants galleys are fast. *And* they're full of cataphracts." He grimaced. "I wouldn't want to face that kind of archery, even in an armored galley. Not when you have to get close enough to ram."

"You won't have to," said Belisarius. "I'll take the akatoi with this ship, using the scorpions. You take the dromon and do as much damage as you can against the corbita."

Seeing John's hesitation, Belisarius pressed on.

"There's no other way, John. I'm not a naval officer—*you are*. I wouldn't know what to do with a dromon. Whereas here—"

He waved at the scorpions.

"I *do* know how to use artillery. Quite well."

Belisarius almost laughed, seeing the look of near anguish on the Rhodesman's face. John, he knew, wanted to finally try out his wonderful new artillery weapons.

John blew out his cheeks.

"You're right, damn it."

He eyed Belisarius skeptically.

"I assume you don't know how to sail a ship, either?"

Belisarius answered with a smile.

The naval officer grunted. He gestured toward one of the sailors standing at the stern. The man trotted forward along the gangway.

"His name's Honorius. Let him command the ship. Just tell him what you want. You can concentrate on the scorpions."

He turned to his assistant.

"Eusebius! Show the general how to handle the firebombs. He's going to command the artillery on this ship. I'm taking the dromon."

John eyed Belisarius' cataphracts. By now, all of them had boarded the pamphylos.

Seeing the avarice in John's eyes, Belisarius chuckled.

"Leave me Valentinian," he said. "I'll want him to aim the other scorpion. You can take the rest."

Less than a minute later, the dromon was pulling away from the ship and heading straight toward the enemy fleet. John was standing in the stern, giving orders to the steersman.

Belisarius did not watch for more than a few seconds. He had his own problem to face.

How best to use his little artillery ship against over two dozen opponents?

A thought came from Aide:

Cross the T.

Explain, commanded the general.

A series of images came to his mind. Scenes of naval battle, featuring ships pounding at each other with cannons. In each instance, the fleets attempted to sail their own ships directly across the coming line of the enemy, in order to bring their broadsides to bear on as many opponents as possible.

Belisarius scratched his chin, pondering. The scenes which Aide had shown him were not entirely relevant to his situation. His ship was armed with only two scorpions, located amidships, not a line of cannons running down the entire sides of the ship. "Broadsides," thus, were impossible.

Still—

The sailor whom John had named as his substitute was now standing next to Belisarius, waiting for orders. The general turned to Honorius, and began gesturing to illustrate his question.

"Can you row this ship at a right angle across the front of that approaching fleet?"

Honorius squinted at the enemy ships. Aegidius' armada was now well into the Bosporus, about a mile distant.

"Easily. They're letting the basket ships set the pace instead of the akatoi. Those corbita are slow to begin with. And if they're packed with cataphracts—and all their armor—they'll be a lot more sluggish than usual."

He leaned over the wall of the fighting platform and began shouting orders to his crew. The ship began taking a new heading, but Belisarius did not bother to watch. His concentration was focussed on the scorpions.

John, he saw, had chosen his weapons well. The scorpions were that type of stone-throwing catapult which were called *palintonos*. The name was derived from the "fold-back spring" design which allowed the two torsion arms to swing forward further than was possible in the more traditional "straight-spring" *euthytonos*. The weapons were mounted on the same type of tripod base which Roman engineers used for cranes and hoists. The scorpions were then fitted onto a swivel attachment atop the tripod. The end result was a weapon which could be tilted up or down as well as swung sideways in a complete circle.

Romans did not manufacture their artillery engines to the same degree of standardization as would be common in future eras. But, from long experience, Belisarius recognized that the two scorpions were both in what was considered the "11-pound" class—that being the weight of stone shot each was capable of hurling. Using that weight of shot, they had an effective range of well over 400 yards.

"How heavy are your firebombs?" he asked Eusebius.

"A little over eight pounds. Not more than nine."

Belisarius nodded.

"We should have a range of almost five hundred yards, then."

Again, he examined the scorpions. The weapons were placed on either side of the wood-castle, far enough apart to allow the engines to be swiveled without the six-foot-long firing troughs impeding each other. Unfortunately, of course, there was no way that both of them could be used simultaneously to fire over the same side. As they—to use Aide's expression—"crossed the T," one of the scorpions would be out of action completely.

For an idle moment, Belisarius pondered alternate ways of emplacing artillery on a ship. Almost immediately, another image came from Aide.

A steel ship, very sleek for all its gargantuan size, plowing through the sea. Cannons—three of them abreast—were mounted in a strange sort of enclosed swivel—

Turret.

—directly amidship. Two enclosed swivels—

Turrets.

—were mounted toward the bow, one toward the stern. Those cannons could be brought to bear in any direction. All nine could be employed in broadsides, to starboard or port. Six could also fire across the bow, and three across the stern.

"Oh, well," muttered Belisarius. "We'll have to make do with what we've got."

The enemy fleet was now almost within catapult range. The nearest ships were off their starboard bow at a thirty-degree angle. Examining the situation, and doing his best to estimate relative speeds, Belisarius decided that they would be able to use both scorpions for at least three minutes before the port scorpion could no longer be brought to bear.

"I'll handle the starboard scorpion," he announced. "Valentinian, you're in charge of the other one. Eusebius, you keep us supplied with firebombs."

He started to give orders to the twelve other soldiers standing on the platform, but saw there was no need. All of them, experienced artillerymen, had already taken their positions. Each scorpion had a six-man crew, not counting the aimer. Two men stood on either side of each scorpion, ready to turn the windlasses which cranked back the torsion springs. That work was exhausting—especially when done at the breakneck speed required in battle—so each man had a relief standing right behind him. The two men would alternate between shots. A loader fit the bomb into the trough while the sixth man engaged the claw which held the bowstring until the aimer pulled the trigger. Those last two men also had the job of helping the aimer move the heavy trough around and seeing to it that the strut which supported the end was properly adjusted for the desired range.

Everyone hurried to their tasks. Within a minute, the scorpions were ready to fire. Belisarius announced that he would fire first. With the help of his crew, he lined up the heavy trough so that the scorpion was bearing on the nearest of the enemy ships. As soon as he saw the target bracketed between the two "ears" which served as a rough aiming device, he yanked on the little lever which served as the weapon's trigger.

The scorpion bucked from the recoil. Not sixty yards away, the firebomb slammed into the sea with enough force to rupture the clay container. A ball of flame splattered across the waves.

"We're at sea," muttered Belisarius. Somewhat lamely, he added: "I forgot."

In land warfare, he had never had to worry about the heaving of a ship's deck. He had fired the catapult just at the moment when the ship's bow dipped into a trough.

Valentinian fired five seconds later. The cataphract had learned from his general's mistake. He timed his own trigger-pull to correspond with the bow lifting to a wavecrest.

His firebomb lofted its majestic way toward the heavens. Quite some time later, almost sedately, it plopped into the sea. There was no eruption into flame, this time. The firebomb plunged into the water at such a steep angle that, even if the clay container ruptured, the naphtha/saltpeter contents were immediately immersed in water.

Harmlessly, in other words. Not least of all because the firebomb landed two hundred yards away from the nearest enemy vessel.

They were still four hundred yards from their foe. Just near enough to hear the faint sounds of catcalls and jibes.

"Again," growled Belisarius. Gingerly, the loader placed a firebomb in the trough. The other artillerymen ratcheted back the torsion springs and engaged the claw. Belisarius sighted—compensated for the roll, guessed at the pitch—yanked the trigger.

He *did*, this time, manage a respectable trajectory. Quite respectable. Not too high, not too low.

And not, unfortunately, anywhere in the vicinity of an enemy ship. Another harmless plop into the sea.

The catcalls and jibes grew louder.

Valentinian fired.

Extravagant failure; utter humiliation. His second firebomb landed farther from the enemy armada than had his first.

The catcalls and jibes were now like the permanent rumbling of a waterfall.

Belisarius glared at Honorius.

"For the sake of God! This damned ship's—"

He gestured angrily with his hands.

"Pitching, yawing and rolling," filled in Honorius. The sailor shrugged. "I can't help it, general. On this heading—which *you* ordered—we're catching the worst combination of the wave action."

Belisarius restrained his angry glare. More accurately, he transferred it from the seaman to the enemy, who were still taunting him.

He pointed at the fleet.

"Is there any way to get at them without having this miserable damned ship hopping around like a flea?" he demanded.

Honorius gauged the wind and the sea.

"If we head straight for them," he announced. "We'll be running *with* the waves instead of across them. Shouldn't be—"

"*Do it!*" commanded Belisarius.

Honorius sprang to obey.

Aide protested.

Cross the T! Cross the T!

Shut up! If you think this is so easy, you—you—damned little fat diamond!—you crawl out of that pouch and do it yourself.

Aide said nothing. But the facets were quivering with some very human sentiments.

SULK. POUT.

Then:

You'll be sorry.

By the time the scorpions were re-armed, Honorius had altered the vessel's course. They were now rowing directly toward the enemy. And, just as the sailor had predicted, the ship was much steadier.

Much steadier.

Belisarius and Valentinian fired almost simultaneously. A few seconds later, the taunts and catcalls were suddenly replaced by cries of alarm and screams of pain.

The two nearest akatoi erupted in flames. The rounded bow of the one Belisarius fired upon was burning fiercely. Valentinian's shot caused even greater havoc on his target. His firebomb must have ruptured against the rail of that ship's bow. Instead of engulfing the bow in flames, the naphtha had spewed across the ship's deck like a horizontal waterfall of flame and destruction.

A deck which was packed with heavily armored cataphracts.

The scene on that ship was pure horror. At least a dozen cataphracts were being roasted alive in their iron armor. Several of them, driven to desperation, leapt off the ship into the sea. There, helplessly dragged down by the weight of their equipment, they drowned.

But they were dead men, anyway. At least their agony was over. Those who remained aboard were like human torches. In their frenzied movements, they helped to spread the flames further. John's hellish concoction was like Satan's urine. It stuck to everything it touched—and it burned, and burned, and burned, and burned. Within thirty seconds, the entire deck of that ship was a holocaust.

Then, the holocaust spread. The steersman, seeing the fiery doom coming toward him, made his own leap into the sea. Unlike the cataphracts, he was not encumbered with armor and could hope to swim.

Swim where? Presumably, to the nearest ship. Unfortunately, by deserting his post he caused the burning ship to head into the wind and waves. The corbita coming immediately behind was unable to avoid a collision.

The flames now spread to that ship. Most of the spreading came from the entangled sails. But some of it came from the frenzied human torches which clambered aboard.

Two ships were now completely out of action.

Neither Belisarius nor Valentinian paid much attention. They were too busy dealing with their next victims.

For Belisarius, that victim was the same as his first. Coming closer to the ship whose bow he had already set afire—now, at a range of three hundred yards—the general aimed his scorpion amidships.

He was deliberately trying to imitate Valentinian's shot. His first shot missed—too low, scattering flames across the sea fifty yards before the target. But, after a quick adjustment of the trough's strut, he succeeded with the next shot. His firebomb ruptured against the enemy ship's railing and spewed destruction across its packed deck.

That ship was out of action.

As he waited for his artillerymen to rearm the scorpion, Belisarius observed Valentinian's next shot. Valentinian was also trying to copy his first success.

He misjudged, however, and his shot went a little high.

No matter. Both he and Belisarius learned another lesson in the brand new world of naval artillery warfare.

Sails and rigging, struck head-on by a firebomb, burn like oil-soaked kindling. Within five seconds, that ship was effectively dismasted, wallowing helplessly in the waves.

Yet—

The cataphracts standing on the deck below were—for the moment at least—unharmed.

Unharmed, and filled with fury. Belisarius could see dozens of them beginning to bring their powerful bows to bear. Less than three hundred yards away—well within range of cataphract archery. In moments, his little ship would be swept by a volley of arrows. The rowers below would be reasonably safe in their enclosed shelters. But all of the men on the wood-castle had only the low walls to protect them.

"Ready!" cried the loader.

Belisarius threw his weight against the heavy trough. The loader and the claw-man helped swivel the scorpion around. As soon as it bore, Belisarius yanked the trigger.

The cataphracts on the enemy ship were just starting to draw back their bows. Some of them loosed their arrows—but, flinching, missed their aim. Most of the cataphracts, seeing the firebomb speeding right at them, simply ducked.

The side of their ship erupted in a ball of flame. There was not the instant destruction which they feared, true. Belisarius' shot struck too far below the rail to scatter the naphtha across the deck in that horrible waterfall of flame. But, soon enough, they would be dead men. And they knew it.

Trapped on a vessel which would burn to the waterline. Trapped in heavy armor. Trapped in the middle of the Bosporus.

Belisarius' ship plowed past them at a range of two hundred yards. He could see some of the enemy cataphracts, through gaps in the black and oily smoke. They were no longer even thinking about their bows, however. All of them that he could see were frantically getting out of their armor.

In less than ten minutes, he realized, he had destroyed half of the Army of Bithynia's cataphract force.

But he did not have time to find any satisfaction in the deed. Belatedly, he realized that his reckless straight-ahead charge, for all its immediate effectiveness, had placed him and his men in mortal peril. Instead of standing off at a distance and bombarding his enemy, he was plunging straight into their massed fleet of ships. There were archers on all of those ships—hundreds of them. *Thousands* of them.

Within two minutes, they would be inundated with arrows.

A voice, pouting:

I told you so.

Sulky self-satisfaction:

Cross the T. Cross the T.

Valentinian had already reached the same conclusion.

"We're in a back alley knife fight, now. Only one thing to do."

Belisarius nodded. He knew the answer to their dilemma.

Valentinian had taught it to him, years ago.

Chop the other mindless idiot first.

He turned to Honorius. The seaman's face was pale—he, too, recognized the danger—but was otherwise calm and composed.

"Straight ahead," he commanded. "As fast as you can. We'll try to cut our way through."

As he brought his scorpion to bear on the next ship in line, he caught a glimpse of Valentinian crouched over his own weapon. An instant later, the cataphract's scorpion bucked. The deck of a nearby corbita was transformed into the same hell-on-earth which had already visited four cataphract-laden akatoi.

Valentinian grinned, like a weasel.

Seeing that vicious grin, Belisarius found it impossible not to copy it. Time after time, in years gone by, as he trained a young officer in bladesmanship, Valentinian had lectured him on the stupidity of fighting with a knife in close quarters.

Valentinian should know, of course. It was a stupidity he had committed more than once. And had survived, because he was the best close-quarter knife-fighter Belisarius had ever met.

He heard his loader:

"Ready!"

The closest enemy ship was a corbita, but Belisarius aimed past it, at the next approaching akatos. He feared the archery of those cataphracts more than he did the bowmanship of common soldiers.

He fired. Missed. Although the ship was hardly pitching at all, it was still rolling, and his shot had been twenty yards too far to the right.

His men rearmed the scorpion and Belisarius immediately fired. Another miss—too high, this time. The bomb sailed right over the akatos' mast.

Windlasses spun, the men turning them grunting with exertion. The loader quickly placed the bomb, the claw-man checked the trigger.

"Ready!" called the loader. Belisarius took aim—more carefully, this time—and yanked the trigger.

For a moment, he thought he had fired too high again. But his firebomb caught the mast two-thirds of the way up and engulfed the akatos' rigging in flames.

Behind him, he heard Honorius call out an order to the steersman. Belisarius could not make sense of the specific words—they were spoken in that peculiar jargon known only to seamen. But, within seconds, as he saw their ship change its heading, he understood what Honorius was doing. The seaman was also learning—quickly—some of the principal lessons of the new style of naval warfare.

That akatos is out of action, but its cataphracts can still use their bows. Solution? Simple. Sail somewhere else. Stay out of archery range. Let it burn. Let it burn its way to hell.

He started to tell Valentinian to pick out the cataphract-bearing akatoi first, but saw there was no need. Valentinian was already doing so. His next shot sailed past a nearby corbita, toward an akatos at the extreme range of almost five hundred yards. Valentinian was as good with a scorpion as he was with a bow. He had deliberately shot high, Belisarius saw, knowing that a strike in the rigging was almost as good as one of those terrible deck-sweeping rail shots.

Another akatos began burning furiously.

"Ready!" called his loader.

Belisarius scanned the ship-crowded sea hastily, looking for one of the two remaining akatoi.

He saw none. Hidden, probably, behind the close-packed cor-bita. Their swift charge had placed them in the middle of the enemy armada.

There was no time to waste. One of those corbita was within two hundred yards. Common soldiers could shoot arrows also. Not as well as cataphracts, true, but—at close range—good enough. Already, arrows from that approaching corbita were plunging into the sea within yards of their ship.

He aimed his scorpion. Missed. Fired again. By luck—he had been aiming at the rigging—his shot struck the rail and poured fury across the enemy's deck.

Valentinian struck another corbita. Then, cursed. His shot had been low. The firebomb had erupted almost at the waterline. The enemy's hull was starting to burn, but very slowly.

Hurriedly, Valentinian fired again. This time, cursed bitterly. He had missed completely—his shot sailing ten feet over the enemy's deck.

Meantime, Belisarius set another corbita's rigging aflame. Then, after two misses, set another aflame.

They were surrounded by enemy ships, now, several of them within bow range. Arrows were pouring down on them like a hail storm. The rowers' shelter sprouted arrows like a porcupine. In his own little cabin at the stern of the ship, the steering officer was crouched low. The thin walls of his shelter had been penetrated by several arrow-heads. But he kept calling out his orders, calmly and loudly.

Arrows thunked into the walls of the wood-castle. Fortunately, due to the height of the fighting platform, the men on it were sheltered from arrows fired on a flat trajectory from the low-hulled corbita. But some of those arrows, fired by better or simply luckier archers, were coming in on an arched trajectory.

One of the windlass-crankers suddenly cried out in pain. An arrow had looped over the walls and plunged into his shoulder. He fell—partly from pain, and partly from a desire to find shelter beneath the low wall. His relief immediately stepped forward and began frantically cranking the windlass.

As he waited—and to give himself something to think about other than oncoming missiles—Belisarius watched Valentinian fire a third firebomb at the same misbegotten corbita.

Belisarius had never seen Valentinian miss anything, three

times in a row. He didn't now, either. The shot was perfect. The firebomb hit the rail right before the mast, spewing death over the deck and destruction into the rigging.

His loader:

"Ready!"

Belisarius turned, aimed—

Nothing. Empty sea.

They had sailed right through the enemy fleet.

A movement in the corner of his eye. He swiveled the scorpion hurriedly, aimed—

A dromon, scudding across the waves, right toward them. John of Rhodes, standing in the bow, hands on hips, scowling fiercely.

His first words, in the powerful carrying voice of an experienced naval officer:

"Are you out of your fucking mind?"

His next:

"You could have wrecked my ship!"

A minute later, after the galley was drawn alongside, the Rhodesman scampered aboard and stalked across the deck. Before he even reached Belisarius, he was gesturing with his hands. Making an odd sort of motion, as if cutting one hand with the other.

"What were you thinking?" he demanded hotly. "What were you thinking?" In full stump now, back and forth, back and forth: "Imbecile! This is a fucking *artillery* ship!" One hand sawing across the other: "In the name of God! Even a fucking general should have been able to figure it out! Even a fucking landsman! You stay *away* from the fucking enemy! You try to bring your artillery to bear without getting close! You—you—"

Hands sawing, hands sawing.

Belisarius, smiling crookedly: "Like 'crossing a T,' you mean to say?"

John's eyes widened. His hands paused in their sawing. Fury faded, replaced by interest.

"Hey. That's a good way of putting it. I like that. 'Crossing the T.' Got a nice ring to it."

Another voice. Sulky. Self-satisfied:

I told you so.

Belisarius chuckled.

"I suppose my naval tactics *were* a bit primitive," he admitted.

Image:

A man. Stooped, filthy, clad in rough-cured animal skins. In his hand he clutches an axe. The blade of the weapon is a crudely shaped piece of stone, lashed to the handle with rawhide.

He is standing on a log, rolling wildly down a river. Hammering fiercely at another man, armed and clad as he is, standing on the same log.

Stone ax against stone ax.

Just ahead is a waterfall.

Chapter 26

After Belisarius and Valentinian were aboard the dromon, Belisarius stared up at John of Rhodes standing on the pamphylos' wood-castle.

"Are you certain, John?" he asked.

The naval officer nodded his head firmly.

"Be off, Belisarius!" Then, with a wicked grin:

"I'll say this much—you may be the craziest ship captain who ever tried to commit suicide, and certainly the most lethal."

He waved his hand about, encompassing half the Bosporus in that gesture.

"You destroyed six out of the eight akatoi and another half dozen corbita. And I sank three corbita with the galley. That's well over a third of Aegidius' entire army and *three-fourths* of his cataphracts. Look at them!"

Belisarius scanned the Bosporus. Even to his landsman's eye, it was obvious that the enemy fleet was scattering in fear and confusion.

A sudden thought came to his mind. John voiced it before he could speak.

"Besides, I think Aegidius is dead. He was probably aboard one of the akatoi, which means that the odds against his survival are three-to-one."

Belisarius nodded.

"That has all the signs of a leaderless army, if I'm reading the ship movements correctly."

John snorted. "They're like so many motherless ducklings paddling every which way." Again, he waved his hand.

"Be off, Belisarius. You're needed in Constantinople now, not here. The dromon will bear you to shore faster than any of those ships can reach land. I, meanwhile—" He patted the scorpion next to him. The wicked grin returned in full force. "—will continue to put the fear of God in those bastards." With a fierce glower: "From a *distance*, like an intelligent man."

Belisarius smiled and turned away. Then, hearing John's next words, smiled broadly. "*'Crossing the T.'* I like that!"

At the general's signal, the war galley's *keleustes*—the rowing officer; literally, the "orderer"—immediately began calling the time. The galley's oars dipped into the water. Swiftly, the dromon headed to shore.

For a time, Belisarius watched the enemy ships milling around aimlessly in the Bosporus. The ones nearest to John's artillery vessel, he saw, were already trying to evade the Rhodesman's approach. One of those enemy ships, apparently, had had enough. The corbita was heading directly back to Chalcedon, on the Asian side of the Straits.

Soon enough, a half-dozen of the corbita were following. Among the remaining ships in the enemy armada, confusion still reigned. A small cluster of the ships—seven in all, led by one of the surviving akatoi—were heading toward Portus Caesarii. Someone among the surviving cataphracts in the Army of Bithynia—Aegidius himself, possibly; more likely, one of his top subordinates—had apparently decided to continue with their treasonous scheme. But, cautiously, they were now planning to land in the more distant harbor.

A wordless cry of triumph coming from Menander drew his eyes back to the main fleet. One of the corbita in that milling mob of ships, he saw, was burning fiercely. John had struck his first blow.

The confusion in the main body of the traitor fleet was dispelled. The majority of the remaining ships, within a minute, were fleeing back across the Bosporus. Only four of them—including, unfortunately, the last of the cataphract-bearing akatoi—decided to make for Portus Caesarii.

Belisarius noticed that Ashot was now standing next to him. Ashot was the Armenian cataphract who led the small party which Antonina had sent to meet him in Egypt. Antonina and Maurice had chosen him for that mission, among other things, because Ashot was one of the few cataphracts among Belisarius' bucellarii who had any experience as a seaman.

"What do you think?" he asked.

Ashot immediately understood all the parameters of the question. The Armenian pointed toward the artillery vessel.

"If I were John, I'd follow the ships retreating back to Chalcedon. Harry them mercilessly. Put them completely out of the action. Leave the ones heading toward Portus Caesarii for Sittas and Hermogenes to deal with. They shouldn't have any trouble."

For a moment, Ashot gauged the eleven ships now heading for the westernmost harbor on Constantinople's southern shore.

"Two akatoi," he murmured, "and nine corbita. To be on the safe side, let's call it three hundred cataphracts and three thousand infantry. Against Sittas' five hundred cataphracts and the two thousand infantrymen Hermogenes brought."

Ashot spat into the sea. "Lambs to the slaughter," he concluded.

Belisarius smiled at the Armenian's ferocious expression. Then, curious to see Ashot's reaction, he remarked:

"Heavy odds, against the infantry."

The Armenian sneered.

"Are you kidding? Against *Hermogenes'* infantry?" The cataphract shook his head firmly. "You've been gone for almost a year and a half, general. You haven't seen what Hermogenes has done with his troops. And the ones he brought to Constantinople were his best units. The finest Roman infantry since the days of the Principate. They'll chew their way right through that Bithynian garbage."

Belisarius nodded. He was not surprised. Still, he was gratified.

"The enemy'll be disheartened, too," added Ashot. "Confused— half-leaderless, probably—scared shitless."

Again, he spat into the ocean. "Lambs to the slaughter. Lambs to the slaughter."

Belisarius saw that John had apparently reached the same conclusion as Ashot. The artillery ship was veering off in pursuit of the corbita retreating to Chalcedon.

"Will he catch any of them?" he asked.

"Not a chance," replied the Armenian instantly. "They're sailing almost before the wind, on that heading. The advantage now is with the heavier corbita and their square-rigged sails, especially since the rowers on John's galley are bound to be tired. But once they reach Chalcedon, those ships are trapped. John can stand off in the mouth of the harbor and bombard them with impunity. He'll turn the whole fleet into so much kindling."

Another spit into the sea. "The Army of Bithynia's out of it, general. Except for the few who are heading for southern Constantinople."

For a moment, Belisarius examined the cataphract standing next to him. The Armenian was now watching the enemy ships sailing toward Portus Caesarii, oblivious to his general's gaze.

Abruptly, Belisarius made his decision.

"In a few months, Ashot, I'll be promoting several of the men to hecatontarch. You're one of them."

The Armenian's eyes widened. He stared at the general.

"You've only got one hecatontarch—*Maurice*. And I don't—" Ashot groped for words. Like all of Belisarius' cataphracts, he had a towering respect for Maurice.

Belisarius smiled.

"Oh, Maurice'll be promoted also. A chiliarch he'll be, now."

Ashot was still wide-eyed. Belisarius shook his head.

"We're in a new world, Ashot. I never felt I needed more than a few hundred bucellarii, before. But among the many things I learned while I was in India is that the Malwa don't have genuine elite troops. Not ones they can rely on, at least. That's a Roman advantage I intend to maximize."

He scratched his chin, estimating.

"Five thousand bucellarii. Seven thousand, if possible. Not at once, of course—I want them to be elite troops, not warm bodies. But that's my goal." His smile grew crooked. "You'll probably wind up a chiliarch yourself, soon enough. I'll need several for all those troops, with Maurice in overall command."

Ashot, again, groped for words.

"I don't think—that's a lot of Thracians, general. Five thousand? *Seven* thousand?" Hesitantly: "And I'm Armenian. I get along well with the Thracians you've got now, that's true. They've known me for a long time. But I don't know that new Thracian boys are going to be all that happy with an Armenian—"

"If they can't handle it," replied Belisarius harshly, "I'll pitch them out on their ear." His smile returned. "Besides—who said they'd all be Thracians?" He chuckled, seeing Ashot's frown.

"I don't have time, any longer, for anyone's delicate sensibilities. I want five thousand bucellarii—the best cataphracts anywhere in the world—as fast as I can get them. A big chunk—possibly the majority—will be Thracian. But they'll be lots of Illyrians and as many Isaurians as we can find who are willing to become cataphracts. Isaurians are tough as nails. Beyond that—" He shrugged. "Anyone who can fight well, and can learn to become a cataphract. Greeks, Armenians, Egyptians, barbarians—even Jews. I don't care."

Ashot had overcome his initial surprise, and was now tugging on his beard thoughtfully. "Expensive, general. Five thousand bucellarii— even if you're not as generous as usual—you're looking at—"

He broke off, remembering. He had seen the Malwa treasure which Belisarius had brought back from India. True, Belisarius had given three-fourths of that bribe to Shakuntala. But the remainder was still an immense fortune, by any except imperial standards.

Ashot nodded.

"Yes, you can afford it. Even with liberal pay and equipment bonus, you've got enough to cover five thousand bucellarii for at least four years. After that—"

"After that," said Belisarius coldly, "there'll either be plenty of booty or we'll all be dead."

Ashot nodded. "A new world," he murmured.

A cry from Anastasius drew their attention.

"There's Sittas! I can see him!"

Belisarius and Ashot looked forward. The dromon was just passing through the double breakwaters which marked the entrance to the small Harbor of Hormisdas, the private harbor of Rome's emperors. Behind the harbor rose the hills of Constantinople. The Great Palace, though it was nearby, was hidden behind the slope. But they could see the upper levels of the Hippodrome. And they could hear the roar of the mob gathered within it.

Belisarius' eyes were drawn lower, to a large figure standing on the nearest wharf.

Sure enough, Sittas. Standing next to him were Hermogenes and Irene.

As they drew nearer, Sittas bellowed.

"What took you so long? Don't you know there's a war to be fought?"

The boar, in full fury.

The mob, too, was in full fury. The seats in the Hippodrome were packed with armed men. Blues on one side, of course, Greens on the other. Even during this unusual alliance, the faction leaders were wise enough not to mix their men.

Balban, watching the scene, was delighted. Narses, standing next to him, was not.

"Almost forty thousand of them!" exclaimed the Malwa spymaster. "I'd been hoping for thirty, at the most."

Narses almost spoke the words: "I'd been *dreading* more than twenty thousand." But he restrained himself. There was no point, now, in getting into another futile argument.

Called upon to settle some petty dispute between the factions, Balban left. Narses and Ajatasutra remained, standing in the fortified loge on the southeast side of the Hippodrome which was called the *kathisma*.

The emperor's loge, that was. Reserved for his use alone. By seizing it, the conspirators had announced their full intentions for all the world to see.

Narses glanced over his shoulder. At the rear of the loge was a barred door. That door was the only entrance to the kathisma, other than the open wall at the front. Behind it was a covered passage which connected the emperor's box in the Hippodrome to the Great Palace.

The door was barred on both sides, now. On his side, Narses saw eight Malwa kshatriya standing guard. On the other side, he knew, would be an even greater number of the Emperor's personal bodyguard, the excubitores, anxiously fingering their weapons.

The passage from the Hippodrome to the Great Palace was now the frontier between Justinian and those who sought his overthrow.

Narses looked away. That frontier would fall too, and soon. Brought down by further treachery.

Ajatasutra's low voice penetrated his musings.

"You do not seem to share Balban's enthusiasm for our massive army."

Narses sneered. "Let me explain to you the reality of the Hippodrome factions, Ajatasutra. Both the Greens and the Blues have about five thousand men who can be considered real street fighters. Charioteers and their entourage. Gamblers and their enforcers. That sort. Serious thugs."

He pointed out over the vast expanse of the Hippodrome. "Those will be the ones you see carrying real weapons—well-made swords, and spears—and wearing a helmet. Maybe even a bit of armor."

His lips twisted further. "Then, each faction will have another five thousand men—at the most—who can handle themselves in a fight. On the level of a tavern brawl, that is. The rest—"

His pointing finger made a little flipping gesture. Dismissive, contemptuous—almost obscene.

"Pure rabble. Carrion-eaters, drawn by the smell of rotting flesh."

Narses lowered his finger. His sneer became a scowl. "I remember a conversation I had with Belisarius, once. The general told me that one of the worst errors people made when it came to military affairs was to confuse quantity with quality. A large, incompetent army, he told me, got in its own way more than it did the enemy's. And then, if they suffer a setback, the mob's panic will infect the good troops."

Narses sighed.

"So let's hope there's no setback. I wouldn't trust that mob in a pinch any more than I'd trust so many rats."

Ajatasutra shrugged. "Don't forget, Narses. We still have four hundred kshatriya to stiffen their resolve. With their Veda weapons. That should hearten the mob."

"We'll soon find out." Again, Narses pointed. The gesture, this time, was purely indicative. "Look. They've finished setting up the rockets."

Ajatasutra followed the pointing finger. At the far northeast side of the Hippodrome, where the race track made its curve, the Malwa kshatriya had erected several rocket troughs on the dirt floor of the arena. The troughs were pointed upward at an angle, aimed directly across the Hippodrome.

Balban wanted to cement the allegiance of the factions with a demonstration of the Veda weapons. The spymaster was convinced that the Romans would be filled with superstitious awe. For his part, Narses was skeptical. In their own crude way, the Hippodrome thugs were not unsophisticated. They *were* residents of Constantinople, after all.

But the eunuch had not objected to the plan. While he did not think the thugs would be overawed by superstition, they *would* be impressed by the sheer power of the devices.

Watching the last few Blues and Greens scampering along the tiers, Narses smiled. The Malwa had assured the factions that the rockets would pass safely over the southwest wall of the

Hippodrome, but the thugs were taking no chances. The entire southwest half of the Hippodrome was empty.

At the base of the troughs, the kshatriyas had piled up bundles of elephant hide, which they were wetting down from a nearby drinking fountain. The Hippodrome was provided with many of those fountains, fed by a small aqueduct. The same water was being used to wet down the large wooden palisades which the Malwa had erected behind the firing troughs. Despite their assurances to the faction leaders, the kshatriya had too much experience with the fickle rockets to take any chances. Most of the Malwa soldiers would stand behind those barricades when the missiles were fired.

"Here comes Hypatius," announced Ajatasutra. "And Pompeius."

Narses glanced down at the stairs leading from the Hippodrome to the imperial loge. The stairs ended in a wide stone platform just in front of the kathisma. For reasons of security, there was no direct access to the imperial loge from the Hippodrome. But dignitaries saluting the emperor could stand on that platform and gaze up at the august presence, seated on his throne above them. And separated from any would-be assassins by a nine-foot-high wall.

Clambering up those stone steps, escorted by Balban, came the two nephews of the former emperor Anastasius. The faces of Hypatius and Pompeius were pale from anxiety. Their steps faltered; their lips trembled. But, still, they came on. Greed and ambition, in the end, had conquered fear.

"*Finally*," grumbled Narses.

A minute later, the new arrivals were hoisted over the wall into the imperial loge. The royal nephews made heavy going of the effort, despite the assistance of several kshatriya. Balban, despite his heavyset build, managed the task quite easily.

Seeing Narses' scowl, Balban smiled cheerfully.

"You are too pessimistic, my friend. Such a gloomy man! Everything is in place, now. The factions are here. The kshatriya are here. The new emperor is here. The Army of Bithynia is on its way. And the Cappadocian is about to slide in the knife in the Great Palace."

Suddenly, from beyond the barred door leading to the Great Palace, shouts were heard. Cries of alarm, from the excubitores. Then, the sounds of clashing steel.

Balban spread his arms, beaming.

"You see? John has unleashed his bucellarii in the palace. What could go wrong now?"

John of Cappadocia's final treachery, when it came, was brutally simple.

One moment, he was standing on the floor of the small audience chamber where Justinian was holding his emergency council, vehemently denying Theodora's latest charge against him:

"It is absolutely false, Your Majesty—I swear it! The excubitores in this room"—he waved at the spear-carrying soldiers standing along the walls and behind the thrones—"are the very finest of your personal bodyguard."

"Which *you* selected," snarled Theodora.

John spread his hands, in a placating gesture. "That is one of my responsibilies as praetorian prefect."

Justinian nodded his head firmly. The five other ministers in the room copied the gesture, albeit with more subtlety. They had no wish to draw down Theodora's rage.

The Empress ignored them. Theodora half-rose from her throne, pointing her finger at the Cappadocian. Her voice, for all the fury roiling within it, was cold and almost calm.

"*You are a traitor, John of Cappadocia.* Irene Macrembolitissa has told me that you have suborned a dozen of the Emperor's excubitores."

Suddenly, the clangor of combat erupted beyond the closed doors of the council chamber. John of Cappadocia turned his head for a moment. When he faced forward again, he smiled at the Empress and said:

"She is wrong, Empress."

The Cappadocian made a quick chopping motion with his hand.

The four exubitores standing at the rear of the chamber strode forward and seized the Emperor and the Empress by the arms, pinning them to the thrones. Ten others, standing along the walls, immediately leveled their spears and stabbed the six remaining bodyguards. The attacks were so swift and merciless that only one of the loyal excubitores was able to deflect the first spear-thrust. But he died a moment later, from a second spear-thrust under his arm.

"It was fourteen!" cackled John of Cappadocia.

Ten of the traitor bodyguards now lunged at the five ministers standing to one side. Four of those ministers, stunned by the sudden havoc, never even moved. They died where they stood, gape-mouthed and goggle-eyed.

"As it happens," giggled the praetorian prefect, "all fourteen are in this room."

The fifth minister, the *primicerius* of notaries, was quicker-witted. Despite his advanced age and scholarly appearance, he nimbly dodged a spear-thrust and scampered toward the door. He managed to get his hand on the door-latch before a hurled spear took him in the back. A moment later, two more spears plunged into his slumping body.

Even then, even as he fell to his knees, the *primicerius* feebly tried to open the door. But the first of the traitor bodyguards had reached him, and a savage sword strike sent the old man's head flying.

John watched the minister's head roll to a stop against an upturned rug.

"I made sure they were all here today, of course. That's my job, you know. As praetorian prefect."

He smiled at the Emperor and the Empress. Justinian was silent, pale with shock, limp in his captors' hands. Theodora had also ceased struggling against the hands holding her, but she was neither pale nor silent.

Furiously, she hissed:

"*Only fourteen, traitor?* That leaves five hundred loyal body-guards to cut you down!"

John of Cappadocia laughed gaily. With a mocking bow, he waved at the great door leading to the corridor beyond. Not five seconds later, the door burst open. Gore-stained soldiers poured into the audience chamber. They were grinning widely and gesturing triumphantly with their bloody swords. They wore the livery of John of Cappadocia's bucellarii.

"All of them, John!" howled one of his retainers. "I swear—*all of them!*"

One of his fellows demurred: "Not quite. There's a number of excubitores forted up in the mint. And all of Theodora's body-guards are still in the Gynaeceum."

"Deal with them," commanded the praetorian prefect. His bucellarii immediately left the chamber.

John turned back to the imperial couple. Theodora spit at the Cappadocian. John dodged the spittle, then returned the Empress' contempt with a cheerful smile, before turning his gaze to Justinian.

"Do it," he commanded.

The two excubitores holding Justinian hauled the Emperor from his throne and manhandled him off the dais onto the carpeted floor of the chamber. Brutally, a third bodyguard kicked Justinian's feet out from under him. A moment later, the Emperor was on his knees, bent double. Each of his arms was pinioned. Another excubitore cuffed away the tiara, seized Justinian's hair in both hands, and jerked the Emperor's head back.

Justinian's eyes, rising, met the eyes of the torturer entering the room through a side door. The man bore an iron rod in his hands. The hands wore gauntlets. The tip of the rod glowed red.

It was the last thing the Emperor would ever see, and he knew it. He barely had time to begin his scream before the rod plunged into his left eye. A moment later, the right. The torturer was quick, and expert.

The Emperor's scream, while it lasted, seemed to shake the very walls of the chamber. But it was brief; very brief. Within seconds, sheer agony had driven consciousness from Justinian's brain. The bodyguard holding his head relinguished his grip. A moment later, so did the excubitores holding his arms. The Emperor collapsed onto the floor.

There was no blood. The red-hot tip of the iron rod had cauterized the terrible wounds as soon as it made them.

Which John of Cappadocia immediately pointed out.

"You see how merciful I am, Theodora?" he demanded. Another mocking bow. "A different man—such as the cruel and despicable creature you have so often proclaimed me to be—would have murdered your husband. But I satisfy myself with mere blinding."

Gaily: "And an expert blinding at that!" Then, with the casual insouciance of a connoisseur:

"It's quite an art, you know. Most people don't appreciate that. It's very difficult to blind a man without killing him outright. Less than one out of ten survive the average torturer." He gestured grandly at the gauntleted man who had mutilated the Emperor. "But I use only the best! The very best! I estimate—" He paused, studying Justinian's sprawled body with exaggerated studiousness. Concluded: "—that your husband has—*one chance in three!*"

Throughout, Theodora said nothing. She did not look at Justinian. She simply kept her eyes on John of Cappadocia. Black eyes, like the gates of damnation.

Even John, in his triumph, flinched from that hell-gaze.

"There'll be none of your haughty ways now, bitch," he snarled. He pointed to Justinian.

"One chance in three, I say. *Unless* he's given immediate medical attention. The *best* medical care."

Sneering: "Which, of course, I also happen to have available. *For a price.*"

Theodora said nothing. The hell-gaze never wavered.

John looked away. His eyes fastened on Justinian. The Cappadocian seemed to draw strength from that piteous sight. Although his eyes avoided Theodora, his voice was cold and certain:

"Now that Justinian has been blinded, he can no longer be Emperor. You know the law of Rome, Theodora. *No mutilated man can wear the purple.* Neither the Senate, nor the populace, nor the army will accept him. As Emperor, *he is finished.*"

The sneer returned in full force. But, still, his eyes avoided Theodora's.

"You may—*may*—still be able to save his life. What there is of it. *If* you offer no further resistance. *If* you publicly hail Hypatius as the new Emperor."

When Theodora finally spoke, her voice matched her gaze. Hell-voice.

"I will do no such thing. If you bring the worm Hypatius before me, I will spit on him. If you drag me to the Hippodrome, I will curse him before the mob."

She jerked her right arm loose from the excubitores who held it. Pointed to Justinian:

"All you have done is blind a man who would someday have been blinded by death. You threaten to kill a man, when no man lives forever. *Do it, then.* Kill me with him. I am the Empress. I would rather die than yield."

She reared in her throne. "There is an ancient saying, which I approve: *Royalty is a good burial-shroud.*"

Hell-gaze; hell-voice:

"Do your murder, then, traitor. Kill us, coward."

John clenched his fist, opened his mouth. But before he could utter a word, one of his bucellarii sprinted into the room. He skidded to a halt, almost tripping over the rumpled carpet. Sweat poured from his brow. He gasped for air.

Half-shouting; half-whispering:

"The Army of Bithynia's been routed at sea! Half their ships burned! Most of the survivors fled back to Chalcedon!"

Gasping:

"They say an army's moving toward the Hippodrome. Cataphracts. They say"—gasp—"the whore Antonina is leading them."

Hoarsely:

"And they say—Belisarius is here!"

Theodora's pealing laugh had no more humor in it than Satan's own.

Hell-laugh.

"You are all dead men. Kill us, traitors! Do it, cowards! As surely as the sun rises, you will join us before sundown."

Every traitor in the room stared at the Empress.

John of Cappadocia was famous for his sneer. But Theodora's sneer, compared to his, was like the fangs of a tigress matched to a rodent's incisors.

"Do it, cowards! Boast to Belisarius that you killed his Emperor and Empress. Do it! Tell the loyal man of your treachery. Do it! Tell the man of honor that you are murderers. Do it!"

Hell-sneer:

"After he spits your heads on his spears. After the flesh rots from your skulls. He will grind your bones to powder. He will feed them to Thracian hogs. He will have the hog-shit smeared on your tombs."

Silence.

"Do it, cowards. Kill us, traitors."

John snarled wordless fury.

"Keep them here!" he commanded the excubitores. "Until I return!"

He stalked out of the chamber, followed by his retainer. By the time he reached the door, he was almost running.

Once in the corridor beyond, he did begin to run. But Theodora's taunt followed faster.

"I will await you in the Pit of Damnation, John of Cappadocia! Before Satan takes you, I will burn out your eyes with my urine!"

After the Cappadocian was gone, Theodora lowered her eyes to Justinian's body.

"Release me," she commanded.

Hesitantly, but inevitably—as if giving way to a force of nature—the excubitores relinquished their grip. They were traitors, now; but they had been too many years in the imperial service to refuse *that* voice.

The Empress rose and walked down from the dais, onto the floor. She knelt beside Justinian. The Emperor was still unconscious. Firmly, but carefully, Theodora rolled him into her arms. She brushed the hair back from his ruined face and stared at the gaping, puckered wounds which had once been her husband's eyes.

When she spoke, her voice held not a trace of any emotion. It was simply cold, cold.

"There is wine in the adjoining room. Fetch it, traitors. I need to bathe his wounds."

For an instant, something almost like humor entered her voice. Cold, cold humor: "I come from the streets of Alexandria. Do you think I never saw a man blinded before? Did you think I would shrink from death and torture?"

Humor left. Ice remained: "Fetch me wine. *Do it, cowards.*"

Two excubitores hastened to obey her command. For a moment, they jostled each other in the doorway, before sorting out their precedence.

A minute later, one of the excubitores returned, bearing two bottles. The other did not.

Theodora soaked the hem of her imperial robes with wine. Gently, she began washing Justinian's wounds.

The man who had brought her the wine slipped out of the door. Less than a minute later, another followed. Then another. Then two.

Theodora never looked up. Another man left. Another. Two.

When there were only four excubitores left in the room, the Empress—still without raising her head—murmured:

"You are all dead men."

Hell-murmur.

All four scurried from the chamber. Their footsteps in the corridor echoed in the empty room. Quick footsteps, at first. Soon enough, running.

Now, Theodora raised her head. She stared at the door through which the traitors had fled.

Hell-stare. Hell-hiss:

"You are all dead men. Wherever you go, I will track you down. Wherever you hide, I will find you. I will have you blinded. By the clumsiest meatcutter in the world."

She lowered her head; turned her black eyes upon her husband's face.

Slowly, very slowly, the hell-gaze faded. After a time, the first of her tears began bathing Justinian's face.

There were not many of those tears. Not many at all. They disappeared into the wine with which Theodora cleansed her husband's wounds, as if they possessed the wine's own hard nature. A constant little trickle of tears, from the world's littlest, hardest, and most constant heart.

Chapter 27

The first rocket awed the mob in the Hippodrome. By sheer good fortune, the missile soared almost straight and exploded while it was in plain view of the entire crowd. A great flaming burst in the sky, just over the unoccupied southwestern tiers.

The faction thugs roared their approval. Many of them rose in their seats and shook their weapons triumphantly.

In the imperial box, Hypatius and Pompeius seemed suitably impressed as well, judging from their gapes. But Narses, watching them from behind, spotted the subtle nuances.

Hypatius' gape was accompanied by the beginning of a frown. The newly crowned "Emperor"—his tiara wobbling atop his head—was not entirely pleased. The crowd's roar of approval for the rockets was noticeably more enthusiastic than the roar with which they had greeted his "ascension to the throne," not five minutes earlier.

His brother Pompeius' gape was likewise accompanied by a frown. But, in his case, the frown indicated nothing more than thoughtfulness. Pompeius was already planning to overthrow his brother.

In the rear of the kathisma, Narses sneered. This, too, he knew, was part of the Malwa plot. The Indians intended the overthrow of Justinian to set in motion an entire round of civil wars, one contender for the throne battling another. Years of civil war—like the worst days of the post-Antonine era, three centuries earlier—while the Malwa gobbled up Persia without interference and made ready their final assault on Rome itself.

As always, Narses thought the Malwa were too clever for their own good. They would have done better to stick with their initial scheme—simply to encourage Justinian's ambitions to conquer the west. That would have served their purpose, without any of the attendant risks of an armed insurrection.

But Narses, slowly and carefully, had convinced them otherwise. The eunuch had his own ambitions, which required Justinian's removal. He would risk the Malwa's future plans for the sake of his own immediate accession to power. There would *be* no civil wars. Narses would put an end to them, quickly and ruthlessly.

The eunuch watched another rocket soar into the sky. The trajectory of this one was markedly more erratic than that of the first. By the time the rocket exploded, it had looped out of sight beneath the northwestern wall of the Hippodrome.

Narses sighed with exasperation. He, too, was being excessively clever. But—he was old. He had little choice. Narses did not have the time to wait, for years, while Justinian exhausted the Roman Empire in his grandiose attempt to reconstruct its ancient glory.

Another rocket. Properly behaved, this one. But the fourth, after an initially promising lift-off, suddenly arced down and exploded in the Hippodrome itself. Fortunately, the section of the tiers where it landed was unoccupied.

Narses sighed again.

Too clever.

He was startled by another explosion. A section of the tiers near the Blue faction erupted in flame and smoke. No one was hurt, however.

Narses frowned. He had seen no rocket.

Another explosion. This one erupted on the fringe of the Blue crowd, killing several thugs and hurtling shredded bodies onto their nearby comrades.

Balban, seated next to the "Emperor" Hypatius, leapt to his feet. He turned and glared at Ajatasutra.

"Did you give grenades to the factions, you fool?" he demanded.

Ajatasutra began to deny the charge, but fell silent. There was no need for his denial.

The truth of the matter was suddenly obvious.

A series of explosions now rocked the tiers, killing Blues and Greens indiscriminately. The giant mob was scrambling to their feet, shouting and brandishing their weapons.

Brandishing them, not in triumph, but at their new enemy—who was even now marching into the Hippodrome through the wide entrance in the unoccupied southwestern portion.

Cataphracts—on foot, for a wonder—flanking a small army of men—and women?—who were hurling grenades at the Hippodrome mob. *With slings!*

Everyone in the kathisma lunged to their feet, now, and pressed forward against the stone wall overlooking the Hippodrome.

Everyone except Narses. Who simply remained in his seat, sighing. Faintly, Narses could hear the battle cries of the newly arrived enemy.

"Nothing! Nothing!"

Much too clever.

Belisarius, standing on the wharf, heard the same explosions.

"That's Antonina!" exclaimed Irene. "The battle in the Hippodrome's already started!"

Sittas and Hermogenes looked at Belisarius.

"The Hippodrome can wait," he stated. "Antonina can hold her own against that mob, at least for a while. We need to make sure the Emperor and Empress are safe, before we do anything else."

Sittas pointed out to sea.

"There are still some ships left from Aegidius' fleet. They'll be landing at Portus Caesarii soon."

Belisarius shrugged. "Let them. Most of that army's been shattered. Aegidius is probably already dead. Even if he isn't, it'll take him time to rally his troops and start marching them to the inner city. We'll deal with them later."

He pointed up the hill. "We must secure the Great Palace. *Now.*"

Without another word, he began striding off the wharf. Irene and his Thracian bucellarii followed. Very quickly, Sittas and Hermogenes had their own troops marching away from the harbor.

The Great Palace was only a quarter of a mile away. With Belisarius in the lead, the little army of five hundred cataphracts and two thousand infantrymen reached the wall surrounding the Great Palace in minutes.

The Great Palace of Constantinople was a vast complex, not a single structure. It was almost a small city within the city. The many buildings of the Palace were separated by peristyle porticoes alternating with open courtyards and gardens. The porticoes were decorated with mosaics, the courtyards and gardens with statuary and fountains.

It was perfectly designed terrain for defense, and Belisarius knew that he had to overwhelm any enemies before they could organize such a defense. So, for one of the few times in his life, he decided to order a straightforward frontal assault.

He looked to Hermogenes.

"Did you bring scaling equipment?"

Hermogenes answered by simply pointing to the rear. Turning, Belisarius saw that squads of infantrymen were already rushing up with ropes and grappling hooks.

He was pleased—somewhat. He studied the wall more closely. It was at least eight feet tall.

"We really need ladders, too," he muttered, "to get enough men over in time to—"

He broke off, seeing the look of restrained exasperation on Hermogenes' face.

"We trained for this," growled Hermogenes. "I didn't want to haul a lot of bulky ladders around, so instead—" He took a deep breath. "Just watch, general. And relax."

Belisarius smiled. Watched. Smiled very broadly.

At thirty-foot intervals, down a two hundred yard stretch of the wall, ten-man squads of infantrymen anchored grappling hooks. Immediately, two men from each squad scaled the wall and dropped over into the gardens beyond. The others divided into two-man teams. Each team began hoisting a stream of soldiers by using a shield held between them as a stepping stone. After the first wave of soldiers went over the wall, the hoisting teams were replaced by fresh soldiers and went over the wall themselves.

Coming from the palace grounds, Belisarius could hear the shouts of surprised defenders and the hammering of weapons on shields. But there were not many of those shouts, and the hammering died away very quickly.

Belisarius was impressed. In less than a minute, five hundred infantrymen had swarmed into the palace grounds and—judging from the sound—had already overwhelmed the immediate defenders.

"With a wall this short—Irene measured it for me—this works faster than ladders," commented Hermogenes smugly. "If necessary,

I could get all the infantry over in less than four minutes. But we shouldn't need to because—"

Belisarius heard a cry of triumph. Turning his head, he saw that one of the gates was opening. In seconds, the infantrymen opening that gate from within had pushed it completely to one side. A moment later, he saw two more gates opening.

Sittas and twenty of his cataphracts were already thundering through the first gate. Other cataphracts positioned themselves before the other gates. As soon as the way was cleared, they too began pouring into the palace grounds.

Once the heavy cavalry had all entered, the rest of the infantry followed. Belisarius and Hermogenes trotted in the rear, with Irene a few paces behind. Valentinian and Anastasius led the way. Menander, Ashot, and the rest of the Thracians flanked them on either side.

As soon as he entered the palace grounds, Belisarius made a quick survey of the area. Hermogenes' troops had already formed a well-ordered perimeter, within which Sittas and his men were drawing up into their own formations. The cataphracts were a bit disorganized. The checkerboard arrangement of the palace grounds—gardens next to small patios next to open-sided porticoes—was hardly ideal terrain for heavy cavalrymen.

Belisarius was not concerned. Enemy cataphracts would be equally handicapped and he doubted if, as individuals, they would match Sittas' elite horsemen. He would use Sittas and the cataphracts as a mailed fist, if necessary. But he was really depending on the infantry.

That infantry—that *excellent* infantry—had already given him the advantage. Their speedy swarming over the wall had obviously caught the traitors completely off guard. Lying near the gates, Belisarius could see the bodies of perhaps thirty men. Most of them, from their uniforms, he took to be John of Cappadocia's retainers. Other than that, the only enemy soldiers in sight were a handful scuttling away in rapid retreat.

Excellent. But—

Here and there, scattered among the corpses of the Cappadocian's bucellarii and a few of Hermogenes' infantry, he also saw the bodies of men dressed in the livery of excubitores. And he could hear, dimly, the sound of combat in the direction of the Gynaeceum.

He turned to Irene.

"Where is Justinian? And Theodora?"

She pointed to the northeast, at one of the more distant buildings.

"They were going to hold an emergency council in the audience chamber of Leo's Palace."

"I know which one it is," said Belisarius. He began trotting in that direction.

"Hermogenes!" he shouted. The infantry general, a few yards away, looked at him. Belisarius, still trotting, pointed toward the building.

"Half of your men—send them with me! You take the other half and secure the Gynaeceum!"

Sittas came galloping up, followed by his mounted cataphracts. Still trotting, Belisarius waved his hand in a circle.

"Sittas—clear the palace grounds!"

Sittas grinned. The burly general reined his horse around.

"You heard the man!" he bellowed. He jumped his horse over a low hedge and began galloping toward the center of the complex. His cavalrymen followed, pounding through gardens, courtyards and porticoes. Vegetation was trampled underfoot, statuary was shattered or upended. The fountains survived, more or less intact. So, of course, did the columns upholding the porticoes—although many of the beautiful floor tiles were shattered into pieces, and a few of the wall mosaics suffered in passing from casual contact with the armored shoulders and lance butts of cataphracts.

At the very center of the palace complex, Sittas encountered two hundred of John's bucellarii. Most of them were mounted. The ones who weren't were in the process of doing so—a laborious process, for armored cataphracts. All of them seemed confused and disorganized.

Sittas gave them no chance at all. He didn't even bother to shout any orders. He simply lowered his lance and thundered into the mob. His five hundred cataphracts came right behind, following his lead.

The result was a pure and simple massacre. The Cappadocian's bucellarii were surprised and outnumbered. By the time they realized the danger, Sittas and his men were almost upon them. At that range, bows were useless. Most of John's retainers had time to raise their lances, but—

They didn't have stirrups. Sittas and his cataphracts went through them like an ax through soft wood. Half of the Cappadocian's bucellarii either died or were badly wounded in the first lance charge. Thereafter, matching sword and mace blows with men who were braced by stirrups, the remainder lasted less than a minute. At the end, not more than twenty of the retainers were able to surrender. The rest were either dead, badly injured, or unconscious.

Hermogenes, meanwhile, led a thousand of his infantrymen into the Gynaeceum. Once inside the labyrinth of the womens' quarters, Hermogenes followed the sounds of fighting. Two minutes after entering the complex, he and his men were falling on the backs of the bucellarii fighting what was left of Theodora's excubitores.

The battle in the Gynaeceum was not as bloody as the cavalry melee in the courtyards, for the simple reason that John's retainers surrendered almost immediately. They were hopelessly trapped between two forces; and they were, at bottom, nothing but mercenaries. Whatever his other talents, John of Cappadocia had none when it came to cementing the loyalty of bucellarii.

Belisarius himself faced no enemies at all, beyond a small group of bucellarii—not more than forty—whom he encountered leaving Leo's Palace just as he was approaching. The cataphracts were in the process of mounting their horses.

There was no battle. The bucellarii took one look at the thousand infantrymen charging toward them and fled instantly. Those of them who had not managed to mount their horses in time retreated also, lumbering in the heavy way of armored cavalrymen forced to run on their own two legs.

Belisarius let them go. He had much more pressing concerns. He plunged into the building. Followed by his infantry, he raced through the half-remembered corridors, searching for the audience chamber.

Hoping against hope, but fearing the worst.

"Who is that?" squawked the "Emperor" Hypatius, leaning over the wall separating the kathisma from the Hippodrome. He stared at the little army pouring through the southwestern gate. Then, goggled, seeing them slinging grenades at the huge mob of faction thugs on the other side of the Hippodrome.

"Where did they get grenades?" he shrieked.

A new battle cry was heard: "*Antonina! Antonina!*"

Ajatasutra leaned over the wall and examined the invaders. His eyes were immediately drawn to a small figure bringing up the rear. Helmeted; armored—but unmistakably feminine for all that.

He smiled bitterly, turning away. He looked at Balban and gestured with his thumb.

"That's what you called the *sheep.*"

Hypatius was now gobbling with sheer terror. Pompeius, the same.

Someone began pounding on the rear entrance to the kathisma, the barred door which led to the Great Palace. Narses recognized John of Cappadocia's voice: "Open up! Open up!"

At Balban's command, the kshatriya guarding the door unbarred and opened it.

John of Cappadocia burst into the kathisma, trailing three of his bucellarii.

"Belisarius is here!" he shouted. "His whore Antonina has some kind of army—" He fell abruptly silent, seeing the scene in the Hippodrome.

"She's here already!" snarled Balban, pointing over the wall. "And she's got grenades!"

Narses sighed.

Too clever by half.

The eunuch rose. Strode forward. Took charge.

"Have you blinded Justinian?" he demanded.

John of Cappadocia nodded.

"Theodora?"

"She's under guard in the palace."

Narses took Balban by the arm and pointed over the wall separating the kathisma from the Hippodrome. He was pointing to the hundreds of kshatriya manning the rockets. The four hundred kshatriya, unlike the thousands of milling and confused faction thugs, were already forming their battle lines. Most of them were opening baskets of grenades. The kshatriya manning the rockets were hastily re-aiming the troughs.

"You've still got your own soldiers and—*if you provide some leadership*—that huge faction mob. *Get down there! Now!*"

Balban neither argued nor protested. Immediately, the spymaster began clambering over the wall.

Narses grabbed Hypatius and shoved him to the wall. "Go with him!" he commanded. "You're the new Emperor! You need to rally the Hippodrome crowd!"

Hypatius babbled protest. Narses simply manhandled the "Emperor" over the stone rampart. Despite his terror, Hypatius was no match for the old eunuch's wiry strength. Half-sprawled over the wall—on the *wrong* side of the wall—Hypatius stared up at Narses.

"Do it!" ordered the eunuch. His eyes were fixed on Hypatius like a snake on its prey. An instant later, Narses tore Hypatius' clutching fingers off the wall. The "Emperor" landed in a collapsed heap on the stone platform below.

Hypatius immediately lunged to his feet and jumped at the wall.

Hopeless. That wall had been designed to keep assassins from the Emperor. A strong and agile man could have leapt high enough to grasp the top of the wall. Hypatius was neither.

The new "Emperor" gobbled terror.

"*Do it!*" commanded Narses.

Hypatius gasped. He turned his head and spotted Balban. The spymaster was racing around the upper tiers of the Hippodrome, heading for the kshatriya rocketeers. He was already forty yards away.

Gibbering with fear, Hypatius staggered after him.

In the kathisma, Narses turned from the wall and confronted John of Cappadocia.

"Where are the rest of your bucellarii?" he demanded.

The Cappadocian glared at him.

"That's none—"

"You idiot!" snarled the eunuch. "Kept them in the palace, didn't you? Planned to keep them unharmed, didn't you? *So you'd have them available for later use.*"

John was still glaring, but he did not deny the charge.

Narses pointed to the chaos in the Hippodrome.

"'Later use' is *now*, Cappadocian. Get them! With your thousand bucellarii added to the brew, we might still win this thing."

John started to protest. The eunuch drove him down.

"Do it!"

John argued no further. The Cappadocian charged down the corridor leading to the Great Palace. Narses went after him, dragging Pompeius by the arm. Before following, Ajatasutra ordered the kshatriya still in the kathisma to join Balban. As he left the kathisma—now unoccupied—the kshatriya were already climbing over the wall and dropping down into the Hippodrome.

In the corridor, Ajatasutra quickly caught up with Narses and Pompeius.

Smiling, the assassin leaned over and whispered:

" 'Years of civil war,' you said."

Narses glanced at him, but said nothing. The eunuch was concentrating his attention on forcing the gibbering Pompeius forward. The new "Emperor's" brother was practically paralyzed with fear.

"If you don't start moving," snarled Narses, "I'll just leave you here."

Pompeius suddenly began running down the corridor.

Narses let him go.

"At least he's headed in the right direction," grumbled the eunuch. "We'll catch him later. He'll stumble into a faint, some-where up ahead."

The eunuch began trotting. Ajatasutra matched his pace eas-ily.

Again, the assassin leaned over and whispered. Still smiling:

" 'The Roman Empire will be in chaos for a generation,' you said."

Narses ignored him.

Ajatasutra, grinning:

" 'Much better than just letting Justinian fight his stupid wars,' you said."

Narses ignored him.

They reached the end of the corridor. Now, they found them-selves in one of the many buildings of the Great Palace. They could hear the sound of fighting coming from somewhere in the outer complex.

As Narses had predicted, Pompeius was waiting for them. In a manner of speaking: the nobleman was squatting on the floor, leaning his head against a wall, sobbing.

Narses leaned over, seized Hypatius by his hair, and dragged the "Emperor's" brother to his feet.

"The only place you're safe now is with me," hissed the eunuch. "If you collapse again—if you disobey me in any way—*I'll leave you.*" Narses released his grip and stalked toward one of the corridors leading to another building in the complex. Ajatasutra strode alongside. Hypatius followed.

The sound of fighting grew louder. Among those sounds, Narses recognized the heavy thundering of a cavalry charge. So did Ajatasutra. Both men picked up their pace.

"Where are we going?" whispered the assassin. "And why"—he pointed with a thumb over his shoulder—"are you so intent on hauling that *creature* with us?"

"I'll need him," growled Narses.

They reached the end of the corridor. They were in another large room in yet another building. Narses plunged through a door against the left wall.

Again, a short corridor. Again, another room in yet another building. Again, Narses led the way through another door. Again, another corridor.

Ajatasutra, though he had an abstract knowledge of the Great Palace's layout, was by now completely disoriented.

"Where are we going?" he repeated.

"I have something to attend to," muttered Narses.

The eunuch broke into a trot. The corridor made a bend. Once around the bend, Ajatasutra could see that the corridor ended in a massive set of double doors. One of the doors was ajar. Beyond, Ajatasutra heard the sound of indistinct voices.

Once they got within ten feet of the half-open door, Ajatasutra recognized one of the voices in the room beyond.

John of Cappadocia's voice.

Narses hissed. "That *bastard.* I *knew* he'd come here first."

The eunuch turned his head. Reptilian eyes focussed on Ajatasutra. "Decide," he commanded.

Ajatasutra hesitated for only a second. Then, with a half-smile:

"You're the best of a bad lot."

Narses nodded. He gestured toward Pompeius, who was just now staggering up.

"Keep him safe," muttered the eunuch. "And deal with the bucellarii."

Narses turned away and slid through the door. Ajatasutra followed, dragging Pompeius by the arm.

Inside, they found a dramatic tableau.

Theodora was on her knees, cradling Justinian. The Emperor, though still unconscious, was beginning to moan.

John of Cappadocia loomed above her, with a sword in his hand. His three bucellarii were standing a few feet away, between John and Narses. Hearing the eunuch enter, the bodyguards turned hastily and raised their weapons. Then, recognizing him, they lowered the swords and stepped aside. Narses slid past them, heading toward John and the Empress.

Ajatasutra relinquished his grip on Pompeius and sidled close to the bucellarii.

The Cappadocian glared down at the Empress. He began to snarl something.

Theodora, her face like a mask, sneered:

"Stop talking, traitor. Do it, coward."

John raised his sword.

Narses, hissing like a snake:

"*Stop, you idiot!* We're going to need her. *Alive.*"

Startled, John turned away from the Empress. His sword lowered, slightly.

"Why?" he demanded. "We were going to kill her, anyway, after she hailed the new Emperor. She and Justinian both. There's no reason to wait, now." He scowled. "And why are you here?"

Narses strode forward.

"I swear, Cappadocian, you've got the brains of a toad."

Closer, closer.

"Think, John—*think.*"

Closer, closer. The eunuch pointed to the Empress. John turned his head, following the pointing finger.

Narses struck.

Ajatasutra, watching, was impressed. The old eunuch stabbed like a viper. The little knife seemed to come from nowhere, before it sank into John's ribcage.

John screamed, staggered, dropped his sword. The knife was still protruding from his side.

Narses stepped back.

The bucellarii bellowed, raised their swords, and took a step toward the eunuch.

One step. They got no further.

Ajatasutra slew the three bucellarii in as many seconds. Three quick blows from his dagger into the bodyguards' backs. Each blow—powerful, *swift*—slid expertly between gaps in the armor, severing spinal cords. Ajatasutra's victims died before they even realized what had happened. The bodyguards simply slumped to the floor.

John of Cappadocia had already fallen to the floor. But his was no lifeless slump. The praetorian prefect's face was twisted with agony. He was apparently trying to scream, but no sound escaped from the rictus distorting his face.

"It's quite a nasty poison," remarked Narses cheerfully. "Utterly paralyzing, for all the pain. Deadly, too. After a time."

Ajatasutra quickly cleaned his dagger, but he did not replace it in its hidden sheath.

"Explain," he commanded.

Narses began to sneer. But then, seeing the expression on the assassin's face, thought better of it. "Do you still have any illusions, Ajatasutra?" he demanded. The eunuch pointed toward a nearby wall. Through that wall, thick as it was, came the sounds of combat. Grenade explosions, shouts, screams.

"It's over," he pronounced. "*We lost.*"

Ajatasutra frowned. Without being conscious of the act, the assassin hefted his dagger.

Narses *was* conscious of that act. He spoke hurriedly:

"*Think*, Ajatasutra. Where did Antonina get the grenades? She didn't steal them from us. She had them *made.* That means she's been planning this for *months.* It means everything that fool Procopius told that fool Balban was duplicity. Not his—the gossiping idiot!—but *hers.* Antonina hasn't been holding orgies on her estate—*she's been training an army and equipping them with gunpowder weapons.*"

Ajatasutra's frown deepened. "But she couldn't have the knowledge—"

He got no further. Theodora's cawing laugh cut him short. The assassin, seeing the triumph in her face, suddenly knew that Narses was right.

He lowered the dagger. Lowered it, but did not sheathe the weapon. "There's still a chance," he said. "From what I saw, she doesn't have much of an army. Balban still has the kshatriya, and the mob."

Narses shook his head.

"No chance at all, Ajatasutra. *Not with Belisarius here.*"

The eunuch shook his head again. The gesture had a grim finality to it.

"No chance," he repeated. "Not with Belisarius here. He's already shattered the Army of Bithynia. Even if Balban manages to defeat Antonina in the Hippodrome, he'll still have to face Belisarius. With what? A few hundred kshatriya? Faction thugs?"

Narses gestured scornfully at the bodies of John's bucellarii. "Or do you think these *lap dogs* are capable of facing Belisarius—and *his* cataphracts?"

Ajatasutra stared at the three corpses. Not for long, however. The sounds of combat were growing louder.

He slid the dagger into its sheath. "You're right. Now what?"

Narses shrugged. "We escape. You, me, and Pompeius. We'll need him, to mollify your masters. We can at least claim that we salvaged the 'legitimate heir' from the wreckage. The Malwa can use him as a puppet."

The assassin winced. "Nanda Lal's going to be furious."

"So?" demanded Narses. "*You* weren't in charge—Balban was. *You* warned him that Antonina was deceiving us. I'll swear to it. But Balban wouldn't listen."

Ajatasutra glanced at Pompeius. The nobleman was leaning against the far wall. His face was pale, his eyes unfocussed. He seemed completely oblivious to everything except his own terror.

The assassin's eyes moved to the Empress. Theodora glared back at him.

Black, black eyes. Hating eyes.

"Her?" he asked.

The old eunuch's face was truly that of a serpent, now. For a moment, Ajatasutra almost drew his dagger again. But, instead, he simply murmured:

"Who would have ever thought *Narses* would commit an act of personal grace?"

Smiling, the assassin strode over to Pompeius, seized the nobleman by the arm, and dragged him to the door. There, he stopped, waiting for Narses.

The eunuch and the Empress stared at each other.

The eunuch's was a gaze of sorrow. Theodora's—

"I will never forgive you. *You are a dead man.*"

Narses nodded. "I know." A rueful little smile came to his face.

"But I might still win. And I'm an old man, anyway. Even if I lose, I may well be dead before you kill me."

The smile faded. Sorrow remained.

The eunuch turned away, and began walking toward the door. Theodora's voice halted him.

"Why, Narses?"

For the first time, there was anguish as well as hatred in her voice. Narses, without turning, simply shrugged.

"Ambition," he said.

"No. Not that. Why *this*?"

Narses turned his head. His eyes met those of Theodora's. There was a hint of tears in her eyes. Just a hint.

Narses fought back his own tears.

"There was no need. And—"

He could not face those eyes. He looked away. Harshly: "I did not stop loving you, child, simply because I planned to murder you."

Anguish fled the Empress. Only the hell-voice remained:

"You *should* have killed me, traitor. You will regret it, *coward*."

Narses shook his head.

"No, Theodora, I won't. *Not ever*."

A moment later, he was gone. Theodora gazed down at her husband. Justinian's moans were growing louder. Soon, he would regain consciousness and begin to scream.

The Empress lifted his head off her lap and set it gently on the carpet.

She had something to attend to.

Crawling on her hands and knees, Theodora made her way to the body of the nearest soldier. She drew a dagger from the corpse's sword-belt.

Then, still crawling, she began making her way toward John of Cappadocia.

The Empress did not crawl because she was unable to stand, or because she was injured, or because she was in a state of shock.

No. She crawled simply because she wanted the Cappadocian to see her coming.

He did. And then, despite the agony which held him paralyzed, tried to scream.

But he couldn't. He couldn't make a sound; couldn't move a 'scle. He could only watch.

Theodora crawled toward him, the dagger in her hand. Her eyes were fixed on those of the praetorian prefect.

She wanted those eyes.

Hell-gaze. Hell-crawl.

It was the last thing John of Cappadocia would ever see, and he knew it.

Three minutes later, Belisarius burst into the room. Behind him came his cataphracts and Irene.

All of them skidded to a halt.

Irene clapped her hand over her mouth, gasping. Menander turned pale. Anastasius tightened his jaws. Valentinian grinned.

Belisarius simply stared. But he too, for a moment, was transfixed by the sight.

Transfixed, not by the sight of the bodies littering the chamber. Not by the sight of Justinian, moaning, blinded. Not even by the sight of the praetorian prefect, prostrate, screaming in a silent rictus, his back arched with agony.

No, it was the sight of the Empress. Squatting over the dying traitor, a bloody knife in one hand, her imperial robes held up by the other. Urinating into the empty eyesockets of John of Cappadocia.

Chapter 28

The rocket soared up into the sky and exploded high above the walls of the Hippodrome. A thundering cry followed, from the assembled mob within.

"NIKA! NIKA!"

"'Victory,' is it?" hissed Antonina. She leaned over her saddle and whispered to Maurice:

"Tell me what to do."

Maurice smiled. "You already know what to do." He pointed forward. They were approaching the looming structure from the southwest. Ahead of them, fifty yards away, began a broad stone staircase which swept up to a wide entrance. The entrance was thirty yards across, and supported by several columns.

"Once we get in there, it'll be like a knife fight in a kitchen. There won't be any room for maneuver. Just kill or be killed."

Antonina grimaced. The entrance they were approaching was called the Gate of Death.

"How appropriate," she murmured.

Next to her, Maurice snorted contempt. "Can you believe it?" he demanded. "They didn't post a guard. Not even a single sentinel."

They were now twenty yards from the beginning of the staircase. Antonina halted her horse and began to dismount.

"There won't be any room for horses in there," she said. Maurice nodded and ordered the cataphracts to dismount. The bucellarii grumbled, but obeyed without hesitation. Much as they hated fighting afoot, they were veterans. They knew full well that cavalry tactics would be impossible inside the Hippodrome.

Antonina drew her cleaver and held it over her head.

"*Nothing! Nothing!*" she cried, and began marching up the steps.

Her whole army surged after her. But, before she had gone halfway up the staircase, Maurice was holding her back.

"You stay in the rear."

Antonina obeyed. Her army swept around her. After they had all gone by, she and Maurice followed.

By the time they passed through the Gate of Death, some of the grenadiers were already launching their first grenades. Antonina could hear the explosions, as well as the battle cry of her own soldiers.

"NOTHING! NOTHING!"

She and Maurice entered the Hippodrome. They were standing on a broad, flat platform. Below them, the wide stone tiers of the Hippodrome—which served as seats and stairway combined—sloped down to the racetrack below.

The three hundred cataphracts were spreading out, filing down the first ten tiers, setting a perimeter. All of them had drawn their bows. In the center, just below her, the grenadiers and their wives had taken their own compact formation. Some of the grenadiers were slinging grenades, but most of them were still occupied in setting up their grenade baskets.

Antonina stared at the enemy, massed on the other side of the Hippodrome. After a quick glance, she ignored the huge mob of faction thugs. Her attention was drawn to the wooden bulwarks positioned on the far curve of the racetrack. She could see the kshatriya muscling around some wooden troughs. She did not recognize the odd wooden devices, but she had no difficulty recognizing the nature of the tubes which the kshatriya were placing in them.

"Rockets," she muttered. She turned to Maurice, standing next to her.

"Tell the army to spread out further. I don't want to give those rockets a concentrated target."

Maurice winced. "That'll make it harder to defend against a mass charge."

Antonina shook her head.

"If all forty thousand of those thugs charge us at once, they'll overwhelm us regardless of how compact we are. But I know that crowd, Maurice. I grew up with them. Forty thousand Hippodrome thugs can swamp less than a thousand soldiers—but not without suffering heavy casualties. *Especially* in the front ranks."

She pointing toward the mob.

"I guarantee you, Maurice, they know it as well as we do. And every single one of that crowd, right this very moment, is making the same vow."

She laughed, harshly. " 'Victory!' is just their official battle cry. The *real* one—the private, silent one—is: *you first! Anybody but me!*"

Maurice chuckled. Then, nodded.

"I do believe you're right." A moment later, the hecatontarch was bellowing orders. The cataphracts immediately began spreading out further. Within a minute, they had established a perimeter which encompassed the entire southwestern arc of the Hippodrome. The grenadiers spread out to fill that guarded space. Soon, the grenadiers were scattered into separate small squads, instead of packed into a tight formation.

Not a moment too soon. The Malwa fired their first rockets at the Romans. One of the rockets plowed into the dirt track below them, sending up a cloud of dust. Another soared completely out of the Hippodrome. But the next slammed into a nearby tier.

For all the impressive sound and fury of the explosion, the heavy stone suffered no worse than scorching. And, because the space was vacated, there were no casualties beyond a few grenadiers injured by flying wooden splinters. Minor wounds, no worse.

The grenadiers roared their fury. For the first time since entering the Hippodrome, the grenadiers launched a full volley.

Hundreds of grenades, their fuses sputtering, flew across the Hippodrome. The volley was not concentrated on any particular target. Each grenadier had simply decided to smite the foe. *Any* foe.

The volley erupted throughout the huge mob of faction thugs. A few landed in the vicinity of the wooden bulwarks sheltering the kshatriya. The Malwa soldiers, accustomed to gunpowder weapons, took shelter long before the grenades arrived. Few of them were even injured.

The mob—

A man of the future, had he been watching, would have called that volley a gigantic shotgun blast.

A sawed-off shotgun, at short range.

"Beautiful!" shouted Maurice, raising his fist in triumph. Below, the cataphracts and the grenadiers added their own cries of elation.

"The hell it was," snarled Antonina. "*Sloppy.*"

Scowling, the little woman stalked forward and began yelling orders at her grenadiers. Her clear, soprano voice—trained by an actress mother—projected right through the shrieking din of the Hippodrome.

Now steadied, the grenadiers began following her commands. Their volleys became concentrated, targeted salvoes.

Antonina aimed the first volley at the kshatriya. All of the rocket troughs were shattered or upended. Again, most of the Malwa soldiers escaped harm by sheltering behind the bulwarks. The bulwarks were solidly built—heavy timbers fastened with bolts. The grenades did no more than score the wood.

But Antonina didn't care. She simply wanted to cow the Malwa, put them out of action. She was quite confident in her ability to deal with a few hundred kshatriya. Her grenadiers, with their slings, easily outranged the Malwa grenades. And the rocket troughs were too fragile and cumbersome to be much of a threat in this kind of battle.

What she was really worried about—despite her confident proclamation to Maurice—was that the huge mob of faction thugs would swarm her with their numbers. There were forty thousand of them, against less than a thousand grenadiers and cataphracts—and the grenadiers would be of little use in a hand-to-hand melee.

So, while the Malwa soldiers coughed dust out of their lungs, crouching from the fury, Antonina began dismembering the mob.

Chop. Chop. Chop.

The next three volleys landed—in series, north to south—on the nearest fringes of the crowd. When the dust settled, and the bodies stopped flying, hundreds of faction thugs were scattered in heaps over the stone tiers. Dead, dying, wounded, stunned.

The crowd, shrieking, began piling away. More thugs died, trampled to death.

The nearest members of the mob were on the northern tiers of the Hippodrome. Antonina sent two volleys that way. The packed mass shredded, disintegrated. The survivors packed even tighter, pushing their fellows back, back. Back toward the far exits. Dozens more were trampled to death.

The kshatriya were stirring again. Small groups of Malwa soldiers were raising the two rocket troughs which had only been upended instead of destroyed. The rest were hurling their own grenades.

But, without slings, those grenades fell harmlessly in the center of the Hippodrome.

Still—

Keep them cowed.

Antonina sent another volley at the kshatriyas. The Malwa soldiers, again, suffered relatively few casualties. But, as before, they were forced to retreat behind their bulwarks, out of action.

Back to the mob.

Chop. Chop. Chop.

Maurice, standing a few feet behind Antonina, smiled grimly. He said nothing. There was no need.

A knife fight in a kitchen.

The first members of the mob who fled from the Hippodrome escaped. Perhaps two thousand of them, less the hundred or so who were trampled to death squeezing through the northeastern gates.

The rest ran into Belisarius.

Marching up with his army, and seeing the Blue and Green thugs pouring out of the Hippodrome, Belisarius ordered half of the infantrymen to form lines on either side of the gates.

"Make them run the gauntlet, Hermogenes," he commanded. "Kill as many as you can—*without* breaking your lines."

"Most of them will escape," protested Hermogenes. "We should box them in. Kill *all* the stinking traitors."

Belisarius shook his head.

"We don't need that kind of bloodbath. Just enough to terrorize the factions for the next twenty years."

He turned to Irene, who was riding next to him. The spymaster had wanted to stay with Theodora, but Belisarius had insisted she accompany him to the Hippodrome. Theodora was safe, now. She and Justinian were being guarded in the Gynaeceum by Theodora's surviving excubitores, five hundred infantrymen, and most of Sittas' cataphracts. Irene could do nothing for Theodora, at the moment, whereas Belisarius had wanted her expertise.

"Can you identify the faction leaders?" he asked.

Irene nodded.

Belisarius whistled and waved to Sittas. The general trotted over, along with the hundred or so cataphracts he still had with him.

Belisarius pointed to the infantrymen lining up on either side of the gates. Already, the soldiers were cutting down those faction members who stumbled against their lines. The thugs who managed to stay out of sword range were in no danger from the soldiers. But, pushing away from the threatening infantrymen, the crowd was squeezing itself into a packed torrent of hurtling bodies. Within seconds, another dozen were trampled to death.

"Let them through, Sittas, those of them that survive the gauntlet. *Except the faction leaders.* I want them dead or captured. Irene will point them out for you."

Sittas began to protest the orders. Like Hermogenes, he was filled with a furious determination to massacre the entire crowd.

"Do as I command!" bellowed Belisarius. He matched Sittas glare for glare.

"Don't be an idiot, Sittas!" He pointed to the southwest. "Antonina has less than a thousand men. Most of them are grenadiers, who won't be worth much in a hand-to-hand battle. If that huge mob attacks them head on, they'll be slaughtered."

Sittas was still glaring. Belisarius snarled.

"*Think*, Sittas. If we trap that mob from this end, they'll have no choice but to pour out the other. *So let them out here.* Hermogenes and his men will savage them on the way out, and you make sure to get the leaders. *That's good enough.*"

"He's right, Sittas," hissed Irene.

Sittas blew out his cheeks.

"I know," he grumbled. "I just—*damn all traitors, anyway.*"

But he reined his horse around without further argument. Within a minute, his cataphracts were forming a mounted line a hundred and fifty yards away. By now, Hermogenes had his five hundred infantrymen lined up on either side of the gates, half on each side. His men stood three feet apart, in three ranks. As the faction thugs poured out of the Hippodrome, they would have to run a gauntlet almost a hundred yards long. Then, they would break against the heavily armored, mounted cataphracts—like a torrent against a boulder. The thugs who survived the gauntlet would be able to escape, by fleeing to either side through the fifty-yard gaps between the last infantrymen and Sittas' line. But during that time they would be exposed to Irene's searching eyes—and cataphract archery.

Satisfied, Belisarius turned away. Some of the faction leaders would escape. Not many.

He began trotting his horse to the southwest, below the looming wall of the Hippodrome. Valentinian, Anastasius and Menander rode next to him. Behind them came the remaining thousand infantrymen of Hermogenes' army.

Belisarius turned in his saddle. He saw that the infantry were maintaining a good columnar formation—well-ordered and ready to spread into a line as soon as he gave the command.

Ashot was right, he thought. The best Roman infantry since the days of the Principate.

He stepped up the pace.

Thank you, Hermogenes. You may have saved my wife's life.

"Forget the rockets!" shouted Balban. The cluster of kshatriya who were trying to erect a rocket trough behind the bulwarks immediately ceased their effort.

Balban turned back to his three chief lieutenants. The four Malwa officers, along with six top leaders of the Blue and Green factions, were crowded into a corner formed by the heavy wooden beams. The three-sided shelter formed by the bulwarks was almost suffocating. Into that small space—not more than fifty feet square—were jammed a hundred kshatriya and perhaps another dozen faction leaders. The remaining kshatriya—those who still survived, which was well over three hundred—were crouched as close to the bulwarks as they could get. Fortunately for them, the cursed Roman grenadiers were still concentrating their volleys on the mob.

Balban stared up at the tiers of the Hippodrome. Those tiers were full of men. Thousands and thousands of men—*armed* men—all of whom were milling around uselessly. At least half of them, he estimated, were simply intent on escaping the Hippodrome through the northeast gates. Many of them had already dropped their weapons.

"We can't win an artillery duel," he announced. "Our only hope is to charge across the Hippodrome and overwhelm them with numbers."

All three of the kshatriya officers immediately nodded. One of them said:

"Most of that Roman force are grenadiers. We'll lose men crossing the track, but once we get within hand-fighting range, we'll massacre them."

"Some of them are *cataphracts!*" protested one of the Blue leaders.

"A few hundred—*at most*," snapped Balban. The Malwa pointed a rigid finger at the mob in the tiers above them.

"You've still got at least ten thousand men!" he shouted. "Would you rather use them—or simply die here like sheep in a *slaughterhouse*?"

"He's right," said another of the Blue leaders. Two of the Green chieftains nodded. Balban's hot eyes swept the other faction heads. After a moment, they too indicated their assent.

"All right. At my command, we'll charge out of here and round up as many men as we can. Then—it's simple. Charge to the southwest. As fast as we can."

He looked at the kshatriya. "Make sure our grenadiers are scattered through the crowd. When we get close enough, we can start tossing our own grenades."

One of the faction leaders pointed to a figure huddled in the corner.

"What about the Emperor? It'd help if he led the charge. Inspire the men."

Balban did not bother to look at Hypatius.

"If your men need inspiration," he growled, "tell them it's victory or death. That should be simple enough."

He lifted his head and bellowed at his kshatriya. It took not more than twenty seconds to explain the plan. It was simple enough.

"*Nika!*" shouted one of the faction leaders. He pushed his way out of the shelter and sprang upon the lowest tier of the Hippodrome.

He waved his sword, shouting at the mob above him:

"Nika! Nika!"

The other faction leaders joined him. They also began shouting, and pointing with their swords to the southwest.

Balban and his kshatriya poured out of the bulwarks. Quickly, they formed a line across the dirt floor of the Hippodrome. At Balban's command, they began marching forward.

Marching *slowly*. Every instinct in Balban—and his kshatriya—cried out for haste. But Balban knew that he had to give the faction leaders time to rally the mob. The Malwa by themselves could not overcome the Romans at the other end of the Hippodrome. They *needed* those thousands of thugs.

So, the kshatriya marched slowly. And began to die, as the

grenade volleys came their way. But they were soldiers, and maintained their ranks.

From the mob in the tiers, dozens of men began leaping into the arena. Then hundreds. Then thousands.

Thugs, all of them. But not all thugs are cowards, by any means. And not all of them are stupid, either. Given a choice between battle and the horror of the stampeding crowd—which had already trampled hundreds of men to death—many of them chose to fight.

By the time Balban and the kshatriya were halfway across the Hippodrome, they had been joined by almost six thousand faction members.

Now, Balban ordered the charge.

"Pull them back, Antonina," said Maurice.

Pale-faced, Antonina glanced at him.

"You've only got three hundred cataphracts," she protested.

"*Pull the grenadiers back*," he repeated. "They're lightly armored and they've got no experience in hand combat."

The hecatontarch gestured at the huge mob marching toward them.

"They'll just get in my cataphracts' way," he growled. "Pull them back and keep tossing grenades. I'll try to hold as long as I can."

Maurice stalked forward, roaring commands. Antonina added her voice to his. The grenadiers and their wives scampered back up the tiers. The Thracian cataphracts moved in from the flanks, forming a solid line in front of the grenadiers. The bucellarii didn't wait for Maurice's order before firing a volley of arrows.

"Aim for the Malwa!" ordered Maurice.

The enemy broke into a charge. There was no discipline to that charge. No formation of any kind. Simply—six thousand men racing toward three hundred.

By the time the traitor army reached the lowest tier on the southwest curve of the Hippodrome, a thousand of them had been slain or wounded by grenades and arrows. The kshatriya, especially, had suffered terrible casualties—including Balban, who was bleeding to death in the arena. A cataphract's arrow had ripped through the great artery in his thigh.

But the traitors sensed victory. Their own grenades were

beginning to wreak havoc. And they were now too close for that horrifying cataphract archery. True, the armored Thracians loomed above them like iron statues—fierce, fearsome. But—there were only a few of them.

The mob poured up the tiers.

"NIKA! NIKA!"

The cataphracts raised their swords, and their maces. Soon, now. The first line of the mob was but twenty yards away.

Thousands of them.

Ten yards away.

The line of thugs suddenly disintegrated. Shredded, like meat. Stopped, in its tracks, by a thousand plumbata. The lead-weighted darts sailed over the heads of the cataphracts and struck the charging mob like a hammer. The entire front line collapsed—backward, driving the thugs who followed into a heap.

The cataphracts stared. Lowered their swords. Turned their heads.

Behind them, marching down the tiers in ordered formation, came a thousand Roman infantrymen. Above those infantrymen, atop the uppermost tier of the Hippodrome, was their commander. Standing next to the commander of the Theodoran Cohort.

It did not seem strange, to the cataphracts, to see two generals kissing each other fiercely in the middle of a battle. Not at the time. Later, of course, the episode would be the subject of many ribald jokes and rhymes.

But not at the time. No, not at all.

The cataphracts did not wait for the infantry to reach them. As one man, three hundred Thracians simply charged forward, shouting their battle cries.

Some of them: "Nothing! Nothing!"

Most of them: "Belisarius! Belisarius!"

And, one enthusiast: "Oh, you sorry bastards are *fucked!*"

An hour later, after clambering over the trampled corpses packed in the northern gates, Sittas and Hermogenes slogged across the Hippodrome.

Their progress was slow. Partly, because they were forced to avoid the multitude of bodies scattered across the arena. Partly, because Sittas paused when he came upon Balban's body long enough to cut off the Malwa's head. And, partly, because they had found Hypatius cowering in the bulwarks and were dragging him behind them.

Belisarius and Antonina were sitting on the lowest tier by the southwest curve of the racetrack. Valentinian stood a few feet away. Antonina was still wearing her cuirass, but she had removed her helmet. Her head was nestled into her husband's shoulder. Her cheeks were marked by tear-tracks, but she was smiling like a cherub.

Sittas dropped Balban's head at their feet.

"You can add that to our collection," he said, grinning savagely.

Antonina opened her eyes and gazed at the trophy. She made a small grimace of distaste. Then, closed her eyes and sighed contentedly.

"How many?" asked Belisarius.

"A hundred and twenty-eight," replied Sittas. "Irene says we got most of them. Beyond that—"

He waved a thick arm, grimacing himself. Not a small grimace, either.

"The place is a slaughterhouse. Especially underneath, in the horse pens."

Hermogenes shook his head. His face was almost ashen.

"Thousands of them tried to escape through the stables."

Belisarius winced. The only entrances to the stables were small doors, barely wide enough to fit a racing chariot.

"Most of them are dead," muttered Hermogenes. "Trampled, suffocated, crushed. Christ, it'll take days to haul the bodies out. The ones at the bottom aren't much more than meat paste."

Hermogenes reached back and hauled Hypatius to his feet. The "Emperor" collapsed immediately, like a loose sack. The smell of urine and feces was overpowering.

"Theodora'll be happy to see *him*," snarled Sittas.

Antonina's eyes popped open.

"No," she whispered. "She's at Hell's gate already."

She turned a pleading gaze up at her husband.

Belisarius squeezed her shoulder. Nodded.

Hypatius spoke. "Have mercy," he croaked. "I beg you—*have mercy.*"

"I will," said Belisarius. He turned his head.

"Valentinian."

Epilogue
AN EMPRESS AND HER SOUL

To Belisarius, the huge throne room seemed more like a cavern than ever, with so few occupants. But Theodora had insisted on meeting him there, and he had made no objection. If the Empress found some strength and comfort in the sight of that huge chamber, and the feel of her enormous throne, Belisarius was glad for it.

She, now, was the lynchpin for the future.

He advanced across the huge room with a quick step. When he was ten paces from the throne, he prostrated himself. Then, after rising, began to speak. But Theodora stopped him with a gesture.

"One moment, Belisarius." The Empress turned toward the handful of excubitores standing guard a few yards away.

"Tell the servants to bring a chair," she commanded.

As the excubitores hastened to do her bidding, Theodora bestowed a wry smile upon the general standing before her.

"It's scandalous, I know. But we're in for a long session, and I'd much rather have your untired mind than your formal respect."

Inwardly, Belisarius heaved a sigh of relief. Not at the prospect of spending an afternoon in seated comfort—he was no stranger to standing erect—but at the first sign in days that there was something in the Empress' soul beyond fury, hatred and vengeance.

✧　　　✧　　　✧

A CITY AND ITS TERROR

For eight days, since the crushing of the insurrection, Theodora's soul had dwelt in that realm. As Antonina had so aptly put it, at the very gate of hell.

Much of that time, true, the Empress had spent with her husband. Overseeing the doctors who tended to his wounds; often enough, pushing them aside to tend Justinian herself.

But she had not spent all of her time there. By no means.

She had spent hours, with Irene, overseeing her *agentes in rebus*—the "inspectors of the post" who served the throne as a secret police—dispatching squads of them throughout the Empire. Those squads assigned to the capital itself had already reported back. The results of their missions were displayed, for all to see, on the walls of the Hippodrome. Next to the spiked heads of Malwa kshatriya—hundreds of them, with Balban's occupying a central position; faction leaders; Hypatius; John of Cappadocia (and all of his bucellarii who had not managed to flee the city)—now perched the heads of three dozen churchmen, including Glycerius of Chalcedon and George Barsymes; those officers of the Army of Bithynia who had been captured; nineteen high noblemen, including six Senators; eighty-seven officials and functionaries; and the torturer who had blinded Justinian.

The torturer's head was identified by a small placard. His face was quite unrecognizable. Theodora had spent other hours overseeing his own torture, until she pushed aside her experts and finished the job herself.

There would have been more heads, had it not been for Belisarius and Antonina.

Many more.

Theodora had demanded the heads of every officer, above the rank of tribune, of every military unit in the capital which had stood aside during the insurrection. That demand, however, could not be satisfied by her secret police. As cowed and terrified as they were, those officers were still in command of thousands of troops. Shaky command, true—very shaky—but solid enough to have resisted squads of *agentes in rebus*.

So, Theodora had ordered Belisarius to carry out the purge. He had refused.

Flatly refused. Partly, he told her, because it was excessive.

Those men were not guilty of treason, after all, simply dereliction of duty. What was more important, he explained—calmly, coldly—was that such an indiscriminate purge of the entire officer corps in Constantinople would undermine the army itself.

He needed that army. Rome needed that army. The first battle with the Malwa Empire had been fought and won. There were many more to come.

In the end, Theodora had yielded. She had been satisfied—it might be better to say, had accepted—the dismissal of those officers. Belisarius, along with Sittas and Hermogenes, had spent three days enforcing that dismissal.

None of the officers had objected, with the sole exception of Gontharis, the commander of the Army of Rhodope. A scion of one of the empire's noblest families, he apparently felt his aristocratic lineage exempted him from such unceremonious and uncouth treatment.

Belisarius, not wishing to feed further the nobility's resentment against Thracians, had allowed Sittas to handle the problem.

The Greek nobleman's solution had been quick and direct. Sittas felled Gontharis with a blow of his gauntleted fist, dragged him out of his headquarters into the Army of Rhodope's training field, and decapitated him in front of the assembled troops. Another head joined the growing collection on the walls of the Hippodrome.

Immediately thereafter, Sittas and his cataphracts marched to Gontharis' villa on the outskirts of Constantinople. After expelling all the occupants, Sittas seized the immense treasure contained therein and burned the villa to the ground. The confiscated fortune, he turned over to the imperial treasury.

The treasury's coffers were bulging, now. Theodora had executed only nineteen noblemen. But she had confiscated the fortunes of every noble family whose members had even the slightest connection with the plot. The confiscations, true, had been restricted to that portion of such families' fortunes which were located in the capital. Their provincial estates—to which most of them had fled—were untouched. But, since most aristocrats resided in the capital, the plunder was enormous.

The same treatment had been dealt to officials, bureaucrats, churchmen.

None of them objected. Not publicly, at least. They were glad enough to escape with their lives.

A POPULACE AND ITS GLEE

The great populace of the city had been untouched.

Indeed, after a day, the populace came out of hiding and began applauding the purge. Throngs of commoners could be found, from dawn to dusk, admiring the new decorations on the Hippodrome. The heads of bucellarii meant little to them, and the Malwa heads even less. But the heads of high officials, nobles, churchmen—oh, now, that was a different matter altogether. Often enough, over the years—over the decades and centuries, in the memory of their families—had such men extorted and bullied them.

John of Cappadocia's head, of course, was the most popular attraction. He had often been called the most hated man in the Roman Empire. Few had doubted that claim, in the past. None doubted it now.

But the populace also spent much time admiring the heads of the Hippodrome factions. For the first time in their lives, the common folk could walk the streets of Constantinople without fearing an encounter with faction thugs. The leaders of those thugs—with the exception of a few who had escaped Irene's eye—were all perched on the wall. And, within days, those who had escaped the slaughter joined them—along with two hundred and sixty-three other faction bravos. Such men might have escaped Irene's eye, and the eyes of the *agentes in rebus*. They could not escape the eyes of the populace, who ferreted them out of their hiding places and turned them over to Hermogenes' infantrymen. Or, often enough, simply lynched them on the spot and brought their heads to the Hippodrome.

The more prosperous residents of Constantinople—and there were many of them, in that teeming city: merchants, shopkeepers, craftsmen, artisans—did not share the unadulterated glee of their poorer neighbors. They were not immune to that glee, of course. They, too, had suffered from the exactions of the high and mighty. But—as is usually the case with those who have something to lose—they feared that the purge might widen, and deepen, and grow into a cataclysm of mass terror.

Their fears were exaggerated, perhaps, but by no means groundless. On any number of occasions, Hermogenes' infantrymen had prevented mobs from beating or murdering a man—or an entire family—whose only real crime was unpopularity. On two occasions, the turmoil had become savage enough to require the intervention of Sittas and Belisarius' cataphracts.

Theodora's rage had shaken the entire city. Shaken it almost into pieces.

It was Antonina, more than anyone, who had held the city together. Partly, by the hours she had spent with Theodora, doing what she could to restrain her friend's half-insane fury. But, mostly, Antonina had held the city together by marching through it.

Hour after hour, day after day, marching through Constantinople at the head of her little army of grenadiers, and their wives, and their children.

"Marching" was not the correct word, actually. It would be more accurate to say that she and her Theodoran Cohort *paraded* through the streets. Gaily, cheerfully—and triumphantly. But theirs was not the grim triumph of cataphracts, or regular soldiers. Their was the insouciant triumph of humble Syrian villagers, who were sight-seeing as much as they were providing a sight for the city's residents.

Who could fear such folk? With their families parading with them? After the first day, none. By the second day, Antonina's parades had become as popular as the grisly display at the Hippodrome. By the third day, much more popular.

Much more popular.

The vicinity of the Hippodrome, for one thing, was becoming unbearable due to the stench. Gangs of slaves were hauling out the bodies and burying them in mass graves. But there were thousands of those bodies, many of them—as Hermogenes had said—not much more than meat paste smeared across the stone floors and walls. Fortunately, it was winter, but even so the bodies were rotting faster than they could be removed.

For another, the vengeful glee of the common folk was beginning to abate. Second thoughts were creeping in, especially as those people sat in their little apartments in the evening, enjoying the company of their families. Reservations, doubts, hesitations—as fathers began wondering about the future, and mothers worried over their children.

The death of arrogant lordlings was a thing to be treasured, true. But, at bottom, none of Constantinople's commoners thought Death was truly a friend. They were far too familiar with the creature.

No, better to go and enjoy Antonina's parades. There was nothing, there, to frighten a child. Nothing, to worry a mother or bring a frown to a father's face. There was only—

Triumph, in the victory of humble people.

Enjoyment, in the constant and casual conversations with those simple grenadiers, and their wives. And their children, for those of an age—who gazed upon those lads and lasses with an adulation rarely bestowed upon rustics by cosmopolitan street urchins. But *those* were the children of *grenadiers*—a status greatly to be envied.

And, most of all, a feeling of safety. Safety, in the presence of—*her*.

She—the closest friend of the Empress. Whom all knew, or soon learned, was striving to hold back the imperial madness.

She—who smote the treason of the mighty.

She—who was of their own kind.

She—who was the wife of Belisarius. Rome's greatest general, in this time of war. And Rome's sanest voice, in this time of madness.

Belisarius had already been a name of legend, among those people. Now, the legend grew, and grew. His legend, of course. But also, alongside it—swelling it and being swollen by it—the legend of Antonina.

"The whore," she had often been called, by Rome's upper crust.

The populace of Constantinople had heard the name, in times past. Had wondered. Now, knowing, they rejected it completely.

"The wife," they called her; or, more often, "the great wife."

Her legend had begun with the words of a famous holy man, spoken in distant Syria. The grenadiers passed on his words to the people of Constantinople. The legend had expanded in a kitchen, here in the city itself. The grenadiers and the cataphracts told the tale.

Soon enough, that pastry shop became a popular shrine in its own right. The shopkeeper grew rich, from the business, and was able to retire at an early age; but, an avaricious man, he complained to his dying day that he had been cheated out of his cleaver.

The legend grew, and swelled. Then, five days after the crushing of the insurrection, Michael of Macedonia arrived in

Constantinople. Immediately, he took up residence in the Forum of Constantine and began preaching. Preaching and sermonizing, from dawn to dusk. Instantly, those sermons became the most popular events in the city. The crowds filled the Forum and spilled along the Mese.

He preached of many things, Michael did.

Some of his words caused the city's high churchmen to gnash their teeth. But they gnashed them in private, and never thought to call a council. They were too terrified to venture out of their hiding places.

But, for the most part, Michael did not denounce and excoriate. Rather, he praised and exhorted.

The legend of Antonina now erupted through the city. So did the legend of Belisarius. And so, in its own way, did the legend of Theodora.

By the end of the week, the overwhelming majority of Constantinople's simple citizens had drawn their simple conclusions.

All hope rested in the hands of Belisarius and his wife. Please, Lord in Heaven, help them restore the Empress to her sanity.

The great city held its breath.

AN EMPRESS AND HER TEARS

The Empress and her general gazed at each other in silence, until the servants placed a chair and withdrew.

"Sit, general," she commanded. "We are in a crisis. With Justinian blinded, the succession to the throne is—"

"We are *not* in a crisis, Your Majesty," stated Belisarius firmly. "We simply have a problem to solve."

Theodora stared at him. At first, with disbelief and suspicion. Then, with a dawning hope.

"I swore an oath," said Belisarius.

Sudden tears came to the Empress' eyes.

Not many, those tears. Not many at all. But, for Belisarius, they were enough.

He watched his Empress turn away from Hell, and close its gate behind her. And, for the first time in days, stopped holding his own breath.

"A problem to solve," he repeated, softly. "No more than that. You are good at solving problems, Empress."

Theodora smiled wanly.

"Yes, I am. And so are you, Belisarius."

The general smiled his crooked smile. "That's true. Now that you mention it."

Theodora's own smile widened. "Pity the poor Malwa," she murmured.

"Better yet," countered Belisarius, "*let us pity them not at all.*"

A MAN AND HIS PURPOSE

In the cabin of a ship, another Empress argued with a slave.

"We will arrive in Muziris tomorrow. You must now decide. I *need* you, Dadaji. Much more than he does."

"That may be true, Your Majesty." The slave shrugged. "The fact remains, he is my legal master."

Shakuntala chopped her hand. "Malwa law. You were bought in Bharakuccha."

Again, Holkar shrugged. "And so? The sale is legally binding anywhere in the world. Certainly in the Roman Empire. Malwa India has not, after all, been declared an outlaw state."

The Empress glared. The slave held up a hand, trying to mollify her.

"I am not quibbling over the fine points of law, Your Majesty. The truth is, even if the Malwa Empire were to be declared outlaw"—he chuckled—"although I'm not sure who would be powerful enough to do so!—I would still feel bound to my obligation."

He took a deep breath. "I owe my life to the general, Empress. I was a dead man, when he found me. Still walking—still even talking, now and then—but dead for all that. He breathed life back into my soul. Purpose."

Shakuntala finally saw her opening.

"*What* purpose?" she demanded. "The destruction of Malwa, isn't it?"

Dadaji leaned back. He and the Empress were seated, facing each other three feet apart, each on cushions, each in the lotus position. He eyed her suspiciously.

"Yes. That. One other."

Shakuntala nodded vigorously, pressing the advantage.

"You can serve that purpose better as my imperial adviser than you can as his slave," she stated. "*Much better.*"

Holkar stroked his beard. The gesture, in its own way, illustrated his quandary.

As a slave, he had been forced to shave his respectable beard. That beard, and the middle-aged dignity which went with it, had been restored by Belisarius. It was a symbol of all that he owed the general.

Yet, at the same time—it *was* a badge of his dignity. Full, now; rich with the gray hairs of experience and wisdom. Foolish, really, to waste the beard and all it signified on the life of a slave. A slave who, as Shakuntala rightly said, was no longer of great use to his master.

Stroke. Stroke.

"How do you know I could serve you properly?" he demanded.

Shakuntala felt the tension ease from her shoulders. Get the argument off the ground of abstract honor and onto to the ground of concrete duty, and she was bound to win.

"You are as shrewd as any man I ever met," she stated forcefully. "Look how you managed this escape—and all the preparations which went into it. Belisarius always relied on you for anything of that nature. He trusted you completely—and he is immensely shrewd himself, in that way as well as others. I need men I can trust. Rely on. Desperately."

Stroking his beard. "What you *need*, girl, is prestige and authority. An imperial adviser should be noble-born. Brahmin. I am merely vaisya. *Low*-caste vaisya." He smiled. "And Maratha, to boot. In most other lands, my caste would be ranked among the sudra, lowest of the twice-born."

"So?" she demanded. "You are as literate and educated as any brahmin. More than most! You know that to be true."

Holkar spread his hands. "What does that matter? The rulers and dignitaries of other lands will be offended, if your adviser does not share their purity. They would have to meet with me, privately and intimately, on many occasions. They would feel polluted by the contact."

The Empress almost snarled. "Damn them, then! If they seek alliance with me, they will have to take it as it comes!"

Holkar barked a laugh.

"Tempestuous girl! Have you already lost your wits—at your age? *They* will not be seeking alliance with you, Empress. *They* are not throneless refugees, hunted like an animal. *You* will be knocking on their doors, beggar's bowl in hand."

With amazing dignity (under the circumstances; she *was*, after all, a throneless refugee): "I shall not."

"You shall."

"Shall not."

Dadaji glowered. "See? Already you scorn my advice!" Shaking his finger: "You must learn to bridle that temper, Empress! You will *indeed* treat with possible allies with all necessary—I won't say humility; I don't believe in magic!—*decorum*."

Glower.

"And another thing—"

Shakuntala spent the next hour in uncharacteristic silence, nodding her head, attending patiently to her new adviser. It was not difficult. His advice, in truth, was excellent. And she had no need to rein in her temper. Even if he had been babbling nonsense, she would have listened politely.

She had her adviser. In fact, if not yet in name.

At the end of that hour, Dadaji Holkar reined himself in. With a start of surprise.

"You are a treacherous girl," he grumbled. Then, chuckling: "Quite well done, actually!" He gazed at her fondly, shaking his head with amusement.

"Very well, Empress," he said. "Let us leave it so: I will send your request to Belisarius. If he agrees, I will serve you in whatever capacity you wish."

Shakuntala nodded. "He will agree," she said confidently. "For reasons of state, if no other. But he will want to know—what do *you* wish? What will you tell him?"

Holkar stared at her. "I will tell him that it is my wish, also." Then, still seated, he bowed deeply. "You are my sovereign, Empress. Such a sovereign as any man worthy of the name would wish to serve."

When he lifted his head, his face was calm. Shakuntala's next words destroyed that serenity.

"What is your other purpose?" she asked.

Holkar frowned.

"You said, earlier, that the destruction of Malwa was one of your purposes. One of two. Name the other."

Holkar's face tightened.

Shakuntala was ruthless.

"Tell me."

He looked away. "You know what it is," he whispered.

That was true. She did. But she would force *him* to face it squarely. Lest, in the years to come, it gnawed his soul to destruction. Youth, too, has its bold wisdom.

"Say it."

The tears began to flow.

"Say it."

Finally, as he said the words, the slave vanished. Not into the new, shadow soul of an imperial adviser, but into what he had always been. The man, Dadaji Holkar.

In the quiet, gentle time that followed, as a low-born Maratha sobbed and sobbed, his grey head cradled in the small arms of India's purest, most ancient, most noble line, the soul named Dadaji Holkar finished the healing which a foreign general had begun.

He would help his sovereign restore her broken people.

And he would, someday, find his broken family.

A FAMILY AND ITS RESOLVE

Ironically, Dadaji Holkar had already found his family, without knowing it. He had even, without knowing it, helped them through their troubles.

Standing next to the stablekeeper in Kausambi, watching the rockets flaring into the sky, he had been not half a mile from his wife. She, along with the other kitchen slaves, had been watching those same rockets from the back court of her master's mansion. Until the head cook, outraged, had driven them back to their duties.

She had gone to those duties with a lighter heart than usual. She had no idea what that catastrophe represented. But, whatever it was, it was bad news for Malwa. The thought kept her going for hours, that night; and warmed her, a bit, in countless nights that followed.

His son had actually seen him. In Bihar, rearing from his toil in the fields, his son had rested for a moment. Idly watching a nobleman's caravan pass on the road nearby. He had caught but a glimpse of the nobleman himself, riding haughtily in his howdah on the lead elephant. The man's face was indistinguishable, at that distance. But there was no mistaking his identity. A Malwa potentate, trampling the world.

The overseer's angry shout sent him back to work. The shout, combined with the sight of that arrogant lord, burned through his soul. From months and months of hard labor, the boy's body had grown tough enough to survive. But he had feared, sometimes, that he himself was too weak. Now, feeling the hardening flame, he knew otherwise.

Stooping, he cursed that unknown Malwa, and made a solemn vow. Whoever that stinking lord was, Dadaji Holkar's son would outlive him.

Holkar had not come as close to his daughters. As planned, Shakuntala and her companions had taken a side road before reaching Pataliputra. They had no desire to risk the swarming officialdom in that huge city, and so they had bypassed it altogether.

Still, they had passed less than fifteen miles to the south. Thirteen miles, only, from the slave brothel where his daughters were held.

In a way, Dadaji had even touched them. And his touch had been a blessing.

The soldiers at the guardpost where Shakuntala had browbeaten the commanding officer, had contributed to his humiliation later. The bribe had been very large, and their officer was a weakling. An arrogant little snot, whom they had browbeaten themselves into a bigger cut than common soldiers usually received. With their share of the bribe, they had enjoyed a pleasant visit to the nearest brothel, on the southern outskirts of the city. They had had money to burn.

Money to burn, and they spent it all. Gold coin from the hand of Dadaji Holkar had found its way into the hands of his daughters' pimps. The girls were popular with the soldiers, and they had paid handsomely.

It cannot be said that the soldiers were popular with the girls. None of their customers were. But, in truth, Holkar's daughters had been relieved to spend two days in their exclusive company. The soldiers were not rough with them; and, young men, unjaded, were not given to the bizarre quirks that some of the local merchants and tradesmen preferred.

After the soldiers left, their pimps informed the girls that they had decided to turn down the various offers which had come in for their purchase, from other brothels. Holkar's daughters had known of those offers, and dreaded them, for they would result in separation.

But the pimps had decided to keep them. They were popular with the soldiers. Steady business.

The brothel-keeper even tossed them one of the coins. A bonus, he said, for good work.

That coin, in the endless time which followed, was his daughters' secret treasure. They never spent it. Sometimes, late at night, in the crib they shared, the girls would bring the coin from its hiding place and admire it, holding hands.

It was their lucky coin, they decided. So long as they had it, they would be together. The family of Dadaji Holkar would still survive.

AN EMPRESS AND HER DECISION

As she watched Dadaji's tears soak her royal skin, the Empress Shakuntala made her own decision. And reaffirmed a vow.

She had never thought much about purity and pollution, in her short life. She had resented the caste system, half-consciously, for the many ways it constrained her. Had even hated it, half-consciously, for the inseparable barrier which it placed between her and her most precious desire. But she had never really thought about it, before. It had simply been there. A fact of life, like the three seasons of India.

She began to think about it, now. Her thoughts, unlike her heart, were very unclear. She was young. Rao, in times past, had tried to teach her some aspects of philosophy, and devotion. But the girl she had been had not taken to those lessons kindly. His soft words had met none of the enthusiastic attention which had greeted his training in other, much harder, fields.

Now, she began to think, and learn.

She had learned this much, already. Watching a foreign general, she had seen Rao's forgotten lessons come to life. Hard fists, and harder steel, were like snow at the foot of mountains. Mountains called minds, which produced that snow, and then melted it when they so desired. Only the soul matters, in the end. It towers over creation like the Himalayas.

She made her decision. As she rebuilt Andhra, she would gather what there was of human learning and wisdom around her throne. She would not only rebuild the stupas, the viharas. She would not simply recall the philosophers, and the sadhus, and the monks. She would set them to work—mercilessly—driving them one against the other. Clashing idea against idea like great cymbals, until truth finally emerged.

That doing, of course, required another. And so, watching her purity imperilled by the racking tears of the low-born man in her arms, and drawing strength from that pollution, she reaffirmed her vow.

I will make Malwa howl.

AN EMPIRE AND ITS HOWL

Malwa *was* howling. As yet, however, only in the privacy of the Emperor's chambers. And only, as yet, howling with rage. Fear was still to come.

The rage blew inward, centered on Malwa itself. The fate of Lord Venandakatra hung in the balance.

"I always told you he was a fool," snarled Nanda Lal. "He's smart enough, I admit. But no man's intelligence is worth a toad's croak if he cannot restrain his lusts and vanities."

"You can no longer protect him, Skandagupta," stated Sati. "You have coddled him enough. He—not the underlings he blames—is responsible for Belisarius. For Shakuntala. Recall him. Discipline him harshly."

Link, then, was all that saved Venandakatra from disgrace. Or worse.

"NO. YOU MISS THE GREAT FRAMEWORK. VENANDA-KATRA WAS JUST APPOINTED GOPTRI OF THE DECCAN.

TO RECALL HIM IN DISGRACE WOULD HEARTEN THE
MARATHA. SHAKUNTALA IS IMPORTANT, BUT SHE IS NOT
AS IMPORTANT AS HER PEOPLE. BREAK THAT PEOPLE,
YOU BREAK HER."

The Malwa bowed to their overlord.

"BREAK MAJARASHTRA. TERRORIZE THE MARATHA
MONGRELS, TILL THEIR BASTARDS WHISPER FEAR FOR
A MILLENIUM. PULVERIZE THAT POLLUTED FOLK."

"FOR THAT, VENANDAKATRA WILL DO. PERFECTLY."

A HUSBAND AND HIS THOUGHTS

The day before his departure to join Lord Damodara's army, Rana
Sanga spent entirely with his wife. Late that night, exhausted from
love-making, he stroked his wife's hair.

"What are you thinking?" she asked, smiling. "All of a sudden,
you've got this serious look on your face."

"Hard to explain," he grunted.

His wife reared up in the bed, the coverings falling away from
her plump figure.

"Talk," she commanded, wriggling her fingers threateningly.
"Or I tickle!"

Sanga laughed. "Not that! Please! I'd rather face Belisarius
himself, with an army at his back."

His wife's amusement died away. "That's what you were thinking about? Him?"

Her face tightened. The Persian campaign was about to begin.
She knew Sanga would, soon enough, be facing that—*terrible
Roman*—on the battlefield. And that, for all her husband's incredible prowess at war, this enemy was one he truly respected. Even,
she thought, feared.

Sanga shook his head. "Actually, no. Not directly, at least."

He reached up his hand and gently caressed her face. Plain it
was, that face, very plain. Round, like her body.

He had not married her for her beauty. He had never even
seen her face, before she lifted the veil in his sleeping chamber,
after their wedding. Theirs, in the way of Rajput royalty, had been

a marriage of state. Dictated by the stern necessities of dynasty, class, and caste. Of maintaining the true Rajput lineage; protecting purity from pollution.

He had said nothing, on the night he first saw his wife's face, and then her body, to indicate his disappointment. She had been very fearful, she told him years later, of what he would say, or do—or not do—when he saw how plain she was. But he had been pleasant, even kind; had gone about his duty. And, by the end of the night, had found a surprising pleasure in that eager, round body; excitement, in those quick and clever fingers; gaiety and warmth, lurking behind the shyness in her eyes. And, in the morning, had seen the happiness in a still-sleeping, round face. Happiness which he had put there, he knew, from kindness far more than manhood.

Young, then, filled with the vainglory of a Rajput prince already famous for his martial prowess, he had made an unexpected discovery. Pride could be found in kindness, too. Deep pride, in the sight of a wife's face glowing with the morning. Even a plain face. Perhaps *especially* a plain face.

The day had come, years later, when he came upon his wife in the kitchen. She was often to be found there. Despite their many cooks and servants, his wife enjoyed preparing food. Hearing him come, recognizing his footsteps, she had turned from the table where she was cutting onions. Turned, smiled—laughed, wiping the tears from her eyes—brushed the hair (all grey, now—no black left at all) away from her face, knife still in her hand, laughing at her preposterous appearance. Laughing with her mouth, laughing with her eyes.

Twice only, in his life, had the greatest of Rajputana's kings been stunned. Struck down, off his feet, by sudden shock.

Once, sprawling on a famous field of battle, when Raghunath Rao split his helmet with a dervish blow of his sword.

Once, collapsing on a bench in his own kitchen, when he realized that he loved his wife.

"You are my life," he whispered.

"Yes," she replied. And gave him a fresh sweet onion, as if it were another child.

"I was thinking of your face," he said. "And another's. The face of a young woman. Very beautiful, she was."

His wife's lips tightened, slightly, but she never looked away.

"I have always told you I would not object to concubines, husband," she said softly. "I am not—"

"Hush, wife!" he commanded. Then, laughing: "The farthest thing from my mind! Even if the woman in question was not the Emperor's own daughter—hardly a woman for a Rajput's concubine."

His wife giggled. Sanga shook his head.

"I was not matching the two faces that way, dearest one. I was—ah! It is too difficult to explain!"

"The tickle, then!"

She was as good as her word. But, for all the gleeful torment, Sanga never did explain his thoughts to her. Not that night. Not for many nights to come.

They were too hard to explain. Too new. Too bound up with new secrets. Too twisted into the misty coils of the far distant future which he had glimpsed, in the chamber of Great Lady Holi and the *being* for which she was a mere vessel.

Eventually, his wife fell asleep. Sanga did not, for a time. He was kept awake by thoughts of lineage. Of the plain face of his wife; the lines of her face which he could see coiling through the faces of his children, alongside his own. Of the beautiful face of an emperor's daughter, destined to be the vessel for the perfect faces of future gods.

The lineage of his life. Life that was. Life that is. Life that will be.

He contemplated purity; contemplated pollution. Contemplated perfection. Contemplated onions.

Most of all, he pondered on illusion, and truth, and the strange way in which illusion can become truth.

And truth become illusion.

A CREATION AND ITS UNDERSTANDING

When the general finally left the Empress and walked out of the palace, the day was ending. Drawn by the sunset, Belisarius went to the balustrade overlooking the Bosporus. He leaned on the stone, admiring the view.

An urgent thought came from Aide.

There is more, now. More that I understand of the message from the Great Ones. I think. I am not sure.

Tell me.

They said to us—this also:

> *Find everything that made us.*
> *Find passion in the virgin, purity in the whore;*
> *Faith in the traitor, fate in the priest.*
> *Find doubt in the prophet, decision in the slave;*
> *Mercy in the killer, murder in the wife.*
> *Look for wisdom in the young, and the suckling need*
> *of age;*
> *Look for truth in moving water; falsehood in the stone.*
> *See the enemy in the mirror, the friend across the field.*
> *Look for everything that made us.*
> *On the ground where we were made.*

Silence. Then:

Do you understand?

Belisarius smiled. Not crookedly, not at all.

Yes. Oh, yes.

I think I understand, too. I am not sure.

"Of course you understand," murmured Belisarius. "We made you. On that same ground."

Silence. Then:

You promised.

There was no reproach in that thought, now. No longer. It was the contented sound of a child, nestling its head into a father's shoulder.

You promised.